I0766946

Chains of a Broken God

Book Two of the Last Son of the Feromage Saga

Written By David Trotter

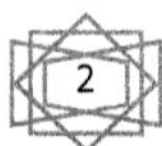

Chains of a Broken God

Book Two of the Last Son of the Feromage Saga

Written By David Trotter
Artwork By Aaron Moschner

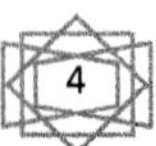

Table of Contents

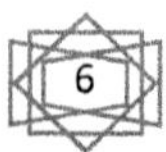

Copyright Page

DEDICATION PAGE

This book could not have come to fruition without the support of many people. Firstly, my family, who are constantly challenging me to be better. Next would be my friends, who are always cheering me on. My core group, Robert, Ellie, Aaron, and Evelyn, and those of IFA, each of you are responsible for bringing life, light, color, and correction to my world. Thank you. And lastly, to each of you who have bought my book, whether by chance, add, or Kickstarter. I hope you enjoy!

SPEAKING OF KICKSTARTER:

Billye Herndon, Dan and Robert Zangari, William T Fee, Brad Andrews, Nikki M Clark, Jerome, Ellie Drees, Irinel Finco, Gerald P. McDaniel, Jessica Johnson, the man, the myth, the legend: Steven Tyler, Brandon Garrett (big bro), Steven Guglich, Arne Radtke, Katherine Shipman, Hugo Essink, Cameron Sjo, Rob Steinberger, Kyle Wilkinson, Shawn Charlton, Isidoro Cortes, Justise Briones, Nyxius, Quentin Foster, N. Scott Pearson, T.J. McDonald, Jacob, Tristan Amant, Will, Alexandra Corrsin, Chris Session, Danniel Kenner, Aaron Moschner, Steven Byrd, Adam Stemple, Bonsart Bokel, Madison, Jolene Trotter (that's my momma), Laura Deason (big sis), and to Rachel Rener and J.A. Andrews who helped share the word.

And to my wife. Yes, this one is dedicated most of all to you. Those long nights and early mornings. The twisting story lines and the overabundance of a singular word I am caught on that week. Thank you. You are far too kind and beautiful to be subjected to the musings of my mind.

And to Darius...I am sorry.

Map of Ordiatea

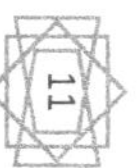

PART 1

LORI

10 Years Ago

Timidly, Lori stepped out from under the arches, her hands trembling at her side as she willed them with all her might to stillness. Blue torchlight flickered off the towering columns, the ancient sconces blackened with use and years. What felt like hundreds of eyes, gleaming with the selfsame, ghostly light, gazed down upon her from earthen seats. A gust of wind tore through the open-air arena - a bowl of natural obsidian, formed from a fallen star, crafted into the place of trial - pulling at her pale gown of flowing fabric.

For the first time in her life, Lori was thankful that her hair was in braids, not whipping around her face and obscuring her view. Black water filled the basin on either side of the narrow berm she walked with practiced steps. A lifetime of preparation had led her here. She would not fail. Sulfuric fumes seeped through the water, disturbing the surface with gurgling bouts of fumes.

It reeked of rotten eggs and molten stone, stinging her already watery eyes and filling her mouth with bile. But she would not stop. Forward she marched, ever forward toward that place that all daughters of Dane's blood must go. Never once had any girl forsaken her duty, never once had any turned away. She would not be the first.

A dozen drums filled the chasm with a hollow rumble. Every step she made was in beat. A lone piper stood atop a wooden tower, playing a somber tune. It was all in perfect time. It was all exactly as it should be. And then they fell silent as the grave.

"Lori, daughter-heir of our ancient forefather," High King Sterkamar proclaimed as Lori neared the midway point. He stood in ritual draping. His hair was as black as the night and his eyes as bright as the stars. Her own father stood by his cousin's side, broader of chest and shoulders, though nearly a head shorter - and that was saying something. "The night is upon us. To walk this path is to turn away from self and embrace that great promise made over three hundred years ago when our first kin came to this land."

Lori knew the words, verbatim. But hearing them here and now, proclaimed by one whose thunderous voice was golden struck by the gods, shook her to the core. Blood of the ancestors indeed. There was no mistaking it.

"Do you swear with your life, your blood, and your soul to forsake all sense of self, to uphold the rites of the promise, and if called upon, to fulfill that promise made by every daughter of Dane from the first to the last?"

Lori was now only feet away from the lord of all of Daneland. She could see the very gold and rubies woven into his beard. She could smell the scent of rich leathers and sweet hay, followed by earthen tones that pleased the senses. The spectacle nearly took her breath away. This was no mortal man, he couldn't be.

Silence hung heavy in the air.

Her father fidgeted, acknowledging her for the first time.

A blossom of heat flared up her chest and neck, burning at her cheeks and eyes.

"I swear it, upon myself, the ancestors, and Ordan, High Father, that I will, if chosen this night, fulfil my duties and the promise made."

Something that looked like sorrow flashed across Lord Sterkamar's silvery eyes. It did not last, as his focus became steel, and his face hardened to iron.

"Then take forth the Oathrod and say the words of the promise prescribed unto our first by the mouth of he who came before us."

High King Sterkamar turned about, his towering frame casting a long shadow across the distance between them. When he turned to face Lori once more, he held a silver rod, in whose head was set a sapphire that shone with a light unlike anything Lori had ever seen.

All her life she had been told of the Oathrod, of its otherworldly design and craftsmanship. But upon seeing it for the first time, all prior descriptions paled in comparison.

Lori swallowed hard, forcing down her fear, her doubt, her anxiety, and stretched out her hand and took hold of the rod. It was warm to the touch, surprisingly so for something that had sat on an alter for what she assumed was at least two or three hours in the chill of Daneland's frigid night - even if it was Spring, hoarfrost still coated the trees and grasses before the sun rose each day.

This was it. This was the moment she had been preparing for her whole life. Others had walked this path, stood in this place. But now was her time.

"I swear," Lori proclaimed, but her voice faltered. She took a calming breath, steadied her shoulders, and started again. "I swear upon this Oathrod, to stand as one called and ready. I swear to fulfil the promise made by my first sister, who was daughter to our first kin, whose blood it is that runs through my veins. I swear this and do so with the intent to break all other oaths and promises, of family and friends, to stand in the place of those who can no longer stand and fulfill the promises made by those who cannot accomplish them further. This I swear upon my name, my blood, and my soul!"

Lori thrust the rod heavenwards, both hands holding firm to the sinuous metal. Heat flushed through her body and an overwhelming rush of emotions came crashing over her. The first of which was embarrassment.

There was no epic display of lights. The heavens did not open to accept her promise. Her ancestor's voice did not fill her mind. She stood, where hundreds of other young women had stood before, without affirmation or recognition from Ordan and Gallae. There was no thrumming of power within her soul. And the brilliant sapphire did not burst into Aethereal light.

Lori was not the first young woman to walk this path. Nor was she the first to walk it back empty-handed.

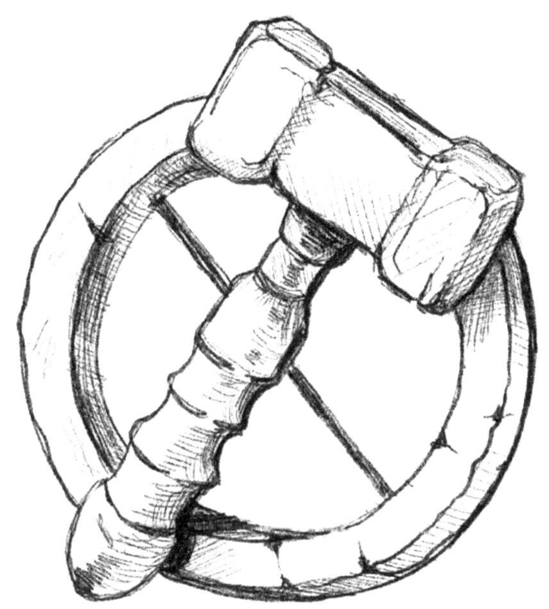

CHAPTER 1: A PLEA FOR HELP
DARIUS

Bronze shields glistened in the moonlight, a wall of over two hundred men in plate and helms. Eyes looked forward, unwavering. Banners hung limp on spears, hoisted high: reds, blues, and greens. Snow drifted from a dark sky, covering sand black as pitch.

Morr. The cursed Island of the Blood Queen and her subjects.

Morr. Home of the damned.

Morr.

"Lines!" bellowed Lord Tareth from atop a painted stallion, one of the only remaining animals left of the siege on the shores of Morr.

Two hundred bronze shields moved in perfect synchronization as two hundred spears dropped a half measure.

"Archers," called out Lady Aoibhinn, her resolve firm in the face of imminent demise.

Fifty or so men formed up at the command, turning their eyes to the mountain fortress teaming with pale fleshed Morreans, affixing strings to great bows.

"Send these bastards to the Halfak's gates!" Lady Aoibhinn cried, thrusting her blade toward the walls.

Thrum!

The sky filled with long, heavy bolts that whistled terribly as they soared toward the walls of the fortress. The bolts were uniquely designed, made to cast fear into the hearts of those who heard them. The cry was high, a screeching of inescapable death.

"Forward to death and glory!" Lord Tareth cried out. Two drummers beat out a marching tempo and the line moved forward, step by heavy step.

"Again!" screamed Lady Aoibhinn. Her call was met by a second wave of death.

Morrean demons screamed and died, falling from the walls of the black keep. It had no secondary defenses, only stacked stone about the height of three men, with two towers erected aside the wooden gates. Those who were enclosed in the courtyard would escape the onslaught of arrows. Those who manned the wall were stripped of what they called life, their own bows too weak to span the distance between the walls and where Lady Aoibhinn had stationed the last of her mighty archers.

"Turtle!"

At Lord Tareth's command, one hundred shields lifted, providing cover overhead. The line moved within reach of the walls, but the Morrean bolts bounced off of polished bronze with the resounding pings of stone on metal.

"Ram!"

An oaken log wrapped with cords and capped with a bronze shield that had been hammered onto its tip was pushed forward.

"Break the gate!"

Thud!

Thud!

Thud!

Crack!

"Storm the keep! The night is ours!" Lord Tareth bellowed. "Leave no stone unbloodied!"

"Archers," called Lady Aoibhinn. "Forward!"

Denathurias, the new Lord of the Iron Mountains, watched with unease as the last of the sons of men stormed the Black Fortress.

"You look unwell, son." It was Angenthor's voice.

Denathurias turned from his perch, hidden away in the trees and hillside, and looked down on his old friend and mentor. Denathurias did not let the white-haired man's age fool him. Angenthor was cunning and wise, but, but that spoke little of his ferocity when the beast within was unleashed. Angenthor and Baenhada had near single-handedly taken the lower keep, attacking with perfect precision and deadly speed. Angenthor, the white wolf, and Baenhada the red, were near-kin, both Feromage of the Canine Tribes. Their third Wolf Brother, Yaenan the Black, had died back on Ethrea and his ring given to his son, who had lived only two seasons.

"It falls too swift," Denathurias answered, his tone naught but a mere whisper in the wind.

"And that troubles you? Have we not shed enough blood?"

"I don't like it," Denathurias grunted. Something was wrong; he could feel it.

"Let the men of the Southlands have their victory." Angenthor placed a hand on Denathurias's should as he spoke. "It will do them well."

"Where are Mireya and her accused priest?" asked Denathurias, though it was more a question for himself than for Angenthor.

"Fled," he scoffed. "And let them rot."

"Magic does not die easy, old friend," Denathurias answered. "It was you who taught me that."

"And what of this has been easy?"

***

Thunder rolled over the moss-strewn canopy of Ranok as lightning lit the night sky. Unlike the hot rain that fell near the shore city of Tur'Mor, a cold and constant rain soaked the forest floor, seeping into the makeshift beds of leaves upon which Darius sat. Next to him, a young girl – lifeless and cold as ice – was wrapped in his coat, her freckled face gaunt and pale. Across the extinguished mound of smoldering sticks, another lay more likely than not feigning sleep beneath a tent of mud-splattered, emerald fabric.

Izebal.

An odd sensation wormed through Darius's guts as he looked on her sleeping figure from beneath the canopy of his own construct tent. Izebal had done this for them, weaving the material from vines of the forest as she chanted Words in the tongue of the Diju, drawing upon the Touch of Ria'Elahm. She had lit the fire within the same tongue, causing flames to leap into existence with a spark of emerald energy.

Magic.

It was still strange for him to see it wielded so.

Throughout Darius's life, magic had been a dark and terrible thing, possessed by those who followed the occultist Blood Queen, Mireya. He bore upon his person two markings of the dark source of Iodaba. The silver streak in his beard beneath his lip and a handprint seared into his flesh at the center of his chest. That scar, the handprint, had been placed upon him by that very Blood Queen herself, just before he had driven her high priest's dagger into her own heart.

Death was too gentle a reward for that damned witch. Darius spat as he recalled that harrowing night and all the nights afterward he had faced. The lost family, years, and will. He had been broken, mind and body. Despite this, the encounter just nights ago had revealed a harrowing truth: he had not destroyed his foes that night.

Slowly, anxiety worked her cold talons into Darius's spine, weakening his resolve, and filling his soul with fear and trepidation. A pain, sharp and deep, throbbed in his lower abdomen. It had been three days since the fight with the Itheanam. And while the surface of his flesh was healed and only a gruesome, puckered scar remained, something deeper was wrong.

"Damnit!" he cursed under his breath as a secondary wave of agony blossomed.

Izebal sprang up, drawing both her wand and her dagger in one swift motion as her eyes filled with emerald light. "What is it? What's wrong?"

Darius dropped his head, shaking it as he let out a hollow laugh. "You're supposed to be sleeping."

"Ethenealal take you," swore Izebal. Sliding her dagger into its sheath, she stood and crossed the distance between the two tents. Gently, she dropped down at Darius's side, tucking her knees into her chest and wrapping her arms about them, leaning the weight of her body into his side. It hurt where she nestled, but the comforting warmth of her body and the sweet scent of her hair were more than welcoming. These last few days, they had become close– far too close.

"Can't sleep?" asked Izebal after a time of silence and rainfall.

"No," Darius answered, glaring into the forest floor as if it could provide answers.

"Has she made any progress? Any signs of life?"

"Since last night?" Darius looked back to the girl, laying so still atop the rusty, golden leaves. And though he did not know her, his heart ached for her. Life was not fair, nor was it kind. He knew that, but none should have to suffer what this girl had suffered.

"It is not your fault." Izebal placed a comforting hand on Darius's arm.

She felt warm and soft, and smelled of sweet honey and herbs. Darius gave up wondering how she always seemed so clean and put together, attributing it all to her ability to Touch Ria'Elahm's light. He was sure he smelled of mud, rotten leaves, and blood. Despite scrubbing himself endlessly in a freshwater spring, he could still feel the oily, thick blood of the Itheanam covering his body.

He shuddered.

Izebal drew her hand away quickly, looking away from him and to the ground.

Darius had not meant to ward her away. Quite the opposite, actually. The hand on him felt good, bringing a measure of needed peace and emotional grounding. His body had betrayed him yet again, leaving him alone. He wanted to curse, to throw his own hands up in the air in frustration. But a sudden surge of white-hot pain in his side kept his hands still.

In awkward shame, he grunted. Rolled his neck side to side, cracking the stiff bones of another sleepless night away in a loud series of pops, and then let out a long sigh.

"We will find our way out," Izebal said, trying to fill her tired voice with reassurance.

The girl, who had been little more than a pale sack of bones and cold flesh, jerked suddenly. Both sprang to their feet, Darius snatching up the enchanted rod of hickory and Izebal simultaneously drawing out her wand and gilded dagger.

Eyes wide, Darius searched the forest, looking for any signs of demon or fiend before dropping once more to the girl's side, scanning her for indications of hurt or life. Her chest rose and fell, sending blood pumping through blackened veins. The amulet on her neck—rather, the gemstone set within the wolf's singular eye— glowed ever so faintly.

"She's starting to convulse," said Izebal as she sheathed her dagger and began rifling through the satchel at her hip. "You need to hold her. Don't let her bite off her tongue."

Already, foamy, grey spittle was beginning to stream from pale lips. Her whole body shook wildly now, and it took every bit of Darius's strength to hold her. Every jerk, every spasm emanating from that fragile girl sent a burst of pain through Darius's side.

"Izebal," he called out. "Do something!"

"Ach'lo nah," Izebal chanted, tracing a hand through the air as emerald runes blazed into existence. "Mah el'han, mah el'han!"

The girl's eyelids flashed open, revealing dead eyes of grey jelly with irises as blue as the summer sky.

"The seal weakens. Death abounds. Blood. Blood. Blood sha—" Her body convulsed once more and went stiff in Darius's arms.

What...what was that? Darius could not speak, his tongue tied in a tirade of confusion.

Something was wrong. Something—

"It's burning her!" screamed Izebal.

Darius, acting out of reflex not thought, snatched the wolf's head amulet, which had nearly turned white from heat, from the girl's chest. The intensity of the pain took him by surprise, causing him to drop the silver to the forest floor as he let out a howl.

"What happened?" Izebal's voice was near manic, eyes wide with terror as she rushed to Darius.

Grunting in pain and embarrassment, Darius answered, "It was just hot. I wasn't—what happened?"

"I asked first," scoffed Izebal, shaking her head as some measure of control began rewinding its way into her voice. She took Darius's hand in her own, her dark skin a striking contrast to his. "Let me heal this."

"Tend to the girl." Darius retracted his hand from Izebal's as he spoke. *I don't need help, not anymore.*

That strange sensation of power, like lightning coursing through his veins, surged through his body, making the hairs on his forearms and neck rise. Ever since Izebal had saved him in the cave, ministering to him the tonic that Alyn had given him, Darius's ability to heal had exponentially increased.

His thumb slid across the rough sides of his silver ring, tracing the raised paw of the bear which represented not only himself but all his forefathers before him. His nostrils flared as he felt the first ray of sunlight, distant and faint, extend itself in his direction. Darius turned his attention upwards, willing those pale morning rays to Bind to himself. Like tiny threads, beams of golden yellow latched themselves to his ring, and from it, Darius drew the power into his own essence.

Waves of ecstasy cascaded over him, so much faster than before. Instantaneously, the burn mark on his hand began to heal as his eyes began to leak golden light. His shoulders shuddered as the power coursed through him, a smile turning up the corners of his lips. The forest, which had been so oppressively dark and cold, seemed to burn away before his very eyes, replaced with brilliant beams of gold.

Darius.

A name that sounded familiar echoed in his mind. That name meant something. Didn't it?

Colors turned and weaved before his very eyes, twisting in beautiful patterns of azure and gold, winding about themselves in infinite loops. Darius drew in more sunlight, Binding two and three times over. Lances of white-hot light pricked at his face and hands, causing him to wince. Waves of rapture washed over his flesh, sending goosebumps across his body.

"Darius!" That strange voice from eternities away called out.

Slowly, tendrils of emerald wove their way into Darius's vision, forming hues of malachite and celadon. As they coalesced, something cold crept up his spine, a sudden sense of wrongness. Eyes heavily lidded blinked, searching for clarity.

The slap that struck his cheek brought said elusive clarity in abundance.

All at once, the rays of the golden sun were severed from Darius's ring. A sharp pain throbbed across the side of his face. Eyes focusing, the form of Izebal outlined as if by a heavy ink-quill and highlighted with vibrant green, stood before him.

"Darius?" Izebal said, her voice pitched high in panic. "Darius, can you hear me?"

"What was that for?" Darius grunted, rubbing at his tender cheek.

"That is twice, messenger boy." Izebal's voice, though leveled out, was wrought with anger and indignation. "You said you would not do that again."

Fueled by his bruised pride and seething embarrassment, Darius grunted and turned his back to her.

"Hey! Do not turn on me, messenger boy!" Izebal snapped. "You and I had a deal. But when you do *that,* it changes you. You get lost in it."

She was right and Darius knew it. Years of training had allowed him to walk that fine line without giving in to the temptation. Worse, he knew the consequences of Binding too much at once. Burning out. Looking at his hands, back still to Izebal, he could see the red patches on his palms and the backs of his hands. It had already begun, and had he lingered any longer...

"You are right," Darius conceded, turning about slowly and facing her, picking up the amulet from the forest floor in a swift motion.

She had been about to say something. He did not know what, but judging by her face, it was not going to be something comforting. Her face froze, as if confused. Slowly, her eyes softened, the green dimming from a bright not natural.

"Thank you," muttered Darius. "I don't know what came over me."

"We can figure it out. Together," Izebal said, stepping closer. "But you must promise me, no more Binding until we can figure out what has changed inside you."

The sensation of ants crawling beneath the skin was still persistent, even after the episode. Darius noted his flesh was still hot to the touch as he laced his fingers together. His head drooped down, a bone-deep weariness pulling at his mind, the fatigue unlike anything he had experienced before.

"It's for your own good," said Izebal, in a tone he took to be soothing but felt more like condescension.

"I was only trying to heal my..." Darius trailed off, his mind recalling what had led up to the disaster. "The girl!"

Izebal jumped at the exclamation, but Darius did not take any heed of her motion. He scrambled past her, his hands pulling at the dirt and rot of the forest floor, fingertips sinking into the cold soil. The sensation was grounding, despite his frantic clamber to the sprawled-out little girl. Whose chest was heaving.

"She's breathing!" exclaimed Darius as hope rushed into his heart. The day had been a ceaseless cacophony of emotions and sensations. Far too many for Darius's addled mind. But this, seeing her breathing, brought such a profound joy to his soul that he could not help but let out a peel of unbridled laughter.

True, her flesh was still pale and ashen, and her lips were still blue, but her heart thudded rhythmically as her sternum rose and fell with each weak breath. Her eyes were still sealed shut, but Darius could see the tips of her fingers twitch. She was alive, and, just maybe, getting better.

"What do you think it means?" he asked of Izebal, unable to contain the hope from elevating his voice. He placed two fingers on the girl's neck, checking the tempo of her heartbeat.

"I do not know," Izebal answered, her voice filled with perplexity as she stared down in wonderment.

"The man, the one you called a master mage, he can save her," said Darius as he wrapped his long coat around her and lifted her into his arms, her amulet still in his left hand." I know it now."

"Darius," Izebal started, but her voice trailed off.

"He will save her." Resolution swelled within his soul.

Why? Why was she so important to him? Why did it matter? She was only a child. True, every life mattered, but why so much this little one's? Darius did not know, and quite frankly, he did not care. He had a purpose, a reason to continue. He could save her.

Find them.

The command echoed through the back of his mind.

Find them!

Darius fought against the demanding call to action. He needed to save her. He needed to do this.

Find them, or blood shall rain!

"Son," memories of Elcon's voice rang out in memory. *"Many have given their all to the greater good. I promised I would help you find meaning and purpose. I did not promise it would be what you wanted."*

"I won't leave her!" Darius roared in defiance of the onslaught of voices in his mind.

"Darius, I'm not asking you to leave her," Izebal said tenderly.

It was all too much: the voices, the memories, the guilt, and the pain. Darius's head swam. All the vigor and excitement that had been there only moments before bled away before an onslaught of all-encompassing darkness. Bile rose in his throat and salt filled his mouth.

"Darius, are you alright? Darius! Dar—"

Brilliant light seared Darius's eyes. And then utter darkness consumed him.

CHAPTER 2: PAIN
AELLIA

The air smelt of sweet incense, the vapors floating lazily as golden rays of sunlight washed over the white linen blankets. Motes of dust floated in the air, like tiny fairies dancing on the breeze. It was neither hot nor was it cold. As a matter of fact, it was nearly perfect. Everything felt so, so perfect. And then the pain came upon her.

Aellia cried out, every fiber in her body screaming in agony. Yet, as she did so, a horrible sensation overtook her. Something pulled at her cheek, lips, and eye. White-hot pain flooded through her.

The room in which she lay phased out of existence.

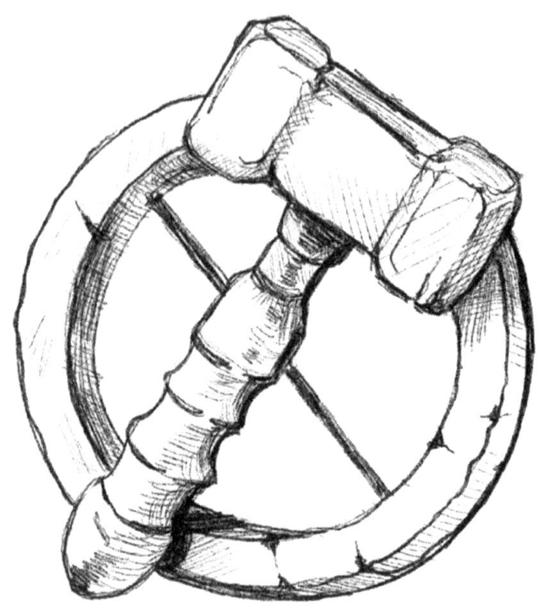

CHAPTER 3: MISTRESS OF DREAMS
DARIUS

Tiny pinpricks of starlight filled a purple, cloudless sky. Snow covered the face of the earth, covering the golden sandals that shod Darius's crystalline feet. Wind howled through gagged peaks, tormenting Darius's ears with its song of ceaseless lamentations. He was once again in the realm beyond, a world of dreams.

"High Father," Darius called out into the eternities. "Why did you bring me here?"

There was no thunder, no demanding voice from beyond.

"High Father, can you hear me?" cried Darius as he strode forward, expecting to find that familiar precipice that overlooked all.

Again, only silence.

What was more disconcerting was the lack of the cliff. There were only endless fields of snow before him. When he turned to look back, he could see mountains that he had never known. Yet, there was a familiarity to them, a dark, terrifying memory that was not his own.

The handprint on his chest suddenly began to burn, the pain of which sent Darius to his hands and knees. Tears filled his eyes, leaking golden light onto the snow about him. As those tears met the white of the snow, hisses spurted forth and they transformed into bouts of steam.

And he was at the foot of the highest mountain.

Darius's head spun, nausea railing against his constitution.

Looking up, he saw a fissure in the mountain, a jagged hole gaping in the grey stone. Stairs carved into the face of the mountain cut back and forth from the ground until they led into that terrible place of darkness.

And he was in that cavern now.

Darius spewed forth upon the cavern floor. His guts felt as if a fire was consuming them, his mind reeling in his aching skull. Again, the scar on his chest burned with agony beyond words. He wanted to tear it from him, rip the very flesh from his body. But he could not bring his hands from the ground, as they bore the whole weight of his body

And he was deep within the heart of the cave, below all else. A stone table with eight sides, eight legs, and eight chairs filled the cavern. Seven of the eight chairs were identical: high-backed chairs of sturdy wood. The eighth was an ostentatious throne, gilded and elaborately carved. Five arches led into the cavernous room, five arches each with a setting for a great gemstone above.

Darius sat now in one of those eight chairs. Across from him sat another. She was robed in white. Over her face was a death mask of silver, and about her head and neck, a white cloth was wrapped. The face of the mask was of a crying woman, pain etched into every feature. The robes were multilayered and ritualistic, the collar high and cuffs of the sleeves drooping. Every thread of the robes was white, save for a strip of cloth that fell from the neck and hung to the naval. It was blood red, and in the middle, embroidered in silver thread, a symbol that sent a cold chill up Darius's spine. An eye, upside down, with flames rising upward.

The figure raised a gloved hand and placed it atop the stone table. She uttered not a sound, but Darius did not miss the clink of metal against stone. When she removed her hand, a silver amulet rested atop the table, an amulet cast in the facsimile of a wolf's head with eyes set of blue sapphires.

"How did—" Darius reached for pockets that did not exist in his thin tunic.

The robed woman tilted her head as if to question Darius's confusion. And though it was utterly impossible, Darius thought the weeping mask smiled back at him. He blinked. The mask was as it had been, mourning and unmoving.

"Why bring me here?" Darius finally asked, gathering his resolve and forcing down his nerves. He had a thousand questions, but he couldn't think straight. So, he asked the first one he could utter.

The woman raised a finger, slowly bringing it to the mask's forehead. Darius felt the whole room shudder. A person of shadow, moving far faster than any human ever could, slid into the room through one of the five archways. Darius instantly recognized the form, not by sight, but by understanding beyond his own comprehension. When he had slain the Itheanam, a face had appeared to him, pale flesh covered with crimson tattoos. Somehow, he knew this was the same face.

"Diabhail," he whispered.

The vision blurred. The masked woman shuddered. And in a way only a dream can confide, Darius knew that name was not a name to utter here. It was painful to her.

More questions came. Who was she? Why did she bring him here? Where was here? What was the purpose?

The dream came back alive, the dark figure moving so fast Darius could barely track his motions. He slid like oil on water, like a shadow. His form flickered like a candle's flame, but there was no light to him. No, not only was there no light, there was darkness beyond comparison, as if all the light was being absorbed by the shadowy figure as he moved around them.

Darius let out a yelp as the shadow figure moved through him, seemingly unaware and unbothered at their placement. This was not happening now. Darius understood. A jolt of pain in the back of his mind came with that understanding. He winced.

The figure vanished.

Chains lay on the table. Five chains. Two shackles for hands, two shackles for ankles, and a collar of black metal for the neck. Runes were now etched into the tabletop.

Rebirth.
Blood.

More pain as he looked over the runes, their meaning searing into his mind.

Vessel.

Agony now surged within him, yet still he strained to look upon the runes.

Lover.
Queen.

No! No, no, no! The word echoed again and again in his mind, but Darius could not utter it, not even once.

Daughter.
Return.

The blood in Darius's vein went cold as ice. He understood with perfect clarity. This was a place of great evil. And this table at which he sat was an abomination.

The silver-masked woman lowered her finger from her forehead and the room blurred. Darius was almost thrown from his seat as if he had been spinning at a great speed and then suddenly brought to an abrupt stop.

The chains and runes vanished in a puff of smoke, and something strange echoed in Darius's ears, though he could not recall what. The sound was familiar but already fleeting. An eerie dread clung to the back of his mind, and already he was forgetting the runes on the tabletop.

The figure in front of him phased in and out of existence, reality blurring.

Darius blinked as if he were warding off sleep. But he knew it was the inverse of such. He was waking. The woman was trying to hold him in the dream. To tell him something, but what?

Urgency was somehow conveyed through the dream, pressed heavily upon Darius's mind. But for what? The link between him and her was growing thin.

"No!" he cried out. But as he did so, he heard himself. Not in the dream, but calling out from his physical body, further separating himself from the dream.

***

"Darius?" Izebal was looking down at him, his head cradled in her arms. She looked worried. Why was she worried? "Darius, come back to me!"

He blinked again. Beyond Izebal, through the canopy of trees, the sky was blue. The air, though still somewhat cool with the oncoming spring, was not icy cold. There was no snow here, only decaying leaves and newly blossoming trees. Darius was back in the world of the living.

"Ethenealal's grace be upon me!" Izebal exclaimed. She then let out a heavy sigh as she raised a trembling hand to her forehead.

She looked exhausted, her face plastered with sweat and worry. Darius, now fully aware of his surroundings, grimaced. The vision was already blurring in his mind. It was different somehow than every other he could recall. Instead of being tired, he felt as if lightning was dancing beneath his skin. His eyes were filled with perfect clarity, the trees and blossoms clear as could be. His ears did not ring in the slightest, and in his state of perfect awareness, he could make out the scurrying of small squirrels and the flutter of birds deep within the forest. Yet it was the thrumming sensation emanating from his left hand that drew the full of his attention.

He sat upright, using his right hand to prop himself. The girl, the amulet, the Itheanam. They were all connected, far more intrinsically than he had realized. The High Father was trying to show him something. That cave from the dream, he knew that cave with a familiarity that was unsettling. Never had he ventured to such a place, but he knew it all the same.

"She wasn't supposed to be there." His words came out raspy; his throat was dry.

"What?"

"The cave. She wasn't supposed to be there," Darius said, his thoughts racing toward the only logical conclusion. "They need her, or someone like her. I've met another in Tur'Mor. A girl with...power. I-I had assumed..."

"Darius, what are you saying?" Izebal asked, leaning in closer.

Darius pushed himself up to his feet, amulet still clutched in his left hand. The skin, though healed, still ached with dull throbbing. He grabbed the hickory staff and his satchel. "Izebal, we have to go now! That girl. I think she is important. Very, very important. I need—" Darius turned about, looking into the trees.

Where had the squirrels gone?

Fear spiked in his mind.

"We have to go, now!" Darius rushed toward the little girl, pulling her up into his arms. "Izebal, hurry!"

"Don't move!" thundered an unfamiliar voice through the trees, followed by a explosive crack and a plume of smoke that sent an instant prickle of dread through Darius's bones.

Quickly, Darius reached out to Bind. However, as soon as he outstretched his hand, something jolted throughout his whole body and a wave of agony singed every nerve in his body. White light arced through his vision before all went dark, and he could have sworn the forming tendrils of blue intertwined.

Nothing like this had ever happened to him before. Never had he felt this pain and disconnect. The sun, though present, seemed so far away in that brief moment of pain. And then the light came back. His veins began to swell with the power of the sun. Yet it was not the same as he had always known. A current of something foreign intermingled with his Binding, causing him to lose hold of it, dropping the rays of sun from his.

A second blast sounded, followed by the gut-wrenching impact of something that wrapped itself around Darius's body, binding him, his hickory rod, and the little girl into a tangled mess.

Mistress of Dreams, Drawn by Aaron Moschner
Cavern Scene

CHAPTER 4: HEALING HOUSE
AELLIA

"She awakens."

"The poor girl."

"She is most fortunate. Look at her face. Nearly healed."

"Ellitheor be praised."

"You did well, sister."

"It is a miracle. An honest-to-god miracle."

"Child, can you hear me?"

Aellia blinked. It sounded like waterfalls were cascading behind her ears. Every fiber of her being felt tighter than a drawn bridge. And her skin, oh, how her skin crawled and itched.

"Daughter, can you hear me?"

Aellia answered, saying she could. But as she spoke, the words that came from her mouth were not her own. They were dull and senseless. Her tongue felt as if it filled her whole mouth, and the salty, bitter taste that coated it was nigh unbearable.

"That's right. You are safe, daughter," said an elderly man whose features were slowly coming into focus. He placed a soft hand on her own. He had short, well-kempt hair, spectacles, and fingers filled with gold and turquoise rings. His smile was kind, his face tender yet knowing.

The surge of fear that went through Aellia's nervous system as his hand touched hers caused the room to spin in her eyes. Nausea filled her already swollen mouth with bile, and she could not help the onslaught of hot tears that ran down the side of her face.

The old man removed his hand very quickly. "I apologize. I did not mean to cause you alarm. My poor daughter. What terrors must you have faced? I pray Gallae's grace upon you."

"She needs sleep."

Aellia looked over and saw what she could only describe as an angel. Hair so red it looked painted. Eyes so blue they must have been cut from gemstones. Upon her freckled chest, an amulet of gold with a faintly glowing sapphire rested.

"Yes, sister." And Aellia knew she was dreaming now, for she saw another angel, the perfect mirror of the first. Red hair like fire, blue eyes like the endless sea, speaking in pitch-perfect harmony with the other. "I have seen one so strong. I would never have thought in my life—"

"Brie," the old man cut in, silencing the angel with the raise of his hand. Without guile or malice, the woman halted her words with a knowing, gentle smile. "Daughter, we are going to help you heal. You have experienced something… incredible. Something terrible. But try to trust me. We only mean to help."

"Come, sister," said Brie. "Let us help her sleep."

"Sister," said the first, stepping gracefully to Aellia's side. She was so beautiful it hurt Aellia to even look at her, as if she glowed with a light from beyond.

Aellia had never been a religious person. Her father had been imprisoned when she was only a child, leaving her mother, and her little brother alone with herself in the streets of Southend. In the cold of winter when the White Fever broke out, all three had caught the deadly illness, leaving Aellia blemished for life, her skin ashen pale and her hair icy white. It had taken her mother and her little brother from her. She could still see them when she closed her eyes, looking like no more than corpses huddled together. She could still hear that last, wheezing cough that rattled Helmar's little chest, the faintest trickle of blood that dripped from his mouth before he followed their mother into the dust. She saw Tomo, and her heart broke again. She could feel more tears pouring from the side of her face, running into her ear and damping the pillow. Tomo, her body like glass, sitting and looking over a purple sky. *"I am not broken, Mirano'ko. I am at peace"*. Tomo's words filled Aellia's mind, memories of that place with the purple skies filling her mind. If there was a heaven beyond, then there were gods, weren't there? How could she deny it? How could she—

More memories came back to her, a thunderous cacophony of sounds and a tirade of images. Tornak, his black eye hemorrhaging darkness, his bitter laugh as he succumbed to the corruption within, just before she had removed his head with Tomo's di'kha. The fight in the cellar. Two demons from Halfak's pits, summoned to destroy her. And Iaenora...

Iaenora!

No answer.

"Sister, be still thy heart." The first of the twin sisters spoke. She had thin, golden chains stretching between rings about her fingers. Blue light shone from her hands, dancing off of the golden links. Aellia tried to move but found her limbs utterly numb.

"Alyn will help you rest, sister," said Brie in soothing tones.

Aellia did not want to rest. She needed to think. She needed to get out. Where was the scepter? Where was Tomo's Di'kha? Where was she? What had happened?

The room began to blur as Alyn's hand descended upon her brow. Waves of cool energy flowed from the touch, soft as summer's rain. Aellia's mind slowed, as did her heart. A soothing warmth filled her body, ebbing away the pain. Sleep came upon her, taking her far, far from this place which she did not know. As she drifted, as if from another place, she heard once more Tomo's voice, *"You are connected to us all now. We can feel you, and I will always be with you."*

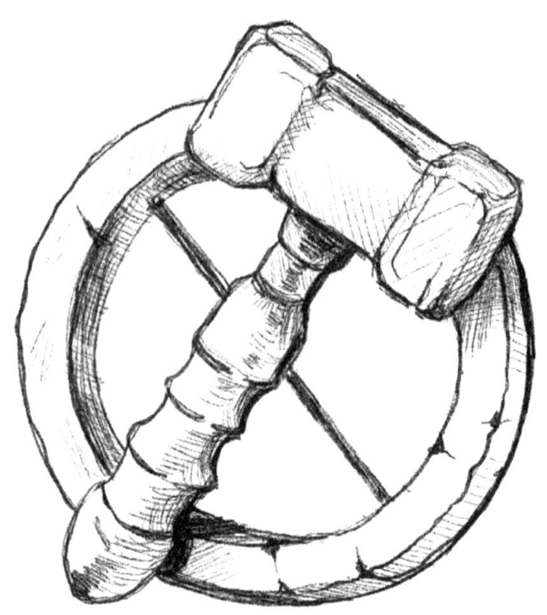

CHAPTER 5: SKOGORTUERS
DARIUS

Half a dozen or so forms moved quickly through the trees, hardly making a sound as they emerged into full view. They were all tall, broad-shouldered men and women with green caps that leaned as if there were about to fall off the sides of their heads, which were shorn across the sides, leaving only a single braided bit of hair running from brow and tied at the nape of the neck. They all wore checkered, forest-green skirts with brown and blue stitching that wrapped over the left shoulder. The only thing that clearly distinguished the genders were the long, braided beards of red, two blonde, and brown that the men wore. Tattoos of blue and black, showing the swirling form of a howling wolf's head, were inked into the shorn sides of their heads, and they had a single piercing in the right ear, where a tooth hung. All of them carried large rifles with short, gleaming bayonets, and an assortment of single-handed weapons at their belts.

"Oye!" shouted the red-bearded man. "What do 'er be doing in the realm of the High Hill?"

Darius stared up at the man. His ears still rang from the blast that had entangled his body with a metallic netting. The shouting man was speaking in such a manner that Darius could hardly make out.

"I'n said, what 'er ye doin' up on the land o' the Lord of Talahmnas?" Anger rose in the man's voice, his neck muscles bulging and his knuckles whitening on the stock of his gun, which was pointed directly at Darius's chest.

"Don't shoot!" Izebal cried out, her voice quivering with pain. "We mean no harm to you. Please, don't shoot!"

"By Ordan's beard!" swore a burly woman with cords of muscles showing on her bare arms. "It do be a bloody-damn Diju! Or me own pa do be a fool!"

The oddly clad troop of men and women all turned their eyes on Izebal, a seething hatred burning within. Darius tried to move, but his arm was bound fast against his chest, the hickory rod intertwined with the net, and the girl tethered to his left side.

"Ye do be right, by blood and stone!" called out another. "She do be a Diju, just look at her!"

"And what do a filthy Diju—" The red-bearded man spat on the ground by Izebal as he sneered "—do be doin' so far from her tents?"

"We just are trying to get the girl to your healer," Izebal pleaded, and it sounded to Darius that she was in excruciating pain.

One look at her face, the tendons raised in her neck and the veins protruding in her forehead, cemented the notion. But why? Why was she in so much pain, and he none at all? The netting was uncomfortable, yes, but it did not cause agony. But that did not change the fact that Izebal was experiencing something horrific. Darius's gut lurched and anger began to boil within.

There was a sharp crack.

The leading female raised her hand again. "Ye don't speak another word, ye filthy witch! Or so help me, by the grace of Gallea, I'll split y'er skull with me own hand!"

"Easy," said the red-bearded man, grabbing the woman's wrist before she could strike Izebal's face again. He then looked from Izebal's whimpering form over to Darius. Their eyes met, and Darius swore he could feel his blood boil.

Darius reached out, seeking the familiar power of the sun. He opened himself to—"Ack!" He arched his back and let out a scream of pain. The cords that wrapped around his body turned red with heat, causing his eyes to cloud. The sunlight that had been so close fractured, the ray shattering like glass just before it touched his ring.

"What in Halfak's damn-bloody gates was that?" swore one of the strangers, turning a confused expression onto Darius's crumpled body as he used the heel of his boot to roll him over.

"That ain't a Diju if I've seen one," said a second, looking between Darius and Izebal.

"Blood and stone! The chut has got a bairn!" called out the first, boot still on Darius's shoulder, bright green eyes filled with fury. "Nee'av! Come over here, take a look at this!"

"Aye, commander!" said perhaps the most muscular woman Darius had ever laid eyes upon. Her neck was as thick as a felled log and her bare arms were corded with muscle and sinews, crisscrossed with bulging veins. She wore a tartan like the rest, but on the base of her pleated skirt, just above the right knee, a silver pin of a two-handed sword behind a ram's head was placed.

"She do be a proper Danelander, that be certain," Nee'av said as she knelt down near Darius's head, looking through the silver cordage that entangled him and the girl together.

"Any markings?" the man barked out. "Any crest or insignia?"

Darius clenched his fist tighter, the wolf's head amulet he had taken off her just moments before cutting into the meat of his palm and fingers.

"None I can see, Orhund," Nee'av answered, eyeing the girl the best she could in her current state.

"You," Commander Orhund barked, looking down at Darius, his boot still on his shoulder. Darius flashed a fury-filled gaze up at the man as he hounded him again, "What're ye doing in Ranok, this close to the border?"

Darius stared directly into the man's eyes, focusing on restraining the boiling rage that was being pumped through his veins by his pounding heart. He took a deep breath through his nose and grunted out, "She needs help. She's hurt."

"Don't touch him!" cried out Izebal at the same time Darius had answered.

"Shut y'er filthy mouth, Diju!" a bearded behemoth lashed out. "I ought to cut that poisoned tongue out of y'er mouth!"

The boiling blood in Darius's veins went cold as ice, his hammering heart thudding into silence.

"Lad's got's some stones, does he?" Nee'av laughed, standing up and barking out a harsh laugh. "Think he's been enthralled by that their Diju. He ain't one, that's a fact."

"He has a child," Orhund answered, eyes still hard on Darius, searching him for...something. Then, he just broke his stare, turning to his band of warriors. "Get'm up and grab two kroichae! Now!"

The whole group sprang into action, grabbing up Darius's satchel that lay next to his bedding, kicking over Izebal's tents she had crafted, and rummaging through their belongings. Subtly as he was able, Darius moved his arm, pinned as it was to his side, and tucked the girl's amulet into his trousers.

"She couldn't be her, could she?" said Orhund to Nee'av under his breath, Darius's enhanced ears picking up their side conversation.

"She ain't look it. Too thin and her bones is all wrong," Nee'av replied in a whisper.

"You ever see yellows like that?" Orhund asked apprehensively.

"It's that bloody Diju, must have a spell on him or whatnot."

"Commander," a younger female warrior said. There was a tattoo of a lark on her neck in blue ink, and her strawberry blonde hair was pulled into two tight, braided rows across her scalp. "What next?"

"Take Tuli and Angul, get word to the Wall, to Pritfort of Iron Keep," Orhund answered. "I ain't taking no chances."

"Commander," the young woman said as she jerked a stiff hand up to the brow of her tilted cap.

Orhund echoed the motion and then dropped his hand, dismissing the woman. She rushed towards two men, whose tattooed faces made them look like demons from one of Elcon's stories. There was a quick exchange, of which Darius heard nothing, and they were off in a silence of motion that startled him. How were such colossal individuals able to move through the forest so quietly? Bitterness filled his guts—bitterness and shame—for allowing them to be taken in such a manner, totally unaware.

"Where are those bloody kroichae?" Orhund barked, the harsh, broken words drawing Darius back to his immediate surroundings.

A woman produced two black collars with long chains dangling from them for a pouch that hung from her waist. As soon as the black iron became visible, Darius saw Izebal go stiff, terror filling her eyes.

"Get the witch first!" said Orhund. The behemoth of a man turned and faced Darius, looking over him like a slab of rotten meat. He snorted and then hocked out a wad of phlegm and said, "We'll get ye right tight, don't ye worry. Won't affect a non-mage the same, but ye will be held fast."

Despite what the man had said, as soon as the black collar was locked around his neck, a bout of icy lightning surged through his body. His joints tightened and his muscles flexed, causing his back to arch and his head to tear back in agony. He tried to scream, to howl at the pain, but no sound came from his mouth. As suddenly as the pain had taken him, it subsided, rendering his muscles useless. He fell in a heap upon the forest floor, face striking with a resounding thud. The last image he saw before he faded into the black of unconsciousness was Izebal, silently screaming as two men wrestled her to the ground and clamped a similar collar about her neck.

***

Darius awoke with a start. His hands were cuffed in front of him, a strong cord running from his wrists to an iron eyelet affixed to the panel of a small cart. Across from him, a beautiful woman in a green dress was propped against a rucksack, along with his satchel, coat, and a stick, stacked neatly. When he tried to recall as to where he had seen the woman before—something about her was vaguely familiar—his mind went blank. And as he tried to rummage through his mind, Darius felt a far stranger sensation, one which scared him far more than he thought possible when he realized what it was. He could not feel the sun.

They rode in an open-top wagon pulled by two horses down a path that appeared to be well-traveled. The trees were cut back so that the canopy did not cover the trail and sunlight beamed down from a cloudless sky. Despite this, Darius could not feel the rays of sunlight upon him. He could not feel their familiar warmth nor the power or need to Bind. He felt hollow, empty, and devoid of all sensation. A hopelessness set upon his soul that he could not comprehend, burrowing deep.

"Oye, Orhund," called out Nee'av, who was sitting behind the driver and holding a strange firearm, unlike anything Darius had ever seen. The weaponry of Tur'Mor had been long and slender,

44

polished and glistening. These were brutish and fixed with bronze fittings. They had great wheels and three octagonal barrels stacked like a triangle. She held the firearm with an eagerness that did not send any feelings of comfort to Darius. "The big'n's awake."

Darius heard her speak, and just as when he had first met Brue and Rauel outside the Temple of Ordan, their strange speak slowly cleared into a more rhythmic and comprehendible tongue.

"He doing anything, Nee'av?" Orhund responded tersely from his position driving the wagon, not even deigning to turn his head back.

"Nah," scoffed Nee'av. "Just sitting there. Haven't ever seen one like him before. The bloody Diju must have a real hold on him."

Darius's head felt as if it were stuffed with cotton. He could not understand why he was here nor what had led to this moment. When he tried to think back to anything further than coming-too only moments ago, a splitting headache overtook him.

"Kroichae, laddie," snorted Nee'av as she used the tri-barrel of her gun to tap the collar about his neck, and then moved it toward the sleeping woman, saying, "Seen that look before. That there bloody witch had you in a spell. This severs anything like that. Who knows how long you've been under her thumb, but we'll get you right as rain, blood and stone we will."

"Tyree is gonna have a trip with you, laddie," said Orhund.

Tyree? Tyree... That name sounded familiar. Why did Darius know that name? He winced as he tried to think. He raised his hands to massage his face, but they were stopped by the cords binding him to the floor of the cart. *What is going on?*

"Easy there, laddie. No need to get work up a bother," said Nee'av slowly. "Just keep calm. We'll be at the Wall soon enough. Blood and stone, I never..." she trailed off with a laugh and a shake of her head. She then reached into the pouch that hung off her hips and produced a small tin can. Keeping one hand on the butt of her firearm, she opened the tin with a deft thumb, took a pinch of a red paste, and placed it under her bottom lip. "Hammer of Ordan, that hits the spot."

Darius faded.

***

When Darius awoke again, stars filled the sky and the sounds of the night danced on a gentle breeze. For a moment, before lucidity took him, Darius found it to be peaceful and wondrous. But as the fog on his mind thinned, the familiar sensation of fear snuck back into his muddled thoughts. Bound and helpless, he was moving forward to an unknown place with no control or power. He felt small and weak, a rather foreign sensation.

"Wall!" cried out a mounted warrior.

"Send 'em up!" Orhund barked.

Darius lulled his head to the side just in time to see three mounted warriors hoist strange pistols into the air, their barrels flaring out at the end like backward funnels.

Boom! Boom! Boom!

All three shots were fired one right after the other, filling the night sky with smoke and fire. Darius nearly jumped from his skin, and perhaps he would have had the cording binding him not held him from doing so. Memories from the back of his mind flashed. The forest. There were men in black leathers. There was a woman, crying. He had been shot. There was a woman crying, dressed in green.

While Darius tried to piece his fractured and missing memories together, the forest in front of him opened into a vast field of flowing grasses and rolling hills. Air, sweet and fresh, cascaded over him, bringing a sensation of freedom unlike anything he had ever known, or rather, that he could recall in his current state. Days, if not weeks, had passed since he had first entered that ancient forest. It had been days since he had breathed in fresh air and seen more than a few feet in front of him. And across that sea green, a towering wall stood in defiance against the world. It was old and grey, appearing as if some ancient giant had lain their sword across the valley. At the center of the wall, two imposing towers and an angular portcullis made up the gatehouse.

Even from such a distance as they were, and with black metal about his neck, Darius could still see soldiers walking the tops of the walls, tiny figures in dull armor that shone in the moonlight. Two long, resounding thuds rang out, low and lasting. Darius turned his attention to the gatehouse, where a cylinder of bronze still vibrated from being struck by wooden hammers. The whole valley seemed to awaken at the resounding sound.

"Best be on y'er best behavior," Nee'av said with a smirk. "Master Tyree will get whatever hold is on your head off."

Darius just looked at her dumbly. He knew something was wrong, he could feel it. But his mind could not focus. Like the dull reverberations from the bell, there was ringing, but no solid thought. He looked once more at the woman in green and could not help but feel some connection to her, some deep sense of protection.

"Don't worry about her, now," said Nee'av, her voice darkening as she looked over. "She'll get what she's got coming to her. Been girls missing, figured it was dirty Diju taken' 'em."

Something about what the woman was saying was not right. Darius knew that, but he could not find the words to argue, nor the will or wherewithal. He felt like a child, confused and helpless. Unable to comprehend the actions of all those around him. And still... it was not right of her to say that of the woman in green.

"Blood and stone," Nee'av shook her head as she laughed. "That witch did a number on you, laddie. Can't speak nor what? Never seen the kroichae do nothing like that before."

"Quit kicking the rock, Nee'av." Orhund's voice was low and hard. "Laddie's mind ain't right. I'm more worried about the lassie. She does nae look right."

"You don't think this chut messed with her." Nee'av kicked Darius in the leg as she spoke.

"Ain't like anything I've ever seen," Orhund answered heavily. "Blood and stone, it ain't."

"Tyree can help her." Nee'av's voice brightened slightly. "Always does."

"She looks half gone," Orhund's voice dropped even lower. "Like a Redeye got 'er."

Nee'av made a quick motion with her right hand, two fingers quickly touching her left breast, sliding across to the right, then back to her sternum and straight down. Her lips moved silently, uttering an unspoken prayer of sorts. Darius had seen something not too dissimilar practiced in the Sanctuary and Temple of Ordan, a sort of warding off of evil. But when he tried to think about it, his mind muddled once more.

A thunderous voice rolled over the valley, amplified by a great horn atop the gatehouse of the wall. "Who approaches the Spanning Wall? Who comes northward to the realm of the Great Wolf of Talahmnas?"

The cart came to a halt and Orhund rose in the driver's seat, answering loudly, "Hail! Orhund of the Skogortuers seeks passage to Talahmnas! I did send ahead to make known my coming!"

There was a long pause of silence. The sounds of the night faded into an uncomfortable stillness. Darius could not sense unease or worry. He could not sense anything at all. He was utterly numb, save for a cool, tingling sensation on his left hand, where a strange bit of silver rested. He cocked his head and peered at it. A strange thing, his memories were. He could recall moments of his life, images, and people. But nothing was solid, like fog over a lake on a cool morning, the hot rays of the sun ready to sweep them away. Nothing save this ring.

An urge came upon him, a sort of primal thing, one which he could not comprehend. An intense desire to extend his hand into the pale light of the moon. To somehow tether himself to her rays. Slowly his hand raised, reading into the cool light. The hairs on his hand, forearm, and the back of his neck raised. There was something he needed to say, wasn't there?

"Oye!" Nee'av hissed. "Put y'er blood hand down or I'll break every bone y'er got! Cursed or not, I'll not have ye causing any trouble, ye hear. Bloody little chut."

Darius held his hand outstretched a moment longer, then dropped it into his lap. What was he thinking? What was going on?

"Forward! To the gate!" called the amplified voice from the wall.

Orhund cracked the reigns and the cart lurched forward, leaving Darius confused and cold once more.

CHAPTER 6: SOME WOUNDS HEAL
AELLIA

Aellia drifted in and out of consciousness. Time passed in a blur, and she could not tell if she had slept for two hours or two weeks. The pain across her face was nigh unbearable, so she found those few lucid moments pure agony. But the fear of the void that overtook her when she slept terrified her more than the pain. Far more, for in that void there was always that man. That terrible, horrible man. Eyes of death seemed to stare directly into her soul, filled with an insatiable, carnal hunger. Images of skin cracked and putrid, covered in crimson ink—rivers of blood that carved wicked ravines into ashen flesh—were burned into her mind, haunting her dreams.

So her days passed into nights and nights into sunrises. An endless cycle of pain and fear, a wheel of torment that she could not escape, that went on and on, driving her closer and closer to madness. She felt as if she were on a precipice, and all it would take to send her toppling over into ruin was the faintest breeze, the slightest touch, the most meager of motions. And it would all be over.

Could it be over?

Would it end?

Aellia thought, if not for the first time, that perhaps the void of nothingness that awaited her was better than this. This constant fear, this constant hurt. She wanted out. She wanted to scream. But she could not even do that. The left side of her face was stitched, her tongue still so swollen it felt as if it pressed upon every part of her mouth at once, and two or three teeth were missing. Something soft was wrapped about her left eye, under her chin, and across her forehead, binding her head together, a binding that Aellia was sure was the only thing keeping her head from falling into pieces.

She blinked, trying to focus on the room she was beginning to believe she would never leave. The ostentatious room had high and painted ceilings; just like the Uppers to paint fat little babies with wings, nude women, and fair men traipsing through golden fields of grain when a quarter of their city was literally starving to death. The paneled walls were hung with tapestries and great paintings in gilded frames, depicting Ordiatian religious scenes such as the Creation of Ethrea, the Sailing from Vanherran, the Calling of Men, and of course, the Fall.

Aellia felt something turn in her stomach as she looked at that terrible scene. Ordan, the High Father of Ethrea, stood over his two daughters, he held a great hammer in his hand, and his wrath was terrible to behold. The two women, as was tradition, had their faces covered in veils of black, matching their robes. They held their heads downward, peering into a circular pit of flame: Halfak's Gates. She had seen such depictions before, but for some reason, this one seemed to ignite something deep within her soul. As she looked closer, she saw six stars haloing the High Father's head, three emeralds and three sapphires.

Aellia tried to sit up, to look more closely at the painting, but a sudden lance of pain sent her head spinning. She cried out in agony, the hurt so sudden and sharp she could not control herself.

The door at the far side of the room swung open moments later, which seemed like an eternity, and through the opening walked that same old man with white hair and garish attire. Despite her pain, Aellia still found it in her to loathe this man.

"Daughter," the old man said as he drew ever closer to her. "Are you alright? I heard you shouting."

He placed a hand upon her shoulder and Aellia wished that she could lash out, strike the man for touching her. How dare he touch her? How dare he put his wrinkled, perverse hand on her body? She tried to swear at him, but her swollen mouth uttered nothing more than weakening, unintelligible sounds.

"Gentle, daughter," the old said, patting her lightly. Aellia's skin crawled and bile rose in her throat to her mouth, tainting her swollen tongue with acrid bitterness. "You are getting stronger, but you're not healed yet."

The old man paused and let out a deep, weary sigh. He rose from the bed and walked to one of the glass doors that faced the inner garden of the mansion. Well, Aellia assumed it was so. She had robbed plenty of manors in the Valamour, and despite their subtle differences, they almost all were built around a central garden or fountain area, adorned with plants and mosaic tiles of bright colors and patterns.

"To tell you the truth," the old man continued, not looking back at Aellia as he spoke, but clasping ringed hands behind his back and staring into the distance. "I am not sure what happened to you. I have my theories. But, nothing like this has happened in this age. Not in a good many. Not even Alyn's Touch has fully restored you. Perplexing, no?"

Aellia wanted to spit at the man, to jump out of the bed and thrust a dagger into his back. What right had he to keep her here? What right had he to touch her?

"Whatever happened to you, daughter, it was not a natural thing," said the man as shook his head, heavy with consternation. "Perplexing. An unusual word. An unusual word. Yet, it does bite. I am perplexed and I am vexed." He laughed, making Aellia feel all the more uncomfortable.

The door opened once again, drawing both Aellia's and the old man's attention. One of those angels from Aellia's dreams—if they were dreams, as she was questioning the lucidity of those moments now—walked into the room.

Dressed in a blue gown of silk, with hair red like fire and a face so perfectly shaped it made Aellia jealous, the young woman who had attended her so often seemed to drift melodically toward her. At least, Aellia assumed the woman was no older than she was, maybe middle twenties. And she was not sure if melodically was the right word, but somehow it made sense in her addled mind, for when the young woman moved, it was in perfect time and air seemed to sing a silent song as she approached Aellia's side.

"How are you feeling?" she asked in such sweet, gentle tones that Aellia could not help lowering her guard. The cool, comforting touch of her hand as it passed over the skin of Aellia's forehead sent goose pimples across her body.

Aellia's dumb silence was apparently expected, for the woman gave the slightest smile and said, "I am going to check your face. I hope you don't mind, but I will be removing the bandages."

What was Aellia to say to that if even she could answer? No, I don't think I'd like that. How would she stop her? It hurt worse than death for her to even try to sit up.

With deft hands, the young woman unraveled the wrappings about Aellia's face. She started with the one that went from the top of her head to under her jaw. The sweet scent of incense and the pungent fragrance of the poultice wafted into the air as the bandages came away.

The healer's lips turned down in the faintest manner, if only for a second, as she removed the cloth from the jaw and cheek. She did not slow for more than a second or two, but the bolt of worry that filled Aellia's gut at seeing that angelic face turn even the slightest bit concerned was disconcerting. But what could she do? Nothing.

"Look, Master Elcon," she said without turning away from her work. "See how the wound festers? The stitching holds, but the flesh does not seem to bind."

"Alyn," said the old man. "It is not your fault. This is something unlike we have ever dealt with before."

The young woman, Alyn, did not answer for a long moment, just stared down at Aellia's face, with large, questioning eyes. Aellia, for her part, could not help but feel a little embarrassed, as if she were intruding in another's private moments. Except, this moment definitely included her.

Alyn let out a sigh and went back to unraveling the bandages. Elcon now stood over her shoulder, staring down at Aellia as if she were some bit of meat a butcher was sizing up to carve. Again. Aellia felt the need to escape, to run away and not look back. Throughout her whole life, there had only been two men she had been comfortable around, other than her father, and they were Felik and Tornak. And Tornak had betrayed her. He had been the reason Tomo had died...

"Gentle, daughter," Alyn said, sensing the rising anger in Aellia's body language. "If you thrash about, it can damage the sutures and cause the wound to reopen."

Aellia glared at the woman with her single unbound eye. However, for some reason beyond her understanding, she could not find it in herself to hate Alyn. She wanted to. This was an Upper, one of the Church's Blessed. She wanted to hate her for not saving her mother or brother, for where was this healing ability when they lay drowning in their own bile? Those wretched, horrid bouts of coughing. They never left her ears.

Unaware of Aellia's darker thoughts, the young woman began to slowly move the wrappings about her left eye. Alyn stopped short, however, as shock and awe filled her face. The old priest, not allowing any space for the healer to work in peace, hurried up to Aellia's side and glared down at her, his own eyes widening in fascination.

Aellia tried to ask what they were gawking at, but all that came from her feeble lips were a smattering of unintelligible sounds. Then, a searing lance of pain. She had, up to this point, been unable to open her mouth in the slightest thanks to the binding about her jaw. It had frustrated her to no end. Now she wished it were still there to keep her from her own stupidity.

"Completely drained," muttered Elcon.

"I have never..."

"Do you mind, Daughter?" Elcon asked. The healer nodded her assent and the old priest reached his bejeweled fingers toward Aellia's face. She jerked, an action she regretted instantaneously, as pain and dizziness filled her head. "By the High Father's throne..."

The old man was holding a multifaceted gemstone of the most pale blue Aellia had ever seen. She had to admit even through the pain that assailed her that the way the sapphire caught the morning light was truly beautiful, but why were they so enamored by it?

"By Gallae's grace!" The healer exclaimed, her eyes widening in shock.

"What is it?" Elcon asked, nearly dropping the gemstone he had just been admiring in his haste.

"Her eye! Look at it!" Alyn gasped as she leaned in over Aellia. A ringlet of red hair brushed Aellia's cheek as Alyn peered down at her, further muddling Aellia's mind as the scent of it wafted to her.

"By the Ellitheor!" Elcon drew even closer, raising his spectacles and calling out, "Maid! Maid!"

Through the door rushed in a little woman, plump and pristine, every bit of her the perfect specimen of posh living and subservient demeanor. Aellia detested her instantly. The desire to reach out and slap her as the little rat scurried to her master's side was only staunched by the insistent knowledge that her arms were as useful as a puppet's without their puppeteer's guiding.

"Go now, to my office. On my desk is a box. Bring it," Elcon said hurriedly, not looking away from Aellia for even a moment. "Take the two Aluth that guard the doorway, they should be able to carry it for you."

The little woman bowed low, raising a golden hammer that hung from a beaded chain to her forehead as she did so, and turned to leave without a word.

"Oh, and have the other item there brought as well. They'll know what it is," Elcon said with a smile, still not turning away from Aellia, his hazel eyes lighting with excitement.

"She is not healed fully," Alyn said hesitantly. "Are you sure she is ready?"

"Daughter, I am not sure of anything anymore." Elcon laughed, leaning back for the first time, giving Aellia room to breathe. He stopped short, then chuckled. "Probably best not to repeat that to Orrum. I hope you know that I do not question the faith. Just... so many changes. So many things coming to fruition so rapidly."

The room went silent, neither having anything to say. Aellia felt a strange awkwardness settle between them. Up until this very moment, the two had been prodding her, studying her, gasping about her, but now, silence. It was unbearable.

"You should not have sent him away," Alyn said after a long moment.

Elcon cocked an eyebrow, a hard line drawing across a wrinkled brow. Aellia had no idea how old the man was. At times, he looked to be no older than his late sixties, but in that moment, had someone told her he was one hundred and five, she would have asked, *is that all?*

"Daughter," he said slowly. "Do not pretend to understand the machinations of our Holy Patriarch."

"Brie said—"

"Is she Blessed, or is she the Patriarch?" Elcon snapped, all humor leaving his voice.

Aellia felt a jolt of fear rush through her. Who was this man? How dare he speak to this divine woman in such a manner? How dare—

"Apologies, High Priest," Alyn said in deference, bowing her head and making the mark of the hammer across her chest.

Elcon's face softened, and his demeanor changed back to the astute, scholarly man that had first interred the room. "Daughter, perhaps it is best you return to the Temple. You have been gone far too long, and the Light of the Ellitheor dims within your Ra'el Aund."

"As you say, High Priest," Alyn rose. "Would you have me bind her once more before I leave? The wound is not wholly sealed."

"Daughter, you have done so much good here," Elcon said, rising to his feet as well. "May the grace of Gallae and the strength of Ordan go with you." He raised a hand as he spoke, touching Alyn's brow with his thumb, and then moved it to either cheek.

Aellia felt a pang of discomfort as she watched helplessly from the bed. She hated that the old man would dare touch that woman that way. It did not matter if it was symbolic or ritualistic. It was wrong, and Aellia hated him for it.

Alyn, in turn, pressed her lips to the largest of the rings on Elcon's hand before turning to leave.

"Despite my ill-humored witticism earlier, Orrum needs to know of this," Elcon said to Alyn's back. "Would you please inform our High Patriarch of this change?"

Alyn stopped but did not turn or look back. "Yes, High Priest, as you would have, so shall I do."

Aellia, unable to hold her head up any longer, let it fall back into the feather pillow, losing sight of the pale dress of the angel that had attended her. Never in her life had she imagined seeing someone like that. It was not a thing of lust. No. It was a thing of purity and raw beauty, something that Aellia did not think existed. Not in this place, this city of greed and pain. But there she went, walking away, causing Aellia to question everything she believed about the Church that had turned her family away, the gods they worshipped.

"Now, daughter, you'll be most pleased," Elcon said with a smile, turning his attention back onto her. "If do say so myself."

Aellia could not move, not anymore. She had lost her will to fight the anger. She hurt, so badly. Her mind, her body, her soul, they were all ablaze. Pain and aguish gnawed at her, causing the ever-darkening tunnel to overtake her vision.

"Daughter? Daughter!" Elcon's voice had moved from jovial to panic. "Daughter!"

From somewhere, far, far away, she heard an oddly familiar voice.

"Aellia!"

Tears burned at her eyes. That voice. No. That was impossible.

But she knew it.

Darkness fell upon her eyes.

Interim 1

Una'pahu

Captain Marcel

Ranella

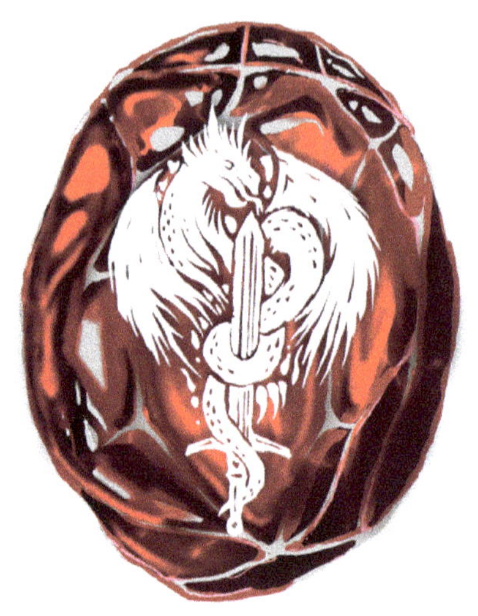

~Una'pahu~

Una'pahu burst out of the trees and onto the forsaken beach, her bare feet carrying her swiftly toward the crumpling form of her Msa'oo. Tears of pain, exhaustion, and terror, all mixed together streamed down her face. She ran so fast, so fast, but not fast enough. She could not change what had happened, she could barely believe it.

Three weeks ago, she set out on a voyage to master the art of the Ta'ala Gau, mystical women who were able to control the waves of the sea. Or, as they were also known, Wave Guiders. But something terrible had happened, something that she was not sure she understood, even now. The ship, the *Pearl of Red Duchess*, had been attacked by the accursed *Black Sister* and her undead crew of Biters, led by none other than Captain Reylelan.

Reylelan. The very thought of her name sent a chill through Una'pahu's spine and warm bile into her mouth. But she could not stop. Not now. For, in the taking of the *Pearl of Red Duchess,* Reylelan had subjected Una'pahu and two of her dearest friends to a living nightmare. Torture, depravity, humiliation, and so many more terrible things. And through those things, somehow, Seamus, her loving, kind, silly Msa'oo, had been transformed into something terrible.

Una'pahu reached him, kneeling in the sand. On his back, charred flesh still glowed red hot, just over the shoulder blades. She had seen wings of flames sprout from there moments ago.

What had happened to him? What had that demon done to her Quickie?

In Seamus's right hand, he gripped the white hilt of a sword so massive no human could possibly lift it with a single hand. And even if they could, how could they possibly wield it? The blade was brilliant white, and in the cross-guard a gemstone gleamed with light, illuminating further the distinction of the right side of his body to the left. Pale skin and red hair on the right, melted and mangled flesh that looked as if it had formed scales on the left. She could not see his face, but she had to imagine it was as grotesque as his back.

"I couldn't stop her," Seamus said. "But I will find her."

The very sound of his voice broke her heart. Where was the joy, the levity? It cracked and seethed from his lips. He did not turn and face her. Just knelt facing the sea, the surf rolling endlessly. Despite the cracked and dry voice, there was also something else. A faint regality that had not been there, a deep strength that reverberated outward in his words.

"Msa'oo," Una'pahu stretched out a hand and touched his shoulder. He flinched at her touch. And though he probably did not mean to do so, this sent a further ripple of pain and anguish through her heart. "It is not your fault."

"I doomed us to this forsaken island."

Seamus had been crying. His words were broken and fumbled, as they always were after he had wept. But there was something else, as she had noticed before. Something deeper to him.

"But I will get us out of this," Seamus said, resolution building as he spoke. He grabbed the hilt of that massive sword more firmly.

Was that light sinking into him? No...

"I will take us back, and I will take back what is mine that she stole from me," Seamus rose to his feet and turned to face Una'pahu.

She gasped.

She hadn't meant to but did so all the same.

The whole left side of his body, from his waist to the missing ear on his head, was covered in purplish-red scarring. But that was not the only thing that caused Una'pahu to gasp. No. He was taller, much taller. Nearly a head and shoulders taller than her now. Muscles rippled from his once lean frame. And his eyes. By the great goddess Gallae, his eyes! The right one was haloed with white. Not white like an eye should be, but white more bright and pure than anything Una'pahu had ever seen. Whiter than the marbled floors of the temples, whiter than clouds in the sky. And then there was his left eye. A slit for an iris, yellow as flame, the pupil black as raven's wings, and the eye itself, red as death.

"It is okay," said Seamus as he looked from her to his left hand. "I am deformed, burned, and broken. But I am still me... sometimes. I can always hear them, feel them."

"What... what happened?" Una'pahu asked, eyes seeing what her mind could not comprehend.

"Well," Seamus started but then stopped suddenly. A smile flickered across his lips. A smile that, despite all the changes, was uniquely Seamus. "Oye! Lightfoot, what took you so long?"

Una'pahu turned about and saw the third member of their little band wheezing as he closed the distance. The bespectacled boy— well, she really couldn't call him a boy anymore, none of them were children now, not in any sense of the word—she had left behind her as she had raced towards the beach had finally made his way to them. He had once been far more plump, more timid. What she saw now was somehow had looked death in the face and overcame it. He had lost weight, quite a lot of it, actually.

"By Gallae, Mother of Grace, Henri!"

"What? What? What is it?" His words spewed out through gasping pants, eyes frantically searching the tree line as he whipped his head about.

"You are hurt," Una'pahu answered, heart breaking at the sight of Henri, battered and ragged.

"Me?" Henri scoffed as his shoulders dropped in a sigh of relief. "You seen yourself? What about flame boy over there?"

"Easy, Lightfoot, or I might roast you," Seamus laughed, joining in with Henri's benign affront.

Despite the levity of the words, Una'pahu could see the hurt behind his jovial eyes. But they were all hurt; Henri had spoken true. They had been through Halfak's pits and back again, their youth burnt away. And yet, they were here together now. They had survived torture and imprisonment. They had survived assault and mental deprivations no human should ever endure, and still they stood.

Unable to hold back the dam of emotions any long, Una'pahu thrust her left hand out and grabbed Henri by the shoulder pulled him toward her while simultaneously grasping for Seamus. Despite the cruel burn marks across his left side, he allowed himself to be pulled into the hug, and even wrapped his arms about them.

They stood there for a long moment, friends holding themselves upright. They stood on that beach and held onto the only things and people they had left. Captain Atura was gone, brutalized and murdered before her very eyes for the sick pleasure of Captain Reylelan. Captain Charlie was gone, his death a mystery and certainty; none survived the sacking of the Pearl of Red Duchess. Even the masked figure called Specter was nowhere to be found. It was only they three. And that was more than enough for her breaking heart right now.

"I can heal you, Henri." Una'pahu finally broke the hug and the silence. "Here, let me help you."

Henri looked puzzled at her words, and in truth, she was still unsure exactly what she could do with her newfound abilities. She could hear the waves and the seas, the streams and the rivers. Like blood pumping through a beating heart, she could feel them. Yet there seemed to be something, the slightest veil, separating her from them. She could touch, feel, sense, but was never truly one with them. Captain Reylelan had tortured her night after night, attempting to break the barrier between her mind and the power that emanated from the rod in her huva-huva. The very rod her mother had sent her to sea with due to her ability to make the strange gemstone set in its head shine with brilliant light.

Una'pahu drew forth the Oathrod, taking hold of it in weak but steady hands, and opened her soul to the essence of the gemstone. Power coursed through the rod and into her body, steady and strong. Waves of strength washed over her weakened muscles and sinews, strengthening her for the task of healing. With all the control she could muster, she released her left hand as she dropped down to the sands and surf, and placed it into the water.

A cold chill surged through her body as the sea granted its lifeforce to her. Millions of lives, past and current, thrummed in her heart as the waves slowly crashed over the deserted island.

Henri's eyes suddenly went very wide.

Speaking words unknown to even herself, Una'pahu rose from her knees. Tiny strands of water coursed back and forth between her and the sea, their bioluminescent strands twisting and twirling in kaleidoscopic patterns. This was not just her doing, it was something else, something beyond her comprehension. And yet it was as natural as breathing.

"Be still, and feel of the love of the Mother of Earth and Water, of all things that live, and have lived, and will for ever live in her. Feel the power of Gallae, in whose heart is the true power of Ria'Elahm."

Una'pahu's voice was powerful and strong, far deeper than her own voice, and filled with sage wisdom. Her hand, which was stretched out toward her friend, pulse with emerald light.

Henri flinched as the light from her hand cascaded over him, soaking him in green liquid. It was not water, for his clothes were not wet. It was not light, for light could not cause his flesh and hair to ripple and toss. In truth, Una'pahu was not exactly sure what it was, but the results were undeniable.

Cuts mended, bruises faded, and gashes closed. The wrappings about his forehead fell away, and all that was left was a puckered scar that made him look far more mature than he had before, not diminishing in any way. Then, as suddenly as it had started, the threads of water that danced and turned, fell away, losing their structure and their shine. The light faded into darkness, and the three were standing alone in pale moonlight once more.

"Now that's a right handy trick." Henri laughed, eyes wide with disbelief as his hands traced his face.

"I guess we're all changed," Seamus said solemnly. "Aren't we?"

"We are." Una'pahu turned and faced him. "And yet, we're the same. We are still together. And that is what matters most."

"And what if I am not safe to be around?" His face darkened as he spoke, worry furrowing his brow as something ancient flashed behind his eyes. Una'pahu even thought for a moment she saw a flicker of fire there.

"Quickie." Her words were placating, she could tell that, but she could not lose him, not again. "Reylelan did terrible things to us. Perhaps I can heal your burns, like Henri." She reached a hand out, but Seamus jerked away from it.

"It wasn't her," was all he said as he backed away slowly from them, as if some dark fear had awoken inside him. "It was me. It was my fault. This was all fault. It was me. It was me. I did this. I should burn. It should burn. It was me. Burn it all! Burn it all!"

"Lightfingers, what's wrong?" Henri said, stepping toward his friend with an outstretched hand.

"Don't touch me!" Seamus roared, his voice cracking under the strain. He breathed out, a single long breath. And then, one, two, three more slower, more controlled breaths followed. "Please...please stay back. I... I don't want to hurt anyone."

"What happened to you in that cave?" Una'pahu asked, she too stepping closer to Seamus, not away.

"I..." Seamus faltered. "I don't know."

And even as he spoke, something heavy fell over him, as if his countenance changed in that very instance. His irises turned a pale white as his back straightened. With a resolution unusual to Seamus's quick-witted manner, he said, "We go on."

Seven generals sat around an octagonal table upon whose surface was a sprawled map of the borderlands between Ordiatea and Calun. Seven generals sat in lavish topcoats and high hats with embroidered symbols of their prestigious ranks. Seven generals sat, fat and proud, glaring down the man who stood with his back to them, hands clasped together with perfect poise. Marcel, the man once known as Felik, stood on the opposite side of the tent, his own uniform starched and pressed, itching at his neck and sending a steady trickle of sweat down his back. Next to him, a dozen or so other captains and lieutenants stood at parade rest, the silver stars at their shoulders polished to a gleam and the toes of their boots reflecting the candelabra light.

Marcel was still in shock three weeks after the fact that his cousin, the Lion of Ordiatea, had rescued him from the gallows for his attempted theft of the King's Jewel. Captain Marcel Moretriou, it had a nice ring to it, he had to admit. But that ring deafened his ears as the knowledge of those who had died for it reverberated through his soul. Mikel had told him of their true fate and of the stand's worth. But to him, he was the soul perpetrator of the Folly of the Fifth, and he did not know if that would ever leave him.

"What you ask is ridiculous!" barked General Beaumont, a flabby man with great white mustaches waxed and curled in popular fashion. His chest was covered with so many unearned metals Marcel was unsure how the fat bastard could even breathe.

"General Beaumont is right, General Thanadius," a woman of equal stature sighed, a gloved hand resting against wrinkled brow. "Have you no discretion for the Rising Star's coffers? This would bankrupt us!"

The Lion turned on his heels. Salt and pepper hair, now tied back in a proper bun, outlined the most fierce glare Marcel thought he had ever seen. Lean and cold, General Mikel Thanadius was taller than most Ordiatians and, unlike his compatriots, had earned each of the five metals pinned to his pristine uniform, the most notable of which was a golden star hanging from a ribbon of royal purple. He was the only general with such a metal, a metal that represented the true worth of Marcel's cousin. A Star of Valor, given to one who had risked life and limb to personally save the life of a ranking officer. Mikel knew war, he understood battle, and he had killed with the very sword that hung at his side. These others were career politicians and noble-born dogs. Mikel was a hero of fearless reputation and notable worth.

"I ask for the means to end the war," the Lion of Ordiatea roared. "Twenty thousand Ordiatian lives have been lost. Twenty thousand. Ordan damn you past Gallae's grace! I don't care if the Rising Star melts the Scepter and Stars to pay for it. We must secure our borders or there won't be a republic to defend!"

Gasps rang out across the table, followed by blusters of profanity and hurtled insults, each of which were flung directly at Mikel. His shoulders did not flinch, nor did his hands tremble. Marcel stared in awe as he shouldered the insults in perfect stance. When had his cousin become so... controlled? One of the leading reasons they had even risen out of obscurity was due to Mikel's brutal tactics and unrelenting spirit. Where had this demeanor of icy strength and resilience come from? Perhaps Marcel was not the only one who had changed over the years.

After a few more personal insults, an eel of a woman, General Gauthier, scoffed, "Have you so little faith in the strength of Ordiatea and of the divine appointment of our government? Ordan himself appointed the first of the House of Tur. and of that line, a true leader still sits, our Rising Star. How dare you imply that he is incapable of defending us as every other Rising Star has in the past."

Marcel wanted to reach out and strangle the old witch.

Who was she to say such things? Who was she to infer that Mikel was saying anything other than the truth? But he knew what she was doing. She, like the other six that remained in their cushioned seats, were trying to remove the one thread that did not match the pattern. Mikel was a soldier first, a man of his men, a leader. They were a viscous, slimy oil, and he was pure water. These did not mix, and the display now made that abundantly clear.

"I am only asking for more conscripted soldiers and that they be outfitted with appropriate kit and uniform," Mikel answered, ignoring a barbed insult. His voice lowered to almost a whisper. "Our last batch of recruits came in rags with rusted pikes and farm tools. Where are the soldiers? Where are those trained in the art of war?"

"Genral Thanadius," General Allard said, his voice too reaching a civil tone. "We have received conscripts at threefold the rates of prior years. Surely you can put these to use. As a man of your lineage, you should see the worth of all men."

Marcel took a single step, one footfall.

"Captain!" Mikel's eyes flashed up, filled with icy fire. "You were not excused from your post. In line, now!"

Marcel's heart thundered in his chest. Embarrassment and anger boiled in his veins. He could feel the red rising up his cheeks and burning at his eyes. But, this was not the time. With the bearing of a military man, he brought his heels back together with a snap, saluted, then then returned to parade rest.

"Half of those conscripted had fallen ill of the White Fever. They are weak and slow. Do you not understand that Calun is rising? Do you not understand that something beyond our sight is happening? If we cannot crush these kingsmen, we will be overrun. A single spider's bite may burn and annoy, but it can be overcome. But what man can stand against ten thousand poisonous fangs?"

"Your ask is valued at over fifty-five thousand gold bars," General Gauthier retorted. "We could conscript all of Southend and half of Un'Mor for that!"

"Would you sell Gauthier Manor for your two sons' lives?"

The question came from seemingly nowhere, catching all of the seated generals off their guard. Mikel pulled his own chair out and sat, starring eyes to eyes at each of the other seven.

"Who here would not sell their estates, give up their gold and their titles for their own children?" Mikel's question was a two-edged sword, Marcel could see it now. These old generals had, maybe, two decades of life left in front of them. Their only success was in their successors. But if they answered yes, then Mikel would have them. If they answered no...they would be ruined. For, despite all else, in Ordiatian aristocracy, the value of a word was beyond the weight of gold, for a word alone could topple a house.

"You know as well as any that my posterity is of my utmost interest," General Gauthier snarled. "Though, a man of your...interests, may not understand the value of a child, those around me do."

Mikel cocked his head, eyes flashing with dangerous glee. "Tell me, then, General Gauthier, as a mother, what would you be willing to sacrifice to see that young Thrallas—twenty-seven I believe—

makes it to the station of colonel by year's end? Would you appreciate it if I were to give him that rank and put him at the head of the last conscript? I was given the same opportunity. You speak openly of my lineage, of my upbringing and my life. Let us speak openly then. I will have no sons nor daughters. But I love my country, as a father should love their child. I will give Thrallas this promotion today, he is in my command. Would you like that prestigious opportunity for him?"

General Gauthier's eyes went wide and her face drained of color.

Before she could retort, Mikel turned his eyes to the next.

"General Beaumont, I believe your daughter is a captain, is she not?" Mikel knew she was. She stood only one person away from Marcel. "At twenty-four, I could promote her to colonel. Would she take the lead of the next march against the Pass? She is an excellent shot, perhaps the greatest I have ever seen. Would you have me outfit her with our latest batch of muskets? Would you trust the powder? How about those at her command to have her back?"

Silence fell across the tent. Marcel fought the urge to look over at Captain Beaumont. She was a beautiful young woman, obviously taking after Gallae's grace for looks, not her parents. He did not move though. No one did.

"Alora!" Mikel barked. "Bring me Papers of Command. I believe we have portions to hand out."

"Stop this madness!" It was General LaCroix, who had been rather silent up to this point. He had two daughters that were seven and three from a second marriage, but his son stood near Marcel. He must have known it would be him coming next.

"What madness?" Mikel's tone was flat.

"General Thanadius, you know damn well this will see you hanged!" LaCroix answered.

"Hanged? For what? Promotions?"

"These are death sentences, and you know it."

"No, General, you know it. Each of you know it, and yet you allow it every day," Mikel said slowly, eyes yet again moving from general to general. There was the lion. It had found its prey and now it would devour. "You'll find me the funds to support this army, or I will see each of you at Halfak's gates. Dismissed!"

"You have no right to dismiss this Council!"

"Are we in the Valamour?" Mikel asked with a wicked smile, looking from side to side of the massive tent as he rose to his full stature. "In a city of stone and gold, you can bury me. But on a field of battle, I am judge, jury, and executioner. You will get me my gold or I will take this army to the very gates of Tur'Mor myself. And before you even speak one word of treason, I want you to ask yourself: who do these soldiers answer to, a man they've never met in a tower or to the one who stands beside them? Dismissed!"

Steam misted off of Ranella's neck and shoulders as sweat rolled down her back in a ceaseless current brought on by the strain of physical exertion. A low roar, starting in her stomach and exploding outward from her gaping mouth reverberated across the snowcapped mountain range of her homeland in the peaks of the Cogadh mountains. Ranella, daughter Telda, of House Tordak, was fourth to the line of Cay, descendant of Ulnak, Advise of Cogadh's nomadic tribes. Her mother, Telda, daughter of Norma, was in the Plainlands with their herd of round-horns, leaving Ranella alone to complete the Great Task. So, despite the pain and strain, Ranella lowered her shoulder once more and pressed the Great Stone ever upward, inching in minute by minute, to the top of Tundal Peak.

"Kalnan's breath!" Ranella swore under her own breath as she strained against the weight of the mighty bolder whose rounded face truly did help, but not so much as to make the task anywhere close to easy.

"T'an, t'an, t'an!" tsked her Lampholder in reprimand, her tongue clicking in an ear-ringing manner.

"How about if you push, Alma?" Ranella snapped, turning her eyes away from the Great Stone and down on to the pretty-yet-wiry frame that was draped in multi-colored robes and adorned with a hat so tall and ornate Ranella often wondered how the Lampholder kept it perched in place.

"Mighty Ranella, it is uncouth to speak such a way of our great deity," the Lampholder said, prostrating herself in the presence of Ranella's glare.

"Up, comrade, I meant no offense," said Ranella, biting back a secondary curse for the slip-up she had allowed. This was a holy task, a divine calling. If she did not place the Great Stone atop Tundal Peak, the favor of Kalnan would be revoked and their sheep would not bear good wool and their ewes would not produce stout milk.

"My lady does me grace, ya," Lampholder Alma answered as she rose from the earth while tucking away a lock of golden hair that had fallen from beneath her high hat of office.

Alma was in many ways the exact opposite of Ranella, and for that Ranella had to remind herself to not be so hard on her. Twice Ranella's age, and half her weight, Alma was thin and mousy, her gloved hands did not know labor other than the trimming and carrying of her ornate silver candelabra, which stood as tall as its bearer. Not only was Alma a small woman, but she was also just always so proper and composed, always attending to the Codex of Kalnan with exactness, and never even once stepping out of line, Belaz be cursed! Worst of all, even being in her middle years and devoutly celibate, all of the young men of Tordak fancied her.

Fueled by a sudden burst of fire in her muscular belly, Ranella heaved against the Great Stone, pushing it slowly up the worn path to its resting place. As she pushed and pressed, Ranella saw the veins bulge in her own hands—strong hands, like her mother's that had served for two decades of winters—the tendons rise in strain. And, as suddenly as the bought of jealousy had wedged its way into her mind, pride and resolution washed it away.

Ranella was the daughter of one of the most respected women in all of Tordak. And when their tribe made their way back, at the end of winter's long stay, it was her mother, and her mother's mother, and so far on, that had pressed the Great Stone to the top of Tundal Peak to usher in the Spring, Season the Divinities, waking them from their long slumber. They were the bringers of life, warmth, and growth. Without her mother, and now her, the tribes of Tordak would not have fields to graze their herds, herbs to cook their meat, or rivers to bring fresh water.

Pride blossomed in Ranella's heart, and a tune came humming through her lips, an old song her great grandmother had sung to her in her infancy, then her grandmother, and down. She heaved with the beat and could not keep back a smile as she heard her Lampholder join her, whistling along to the gentle melody.

Hours passed, whistling and humming turned to full on singing. Alma was a perfectly pitched soprano and Ranella was a well-harmonizing alto. They sang songs of the fields and valleys, of the mountains and streams. The tune helped ease the burden of the Great Task, and a burden it was.

The sun had nearly set when the two women came to a stop. A great arch of stone stood before them, the ancient rocks covered in flags of vibrant colors, though many had faded and worn with time.

Two basins sat on either side of the archway, great braziers of cast brass etched with the ancient writings of the first peoples of Cogadh.

Solemnly, and without preamble, Alma stepped with ceremonial poise toward the brazier on the left side of the arch.

"Great Kalnan, bringer of heaven's golden warmth, we beseech thee awaken and rise once more from your slumber beneath the mountains," Alma chanted as she touched her candelabra to the brazier. The blaze that erupted was sudden and violent, sending up great bouts of blue-red flames. Despite this, Alma did not flinch. And why would she? She had made this journey a dozen times with Ranella's mother. Why would this time be any different?

Slowly, Alma turned from the left brazier and marched to the right. "Great Kalnan, bringer of heaven's golden warmth, we beseech thee awaken and rise once more from your slumber beneath the mountains. Come once more and hear the plea of your creations, for by your hands of stone were all children crafted. By your heart of fire, were all things given life, and by your will do we serve."

Another torrent of flames jumped into the air as Alma touched her candelabra to the brazier. After the flames settled to a steady blaze Alma turned and faced Ranella was teary eyes and a proud smile on her beautiful, though slightly sooty, face. "Ranella, daughter Telda, by the grace of Kalnan, bringer of heaven's golden warmth, go forth to the peak of the mountain. Place the Great Stone, so that all may have life, light, and warmth once more."

Ranella, nearly forgetting, quickly raised two fingers to her lips and then pressed them to her brow, saying, "Long have we strained through this winter, may this offering be an offer accepted by the Divinities."

Ranella had wondered at that part of the ceremony when her mother had told her. It was obvious that the Great Task must be completed, for every year that it was, their peoples had life, light, and warmth. To her knowledge, Kalnan was the Old One, the only divinity they worshipped. She had to bite back the questions that threatened her mind, and accept the words which her mother had told her. But, now that she was here, saying those words, she could not help but feel those same questions coming back to her mind.

"Go forth, comrade of all, and deliver us from the dark of winter's heart," Alma continued, not noticing Ranella's hesitancy.

"As commanded, so I do," Ranella answered, shoving her questions away as she shoved the Great Stone forward through the archway.

The rest of the journey, only a few more painstakingly steep steps, was over so quickly that Ranella was caught off-guard when she saw the Peak and the Alter of Kalnan.

All breath left her lungs as the imagery before her unveiled itself. For three days, all Ranella had seen was the smooth, grey face of the Great Stone, and the earthen path at her feet. For three days, she had pushed and pushed and pushed, every fiber, muscle and sinew in her body screaming in strain and exertion. And now, the whole world opened before her very eyes.

Towering above all other peaks, Tundal mountain was the tallest of all mountains in Cogadh, taller than all but the very highest of Northern Daneland. Unlike those of Northern Daneland, these mountains proffered a view of Kalnan's mighty hand. Looking down from the peak, she could see the valley formed from his palm, and the five ravines that were his fingers, cutting their way through the other unnamed mountains of Cogadh. Only Tundal was granted a name, given at the end of Kalnan's great work, where he created the first woman, giving her his ability to create life. Tundal, bride of Kalnan, was said to be lain to rest at this very peak after giving birth to twelve sons and fourteen daughters, living to the ripe old age of one hundred and ninety-two, solidifying the race of humanity and her place with them.

Slowly, Ranella pressed the Great Stone into a small divot of cast brass, where underneath lay the bones of Tundal. For, as in her life, she bore the great task of bringing life into the world, so do now her daughter's daughters bring forth life by completing the Great Task each year, and then bringing the stone back down the mountain so that she can rest in the arms of her creator and lover, Kalnan.

As the stone came to rest on its perch, Ranella let out a breath of completion. She had done it. She had completed the Great Task and delivered the Great Stone to Tundal Peak. Her people would have warmth, light, and life. In a bout of self-satisfied fulfillment, Ranella let out a long cry, an undulation of notes that harmonized with winds, snows, streams, and stones. There were no words, for words were not needed in the worship of Kalnan, but there was spirit and joy. Her sacrifice was complete.

PART 2

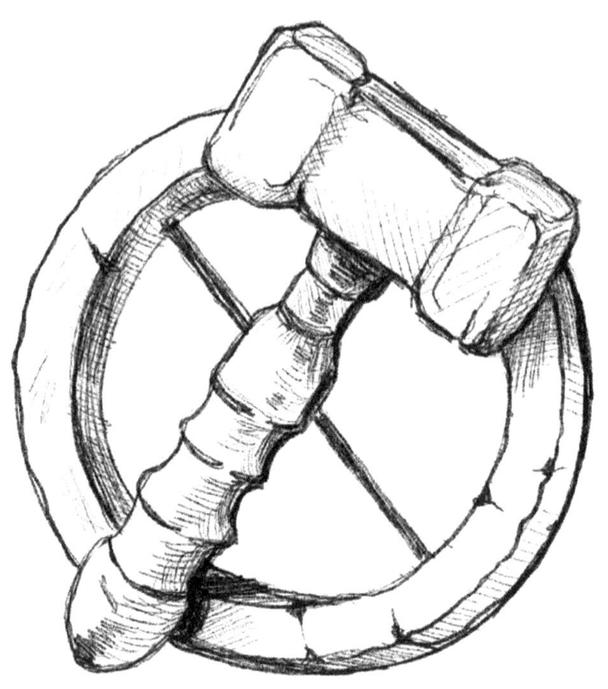

Chapter 7: Jrotnhalm
Darius

Darius was pushed out of the wagon and dragged onto his knees into the muddy grounds of the gatehouse inside the gatehouse of the Spanning Wall. The black iron collar latched onto his neck was so cold it felt like tongues of fire licking his skin, an odd sensation that continued to fog his mind. Next to him, the woman in green was laying, sprawled out in the muck, her beautiful garments tarnished with mud and the gods knew what else. A spike of anger rose in Darius, but it was extinguished instantaneously by a pulse of pain from the collar, causing his tendons to rise and his veins to bulge in agony.

"Don't try nothing stupid, laddie," said Orhund as he grabbed Darius by the arm and hauled him to his feet. "The more you resist, the more the kroichae burns. Keep that in mind as these next moments pass."

Bitterness seethed within, but Darius forced control over his raging emotions, not wishing the return of the biting pain of the kroichae. What kind of people made such a thing? More importantly, how?

"Report?" came the same voice that had echoed over the valley as the wagon approached the wall.

Orhund bowed, raising a clenched fist to his brow in doing so, "Lord Commander Krarraek, Tuli and Angul were sent ahead. Did they inform you of our finding?"

"Aye, Commander Orhund," answered one of the largest men Darius had ever seen, and he had been kin to mighty Angenthor. The lord commander's hair was red as flame, his eyes green as grass. He had on a skirt of pleated plaid, and over his right knee was a golden pin, a tower encircled by a wreath of knotted cords. He used the butt of an axe unlike any Darius had ever seen to support himself as he walked forward. His limp, however, did not make him appear weak, as if not even injury could slow him. His voice was deep and rough, his eyes hard as steel. He scanned over the retinue in front of him, and Darius could not help but feel slighted by his gaze as he looked at him with indifference. "Damn, dirty Diju. And look at this one, got the Hammer of the Church right on his chest. Blood and stone! Just what we needed. Bah!"

"Lord Commander," Orhund pressed, beckoning to Nee'av with his off-hand. "We found a bairn with them. She do be of the age, but we can't tell for certain."

"By Ordan's stone!" Lord Commander Krarraek barked after taking no more than a passing glace at the pale face of the little girl. "We don't have time for second-guessing. Get 'er to Master Tyree. That old codger be the only one who can help her. Word has already been sent to the High House. Best find faith and pray that we do have her!"

"Aye," Orhund said with a sharp nod. "And what of these?"

"Ain't no Diju going past my walls," Krarraek spat. "Take her to the dungeon. She can rot there 'til we get the rest of this sorted away."

"And what of him?"

Krarraek stepped forward, eyeing Darius for a long, hard moment. Darius could see the muscles beneath his thick beard working as he thought of what to do next. "Bah!" he shouted at last, as if disgusted by his choices. "He's got something on him, a spell of sorts. Send him up with the bairn. Perhaps the old coot can conjure up something to break it after the girl's seen to."

Orhund nodded again, this time more hesitantly, before motioning to Tuli and Angul to haul Darius back into the cart. They tossed him in bodily. He landed hard on his left shoulder, and his head smacked the panels hard, sending stars through his vision.

"No troubles," the Lord Commander hissed. "Don't leave his side. And keep that damned kroichae tight. I'll have no bloody foreigner running through Talahmnas on my watch. Now, go! It won't be my stones taken if it be too late for the bairn. Get her to Tyree!"

"Aye, sir!" Orhund snapped. He turned sharply on his heel and hoisted himself into the wagon, whipped the reins, and rode hard toward the rising hills.

Darius's head bounced on the floorboards at every bump, and there were many as they wound their way ever upward. He had no comprehension of time or distance. He had no bearing as to where he was nor what he could do. Everything was a blur of pain and confusion, and any thought that even edged toward escape or removing the black iron sent waves of agony and nausea. So, he laid his head upon the floorboard and waited for whatever fate would come by the hands of this Master Tyree.

When the cart finally stopped and Darius was hefted out, the very faintest hints of dawn were upon them. The sky, still dark blue, had hints of purple welling deep within, along with shades of pink and gold. Stars still pricked the heavens, and two—a deep blue and brilliant green—stood in stark contrast to the rest. They were large, far closer to the world than any of the others in the sky, and they filled Darius's mind with wonder.

He blinked dumbly as he looked upon them, as if they held some hidden meaning to him, some connection of which had forgotten.

"Inside, laddie," Orhund said as he pushed Darius toward a building that was perhaps the most peculiar thing he had ever seen.

The structure seemed to have been built as a small stone shop at least a hundred years ago, then added on to several times over. With each addition there seemed to be no uniformity whatsoever. A strange tower rose from the back of the building with a deck on one side and a bulbous protrusion from the other. There was a glass dome in the center of the roof and a long gazing glass on an observation deck near the front. A large sign, whose paint had long since chipped away, swung over an egg-shaped door, upon which dozens of runes were roughly scratched as if with the tip of a knife rather than a carpenter's chisel. And, from the base of the hill to the door, a gentle gradient was formed of a smooth, plaster-like substance that Darius had never before seen.

Darius made his way up the smooth slope, the tips of his boots still somehow managing to catch here and there, sending him staggering. His legs felt as if they were caked in mud and his boots filled with lead.

Thump thump!

Darius's eyes shot up to the door. What was that?

"On with ye," Orhund shoved Darius forward, sending him sprawling onto the ground.

His elbows landed with a hard crack, his wrists still bound together. At least he had kept his face from striking the cement path.

"Blood and stone!" Orhund swore, his voice exhausted. "Listen here, laddie. I am gonna cut them cords from y'cr hands. Don't try nothing funny, y'er hear?"

Darius, eyes rolling and head muddled, nodded in assent. He was not even sure he could have crushed an ant if he wanted to, much less have the strength to strike at the fierce and muscled commander.

Orhund set the young girl down gently and reached behind his back, drawing a long, single-edged knife with an antler handle and brass fittings.

"Don't ye move," Orhund emphasized each word with an edge as sharp as the forearm-long knife he held.

He knelt beside Darius and slid the blade between his wrists, cutting away the cords with ease. Blood rushed into Darius's fingertips and he reflexively opened and closed his fingers, pumping the warmth through his hands and into his arms.

"That's quite some ring ye got there," Orhund said, tapping Darius's ring with the tip of his long knife.

Darius looked into the man's eyes, wanted to speak, but could not form a single reply, not even a nod.

"Damn Diju," Orhund swore, using the flat of the blade to turn Darius's head this way and that. He was eyeing him. Searching him for... something. But Darius knew not what that was. "Bah! Up with ye!" Orhund grabbed Darius by the hand and helped him to his feet, while he swiftly slid the knife into its sheath at his back. "We don't have all day now. To the door with ye, I'll get the lassie."

Darius moved once more, trudging forward, each step a mental battle.

Once at the door, Darius stared in stupefaction. His lips felt dry and swollen and his eyes ached. Something in the back of his mind itched, though he could not tell what it was. Everything was a haze, a muddled fog of dissociation. Yet, he knew something deep down. He needed to show these people that he was not at fault. His hands, though bound, drifted to his pocket where something lay concealed. The key to his innocence.

A loud knock rang out thrice over. Darius blinked. Orhund was next to him, holding the young girl with one arm, her body slung over his shoulder like a sack of potatoes, and with the other, he was gripping a wolf's head knocker of iron, clanging it over and over. The harsh clangs rang over and over in Darius's ears, making him want to vomit.

"In with ye! By Ordan's stones! Stop beating on me door!" an elder voice called out from inside the shop, nearly reaching manic tones of aggression.

"Don't touch anything," Orhund seethed and then pushed open the door to Master Tyree's shop.

The pungent odor that assailed Darius's nostrils as that door swung inwardly nearly took him to his knees. His eyes immediately filled with tears and his breath caught in his throat. He took several sharp breaths, coughing and spitting. It smelled of tanning solution, alchemical concoctions, and the most ill-matched series of perfumes one could imagine.

A hand pressed Darius forward into the eclectic shop. Shelves and tables littered the area, heaped with papers and books, jars and vials, skulls and bones, and a multitude of fauna and flora, many of which Darius had no knowledge of. That being said, there was not a single thing on the floor, not one out-of-place book, tool, or bone. The walls were draped with tapestries, maps, busts and mountings, but the floors were pristine. This unsettled Darius for some reason beyond his current understanding.

Thump thump!

There it was again. That strange sound... or feeling. Darius could not understand what it was, but it seemed to be coming from inside the shop. Drawing his mind.

"Ah!" the voice from moments ago called out. "What did ye bring me from Ranok this time, Orhund?"

The man's voice cracked as he spoke, and when Darius spotted the old mage behind his desk, he understood why. His wizened face looked as if it had been held against a smelting pot, a burn having claimed his left ear, half his cheek, a chunk of his shoulder, and the length of his arm. And shockingly, that was not the most prevalent feature of the mage. Hair like a barn owl and a forked beard of snowy white, patchy on the left side, flared off of his head as if he had just been struck by lightning. His eyes were covered by the most peculiar contraption of brass cogs and multi-colored lenses. Tattoos of bright blue—runic symbols and strange geometric patterns— adorned his neck and arms, many of which were marred by the puckered burns. He wore a sleeveless tunic and massive gauntlets with cogs and pistons that had strange tubes running to a device on the back of his chair that emitted a low thrumming sound.

The whole room suddenly spun in Darius's eyes as sounds evaporated like mist. A surge of hot pain emanated where Itheanam's horn had punctured his abdomen and lanced throughout his whole body. Doubled over in agony and nausea, Darius vomited.

"By Ordan's thrice braided beard!" the old mage swore. "Why in the burning pit does he have a kroichae on?"

Orhund, whose face was turned in a sneer of disgust, stepped away from Darius and answered the old mage, saying, "He's under a spell. A Diju has Touched him. Just look at his eyes!"

"Blood and bloody stones," Tyree barked as he pushed himself back from the table. But, to Darius's surprise, the old man did not stand. His chair moved with him, then propelled mage toward them on four wheels. And for the first time, Darius got a good look at the man's legs... or at least, what was left of them.

The left leg stopped just below the melted knee, a stump of puckered flesh that threatened to turn Darius's sour stomach once more. The right had a gash that started just above the knee and trailed down the withered appendage into a wool sock tucked into a laced boot.

"Get it off him!" Tyree shouted as he hurtled toward them in his wheeled chair, the back of which emanate a soft glow of sapphire and emerald light, along with the whirling and clicking sounds of many cogs and sprockets turning.

"But master—" Orhund started as he moved the girl from his shoulder into both his arms.

"ye got a cock in y'er ear?" Tyree snapped. "Lay the girl on the table and get the damn thing off him! His veins is turning black!"

Orhund looked as if he had been slapped, if only for a moment before he sprung into action. He rushed to a relatively clean table and gently laid the young girl down, her body still covered by Darius's coat. Next, he dug in the small pouch about his waist and retrieved a small key, a key which slid into the back of the kroichae at Darius's neck.

Click!

Instant relief washed throughout Darius's body, the shock of which dropped him to his knees, just missing the puddle of vomit. His hands struck the floor, opening just in time to catch himself. And in doing so, dropping the silver amulet he had held so tightly.

The sharp clink of silver on wood did not go unnoticed by the two men that seemed to tower over him now. Their eyes went wide as the amulet came to a clattering stop, gemstone eyes glaring back at them.

"Bloody pits of fire," whispered Orhund.

"Go!" Tyree said slowly. "Damn it! Go! Go! Go to the Lord of the High Hill! Go now!"

"But, the girl—"

"Go!" Tyree bellowed, his voice cracking with thunderous command. "By Ordan's beard! We found her!" He blinked, looking between the necklace and the little girl, and repeated himself in a little more than a whisper, "We found her!"

Orhund did not argue this time, but turned on his heel and rushed out of the shop, his face a mixture of excitement, concern, and determination. The man moved through the shop, dodging tables and stacks of books and cases with a grace that did not go unnoticed by Darius. Who was, thankfully, beginning to gather his facilities and along with them, his memories.

"Izebal!"

"Laddie," Tyree said, his full attention on the girl at the table. "I need ye! Hurry! She don't have much time!"

"Listen, my... my friend, she, she is," his mind still felt as if it were filled with cotton and thorns. "She needs me."

"She can wait," Tyree snapped with indignation. "This lassie, she will die if you do not help me! We don't have time! No time! Go and get me that crystal! The big purple one on that there shelf, laddie. The one that be next to the ruby talon!"

Darius turned about in a haze, his mind racing. He had to get control of himself. The room seemed to be spinning. He could not let her die now. Not now, not after everything he had done. He could not lose her, not like his father, his brother, his mother. But who was he afraid to lose? This girl or Izebal? Or both?

When did the room become so hot?

The crystal, get the crystal.

As Darius rushed toward the crystal, he heard Tyree throw open a drawer from the table where he sat earlier. Palming the cold gemstone, he turned to see the old mage tossing aside various utensils and artificiary tools, then proceeded to set a cluster of small gemstones onto the table, all radiating one of the Sources' Light.

"Aetora or Ria'Elahm, laddie?" Tyree asked, breaking the momentary silence.

Darius did not answer. He looked over the stones, somewhat baffled by the sight of them. He had never seen the two different Lightsources together before, and this manic mage had them clustered into a drawer.

"Snap out of it, laddie!" Tyree barked. "Now, ye do answer me! Do ye draw from Everlight or Lifesource? I need t'er know to make the Jrotnhalm work."

"Neither," Darius mumbled, refocusing on the frayed-haired man.

"What d'er ya mean?" Snapped the old mage. "I do gots a half-dead lassie and a half-brained goat licker to help me! What in Ordan's creation did I do t'er deserve this?"

"I don't think I can help you in that way," Darius replied levelly.

"Laddie, y'er eyes do already begin to light—" And then old mage stopped and looked into Darius's eyes with wonderment. "Bless my beard!" he cackled, running his free hand threw wisps of white beard. "Feroblooded...but no..."

"I can't Touch the Sources," Darius pressed, urgency swelling his voice. "But surely I can help somehow. Please, I can't let her die!"

Tyree, shook his head furiously and then pulled his googles down over his eyes, making them appear three times larger than before. With the uncovered hand he marked a rune on the girl's chest, a single line downwards, with two crossing lines and then a dot to the right. With the still-gauntletted hand, he took the crystal from Darius and placed it under a series of glass tubes and faucets. He turned a brass wheel, and a flame ignited under a beaker, which caused a white, foaming fluid to bubble. The fluid rose and began to wind between twisted tubes that gradually narrowed in diameter until it came to a spigot. Carefully, Tyree released the fluid into the hollow geode. It hissed and spluttered as it touched the purple crystals, eating away at them until all were a homogeneous solution.

"Laddie," Tyree's voice was steady for the first time, his eyes focused strenuously on the geode solution. "When I tell ye to pull me back, y'er not to question, but yank with all the strength y'er got, ye hear?"

"What?" Darius asked, his heart rate rising, eyes darting from the various scenes taking place. The solution was steaming ferociously now. The rune that Tyree had marked upon the girl's bare chest was beginning to blaze, and the sapphire stones infused with Everlight were leaking slowly onto the table. Streams of liquid blue light crept towards the girl, flowing along the grain of the wood, glowing gently, and up onto her flesh, where the streams found their way into the painted rune.

"Jrotnhalm takes focus, laddie," Tyree breathed out sternly. "Y'er to pull when I do say pull. That is all ye have time to know! Now, be ready!"

Tyree lifted the geode over the girl's chest and began to pour, chanting loudly, "Ae rok jnal! Fae'lur yahl! Khal'al thu! Khal'al thu! Urdan'ae fru'ul! Ga'aena fia'jr! Unnda'yahl! Unnda'yahl!"

The tattoos on Master Tyree's own flesh glowed vividly, like lightning igniting in the night sky. White speck danced across Darius's vision, and he raised an arm to block the burning white beams erupting from the girl's chest. A low rumble echoed forth, as did the sounds of battering winds, ripping and tearing at the papers near the table, sending them flying in a whirlwind. Darius felt himself being forced backwards, so he drove his heels into the ground and turned his eyes back towards the little girl and gasped in shock.

Master Tyree, supposed High Mage of the Northernmen, had his arm elbow-deep in her chest. It was plunged into a pool of white, light-formed runes. He was chanting, words Darius could neither hear nor understand, as he slowly pushed his arm further downwards. The strain on the old man's face was palpable, sweat beading on his furrowed brow. Yet, he had a wild determination in his eyes, a determination that Darius found somewhat admirable. He did not know this man, but Tyree had jumped in just as willingly and just as fervently as he had to save this nameless girl.

"Ready y'erself, laddie!" screamed the old mage, sapphire light pouring from his lips as he called out. "I do got her! Ready!"

Darius pulled himself around the table to where the old man was set, all the while the wind beating upon him, papers slicing at his face and hands. Darius placed his hands on Tyree's shoulders, gripping them tightly, and stared down into the pool of runic light.

With a sudden jerk, Tyree lurched backwards, knocking his head into Darius's nose, sending a spirt of blood flying. Darius released the old man, bringing his hands to his face and letting out a yelp of pain as stars formed in his vision. Tyree screamed, his whole body going stiff. Darius jumped towards the old man, the gale nearly taking his feet out from under him, latched onto his shoulder with one hand and drove his boot into the table.

"Not yet!" Tyree groaned, morc light leaking from his mouth, as well as from his clenched eyes and bleeding nose. "Don't ye give up on me, lassie! Ae rok jnal! Fae'lur yahl! Khal'al thu! Khal'al thu! Ae rok jnal! Fae'lur yahl! Khal'al thu! Khal'al thu!"

Tyree's arm slowly began to rise from the pool of light, and to Darius's surprise and absolute horror, a hand gripped the old man's, small and tender, and formed utterly from mist. "I got ye, ya little pup! Come now! Come on!" Tyree cried out as he pulled backwards, the hand rising. "Blood and stone, laddie, pull!"

Darius thrust his leg straight, the heavy table not budging a hair as he pressed against it. He pulled on the old man, and it felt as if he were trying to pull upon a mountain. From the ceiling, he could see the sunlight leaking through. He opened himself and reached of the rays of light that he knew would grant him strength. But nothing happened.

Horrified, Darius looked to his hands. *Where is my ring?* Confused, he saw it there, nestled on his finger, but he could not feel the Binding. Fury welled inside him, the will to fight against the odds.

Again he tried. He would not let this girl die. He would do what he set out to do. He would accomplish something, save someone. He had to. He had to.

Pain ripped through his body. Flashes of white and blue spotted his vision. But strength came. Not as he had known before, but stronger than any mortal man could hope to be. But the exquisite pain cut into him like daggers and currents of energy scorched his nerves.

Both men screamed and strained, pulled and spat, for what seemed like an eternity. Darius's shoulder felt like it would rip out of its socket, and the muscles in his leg screamed in agony. Yet, when he looked at that little girl, lying on the table, and when he saw the ferocity of the old mage, steel filled his veins and he pulled on through the pain.

A whooshing thrill of wind filled the air. All the lights in the room flared wildly. Then there was darkness, then there was silence.

A figure appeared, or at least the form of a person materialized before them. Tyree held her, a pale, translucent girl, who looked like the one on the table, but made up of mist and light. However, there was something wrong with her. In her heart, there was blackness, dark, oily blackness that emitted a low, eerie, maroon afterglow.

"Touched by a Soulless One indeed," Tyree said mournfully.

The aperture nodded her head weakly in agreement.

"Be still, lassie, this I can fix. Be still." And he took two of the gemstones from the table, one sapphire and one emerald, both of which still held light, and touched them to the black heart. Sounds of glass errupting rippled outward, an unnatural, blood-curdling sound that made the wound on Darius's chest flair with pain.

Darius pulled open his trench coat and stared down at the glassy handprint. It felt as if gouts of flames were bursting from his chest, searing away the flesh. He heard in the back of his mind a scream, that same scream Mireya had bellowed over a thousand years ago. His eyes went dim and he faded into darkness.

A jagged peak rose in the distance, cut against a midnight sky. Upon its face, a jagged maw of stone opened and blackness, far darker than night, seeped from within the cavernous pit. A cry from within. A screaming woman. Laughter, evil and cruel, booming outwards.

A face marked with crimson ink filled Darius's view. Eyes of black ringed with red glared down upon him as he fell upon the snowy earth. Darius raised a hand to protect his face, but it was not flesh and bone, instead crystal and light.

"My Queen shall return!"

"No!" Boomed a thunderous voice from the heavens.

Ominous laughter filled Darius's mind. Terrible, endless bouts of malicious laughter.

"You must find them!" the voice boomed.

Thump thump... Thump thump... Thump thump...

"Easy now, easy," Tyree said soothingly.

Darius opened his eyes slowly, blinking away the tears that blurred his vision. His head felt as if it were a drum being beaten over and over again. The air was so thick with smoke and vapors that made it difficult to breathe.

After heaving himself upright, Darius searched the wreckage until he saw the old mage, who was leaning over the girl's motionless body. Above the body, in the careful arms of the mage, a specter of light glistened. Next to the girl's body, three cracked gemstones lay, all of them clear and totally devoid of light.

"Unnda'yahl... Unnda'yahl," chanted Tyree in soft, lulling tones as he laid the misty figure onto the body of the girl.

As two entities merged, the physical with the aethereal, the runic symbols pulsated once, then twice, then blinked out. Tyree let out a long breath and then chuckled to himself as he turned his head and looked towards where Darius now stood.

"Ye got some stones, laddie," the old mage said as he shook his head. "Ye do got them for sure."

"Is she going to be okay?" Darius asked as he hurried to the mage's side.

"That she will, I do believe, laddie. I do believe," Tyree answered as he pulled the torn blankets over her body.

"What was that?" Darius asked, eyes still focused on the girl, whose flesh seemed to regain color by the moment and whose hair was already turning a brighter shade of red, all veins having lost their sickly back trails.

"That do be a Jrotnhalm, laddie," answered the mage with a chuckle. "Y'er not from these parts, are ya, laddie? ye act like a soft-handed Ordiatian, but look like a near-kinsman. But ye got stones under ya, that do be certain. She wouldn't have made it without ye. That do be the honest truth, on Ordan's hammer and Gallae grace it do be that."

Darius did not reply, but just stared at the girl, watching as freckles seemed to sprout across her nose and cheeks. Her lips turned red and her eyes began to move behind closed lids.

"She do wake," laughed Tyree as he clapped his hands together. "Laddie, ye don't know what ya did do, by my beard I do not know that ye do, do ye?"

"Wha- what?" stammered Darius in confusion, trying his best, and failing, to understand what the wizened old man was saying, or anyone in this land for that matter.

"The lass, this lassie, she do—"

The door to Tyree's shop banged open.

"Hail, Lord Ruthvin, Lord of the High Hall and Defender of the Borderlands!" cried out Orhund as perhaps the most imposing man Darius had ever before seen marched into the disheveled shop.

CHAPTER 8: ONLY A MEMORY
AELLIA

"Good morning, daughter," Elcon said as he knocked on the door to her room. *Her room?* She was already beginning to think of this place as hers. A shudder wriggled its way down her spine at the thought.

Aellia looked up at the man. He wore robes today, along with an apron bearing the image of Ethra embroidered in golden thread.. Unusual for him.

"Happy Orday," he said with a wink as he moved across the floor, his silk slippers making an obnoxious whooshing sound with each step. "I had hoped you'd have recovered enough to attend services this morning. Alas, it does not appear to be in the greater will."

Aellia burned with indignation at the remark. How dare he!

"I did, however, want to leave you with something." His grey eyes lit with excitement. "I had meant to give this to you yesterday, but...something unexpected occurred."

Yesterday? What had happened yesterday? Aellia tried to think back, but her mind was utterly blank. She could not remember anything, and not just from the day before. Large bits of her memories were missing, and those that were still there were as fractured glass.

"Are you alright?" Elcon asked as he sat at her side upon the bed.

"Do I look alright?" Aellia scoffed, not trying to hold the disdain back from her words. However, the insult that was so perfectly timed and aimed, fumbled out of her stitched mouth in an incoherent mumble.

"Daughter, I cannot understand you," Elcon tutted with a shake of his head. "Your mouth is still not healed."

He patted her hand as he spoke. The touch of his wrinkled fingers, the way the skin seemed to just drape over the bones of his spotted hands, made Aellia's stomach sour.

"Ah, but that brings us to this," he exclaimed as he produced as small box from the hanging sleeve of his emerald robes.

As soon as the box slid from beneath his robes, Aellia knew what resided within. Her heart thrummed in her chest and she could not hold back the smile as it pulled at her deformed lips.

"This was found on your body, when we pulled you from the Temple that fateful night," Elcon said, his own voice rising as he began to unlatch the small brass clasps of the stained box. "I have to admit, we were rather perplexed at its discovery. I am hoping that, as you recover, you can help fill in the gaps of our understanding."

Aellia pushed herself upright, wincing against the waves of pain, unyielding resolve steeling her mind as she reached out. And she heard.

Aellia!

All sense of hesitation, reservation, and caution fled Aellia in one single instant. These feelings were replaced by an selfish need, an unrelenting desire to hold the Oathrod once more. She needed to take hold of it, to secure it once more in her own hands. She needed it, more than any other thing she had ever had.

"Iaenora!" she gasped, her hand shooting out as the lid clicked open.

All at once, power surged through her body. She felt electricity kiss her palm and her fingertips, then rush up her arm. Her eyes flashed with new sight and her tongue stung with the vile taste of acid. Nausea warred with an all-consuming thrill. Every fiber of her being felt as if they were tethered to a lightning rod as a bolt struck true.

Violent gusts of air battered at her ears as currents of wind ripped and thrashed about Aellia. The bed sheets were striped from her body and flung away from her, along with papers, lamps, and various other articles. Up, up into the air she rose, her limbs slowly gaining strength.

Her eyes, her eyes saw. They saw with a clarity she had nearly forgotten—though something was wrong. To the left of her face, she saw nothing. Only darkness. Her left eye was gone, only a grey jelly remained. She could see nothing in her periphery. Terror welled within her, a fear of the darkness that would not abate.

How? Why? How was she not healing? All of this power, all of this energy. Why wasn't she being made whole?

Aellia! Aellia! Can you hear me?

Aellia could not focus; she thrashed about wildly now. There was other screaming. A man's voice, panic rising higher and higher.

Aellia, you must let go! Our bond, you're pulling too hard. Let go your anger and fear. Let go.

Let go? How... no, why? Why should she let go? She had power now. She was no longer helpless and alone. Her limbs knew strength and her body was whole once more save for her eye.

Slowly, Aellia raised a hand to her face as the gale beneath her thrashed the garish room into a swirl vortex of clutter. Her fingers traced the outline of a cold ravine in her flesh, starting at her lip and trailing upward in a jagged line until they touched something soft. A bandage still covered the left side of her face, the careful wrapping that concealed her gouged eye.

Aellia drifted for a moment, a single heartbeat that stretched on for eternity, before quelling the tempest within. Downward she sank until she felt the soft mattress beneath her bare feet. Papers and clutter were strewn across the opulent room, but Aellia paid them no heed. Gently, she unwound the wrappings, her good eye glaring at the old man, who was now several feet away from her, being helped to his feet by two Aluth.

One of the two, a thick man with hard eyes peering behind the layered covering, took a step toward her. However, before she could outstretch her hand and send a powerful gust of wind at him, the old priest placed a restraining hand on his shoulder, commanding him to hold his ground.

"We have waited generations for this moment," the old priest said in reverent tones. "Do not presume to understand what that young woman can do."

Despite her loathing of the man, she felt a prick of something akin to gratitude or respect for the old priest's words. The sensation nearly made her sick.

"Is that you?" Aellia snarled in her mind.

"He is a man of the Order of the High Father and Holy Mother," Iaenora retorted. *"And he saved your life."*

"I thought you flew us to safety?"

Aellia stopped suddenly, the bandages still in her hand. That memory was not hers. She had not been conscious when she had flown to the Temple of Ordan and... by the gods. She had fought Aluth—and won!

"We are bonded," Iaenora echoed in her mind. *"There is no you and I, only us. I am you, and you I, and we one."*

Aellia's head hurt, and now not only from the battering of the winds and storms or the knife wound, but Iaenora's rambling rhetoric. That being said, she was determined to get these cursed bandages from off her eye.

She moved quickly, unraveling the linen that bound her head. Round and round the wrappings went until something hard fell into her lap, and the last inches of bandages fell away.

A small stone, perfectly cut, surged with brilliant sapphire light. It looked unlike anything Aellia had ever seen before. She had seen illusive Fragtorches, bizarre light rods crafted by the secretive Asterverians, and the amulets of Everlight that so often hung from Blessed necks. Those had each shown with a bright azure light. But this stone pulsated as if a tiny thunderstorm raged within its crystal heart.

"By Ordan's throne above!" gasped the old priest, who had unexpectedly drawn close to her.

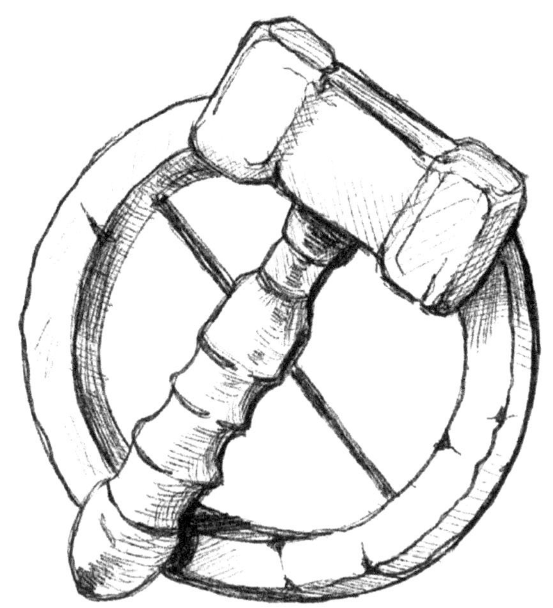

CHAPTER 9: THE HIGH HALL
DARIUS

Darius, whose weakened limbs still had not regained their true strength, nursed his aching head as he sat in a high-backed chair. The fabric pricked at his skin, the frayed embroidery poking through the worn vest and thin fabric of his shirt. His trench coat was draped over an odd hook by the door, which was guarded by two silent sentries in black and silver pleated skirts and heavy breastplates and helms. Across the room, the young girl whom he had carried through Ranok for countless days sat at a table while the old mage, Tyree, and the man whom he now knew was her father, were talking in a hushed tone.

Darius watched the small party through steepled fingers that pressed firmly against his brow, and could not help but smile. The ceaseless pounding be damned. The man, announced as High Lord Eric Ruthvin, stroked the back of her crimson hair.

She was safe. She was home.

A weight that had set so heavily upon his heart and soul was lifted. And yet, as he watched the man tenderly comfort his daughter, Darius could not help but feel the small nick of hurt.

It had happened all so suddenly. The doors had been flung open. There was yelling and swearing. Darius had been moved bodily out of the High Lord's way by the sentries that now guarded the door, tossed like a rag doll across the floor and had cold blades pulled on him. Tyree had shouted a slew of incoherent curses and commands. And Lord Ruthvin, a man who towered even over Darius, had swooped up his daughter without a glance back. He held her, rocking back and forth, whispering something into her ear as he did so.

Tyree, after his initial tirade of useless commands, had threatened the silent guards that if they did not stop harassing Darius that he would melt them down and put them back on his shelf. An odd threat, but not one Darius took a second thought of in the moment.

Without hesitation or argument, the two guards immediately ceased any form of aggravation. To add to his bewilderment, in the same instance, the two helped Darius to his feet and helped him to the chair where he now sat without a word or complaint. After doing so, they took his coat and satchel in a stern but cordial manner, and took their place at the doorway, hanging his most precious belongings over the horn of some beast he did not know.

His rough treatment, however, was not the source of this strange new pain her felt deep within his heart and soul. No, it was something else. And, maybe it had some effect on him, but was not the root cause, if he were being honest with himself. Darius hurt because he was losing a part of him, again. Like his father, then his brother, and then the rest of his kin, this person, this young woman who he had carried and cared for, who he had fought an Itheanam to save, and then protected throughout the long journey of Ranok, was home now. And he was alone again.

Suddenly, as if struck by lightning, and intense wave of emotion overtook him as the realization that Izebal was not there at his side came to him. She was...somewhere. Darius could not make his mind remember. He saw shadows of memories, but that black collar had done something to him, more than dampening his abilities. It had blurred his mind and distorted his sentience, as if he had lived these last few hours in a dream.

Well, that dream was over, and he needed answers.

"Eh!" grunted Darius as he forced his tired body from the chair, his tired legs finding renewed strength through a simmering rage inside.

The two men turned their heads. Surprise painted both their faces, as if they had not expected to be interrupted. *Well, they might as well get used to being uncomfortable*, thought Darius as he hobbled forward, his right leg dragging slightly, the wound in his abdomen pumping hot pain through his body.

"Where is she?" Darius growled.

"Where is who?" Lord Ruthvin returned, his heavy golden brows knitting, which caused the ornate tattoo on his forehead to fold into an unnatural tangle of knots and symbols. His hand fell from the table, drifting down to where a basket-hilted broadsword hung, one of two weapons the High Lord carried, the other being a massive spear that was strapped to his back, the head of which was covered by a leather sheath. Realization suddenly lit behind the High Lord's eyes crystal blue eyes. "Ah, the witch. She is locked away now, laddie, and you are free from her spell."

"She is not a witch," Darius snarled, his words coming slow but firm. He raised a hand and pointed a finger at the young woman. "She saved her. She'd be dead if it weren't for Izebal."

Lord Ruthvin's eyes softened and his face relaxed, his regal bearing one of majesty and might, "My friend—and I hope you know, you are friend to me and my house for what you have returned to us—you were under a heavy spell. The kroichae broke that spell. Your memories, however, must still be muddled."

The man placed a massive, tattooed hand on Darius's shoulder and smiled kindly at him. As Lord Ruthvin's eyes met his, the lord's expression changed. He studied Darius for a long, uncomfortable moment.

"He do be from Tur'Mor, he do be an Emissary of the Church Ordan," Tyree spluttered, wheeling around the table and pointing a gnarled finger at the golden hammer on the lapel of his vest. "But what news need we have of the Church?"

Lord Ruthvin rose to his full stature, nearly a head taller than Darius and a good hand's width broader on either shoulder, and shook his head as if perplexed. Suddenly the man burst into a torrent of loud and raucous laughter. "By Ordan's beard! My daughter is home. By Gallae's grace, she do be returned. And here, we do split hairs over this and that. My friend from the Church. I hope you do not take this as rudeness, but I am to go to my bonnie lass. She do miss her daughter and will burst with joy when she sees her alive and well. Come now, Little Ery! We needs be off." He turned to his daughter and took her up in a swift motion in one arm, the girl clinging weakly to his broad neck. "As for you, friend, y'er welcome to my home and table. Come tonight. We'll sort all this out. You too, Master Tyree. I am in need of your wisdom and council."

"As you wish, me lord," Master Tyree said, placing a withered left hand against his chest and bowing slightly in his wheeled chair.

"I mean it." Lord Ruthvin turned his gaze down to Darius. "Y'er an enigma, my friend. I want to know more, but I do have to get me daughter home. I am sure ye understand. Kuln, Kren, to the High Hall!"

The two silent sentries turned on their heels and a mechanical motion and exited the shop. Lord Ruthvin nodded once more to Darius before rushing past him, a smile as bright as the summer's sun blazing across his face, his daughter held tightly to him.

"Enough to bring a tear to an old man's eye, it do be," Tyree said as the door clattered shut.

Darius, the reverent moment past, found himself hurtling back toward the reality of the situation he was now in. "Listen, I have to get Izebal back."

"Hold y'er stones, laddie," Tyree chuckled, wheeling past him toward the shelf where Darius had retrieved the crystal used for the Jrotnhalm. "Y'er not in Tur'Mor anymore, but Daneland and the great city of Talahmnas. Heed the words of the High Lord, and all will work in y'er favor."

"She is in a cell," Darius barked as he stepped toward the mage. "She has one of those, those damned collars on her, like dog! She is in pain!"

Master Tyree shoulders rose and then fell heavily with a long exhale. "It won't do ye no good to go rushing down there now. Listen, laddie, listen to the words I speak now. Y'er best hope is in the High Lord. ye did him a great favor, more than any could even hope to believe. But the Diju... long has the feud between the Clans and the Wandering Ones been. Y'er gonna need all ye can get if ye ever want to see her again."

Darius felt something drop in his guts, as if a molten ball of steel had been forced down and his throat burnt all the way, and now

seared his insides. Dread and anger boiled within him. And his heart ached with an agony he had never before known.

"Laddie," Tyree turned his chair, the crystal returned to its place on the shelf. "Eric do be a good man. If what ye say is true, if that w- Izebal, if she did in fact help save his daughter, y'er best case is to go to him tonight and explain. He'll hear y'er words. I know him."

Darius glared at the old man, the hurt and anger within threatening to rend in mind and soul, and took two long breaths before asking, "And if he doesn't?"

Tyree's whimsical face turned hard as steel, and Darius saw the face of a man who hand known violence. "Laddie, y'er just one man."

Darius snorted, turned away from the old man, and took up his coat from the rack. "Well, what are we waiting on?"

"Stones of a mountain toll!" Tyree cackled loudly. "Blood and stone, laddie!"

Darius did not feel any of the amusement the old codger seemed to exude. He exhaled slowly, his back still to the mage, and pulled the familiar coat over his shoulders.

"Easy," Tyree said as he wiped tears of laughter from his weeping left eye with a bright blue handkerchief that was embroidered with golden owls. "Let me change and we'll take my carriage. Blood and bloody stones, this laddie do have a pair, don't he?"

Darius did not consider himself an impatient man, but the time spent waiting on the old mage to get ready in one of his myriad back rooms was near maddening. To pass the time, Darius had first slumped back into the old high-backed chair, but found that utterly infuriating. Next, he ambled through the shop, looking at skulls, tubes, crystals, petrified plants, apertures of unknown usages, and a multitude of other oddities. He found himself thinking of Elcon, and how much his old friend would have liked to have seen all of this. He could almost hear the calm, collected voice of reason the high priest had, that matter-of-fact tone he used so often, explain what these bones were, what this crystal could mean in the scientific world, and how great the wisdom of the Ellitheor was to give such to mankind for their betterment and usage.

It was in these musings he came back across that old box, locked tight and buried beneath a mountain of clutter. His attention was immediately drawn to the strange box. A jolt of energy ran up spine and his palms went clammy. Slowly, he stepped toward the box.

Thud thud!

Thud thud thud!

Darius's eyes widened, his instinct to fight flared within his mind. Yet, at the same time, something external, something powerful, pressed on the soul. An urgent need, an all-encompassing need swelled within him. Something was in that box and he needed to get to it.

"Laddie!"

Darius nearly jumped out of his own skin. His hand shot out, he could feel the rays of the sun, which poked through the domed ceiling, bend toward his ring. His perception sharpened and the whole room seemed to snap into focus.

"Ordan's beard!" Tyree gasped. "Y'er eyes! By gods on high!"

"What?" Darius wheeled around on the befuddled mage. His skin felt as if lightning was coursing through him, every nerve alight with pain and pleasure. The ecstasy was nearing its zenith already, and he wanted to fall into that cold dark well just beyond his consciousness.

"I never..."

Darius, suddenly lucid, grappled against the torrent of blistering heat the coursed through his veins, the endless cascade of power that he had tethered himself to in an instinctual reflex of fear and weariness. Countless lines of golden sun had threaded through the dome of glass and latched themselves to the silver ring, hemorrhaging power into his veins at an alarming rate. The power crackled against his skin and nerves, an unwanted side effect of that strange elixir he had ingested.

"Laddie, are you alright?" Tyree's voice was no longer whimsical, his question filled with concern.

Darius grunted in agony, falling to his knees. His left had clutched at his right forearm, as if he could staunch the flow of power. Noises assailed his ears, bugs crawling, boards creaking, the whine of Tyree's mechanical chair. It was all too much.

"Daulkae nox, farum!"

A mist of darkness began to seep through the shop, choking out all forms of light. Brazers went cold, rune-bulbs disappeared, and windows were coated with a thick film of oily black. And all of this emanated from a strange fluted staff of bone-white with a massive sapphire encased by the wings of a snowy owl at the head held by the gnarled hands of Master Tyree.

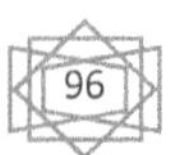

The severing of the Binding was harsh and cold, the loss of power nauseating. Darius fell onto his hands and wretched over and over, though nothing came up. There was no soothing the acidic burn in his guts. Pain remained as all sensation of pleasure fled from him, as the light had from the mists of darkness.

A long moment of silence fell across the room, the only noise being Darius's labored breathing. Slowly, the mists began to retract, flowing toward Tyree like water draining from a washtub.

Darius stared up at the old man, his labored breaths coming in short, dogged pants. "Thank...you."

"Questions upon questions," Tyree mused as he waved around his short staff, the tattoos on his hands and chest shining dimly with Aetora's light. "But one thing do be certain, it weren't the Diju whose power did this to you, of that I am now sure. I had thought... but no. This do be something altogether new and different. Blood and bloody stones it do be, don't it?"

"I tried to tell them." Darius slowly rose to his feet once more. "I tried to say I was different. But I never got the chance."

"Well, there will be time enough for questions and answers," Tyree said as he slid the strange staff into a copper tube until only the crystalline head stuck out by his side. "But tonight, we go to the High Hall. And all this—" He waved a gnarled hand toward Darius. "m—Can be handled there."

"And if I refuse?"

"If ye do want your bonnie lass, y'ed better wizen up good and smart. Y'ev got stones, but do ye have brains or wool between those ears of y'ers?" Tyree asked with a sardonic smirk.

Darius looked at the old mage, really looked at him. Behind the whimsy and the near-manic mannerisms, he saw a power there, a strength of will that could not easily be broken. This angered him, more than he would have liked to have admit. Darius wanted so badly to just turn and walk away, but one glance at the collar of black iron that rested upon the table turned his will to water. Like a dam bursting, his resolve washed away and, and, and he acquiesced.

"I will go. But if she is harmed any manner—"

"You'll do what, laddie?" Tyree quirked a dark smile, as if he were goading him even now to act. "Burn place down? ye think ye can, don't ya? By blood and stone, laddie, I do like you! ye got real fire in your belly, ye do."

The sheer amount of utter rage that well up inside Darius's soul was nearly palpable. He could taste the anger on the tip of the tongue he now bit down on to stop him from spewing incredulous slurs. His hands balled into fists at his sides, and it took every fiber in his being to not raise them in anger against the old mage.

Why? Why was Tyree acting this way? What had Darius done to deserve such behavior? All he had done was save the daughter of these burning people's lord. Why on Ethrea's green planes were they treating him this way? And Izebal? What had she done other than simply exist?

The sun, which Tyree had blocked out, seemed to reach for him once more. It would be so easy, to Bind, to lash out and strike the man down. Rush to Izebal's side, to free her and escape this Halfak forsaken place.

"Y'er thinking," Tyree smirked. "If I could just Touch the light, eh laddie? Well, try it. Make an old man's day, won't ye?"

"Why are you doing this?" Darius teeth ground together as he snarled out the question. He could taste the venom mingled into the words. He did not care.

"Y'er looking at this all wrong, laddie," Tyree tutted as he patted the head of his staff. "Y'er welcomed into the High Hall itself, offered a seat at the table. Y'er an honored guest. But make no mistake. Y'er a stranger, traveling with queer folk, in a land that don't take kindly to neither. Now, ye've been told that y'er friend won't be harmed and that you'll be able to talk for her tonight. Stones ye got, but like I asked, do ye got brains? If this were y'er home, and strangers showed up from nowhere with abilities none have ever seen, what would ye do?"

The cold, calculated question cut Darius to the quick. A memory, fleeting, lighted upon his mind. His grandfather speaking about a campfire when he was only a child sitting in his father's lap. Tales of strange people from a far shore called Morreans. Come to terrorize their home and their way of life, preaching a dark religion of blood and death, and sacrificing all who refused to bend the knee.

Darius's hands fell, his fingers unclenching. His thumb gliding trepidatiously across the cold of his silver ring. Slowly, his heart rate lowered and he allowed his mind to look beyond himself at the bigger picture. However, even as he did so fear of what was happening to him on the inside sunk its icy teeth into his veins. He was losing control, not just of the current situation, but of his abilities. Now was not the time for brazen acts. He needed to gather his facilities. He needed a plan.

The old man was right. He was a stranger to these lands, and though he had brought back the daughter of a lord, how would it have looked to him if these had been his own kin and that had been his own daughter? The throes of embarrassment caught in his heart and he winced at the thought. He had no daughter, no family, no one.

"There he goes," Tyree said slowly. "Easy now. Easy. Now, let us go to the High Hall, for there do be much to talk through, least of all those eyes of y'ers."

Darius scoffed out a hollow laugh and said, "It's always the eyes."

***

Around the back side of Tyree's shop there was a small shed with a sloping ramp of smooth stone leading to a large sliding door. Tyree produced a small bronze key with a glowing gemstone affixed within the teeth and slid it into a lock. With a sharp turn of his wrist, a series of clicks and clanks began to fill the air as the great door rolled upward, disappearing into the closure above.

"Those soft-handed Ordaitians think they do be clever, playing with cogs and steam, underground trains and sky balloons. Don't think we don't know about 'em. Clever as they do think they be, ye best believe they'd piss themselves purple once they figure out what I've created here!" Tyree cackled as the opening door revealed a large carriage unlike anything Darius had ever before seen.

The carriage, if one could describe it as such, was painted entirely black with four large wheels and glass-plated driver's box, but no place to hitch a team of horses or oxen to it. The wheels, upon closer inspection, were coated with some dense material that felt strange to the touch, as if it would be soft but had little give to it. Great springs sat under the carriage and wheels, and an axle ran toward the rear of the behemoth and was affixed to a contraption of cogs, pistons, and tubes that utterly baffled Darius's mind.

"I do call it a Mechanized Animal-less Carriage, or M.A.C!" Tyree announced proudly as he wheeled past Darius in his chair.

Sudden realization struck Darius like a gong. With widening eyes he watched Tyree lower a ramp on the back of the M.A.C. and ride into the heart of the metal beast. Fear coursed through his veins at the thought of boarding something so unnatural. He knew the fear was unfounded, but he couldn't help but feeling queasy at the thought.

The damn thing propelled itself. No horses, no oxen. It would just...go!

A thousand concerns and questions filled his mind, but Tyree left him no time to contemplate them. "Up with ye, laddie. The Lord of the High Hall waits for no man when it comes to eat'n! Up now!"

Steeling himself, Darius climbed up the ramp and found two open seats, backs to either side of the carriage facing one another. They were long benches, covered in plush velvet and were extremely soft to sit on, and every so often, there were straps with bronze buckles that he needed no instruction to understand what they were for. Quickly, he locked himself into the seat. Unsurprisingly, he found that this minor thing did little to calm the fear thundering in his heart.

"Now, watch as this little bird sings!" said Tyree as he drove his staff into a panel on the floorboard. A series of lights flickered on, illuminating the deathtrap of steel and velvet with a faint golden glow. The apparatus at the back of the MAC whirled into life, cogs spinning, pistons pumping, and chains humming in a deafening symphony of terror.

"Ain't figured out how to muffle it all yet," Tyree called out over his shoulder, his voice punching through the deafening roar of the machine. "But other than that, she runs like a dream... unlike me. I ain't ran in forty years! Bahaha!"

Darius looked up at the old mage, about to say something, anything, to get him out of this death box. Before he could do so, Tyree yanked back on the staff's head and the machine began to roll backwards out of the shop, the ramp lifting up and sealing the black box shut tight with an ominous *thud!*

***

The ride to the top of the High Hill upon which sat the High Hall was surprisingly smooth. The cobbled road scarcely jarred them at all as they sped ever upward. Darius spent most of the ride with his eyes clenched shut and his back pressed firmly against the soft seat, so much so that when they stopped, there was an impression in the velvet, along with a thick sheen of sweat. And when Tyree's M.A.C. came to its final stop, after three or four checkpoints, Darius did not hesitate in the slightest to unlatch the seat's belt and fling himself onto solid ground, all but falling to his hands and knees and kissing the earth.

Thankfully, he did not, for where they had parked was in some form of stables with about two dozen stalls with thoroughbred stallions and mares, lining the opposite wall from where they had stopped. The ground was strewn with hay and smelled sweet with honeyed oats and manure.

A porter stood outside the horseless carriage, apparently unfazed by the strange contraption. He wore a grey shirt and one of those strange over-the-shoulder skirts the Skogortuers had worn—a kilt Darius thought he heard one of them say. However, the porter's was not the drab colors of the forest, but bright blue with checkered patterns of black and silver running throughout it. He wore long stockers, with tiny flags about the calves that matched his kilt. And at the left breast, where the kilt connected, a bronze circlet was pinned bearing the image of two swords in the middle. This was not the most striking part of the young man's appearance. That designation would go to the oddly cropped hair, like a bowl had been placed on his head and crude sheers had shorn away the rest, and wispy mustaches that fell off his upper lip.

"Master Tyree," the young man said with a bow that revealed a large knife sheathed at the small of his back with an antler handle. "Welcome to the High Hall." The young man then stumbled, looking toward Darius with furrowed brows. "And, um, Mister Darius, honored guest of our lord, welcome, to Talahmnas and the Hall of the Wolf."

"Bah! Come on ye freckled flop! ye ain't needin' no formalities with me, and that ye should well know." Tyree pushed the lever on his wheeled chair and zoomed past the porter toward the double-oak doors at the end of the stables.

"Uh, this way, sir," the young man said, a bit of red spreading up his neck and cheeks as he ushered Darius toward the flight of stone steps that led to the same door Tyree was whirling toward.

Darius followed the young man, who walked with a trained poise, every step a practiced thing. The stables were long and elaborate, and Darius did not miss the intricate carvings and sculptures that adorned the gates, walls, and beams. It seemed a little too much in truth. These were horses, and the artistry here could have rivaled the Sanctuary in Tur'Mor. That being said, Darius could not help but admire the work, wishing, if only for a moment, he had stayed his hand in the Sanctuary's courtyard. Where would he be now? Would he still be working stone, serving meals with Ranun? Poor, kindly Ranun. A heat burned in his heart as he pictured the old priest, lying on the street, dead and bleeding.

"Ye alright, sir?" the porter said, reaching a hand out and catching Darius by the arm as he stumbled.

"I'm fine." Had he had been more self -aware, he would not have been so gruff with the young man who had just been doing his duty. But, he had not had time, not in the slightest to even mourn for the old priest. True, he had not known him long, but he had been kind and true. A good man who did not deserve his demise. And what of that girl in the market, the one he had saved? There was something about her.

I wonder if Elcon had found her? Would she have understood the hammer, the words he had crudely carved into the haft of it? Why? Why had he done it and what had they meant?

Honestly, it was all becoming too much. Everything seemed to be happening at once. To make matters worse, he could not dwell on either of those two, but needed to focus on Izebal and the damned letter, sealed to someone called the Apostle. It was just all too much.

"Enter well, friend of Clan Ruthvin," the porter said as he turned the gilt handles and opened the doors.

"Yes, yes," Tyree cackled as he wheeled past them once more. "Enter well. I've been entering well since before your pappy was born, laddie! Now, Darius, on with ye. We don't want to keep the old wolf waiting!"

The porter, who up until this point had managed to not break decorum, let out a small chuckle, a snorting chortle of sorts. And proceeded to turn beat red.

"There he is!" Tyree said, looking over a scarred shoulder, his white beard flaring out like an owl's wings. "That's what I like to see! A lot of respect and a little good-natured fun! I'll be sure to tell Eric of y'er insolence."

Darius looked down at the trembling young man and whispered, "Is he always this ..."

"Crazy?" the porter said, his words exasperated words coming out in a huff. "My da said he were born on a rock, and his head got thunked. I do think he is right."

Darius shook his head and let out a small laugh, his eyebrows raising in amusement as the old mage zipped down the long corridor before them. And long it was. The hall, whose entire length was covered with a black carpet with silver embroidery, was lined with polished sets of armor that ranged from styles not too dissimilar to the ones worn by those before his cursed slumber, to what was called by Elcon the High Age: gilt metal suits that encased the entirety of the wearer, adorned with fanciful helmets with great plumes of bright feathers. Along with the suits, weapons of every type conceivable were hung upon the walls, blades crossing in fanciful patterns. Tapestries and paintings also hung from the walls, most of which depicted busts of noble-looking individuals, that, over time, grew to look more and more like the Danelander Darius had met inside Tyree's shop.

Opulent was not the correct word to describe the hall; ostentatious would have sufficed better had Darius the mind for words. His eyes darted back and forth, wildly scanning as he stepped ever faster to catch up to Tyree's wheeled chair, his mind brimming with thoughts and emotions.

The walls and floors were not the only things to draw the senses. Rich scents of wood and spice filled Darius nostrils as he moved down the chandelier lit hall. On top of those, the fragrant aroma of freshly baked bread and smoked meats wafted over him, causing his mouth to water and his stomach to let out a long and low rumble.

How long had it been since he had eaten a real meal? Tasted fresh bread? Had anything other than campfire cooked deer and harvested berries and mushrooms?

A woman dressed in a grey dress with a white apron and bonnet seemingly appeared out of nowhere before them, where the hall they traversed connected with another running perpendicular, which carpet was not black, but royals blue with silver threading making up many symbols that Darius could not make out.

"Master Tyree, honored guest," the lady said as she placed hands to the side of her dress, which seemed to be starched so severely that it did not move at all, but hung like a cowbell from her shoulders to the floor, making it appear that she floated about as she walked.

"Mistress Miphia," Tyree said with a courteous bow of his head, his right hand coming to his brow in doing so. "A pleasure this fine evening."

"Our house has much reason to rejoice," the aged woman said, her plump cheeks rosy and her eyes showing the remnants of a long cry. But, it was joy that had caused the tears, for despite her perfect mannerisms, Darius could see the smile brimming behind her wrinkles. "Little Ery, home once more. The bonnie lass was all but starved, her poor little body withered to not but skin and bones. But home, home once more, she is! Blessed Ordan and Gallae, blessed be indeed."

"A good night, ma'am, a good night!" Tyree chuckled as he wheeled up to the maid. "And how is our Lady?"

"Master Tyree!" Miphia said, an over exaggerated gasp on her lips. "You know I am not to speak of the Lord and Lady of the House."

"I do, I do," answered Tyree.

"This way then, Darius," Miphia said with a gesture of her hand toward a single door, no less ornate than the set of double doors that had led into the house. "You'll need a wash and change, before being seated at the table."

Darius could not help but feel a well of frustration filling within. It was not this woman's fault, he knew that, but it still irked him deeply. He had one thing on his mind, and one thing alone: freeing Izebal.

"If ye don't wash, ye don't eat," Miphia said firmly, looking over Darius with an appraising stare. An appraising stare that apparently found Darius lacking. "These do be your rooms anyhow. You'll find water and soap, and I'll have one of the Sylians find you some fresh linens. Dinner is being served now, so don't dawdle. The Royal Family is dining, but I will make certain you'll have plenty to spare if ye don't waste time. ye hear now?"

Thoroughly scolded, Darius could find little else to do other than comply. What other option was there? To argue with the house help? To make a scene? In truth, Darius figured he was bit ripe and the notion of a bath, no matter the situation, was not unwelcome. Tyree's words came back to him, urging and imploring him that the best way to secure Izebal's freedom and resume his journey was to simply comply. But simple was an understatement, he still had pride enough within him. Pride and anger aplenty.

And what good would that do him now?

"I'll be back shortly to fetch you, laddie," Miphia said, her grimace at his appearance swiftly replaced with a warm smile.

Darius nodded his assent, not trusting his mouth to open in fear of what might come out. Over and over again he had to remind himself that she was simply doing her duty. She probably didn't even know about Izebal or his plight or anything other than the fact that he had apparently saved the daughter of the Lord of the High Hall. So, pushing the frustration deep down, Darius walked through the door and into a pentagonal room of bare wooden walls and a lofted ceiling, whose great timber rafters were naked to the eye.

The door closed behind him with a click. A heavy sigh left his mouth, and with it all the weight of the world seemed to come cascade down. His mind raced and his head ached, causing bouts of dizziness to blur his vision. Heart thundering and head pounding, Darius unlatched the cogs of his heavy, mud-caked boots, and stepped out of them onto the wood panel floor. Even through his wool stockings, he could feel the cool seeping in, a soothing sensation that sent an immediate calm through him. Next, he took off his coat and satchel, hanging them on a rack by the door before stripping off his tattered shirt and vest, taking only the briefest pause to admire the golden hammer that had perhaps saved Izebal and his very lives.

Holding the vest in his hands, he scanned the room more closely. A large rug of what appeared to either be elk or moose sat in the center of the room. On one wall was a wide bed with woven blankets and down feather pillows. Opposite of that was bronze washing tub with a curtain hung from a runner that could provide some measure of privacy. A basket sat empty beside the plush bed, so that was where he tossed the shirt and then his trousers, socks, and small clothes. A small iron stove kept the room warm, and atop it a tea kettle was set. Next to the stove was a stand with two cups, a pitcher of water, a flute of wine, red and dark, and an assortment of dried meats and carved cheese.

Darius mouth suddenly felt very dry and his stomach rumbled loudly. Need consumed him, and without further thought, he tore across the room and into the small, but elaborate pile of food and drink with animalistic fervency. Everything tasted *amazing!* The wine was rich and full-bodied, the cheese sharp, the meat robust.

The tiny pieces of bread had been dried and covered with oil and herbs that excited the senses.

No sooner was the small assortment of food and drink devoured than a pang of guilt struck at Darius's heart. Here he was, in a warm room, gorging himself on food and drink, while Izebal set locked in a cage with people who hated her for no other reason than her appearance, for her being a Diju. And why? Because she practiced magic? Tyree practiced magic here, and he was held in the highest regards. A pit formed in his gut, souring the delectable meal he had just consumed. There was only one thing that he could think of that differentiated her from these Danelanders, and the thought of it made him sick.

Darius stomped over to the basin, turning the knobs that would pipe warm and cool water into the tub. Slowly, as the water rose, so did his frustration at the predicament he found himself in. What was he to do? What could he say?

Turning about, seeking any kind of answer, he found his own frazzled features staring back at him. But not how he had remembered himself. The clean edges of his beard and hair were gone, gnarled, matted bits of black sticking out at sporadic angles. His eyes were sunken, and dark circles sagged beneath them. His check bones were sharp and his stomach too was sunk in, showing lines of dirty ribs and a nasty, pale scar over his abdomen. But that was the only scar he saw; that, and the shimmering hand left by Mireya. His whole body was free from the myriad lines and markings he had come to know. It made him feel oddly childlike, innocent, though the memories of battle and death were never far from him.

His hand darted to his shoulder without thought, swiftly feeling for the raised flesh that had always been, since the time of his swearing of the Oaths. A great sigh of relief escaped his lips as his fingers traced the bear paw that match that on his ring, a comfort of normalcy he had been missing. He was, if not different and less scarred, still Denathurias of the Iron Mountain Tribe. The Black Bear.

A low knock at the door had Darius whirling about and dropping into a fighter's stance.

"Bringing in fresh clothes, do ye be proper?" came a mousey voice, far too young to be Miphia, but carrying the same tone and accent.

"A moment," Darius answered and he swiftly stepped into the tub and pulled the opaque curtain around it. The water was far hotter than he had expected, and he had to bite his tongue so as not to yelp in pain.

"Come in." The words seethed through clenched teeth, no small amount of discomfort showing through.

"Sir, do ye be alright? May I help?"

"No!" Darius exclaimed, perhaps too loudly. "No, I am fine. Just, leave the clothes on the bed."

"As ye would, sir."

The door opened and through the curtain, Darius could just make out the blur of someone gliding toward his bed, laying out a few things, and then whisking the basket away and also taking his trench coat. Before he could understand what had happened, before he could tell her to stop, she was gone.

Blast it all. Hopefully she left the satchel, thought Darius as he slowly peaked out from behind the curtain and glanced over the room. To his immediate relief, the leather bag still hung from the hook he had placed it one, but every other belonging he had was now gone, save for the ring about his finger.

Thanks to the not-so-meager portions of cheese, meat, and spiced wine, Darius was more alert and aware than he had been in a very long time. To his shame, it also allowed for his temper to get the better of him. A slew of low curses rumbled from his lips as he stomped to the bed, sending water droplets cascading over the wood floor and elk-skin rug.

The swearing did not lessen as he pulled a cotton towel from the edge of the bed over his shoulders and through his hair. The sensation of soft fabric and intense rubbing helped sooth his aching head and calm his nerves. Slowly, his breath lengthened and his cursing tapered off, replaced with a smoldering calm.

"Are you ready, sir?"

"A moment more!" Darius growled as he finally caught sight of exactly what the young maid had left on his bed.

Laid out in perfect symmetry, the focal point being a black and silver kilt with royal blue plaid throughout, we six items. Other than the kilt was a fine silver shirt that had cords lacing up the chest, one of those small belt bags and belt, a pair of grey woolen stockings, and polished black shoes.

"High Father above. Is this some unspoken trial you have laid before me?"

"What was that, sir?" came the mousey voice from outside Darius's door.

"Nothing," said Darius quickly. A little too quickly, for he heard the maid snicker.

So be it. I'll play their game, but only for Izebal. He paused in his silent rambling as he wrapped the kilt about his waist, threading the buckles on his right hip into place.

His self-assurance that it was solely for her benefit seemed a meager thing. There was something about being away from her that made him feel... strange. Like some part of him was missing. Though what that part was or what it meant was still not clear to him.

Shrugging it off, burying those thoughts and feelings as he had buried so many others before this one—he had a purpose he must fulfil, that was all that mattered—he tugged the shirt over his body and looped the belt about him. He was not sure if he had hung everything right, he had only seen a few of these things, but had noticed that each of them had the pleats to their rear, and the leather pouch—his having what looked like tufts of rabbit fur hanging from it—about the groin, and a knife at the back. He had not been given a knife. No surprise there. So, he pulled on the socks and then laced the shoes. An oddly frustrating motion, having used the cogs on his boots for so long and buttons for his trousers and shirts, his fingers did not immediately recall the motion of tying small knots.

Irritated, slightly confused at the situation and his own personal thoughts, and feeling uncouth, since it was little more than wrapped skirt about his waist, Darius turned to the mirror and oils, working quickly at his beard and hair. The silver bolt below his lip glistened in the lamp light. Strange how it aged him, and yet he was only just a young man, and it had been a long, long time since he had felt this insecure.

"Sir, we must be on our way," the maid's voice rose an octave higher than before, a trimmer of worry in her ever-pleasant demeanor. "The Lord and Lady have finished their supper. They will be most offended if ye do not hurry in for a least the last moments."

"I wouldn't have bathed and whatnot had I not been asked." Darius's words were far too quiet for the maid to hear. *When did I*

become such a weak, sniveling, windbag? Focus. You need to focus. Tell them the truth, show them Izebal had nothing to do with their daughter's capture. Moreover, prove that without her, both he and the little girl would still be in that cave. No. Not simply in the cave. Their souls would have been consumed by that Itheanam, and their bones grafted into that corrupted spawn of Iodaba. Instead, he answered, "Coming."

Darius was led into the feast hall by the small maid who had waited out by his door, and the sights and smells nearly overtook him, causing him to pause in the doorway in a slack-jawed stupor. Cascading aromas threatened to bring him to his knees. Buttered bread, meats cut into slabs and hunks, mouthwatering mounds of beef and lamb, steamed vegetables, and a vast array of cheeses, many of which Darius had never before seen in his life. Spiced wines and honey ale tantalized the senses, filling the air with a pungent fragrance. However, it was not the food and drink that had stunned him. It was the colossal chunk of meteorite at the head of the table, into which was carved the throne of the Lord of the High Hall. And in the meteor's surface, lines of silver shone bright.

"Moonstone!" gasped Darius.

CHAPTER 10: WHAT IS LIFE
AELLIA

Aellia, can you feel it? Can you feel the Everlight coursing through us?

Could she feel it? What kind of gods-damned bloody question was that? Could she feel it? It felt as if a thousand bolts of lightning were striking her flesh while simultaneously a thousand more were blossoming from her chest. Her whole body shook with the power of something beyond her comprehension, but not beyond the mind of Iaenora, who reveled in the course of the Everlight's Touch.

I can feel her. So close, so pure.

"I feel like I am about to explode," Aellia answered in her mind, for her jaw was locked tight and her tongue still thick from her healing wounds.

Yet, even as she sat there, power coursing through her veins, Aellia could feel the injuries that had afflicted her beneath the bandages begin to mend. It was a disconcerting feeling that sent spasms of twitching muscles and deep cramps throughout her body. She writhed and flailed upon the bed, kicking away sheets and flinging pillows in her frantic thrashing.

"Daughter," the old priest said, raising the amulet that hung about his neck that bore the likeness of Ordan's great hammer, Ethra World Bringer. "By the power vested in my by the High Father and Holy Mother, I bless you. By their grace and mercy, I command this power subside."

The amulet he held so firmly made a small *clicking* noise as it opened. A gemstone, once concealed by the golden head of the hammer, was revealed. All at once the power that threatened to consume Aellia began to be drawn toward that stone. Everlight streamed from her flesh, running like a river of light, into the amulet which Elcon held in ringed fingers.

The sensation was both the most relieving Aellia had ever felt and disconcerting. Something cold settled in the pit of her stomach, a fear she could not explain at the old man's ability to draw the Everlight from her. In all her life, not being one of religion, she had never heard tell of a male being able to Touch the flows of Everlight, save for the High Patriarch.

"Do not be alarmed nor afeared, daughter," the old man said. He was panting as if he had done some great and strenuous thing, but all he had done was hold a little golden hammer and say some words. "This is a Sy'ey Aund, a mouthful I can attest, but an invaluable tool of the clergy. This one in particular can channel the flows of Aetora and Ria'Elahm."

"What in Halfak's blazes did you do to me?" Aellia asked through gritted teeth. She felt as if the life had been drained from her, the strength sapped from her limbs, and a blanket of wool cast over her thoughts.

"I can assure you, nothing harmful," Elcon said in a tender manner.

Aellia was not buying his act. This pompous old windbag had just siphoned of her Light. She felt hollow, weak, powerless.

"One of my responsibilities as Shepherd of Tur'Mor, is to help guide young daughters who are blessed by the Touch of Aetora to find their full potential granted by the Ellitheor. However, many do not have the strength or skill to properly harness this great burden in their youth. This here—" He extended the amulet toward her as he spoke, removing the chain from about his neck in a nonchalant manner Aellia expected was used to trick young girls into feeling a sense of comfort. Not her. "—is a Sy'ey Aund. A tool crafted by

heralds long past, to aid us mere mortals in our journey to return to Vanherran and into the presence of the Ellitheor once more."

Aellia gritted her teeth, teeth that she could feel were totally healed once more. Her gums no longer ached and as she slid her tongue across them, not a single chip or gap could be felt. However, despite all the powers and abilities of herself—Iaenora mostly—and the twin Blessed, her left eyes was still ruined. She ran a finger across the jagged scar. The wound trailed from just above the eye until just above the lip. It was cold, dead, and painful. But her eye, her ruined eye, seemed to pulse as her fingertip brushed it.

"I'll admit, daughter," Elcon said with a low shake of his head. "That one will probably never heal. I've not seen a wound that was unable to be healed by Alyn's Touch before, short of death. Curious indeed."

Curious? Curious! Her face had been flayed open, and this old man was musing about it?

Aellia, be still! This man has done nothing but help.

Not her. Not now. Anger welled in Aellia chest, a sickening, inky pool of venomous hatred. *Get out of my head, Iaenora. This isn't your fight.*

We are bonded, Aellia. Every fight is our fight.

He has held me here against my will. Who knows what he has done to me, what kind of experiments he has ran on me. I've heard what these Priests of Ordan do in the shadows, what their false religion hides!

Do we go back to this, then? Iaenora's voice was frustratingly calm, nearing patronizing. *This man has spoken to the Voice of Ordan, the physical receptacle of the last remaining link of the High Father to this land.*

I don't care who he's talked to. Something about him isn't right.

"Daughter, you don't look well." Elcon spoke with more caution than before, stepping ever so slightly forward toward her.

"Don't touch me, priest!" Aellia spat. She immediately regretted this motion, as the well of anger transformed into a pool of nausea, sending a ripple of cramps through her stomach and turning her bowels.

"Gentle, gentle. I am only here to help," Elcon said. "As a token of good faith, beyond returning to you your scepter, I have brought you this."

Elcon snapped his fingers twice. The door opened and two Aluth walked back into the room, again carrying a box of dark wood. They did not speak—Halfak burn it—they didn't make a sound as they walked, their wrapped boots padding noiselessly across the floor.

The one holding the box, who was slightly taller than the other Aluth with rich brown eyes that caught the light in a dazzling manner, handed it over to Elcon. Without a word or command, the two turned on their heels and exited the room once more. Aellia had to admit, there was an ominous beauty to these Aluth's movements. She suddenly became very grateful that the Crew had escaped the Church's notice over their years of thieving and redistribution of wealth in Southend. However, as swiftly as that relief came upon her, so did the hurt of her loss, of Felik and Tomo, of Belthezar and Felohme, and even Tornak, the traitorous bastard. How she hated him. How her heart lurched at the memory of cleaving his head from his shoulders. He had been a boy, just a boy, but had cost them all everything. Now, it was only her, alone and broken.

"I believe you'll recognize these," Elcon said as he flipped a small, central latch on the dark box. With steady hands, the old priest opened the lid.

Aellia's heart turned a somersault, and she could not hold back the ensuing tears that forced their way through her stoney demeanor and out onto her cold cheeks. For in that box, cleaned and polished, lay Tomo's Di'kha and her dagger. The last two remnants of her former life.

"Daughter, I speak honest truth when I tell you, you are no captive here. I know what it must look like to you, but I will do everything in my power to help show you the truth," said Elcon, his voice low and grave.

"Why? Why help me?"

"Have you not seen enough? Have you not placed the pieces together, daughter?" Elcon asked, and though there was no condescension in his voice, it still pricked Aellia's heart. "I am called to watch over the people, in the very name of the High Father and Holy Mother. You, daughter, are chosen, beyond Blessed. I have never met anyone with your unique capabilities before in my lifetime. You are a gift, a gift from the very Ellitheor."

See, Aellia, Iaenora echoed in her head. *This man knows that we are good. He has felt the Voice of the High Father. He knew the Keyholder.*

Despite her intuition, all of her hesitancies and fears, Aellia lowered her guard and extended her hand. Slowly she took hold of the red-wrapped hilt, her fingers finding gruesome memory in the grip. Longingly, she eyed the swirling dragon of cast gold that made up the crossguard and the matching loop for the pommel. The curve of the blade glistened like dew in the morning sun, perfectly polished and honed, save for a deep notch where a demon's blade had chipped away the folded steel.

There was no explosion of light, no concourse of angelic singing as Aellia hefted the blade out of the box. Just memories. Cold, dark memories, and pain. Tears that had flown freely dried as pain turned all sadness to hatred.

Aellia, be still your soul. This is a great blessing to you. I know what this means to you.

No, you don't. How could you? How could you know? You never met her, you never saw her smile, you never heard her laugh nor her weeping in the night. You never held her, or had her hold to you, when all hope had fled or when the nights were long and cold.

No. But I know you. I share your memories, your emotions, and your feelings. I cannot say I remember, but I can recall.

That was not right. This was private, not something Aellia wanted to share with anyone, not even Iaenora. But try as she might, she could not find a way to seal off this portion of her soul from the Sage of Wind and Skies.

"It did not have a scabbard," Elcon said, breaking the silent conversation between the two. "So, I had one issued for you. Constructed by our very finest craftsmen. And, and I rather think you shall enjoy it and its...unique features."

At these words, Elcon slid some hidden lever on the box. A low *click* rang out, followed by a secret drawer in the box sliding outward, revealing the hidden contents inside. And what contents they were. Two vambraces of polished silver, with veins of sapphire running through them. They looked as if they had been melted and reformed, far more alive than simple polished steel. Aellia knew these at once; they were hers. A vague memory of wearing them as she had Bonded with Iaenora flashed in her mind's eye. However, it was the blood-red scabbard set with golden fixtures that caught Aellia's full attention. A set of three leather straps connected to the scabbard, allowing for the blade to be worn at the back or hip, perfect for flying, out of the way, yet easy to draw. Placing it back

may be another story, Aellia thought for a brief moment, but figured she would have ample time to figure that maneuver out. And next to that scabbard, a small sheath was fixed, the perfect size for her most prized dagger, which lay next to the Di'kha.

"Go ahead, daughter," Elcon said with an encouraging smile. "Take them, they are yours."

Aellia thrust forth her left hand, snatching up the scabbard and strappings, leery of some trap. Elcon did not resist. He simply smiled and waited in an infuriatingly patent manner. Noticing this, Aellia, rather sheepishly now, slung the scabbard over her back and fixed the buckles across her chest and shoulder, sliding the dagger's sheath to under her left arm against her side, then retrieving her two vambraces.

"You look like an angel," came a dreamy voice from across the room.

Aellia's eyes shot up, quickly assessing the room once more, as her hand grabbed at the dagger she had only just slid into its sheath.

"She does," Brei intoned as she walked in behind her twin in perfect poise and harmony.

"And what shall we call her?" Ayln smirked, making her face all the more beautiful. "For I have not heard of angels in this age."

Aellia let go of the hilt of her dagger, her hand slowly falling to her side. What had she been thinking? Who was she going to fight? An old priest? The Blessed who had saved her life?

Breathe, Aellia. Breathe and be calm.

I swear to whatever god made you, if you do not find silence, I shall!

Aellia, was that another joke? I thought you had altogether lost your humor? Perhaps it had been blown away in one of your self righteous storms of anger.

"Blessed Ones, what brings you here today? I was not aware of further healings needed?" Elcon asked, seeming somewhat perturbed by the entrance of the two sisters. Not something Aellia had ever noticed from him before when they had arrived, announced or not.

"We come bearing tidings of the utmost import, High Priest," Ayln said with a shallow curtsy. "The Patriarch Orrum is here, and requesting audience."

"Patriarch Orrum? Here?" Elcon said, dropping the case onto the ground with a loud clatter. "Why? Have you met with him?"

"No, High Priest," Brei said with a curtsey as shallow as her sister's. "We had been on our way from our chambers to meet with the Sisterhood in the Valamour, when I had premonition, though not a full vision, of our Grace's coming. We thought it prudent to inform you. I could not sense his need, but it seemed urgent."

"Thank you, daughters, your perception and forethought are a blessing in and of themselves," Elcon said, making the Sign of the Hammer with his fingers. "And, dear Aellia, I do apologize for the commotion and the abrupt need to depart now. But, I am afraid I must go and make myself ready. Rest well. If you'd like, there is Aympher Tea and Grayuun Tea over there, hot and ready. Just needs to steep. I must go now. Farewell until tomorrow. I will see you soon. Get some rest."

Elcon, Ayln, and Brei seemed to move in a blur of motion before Aellia's eye, none of them taking another thought of her or her presence. And, for once, this actually bothered her. She had lost count of days here, but to be utterly ignored because some old man in a hat was arriving was absurd. She was, well, she was the Sage of Winds! She harnessed the powers of an ancient entity sent to protect all of Ethrea.

We are the Sage of Winds and Skies. Not just you, Aellia.

I know that! spat Aellia as she crossed her arms in frustration, the door closing swiftly behind the departing three.

I thought you liked being alone?

I like not being left out or treated like second best. Bah! It's always this way with these Uppers. Don't you see? I hold all this power, these so-called unknown abilities, and I am just tossed to the side because of another old, rich, windbag.

He is the Voice of the High Father, Aellia. He is no normal man. Show some form of reverence.

Or what? I'll be cursed? Maybe I'll have a little voice shoved into my brain that is always telling me what to do and not do?

That might be helpful, you know.

"Ugh!"

Aellia grimaced as her hand flashed to her face. She should not have uttered any actual noise. The scar there felt as if rivers of fire flowed beneath the surface of her skin.

Why can't I heal this?

It has been Touched by Iodaba's corruption. Something that should not be possible.

What do you mean?

Aetora's Light is spirit and mind, it is cognitive reasoning and life, in the sense of understanding. Ria'Elahm's Light is matter and life, all things living and growing, from the motes of space to the great stones of the mountains and the very waters of the deep. These two are things of Creation and Life. Iodaba is the antithesis of such. It is death, decay, poison and corruption. It is rust where Ria'Elahm is ore. It is loss where Aetora is memory. It is death in essence, and the essence of death. It should not be able to be harnessed as such, forged into metals of any type. Neither I, nor any of my sisters, knew such evil during the Days of Dread. Priestess and priests of the Fallen Ones could spew for the corruption of Iodaba, even fuse it into their mindless minion's souls for a time, but never make physical weapons with it.

Well, damnation. Looks like we have a new problem to worry about.

We? Are you saying you believe in the Ellitheor? That you accept our divine mandate and calling?

Well, it's kind of hard to ignore the literal shard of a Sage that has bonded to my mind and soul.

Blessed day! Aellia, I knew it! I knew you would begin to understand our purpose.

Hang on. I said it's hard to ignore the fact that there might be powerful beings and maybe even...I don't know, something more. But I never said I believed in gods and divine purpose. And at the same time, how can I ignore what I have seen with my own eyes, felt in my own soul?

Faith is not knowing, Aellia. That is knowing. Faith is trusting in what you cannot know, but what you feel to be right. We are bonded, Aellia. I know you, perhaps more so than any other being out there. We can do this, together.

And what exactly is, 'this'?

We must find my sisters and help them awaken. You've known the one that is called the Keyholder. He and eleven others have the power to awaken us. They have sworn oaths, ancient and powerful. It was the contingency plan of the High Father, set in motion before the Day of Dread, before we sealed away the Fallen Ones, in case our sacrifice proved incapable.

Are you talking about that creep on the stairs?

Aellia, not everyone is, what you call a creep. Some people truly mean well and good.

Then they're fools.

Perhaps. Or perhaps they have something you have forgotten.

And what is that?

They have hope and mercy.

"Ha!" Damnit! Why laugh?

Why did you laugh?

I thought you could read my mind.

It's not like that, Aellia. Just as you cannot read mine. Not yet leastwise.

Right. Well. I just find it funny that you attribute mercy to the man that I watch beat two Kh'ar robbers senseless. With a masonry hammer.

Well. Mercy takes on many forms in many places, scoffed Iaenora. *Do not think that I spent my centuries living only mending and healing. I was a warrior. I flew on the front lines, just over the banner of my brother.* Iaenora went uncharacteristically quiet, biting off that last word. Aellia felt a swell of embarrassment and guilt in her mind. But, it was not her own. Not this time.

Your brother? What happened to him?

Iaenora did not answer.

Oh no you don't! You have pinched and pried almost every secret I have out. Don't you dare start holding back from me now!

Suddenly, the whole room shook, and an ensuing darkness overtook all round Aellia. Aellia reached for the scepter, forgetting the conversation and focusing on trying to draw some form of Light into her. That bloody old priest had sucked all the light into his weird necklace! She had nothing, nothing to call upon. The air became cold. So cold. Her eyes became heavy.

"Iaenora," Aellia groaned, her throat straining against two cold tendrils of inky black. "Help me."

Silence abounded.

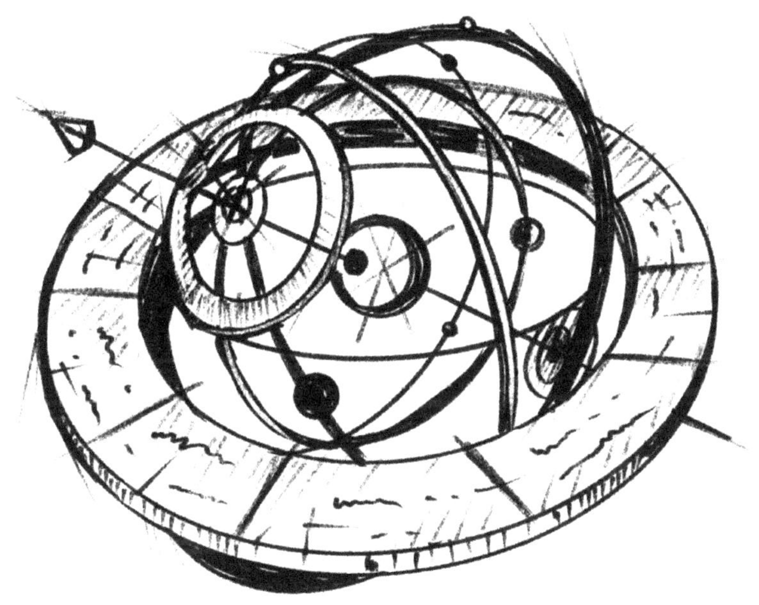

Chapter 11: Conversations A Plenty
Elcon

"Thus you see the tremendous importance of this endeavor, old friend," the High Patriarch said, his back to where Elcon sat behind his own desk in his study, in the high-backed chair he loved so much, a love that he did not feel so connected with at the present moment. "If this were to go awry, if the people were to know, Elcon, there could be pandemonium in the streets."

"Yes, yes," Elcon said, tossing his finger in a flippant gesture as his elbow rested on the desk. How many times would they go over this? How many hours would be consumed by this very discussion? Precious hours Elcon did not have to squander. "But what are we to do, Your Holiness? The schism you fear is already deepening, not something heretofore resolvable."

"It is not so deep as of yet, old friend," the Patriarch said, turning his brilliant blue eyes onto Elcon, who straightened up as a chastened child. "Or else you stewardship is lacking. Something I find far to difficult to envision."

Elcon did not miss the twinkle in Orrum's eyes as he spoke, the jest of envisioning blatantly bespeaking his Gift. "Father, I toil without ceasing, as you so claim, but the streets are thick with the unrest of those who have strayed from the flock. Every day our congregation lessens, and those who call themselves Kingsmen, who pollute themselves with false lineages and corrupted doctrines, win away the hearts of the young and impecunious. It is not on idle ears that the reports of our very own General Thanadius fall. Our good Mayor, Xandar, too, does come to me in supplication, seeking guidance against the rising tide of those called Kh'ar Robbers. By Ordan's blessed name, his own brother was abducted by that lot of heathens who worship—worship!—the Fallen One's very accursed names."

"What happened to Alec Adelmo is travesty, and the rise of the Calun Nation has many hearts weakened," the High Patriarch said as he walked the long length of Elcon's desk, his gloved hands brushing against a few of the apparatuses he had been tinkering with, then inevitably landing firmly upon a heavy tome of green-bound leather with a golden hammer inlaid on its cover. "It is this, these words, that bind us together and keep us strong. Do not forget the covenants you made with the High Father and Holy Mother. We are duly sworn to abide by their teaching and words, words that have become abundantly clear in my eyes. Would that I had not spoken in haste, that I had stayed my hand and not sent that boy away. May Gallae's grace and mercy be upon my soul for that."

"You acted in a manner that was in accordance with your office," Elcon said, rising for the first time since entering his opulent study. He walked over to the High Patriarch and laid a ringed hand upon his robed shoulder. "We have all done the very best we could, given the nature of our callings. And we, together, agreed that it was the best in the interest of the Holy Church to send Darius on. A decision for which we do not know the ends, but have since understood the beginnings. Think of what we have discovered, the truths uncovered."

"Yes," Orrum said, nodding his head slowly in appreciation. "Yes, what your three found was beyond helpful to our cause."

"Ironclaw and Darkknife will be pleased with your words of acclamation."

"Did something happened to the third?" Orrum asked, genuine concern showing through on his weary face.

It was Elcon's turn to crack a wry smile. "Billtooth doesn't care much for anything anymore, other than violence. Doesn't have the taste for it."

An awkward pause hung for but a moment before Orrum rolled his eyes. "You were always better with a blade than a joke. Subterfuge over comedy, old friend. It suits you far better."

"Alas, I do believe you are right," Elcon said with a hollow, half-embarrassed laugh. It felt good to have a conversation with one's equal—if not more so—in intelligence and understanding. The two had been friends for nearly as long as he and Ranun had. Funny how life has a way of putting those in your life at the time you need them the most.

"Do not think I forget you are Von, my friend. A man wed to the sword, to then be covenant to the Church," the High Patriarch said solemnly. "Many lives you have lived, and each of those have led you to be here, to be where the Church needs you, where I need you. Be like he of whom your name bespeaks, be like he who stood when other men found fear in their hearts. Be implacable and bold. Be firm and true. And most of all, be loyal to the cause in which we are bound together."

Elcon swallowed hard at hearing his sworn-name given, Von. Von, the only human who was said to follow the Apostle of Death when all other turned home. He alone left all he had to go, and nevermore was he heard from again. But his name would live on. It would be worn by those sworn to the sword, wed to it, who had mastered not only blade-craft, but themselves. Von, the title held before the name of bearer, for it came before self and all else. Von, the one thing from Elcon's old life that would never leave him. He was, is, and forever would be, Von'Harr, blademaster of Ordiatea.

"Well, I must be off," Orrum said as he checked his pocket clock. "May the favor of the Ellitheor be with you."

"May Ordan strengthen thee and may Gallae's grace attend thee," Elcon said, stooping to a knee before the High Patriarch.

Orrum took from his pocket a sealed missive, not too dissimilar to the one stamped and given the young Darius before his departure those many long nights ago, had handed it to Elcon as he rose to his feet. "Grace and abundance be upon you and your house. May prosperity reign and the Kingdom come."

"Amen."

"And Amen," Patriarch Orrum said with finality.

Elcon walked his old friend silently through the study and to the locked door. With a turn of a crack and the pull of a latch, the door swung outwardly. The High Patriarch nodded a final farewell—it was uncouth to speak once more after the formal vale of the priesthood—and stepped into the outer chamber where he was meet by his steel-clad Aluth.

Slowly, Elcon let out a long sigh. He reached into his coat pocket and pulled out an embroidered kerchief and dabbed at a bead of swell rolling down his temple. His hands shook, a slight tremor brought on not by fear, but by age. The sweat, too, was that perspiration of exertion. Kneeling and rising, that had been all he had done, and yet, sweat streamed freely and his joints felt as if they would burst into flames. Von. He had been von, but no longer.

The comforting cushion of his chair brought near instantaneous relief. Yet, as he sank into the lush fabric, his eyes drifted to the door where the High Patriarch had just exited, or, more correctly, to just above. There, mounted on a lacquered mahogany board, whose edges shone bright with inlaid gold, hung a polished rapier of exquisite design. Elcon's eyes watered with tears as he looked over the fine length of shining steel, the opal stone set into the pommel that provided the perfect balance and counterweight. The ornate craftsmanship of the basket about the hilt. And then, of course, there was her little sister, the parrying dagger he had named affectionately Gallae in his heathen years, for the many times she had saved his neck. Such beauty and meaning hung upon that wall, a life lived in the vibrance of youth, hung away, just out of reach, yet always there to remind him.

Micaela, her steel hair bound up in a tight braid atop her head, walked into the room with militaristic poise. A silver helmet was tucked under her left arm, the plumes trailing behind her nearly to the floor. She wore a breastplate of polished steel and riding trousers common amongst the heavy cavalry. At her side hung a curved saber that carried none of the adornment of the two blades Elcon had just been admiring.

"I come as one called to serve," the Avajan'Aluth announced upon her entry into Elcon's study. An entrance that nearly had Elcon jumping from his seat in alarm.

"By Gallae's grace, Micaela! What are you doing here?"

The Avajan'Aluth noticeably cringed at the usage of her name. Something Elcon swore to himself he would stop doing. But by the gods, the fire in her eyes when provoked ignited something in him he had not felt in ages before meeting her.

"I report as called upon," the Avajan'Aluth continued, fighting through the noticeable frustration. "By your own words, to report if there was any mention of the happenings of Hallowed Night."

Hallowed Night! The moniker he and she had chosen to bequeath to the night upon which they had found young Aellia. It had been weeks, and not one word had bled onto the streets of Tur'Mor to either of their knowledge. Thankfully, the launch of the Mayors first patronable skyship had taken much of the attention off of them. But it was inevitable, Elcon had known it, that someone somewhere must have seen something that had happened that fateful night.

"Speak, Avajan'Aluth, my ears are yours," Elcon answered, his stunned demeanor causing him to fall back into formality as rescue from wordlessness.

"As my Shepherd guides, so shall I go," Micaela answered with a bowing over her head and a sudden dropping to one knee. She then rose swiftly, showing no sign of pain or unease. "Three of my Aluth stationed near Darhdall Alley overheard someone talking. It seems that the High Priest's sisterhood have failed in totally adjusting Regent Aldorian's memories. He has turned to drinking rather profusely. And in his drunken stupor, he tells tales of events he should have no recollection of."

Elcon's heart sank as his fury began to smolder within his very core. That fat curd had been a thorn in his side for far too long. Why couldn't have simply kept his mouth shut? It was all supposed to be a dream in his mind, Shanavaral had overseen the procedure herself.

"What do your ears hear?" Elcon asked, his voice a menacing whisper.

"It is said that he frequents an old tavern of sorts," Micaela paused for a brief moment, contemplating. "A tavern that had once been a rather unseemly place that burned down in fire not too many nights before the Hallowed Night. The proprietor had procured a new location across the street and reused the old moniker, The Twisted Stool."

"A brothel?" Elcon said the words without thinking, his mind racing. Where had he heard that name before? Why did it stick out in his mind so? "Have you heard any of his ramblings?"

"Only that he claims demons took him in the night, and that an angel of vengeance fell from the sky, striking down his guards for crimes they did not commit," Micaela continued, though her eyes had narrowed slightly on Elcon. "An angel described as a petite woman with ice for hair and eyes of lightning."

"And what does Mayor Xander think of this? Does he not fear that having one of his Regents roaming around the city inebriated would be bad for his reelection campaign?"

"Chief Inspector Aurelius Hallock has been spotted many a night, tailing Aldorian in the shadows," Micaela cocked a slight smile. "That man, now there is a man who knows his ways about the streets."

Elcon grimaced. It was true, Aurelius Hallock was the best of the best, and one of the few men more loyal to the Mayor than the Church, a frustration that had gnawed at Elcon for quite some time.

"His Silver Stars, too, are about," Micaela continued, clearing her throat. "But they are of less concern. Brutes and bullheaded, the lot of them. It does beg the question: what do they know that we don't?"

What do they know, indeed? It was no question. Elcon knew exactly what they were truly looking for, and it was upstairs in hands of a woman just only out of adolescence. But did they know what it truly was? That was the real question. Did Mayor Xander know that he, in his very residency, had housed one of the six divine scepters? Did he know what it had meant or what they were capable of? And if he did, what was he planning on doing with it?

At this point, Elcon's mind was nearly numb. So much had happened, so many things weaving and intertwining. It was becoming too much. Had he lost his edge, his most powerful tool? The very mind which he had honed over years of learning, subterfuge, political intrigue, religious understanding, and mastery?

No. No he had not. He would find the underlying cause of this. He would figure this out.

A quiet knock sounded at the door. Micaela looked at Elcon, concern rippling across stoic her face, just behind the eyes.

"High Priest," came the melodic voice of Brie—or was it Ayln? Elcon had such a time telling the two apart. "May we enter?"

We? He guessed it did not matter which had spoken first. "Enter as you would, Blessed Daughters." By using their formal title, he denoted the propriety of the engagement before they had even entered his study.

The crank turned and the handle shifted from the outside. That would be one of the Aluth, making sure the Blessed did not do any labor outside of their calling. An oddity, Elcon mused, that these two groups, Blessed and Aluth, were both wholly subservient to the Church, and yet, while one group was supremely esteemed as one as near to divinity as a human could be, other than the High Patriarch himself, the other was considered as lowly as those who clean the floors. Albeit, far, far more deadly.

Brei and Ayln Candius burst into the room, somehow both in graceful unison and frantic disarray. "High Priest," the two curtsied in unison. "We hate to come so unannounced, but it is a matter of urgency."

"Speak freely," Elcon said, worry coursing into his heart, muddling his already frazzled mind.

"The girl," Ayln stammered out, fumbling over her words, face distraught.

"She is gone," Brei continued.

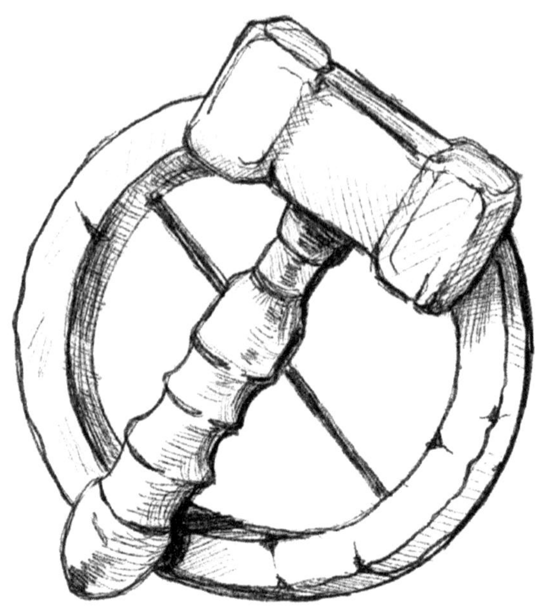

Chapter 12: Dinner and a Show
Darius

"Moonstone!" Darius gasped in raw amazement. Never before had he ever seen such quantities of celestial stone. His tribe had scavenged the whole of known Ethrea in search of even the most meager deposits of the precious ore. Yet here, here was a piece of Moonstone than he could forge enough weaponry to arm a thousand of his brethren. If only they'd had this before the storming of the Black Fortress of Morr.

"There's the laddie!" shouted Tyree as bits of meat fell from his feathered beard. "About damn time, too!"

If there had been any formal announcement or introduction planned, that proclamation had utterly ruined it. As for Darius maintaining a level of decorum, well, that was ruined by his gaping maw.

Embarrassed to his core, Darius snapped his mouth shut and continued in after the little maid in her motionless grey dress as she seemed to glide across the granite floor, not scuff nor tap audible. The table itself was nearly as much of a spectacle as the meteorite, if it were not for the veins of moonstone threaded throughout. Formed from the trunk of a great oak, the lacquered table was set with twenty plates on either side, and the head, which was formed from the crotch of the great tree, was so wide that two men could stand with arms outstretched and just barely touch the sides. The legs of the table were carved into what looked like wolves' paws—fitting— and were as thick as the ham of a man's leg. The chairs set about the table were magnificent pieces of work, high-backed and glinting with silver gilding, the seats of which were of the black and silver of the High House's tartan.

Two hogs were plated, an apple in the mouth and everything. Their sides had been carved away, ribs on full display with cold juices coagulating on them. This meal had sat for a long time, but Darius felt no guilt at his tardiness. These had eaten. They were fine. And, upon a secondary glace, he took note of each of the additional guests seated around the now standing Lord Ruthvin. He also took note of the two massive dogs, black as tar, laying down and chewing on a thigh bone of an ox, drool slopping onto the floor as the bone cracked under their mighty jaws.

Starting at the farthest from the Lord of the High Hall, those two silent soldiers, Kuln and Kren, sat straight and unmoving. Something within their helmets sent a shiver down Darius's spine, though he could not quite make out what or why.

Past them, on the left side of the table, was Tyree in his wheeled chair. He had not changed since they had arrived but looked as if he had eaten his fill. His bright eyes were filled with merriment and delight.

Next to Tyree sat a striking young woman with braided golden hair and blue eyes that were certainly inherited from the Lord of the Hall. She was tall and lean, face hard and eyes forward. She was pretty, though a fire burned behind those eyes, and Darius knew she had skills beyond the words of a mere court gossip. Further adding to this assessment on her left forearm Darius could see the telltale signs of one who practiced archery for more than sport. She sat proud and regal in a lady's dress, appearing absolutely in her element.

On the other side of the table sat two more young women, one of whom Darius immediately recognized as the girl he had saved. However, she looked a totally different person. Her features were soft now, not gaunt. Her eyes were bright and her cheeks rosy, becoming all the more so when Darius's met her gaze. He gave her a little smile, and a portion of his worry seemed to relinquish at the sight of seeing her healthy and happy. Like Ery, her older sister next her, was also redheaded and fair of features, though she had many more freckles on her nose and cheeks. She was a pretty young lady, probably in her mid-teenage years. They both wore matching dresses of blue and were not nearly as bold as their elder sisters, giving both of them a more juvenile appearance.

Lastly, a woman Darius could only describe as imposing—and presumably the Lord's wife—sat at his right-hand side. She had bright red hair, not dyed like those of the Tur'Mor, but natural and frizzy, pulled into twin braids down the side of her head. She was a handsome woman with a strong jaw and muscled shoulders that were bare, showing off twin tattoos. Her dress was shimmering blue, tight against her bosom and wrapped about her arms above her biceps, leaving lace draped onto solid muscles. About her torso, from her left shoulder draping across her breasts and abdomen and falling at her hips was patterned shawl matching Lord Ruthvin's kilt, and over the shoulder was a circular golden brooch with a sword through it. On her left hand, covering a series of tattoos, a silver netting was set, connected rings and chains that brought memories to Darius he had long since forgotten.

"Friend of my home, welcome, to Talahmnas!" announced Lord Ruthvin as he raised a horned tankard into the air in salute.

The maid quickly pulled a chair out. It was stationed between the eldest daughter and the head of the table, directly across from the lady of the house. Darius, unsure of any customary response, resorted to his most common reply: nothing at all. He sat silently; hands set tense upon the arms of the chair.

"Come now, laddie! Ye're our honored guest," Lord Ruthvin thundered. He then plopped into his chair and threw back the tankard, sloshing ale down his braided beard. He then let out a loud belch.

"Eric!" hissed the lady of the house, shooting daggers at her husband. Her steely green eyes no doubt could do more harm than real daggers.

"Oh! Of course, forgive me, love!" Eric said, palming his head, jostling the silver crown. "Where do be me manners? Anywho, Darius. This do be me bonnie lass, Sophie. Gem of the land, she is. Bore me two good sons, thick as thieves and thicker in the head if ye know what I mean? Then, three daughters graced home. Lori, the one that looks like her old pa, Ella there, sweet as pie and pipes like the heralds on high, and then, Little Ery, who you did already meet."

The young girl blushed profusely at the mention of her name. Though she was not the only one to show discomfort. Lori, who was sitting right next to Darius, rolled her eyes and shook her head, while Lady Sophie twitched ever so slightly at his less than regal remarks.

"Our family is graced," came Sophie's more proper response. She was not drunk, and Darius highly doubted this woman had ever allowed herself to become so. She was so stiff and proper, the image of propriety and sophistication, albeit a very muscular one. "My husband has perhaps celebrated a little too much at the return of our daughter."

"Can ye blame a man?" Eric thundered jovially. "Saved from death and Halfak's gates. Brought home to us by a stranger bearing the mark of Ordan. Ain't thought I'd ever see nothing like it."

"What my husband means to say," Lady Sophie cut in at her husband's faltering rambles. "Is that we are most gracious for the return of our daughter."

"Tyree said ye were able to help in the Jrotnhalm," Eric blurted out. "Is that true?"

Darius blinked, not certain what the High Lord was asking. He was, thankfully, saved by the wizened voice of the old mage, Tyree. "That he did, that he did! He's as strong as an ox. Don't let those soft hands fool ye none. He's got stones under his belt, he do!"

Darius felt a flair of heat up the back of his neck and could not help but notice Lori stifle a laugh. Ella looked mortified. Lady Sophie remained poised, pressing through the comment with artful tact. "How did you come to find our little lass? I've heard from Master Tyree and a report from Orhund. But, we would like to hear it from you."

"Ah, come now, Sophie," said Lord Ruthvin. "Look at the lad, ain't hardly got any meat on them bones. Let 'im eat in peace. Stories come best by a full stomach and to the smoking of pipes and the sounds of a crackling fire."

"No," interjected Darius, eyes still downcast. He raised his head, meeting first Lord Ruthvin and then Lady Sophie's gaze. "She is right." He nodded to the lady, and then, calling upon all the lectures he could, delivered by the mouth of perhaps the greatest orator he knew—Elcon—Darius pressed on. "There are many things that need to be discussed. Foremost, the release of my companion, Izebal, whom yours have labeled a witch."

The room went utterly silent.

Ten. Fifteen. Thirty seconds passed, and still, no one talked. But Darius refused to break. He refused to give up his advantage. For a fool, when silent, could be considered wise. He knew what he wanted, what was the point of arguing any other topic? His reasons for being in the forest were irrelevant to this conversation. He simply wanted Izebal free from bondage. From there, well, he would figure out the rest.

It was Lord Ruthvin who spoke first. Before doing so, he reached up above his head and took hold of that great spear that had hung from his back in Tyree's Shop. It was mounted, fixed directly into the meteorite above the carved throne. And as Lord Ruthvin grabbed the haft, Darius saw tendrils of silvery-white light arc between the now-naked head of the spear and veins of Moonstone. His eyes went wide, and he almost broke his silence, but Eric started in, saying, "It is a funny thing, Outlander. That one such as y'erself came us in such perilous times. I don't be accusing ye of anything, so don't go jumping to conclusions now. What I mean to say is, it is a mighty strong coincidence that not one of my Skogortuers could find hide nor tail of my little lassie. But you, a total stranger, who does accompany himself with the likes of the Diju, did bring her here."

"Say what you mean," answered Darius. "You know what I want. Ask. As long as it gets Izebal free, I'll answer. But I want your word. If I answer your questions, play this game, you'll let her go."

Had there ever been warmth and merriment in the room? None at this point could say one way or the other. All were tense, eyes hard locked either on Darius or down at their plates. Lori moved first, shoving against the table, sending her chair sliding backward with a deafening scrapping noise.

"Thank you for bringing her home," her voice was hammered steel and a mountain's song, fair but very dangerous. "Father, I will retire to my chambers, if it pleases you?"

"Lori is right," said Lady Sophie as she rose from her chair as well, though not as dramatically. And somehow, that was even more menacing. Darius could feel his heart hammering in his chest now, the ringing near deafening in his ears. "Ella, Erskina, off now! To bed with the two of ye."

"But Ma," Little Ery squeaked. "I wanted to know how he found me. I don't remember anything. I just want—"

"Ery," said Lord Ruthvin. "Listen to y'er mother. The three of ye to bed."

"I'll be going, too," Lady Sophie said. "I need to speak with me brother."

Eric looked hard at his wife, thick brow furrowing.

"Not about this," she said quietly.

Realization dawned in the High Lord's face. "Ah, yes. I understand. We'll talk tonight. Love ye, me bonnie lass."

Lady Sophie leaned over and kissed her husband on the brow. "Play nice. He is still a guest. And remember, he did save our daughter."

"And Darius." Lady Sophie turned her eyes on him once more. "Thank you, for what you have done for us. I implore you listen to my husband and do not judge too swiftly. These are dark times, far darker than you Outlanders believe."

Darius nodded his assent, not daring break the momentary peace silence had brought.

Once the lady left, following her daughters up a spiral set of stairs that wound behind the massive meteor and up into their chambers above, Lord Ruthvin turned his attention back to Tyree and subsequently, Darius.

"Alright then," he said cooly. "Master Tyree, you best be laying down a foundation for our guest. He needs to understand what he has tangled himself in."

Tyree, to his credit, actually took this command with an air of seriousness that was worn all too well on his otherwise wizened face. Hard lines were formed of aged wrinkles, dark drooped eyelids lost their crazed edge and became heavy with the burden of knowledge.

"Darius, lad, this is a dense bit of knowledge. ye need to understand firstly, that we do appreciate you bringing back Little Ery. She is, well, most invaluable to us," Tyree said slowly, as if he were searching for the exact right word every time his lips parted.

"It is more than a father's love," Lord Ruthvin cut in, his own grave face looking to be near tears. "Don't get me wrong. I love her fiercely. But, it do be more than that. You'll see. Continue."

Tyree did not look offended nor upset at Lord Ruthvin's interjection. If anything, a bit of relief rested on his face. "Every daughter of the line of Dane, from Dane Stronghammer's own daughter, progenitor and protector of the Danelanders, to every daughter born of that line, a test has been issued. Lori and Ella have both walked that path and were not called to it. Little Ery was to test after the Ulkeniheim, which was to take place at the next full moon.

"Yet, strange things began to happen. Dark things. Terrible things. Sheep would be found skinned alive. Oxen in fields still standing, but their skulls ripped from their shoulders. And then, the true terror began. Girls—wee bairns all—snatched up in the night. Gods above. We'd find 'em in the trees, swaying in the morning breeze, not an organ in their torsos."

Darius's stomach curdled and his mind flared with rage.

"Draugr we thought, perhaps even Redeyes, devilish shites," Tyree spat, taking no notice of Darius's changed demeanor. "But it couldn't be. They don't discriminate, the chutting pig lickers. That left the Diju. Diju have long been after our young girls, any that could Touch the Lifesource. And not many can, mind you. But every girl that went missing until Little Ery had the Spark in them. Every last one of them."

"It wasn't Izebal," Darius snapped. His ring tingled on his finger, he itched to Bind. The bear in his mind wanted out, wanted to be free. Needed to be.

He breathed out slowly. *What is wrong with me?*

"Laddie," Tyree said slowly, his hand hovering over to the head of his scepter. "I ain't saying it was her specifically. But, ye got to admit, we had a good strong reason to suspect."

"Can the girl Touch? Do you know?" Darius asked, trying his hardest to force his thundering heart to calm. Why was it so hard to control himself?

"The test was to determine that," Lord Ruthvin sighed, leaning back in his chair. Apparently he was not all that concerned with the war raging behind Darius's eyes. "Not a daughter of my father's kin has ever had an affinity for the Spark."

"This girl does?" Darius blurted out the question. The wolf in the forest of pale blue light. The reason the Itheanam had not yet

consumed her. That part made sense. However, the pointed accusation toward Izebal made did not ease his anger. They were judging her based simply off of her appearance. They had no idea who she was or what she had suffered through. It was deplorable.

"We don't know, how could we?" Tyree said as if Darius were daft. "The Ulkeniheim isn't for days and she ain't been tested. Didn't ye hear what we just said?"

"Master Tyree," sighed Lord Ruthvin. "He is a guest and doesn't know our ways. Where he comes from, one out of every thousand girls is born into the Light. Not so many here, not since our long exile."

"That be true. That be true, indeed. Forgive me, laddie, its been a day, now hasn't it?" Tyree said with a wink.

"But," Lord Ruthvin cut it. "We get ahead of ourselves. We've talked a lot about me and mine. I am far more curious about you, lad. How did ye come to find her. And don't just say ye stumbled across her in the woods. We searched them trees for two weeks, night and day."

Darius weighed his options: stubbornness or truth. He knew only one would even give Izebal the slightest glimmer of hope for release, so he chose the only real option. Truth.

"For you to understand, I need to go back." Darius chose his words carefully once more. He needed to explain why he was here, when in truth, all he knew what that he had been sent out of Ordiatea on an errand with a missive and a prayer, to find one called the Apostle. So, the trick was now, how to share, but not overshare.

When he spoke next, he did so deliberately. He told them of his time spent in the Bread House of his late friend Ranun, and his demise at the hands of the robbers. He told them he had worked for one of the high priests, but did not name Elcon by name, just title. He told them he had been sent from Tur'Mor by command of the Church, to deliver the sealed envelope to one called the Apostle in Northern Dane. He did not mention his stay at the Fourth Eye Inn but did share how he had been set upon by Hunstmen that drove him into the trees.

"Why would Huntsmen be after a member of the Ecclesiastical Order?" Lord Ruthvin asked. He had been listening in utter silence, his left hand resting on the head of one of the two gigantic, scratching aimlessly. "They don't bother themselves with the religious sort. Kind of counterproductive, if you get my gist."

Darius had long since realized that the Church knew far more than what Ranun had originally told him. They were aware of true magic, of witches and beasts of the dark. They had known of Morreans, though they had a separate name for them. And yet, all of Tur'Mor had treated such as fables and child's fantasies. What had it benefited the Church to keep that secret alive, that false notion so embedded in the minds of its people? Darius had not stopped to think about that before.

No. Now was not the time for thinking about fables and tales, he needed to focus. Izebal. Freeing her was his highest priority now. "Honestly, I don't know," Darius answered in truth. "But because of me, Izebal's whole troupe had been decimated. A horde of Huntsman had set to burning their tents and chaining their children. I did what I could, but I was too late to save them. I couldn't save them." His words trailed off as a lump formed in his throat. He saw the faces from that night, since shielded from his memories, crying out in pain and pleading for salvation. He had failed to save them but brought retribution heavy upon the heads of those who had murdered them. A fire filled his bosom as he recalled that harrowing night. "Izebal's people were slaughtered. Only she escaped. We fought our way free and fled further into Ranok. And in the heart of the old wood, I had a dream where I saw a tree. I was led there by the likeness of a wolf. That was how we found her. Lord Ruthvin, I believe your daughter called me. I had questioned the origin of that dream, but I think I know the reality of it now."

A stillness settled over the room, a hushed moment of thought. That peaceable stillness did not last, as Tyree blurted, "Y'er forgetting something, laddie. Ye totally left off you fighting the Soulless One in the cave where the lassie lay still as stone!"

Lord Ruthvin, for the first time, looked utterly taken aback. "You what?" His voice rattled the banisters, or so it seemed. "Ye mean to tell me that you, a priest's errand boy, fought a Soulless One?"

"Not just fought, me Lord. Bested and killed," Tyree said, adding an additional wink at Darius for good measure.

"I got lucky," Darius said. He lifted his hand, showing off the silver ring about his finger. "This is what my people called Ellitheor Silver."

"Ordan's hairy stone!" Lord Ruthvin barked out in laughter. "Ye got Moonstone. Gallae's grace ain't that lucky, laddie. But still. How did a ring take down a Soulless One?"

Darius couldn't help it. A smirk pulled up the corners of his lips, a dark, terrible smirk at the memory of seeing the Itheanam writhing and withering away. "I shoved it down its throat. Did the trick."

"Did the trick indeed!" Tyree clucked. "But now, no y'er gonna tell us the rest of it. Y'er not no thin blooded Ordiatian, that much is clear. ye got something in ye, though what I don't rightly know. How did ye survive unscathed?"

Darius couldn't help it. His smirk turned into a laugh, though not one of mirth and merriment, but of dark recollection. Absentmindedly, his hand fell to his abdomen where, hidden from view, a puckered scar still burned in his flesh.

"I was near death's door when Izebal found me," Darius answered. "She gave me an elixir that healed my wounds, and not just those that bled, but all my scars, aches, and pains. They washed away, as if they had never happened. All, that is, but three."

"Oh?" Tyree asked.

Darius touched just below his lower lip, "took a hex to the face by a nasty blood witch, hurt like Halfak's flames, but this streak of silver is all I have left to show for it."

"Bah! Makes ye look refined," cackled Tyree. He then hefted a mangled hand to a melted face. "My scars don't do me any such favors."

"No, old friend," laughed Lord Ruthvin. "But they tell a story all the same. I only see one bolt of iron you, laddie. Did the others turn y'er undercarriage grey?"

Both Tyree and Lord Ruthvin burst into a fit of laughter at this. Darius did not find it so amazing as these two, but had to admit, this was better than the steely silence of before. Perhaps, if maybe he could just play his cards right, he could convince them without a fight to release Izebal. He just needed to keep his cool and talk.

"No," Darius answered. "I got one in my guts from the Itheanam and one in my chest...well, from another witch."

"And ye still want the Diju free?" Tyree asked. "Seems like you'd be done with the lot of them!"

"It wasn't a Diju." Darius ground his teeth. "I get you have your history, but not everyone that looks a certain way is evil."

"Hold your horses, laddie," Tyree said, doing his best to stave off another bout of laughter. "It's just, ye seemed to have a rough run with dark sort, what makes ye so insistent on freeing this one?"

"She didn't do anything wrong. I came to your hall, I answered your questions. What more do I have to prove that I am not a threat?" Darius fumed. Anger unlike he had known before seemed to swirl within his stomach. Something was wrong with him. He was off. He could... he could feel the beast within.

No! Not that. I can't let it out here. Not now!

But the bear was there. It was hungry.

In a panic, Darius's eyes flashed to the Moonstone meteor. Anger burst into fear. The veins of silver seemed to writhing and wriggle. Arcs of white light that had not been there before danced across the slick onyx surface. Darius's mouth went dry and he tried to back away. Driving his heels into the floor and heaving, he overturned his chair and rolled across the floor, popping up into a warrior's stance.

The desire to pull upon the moon's light, to Bind once more, to say the words, was palpable. His heart thundered in his chest as his muscle went taunt as a bowstring.

"Oye! Easy there, laddie," Lord Ruthvin said, rising swiftly, haft of his great spear tight in his hand once more. His two hounds, who had been lazily lounging were up now, hackles raised in feral expectation. "What's gotten into ye?"

"The Moonstone, what's happening to it?" Darius blurted out through labored breaths.

Lord Ruthvin turned around and stared up at the meteorite that blazed in brilliant white. The old mage cocked and eye, peering at the meteor, and then shrugged. At that, Lord Ruthvin turned back to Darius and asked, "What do you see, lad?"

"Fire." The act of talking scorched Darius's throat and lungs, as if her were burning from the inside out. "Blazing white fire."

Lord Ruthvin let out a breath, outstretched his hand, and touched the blazing pillar. Nothing happened. No cry of pain nor ecstasy. No flinching from heat or jolt of power. Nothing.

The room seemed to fold around Darius, the walls rushing forward to meet him. The air became exceedingly thin, causing his already aching lungs to labor for every panicked breath.

"Master Tyree," Lord Ruthvin barked. "What do your mage eyes see?"

Master Tyree said some unintelligible phrase that sounded more of grunts and glottal humming than actually speaking, all nonsense and muttering. However, when his eyes burst into azure light, Darius raised a hand to shield his eyes.

"There do be a lesion on his Cognitive Reflection, marring both the physical and the Aethereal," said Master Tyree. He wheeled closer to Darius. "Something is causing dissonance inside. I think the Moonstone do be affecting him, but its something else, something deeper. A blackness is on his soul, a rot deeper than flesh."

"Can you help him?" Lord Ruthvin asked as he took a step toward where Darius was doubled over.

"He needs something to dilute Iodaba's blight, but it do be deep within," Tyree answered, a bit of panic seeping into his voice.

Darius, feelings as though his whole body would be consumed, reached for the only thing he could think of to ease the pain. Summoning what meagre strength he could, he tore the ring from his finger, letting it fall to the ground with a hollow clink.

In an instant, the whole of the room dimmed. The feeling of licking flames dissipated and the horrific illusion that had filled his vision, the blazing pillar, returned to a black meteor.

"Well," Darius grunted through clenched teeth. "That's new."

"Blood and stones, laddie!" Tyree barked at Darius. "ye about near scared me to death! What in Halfak's damned gaits was that?"

"I don't know," answered Darius. He turned his attention away from the old mage and toward where his ring lay motionlessly upon the floor. Why? What had happened? Was this due to the potion? He had been feeling different these past few days, but nothing like this.

"Tyree, is the lad stable?" Lord Ruthvin's eyes were hard and his expression stern. He gazed down at Darius, one hand back to stave off his two hounds that still were rumbling with low growls.

"That do be a question for him, not me," Master Tyree answered. Slowly, the light in his eyes faded, returning them to a watery blue of natural appearance. "But, I don't see any immediate concern now that that ring be off him."

"Right then," the Lord of the High Hall turned once more to Darius, expression softening. "A lot has happened, a lot. My better judgement says to lock ye in the dungeon, but me heart says y'er not a threat to me or mine. Don't prove me wrong. Go, find sleep tonight. We will continue this in the morning's light."

"No," Darius grunted.

"Excuse me?" Lord Ruthvin looked as if he had been slapped in the face.

Darius stretched out his hand and took hold of his ring. He was reasonably certain he had control, and that if he just didn't open himself to the Binding, he would be okay. Those around him stiffened, though he was not sure if that was due to his objection or to him taking back hold of the ring.

"I am not leaving this room until I know that Izebal will be freed."

"Stubborn indeed, Master Mage," laughed Lord Ruthvin after a long pause of contemplation. "I see ye won't be dissuaded, and ye ain't gave me a reason to doubt ye yet. So be it, Darius. I will send for her immediate release. I'll have her brought to the High Hill.

So be it? That was it? Darius starred at the man, looking for any sign of trickery. But he could find none. The lord of the High Hall looked utterly sincere.

Darius, unsure how to respond, nodded his head.

"Not a man of many words, are ya?" laughed Lord Ruthvin. "Come then, get some rest. Y'er gonna need it, for if ye want to travel to the Northern Mountains, to the city of Dane, y'er gonna have to prove y'er steel."

Darius eyes narrowed on the laughing man.

"What did ye think," continued Lord Ruthvin, finding way too much amusement in Darius's puzzled expression. "ye think you'd just tramps y'er way across the whole of Daneland without thought or worry? No, laddie. But lucky for you, the Ulkeniheim do be fast upon us. Sleep well, for tomorrow we'll test y'er metal and see the true quality of y'er spine. For you'll rise to meet, or be turned away. Thus is the way of the Danelanders, and thus you shall abide."

CHAPTER 13: DRAFTING
AELLIA

By Gallae's breath, the wind upon her flesh was euphoric. Aellia laughed aloud, and in her mind, so too did Iaenora, joining in the rapture that only freedom and flight could bring to one's being.

They soared together, high over the streets of Tur'Mor. Aellia's right eye leaked tears down her face, whether from the wind or from bliss, she couldn't tell. Her left eye saw not a thing. There was only blackness and pain, and deep, unsettling fear. Fear of the dark, fear of what she could not see, and a fear that was more than her own. For what could do this to a being of power such as Iaenora?

The blade of the Dorr A'Gadh.

Iaenora's voice took her by violent surprise. Aellia almost fell out of the sky, so hard her heart skipped.

"Don't do that!" Aellia was furious. Why was this so difficult? She had been bonded to Iaenora for what seemed like an eternity. However, at times of contemplation or exacerbation, when the formless spirit would speak to her, it would send a jolt of panic through her like lightning.

I am sorry, I did not mean to startle you so.

"It's fine," grumbled Aellia. "Just, warn me next time."

How would I warn you of when I am about to speak, if not by speaking, which is the catalyst for your fear? Perhaps that high priest could help you understand our bond better?

"Do you really think I am going to just stay where that old creep can stare at me in my sleep?"

In truth, the 'old creep' had not done anything untoward to her, despite how she loathed to be around him. He had returned not only the Oathrod to her without question but also her favorite dagger, her vambraces, and Tomo's Di'kha. The Di'kha was strapped to her back, the dagger affixed on her chest, by a sheath the old man had custom made for her. Why? Why was he helping her?

No one did good for the sake of good. Aellia had learned that the hard way. Years on the streets, the slums, and gutters had taught her that. Friends had sold their bodies for a little more than a cup of soup and a bed to rest their head, even if it was in bad company. No one cared about anyone, unless there was coin to be made. That was just the way of Tur'Mor.

I do not believe that he intends you harm. Iaenora's words were not exactly condescending, but Aellia felt a prick in her heart as spoke them. *Also, he is one who councils with the Voice of Ordan. Perhaps he can help us on our quest to find my sisters?*

Find her sisters. Right. That was what Iaenora wanted. But what did Aellia want? Why was she running? More importantly, where was she going?

A massive seagull squawked, startled by Aellia's presence in the sky, subsequently startling Aellia out of her thoughts and thrusting her back into the present.

She was over Southend now, just beyond the junction of Wellers Avenue and Beckran, deep into the slums of Tur'Mor. Dozens of stucco coated housing units, stacked three to five stories high, slouched together in a lane on the left side of the muddy road, while a wrought-iron fence ran across the other. Behind the fence, three stacks rose into the air, bellowing clouds of acrid black smoke into the air. Aeneas' Foundry. Aellia knew it well. Many of the patrons of the Twisted Stool toiled their lives away casting and molding metals, breathing in the toxic fumes, and dying sad, miserable deaths.

What are you doing?

"Can't you read my mind?"

You know how this works, Aellia. We share the bond, but you have to let me in.

Let her in. Aellia had done that once, beneath Aldorian's Manor. She had never felt power such as that before. And though she could not lie to herself and say she did not crave that power, the cost was too high, too painful. For when she truly allowed Iaenora in, to become one with her, she had to allow herself to be vulnerable. To open herself and share the most intimate parts of her being, her mind. And that she could not do again.

"I know," Aellia answered solemnly as she descended to the ground.

Bouts of air sent muck and debris scattering about as Aellia stopped her just a finger's span from the road. It was Spring in Tur'Mor, so rain had been frequent and heavy. She had not seen it, locked away in the High Priest's manor, but the tell-tell signs were all about her now.

Do you not fear being seen, bonded one?

"Are you nervous?" Aellia scoffed, actually amused at the idea of a near-deity being afraid of something so insignificant.

Aellia, in my short time in my physical form upon Ethrea, many worshipped my family, building temples and shrines to our names and our Gifts. Others feared us, feeling threatened by our presence. They would, in the most dire of times, hunt us.

"And what could they do?" asked Aellia with no small amount of amusement in her voice. She had thrown grown men like rag dolls, called thunder down from the sky, and sent tempest blasting from her very hands.

Men are clever and cruel, and their machinations know no bounds.

"And you wanted me to stay in that priest's house?"

These are not same. I speak of dark and evil men. You fear any that try to help you!

Aellia grimaced at the remark. It was true. She hated that Iaenora was right, she hated that she could not trust others. More than anything, she hated that every time she loved or trusted someone, they either died, like her mother, brother, Felik and Tomo, or they betrayed her.

"It doesn't matter," Aellia snapped as she looked about the empty street. "There's no one here to see us."

It was strange to see the street so empty. What was stranger still, was the absence of beggar's calls and housewives yelling, the sounds of strays yapping and children running.

"Something's wrong." Aellia spoke aloud as she slowly drew the Di'kha from her back.

Slowly, Aellia walked down the street, peering down alleys and paths. Not a soul. Windows were shuttered and all was still. There weren't even carts or mules about.

Something caught Aellia's attention. Across the way, a massive bulletin with an iron lamp on either side displayed several painted images, the largest of which she could make out from where she stood. Anger boiled in her veins and her skin began to crawl with disgust as she drew ever closer to the board.

The likeness of Aldorian's bust, fat and proud as ever, was pinned to the center of the bulletin. Aellia's stomach soured. Felik, ever the planner, had forced Aellia to learn her letters and numbers. He had said, "If you are to portray a lady, you must be able to speak, write, and act like a lady." In this moment, she was both deeply appreciative of that tutelage, and even more deeply disgusted.

In large block letters above the prude's likeness read the phrase, NEWLY ELECTED REGENT, ALDORIAN, PROCLAIMS NEW STATUTES. Underneath his bust, the following bullets were inked:

By strict decree, enforced by the Silver Stars of Tur'Mor, the following statues will be enforced with exactness:

- *No solicitation during working hours*
- *Beggars will be jailed if found*
- *Every shop selling wares or services must have an official license sealed by the Regent's Official Office*
- *Children left unattended will escorted to the Southend monastery, where parents can claim*
- *Children unclaimed will be moved to more permanent residencies*

"What in fiery gates of Halfak is this?" Aellia swore, her good eye fluttering from top to bottom of the bullet titled, *proclamation of Integrity and Cleanliness, For The Betterment and Investment of Southend.*

I have to admit, bonded one, this is quite disturbing.

Aellia did not answer Iaenora but turned her attention to the rest of the board. Her eye flew left to right, scanning everything. There were job opportunities, sales, and warnings, such as were upon every board, and then there was a terrible depiction of

someone she knew, but looked far more horrific than she could fathom. Herself. Irises that blazed with specially painted iridescent blue glared menacing at her. Veins protruded across her forehead and her hair stood on end. Another set of block letters printed the following, *Public Enemy No. 1. Extremely Dangerous. Do Not Engage. Report to the Regent's Office Immediately.*

Aellia! This is terrible!

"I know!" Aellia answered. She reached out and tore the thick paper from the bulletin. Gazing at the crude likeness of herself, she said, "They got my ears all wrong! And please, tell me my forehead is not this big."

Aellia! Iaenora gasped. *This is serious. You're a wanted woman. We really need to be more inconspicuous.*

"Felik never got a full spread on a bulletin before," Aellia scoffed, not even listening to Iaenora's pleading words. "Just a rough sketch once. But, come on! Look at the coloration. That fat windbag must be scared stiff!"

Aellia folded the paper quickly, crumping parts as she did so, and tucked it between the strap on her waist and her shirt, laughing all the while.

I really do think we need to be careful—

Aellia heard them too. Three or four coming this way. They walked with purpose, wearing heavy boots. The group of men laughed as the advanced toward Aellia, talking of this and that. Their voices were distinctly Southender, but their phrasing made Aellia think of Uppers.

"*Silver Stars*!" cursed Aellia, panic gripping her chest. Her good eye darted about, looking for any place to hide. She would never blend in. She was wearing one of the high priest's shirts, her vambraces and the straps of the sheath holding it to her petite frame, a loose pair of britches she had pilfered, and had bare feet. And, she had a sword strapped to her back. Something very illegal for anyone who did not carry a permit. Something no one in Southend could hope to obtain.

Aellia reached into herself, feeling the pulse of energy that flowed from the Oathrod into her very being. She reached out and felt the wind, the air. She felt the sky calling to her.

Don't do it! If they spot us, they'll alert the guard!

The trance was broken. Aellia blinked. "What? What are you talking about? These people don't even believe in magic. What are they going to say, that a girl just up and flew in front of their very eyes?”

I do not understand this place or this time. I have lain dormant for…I do not even know how long I have slumbered. But this much I know. Mankind has always feared what they do not know. This, and that no matter the people, there are always those searching for our Gifts, so that they can turn and corrupt. It is the way of the Fallen Ones and their dark forces.

“Well, what should I do?” Aellia asked, panic reaching a near boiling point. She looked to the houses across the street. They were all shut tight, windows having bars over them, another perk of living in Southend. Frustrated and nerve wracked, she hissed under her breath, “They’re getting closer!”

You should have stayed. We are not ready for this yet.

“Is now really best time for a lecture?”

Try Drafting!

“Try what?” Aellia said, crouching down behind the bulletin. The group was nearly upon them. She peeked around the end and saw three men and one woman, all in black leathers with a silver star pinned to their chest. They each had billyclubs hanging from their belt loops and tall hats with a like star upon their center. One of the men, the largest of the group, carried what looked like a shepherd’s crook.

We are of the wind, Aellia. When I was in my physical form, I could, momentarily, shift the very essence of my being into the air. I called it Drafting. This would allow me to move through space in a non-physical manner. But, Aellia, I must warn—

“There’s no time!” Aellia hissed, frustrated that the spirit hadn’t told her of this sooner. But then again, when had there been time? “Tell me how to do it.”

Drafting takes utter oneness with the wind, Aellia. You can’t force it. You need to let go.

“What I don’t need is a lecture,” Aellia snapped.

I cannot teach you. Iaenora actually sounded sorry. *I can do it for you. But you have to let me in.*

No! Anything but that. She would fight these four. It would be easy. And why not? They were little more than thugs, preying on the poor and downcast. Just as she had thwarted the Kh’ar, she would overpower these.

I know what you're thinking. Even if I can't directly read your mind. I will not let you hurt innocents! You cannot have my power for that.

Aellia felt a sudden chill flow through her body. Or, perhaps, it would be better stated that she felt a sudden leeching of power. That ever present flow of Everlight was suddenly dammed up, just out of touch.

"What are you doing?" Aellia was nearing frantic levels of panic now. "Why are you doing this?"

We need to learn to trust each other. I have nobody. But you have no power without me. Let me in and I will save us. Shut me out and let us hope that your skill with that sword has improved since the fight beneath the cellar.

Aellia pressed her back against the bulletin board, trying to make herself as small as possible. The guards were close now, too close. Her hand drifted to the hilt of Tomo's sword. However, as it did so, she caught a glimpse of herself in a puddle. She looked small and scared. What was she thinking? Taking on three Silver Stars. Fighting? She was still recovering from her last fight, a fight that had nearly killed her.

"I am scared," Aellia whispered.

I know.

Aellia let out a slow breath. And with that exhalation, so too went her fears and doubts. She tried to clear her mind, to make space. She feared having someone else close to her. But there was no other way.

The girl's eyes who stared back from the puddle at Aellia burst into brilliant sapphire light. And then, in a tempestuous gust of wind, she vanished from view.

Aellia shifted.

She could not feel her hands or toes. She could not see shape or form. Her mind could not comprehend it. There was only solid matter and air. Voices carried on that wind, startled ones, though she could not make out what they said. Aellia was not there now, not in control.

Aellia sat in the back seat of her own mind. Like passenger upon a carriage, she rode forward. Iaenora was there, her mind was so strong and powerful. She was a ray of azure light, a form Aellia could not see, but could define in every way imaginable. She was tall and lean of build, long white hair that flowed like the wind off of her

noble head. She had eyes of light and skin like marble. And yet, she was of no physical sustenance, nor did she occupy space. Neither of them did. For they were not, and they were the wind.

The ground rushed up to meet Aellia. Where there had been nothingness, her feet met stonework. She rolled forward onto loose stones, her torso thudding wildly as she tumbled end over end. If there had been any air in her lungs, it was thoroughly battered from her body, leaving her gasping and coughing upon her hands and knees.

"What in Halfak's pits was that?"

Drafting... Iaenora said lightly, her voice returning to it normal, chipper tone. *I thought that was rather obvious.*

"No, damnit," Aellia gasped. "I saw you!"

You what?

"I saw you, as in, you you. When we were the wind, I could see...you!"

You saw my Cognitive Shadow. My Aethereal Essence is still bound to the Dimdreal, and my physical body has long since decayed.

Aellia, so utterly overwhelmed, heard what the Sage was saying, but could not make heads nor tails of it. Her stomach clenched and she vomited.

Ah, Iaenora said wistfully. *I remember when I first discovered my ability to Draft. It was a rather tumultuous experience.*

"I feel like I've been torn in half," Aellia groaned, rolling away from where she had been sick and lying flat upon her back on cool, wet stones.

Well, not to diminish your feelings, technically, you were separated at the very Aethereal level, every particle of your being shifted from one form to another.

"You know," Aellia said, opening an eye and expecting to the angelic Sage standing over her. She wasn't there, obviously. "You're really full of yourself."

Aellia! How dare you? I'll have you know, that of all my sisters, other than Zaevot, I was considered the most peaceable and humble. But, to a mere mortal, such as yourself, it is hard to comprehend our ways.

"Our ways?" Aellia asked, frustrated with herself that she was actually becoming intrigued by what the spirit was saying. Maybe it

was the thrill of the flight she had just experienced or the adrenaline of almost being captured. Either way, she did not really care.

Now is not the right time. Iaenora paused for a long moment. When she spoke again, her voice was back to a more chipper tone, light and airy. *I am afraid I am rather lost. I was not able to totally control our escape. You do have such a tight grip on your mind. Whatever is in there, we really should talk about it.*

"No!" snapped Aellia before she could stop herself. "Not right now, anyways," she added on rather sheepishly.

Either way, do you know this place?

Aellia, having somewhat regained her facilities, attempted to raise herself from the ground. She was in a courtyard, the loose gravel upon which she now knelt was marked with pavers of exquisite design.

Damnit. That meant she was out of Southend.

Raising her head, high walls adorned with the likeness of ivy rose towered over her, solid white walls of glistening, veined marble, save for an ornate gate bronze. A gate of which she was knelt upon the wrong side.

Immediate recognition clicked in her mind, along with a bone chilling wash of fear. She knew the pentagonal symbol on the opposite side of the gate, even if she could not see the crest. This was the Asterivea.

"We have to go, now!" Aellia made to stand, but even as she did so a firm hand grabbed her shoulder.

Aellia reached for the dagger at her side. It was too late. A hand took her by the arm as a jolt of pain coursed through her body, rendering her body limp.

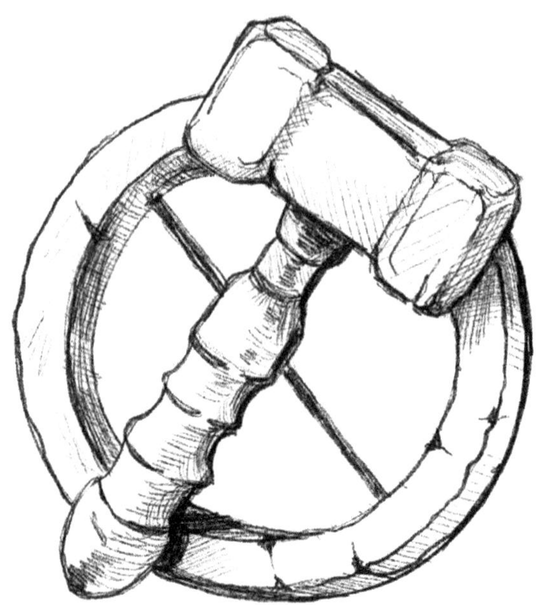

CHAPTER 14: BREAKFAST
DARIUS

Darius saw two mountains rising high in the distance. One a beautiful, snow-capped vision of strength rising majestically into the heavens. The other was broken and jagged, the top a mess of roiling lava that spewed itself over the landscape beneath. From the first, rivers and life flowed at the foothills and valley. From the second, only char and death abounded.

Footsteps behind him sent him whirling about, fists raised to fight. Fists of crystalline flesh with golden veins running beneath. Standing before him was the woman in white with the death mask of silver.

She cocked her head, as if to question his actions, silently scolding him for attempting harm to her in any way. Something about the woman unsettled Darius. Never before had he seen others in this place, other than the High Father, and that was more of cloud that looked like a face if he was being honest with himself. But this, this was an actual person.

She drew closer, raising one of her gloved hands and placing it on Darius's right fist. A shock of heat moved between their hands, passing from her and into him. It continued from his fist until it reached every facet of his being, consuming him in warmth.

"What was that?" Darius asked, eyeing the woman suspiciously.

She did not answer.

"Can you talk?"

She stepped back from him and began to make a series of gestures with her hands. Darius stared at what she was doing, but could not make any sense of it.

"I, I don't understand."

The woman raised a hand to her, tapping her forehead with two fingers. She then laid them upon her left palm in a gentle motion. Next, she proceeded to mimic the rocking of a child.

"Dreams? Something about dreams?"

The woman nodded her head in affirmation. She then touched her chest and repeated the gesture.

"You are dreams?" Darius was a little confused now, feeling he had lost some of the ground he had gained.

The woman mimed a box with bars in front of her and then clasped at the air shaking her head.

"You're trapped in dreams?" Darius asked.

The woman looked taken aback. However, instead of shaking her head no, she became much more animated, nodding yes vigorously. She pointed to the sash of red about her neck, the one that bore the image of the upside-down eye. She made a motion, as if she were being hung by the cloth, though she never actually touched it.

"That holds you here?" Darius pointed to shawl, taking a step closer.

The woman took two sudden steps back, putting more than an arm's distance between them. She raised her right hand in a fist, touching her fingers to her chest and lifting her little finger. She then extended to her first two fingers on both hands and made a warding off gesture that definitely meant, *Do not touch it.*

"Right, don't touch the red cloth, got it," Darius grunted. What did all this mean? What was going? Why was she here?

The woman drew a rod from her belt, a silver rod, whose surface was an amalgamation of twisting veins and sinew. At the head of the forearm-length rod was set a thumb-sized stone of translucent opal, the color of which seemed to shift as she drew forth the rod.

Darius took an involuntary step back. There was something unnatural about the way the light refracted in the head of the scepter, sending flecks of purple, gold, and black shifting across the multi-faceted gemstone. It sent a chill down his spine just to look at it.

The masked woman took another step forward, and this time, Darius stood stock-still, his heart hammering in his chest. As it did so, he noticed something, barely perceptible, that further deepened his concern. The wound in his side pulsed with hot pain, and as it did so, flecks of black marred his golden veins.

Darius's eyes widened at the sight. The woman moved even closer, excited by the revelation. With a swift motion, she took hold of Darius's forearm with grip tighter than steel, and turned his arm over to study his veins.

"What is it? What is happening?" asked Darius, unable to keep the panic out of his voice despite himself as he watched what looked like black ash flowing along channels of golden light.

Silently, she pressed the head of the scepter into the wound on his side. A flare of agony erupted from the connection, sending Darius to one knee. Motes of white and black burst before his vision as he let out a howl of pain.

The woman cocked her head, the mournful mask reflecting Darius's wailing throws. But she did not lose her grip, not on his arm nor on the scepter pressed into the wound. She seemed now to tower over him.

Why? Why was she doing this? Darius could not comprehend what was happening. All there was, was pain.

Wanting nothing more than to roar in pain, Darius thrashed his head about. However, to his surprise, he noticed the black motes dissipating, as if they were retracting back into the wound. His hands and arms were clean, veins pumping golden light.

The mountain of magma burst forth into the sky, rocking the world and sending plumes of ash cascading over the mountainside, directly into Darius and the woman.

Darius bolted upright, throwing blanks across the room as his howling carried from dream into waking. Sweat soaked his back and brow, and as in the realm of dreams, so too did his heart thunder in his chest now.

Panic still gripping his mind, Darius thrust for his forearms. His veins stood on end, but no flecks of black could be seen, just blue veins carrying blood. Unsatisfied, he leapt from the bed and careened toward the polished mirror while tearing his nightshirt from his body.

The handprint left by Mireya's tainted touch still glistened a scaly white. Normal. But the puckered scar from the Itheanam's horn, there was something off about it. Darius heart skipped a beat. Small veins of black, emanating from the core of the wound, trailed into his abdomen. They did not stretch far, maybe a hands breadth or so, but they were there all the same.

"Gallae, goddess of grace," gasped Darius in harrowed fear. "What is happening to me?"

The more he stared, the more grotesque the visage became. His flesh was no longer just scarred, but looked as if it were being eaten away. And yet, through the gore, something else was apparent. Small lines, almost like a barrier, of faint light sapphire shone.

The potion the sisters gave me, the potion of light, it must be that, Darius thought as he went to touch the wound with his finger. He paused, just short of touching it, thinking better of it. What if it spread?

Another thought then filled his mind. What if this was the cause of the strange feelings from yesterday? He had been so on edge, so quick to anger, to fury. Never before had he felt the way he had, as if something was poisoning his mind. Perhaps something was poisoning him.

Forcing himself to take a calming breath, Darius slowly stepped away from the mirror. He had been acting brash, bulling about and demanding. He was better than that. Though he had only had but a few short years under his belt as a leader of his tribe, he had had years enough to know the position Lord Ruthvin was in, and how the man was doing all he could.

Actually, now that he stopped and thought about it, he was rather impressed with the Danelander. The whole of his time in Tur'Mor, if ever spoken about, Danelanders were not spoken well of. Brutish, bullheaded, traditional, and strange. Those were the words used to describe them, and even him, once. He had done to them the very thing he was accusing them of doing to Izebal—

Izebal! Darius whirled about. The realization that he had slept at all the night before struck him like a bell. He had every intention of

waiting through the night. Lord Ruthvin had said that he would send for her, have her brought here. Darius was going to wait up for her.

Guilt stabbed at his heart, further souring his mood. A mere dream had caused him distress. He had woken in a sweating panic because of a dream, while Izebal had been held in a cell, laden with chains and an accursed kroichae.

Quickly, Darius found another layout of clothing, this one slightly different from before. More earthen tones and the shoes were ankle-high boots of soft leather and thick soles. In all, it gave him a much more subtle and rugged appearance, for which he was thankful. Though, if truth be told, he wanted his sturdy trousers, boots, and his trench coat back.

"Good morning, sir!" came the chirping tone of another grey-clad maiden. "This way."

She, like all the others, moved as if she were hovering over the floor. Her bell-like skirts did not move a whit, hanging perfectly straight as she glided forward toward the main hall.

"The Lord do be expecting you," the maid said with a bow that did not extend past her waist. "In you go, sir!"

Darius, unsure still to the appropriate protocol, thanked the young woman and stepped into the main hall. This time, the hall was packed with people, every chair taken. Lady Sophie sat next to her husband in her customary seat, but her daughters were not beside her, nor anywhere to be seen.

Darius missed a step, stumbling forward into the room. The power wafting from Moonstone was nigh unbearable. All turned their attention on him as he entered, silence washing over the noisy ensemble in an instance.

"Morning!" Lord Ruthvin said, rising from his seat carved into the great meteor of Moonstone. "Nice of ye to finally join us!"

Darius, still wrong-footed from his stumble, grunted for a response.

"A way with words to make Haljorn the Horn jealous," cackled Tyree from beneath a tankard of ale.

A low grumble of awkward laughter rolled around the table, but ultimately fell flat. Of the crowded table, Darius recognized Orhund and Nee'av, leaders of the Skogortuers that had apprehended himself and Izebal. There was also the behemoth of a man with flaming red hair known as Lord Commander Krarraek Pritfort, who sat across from Lady Sophie at the left hand of Lord Ruthvin. He recognized them for the siblings they obviously were, though he had to admit, Lady Sophie had the looks and he had the brawn.

Others at the table he did not recognize. A brown-haired man with hair on him to make look as much a bear as Darius in his Feroform. Another with greying hair whose whole of his left side was a tapestry of blue-white ink carved into weathered flesh. A lean woman with skin far darker than the rest and the side of her head shorn bald, sat with hard black eyes locked onto Darius, and when she turned to talk to the man sitting next to her, the earrings in her left ear, which were wired bones with crude runes carved into them, clacked together noisily.

"All righty then, let us eat," Lord Ruthvin called out, his voice merry and bright. He then gestured to an open chair by Lady Sophie and said, "But first, let me introduce y'all to Darius, friend of my house and retriever of me very own wee Ery!"

Darius, feeling as if every eye in the room was burrowing into his soul, stood firm in his place. He could feel the hairs on his neck and arms raise, the blood quicken through his veins, and his heartbeat racing. As it did so, strange sensations, much like the touch of shock from woolen stockings, spread through his body.

Lord Ruthvin, not to allow the moment to sour, pushed his way forward and walked to Darius's side. With a firm pat, the Lord of the High Hall slapped him square on the back, and proclaimed, "A friend of my house, and one to put forth his name and merit for the Ulkeniheim!" With that, one by one, those that sat around the table rose and made their to great Darius.

As they came and formally introduced themselves—many of whom were Pritforts, MacNals, and Bjorndanes—they each proceeded with the same ceremonious thing. "Hail, I am so and so of such a place. May your bones be strong and your days long!" Darius noted that each person's kilt directly matched the names provided, and each of them had a pin placed near the hem over the knee, most of which were silver, with an occasional bronze pin here and there, or the rarer golden pin.

When at long last the crowds had passed, the woman with the shorn head and dark complexion rose lackadaisically and made her way toward him. She did not wear a pleated kilt as the others, but baggy trousers stitched of plaid. About her waist was a silk sash that clashed with the dull patterns and pinned to it was a golden crest of a broken spear wreathed in flames. Her chest was bound with wrappings and a brown leather vest that only fell to her ribcage was all she wore. Her tattooed bellybutton had a bar of iron through, which instantly caught Darius's eye. He had never seen something like that before. He was immediately intrigued by her, from the top to the bottom, she was an enigma for certain. Of that much Darius was sure.

"Hallowed met in the lands of the damned," she said with a voice like a baleful wind blowing through a field of dying grass. And her accent. What was that? It was unlike anything Darius had ever before heard. "Water I have not, but shade I would offer, if only to ease that passing sun."

This was a warrior. And if the scars on her forearms and hands were not sign enough, the way she stood, the way she walked, like a hunting wild cat, and the way she stared undaunted up into the eyes of a stranger who was head and shoulders taller than she, were all clue enough.

Darius, taken aback back her statements, answered in the only way he could think. "Well met."

"Well met," she echoed. When she blinked, tattooed eyes started continuously back, inked directly into her eyelids.

Lord Ruthvin, who still stood at Darius's side, burst into laughter, "Well me indeed!" He thundered, slapping Darius on the back once again. "This do be Al'elahdrak Ruthvin, my sister's adopted daughter."

"Call me Talon," the woman said with a bow of her head, sending the bone earring clattering once more.

"Darius," Darius grunted back, extending a hand.

When her hand clasped his, he was immediately taken aback, not only by the strength of which she grasped his hand, but by the hard, coarseness of her flesh. Her whole hand felt as if it were a single callus.

"Let us then break bread," Lord Ruthvin thundered loudly. This was met with uproarious approval, as those who had found their seats once more banged mugs fervently upon the table, so as to amplify their affirmation.

"You can sit there," Lord Ruthvin said, pointing to an open seat by Lady Sophie's side.

Darius nodded and said, "As you would, Lord Ruthvin."

"Bah! Enough with that. My subjects call me Lord Ruthvin. In this hall, we are clan. Blood be blood. Call me, Eric." said the lord, throwing an arm wide over the throng. "You've earned that twice over. But come now, let us eat."

The meal from that point on passed normally. Little was said toward Darius, with most of the conversations focused on the Ulkeniheim. From what Darius gathered, it was a rather large celebration that had been canceled due to Little Ery's disappearance. Everyone seemed rather pleased it was being reinstated, with many piping off about the need for tradition and whatnot.

Darius let most of the words roll over him. There was too much noise. Luckily, the Moonstone was not reacting with his blood as it had done so the night before. He could still feel it, a low thrum in his blood. But he did not have those mounting urges, the feral call to Turn.

"Darius, lad, are you listening?"

Darius jerked his head toward Eric, who was looking at him with puzzlement plastered across his broad face.

"Sorry," Darius muttered. "I'm...distracted."

"Well," Eric said with a coy smile. "Hopefully this next bit will hold y'er attention. Though, it do be a shame. Looks like the porridge has turned and gone cold on ye."

"What bit?" Darius asked, concern creeping its way into the back of his mind once more.

"Well, I meant to wait," Eric said as he began to rise once more, his voice increasing as he did so. "But, I figured, why not get it out and over with. We do all be clan here. So this will before all so that all will know. Bring her in!"

The double-doors on the far side of the moaned as if under tremendous strain. Hinges creaked loudly as the doors began to move inward, pressed open by the now visible guards in the heavy metal suits with eyes that never blinked. Darius felt his heart drop into his stomach. Standing there in the hall, the light of the sun pouring in behind her, was Izebal.

The range of emotions he felt at seeing her, well, he did not know he could feel them all so vibrantly. Fear. She was bound, the kroichae about her neck had two chains whose ends were held by those wearing the garb of the Skogortuer. Pride. She stood tall, undaunted and unbroken. Pity. Despite her proud stance, Darius could see the pain behind her eyes, the hard outer layer she put on for others to see. Anger. For those who sat around this table and ate and drank, including himself.

"Hail, Lord of the High Hall," called out one of the Skogortuer. "We bring you the Diju, as requested!"

"Good," Eric said.

Darius felt a torrent of rage and hatred, just below the surface, threatening to burst the dam of restraint he held on his heart. He wanted to lash out and everyone and anyone. He wanted to rush forth and rip the chains off of her body. To take her far, far away from her.

"Now, take those off her," Eric continued, utterly baffling Darius. "Our friend here has said she was one who helped save my daughter."

"Eric," Krarraek said, he meaty fist clenching a spoon so hard the metal bent around his fingers. "She do be a Diju." His words were little more than a hissing whisper.

"Darius, did this woman help save my Little Ery?" Eric asked, turn all the attention of the room onto him with a singular question.

"She is innocent. She's done nothing but help." Darius tried to make his words come out right, but they just would not. "She saved us both!"

"I believe you," Eric said in such a matter-of-fact tone that Darius could not help but feel a deluge of relief wash over him, clearing away the hate that burned so fiercely just moments before. For, as the Lord of the High Hall said he had believed him, he too believed Eric. "Release the chains from her and take off the kroichae. It is not needed here."

Orhund and Nee'av both bristled at this, but neither said anything to the contrary of the lord's command. Krarraek looked as if he could spit fire, but he too held his piece. Tyree, on the other hand, was nearly leaned out of his wheeled chair, eyes wide with anticipation and fascination. And Talon, she leaned back in her seat, watching it all with cool demeanor.

The two Skogortuer looked to Orhund who echoed Eric's command. With a sharp solute, they turned and began removing the chains from Izebal's wrists and unlocking the black iron from her neck. All the while she stood poised in perfect stillness. Her eyes looked forward, not at a single person in the room. She was like an angel, and Darius could not help but look on in awe at her.

"Come," Eric said, trying his best to sound as joyous and at ease as he was before. "Come sit by our friend Darius's side. Eat and drink. I fear your treatment in Talahmnas has not been the best. I hope to rectify that, starting now."

Izebal walked forward, the two silent guards just behind her on either side. One reached a hand out and slid her chair back. She stepped into the opening, her hand just brushing Darius's as she reached for the armrest. Her skin was cold and clammy, and when the tip of her finger touched his hand, he almost thought she was trying to grasp for him. The scrape of wood on wood as the chair pressed her into place ended the brief moment, but left Darius confused.

All eyes were fixed upon Izebal, the room silent and still. And while Darius normally would have found solace in the turn of attention away from himself, his instinctual nature nearly had him back upon his feet.

"Kinfolk are we all in this room," Eric said in a somber tone, leaving behind any feigned attempt at levity. "So, I will speak to you as the elder brother should. Krarraek, blood of my betrothed, you have the first voice if there is concern you'd like to address."

Darius felt his heart tighten like a vise. He suddenly understood how hot iron felt just before it was to be struck, laid out helplessly upon the anvil.

"Brother, we do call you lord and expect ye to protect our lands," Krarraek said. His voice was like stone grating against stone, deep as a gorge and cold as the snow-capped peaks. "ye know what we've faced these past months. Y'er own daughter was taken. I just find it a bit strange that we'd let these two sit here in this place without no thought nor care."

Three or four others grunted their approval of the man's words, though none dared speak out yet. Eric leaned back against his throne, raising a hand to stroke his golden beard. For several long moments he sat in silent contemplation, the whole room waiting anxiously for his verdict.

"What say you, Master Tyree?" Krarraek pressed. "You've advised three lords of this all. What say you of this, Diju witch?"

"Krarraek!" snapped Lord Ruthvin. "Unless we do find fault, she do be a guest in this hall now."

"My lord," Krarraek said, an expression as if he had downed a whole tankard of soured goat's milk curling his lip.

"What say I?" Tyree answered, paying no heed to the tension of the room. "I say this one here, he do be of good stock. I don't rightly know what he do be, but he showed stones yesterday. And actions are the merits of a man, are they not, Master Pritfort?"

"Aye, that they do be," Krarraek assented. "But I asked of the girl, not the lad."

"Woman."

Darius nearly jumped out of his skin at the sound of Izebal's statement. It was not a loud declaration, nor was it meek. It rippled with authority and dominance, while still maintaining a level of respect.

"Excuse me?" Krarraek barked, slamming a hand down on the table. "I was speaking to the mage here."

"That is a dreadful tongue you have there, sir," Izebal answered blithely, crossing her own hands in front of her upon the table, as if everyone in this room were not judging every action and reaction she made. "What it I could clear the air? Prove to you all of our intent and innocence?"

Silence fell once more over the room. It was Master Tyree, this time, who broke it first.

"Innocence, perhaps, might not be the best word, lassie. But, I do have a keen ear and keener eyes. What mysteries do ye keep that so embolden ye?"

Izebal reached to her side, pulling up the small satchel that hung from her hip. She placed it on the table for all to see. Darius could not help but smile. He knew of that leather sack's secret.

"May I?" Izebal asked, looking directly at Lord Ruthvin.

"If y'er try'n any funny business, this ain't the place nor time. But I gave ye my word. Y'er a guest here unless you y'erself prove otherwise." Eric, for the first time, sounded a little unsure.

"I seem to have misplaced my amulet," Izebal said suddenly, as if the thought had never crossed her mind until that exact moment.

The woman, Nee'av, turned her head away. It was then that Darius could see the golden chain about her own neck. An intense bout of anger sparked in Darius. How dare this woman touch her things? How dare she wear something of one she deemed a witch and a sorcerer!

"Give it to her," said Darius, his voice low and steady, belying the raging fire within.

No one said anything. No one moved or acted.

"You don't know me," Darius growled. "You fear her, because you know what a Diju can do. But you don't know me. Give. It. Back."

Something he said must have struck a nerve, for the Skogortuer bristled like an iron badger, face flushing red. "Ain't naught ye can do it me, lad. Best ye remember that here."

Before Darius could speak next, Orhund cut in. "Nee'av, hand it over."

"What?" Nee'av looked as if she had been slapped.

"You heard me." Orhund's voice was level. It was clear he was not happy about what he was saying, but he too had chosen to draw a line in the sand, and that line was on the side of Eric.

"By blood and bloody stone! Y'er all mad! She's a bloody Diju and we're all gonna act like it's roses and sunshine because they said they did something? We found them, in the forest, harboring the lassie! Who's to say they wasn't the ones who stole her outright?"

"Nee'av!" Orhund looked pained now, but he pressed on. "Take it off. If our Lord Commander sits at this table, we obey."

Fire blazed behind the woman's eyes as she unclasped the golden chain. In a fit of insolence, she hurled the amulet at Izebal's face. Without thinking, Darius caught the necklace, chain and all, right before it struck true.

Darius lowered the amulet onto the table right in front of Izebal. He could feel the need calling to him, the strange unnatural and rhythmic pulses of energy caused from the injury he sustained, and the tonic used to heal him. The silver of his ring went ice cold, as if it yearned for him to Bind once more. But he pressed this down, tucked it away behind a wall of self-control. If he did Bind now, it would most certainly undo everything he had worked for the past twenty-four hours.

"Out!" Eric was already on his feet as his voice came thundering out. "Out of my hall!"

"My Lord! I have only ever served this land!" Nee'av answered, looking shocked at the Lord of the High Hall's response to insolent behavior.

"I said out!"

Nee'av, for perhaps the first time that day, showed some level of restraint. She took in a deep breath, placed her hands upon the table, and scooted her chair back. "I live only to protect and serve."

"You are dismissed," Eric said cooly. He then turned his attention to the rest of the room as Nee'av made her way to the still-open doors, her head hung in shame. "If anyone else feels likewise, go ahead and leave."

"Brother," Krarraek said in little more than a whisper, he showing constraint for the first time. "Be easy on them. They do only seek the best of the kingdom. ye know that."

"Captain Orhund," Eric said, his voice returning to a calmer tone. "Y'er welcome to stay for my brother's words. But I warn you, we are in a precarious time. I would know that I can trust those who eat at my table to listen to my command."

Orhund rose from his seat in a proud manner. He placed his right fist on his gut and then raised it so that the back of his hand touched his brow, saying, "By my body and mind do I serve."

"All is well then?" Eric asked of the table.

A low mutter of agreement rippled across the room.

"Perhaps it best we listen and learn of what the young woman has to say," Lady Sophie said, adding her voice of regal reason to the throng. "I, for one, am rather curious as to what she has that in that sack of hers."

"Agreed," Eric said, shooting his wife a thankful smile.

"The woman Nee'av was right," Izebal said as she picked up the amulet and placed it around her neck. "It would appear to most that we are indeed at fault. We were found in the trees by Captain Orhund. We did have your daughter with us at that time. And I am, as pointed out, a Diju. And not just any, either. I am one who seeks the Words, I have the knowledge of a good many Words, and I have the Spark of Ellenethenal in my veins."

Many at the table seemed confused by Izebal's statement. However, Darius noted that Tyree was not one of them. He did not miss that the old mage's hand slid the haft of his scepter as Izebal began to speak.

Suddenly, Darius felt an unsettling feeling. Izebal was so calm and in control, acting as if she were exactly in her element. Fear pricked at his heart as he recalled the night in which he had been struck by another witch's hex, leaving the tarnish silver in his beard. But no. Not Izebal. She had saved him.

"Let me, however, show proof of what we found deep in Ranok's corrupted heart." Izebal flipped open the satchel. A pulse of green light flowed from her amulet into her fingertips as she said a word that Darius could not comprehend. Green runes of light formed over the seal. Izebal plunged her arm into the abyss that was her bag, retrieved the ashen skull of the Itheanam, and thrust it onto the table with a resounding thud.

"By Ordan's beard," gasped Eric. "He was telling the truth."

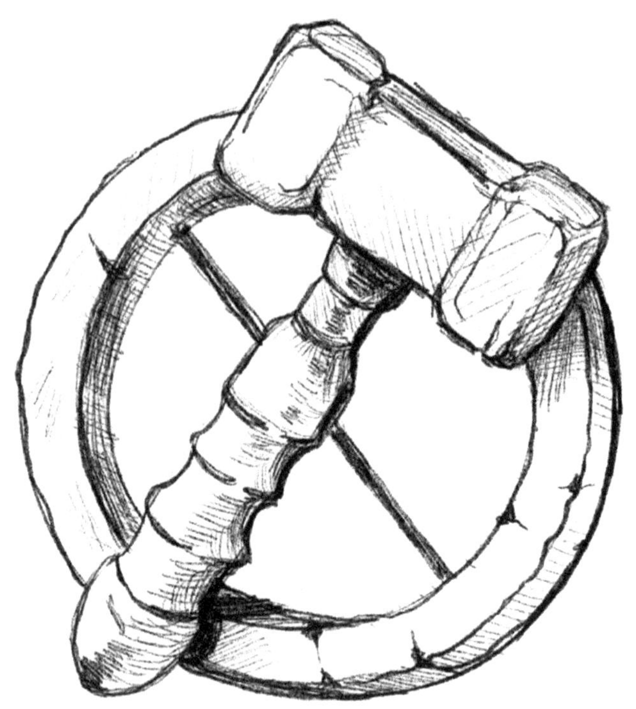

CHAPTER 15: HORNS
DARIUS

"Horn of the dark creature called Itheanam, taken from the body consumed by flame. Hard won from deep in the caverns where your very own daughter was found," Izebal said, her words drawn out with dramatic effectiveness. All eyes were on the ash-colored skull. Izebal scanned the room, letting an ominous silence linger, if only for a moment. "So it was when I found it, laying before Darius's own fallen form. I understand that you have no reason to trust a Diju—" Her voice harbored no warmth, coming out clipped and harsh. "—but trust me when I say Darius meant no malice or deceit in that cave, nor in the returning of your daughter."

With that, Izebal lowered herself into her chair, chin high and eyes sharp. Darius could see that her hand shook from nerves, a

slight tremor in her fingers in the face of a dozen detractors that hated her simply due to her bloodline, but that was it. To all else, she was as stone, perfectly poised, as if this were her hall and all these were her subjects.

"Don't touch it!" shouted Tyree, bursting the dam of silence with a deluge of frightful words. "Its been a century since a Soulless One has been seen in these parts! Don't touch it!"

Looking about the room, Darius hardly thought the warning necessary. Everyone looked as if they had been cemented to their seats, eyes wide with emotions ranging from confusion to outright hysteria. Krarraek looked as if every vein in his bulging neck was about to burst. Lady Sophie, while more in control than most, scooted away from Darius toward her husband while a hand fell to her side, gripping a sheathed saex.

"It won't hurt you," Darius grunted with a shake of his head, trying his best to cover the blossoming amusement that was swelling within. "It's been severed from the body, there is not a trace of Iodaba left. It's just a horn and skull now."

"Draugr and troll, goblin and wylven, we face without flinching," Erik said, rising slowing and placing both hands firmly upon the table. He glared down at the white skull with the spiral horn of silver that protruded from blood-red runes of the Morrean dialect. "What is this evil that has each of you turned to jelly in y'er legs and has y'er stones sunk into y'er hips?"

"My lord," Tyree said with uncharacteristic caution. "These do be of the worst kind. Draugr do be of the undead, trolls do be mindless brutes who feast on flesh, goblins are spawns of darkness, and wylven be creatures of blackest night. Only do the accursed Redeyes of Beyorne Forest come close to the evil that sits upon that table."

"Never once have I seen anything like that," Orhund said with a snarl. He raised a golden hammer pendant from a chain in his shirt to his lips and then dropped it back once more. "It's evil. I can feel it in me bones."

"Evil isn't the half of it! Soulless Ones are not born, but made. Something dark did this. Did something that shouldn't be possible after the Sealing."

"Speak clearly, Master Mage," said Krarraek. "Not all of us do be steeped lore and mysteries. What in the pit is that thing?"

"It's an abomination!" Tyree's voice cracked as he bellowed. "A demon spawned of blood and death! A soul for the Soulless! A curse upon the land!"

Darius, who was rather amused at the outburst of the Danelanders at seeing their first Itheanam skull, sighed and said, "It's dead. That is what is. Nothing more."

"How are you okay with this?" Tyree gawked.

"I told you before," Darius said with a shrug before proceeding to grab the mug that sat in front of him and taking a long drag of ale. It was full-bodied and earthy, with a strong scent of honey. He set the tankard down and reached into his own satchel. Looking directly at Lord Ruthvin, Darius plopped the sealed envelope before him and said, "I've killed these before. As Izebal said, we mean you no harm. We just want to get to the Capital and deliver this letter. That is all."

Lord Ruthvin reached forward and took up the envelope, sealed by the signet of the Patriarch of the Church of Ordan. Darius was unsure just how faithful these Danelanders were. True, he had heard them swear by the Ellitheor, he had seen a few pendants and chains, but that was all. In Tur'Mor, great edifices were constructed for the gods; fountains portraying Ordan and Gallae in marble littered the streets; and massive cathedrals of worship were built up upon the tops of hills as a sign of deference and as a place to gather together in holy servitude. Darius could only hope that respect for the Office of the High Patriarch reached this far from his seat in Templetown.

"I don't get in the way of the Church," Erik said slowly as he glanced over the sealed parcel. He tossed it back to Darius. The envelope landed with a solid thud upon the table, its contents heavier than they appeared. "But no one goes through me lands without the proper rights, and this is the real meaning of this conclave."

"That's it?" asked Darius. "No more questions about myself? Izebal and I are free?"

"Talahmnas is a free land, I told ye, laddie," Erik said with a smile. "We Danelanders hold true to our word. You prove y'erself in the Ulkeniheim, and all will be well. The lady has shown herself true and honest. So, as I said, she is a free woman, free to traverse these streets and this hall. So I have said, so it shall be."

At this command, the room went utterly silent. Eyes darted between Izebal and Lord Ruthvin, but none dared to issue further complaint. And, to drive the point further, Lady Sophie rose to her feet, a long sash of patterned wool in her hands.

"For returning our daughter, you have our utmost thanks." Lady Sophie extended the cloth to Izebal. It was then that Darius caught the silver form of a wolf's head with an eye of sapphire pinned to the plaid. "Along with that thanks comes our deepest apologies for the way you entered Talahmnas. Please, take this as a sigh of welcome and kinship, for as long as you wear this, no one will ever mistake you again in these lands as anyone other than kin and clan."

Izebal stood and nodded to the Lady of the High Hall. She then lowered her head and allowed Lady Sophie to wrap the patterned cloth about her, pinning it over her shoulder with the wolf-head amulet. A simple "Thank you," was all she spoke before returning silently to her seat.

"Blood and stone," Erik said in a grandiose voice, as if he were beginning a tale of ancient times. "That is the way of the Danelanders. For nineteen generations, our clans have defended this land with blood and stone. Blood of our fathers, and stone of the gods. The Ulkeniheim is the great leveler of men, a test to humble even the proudest of entrants. Each of you that sits at this table has proven y'erselves - bronze, silver, or gold, it matters not - to be of the blood and stone. I put forth young master Darius to stand before the tribunal of the clans, to prove his blood, and gain the right to travel our lands. Do we have an accord?"

"Aye," Krarraek stood, eyes filled with a heaviness beyond words. "I would speak for the Pritfort clan. Let the laddie play the game and prove himself. Until then, I reserve me judgement to myself."

"Aye, I speak for clan Bjorndanes, let him stand and test his metal!"

"Aye, I would like to see the wee laddie out of robes and in proper wear. Let us see if he can best a test of men, not just beasts in the dark. I speak for the MacNals, let him play!"

"So none do oppose?" Erik said, measuring the room with hard eyes and a gleeful smile that sent a chill of worry up Darius's spine.

"None!" shouted the room in unison, though some were less fervent than others.

"By my throne, given to me to guard this land, I call upon Darius, Slayer of the Soulless, to stand in the ultimate trail of character. Would you deny yourself this?"

Darius met Erik's eyes with what he hoped was an unyielding expression of self-confidence. "I accept your challenge."

"Ye have two weeks, laddie," Erik said with a nod. "Best make y'erself ready."

The next few moments were a haze of cheering, ale drinking, and raucous music. Where had the pipes and drums come from? Surely from outside, but they were so blaringly loud now in Darius's ears. Were all Danelanders accustomed to random bouts of singing? The Hall doors were thrown open, and many more poured into the High Hall, surrounding the table and shaking Darius's hand, offering their thanks for the return of the daughter princess.

Despite the cloth pinned about her, no one drew close to Izebal, who had managed to slide the Itheanam horn into her satchel once more and sink into the shadows, away from all of the side-glances and hateful eyes. At least, that was where Darius had seen her last. He had tried to wind his way to her several times, but at each attempt, he was met by another hairy man who wanted to shake his hand or a babbling woman who had plenty of daughters not too many years his junior. Now, when he looked her way, he felt a twinge of sympathy for her. Tyree had wheeled himself to her side and was most certainly ranting about something as half-cracked as he was.

"Excuse me," said Darius, not caring where the man was in his story or even what he was talking about, as he pushed his way toward Izebal.

"And that is how the wylven took me leg! Gnawed it right to the bone!" Tyree cackled, a tear welling in his gleaming blue eyes.

"That is a rather interesting story, Master Tyree," Izebal said with a laugh that sound like the flow of a joyous melody.

Darius stopped in his tracks, eyes widening. She was talking and laughing? No. This must be some kind of mistake. Only moments ago she looked as if, given the opportunity, she would vanish in a puff of smoke. Could she do that? Darius did not have time to dwell on that thought, for Tyree had spotted him and beckoned him forward with a waving hand.

"Come, me boy! Come and talk with a crazy old mage!"

Darius strode forward, trying his best to mask the concern—and a fair amount of his own stress at the overcrowded room. Everything had happened so fast. He was still in shock, of that he was certain.

"Come on now, y'er stones don't be dragging ye down that much, laddie! Put a little pep y'er step!" Tyree cackled.

Izebal blushed at this. Blushed! She hid it well though, raising a cup of something Darius was certain contained no alcohol to her ruby lips and drinking.

"Sorry, I—"

"Ain't no need for apologizing! It do be time for strategizing!" Tyree belted out, along with a deep and long belch, his own tankard drained and tossed to the ground with a loud clatter.

One of those grey-clad maids swooped right in. Not two times did the cup *clank* on the floor before it was swept up. The maid extended another tankard of golden mead and left with a bow that did not crease any of her clothing.

"Fine ladies, them are!" Tyree said with a shake of his head, his forked beard frothed with foam. "Anyhow. I was just welcoming young Izebal to the clan and letting her in on one or two pertinent bits of information."

"I especially appreciated the story of how your mother met your father," Izebal said with a sly smile. "A very colorful tale indeed."

"Like two pigs chuttin' in the mire!" Tyree spouted out with laughter.

"Does everything here happen so...?" Darius started.

"So what? So effectively? Efficiently? Acceleratingly? I'm running out of ingly's, laddie!" asked Tyree through a torrent of snorts and bursts of laughter.

"So fast and haphazardly," Darius grunted, casting his eyes about the room. "I feel like I am in a whirlwind."

"Laddie, that's life," Tyree said with a knowing look. "And if y'er afraid of a chaos, ye got a long and tiresome road ahead of ye."

Darius huffed as he crossed his arms. He was upset at the noise, the revelry, and most of all, at how well Izebal of all people was taking this. Moments ago, she was in chains, held against her will. Now she was laughing and talking. This was all just too much for him to take in. He needed some air, desperately.

"Laddie, y'er looking a wee bit green," said Tyree with a raise of a wizened eyebrow.

"I just... I need to step out."

"Are you alright?" Izebal asked, concern ebbing its way into her steady voice.

"I'm fine." Darius hadn't meant to snap at her, but everything seemed to be spinning. His hand itched. And the stone—What was it doing now? The whole room seemed to pulse with every uneasy breath.

"Take a walk in the garden, clear y'er head," Tyree said, all humor gone from his voice. "I'll keep the hounds at bay. Of with the both ye. It's been a long two days, I'm sure."

"Thank you," Darius said in earnest. "We won't be long. I just need to breathe."

"We'll have to continue our conversation," Izebal said with a smile toward Tyree. "I was not aware that others knew of the Words."

A loud bit of commotion turned their heads. An approaching group of bearded men sent a stone into Darius's guts. He had no desire to have another talk with anymore Danelanders at the time. Tyree whipped his head back and forth between the oncoming men and Darius.

"Ah, yes," Tyree said, his wide smile flashing back across his scarred face. "That we will. I have a good many more questions for ye as well. But be off with ye! Go now!"

"Oye, ye big lumbering oaf! Is that ye Krarraek or did someone let Beyorne red bear in here?" Tyree wheeled away, cutting off Krarraek's advance, catching the behemoth in what was certainly an unwanted conversation.

Izebal took Darius by the arm, wrapping her hands around his bicep, and lead him through the throng of drinking and clamoring Danelanders. She walked with such poise and command. It baffled him. Had he not been so overwhelmed with the noise and tumult, he would have gawked at her. She, on the other hand, seemed to take little notice of his situation, pressing firmly toward the doors and away from everything and everyone all at once.

With a burst of chill spring air, Darius stepped out of the High Hall. Sweet scents of pine, grass, and burning fires filled his nose. His eyes watered at the morning sun, which had now risen high into the sky, illuminating the vast landscape of Talahmnas, a view the swept Darius's breath away.

The High Hall had upon its main entry an immense colonnade of great timbers set into cut granite. An eave of thatched gold sat upon the carved timbers, not too dissimilar to that of the Sanctuary's.

Darius was once again reminded of both the similarities and vast differences of the two cultures.

From beyond the colonnade, a garden of worked hedges and granite statues were set into perfect rows of geometric patterns, turning at hard angles and displaying the craftsmanship of the Danelander's stonemasons. At the far end of the garden and all the way around the top of the High Hill, a railing had been erected. It was all so beautiful, and all so intrinsically Danelander, that Darius could not help but let out a laugh as he stared out in admiration.

"A woman could get jealous if she saw the way you stared at stone," Izebal said, digging into his ribs with her elbow.

Darius felt a flush of heat wash over his body. What in Ordan's creation was going on here? Had he gone mad? The whole world seemed to have shifted overnight, and he could not make two ends meet in his mind as to how or why.

"It was a joke," Izebal said with a sigh, patting him on the cheek and stepping back from him. "You need to lighten up, messenger boy. We are safe for now. Be thankful of that."

"Lighten up?" Something in Darius finally broke. "Lighten up? Izebal, they put us in chains as if we were thieves. They imprisoned you. How can you be okay with this?"

Izebal turned, her expression pensive. A tired smile crossed her ruby lips. "Darius, I have spent my life in fear of these people. I was expecting much worse than a night in a cell."

"So you think I should just play their game? Act like none of this is of any consequence?" Darius's voice was low and growling, every word hurting his throat nearly as badly as the situation hurt his mind. He could feel the vein on his forehead lift, the pulsating beat of his heart as blood surged through his body.

"Do not put words into my mouth, messenger boy," Izebal said coldly. "I am only stating the obvious. We have a goal: to get to Dane. If we try and sneak there, it could take weeks or months, evading these skirt-wearing oafs. I still hold little love for them and their ways, make no mistake. But, I have to see the reason in this thing. Why can't you? What is so wrong with playing their little game?"

What was so wrong with it? It made sense. Prove himself, and they would have unfettered access to the realm. But that was just it. He did not feel like he needed to prove himself further. Hadn't his prior actions spoken well-enough of his intentions?

"All I am saying is that we chose the better path," Izebal said. She then lowered her voice. "Ethenealal spoke to me last night. I dreamt and saw a great tree, in whose roots were woven the Pattern of Life. I saw and heard a Word, lost to time. It was spoken to me by one in white whose face was concealed from my view. Darius, I do not idly stand by this path, but intend to walk it with open eyes."

"You dreamed of a woman in white?" asked Darius, his full attention drawn immediately to Izebal's words.

"I did not say woman." Izebal looked at him with deep, questioning eyes. "How did you know?"

Darius looked around, assuring himself of their seclusion. "Izebal, I have seen her. She is bound in a place she cannot leave. I think...I think I need to help her, like the girl in the forest and the other from the streets of Tur'Mor. I am being called."

"I would know more of these dreams," said Izebal, stepping closer to him. "But not here. Please, accept this test of these Danelanders. Perhaps there is more happening here than we know."

"And what of you, what shall you do?" asked Darius.

"I shall see just how 'free' I truly am here." Izebal scoffed, her fingers running the length of the patterned scarf. "I will go to the groves and commune with Ethenealal, seeking wisdom and guidance."

"So, you're leaving, then?" Darius felt his heart tighten at the realization.

A soft smile spread across Izebal's lips. "You grow bold, messenger boy. I shall return. Give me a day or two. There is a grove in Beyorne to the north, over the Granite Mountains. I will request a horse. I should not be gone more than a few days."

"What if they refuse to give you one?" Darius asked, perhaps too quickly, too hopefully.

Izebal just shook her head. "I believe they are as bullheaded as they claim. The man, Erik, gave his word. They are honest, to a fault."

"What of Morreans, or goblins?" Darius asked, his argument notably weak. Izebal was a powerful sorceress, able to conjure spells through her abilities with Words and Ria'Elahm.

"I'll be fine. This will not be my first sojourn into Beyorne. My troupe would hold a festival there every harvest moon. I am quite familiar. I am more concerned with how you will behave yourself in this place while I am gone."

Darius grunted. He was clearly not happy with her decision to leave. But how could he tell her that? What was his place? He had no right, no claim to her. That did not, however, stop a deep and troubling concern for her safety and wellbeing from welling up in his chest, obscuring the small jab she made at him. He found no humor in the moment. Only apprehension at the situation, a perturbing unease at the thought of being separated once more. And then there were the dreams. Surely they meant something.

"Don't look so down, messenger boy," Izebal said with a half-hearted smile that did not reach her eyes. "Just promise me you won't leave without me."

"Tell me again, why didn't we just go around this place?" Darius sighed in frustration.

"The girl," Izebal answered pointedly. "We saved her. That does not count for naught. We did the right thing."

Darius looked upon Izebal, a living thing of vibrant beauty, compassion, and honor. He needed to say something before she left once more. How many times would she return to him? But what to say? He did not even understand what he himself was feeling toward her. It was all a swirling mix of adoration, respect, awe, and something deeper. There was an attraction. He could no longer deny that. When she had entered the High Hall, that was the moment he realized just how much she captivated his heart, mind, and soul.

Fear filled him.

What had he just admitted to himself?

CHAPTER 16: THE TOWER
AELLIA

Aellia's arms screamed in agony, her shoulders sore from the way her wrists were bound together against the pole that crossed under her armpits and down her back. She had been lashed to a cross and set into the floor of a dark cell. Everything smelled of earth and running water; that and the malodorous stink of rodent droppings.

Wailing moans echoed off of the walls of the subterranean tunnel, men and women alike pleading hopelessly for their lives. They cried out constantly, begging for the reason of their capture or for mercy for their sins. They proffered prayers up to Gallae, pleading for grace. They offered prayers up to Ordan, demanding justice. Their prayers made Aellia wanted to smash her head against the straw-strewn floor. If only she could get off of this bloody cross.

The steady flop of soft-soled shoes on stone reverberated off the walls. Someone was coming. Multiple someones, though Aellia could not make out how many. As they approached, she would have thought the pleading and begging would have increased. On the contrary: the cells beside her went deathly silent. A heaviness filled the air, and despite all her rage, she could not keep out the sense of impeding doom that gnawed at her will, chewing away at the meager strength that remained.

I should have stayed.

I told you.

Iaenora, is that you?

Who else would it be? Do you harbor another ancient being in your mind?

Yes. That was Iaenora. Had there been any doubt before, Aellia held none now.

Where are you?

We are bonded.

I mean, where is the scepter? Are you close?

Our link is strong, therefore we must be close to the Oathroad.

We need to get out of here. Any ideas?

Ah, so now the lone warrior seeks sage advice.

For Gallae's grace! Aellia groaned in her mind. The footsteps were getting closer. They needed to act and Iaenora chose now to lecture?

I will teach whenever and however I can. You must learn to accept me or we can never complete our great task.

I don't want to complete a great task. What I want is to get out of this cell! What about Drafting?

That would require contact with the Oathrod to draw upon Aetora's light.

So, we need to get to the scepter. If I do that, you can get us out of here?

Aellia. This place is very, very old. I can feel the ancient wards carved into the stone. It is a place of deep secrets. Who are these people?

Are you serious? They're almost here! I don't have time for a lecture in Ordiatian society and secret cults! But trust me when I say this, it will not bode well for either of us if they take us.

I believe we are already taken. I do wish you would have listened and not sojourned away from the goodly high priest. He was such a nice man.

He was a creep! He captured us!

He healed you, Aellia. You need to learn peace in your heart. Not everyone is out to hurt you.

No, those who cared are dead.

I care.

Not enough to get us out of here.

Do you hold the Oathrod?

The footsteps stopped. They were right outside her door, or what she supposed was a door. Her back was to it, the cross leaving her legs splayed out on the floor in a seated position, arms strung over the sides and wound tightly to the upright mast.

A keychain clattered, followed by the insertion into a lock and grinding of many small gears. So there was a door, and it was locked. Getting off of the cross would have amounted to little more than a minor increase in comfort.

"Cha'lin nah alhe felro, Calun?" announced one of the people that entered the room. Their voice sounded strange, not quite human. It had a metallic sound, along with some kind of distortion.

"Do you speak the language of Ordiatae?" asked the same person, this time speaking High Republic, a snooty, airy dialect spoken by Uppers. The sound made Aellia's skin crawl.

"Why would you lead with that?" Aellia answered sardonically.

Why are you trying to make them mad?

They tied me to a cross!

"We are going to untie you," the voice continued in its strange, inhuman tone. "Do not try to harm us. We have no desire to harm you."

"Sounds like something someone who hadn't just abducted and imprisoned someone would say," Aellia scoffed.

"Be still," another voice reverberated, more feminine but still distorted. "This will not hurt you unless you move."

There was a low *click* that Aellia immediately recognized as the open and locking of a folding knife. Her heart rate quickened. The cold touch of steel slid along her wrists, but it was the spine of the blade, not the edge. With two swift slices, the cords fell away.

Aellia tumbled forward. Her arms were totally numb due to lack of blood flow. Her face almost struck the floor, but a quick hand caught her a hair's breadth away.

"You are weak." This was not a question, but a gruff statement.

Aellia lulled her head to the side and looked at the gloved hand that held her, silver and blue silk protruding from loose-hanging sleeves of similar material.

"If you're looking for a thank you, check another cell," said Aellia with a jerk of her shoulder, pulling away from the gloved hand.

She rose to her feet, her aching limbs beginning to find feeling once more. It felt as if hundreds of tiny pinpricks were running up and down her arms. As she turned about, the sight of the three nearly stole her breath away.

Aellia had always considered the Church of Ordan a cult. But they held not a candle to these three. All were draped in fine robes of elaborate design. They wore strange aprons with foreign symbols embroidered into them. And on their faces they had masks of silver with blue lenses over the eyes.

"Be not afraid," said the Asterverian that was clearly female.

"Be not afraid?" Aellia took a step away from the three, but she could not go far. Her back ran into the damp wall of her cell. She was trapped, with no way out.

Anything, Iaenora? Anything at all?

They do not seem to hold weapons of any kind. Perhaps they do mean no harm.

Aellia grit her teeth. She did not like the way 'perhaps' sounded, especially when it came to her personal wellbeing. Felik had always said words first, run second, fists last. Well, there was nowhere to run and Aellia highly doubted she could talk her way out of this. Fists it was then.

"Do not try anything foolish," said the largest of the Asterverians. "The Illuminated One seeks only to ask you a few questions. Answer those in earnest, and you will be free to go."

The big one was all chest and shoulders. He favored his right knee. The little one was so thin that their fitted robes draped around them. A swift kick to the big one's knee and a jab to the throat would put him down. The little one, well, she could just bull over them. And the female. The way she stood concerned Aellia, in the fact that she seemed absolutely devoid of concern. Ignorant people always had a tell. Confident people overcompensated. This person knew something. Aellia would have to take her out first.

"Don't—" started the big one, but it was too late. Aellia was already moving.

Aellia dove at the female, grabbing onto the front of her robes and rolling her body over her.

Zap!

Electricity surged through Aellia's body, momentarily blinding her. She fell limp to the floor, body convulsing uncontrollably.

"We did say not to try anything," scoffed the little one.

Aellia grimaced up at them. She had a thousand curses she wanted to heap upon them, but she could not find the strength to utter a single word.

"Here, take my hand," said the big one, extending his hand downward toward her.

Aellia, confused as to what had happened, and seeing no other reasonable option, grabbed onto the big guy's hand. He lifted her as if she didn't weigh anything at all—a motion that made Aellia feel slightly insecure. She knew she had lost weight due to the injuries, but to be moved so effortlessly was disconcerting.

Apparently, the big man was just as surprised at the ease of the process. He stumbled backwards a step or two, having put too much force into the motion and sending his body off kilter. His back thudded hard against the wall as Aellia was sent soaring into the ceiling. Luckily for her, or perhaps unluckily, she was still holding fast to her captor's hand.

Using the moment of the crumpling big man, Aellia ran across the cell's ceiling in an arc, then pushed off with a quick twist. The force of the descent, coupled with the connection of the man's hand, allowed Aellia to drive a knee squarely into her holder's face. The mask cracked—as did the wearer's nose—in a squelch. Blood splattered Aellia's knee as tiny shards of metal tore into her flesh.

Blue light erupted from the fractured mask, tiny crystals of Everlight bleeding their light over the man's mangled face. Aellia had forgotten just how hard she hit now; memories of how she had tossed that Kh'ar thug across an alley and into a wrought iron fence filled her head with sickening clarity.

To the man's credit, he did not stay down long. The Everlight that leaked over his face was mending the many cuts, drawing the blood that smattered his face back inside the flesh as tiny shards of the mask fell to the floor. He had a dark complexion, probably from northern Telnor, with a blocky jaw and, from what Aellia could see, deep brown eyes, though only one was visible. That being said, there was enough anger in that singular eye for the both of them.

"You little prick," his voice had lost the strange reverberative quality that Aellia realized was produced by the masks they wore. It was a stone-grinding bass, filled with malice and venom. "I will break you!"

"No!" shouted another of the Asterverians. "We have direct orders from On High. We cannot kill her."

"Who said anything about killing?" Blood still tinged his too white teeth as a wicked smile spread across the revealed part of big man's face.

For the love of the great goddess, do you ever try talking first?

"Not now, Iaenora," Aellia shot back as she slid her back across the smooth wall, inching closer to the door and away from the three.

"Uh uh uh," tutted the feminine sounding Asterverian. "I wouldn't do that if I were you."

"Just let me go and no one else needs to get hurt," Aellia answered, her body still slinking to the doorway.

The Telnorian marched to the door, hefting a chair as he walked and plopped himself down. He intertwined his gloved fingers and stretched his arms outward, cracking his knuckles in a loud series of pops.

"You are an enigma, young lady," said the third Asterverian. She sounded much older than the other two, and far kindlier. "Here at the Asterivae, we do not seek to destroy, but to study and create. Come, let us talk peaceably. Clearly you are of great power and far beyond our skills and capabilities."

The big Telnorian did not like this statement, Aellia saw him squirm. But to his credit, he did not argue or rise to the statement. Aellia found herself unusually drawn in by the older woman's speaking and was surprised to find her hands opening and her muscles relaxing.

"That is better," she crooned. "Just relax. We only wish to talk."

"Why am I here?" Aellia tried to hold on to the flame of rage, to stoke it in her mind. But every time this woman spoke, less and less anger burned within.

"Dear child." The woman cocked her head as she spoke. "You infiltrated our gardens, passed our guards without them even noticing. A feat, might I add, that was very impressive. Rest assured; they are being taught the measure of their mistakes."

Aellia slid down the wall until she felt the hard floor catch her. All was fine. This was fine. She just needed to let go.

"Come come, this better, isn't it?" the woman spoke, and as she did so, Aellia could have sworn she saw patterns of blue light emanating from the slitted mouthpiece of her mask.

It was better. No hurting. Not fighting. No useless struggling.

"Walk with us, would you?" the woman said in the kindest voice Aellia had ever heard.

What a good idea. She should walk; her legs were sore from sitting. A walk would do them well.

Aellia

"Okay," Aellia answered. For some reason, her tongue seemed very heavy and her head felt as if it were stuffed with cotton. But the walk would help. She knew it, beyond a shadow of doubt, the walk would help.

"That is a good girl," the woman's voice was sweet as honey. No, sweeter, sickeningly sweet. It made Aellia's whole body shiver. But, oh, how she wanted to hear it again, over and over and over again. Aellia would be good, she would do anything for that voice to praise her.

When Aellia tried to answer, she found her tongue could not move, nor her jaws open. That was okay. Perhaps if she was very good she the woman would speak to her again. Say she was good. Tell her what she would have her do.

Aellia.

Time passed. Aellia was not sure of how much of it passed, but it had passed. She had been walking, up flights of spiraling stairs. She had been walking, across carpeted floors and under great arches held by colossal pillars of carved marble. She had been walking for what felt like an eternity, for what felt like no time at all.

Something sweet passed through Aellia's senses, like lavender blossoms and fresh linens. It made her head light and feet tingle, giving her the absurd desire to twirl about like a girl at a maypole. The dark cell seemed slip from her view as her bare feet carried her along gleaming floors. Sunlight streamed in through towering, stained-glass windows, lighting upon a fountain of pure gold whose water dazzled the eyes as it cascaded over three beings of regal stature.

"These were the first," said the woman is soothing tones. "They were seekers of truth and light. So are each of us. That is the purpose of this place, our credo, and our society. You will become a much desired part of this world, and as we seek to understand you, I believe much of great worth will be divulged."

Aellia rolled her head on her shoulders to meet her master's masked face. Master? When had she begun to think of this woman as her master? But what other title would make sense? Something in her mind railed against the idea of calling another human 'master' but she simply could not be bothered with that notion, not when this woman spoke so sweetly to her.

Aellia!

That voice. She knew that voice. It was strange and yet familiar. An impossibility. A part of her soul yearned to hear it once more, heart aching for those familiar tones and inclinations.

"This way," said Aellia's master. The woman was standing before a pair of doors, painted violet. The knobs were polished brass as were the hinges. Aellia had to squint as she looked upon them, every bit of metal catching the light in an overbearing brilliance. "Once inside, you will find that you will be much more yourself. Take your time. Breathe. I will return to you when the time is right."

Aellia cocked her head and the sound of the woman's voice. What had she meant? Was she leaving her? Aellia's heart began to race, panic creeping up her spine. She couldn't be far from her master, that was wrong. No! She wanted to scream the word, to shout at the top of her lungs. But not a sound came out, and when instructed, she stepped through the double doors silently, obediently.

The doors shut with a soft thud. A key turned in the lock, and as it did so, a quick *pop* sounded in the room, followed by a low buzz. Small glass orbs flickered to life, shining with a faint blue hue, illuminating the large sitting room adorned with a lounging settee of pale lime coloring with frilled lacework, a small table set with a fine tea set, and an overly ornate mirror set in a bronze frame.

In an instant, the fog that had set on Aellia's mind vanished. And in that vacuum of space, nausea filled her stomach. Aellia grabbed at her midsection as she stumbled toward the settee and flopped down onto her back. Her head felt as if it was filled with stinging nettles, and her hands and feet prickled with some strange sensation, as if she had sat on the edge of a stool for a long period of time and now all the blood was rushing uncomfortably fast to her extremities.

Aellia felt hot tears slide down the right side of her face, trailing salty streaks from her cheeks down onto her neck. The left side of her face did not weep, did not see, could not see. It could not see the domed ceiling nor the gold-leafed trim. It could not see the gossamer paintings of the Ellitheor, nor their heralds, the angels of myth and legend. But with her right eye, Aellia looked upon it all, laying upon her back, staring hopelessly upward.

Aellia.

She sat bolt upright, whirling her head about. That voice. She knew that voice. It came to her, not as if it were in her mind, but from without her body, from without this room, pleading.

Impossible.

With trembling hands, Aellia searched her body, patting herself down in hopes of find the Oathrod. Tears of bitter grief turned to hot tears of anger. Again, she was trapped. Again, she was held against her will. Again, she was defenseless.

No.

The word was fire in her heart, her mind, her soul.

No.

She was not defenseless, nor weak, nor helpless. She was the wind and the storm. She could feel that power still beneath her flesh, rippling waves of light smoldering her along her nerves, prickling her skin, sourcing the very essence of her being.

"Iaenora," Aellia said as she rose to her feet. She cast out her hand, pushing away the doubt. "Come to me!"

A pulse. A wave of power. The lights snuffed out then blared so brightly that the bulbs that contained them burst asunder. Sapphire light rushed toward Aellia, cascading over her, seeping into her. Air whirled about her body, tossing the tea set, the plates and saucers shattering against the wall.

They had made a mistake leaving her here. They had mistaken her for weak. Aellia was not weak.

The bond strengthened. She could feel Iaenora's presence substantiating within her body and mind.

A scream, a cry of panic and pain reverberated throughout the massive foyer on the other side of the inviolable doors. Wood shattered as the Oathrod crashed through those very doors, sending splinters into the whirlwind.

Stop leaving me! Iaenora's voice thundered in Aellia's mind, sending a grim smile across her face. Power, it filled her body. *They put me in a box!*

"Me too," Aellia snarled in dark delight as she stepped toward the door. They had put her in a box. But they had underestimated her, took her for a weak thing, because she was small, because she was scared. Because she was not rich nor perceptibly powerful. "Let them see me now!"

Aellia thrust her hand forward, sending all the wind, the debris, the settee and its cushions, the tiny shards of the painted tea set, hurtling into the door, bursting them apart.

Bright light bathed Aellia's body as the wind lifted her from her feet and carried her over the shards of glass and slivers of wood. She scanned the room, her right eye seeing as a mortal; her left lit with Aetora's power saw things no human could. Tiny details were discerned in an instant fell into perfect synchrony. Before her rose that towering fountain of gold, the waters no longer appearing mystical. Just water. Just gold. So much gold. The statue alone could have fed all of Southend for a season and then some. Two winding sets of stairs worked their way upwards on either side of the three golden individuals. They were white marble, blue-veined, and magnificent. Balusters and rails leafed in gold and carved of polished wood lined the double staircases, whose bottom steps flared out like two great fans.

Aellia's focus rose upward, gazing upon dozens of hanging chandeliers and apertures she could not understand. Large crystal tubes and floating orbs of so many colors and patterns it boggled the mind. Bronze compasses and squares, golden charts and baubles. She could feel herself lifting skyward, floating up and up. The spiraling stairs wound upwards. Upwards to what she knew was a domed roof of glass, supported by steel arches. Glass that had been smeared with Tomo's blood. Blood spilt by Tornak. Her lover and her so-called friend.

Floor upon floor passed by her as she rose ever upward, each open to look down upon the open atrium, each a maze of bookshelves and tables. Dozens, no, hundreds of masked figures in robes of varying hues were rising to their feet, pushing away from their tables and papers, scrolls and devices. They were clamoring about. Calling for this and that. Aellia did not stop her ascent, did not pay them any heed. She was no one's prisoner, and she would show the world what would happen to any of those who would try and cage her again.

The ceiling was only a short distance away now. The tower narrowed slightly with every floor, and what at the base had seemed so vast was now only wide enough for the dangling chains which supported the vast array of hanging objects now so far below her. Aellia stopped, alighting on a steel hoop thicker than her body that was bracketed into the ceiling. She stood there, the black metal cool on her bare feet. It was all so massive.

Voices sounded below her, people shouting and yelling. Sounds of ladders and metal boots. They were all so small. So insignificant.

Aellia, we need to return to Elcon.

Aellia stiffed that the words, her body going rigid with fury and indignation. She had just escaped her captives, why would she want to return to one?

"No."

Aellia, hear me. We must find my sisters. There is one who speaks with the man Elcon who can help us. He has a connection to Ordan, I felt it. We must find my sisters.

"I said, no!" Aellia turned her gaze upward once more, glaring at the ceiling. It was not painted nor adorned with gold or jewels, no murals or art. This was practical. A series of heavy beams meant hold the top of this tower and all that dangled below. "I am leaving this place, all of it. I have nothing left here. Tomo is dead. Felik is dead. Belthazer and Felohme too."

Aellia. We are bonded. We are more than this. We must be.

"I didn't choose this, any of it!" Aellia's voice rose in anger, in bitterness and hurt. "Let me be free!"

When Iaenora spoke next, her words were calm, but pained. *"We are the wind and storm. Our soul yearns for that which cannot be held nor contained. To drift and blow, to flow over endless fields and never cease. Would that we could, would that you and I could lose ourselves in the void and become nothing but that which cannot be held nor seen. But the wind carries life, summer's warmth and winter's chill. We carry the birds of the air, which drop the seeds of Spring. We are least of all, the one that cannot be glimpsed nor touched, but without us, there is no life, no air breath, no wind to feel, no storm to rage. We are all of those things, and so much more. I chose you, not because you were the strongest, but because, like the storm, you are a force beyond what the eye can see. You always have been.*

Aellia blinked, allowing the words to wash over her, to sink into her mind. She wanted to rail against them, reject them. But they struck too true to her heart, piercing through her pain and her guilt to her very core.

Aellia realized something, something she had not had the chance to consider before this very moment. Something that, through all the fighting and loss, had changed deep within her. And that realization caused her to tremble more than all of the pain and torture she had suffered over the course of these past weeks. Aellia did not know who she was anymore. And that scared her more than she could even begin to comprehend.

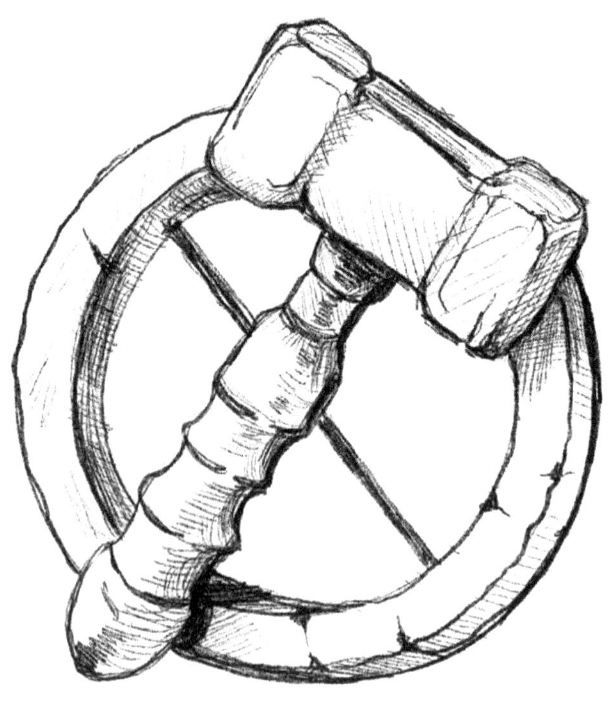

Chapter 17: Ink and Cream
Darius

Darius rode in silent appreciation of the horse-drawn carriage that carried Izebal and himself down the High Hill. When the festivities had ended and the High Hall cleared of the clans' leaders, Tyree had excused himself to return to his shop and invited the two of them to come and visit him. Izebal had agreed to the old mage's request without any rebuttal or hesitancy.

Darius was still not sure what to think of the two of them. An unlikely duo, but it also made sense as he thought on it. Since entering Talahmnas, Darius had yet to meet, or even hear of, another mage in the city. It seemed that there were fewer of those who could Touch Aetora here than in Tur'Mor, and to that day, Izebal had been the only person he had met who could Touch Ria'Elahm. Tyree must have been beside himself to have another person who could do similar things. Ordan above knew that Darius wished he had any of his brothers left to share his burden.

Months had passed since he had awakened, and the bite of loneliness had not abated in the slightest. If anything, it had grown more difficult to bear. He missed his father and mother, his brother, and all of his kin. He missed the fanciful tales told by Angenthor, he missed wrestling with red-headed Baenhada.

"Are you alright?" Izebal seemed concerned. "You've been quiet since the garden."

Darius shrugged, his fingers laced together in his lap. He wished he would of have said something up on the hill. Thinking back, the timing had been perfect. She smelled of spiced honey and lilac, a lovely scent. He could tell her that much, couldn't he? However, he hadn't the courage to say anything.

Courage. What a fickle thing.

He could fight monsters, demons, and witches. He stood against the darkness, raged against Mireya's armies and Diabhail's consorts. Yet, in the face of one whom he cared for, that was when his resolve failed him.

"What are you thinking about?" Izebal prodded. "Come on, you can talk to me."

"My kin," Darius answered. It was the truth, if only half of it.

"Tell me of them," Izebal said. She leaned back into the soft seat of the luxurious carriage and stared out the glass window. "We have time, and this is far more comfortable than the wagon I was carried up the hill in."

Darius could not help but let out a little laugh. When he looked up at her, his heart warmed. Radiant beams of sunlight refracted off of the glass, showering her in warm, golden light. Her dresses fit her so perfectly, and the gold coins that hung from her scarf tinkled as the carriage rolled smoothly forward. Darius wanted this image to be burned into his mind forever. She was, perhaps, the most beautiful woman he had ever seen. And ever since he had admitted that to himself atop the High Hill, he could not but notice little things about her. The way her chin turned ever so lightly, making her lips quirk to the left. The silver tattoo at her neck of the three loops intertwining in a mystifyingly endless pattern. The way her collarbones stood out just so above her chest, and how that entrancing golden, amulet fell ever so perfectly at her bosom. Everything about her was so majestic, so beautiful.

A sudden realization dawned on him, as he sat in that carriage. What would happen to them once they arrived in Dane? Where would she go? What would become of, well, whatever they were?

Darius had little experience with women—warring against Mireya and her thralls, and subsequently being cursed to a millennium long slumber, had left little time for pursuing romance—but he had learned from his father that being honest, kind, and straightforward was often the best approach. What had he to lose, anyway? Izebal was leaving, and who was to say they would ever see each other again. Why then say anything and further complicate and confuse the situation?

"My father," Darius started, realizing he had lost himself in a stupor of thought, again. "When we were out hunting, would always find a stone with some kind of unique property—-quartz, oval, smooth, calcified—and would bring it back to my mother. He always told her that it was the little things about her that he loved, how every part of her was unique and different."

Izebal blink. The most radiant smile shone brightly across her face. "I would not have thought that..." She flushed and fell silent.

"Thought what? That my father was a romantic?" Darius laughed, feeling a bit of tension easy as his mind was filled memories of his father's warmth to his mother. "Because I am as warm as a river stone?"

"Well," Izebal said, her blush still coloring her cheeks. "You're just so, you know, stoic."

Darius scoffed, his thick eyebrows raised in questioning.

"Oh, come now," Izebal squirmed. "You can't be serious? You've more trouble opening your mouth than an Itheanam's skull. With your bare hands."

Her smile faded. "What was your father like?"

Darius fumbled to find the right words. How would you describe a man who had meant everything? Who was your whole world, your exemplar, and mentor?

"He was firm. He had a passion deeper than the Shimmering Lake and stronger than the Iron Mountains." Darius let out a laugh, hands aimlessly fidgeting with his ring, his father's ring. "He had this way with the children in our tribe. They loved him. He could tell the very best stories. Once, when I was a child, he and my uncles took down a bull occex with horns the width of my legs. That night, at the fire, we ate as he painted the most vivid picture of the hunt. How I longed to have been with him, to share in that glory."

Izebal's eyes glistened with tears. "He sounds like a wonderful man."

"He was." Darius felt a pit in his gut open, a deep sorrow furrowing though him. "But he is no more. Slain by the hands of Mireya's high priest, Diabhail. Every good thing in my life was taken by her and that damnable man. Everything."

Silence fell between them. Darius's heart was heavy with the bitter sorrows of loss, so much so that he could not see the pain in Izebal's eyes, the way her body shifted from him. He was hurting, but so was she.

The silence persisted until they reached Tyree's shop. As the carriage came to a gentle stop, before Darius could rise, Izebal reached a hand out, taking hold of his.

"I am sorry, Darius," she said. "For what it's worth. I would not wish what happened to you on anyone. But it is why I must go. We need answers to all of this. I need to regain my strength and connect with Ethenealal. If what you saw in that cave was true, a vision of Diabhail's own likeness, we need all the strength we can muster."

The warmth of her hand on his sent a rush through his body. Darius knew that in this moment he had a decision to make. And though it pained him, he knew what he needed to say. If there was any hope of a future... he stopped that line of thinking, steadied himself, and answered. "I understand. You must do what you must, and so do I."

The smile that spread across Izebal's lips filled Darius's heart with warmth.

"Thank you," she said softly. She rose from her seat, leaned forward, and kissed him lightly on his cheek. "For trusting me."

Izebal stood upright, strained out her skirts and adjusted the pouch at her waist, and said, "Well, best not keep the old codger waiting."

Darius did not move as Izebal stepped out of the back of the carriage. His heart thundered in his chest. What had just happened? A thousand competing thoughts warred in his head all at once, the noise debilitating. Yet the bright spot on his soul could not be overshadowed. Somehow, for some reason he could not fathom, Izebal had just kissed him.

But what if it was just a Diju thing? Did it mean anything? Was she just being friendly?

"Oy," Izebal called out. "Messenger boy, are you coming or not?"

Darius jumped out of his seat, whacking the top of his head on the ceiling of the carriage with a loud *thud!* Izebal laughed openly, her voice like an angel's song. Heat flushed his face as he muttered a curse.

"Are you alright?" Izebal asked through stifled laughs.

"Fine," he grunted in response. "Let's just get this over with."

The embarrassment and pain mingled with the frustration and confusion of the day. His mind still struggled to track how certain events had led to this moment. Captured to honored guest. Chains to regalia. And now, he was being prepared to compete in some ceremonial game to prove himself before a group of people he could not care less about. And yet, there were oddities about these Danelanders, certain mannerism that reminded him all too much of his own people. Little things, like way they held so tightly to individual honor and personal strength, a far cry from those of Tur'Mor. They seemed to only care about coins and political prowess.

These thoughts weaved their way through Darius's mind as he walked up to the door of Tyree's shop and opened it to the clattering of the bell.

"'Bout bloody damn time," came the raspy, wizened voice of the old mage from behind his work bench.

Darius snorted at the assaulting smells of the shop. Preservatives, solutions, rust, and a multitude of fungi. It was a rather sickening concoction, one that was tinged with a sickening sweetness that he could not place, but made his stomach tie in knots.

"Ye'll get used to it," Tyree said, lifting his spectacle-laden head up from his studies. Half a dozen colored lenses flared out in a multitude of directions, held by brass wires and turned by tiny cogs and sprockets. "The smell that is. I never do get used to stuff. My life's work, it is. A marvel."

"A mess," said Izebal, her words filled with wit, not spite. "How do you find anything in here?"

Chains. She had been in chains, and now she was trading quips?

"Everything has its rightful place, lassie," answered Tyree as he pulled off his thick gloves. "But, that's not why y'er here, is it? No, no. Lord Ruthvin has in trusted me in y'er training, laddie. I'm to make a man out of ye in just a few short weeks. Blood and bloody stones, what was he thinking?"

Darius forced himself to calm down, focusing on what he knew. Or at least what he had been assured. Free passage through Daneland would see him swiftly to his goal. What would a few days in one place truly hurt if it got him to where he needed to be must quicker? He guessed he would just have to learn that for himself. And, if it all went wrong, it would not be the first time he had fled away on his own. As long as it did not end as poorly as last time. He had no more Everlight elixir to save him.

Even at the thought of the fight in the cave, the wound in his abdomen flared with pain. Darius grunted as he doubled over. He reached out for anything to stable himself. Luckily, his hand found a table, and held to it as if it were a cliff's edge, and he was dangling over the abyss.

"ye alright, laddie?" Tyree was already wheeling toward him, all humor gone from his voice.

"I'll live," Darius grunted in reply, his eyes held tightly shut against the already subsiding pain.

"There must be something we can do about that," Izebal said, her words more directed at Tyree than at Darius.

"That, lassie, do be beyond me," Tyree shook his head slowly as he spoke. "I'd never thought one could survive the lance of a Soulless One, much less walk away from it. As for the pain, I do have something that might be able to help. But…"

The old mage's voice trailed off as he looked away. Intrigue took hold of Darius's mind, his whole focus now fully upon Tyree.

"What?" he asked through gritted teeth.

"It is a hard sedative, derived from the root of the Krulak bush from Tuawtia," Tyree answered, his voice unsure.

"A what?" Darius retorted, the words meaning nothing to him, leaving him feeling ignorant once more. But he did not care. He just

needed to ease the pain. Everything else he could work through. How else was he to complete his journey? How could he awaken the Sages and break the chains that bound him if he was constantly doubled over in agony?

"A psychedelic sedative with dissociative properties," Tyree said, waving around a withered, wrinkled hand. "ye know. It alters the brain and makes one tired as a stone. Deadens the mind, puts ye in doldrums of sorts."

Well, that wouldn't work. Pain was as an old friend. But the thought of losing his mind—his consciousness—once again filled Darius with dread. He had spent a millennia sealed in a tomb and had woken up as if only one night had passed. Fear of losing control outweighed the boiling pain of reality. So, he would suffer.

"No," Darius said firmly.

Relief seemed to wash over Tyree, along with a bit of shame. He had slipped up. Darius saw that now. The old man hadn't wanted him to know of the strange root and its abilities. It wouldn't matter. Darius wouldn't touch the stuff. Drink, a momentary reprieve was appreciated. Losing himself was unacceptable.

"I do have, however, a tonic that should numb the pain if applied directly," Tyree said, his demeanor brightening.

"Why didn't you lead with that?" snorted Darius in response.

"Ye get over the hill of a hundred years and then talk to me about how well y'er brain holds the little things!" Tyree snapped.

Darius raised an eyebrow at the old mage. He had told him of his plight, the ceaseless slumber that had taken his wits.

"That don't count," Tyree spat. A wild smile formed on his wrinkled face, eyes flashing with azure light. "Ye was asleep. I've been out, busting my stones every bloody day. Ain't no rest for a master magus."

"Would you two please just stop?" Izebal's voice was nearing exasperation. She held a hand to her temple and was shaking her head in dismay. Though Darius was sure he saw the hint of a smile flash across her own lips.

"Right, right," Tyree said as he wheeled away from Darius and began rummaging through an open box. "This is to be applied twice a day, every day. It will help the pain and lessen the chance of spreading. It's not a miracle though, whatever has happened to ye, y'er gonna need to get fixed outright, eventually. But this should help."

Darius took the circular tin from the old mage's proffered hand. He spun the lid and revealed a lavender-colored cream whose aroma nearly stole his breath away, sending what felt like a crusting of hoarfrost down his nostrils, coating the back of his throat.

"A bit potent," Tyree laughed. "Best put some on and close 'er up tight. Hard stuff to come by."

Darius, not for the first time, wondered just how many oddities and concoctions were held up in this old shop. Again, the pang of regret that Elcon was not here to see this stung at him, nearly as sharp as the scent of the cream he held.

Not to delay the inevitable, Darius dabbed a finger into the purplish cream and lifted his shirt. The wound was an angry red, the raised white flesh lined with black veins.

"Wait!" Izebal exclaimed as she eyed the angry scar tissue. Her hand dropped to the satchel at her hip. Swiftly her fingers traced the rune-seal to undo the binding, and with deft precision, her hand retrieved what looked like a silver quill and a small vial of emerald ink.

Darius eyed the fine point on the quill and the vial which Izebal held. He had seen her draw runes of the ancient Words of her people. It did not take much to connect the dots as to what she was about to do. Reflexively, Darius stepped away from her, his eyes darting back and forth.

"Diju indeed." smirked Tyree. "I didn't think of that. Foolish of me. Ain't no Danelander whose had the Touch of Ria'Elahm in over ten generations. That, lassie, just might work."

"Why didn't you tell me it had gotten this bad?" Izebal's words were little more than a whisper, but the glare in those emerald eyes sent a shiver down Darius's spine.

"Bah! Ethenealal's breath! You are a stubborn and bullheaded man!" Izebal's eyes flashed around the room. She muttered something under her breath about not having time for this and something else about groves and Lifelight. When her eyes rested upon Tyree's workbench, she pointed a stern finger and barked, "Lie down, Messenger Boy, and take your shirt off!"

Darius blinked in surprise.

"I'd do as the witch with the magic ink says, laddie," whispered Tyree in an unusually somber manner, though his eyes twinkled with humor.

"I'll be fine," Darius retorted, feeling a sudden lance of indignation. He had had about enough of this being pushed around and commanded, even if it was by Izebal. "I have the cream, I'll—"

"Darius!" Izebal's voice cracked like a whip. "I did not walk through Ranok and into Daneland, suffer chains and humiliation, just to have you die from Iodaba's blight! Take. Off. Your. Shirt. And. Lie. Down. Now."

Darius moved with such conviction as he had never before felt. Without even realizing what had happened, he found himself lying upon his bare back, looking up into the domed glass of Tyree's shop with Izebal studying the puncture wound with concerned eyes. A flush of warmth rushed up his body as her cool fingers traced the outside of the scar tissue, pleasant but concerning for obvious reasons.

"This is bad," Izebal spoke without looking up from him, her hand digging once more through her satchel. "Master Mage, do you have coal and paper? I need to sketch this out before I start."

"Two moments, lassie," Tyree said as he wheeled over to a cabinet of drawers. He thumbed through them swiftly, his gnarled hands moving with practiced precision. When he returned, triumph was plastered across his wizened face. "Coal pens and parchment, for the lady."

"Thank you," said Izebal, not even looking at him as she took the materials and set it next to her grandmother's book, which she had sourced out of the satchel while Tyree had been searching.

She worked rapidly, whispering under her breath different things that Darius couldn't understand, but realized were Words. After a few crumpled sheets of parchment—and some words that Darius definitely understood the meaning of—Izebal seemed to have found the correct Word to use in her book.

"I do not have much of the Lifelight left to me," Izebal said as she pulled her amulet from her blouse. She was right; the stone that once had shone so vibrantly was now dull as a normal gemstone. "The collar drained much from me, but I should have enough to ink this rune. It will be but a barrier, not a solution. Like the cream, it will help, but not solve the problem."

"If you use your Light, you'll be without your powers," Darius said as he began to raise himself from the table.

Izebal placed a firm hand on his chest, stopping him from sitting upright. "I am going to the groves. I will replenish my Light there.

But, if this is not contained, I fear you will not live to see my return, much less compete in these games for passage."

"The lassie is right, lad," Tyree said. "If y'er not healed up, I don't know how ye could compete. Ain't seen no one face bigger odds than that, maybe other than the Red Dread."

Darius had little care of Danelander lore or history right now. "Izebal, what about you? You'll be defenseless."

Izebal smiled at him as if he were an ignorant child, "You are a dense man, Darius of the Iron Mountains. I am never defenseless. I shall be fine. Now, are you done complaining? If so, I can get to work."

Darius harrumphed, but did as he was told.

From where he lay, he could not see what Izebal was doing, so as she wiped around the edges of the wound with something cold, he nearly jumped out of his skin.

"Ethenealal's grace! That was only to clean the skin to keep back infection," Izebal chided. "I haven't even began to prick the flesh. Master Mage, do you have something for this messenger boy to bite down on?"

"Come to think of it, I have just the thing!" Tyree said with a gleeful cackle as he wheeled off yet again.

"Darius, you're going to have to hold still," Izebal said quickly, her voice housing no humor now. "If these lines are done wrong, well, it could go very badly."

"Badly?" Darius swallowed hard.

"Just," Izebal said calmly, "try and not flinch. It will sting... a lot." A hand reflexively lifted to the shimmering mark on her own neck as she took out her dagger and cut the quill even sharper.

"Our kin—those of Galacia—still practice the carving of runes, but I have heard they do not have use the ink as the Diju do any longer. A pity." Izebal's voice was calm and steady. Darius realized this was more for him than her. Again, he found himself in awe of this woman. Again, he found himself falling even more for her. "They are such powerfully blooded people, one of the few Matriarchies left."

Darius understood what she was doing, but it did not lessen the pricks of pain as the tip of the silver quill bit into his flesh. Time and time again, the surface of his skin broke, and every time there was a disturbing sensation of something unnatural sinking into his flesh. He did not know how long the process lasted, what all Izebal said in

her soothing voice, or if the pricking or the wound itself hurt more at this. When the seemingly ceaseless pricking ended, two things became certain:

One, there was a near instantaneous relief to the aching of Iodaba's spread. It still burned hot in the central wound but did not radiate outward any longer. Two, for the first time since leaving the cave, his mind was snapped into a clarity he had nearly forgotten he could possess.

Darius shot up, an intense focus seizing his mind. His eyes darted around the room, taking in everything as if for the first time. When they met Izebal's, nothing short of pure elation filled him.

"By Ordan! What did you do?" he exclaimed joyously.

"I take it the rune worked?" Izebal asked coyly, a smile spreading across her lips.

"Worked?" said Darius. "I feel like a new man. Not since that elixir have I ever felt so alive."

Tension seemed to melt off of Izebal's face, replaced with what looked to be an arrogant smile. "Perhaps next time, you won't be so bull-headed as to allow something like this to spread. You're lucky you have your ring. I do not know how else you were not consumed by the blight."

In his state of clarity, a realization came over Darius. "It is still in me though, I can feel it."

Izebal's smile faltered. "Yes, you are marked. And, unfortunately, the runes I drew will fade in time. I could continue to touch them up, adding more Lifelight to them, but—"

But they would fade. In time, Darius would be consumed by Iodaba's Touch if he could not find a way to extract the poison in him. The handprint seared into his chest chose to use this moment of fear and realization to reverberate, sending a spasm through his torso.

"What is it?" Izebal asked, eyes flashing with alarm.

Darius grit his teeth against the pain, that old familiar ache, and grabbed the buttons of his shirt. Steadily, he thumbed them closed, focusing his mind on the memory of his first attempt at buttoning in Ranun's Bread house. How long ago that seemed. How much it felt like just yesterday. He would get through this. He always did. He was a survivor.

"Darius?" Izebal pressed. "What is wrong? It's that scar, isn't it?"

"I'm fine," Darius answered. He knew his face was contorted; he knew his hands shook. But what could any of them do for it now? Hadn't they done enough? They had saved him, relegated the pain to a single location. He was alive. That was enough. It would have to be.

Izebal did not argue further. Darius could see the hurt in her eyes, the way his words cut her. He didn't mean to hurt her, or anyone. But people seemed to always be the unwilling benefactors of pain when he became close. Maybe this whatever it was with Izebal was a mistake. He should've stayed the course. He shouldn't have brought her here. He would only cause her pain.

"Oy, laddie." Tyree's insufferable voice cut through the tension like a hot knife through butter, no, like a scalpel through flesh, severing the nerves as it glided along Darius's resolve.

Darius shot him a withering look, one that had struck fear into the hearts of fiercest of warriors. Tyree, damnable man, did not even flinch.

"Y'er gonna have to do more than piss venom if y'er gonna survive the Ulkeniheim, laddie," Tyree wheezed out through a laughing fit that melted into a series of wet coughs. "ye ain't the Red Dread, that's for damned sure. Y'er not even worthy of Silver, if'n ye ask me."

The sound was disgusting, but it had snapped Darius out of his mind. What was he doing? He had real concerns, a purpose. And here he was feeling all sorts of sorry for himself. He needed to get to Dane, reach the Apostle, and figure out what all of this truly meant. What he needed was answers. Like, who was this Red Dread?

"You're right," he grunted. "When do we start training?"

"Wrong question, laddie," Tyree said with a smile as he wiped the spittle away from his forked beard with a vibrant bit of cloth. "What are we training for, that do be the real question."

CHAPTER 18: NOT HER MEMORIES
AELLIA

Aellia looked up at the dark ceiling, still perched in the colossal metal ring. There was a great commotion below her, voices raised in hurled commands and demands. She paid them no heed.

We can go, leave this place.

Aellia could leave, she knew that. She could drop from her vantage point and soar out of those staggering doors, flying far from this cursed tower. But on the other side of these planks of wood was where Tomo had died. Alone. Betrayed.

Aellia, please. There is nothing left for us here. We can become more, what we're meant to be, together.

What we're meant to be. What were they meant to be? And what say did Aellia have in any of this? She hadn't wanted to become a Sage, she had just been trying to escape with her life. She looked down at the sinuous rod of silver, studying the way the metal seemed to grow around the sapphire stone at its head. She gazed into the shining gemstone, whose cut edges refracted light all about it. As she did so, she felt a pulse move between them and she was carried away from that place..

Aellia drifted in a plane of pure light. Skies of the most stunning shade of blue filled her vision. Grass flowed below her, green as cut emeralds, the blades of which looked like blown glass. She extended her hand, running fingers through the flowing greenery, caressing the long blades. To her surprise, it felt like the finest silk she had ever laid hands on, bending and flowing at her touch. And the vibrant smells of this place, so exquisite it sent a thrum of pleasure through her senses. The earthy scent of nature in full blossom, of roses and lilies, of running streams and trickling falls.

Aellia had died, she knew it. It was the only reasonable explanation. However, what had she done to inherit a place such as this for her eternity? Perhaps the gods weren't so cruel as to punish her for her actions. Perhaps they truly had looked down upon her plight, upon the hurt and death she had endured. Perhaps she could be at peace?

Cautiously, slowly, Aellia drifted downward, her bare feet landing upon solid ground. Blades of silky grass tickled at her feet. Feet that were not of corporeal flesh, but composed of crystal. And beneath the surface, veins of sapphire light flowed.

She was not shocked at the sight, nor was she appalled. It seemed to just make sense to her. This was death. Why would she maintain her mortal form?

"Aellia."

Aellia turned about, not sure what to expect. What she saw made her knees go weak.

Before her, arrayed in a tunic of white linen embroidered with golden trim, stood a youthful female of exquisite sorrow and beauty, of which Aellia's mind could barely comprehend. She had hair of molten bronze, flowing from under a regal crown of living gemstones, parting around ears that were long and pointed. Her body was lean and majestic, every feature looking as if carved from marble, delicate and soft, and yet hard as stone. It was her eyes that truly took Aellia's breath away. No irises, just black pools filled with starlight set into an angular face. The split of her tunic, just below her collar bones, revealed what could only be described as a tattoo. A gemstone was carved into her flesh, a brilliant sapphire that looked shockingly similar to the one...

"Aellia." As the youthful female spoke, her lips turned upward into a shy smile, but that smile was a mask hiding indescribable hurt. Pain and exhaustion were etched into her features. Her voice, despite the pain, remained steady and sweet. "It is a pleasure to meet you in the flesh. I am, as I am sure you have already surmised, Iaenora. Welcome to the realm of Aetora's light."

"How?" Aellia gasped. Her hands began to shake, her mind railing against what her eyes saw. It was impossible, inconceivable even. "How am I here?"

"Wrong question," Iaenora said with a shake of her head, which sent her hair rippling across her shoulders and down the length of her back.

"What do you mean?"

"Again, wrong question." Iaenora's pained smirk managed to simultaneously send a ping of sorrow through Aellia's heart and piss her off to no end.

"Then tell me!"

"Why?"

"Because I want to know," Aellia answered, her voice rising in frustration. "I want to understand what in Halfak's blazing pit is going on!"

"Aellia," Iaenora cocked her head. "Why is the question you need ask. Why are you here? That is the question."

If Aellia had access to one of her knives, she would have flung it at the angel…sage. Whatever Iaenora was. It was all just too much.

"Aellia, I brought you here at great cost." Iaenora began to speak again, not even acknowledging Aellia's frustration. "I have tried and tried again to coax you into making the correct choice, doing the right thing. Alas, my endeavors have amounted to your capture, twice. By two different groups of people. Really, it is rather impressive to be so self-unaware and jaded that you have fallen into the hands of such awful people time and again, when if you would just listen to me, we would be well on our way to fulfilling our duty."

"Listen to you?" Aellia snapped, her limbs went rigid and her eyes began to sting. "Listen to you? You leeched onto my soul and infested my mind! Listen? I can't not listen to you! You're literally bonded yourself to my brain!"

"Actually, you bonded me to your soul, if you want to be accurate," Iaenora said with a shrug of her perfect shoulders.

Fury blossomed in Aellia in such a way she had never before felt. This was not the same as the hatred she held in her heart toward Tornak, the disdain toward Uppers. This was different. Those were deep, seething embers that perpetually scorched her

heart and soul. This was a flaming lance of injustice and downright ignorance that hit her square in her pride.

"Me? Me?" Aellia guffawed. She stepped forward with each proclamation, her wooden legs straining with each heavy footfall. "I didn't choose any of this. I didn't want to be a Sage, I don't want to fight your battles, your dark gods! I had friends, they died. I want them back! I wan—"

The words were choked off by a lump that formed in her throat. It burned, it hurt so deeply. Her hands, which had began to rise, quivered uncontrollably, hovering in front of her. She stared down at them. Crystalized flesh, and under the surface, veins of sapphire weaved threads of light throughout her body.

Iaenora shuddered, as if something caused her great strain.

"Aellia, listen to me," Iaenora's voice was little more than a pleading whisper. "I cannot keep us here long, but you must understand. We cannot fail. The world depends on us, on you. I get that you are hurt, that you have suffered such terrible loss. I understand that a darkness sits on your heart, plaguing your soul. But you are not alone. There are others, others we must find and bring to the Keyholder. We have a solemn responsibility."

"No." Aellia said the word, she heard it come out her own mouth. But it did not make it feel any more real. When she looked up from her hands and saw the confusion on Iaenora's perfect face, she pressed on. "No. You have a responsibility. I am done. Find someone else. You said you chose me. You chose wrong."

Silence hung between the two of them, harrowing as the night is long. Aellia could feel her heart pounding in her chest and a void forming in her guts. She wanted this thing, this vision, to end. She wanted it all to just go away.

"Aellia, at many times and in many things have I erred throughout my life," Iaenora spoke slowly, her eyes fixed upon Aellia's own. "But in this, I can assure you, I have not. You are who you are supposed to be. You are as the very air: not perfect, nor fleeting, though you move from place to place. You are necessary, and though you may feel invisible or minuscule, you are the very lifeforce of existence for those around you. Do not think so little of yourself, Aellia of Livithia, for you are mighty beyond even your own comprehension. Let me show you."

Iaenora leapt from the metal ring, winding herself through the air as gracefully as a diving hawk. Lights and imagery were not but blurs to her eyes as she swooped in a great arc. She could feel the essence of Everlight pulsating through her body, fueling her as she began to climb rapidly toward the ceiling.

A burst of power at the last second transformed her physical body into the very air she commanded. Iaenora Drafted through the tangible ceiling, her body passing through imperceptible cracks and crevices. When she rematerialized, she stood in a grand chamber domed with glass and supported by great bronze arches.

Aellia knew this place at once. The grand telescope, the tables and chairs. It had been here, in this very room, that Tornak had ended Tomo's life. Pain welled within her chest as that imagery played in her head over and over again.

Iaenora outstretched their hands as she drew in a steadying breath. It took every ounce of strength to maintain the balance of control in Aellia's body. This was not the Daulkaefar body she had been born to. It had limitations she was not accustomed to. It was weaker, prone to fatigue, always tired and shaking. It felt heavy, both physically and mentally. But she needed to show Aellia that it was strong.

Pale strands of light emanated from her fingertips. They flowed outward, winding about the many busts of men and women whom, though she knew them not, must have been of great importance. The strands fell across the tables and chairs, wound their way toward the telescope with its many lenses and apertures, until they covered nearly the whole of the room.

"What are you doing?"

Iaenora's mouth spoke, though it was Aellia's question.

"Great power was here," Iaenora answered, straining to maintain control of their body as she pushed more and more of her power out, seeking any trace of what she knew she could sense.

Footsteps echoed outside the bronze doors, followed by the distant jingle of keys on a ring. Iaenora had to hurry.

"You took over my body to just get us captured again?" Aellia's words pressed upon Iaenora's mind with all the force of a crashing wave. She grappled for control, the sensation of fear driving her now more than anger.

"We are not animals to be caged," hissed Iaenora. "Stop fighting me and let me show you! By Fenron's Blade, why could not Auyxus be here now?"

Figures of light suddenly sprouted out of thin air, strange wisping things that were neither material nor immaterial. They looked as if they were spirits, casting about, but they seemed to take no heed of Iaenora as they went about their ambling.

Aellia nearly screamed in fright as ghosts materialized out of light around her. Her fear turned to wrath, however, as one of the specters' form became apparent. Tornak.

He stood there, arguing with...nothing. Where there should have been another, only a haze of dissonant light vibrated. Tornak was arguing with that haze of incorporate fuzz. Aellia could hear no words but could make out gestures.

Suddenly, the room flickered. Only Tornak stood there now, his body rigid. He looked up at the dome and watched something, something that struck Acllia with understanding and grief at once. This was it. Tornak was watching Tomo die. Just. Watching.

Filled with grief and pain, Aellia cast her eyes up at the dome of glass. She feared to see her there, to see Tomo's body sprawled and bleeding. To both her relief and bewilderment, Tomo's body did not appear on the glass. Aellia blinked back tears of bitter confusion as she looked upon nothing, just glass.

A blink of blue light appeared where Tomo should have lain. Tornak's shoulders fell as if he knew what had just happened. The light seemed to trickle down, through the glass of the dome and land on one of the tables, coalescing into a sphere of azure. Suddenly, as if snuffed out like a candle's flame between one's fingers, that blue orb dissipated at once.

Aellia found herself back in total control of her body.

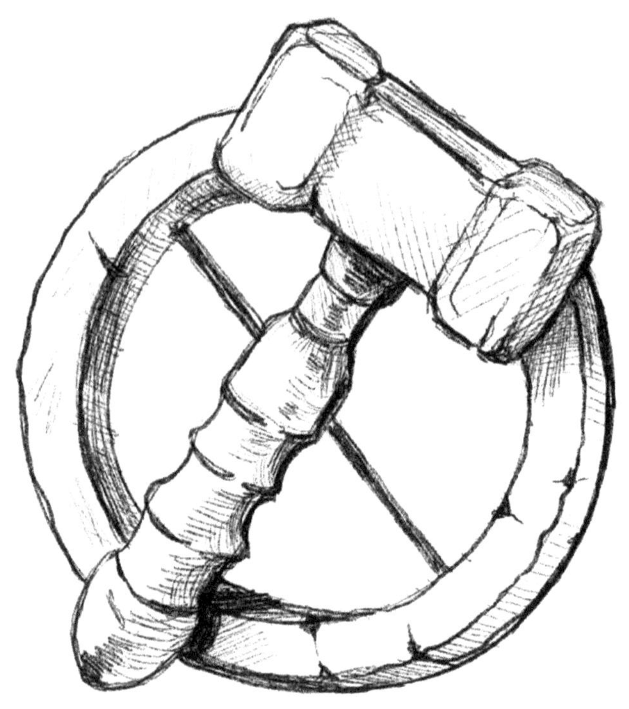

CHAPTER 19: GOLD AND IRON
DARIUS

Darius stood catching his breath in a large field of manicured green, eyes darting between the various pits of sand and stone laid about. Bleachers of wood rose above him with large banners of clans fluttering from bronze poles. Darius wore a loose shirt and a drab kilt, both soaked with sweat, as were the forearm bracers of worked leather strapped to his arms and the soft little shoes of sheep skin laced tightly about his feet. He felt utterly ridiculous but found a small amount of solace in the twenty or so other young Danelanders dressed in similar garb strewn about the green. They, however, did not look nearly as exhausted as he felt.

Izebal had left on her journey. She had kissed his cheek as she parted. It had seemed like a dream. He had said nothing. Not a single word. She had smiled as she parted, but Darius saw the hurt in those brilliant, emerald eyes. He had done that to her, put that hurt there.

"Move y'er lumbering arse, ye great buffoon!" Tyree barked from his wheeled chair. "I'd get up and run circles around ye if the good lord of the house did tell me to train ye!"

"It's been hours," said Darius, his throat raw from exertion. The cool morning had been burned away by a cloudless sky and blazing sun. Darius, not for the first time since arriving at Dwallen Fields, ran his thumb across where his ring should be. Yet again, fear gripped at his chest as the realization that it was not with him struck. "And why can't I have my ring?"

"Y'er ring?" Tyree let out a cackle. "Y'er trying to prove y'er manhood and ye want to use some enchanted piece of jewelry? Come on, laddie. I thought ye smarter than that. Leastwise, a bit more pride in ye."

"This is pointless," Darius snapped. "The ring, my abilities, is exactly why I don't need to be doing this. None of you manly men seemed to care when I used it to save Little Ery."

Tyree crooked an eyebrow.

"What?" Darius was not in the mood for playing games. He wanted to lash out at something. To strike, hack, anything except bloody-damned running.

"Tell ye what, laddie," said Tyree thoughtfully. "Y'er looking like y'er two steps from a short drop. So, I'll give ye the choice. Stones or fists? What'll it be?"

"What is that supposed to mean?"

"Ye tell me," Tyree answered. "Stones or fists? Simple choice for a simple man."

"But what do they mean? What am I choosing?" Darius asked, not wanting to be blindsided again.

"Y'er about to choose more laps if ye don't spit it out," Tyree answered with an evil grin.

"Fists!" Darius yelped. Anything but more running.

"Y'er gonna need these then, laddie," Tryee said as he tossed a bundle of white strips of fabric toward Darius.

"What do I do with these?"

"For the love of the gods on Vanherran, ye sure do ask a lot of bloody questions!" Tyree smacked his forehead as if Darius had just asked what color grass was.

Was he missing something? Darius looked about him, wondering if everyone else was as confused as he. The other young women and men seemed to be drilling in either small groups or one on one as he was with Tyree. Their instructors, however, were barking exact commands and instructing them how to do any myriad of feats of strength, skill, or stamina that could be used as the three tasks to perform in the Ulkeniheim.

"They're wraps, laddie," Tyree groaned in exaggeration. "Ye don't want to break y'er nimble little fingers, do ye? Ain't ye ever worn wraps before?"

The Aluth had worn wraps of sorts. Long strips of linen they would weave between their fingers for support. These were cords, round and thick, how was he to wrap these through his fingers.

"Oy!" Tyree called out. "Talon, a hand for the Outlander?"

Darius's eyes darted across the field, trying to find this Talon before they made their way toward him. He expected one of the thick, burly and bearded men who were training the young men who were not yet permitted to grow out more than horrid little mustaches that plagued nearly every upper lip that Darius could see.

On the contrary, the tan complected woman from that morning rose from where she had been sitting, legs crossed and hands held in front of her in what Darius assumed was some ritualistic trance. She did not wear a kilt, as even the young women out here wore, but baggy trousers of plaid stitching. A green sash was tied about her otherwise bare stomach that then wrapped up her ribs and around her bosom as a binding. Across her lean, muscular shoulders, the tops of her arms, and full of her striated back was the inking of a black dragon.

Darius understood at once the danger this woman imposed. She walked as a cat stalks a mouse, her grey eyes seeing not only her prey, but all that went on about her. The cool smile on her scarred face was not a pleasurable one, but that of one whose confidence is gained through trial. Notwithstanding these things, he was still taken aback at the deference the others around her showed her as she strutted toward him.

"The savior of Daneland's daughter." Talon's voice was clipped, but her accent was fully Danelander, and it was jarring to Darius's ears. As if his eyes could not come to reconciliation with what his

ears were hearing. She shot out a hand in greeting, "A friend of the Wolf is a friend of mine."

Darius grabbed for her hand, but she moved like a viper, clasping his forearm with vise-like grip, nails biting into flesh. She wrenched him forward, driving her shoulder into his chest. Darius's head fell forward, just so that her lips were right by his ears.

"Prove to me y'er more than a story, and I'll believe ye," she hissed into his ear. "Prove y'erself a liar out here, and that's all ye'll ever be."

Darius coughed as he tried to catch his breath. Had it not been for the endless running, and the lack of his ring, he would have never been taken so off his guard. That is what he told himself anyways, as some meager bandage against the wound in his pride at being doubled over by a woman half his size and a third his weight.

What the bloody stones was wrong with these people?

... Darius went sour in the face.

Damn. And now he too was beginning to swear like them.

"Talon here was one of the best there ever was," Tyree said with pride. "Trained her meself. One of the few womenfolk to ever get the golden circlet."

Talon raised a hand to a circlet of gold pinned wrappings just over her shoulder. It bore the image of a diving bird, talons flared for the kill. Poetic.

"Her grandfather was a Tauwtian acolyte of the Sand Vipers sect, a devotee of the cult Uuradan," Tyree continued. "His was the hope to bring the Eternal Flame to all of Ordiatea. Guess Danelander women have more to offer than an eternal dragon god, eh?"

Dragons? Now Darius knew this old man was crazy. The laws of nature did not account for dragons. How could giant sky lizards exist? *Now I sound like Elcon.* Darius laughed in his head at the thought. Dragons? He had delt with worse.

"Got the ink to prove it," Talon said with a wink. She was all smiles and levity now that she had asserted dominance over him. She turned about to show the eerily beautiful markings on her back and shoulders.

"Do you still practice?" Darius asked, unsure as to where this conversation was headed now.

"Practice?" Talon lifted an eyebrow. "Do I look like a cultist?"

"I did not mean offense." Darius tried to backpedal, but Talon let out a hearty laugh, catching him further off guard.

"Me grandpa was a sand-bellied lizard worshipper," Talon shook her head. "Me da and ma are Danelander blooded through and through."

"Alrighty ye two, enough lip slapping!" Tyree exclaimed. "Talon, this laddie here needs some help with cording himself up. Don't want him breaking no dainty fingers, do we?"

"Ain't never wrapped before? Bloody-damned Outlanders," Talon said with a sigh and shrug of her shoulders. "Guessin' ye to want me to rag-doll'em too, then, are ye?"

"A little lesson wouldn't hurt, if ye have the time," Tyree answered with a gleeful smile, fingers combing through his forked beard.

Darius felt his heart sink. Another lesson. He had learned well from the Avajan'Aluth that size was not everything. That woman had bested him time and time again, and that was with his ring and before his injury. This woman looked tough as iron, and coarse as sand. However, the thought of fighting instead of running quickly overcame the discomfort of potential embarrassment. He had learned swordplay from the Avajan'Aluth. He could learn from this woman as well. It was as his father had always told him.

"Son, you can always learn from every situation. How to or how not to do something."

"Take the cords, wrap'em about your palm from the base of y'er thumb to the bottom of y'er fingers, four or five lashings should suffice," Talon said as she unwound the bundle of white cords, handing one length to Darius and keeping the other for herself. "I'll do the non-dominate hand after ye try. We'll see which one holds better, eh?"

Darius wrapped it about his right hand to the best of his abilities, making sure the cords were tight as possible without totally cutting off the blood flow. Next, Talon walked him through the rest of the wrapping technique, leaving Darius's entire hand bundled into a fist, totally covered in white binding. His wrist, too, was bound tight, so that little to no motion could be made. He had effectively had his hands turned into bludgeoning clubs of white cords.

"Seems a bit crude," he said as he looked over his right hand.

"I'll get y'er dominant one, sit tight and watch," Talon said as she sat down right next to him.

Her scent hit him, that of wood char and ash, sweat and dirt. It was not a bad scent, but one that spoke of labor and physicality. She took his hand in hers; they were rough and calloused, and moved with practiced efficiency. Within seconds, his left hand was done up tight. And though he hated to admit it, it felt more secure than his right.

"See that there sand pit?" Talon pointed a few yards away with her chin as she tucked the last strand into the base of Darius's wrappings. "We'll spar there. They always do some kind of fighting in the Ulkeniheim, might as well start with Skulkien."

"Skulkien?" Darius asked as he rolled his shoulders in preparation.

"There are a couple different forms we train with here," Talon said as she rose dexterously to her feet. She didn't come to Darius's chin, save for the braided hair that was coiled like a viper. "Skulkien is the art of pummeling. Heavy blows. No grappling, grips, or kicks. Strikes to the body, legs, and arms are permitted. Strikes to the groin and head are considered low but not illegal. Makes ye look like a soft-handed, goat-romping chutling. Skulkien is about pure physical dominance. ye should find it right up y'er alley, big man."

Darius felt a flush of heat at the words at the back of his neck. He was hopeful his already blustered appearance, thanks to the miles of running he had already endured, kept any real sign of embarrassment away. But hope wasn't certainty, and he heated how easily such things ate him.

"So, we just..."

"Beat each other until one of us yields," Talon said with a crooked smile as she stepped down into a pit of coarse sand. "Tap, tap, boom."

Darius stepped in after her but turned to look at Tyree. Was he really about to get into a fist fight with this woman? He hoped the old mage would say something, stop this before it started. With the Avajan'Aluth, she had held a long steel, something dexterous and sharp. It gave her an edge. What did this Talon have?

"Tap fists and square off," was all the old mage said, wild blue eyes lit with zealous fervor.

Talon raised both hands, extending them toward Darius. Darius, in turn, let out a low sigh and tapped her fists with his own.

"Fight!" Tyree cried out.

Talon was a blur. Blow after blow struck Darius. First to the right side of his body, just under the ribs, the second to the left, and then a double to his gut. The wound in his abdomen exploded with pain, sending bursts of light through Darius's vision. He let out a grunt of pain that was cut short as two more blows caught him in the right side yet again, sending him to one knee.

"Come on, Outlander," Talon said through measured breaths. "Move y'er giant arse or be leveled."

Of course she would strike before he was set. It was his own fault. He hadn't taken this seriously. He wouldn't make that mistake again.

Standing upright, Darius raised his right fist as he moved his right foot in front of him. He tucked his elbow tight and placed his left knuckles against his cheek.

"There it is," Talon said, manic glee lighting like fire in her eyes. "There's the fighter. Now, hit me! Hit me!"

Darius stepped in, fainting right and cut left, striking low. Talon moved like a bird of prey, dodging while landing two quick jabs. These were not like the others: they were measuring thrusts, checking his stance, his positioning. They still hurt like Halfuk. Darius grit his teeth. If they wanted a fight, he'd give them one, propriety be damned.

Talon bounced back and forth, Darius swinging wide, wild strikes, each just grazing her body or missing all together. She bobbed in and out, landing body strike after body strike. Darius was catching her rhythm though, watching her steps. Just as he thought he saw an opening, she darted quick left and then right, slinging her left hand like a barb at the end of a whip. It caught Darius just below the ribs. There was a loud crack followed by a rush of pain. Darius smiled. Talon was on his right side. With his forward hand, he struck.

The blow caught Talon dead in the chest. She had left herself open, probably thinking her strike would have taken him to ground. Perhaps it would have taken a normal fighter down. Perhaps this wasn't the lesson intended. But he was a warrior, and a bloody good one. Even without his ring.

Talon slid across the sand, the strike having taken her off her feet and sprawling through the air. When she came to a stop, Darius heard the slow clap of withered and ringed hands.

"Blood and bloody stones, laddie," Tyree said. "Y'er slow as an ox shitting in the winter, but paint me pink and send me to a brothel, ye hit like forge hammer."

"Lucky shot," wheezed Talon, who had risen to her feet now and, to Darius's surprise, was smiling widely. "I thought ye weren't gonna hit me for a minute."

"Wasn't that whole point?" Darius asked. His side stung, and he found himself hugging at it.

"Bruised a rib?" Talon asked, as if she hadn't been the one to do it.

"Ya," Darius grunted in reply, not saying that he felt it break, not just bruise. "I just need my ring and—"

"Wrap'em up and get ready for round two," Talon said with a shrug of her shoulders. She pressed a wrapped fist to the bottom of her jaw and cracked her neck in a loud series of pops. "Let's see if ye can learn a thing or two about the actual play."

Darius was instructed for the next several hours in the play of Skulkien. And when Tyree finally tired of watch the two go at each other, the old mage said it was high time for lunch. Which Darius learned was dried meats and hard cheese with goats milk for him. It tasted like a gift from the gods. It tasted less so as he spewed it up an hour later running around the outer ring of Dwallen Field.

Why in the flaming pit am I doing this? Darius swore to himself as he lifted himself from the ground not for the first time, wiping spittle and froth from his lips as he took off once more. Yes, he knew he needed to get to Dane. Yes, he knew that he needed to fulfil his purpose of finding those like girl from Tur'Mor and that this Apostle would be his best bet in doing so. But, why was he trying so hard? Why was he allowing himself to be put through this? Couldn't he just take it a little easier on himself?

Memories of his father came back into his mind, washing away the worn path around Dwallen Field, replaced by timbers as his father swung his ax, splintering great longs asunder with mighty blows. He remembered that moment. He had questioned his father to why a chief should have to split wood when they had lower tribesmen who could be doing it. "Anything worth doing is worth doing right. Don't expect someone else to do what you wouldn't, son. Be a man in all you do, or don't waste your time doing it." He hadn't understood just how much those words would impact him at the time, but they had sunk deep into his soul.

He would do this, not just for himself, but for his father, for his mother and brother. He rose to this, not just because he had sworn an oath, but because it was the right thing, and who else would do it? And if that meant running some laps and playing the game, so be it. He would do it.

"What in the bloody damned pit are y'er doing, laddie? Stones caught in y'er limb? Why aren't you running?" Tyree's voice shattered the memory and green grass with a worn trail flooded his view. "Run!"

***

Darius sank into his tub. The hot water, infused with herbs and tonics, pricked at his flesh. As he slid down, he felt the bones in his body take a collective sigh of thanks as the pressure of his joints dissipated in an instant. All was calm and peaceful. He blinked.

Snow fell upon Darius's naked body, melting as it touched his shoulders of crystal. Skies of deepest purple were split with silver lightning. The scent of char and ash wafted through the air. Darius had been transported yet again to the strange place of dream and vision.

Thunder rolled across the expansive sky, rumbling the blasted earth upon which Darius stood.

"Denathurias, son of the mountains, why did you hide yourself?" boomed the voice from the heavens above.

Darius turned his eyes toward the forming clouds, staring into eyes composed from the light of the two great stars, one emerald and the other sapphire. Confusion filled his mind. He had not hidden himself.

"I do not understand," he replied. Something felt off. The air was hot, not cold. The smell of char was not just of earth, but of scorched meat and hair, an acrid smell tinged with the sweat of burning flesh.

"The time is far spent, there is little remaining," the Voice echoed. "You have been tainted."

Darius looked down at his body. A thunderhead of swirling black pooled in his abdomen, rimmed by shimmering runes of silver. Maroon lightning crackled in that black ink, sending a chill down Darius's spine.

"Can you heal me?" Darius asked, turning his eyes upward once more. "Can you not remove this corruption from my flesh?"

"I am bound!" The thundering Voice sounded almost mournful.

"You're a god!" Darius's golden heart raged within his chest. "Why can't you save me?"

"I am bound!" the Voice boomed so loudly it sent Darius stumbling backwards. "Find them! You must free me from these chains."

"How? Am I not doing that? Am I not seeking out those whom you had chosen?" cried Darius into the tempestuous skies. "What are you not telling me? What chains can bind a god?"

A long silence filled the void between man and deity. Darius was about to call out again, to rage in anger—anger about how alone he felt, about how little guidance he had, anger toward the Ellitheor for their own indifference to the plight of man—when a blinding bolt of lightning split the sky. Darius raised a hand to shield his eyes, but it was of little merit. The heat of the strike was so that it felt like every particle of skin, crystalline or not, would be consumed by fire.

And then the skies opened. A fissure of light hovering in open space between them.

Darius stepped forward, peering into the fractured air, and what he saw caused him to tremble to the very core.

An elderly man knelt upon a cavern floor. His bald head dripped with sweat and fatigue, his bearded face was a mask of pain and anguish. He wore a robe of emerald that though once would have been a thing of beauty was now stained and tattered. His arms were extended outwards, fastened to what Darius now saw was a circlet of runes etched into the ground. Three chains bound his left arm downward, chains of emerald light that weaved into his very flesh. Two chains of sapphire held his right arm down, and a third laid shattered upon the ground.

Darius stepped closer. The main lifted his weary head, a morose smile spread across his cracked lips. His eyes were of fire and his flesh of white gold, dimmed, but golden none the less.

"Denathurias," the Voice said. "Welcome to my prison."

"Great High Father above," Darius gasped, eyes growing wide in shock.

"Oh, I do not feel so great," said the Voice. "And have not, not for a very, very long time."

Strain etched the face of Ordan.

Ordan. The High Father.

Darius's heart thundered in his chest. He had assumed. To meet a god, though, to stand face to face with one. He suddenly felt very light, his feet barely holding him to the floor.

"How?" The word fell out of Darius's mouth. All of the anger and the frustration from just moments ago was gone, replaced by awe and confusion.

"How?" Ordan smirked, though it did not each his eyes, one of emerald and the other of sapphire. "How did I end up here? How did I bring you here? Too many questions and not enough time."

The chains around Ordan's arms pulsed. One of the green ones faded ever so slightly, becoming dull and a thing of metal not light. Ordan looked down at it and frowned.

"You must find them." His voice was pleading, filled with exhaustion and pain. "If they fail, I have failed, and all is lost. You must find them."

"I don't understand? What am I to do?" Darius asked, stepping closer.

"You must find them, or blood shall rain!" Ordan boomed, strength filling his voice once more. The chains at his arms rattled at his cry. And, to Darius's horror, small cracks he hadn't noticed before, just below the chained god, spread. It was like shattered glass, and from those cracks, tendrils of ink-black smoke tinged with maroon rose.

And Darius understood.

The tales told of how Ordan had cast his own daughters through the Dimdreal after they had turned their hearts to Iodaba's Touch. Ordan had done more than just cast them out, he used his own body, his essence and soul, to seal that binding.

Understanding came in waves, crashing over Darius's racing mind, as he looked upon the broken god kneeling before him in the dark cavern, alone and weary. The seal was breaking, Ordan's strength was failing, and somehow these individuals, like the girl from Tur'Mor, were connected.

The girl. That chain.

"Find them!" Ordan bellowed as another series of cracks splintered the ground beneath him.

Darius gasped for air, choking on the hot water that filled his lungs. He flailed about, striking his hands and feet on the bronze tub, his eyes unable to focus on anything. Panic nearly over took him, but a strike of his chest onto the front of the tub expelled the water from his lungs, subsequently sending him into a coughing fit until he could see straight once more.

He was back in his room, and more confused than he had ever been in his life. And then the pounding at the door commenced.

Interim 2

Betrugyn

Hallock

Una'pahu

Tassi

Lori

Betrugyn watched in grim satisfaction as the man once called Rahnaluz raised his steel against his failed squire. They both looked grotesque, their marbled flesh near grey in coloration.

Grafting was tricky business, one which his fellow Dorr A'Gadah seemed less than intrigued by, but that utterly enthralled Betrugyn. Simply put, Grafting allowed him the ability to take any expired body, man or beast, transplant the heart with a corrupted crystal infused with Iodaba's anti-light, and make something whole once more. Now, they did lack many of their more natural inclinations and predispositions, and one could not help scaring. But, upon further experimentation, Betrugyn had learned that many of their memories and personality traits were still there, deep within their brain.

And that was the trick. Saving the brain. It was, perhaps, the most difficult part. The boy had been much easier. A severed head was of minor difficulty to mind. Betrugyn himself had experienced a near complete decapitation in his early years. But penetration of the cranial cavity was far more challenging. Hence his fascination with the man once called Rahnaluz.

It had taken nearly every bit of anti-light he could muster, exhausting his secret stache for what could have been a disaster. But it was no disaster. This was a glorious success. Betrugyn smiled as he watched the older man move around the young boy, striking him with precision. The blade pierced deep into the boy's stomach, eliciting a grunt of pain.

"Dah! Again!" Betrugyn chided. "Keep your steel high, you dog! I have put too much into you to have you wasted."

The squire stepped back, Rahnaluz's blade sliding bloodlessly out of his abdomen, and raising his own steel in a high-guard position.

"Now, strike!"

Steel clanged on steel, the two moving faster than any man could hope to. These. This was the way. He could use them if he could just -

A sound like shattering glass filled the gymnasium. The air seemed to ripple. A solid formed of a greenish hue veined with black and maroon anti-light.

Xi?

What was she doing to her?

The air shattered and through it stepped the Poisoner, Xi.

"Playing with puppets, I see," her words were clipped, and spoken by one whose throat was raw and festering. From beneath the mask she wore, sores could be forming upon her cheeks, red and irritated.

What in Halfak's pits had she done to gain this reward? Mused Betrugyn before thinking better of it. None of the Dorr A'Gadah shared what had drawn them over to the worship of the Great Khadais, and they each carried their own scars for that choice, though not all on the outside.

"My comrade, what brings you to my humble abode?" Betrugyn asked instead.

"They are clever," Xi said without acknowledging Betrugyn in the slightest. Another commonality amongst the Dorr A'Gadah, there was little love between them. "How do you get them to listen so well?"

"Listening is a choice," Betrugyn said, kicking his boots up onto his table and reclining back in his chair. He looked across the room

to where a grand clock, whose housing was busted, stood lopsided against the wall. It was half-pasted eleven. Far too late for visitors. "I removed that option."

"Ah," said Xi, though he could tell she held little interest now.

"So, again, I ask, what brings you here, comrade?"

"It seems to me," her voice was like nails being dragged down a slate. "You are not loved by Edous. I saw the way he looked at you."

"Ha!" Betrugyn actually laughed. "Now, why would you care how he looks at me. Are you growing jealous, Xi?"

A curling bit of vine that extended from the cuff of her sleeve shot out into her hand forming a rod with thorns black as sin, tipped with oozing venom. "I come to you to seek, how would the little bitch put it, ah, parlay."

"No love for Reylelan?" mused Betrugyn, only slightly put off by the thorny rod. His own hand floated near his favorite dagger, the flame-like edge calling for violence.

"I can respect a man who creates, I can ever respect a man for dominating," Xi said. "But I loathe coercive menticide."

"Not one for the eyes, eh?"

"I would cut them out if didn't know that they would grow back," Xi spat. "What she does not sit well with me."

"And harvesting body parts to feed your plants, which is good, dah?" said Betrugyn.

Xi let out a long, raspy sigh. The thorns slid back into her arm, and not for the first time, Betrugyn wondered what she looked like naked. Did the vines cover her? Did they consume her flesh, or was it all beneath the skin? She was flat and thin, but the mystery of it all made him famished.

"I'll admit," Betrugyn said at long last, letting his eyes fall away from her. "It would not hurt my blackened heart to see Edous stumble. If not, just for once."

Xi looked excited, her black eyes flashing brightly. "Not a word to the others?"

"Am I daft?" Betrugyn asked, affronted.

"Will you swear to me, Betrugyn, that you will work together, to make sure the will of the Great Khadais is seen. That the Favored Ones will find their place once more. And that you and I will be one in mind to help bring about their return, and rise next to them together?"

Betrugyn thought for a moment, looking at the woman whom he had served next two for over two centuries. He had been the last to join the Dorr A'Gadah, an ancillary task boy, deprived of his humanity and forced to complete the most debasing of tasks. Xi was second to Edous. Could they rise together? Was this even possible?

"Yes," he spoke without thinking, without hesitation, excitement thrumming through him.

"Seal it?" Xi took out her hand and removed her glove. Tattoos that looked like vines wrapped around her fingers, knuckles, palm, and wrist. She, with a long fingernail, drew a line across her palm until blood pooled, black and red.

Betrugyn, both surprised at the suddenness of the situation and the elation at the prospect of perhaps doing more than upsetting Edous for once, slid his own glove from his hand and drew his flamberge dagger across his palm. "Sealed."

The two clasped palms. A shock went between the two, a rush of pain and pleasure. Anti-light coursed back and forth, sealing the dark promise that they would work together.

Betrugyn did not know what would happen if he broke this promise, and frankly, he did not care anymore. Two hundred and forty years in service to the great Khadais, and all he knew was pain and emptiness. He was sworn to his bidding, but not Edous. despite how much that pompous asshole marched around proclaiming he was the avatar of Khadias, Betrugyn knew otherwise.

Xi let out a moan as her eyes sparked with maroon power. That sound was maybe the most beautiful sound Betrugyn had ever heard. His heart, which he had thought dead, beat once more. Those rashs weren't rashs, but radiant marks of a woman of power. The hunger for the anti-light, the need to consume, filled his bosom. And if he were not mistaken, so too did it consume her.

In a flurry of motion, Xi ripped the shirt from Betrugyn's chest, running tattooed fingers down his body. Need and passion filled him. It had been so long.

She bit his neck. He could feel the heat of her breath. The sting of poison biting even deeper excited the senses. The aroma of her body was intoxicating.

Xi pressed him back into his chair. He let his body fall, not caring how it landed.

"I can see you want me," Xi rasped. "Take me."

"Take you?" Betrugyn asked, cocking an eyebrow and running a hand through his strewn hair. "Get on your knees and take me."

"And you say you heard a ghost whoosh away?" Hallock was not even looking at the City Guard as he took down notes on a padfolio. He had been at this for hours now, searching high and low for any signs of the mayor's missing brother. "You didn't see anything?"

"Right, Chief Inspector. Swear on my badge," the young woman said with a shake in her voice. "We were patrolling through here and Beau thought he saw something. But, when we got close, nothing but a strange whoosh! All these bulletins were just ripped off all at once, tossed around like a gale storm hit. Listen, I ain't saying nothing untoward about nothing. Gallae's grace keep me, I've been a devote devotee my whole life. My sister serves in the Sanctuary. But, Chief Inspector, by my soul, things have been off in this city. Young girls gone belly up is one thing, could be any twisted freak. We've heard it's more, it's all about the precinct. Kh'ar Robbers, the King's Jewel. Now the mayor's own brother."

"What about the mayor's brother?" Hallock looked up for the first time, a hard expression his mustachioed face.

"Inspector-"

"That's Chief Inspector, Constable Bragg." Hallock was not one for enforcing his title, but these were walking a tight line. No one knew of Alec's missing status.

"Apologies, still a little flustered is all," Constable Bragg said, turning her hat in her hands. "But word on the street is, that no one's seen Alec near a month on now."

"He has gone to the Front. He left with the Generals via the military's Class A Skyships. It is a well-documented actuality. One would think one in your position would be focusing on why young women have been turning up in the gutters with holes in their back. Not on the whereabouts of our good mayor's brother." Hallock answered with a heavy finality in his voice while snapping his padfolio shut for an added emphasis.

"You're right, sir! I meant no offence, sir!" Constable Bragg snapped her heels together quickly, and proceeded to fumble her hat, trying to salute while it was still in her shaking hands.

"Sergeant, a final word!" Hallock barked, ignoring the constable's embarrassing show. He knew he'd have Halfak to pay for beating down these from Chief Constable Konsuer - he was out of his jurisdiction, and these weren't his men - but he needed answers, and fast.

"Aye, sir," answered a burly man with curly black chops almost as fine as Hallock's, a feature that made Hallock all the sourer for abusing his rank as appointed authority from the mayor himself. A good-trimmed mustache was a clear indicator of a good-trained man, and this one's was trimmed to perfection.

"I wanted to thank you and your team for staying over and answering my questions," said Hallock nonchalantly. "If any of yours hears anything else regard the break in at the Mayor Residence or has any leads around the stabbings, please inform my office."

"Chief Konsuer rolls everything up as it should be," the big man said gruffly. "I'll be right honest with you, I could spit farther than I care about where Uppers and their family spend their days. But this killer - the people of Southend have gone to calling'em the Butcher of the 'End - ain't no signs of him up. Got one of little girl with blue eyes who scared Regent Aldorian, but nothing of a knifer whose done put at least twenty-three women in the ditch. It ain't right. You've got pull at the top, how about a word for us little people?"

Sergeant Tailor was no little man, and his comment left little room for miscommunicated sentiment. He walked a dangerous line, but Hallock had to admit he respected these who would, in the face of their betters, voice up about those they were sworn to protect.

"I'll see what I can do," Hallock said, giving crisp nod as he pulled his gloves back onto his hands. "Butcher of the 'End? A bit melodramatic, don't you think?"

"For me, maybe." the big man shrugged. "For the mother's who will never see their daughter's grandbabies, not at all."

Hallock sat in deep contemplation, the click clack of the carriage providing a tempo for his thoughts. He had been at this for weeks now, and still no such luck. Only questions upon questions. More infuriating than that, Xander's election campaign was taking all of his time, leaving Hallock to work at this far into the nights, missing precious time in his books.

Everything about this case boggled his mind. Girls knifed down in the streets. Halfak burn it all, there had even been a noble born in Livithia, taken in their estates. If the common folk ever caught wind of that. And then there was the Kh'ar. They were an infestation of wood lice! They just got everywhere, multiplying and destroying everything. And for what? Why would they want a king? Did they really think that would change anything for them? If they really wanted power, they'd buy up foundries. The future was in steel and steam. Ten years ago, no one would have believed that man could fly. Five years ago it was said that no more than one or two people could be lifted into their air by balloon. Now there were Class A Skyships, armed with long guns - also called Nemesis, Class B for troop transport - called Fens, which he supposed was short for Fenron, and it was said that those in the Asterivae were close to coming up with a civilian class carrier that would revolutionize long distance travel.

Hallock shook his head. His mind was wondering, and not for the first time. He had always wanted to be an Engineer. He had a brilliant mind, one of the sharpest in the Academy. But war led to police work, which turned to investigation. Strange how life's turns can take one in such vastly different direction. He was nearing sixty now. There would be no years of tinkering and building. His path was set. At least he had his books.

"Sir," called the carriage driver. "We've arrived."

"Speak of the Fallen, and there they shall be." The words were more a mumbled idiom than an actual swear.

The carriage came to a gentle stop and the coachman could be heard descending to lower the step and open the heavy door. Chief Inspector Hallock was not an anxious type, but Mayor Xander had made it clear that he was to be protected at all times. This carriage was only one of the many discomforts he was forced to endure. And no, the carriage itself was not uncomfortable to ride in, but the repute that came with riding in a banker's armored wagon, fitted with a gunner, driver, and coachman, was all a little too rich for his blood.

"Chief Inspector!" said the coachman as he opened the door.

A waft of salty air filled his nostrils. When one spends so many of their days in the Valamour, one can forget that Tur'Mor is a seaside city. When traveling to the Northwestern quadrant, that is disabused. Vineyards and fields, lavish villas and rolling hills extend all the way to the white walls of Tur'Mor, farther than the eye can see.

Hallock stood and looked out, admiring for a moment the beauty of the landscape. Tur'Mor certainly had its blemishes. But who could say that it was not a marvel in and of itself. Like four different worlds combined into one gigantic ring of protection. How their forefathers had planned it out was beyond him, and he almost believed the fairytales of elves and dwarves help construct the heart of the city.

"You alright, sir?" asked the coachman.

"Children truly do experience life as it should be," Hallock said wistfully.

"If you say so, sir," the man said, lifting his tricorn hat and scratching at his brow. "But I don't think I'd much like going back into the schoolhouse again."

"Right you are," laughed Hallock hollowly. "Right you are. Well, I will be about my way now."

"Aye, sir. A moment if you could," the coachman looked a little nervous now.

"What is this about?" Hallock's face hardened and his hand went instinctively to his belt where a two-barreled pistol was concealed.

"Not my doing, sir. Only following orders."

The coachman looked more uncomfortable than scared. This, and the lack of sweat, told Hallock there was not imminent danger. No, this was something else. From a distance, a second carriage popped into view, all green and gold, bearing the blazing Hammer of Ordan on both doors. Hallock's guts went sour.

"Who dared set me up?" Hallock snapped, more made at himself than anyone else.

"Sir, the Church is only-" the coachman mumbled. His face went pale as sheet; chagrin written all over his features.

"I am guessing you should not have said that?" Mused Hallock, shoving his hand into his coat pocket instead of gripping his pistol.

"I am just trying to do my job, sir. I have a family."

"Oh, for Gallae's grace, I'm not going to have you strung up for collusion with the mayor," Hallock sigh, rubbing at his forehead with his left hand. Why? Why the infernal Church and their incessant pestering? Why now? Didn't he have enough on his plate? "Seeing it is about my personal wellbeing. Though I have told the man I am capable enough on my own."

The green and gold carriage rolled up quickly, the white horses pulling it moving faster than Hallock felt necessary. When it came to a stop, it bounced on lifted springs, surely jolting those inside.

However, to his surprise, not a single complaint or exclamation was produced, just utter silence.

When the door answered, this little mystery was solved. Four individuals wrapped in white stepped out. They had silver vests and hooded cloaks of white. Their faces were wrapped, so as only their eyes could be seen. Three of them were dressed exactly alike. The forth one wore a strip of blue about their neck, right wrist, and their right thigh.

This was an extremely peculiar thing. Hallock had never seen an Aluth wearing anything like that before. He stared at the plan cloth, tied unceremoniously about the individual's neck, arm, and thigh, and contemplated a myriad of different things it could represent, but came up with nothing that made in logical sense on the spot.

"I assume you will be my escorts?"

All of the Aluth drew the swords at their sides and brought the flats of their blades to their forehead in unison.

"I'll take that as a yes."

The one with the blue cloth stepped silently toward Hallock and handed him an envelope sealed with golden wax. Hallock's eyebrows lifted as he noted the seal was made from the High Patriarch's own ring. A bit of excitement fluttered through his chest. These were no ordinary Aluth. This was something different. And maybe, these Aluth weren't sent to tend to him as a child.

With a quick swipe of his thumb, Hallock broke the seal. He unwound the ribbon that laced the envelope and then retrieved the parchment from inside.

Chief Inspector Hallock.

It has come to the attention of the Church that you are, by command of our mutual friend and brother in Ordan's holy faith, pursuing events of rather unorthodox nature. We understand that there have been a great many events that transpired over the past few weeks that have left the people of Tur'Mor, and all of Ordiatea, in a state of turmoil and unrest. As a Church, we are saddened by these dark event, and our hearts go out to the families of those who have suffered. We have informed Mayor Xander that we are working directly with the Rising Star and the Council of Six to oversee these things. We appreciate your efforts and your diligence. Please turn over your notes and anything you may have pertaining to this case to these who have provided this missive. They have been instructed to take nothing that does not directly tie to the following events;

Firstly, anything pertaining the unfortunate souls of those young women knifed down. We know this is a dark stain upon us all. Know that it is being addressed at every level.

Second, anything pertaining to Regent Aldorian. He has suffered a traumatic event and the Sisterhood of Un'Mor will see it his swift and peaceful recovery.

Lastly, we ask you to turn over anything pertaining to the young woman who assaulted the Regent in his home. She is a threat that has been deemed necessary for the Church to intervene in directly.

Thank you for your continued and tireless service to the Empire of Ordiatea and your dedication and supplication to the Faith.

Patriarch Orrum, Voice of Ordan, Shepherd of the Nations.

Hallock stood stalk still. The paper was in his hand, but he surely had not just read what was upon it. 'Turn over his research?' 'Being addressed at every level?' 'Necessary for the Church to intervene in directly?'

No. No, this time the Church had gone too far. This time they had overstepped their bounds. This was going directly to Mayor Xander. This was inexcusable -

Hallock looked over and saw the coachman, driver, and gunman in a line. They were standing perfectly still, just... looking.

"Oye!" Hallock yelled. "What is this rubbish?

The Aluth looked up at him, as if they were confused. They walked over toward him. This time, Hallock did not stop as he grabbed for his pistol. His thumb at just undone the button hold the little double-barreled wheellock in its holster, when the Aluth with blue strips of cloth placed a gentle hand on his shoulder.

"Look here," Hallock said, his voice missing the resolute bravado he always spoke with. "You're going to have to take this back to your

leader with an apology and empty hands. I am not turning over anything. I have been commissioned by our duly elected mayor to oversee the very things on this here missive."

The Aluth looked him directly in the eyes, and Hallock felt something go cold in his spine. He had not noticed earlier. How had he not noticed? The Aluth had bright blue eyes.

But, only the Blessed could Touch the Everlight? Hallock's mind whirled as panic gripped him.

The Aluth move swiftly, lifting it's left hand. In the palm of it's gauntlet, a small sapphire stone was set in a strange apparatus. Inside the stone, light swirled about. Everlight. Hallock knew what it was, but he had never seen it up close like this, not outside of... another memory popped inside of his mind.

He was in the Sanctuary.
He was a boy, sitting between his mother and father.
An elderly priestess was holding something blue and shiny.
He was confused by it.
It was so bright. How did it not burn her hands? Her eyes glowed with a matching light. How did they do that? How was any of this possible?

Hallock sat in deep contemplation, the click clack of the carriage providing a tempo for his thoughts. He had been at this for weeks now, and still no such luck. Xander's election campaign was taking all of his time, leaving Hallock to work at this far into the nights, missing precious time in his books. Xander's primary rival, he had been getting money, lots of money. Hallock would figure this out, if it took him until the night of the election, he would figure it out. And when he did, Xander would win again, and another four years of prosperity would ensue.

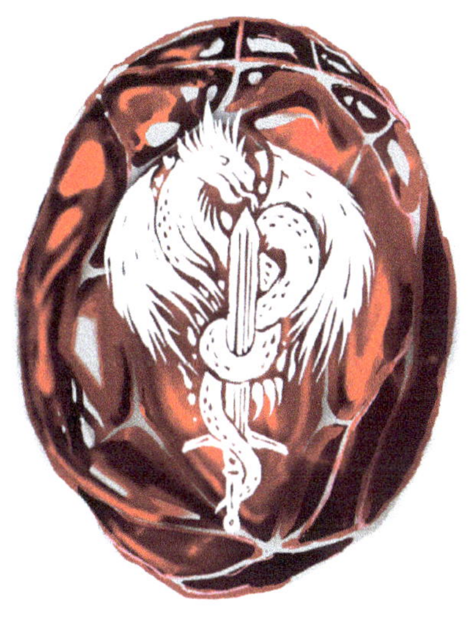

Una'pahu followed Seamus and Henri back into the cavern where all of their lives had changed forever only the day before. The sulfuric smell assailed her nose, but she refused to stop now. Not after everything that had happened. Especially to Seamus.

He walked at the head of the group, leading them down the winding path of melted floor. Yet, her eyes were not on the cavern walls but upon the scars that marred his back. Two great marks, as if a knife had been racked down his shoulder blades, black as death seemed to suck the light from around them. Una'pahu had seen wings of flames extending from those scars, but even now, looking at them, she could not bring herself to believe it.

What had happened to him? She asked herself for the thousandth time. What had that viperous bitch done to her Quickie? He was a stranger now, hollow and devoid of the laughter and merriment she had always known. His once lanky frame was corded with lean muscle and his left side looked as if it had been dipped into to heart of the volcano. His once disheveled - hair that she once ran her fingers through in moments of deep quite upon the rocking oceans - was long and curled, falling to the tops of his broad shoulders, where a massive sword was lashed.

Una'pahu had tried to talk to him about it the night before, but he had been a stone, uttering only that it was all his fault. And when she pressed, a fire lit behind his eyes - not a figurative fire, but some real flame - and he had demanded she leave his side. Almost at once he began to weep, apologizing profusely for his actions.

She had slept by Henri that night, the two old friends together under the stars while Seamus walked the shoreline well past the time her eyes had grown too heavy to hold open.

Down the wound, deeper and deeper, the heat of the cavern starting to make sweat pool on the small of her back where her huvu'huvu was wrapped. She reached toward it, and as she did so, she felt the familiar pulse of energy from the scepter at her side.

Una'pahu slid the rod from her belt, thumbing thing green gemstone as she gazed into it. For generations this had been in her family, an heirloom passed from mother to daughter with a promise that one day, a daughter of the sea would rise that would be more than met the eye. That the spirits of the ancestors would confine in her all their powers, all their knowledge, and with that, the burden of all the realms.

But she had no more power than any other Ta'ala Gau. If she was being honest with herself, had she had her grandmother's abilities, she could have saved everyone. Master Charlie, Captain Atura - a sharp pang of guilt stung at her heart when she thought of the captain. She had given her life to save Una'pahu, but why? What was the reason? Why was she any more important than any other Ta'ala Gau? She could feel the ocean, she could hear the waves, even guide them. But she could not command the depths. She could not bring forth the many waters by a mere raising of her hand. She had been weak and powerless in the face of Reylelan, so much so that the witch had escaped from the island with the Heart and the one Seamus and Henri had called Specter.

"Down here," Seamus's voice was a low grumble, like water cascading over a great fall. It was somehow both dry and broken, and also a thundering force that made her insides weak.

Despite his scars, Una'pahu still loved her Msa'oo. She had been wrong to turn away from him for her training. Had she stayed, she could have protected him from... well, whatever had happened.

I will not leave you again, Msa'oo, this I swear.

"Ah, and how shall we lift the bridge? Do you have another pair of glove, Quickfingers?" Henri asked, cocking an eye while rubbing his glasses on a bit of cloth.

"No." Seamus answered flatly. "We won't need a bridge."

"No, no!" Henri stopped dead in his tracks. "You should not do that thing again. You don't know what it means. What you could become."

Seamus turned slowly to face them. He seemed larger than before, as if he were no longer human. A opal glow shone in his eyes, his irises seeming to actually be illuminated somehow. "I will take you across. It is the only way."

"But why? Why do we go into this damned cave? What could there be?" Henri protested, seemingly unphased by his closest friend's transformed countenance.

Seamus scoffed.

"I am serious, Quickfingers, what do you hope to find down here?"

"I don't have any hope," Seamus answer coldly. "But I need answers. And, I am not sure if you noticed, but we're on a godsdamned island out in the middle of nowhere, with no way off, and no hope of contacting anyone. Actually, that is not entirely true. Reylelan knows we're here, and if the Heart isn't enough, she'll come back. Do you want to face her and her horde of Biters again?"

Henri blanched. "Point taken."

"Seamus, please, we need to talk," Una'pahu pressed forward, reaching out toward him.

Seamus stepped away, fixing her with a pained expression. She could see him trying to harden himself. Una'pahu did not attempt to hide the hurt it caused her.

"Seamus, please..."

For a moment, it felt as if he would stop and actually talk, but then something inside him hardened further. "On the other side of the ravine, there is a cavern not made of magma, but by the hands of the ancient Iarathor of four centuries ago, before the reign of Uuradan the Black."

"What are you talking about, Seamus?" Una'pahu heard her voice break as she asked, no, pleaded. She just wanted her Msa'oo back.

"Seamus?" he paused, as if confused. "We need to go further. The Specter left this behind," he held up a silver disk with a crack in its face. "If we can fix it, perhaps we can communicate with the one who holds the other half."

"Seamus, you're scaring me."

Seamus's face softened, a weariness beyond words falling over every feature of his body. He let out a long, hard sigh. "Una'pahu, I am not who I was anymore, not truly. I can't explain it, but perhaps in due time, you'll be able to see. For now, we must get to Khundal'Khal."

No. No this was not okay. Una'pahu grit her teeth, reached out and grabbed Seamus by the arm, turning him around to face her. When had he gotten so tall? He stood like a statue of death, his face and arm melted into scale-like patterns. He was still Seamus, he had to be in there, but there was something - someone - else there as well.

"Seamus, until you tell me what happened, I am not going another step," Una'pahu put every bit of force and control she had let into her voice, forcing a direct steadiness to what should have been a trembling tone.

Seamus took in a deep breath and then exhaled long and slow. When he opened his eyes, the green of his irises was all but gone, a crystal white glistening brightly in their place. Somehow, the scar looked less morbid that it had even moments ago and his red hair shone in the dark tunnel, as if it were illuminated by the sun. And Una'pahu thought she sure was seeing something, for it seemed to float about him, as if tossed by waves upon the sea.

Decisively, Seamus reached his hand over his shoulder and took hold of the white-leather hilt of the massive sword. A breeze, hot and dry, rushed up the tunnel as he took the hilt in both hands and drove the tip of the blade into the ground. A dull *thud* echoed as metal struck stone.

"I am what I am," Seamus's voice was a blend of his own and something far older. Not wearied by time, but enlightened by it. It was vast and deep, powerful as the sea, and twice as mysterious.

"The sword did this to you?" Una'pahu asked, biting back her fear and looking up into his endless eyes. "Throw it away, be rid of it."

"No!" Seamus thundered. "There is a war in my soul. This blade seals away the baser parts of me. I am not the Seamus you knew, not anymore. I care for you both, but I am not what I was." His face suddenly lost its certainty, its overbearing poise. Sorrow knit its way across his eyes, which turned a shade of green evocative of grass. "Snapdragon, I am lost," his voice was pleading. "I am not sure how long I can hold on."

"Seamus, drop the sword, just let it go!" Una'pahu felt as if a hot lump of iron were ramped in her throat. She wanted to scream and weep. She wanted to take that cursed blade and throw it far, far away.

"No, you can't," Seamus said, wincing as he spoke. "It is all that keeps the fire at bay. It must not leave me. I must protect you."

"Agh!"

"We must not fail," Seamus's voice returned to deep baritone, somehow both rich and raspy. "We have a sacred duty to protect this land. We are honor-bound. My father - "

Seeing her loved one so tormented, so torn, she struck out at the blade, swatting at the flat of the sword. However, as soon as her flesh struck the white metal, a surge of pain cascaded through every fiber of her being. It felt as if she had been struck by lightning.

Just before she thought she would lose all consciousness, the scepter at her waist pulsed with a brilliant green light, matching the frequency of the blade. A burst of power, far greater than what she had just experienced pushed everyone backwards. Seamus roared as he was flung down the tunnel, his sword clattering away from him, sliding down the magma tube. Herni cried out, whether in fear or pain, Una'pahu did not know, as he was launched off his feet and into the wall. Una'pahu, however, stood firm, as gentle waves of green light rolled from her hands and eyes, and flowed over the walls, illuminating the tunnel with an eerie green.

Una'pahu looked down at her hands. They trembled with an uncontrollable shake. The tattoos on them glowed ever so faintly, pulsing in time with the scepter. She could feel power thrumming through her, strengthening her limbs and mind. But it was also distant and separate. It had always been distant. She had never truly been able to be one with the power, as her teachers had said she would. She had only ever been able to direct it, and that with great effort, as when she fought that fiendish sidepiece to Reylelan.

"What in the kraken's depths was that?"

Henri's distressed voice nearly caused Una'pahu to jump out of her own skin. She whirled on him, eyes flashing with power. The scepter, it was full. Somehow, touching that blade replenished the store of Ria'Elahm's power within the gemstone, and more so. Never had she felt the power this way. It was almost like it was alive. Calling to her.

"Oye, Snapdragon, did you hear me?"

Una'pahu shook her head, clearing it for reason and thought. She needed to answer him. But how? How could she, when she herself did not know what was happening? Ever since Reylelan, everything she had ever known had been turned on its head, and she could not make sense of any of it.

"Agh!" Seamus's voice ripped through the tunnel. It sounded pained beyond measure, as if some great torment had inflicted him.

"Didn't he say he couldn't let go of that sword?" Henri asked, eyes filling with dread. "Why did you have to go and slap it?"

Una'pahu started running down the cave, scepter held in her right hand like a dagger. She did not need to respond to him. Wasn't it obvious? That blade was doing... something to Seamus. She needed to free him from it. Didn't she?

All thoughts of concern for Seamus were ripped from Una'pahu's mind as she stumbled upon his heaving form. He writhed upon the ground, back arching in an unnatural manner. His bare feet dug into the ground, sharp bits of rock tearing at his flesh, leaving smears of blood upon the wrapped stone. However, it was his eyes that held her. They truly blazed with fire now.

Click Step Click Step Click Step

The sound was like music to Tassi's ears. Who would have thought that a simple noise would bring so much joy?

Not Alessandro Tassi, that was certain. Yet, here he was, barely able to contain a grin as he walked on his new leg as if it were his own flesh and blood. Three weeks or more had it been since he had been gifted the prosthetic, three weeks of painless life. Something had not known for nearly two decades.

"Please, I'm begging you, I don't know about any bloody Kh'ar," whimpered the lordling.

That sniveling little roach. Couldn't he just be silent for two burning minutes? Tassi turned on the man. The poor bastard looked worse for wear. Down to not but his small clothes, tied to an old whicker chair, and beaten so badly that one eye was sealed shut and the other oozed something red.

"Please, no more... I, I have gold, please, I'll do anything," he whimpered.

"You see, gold don't do me a whole lot of good here," Tassi said with a long, exaggerated sigh as he took out a heave purse and threw it at the feet of the nobleman. Bars and siglats alike clattered across the blood and piss-stained panels.

"What I need," Tassi said, step smoothly back toward the man, while drawing forth his trusted hunting knife. "Is information. Information my employer believe you have."

"I don't know anything. I swear on Ordan's throne!"

The boy was probably twenty, maybe twenty-two. Blonde with fair skin. An anomaly here in Ordiatea. Should've stayed north. Though, he didn't look like any Danelander Tassi had ever met. Too pretty. Well, he was too pretty. Now he was missing a few teeth.

"Gallae, Mother of Grace, watch over this soul. Protect me from harm and keep me from evil."

"Lad," Tassi said gruffly, using the flat of his hunting knife against the boy's chin to lift his head as that their eyes could meet. "Prayers ain't for shit. I need answers."

"Keep me in thy arms of - AGH!"

Tassi slammed the tip of the knife into the lad's hand. Bones crunched, blood splattered, and wood cracked as he drove it deep into the arm of the chair.

"Now, I have a good many knives," Tassi said before standing up and walking back to where a strange metal instrument lay. He picked up the brass orb, all wheels and cogs, with tiny little pistons and gemstones that glowed slightly. "But I've been told this little beauty can do a right bit of pain. Now, I'm not sure exactly how it works. The Hoods just gave it to me. Showed me how to turn it on. Funny thing is, they never told me how to turn it off. I guess there's no time like the present to try out."

The boy's left eye went wide and color drained from his face. His breathing became rapid and strained. He jerked back and forth, the knife tearing deeper into his hand, despite the bindings on his wrists.

"Ah, not a fan of the unknown, I see. Me neither. I hate messing with Hoods. But they pay well and let me do my job without any hassle," said Tassi lackadaisically as he strolled back, tossing the orb up and down as he walked. "Last chance, lad."

***

Tassi walked into a dark cell. A man sat in a wicker chair. He had been stripped to his small clothes. He had a strange branding on his chest, just over the heart. An upside-down eye with flames on it. The man had a hood over his head, one which Tassi removed none to gently.

"Good morning, sir," Tassi said with feigned politeness. "I am here to ask you a few questions. Won't you indulge me? I'm sure you heard your friend next door. He was not very good at answering questions. Let's not be like him."

Tassi tossed a bronze orb that dripped with blood and small chunks onto the man's groin, causing the man to let out a grunt of pain. The grunt turned to a scream as he realized what coated the ball.

"Please! Please! I don't know nothing!" He cried out. Piss had already begun to soak floor.

"Well, let's start with something nice and easy. Where did you get that nice little mark there on your chest?"

The man blanched. Had there been any color in his face, it was gone now.

"Ah, so you do know something," Tassi said with a knowing nod of his head. "I know something too. I figured out how to turn that little devil off. But, mark words, you don't want to see what it does before I do."

"No!" cried the man.

"No?" Tassi finally snapped, striking the man across the face with an open palm. "I've killed three men today! Three! If there was a god above, I'd curse his name. I'd spit on his throne. I'd piss on his fields of gold! Three men died at my hands! Three! I don't have the patience anymore. You speak, or I start carving bits of meat from your bones and feed it to swine. Do you understand me?"

The wept openly, trembling in fear and desperation. And then he broke. Tassi could see it happening. He could see the will die within the man. They always broke eventually; this one didn't even need any carving.

"My father is a man of the Blood, a true man of culture. We are a lordly house. All we want is to have back what is ours. Its been stripped from us, squandered by who? Peasants and foreigners! Damn them! Damn thcm all. I served the great Khall'ah Kh'ar! We shall return, true Kingsmen!"

"So, it's true then?" Tassi said coldly. "There are bunch of pompous pricks who think they're going to sell over this land to the Calun nation?"

"What?" the man looked aghast, as if tying him practically naked was a minor offense comparatively. "There is no Calun. It is a lie. Calun is not our enemy, it is the last of the True Blood. We betrayed our oaths. There they still believe the old ways. Their king is our king. A fraud sits upon the High Council. The Rising Star? Bah! What a load crock! We deserve a king. And those of the Blood deserve to rule alongside him!"

"How are you getting messages out of the city? Who is your contact? I need names!" Tassi roared. But it was too late. He could see it in the boy's eyes. Where there had only moments ago been a broken man-child, there was now a delusional zealot, bent on some greater good. Damnit. Tassi sighed as he slid his hunting knife from his sheath. "Four."

PART 3

~LORI~

Five Years Ago

Rain muddied the fields of emerald clovers, cascading down and soaking Lori to the bone. She shivered despite herself, her aching hands gripping the hilt of her sword and handle of her small, studded, leather-wrapped shield with furious intensity. Her chainmail was heavy on her shoulders and the hauberk beneath it clung uncomfortably to her skin, but she was thankful to it. Helatha's spear-tip had taken a chunk from her shield, then glinting uncomfortably close to her collarbone, as it slid the length of her chest.

"Eyes up, princess," the young woman called out. "Daddy ain't here to protect you now!"

Lori's blood boiled at the taunt. Still, she had to admit, that had been clever footwork on her opponent's part. And even though the tips were blunted, it still stung like Halfak's pit when the head of the spear hit her chest.

"Focus, Hela!" barked Lady Freybjron, her hazel eyes hard as unforgiving as the storm they fought in. "No Berzerk fights first with words. Iron and blood, that is what we are. Now, square up, the both y'er!"

"Ma'am!" Lori and Helatha called out in unison.

Helatha was a hand's breadth taller than Lori and had shoulders to match any low-blooded Danelander lad. She was of Clan MacLaihdir, a minor family with old blood-ties to Clan Pritfort - Lori's own mother's clan. Lori had known Helatha her whole life, Talahmnas was big, but not that big. Her mother had forced her to learn all the genealogical ties to every house, both major and minor, along with their accompanying crests, sigils, and standards.

"It's the mark of a proper lady," her mother's voice echoed in her ears as she turned her body sideways, providing the narrowest of fronts for her opponent. "To know who your liegemen are, your kin, and their families. A good leader is not one who takes their people for granted but elevates them at every given chance."

But Lori wouldn't be a true leader. She'd be married off to either the Sterkamar or the Blackwater clan. When she had voiced this to her mother, she received a verbal degradation that could have my the Stone of the Ancestors blush.

"Taisuch!" Lady Freybjron exclaimed from her vantage box, erected just over the field.

Helatha roared a fierce battle-cry as she hoisted her spear in both hands and charged. Lori, who had let her mind wander yet again, barely had time to raise her shield as the merciless onslaughts of jabs ensued.

Each strike sent reverberations through her arm, the next more exquisite than the last. Lori winced, but bit back the pain. Two years of training of going expressly against her mother's will would not end in defeat here. Only ten young women were chosen each year train for the title of Berzerk, and Helatha was the only thing standing between her and the indentureship.

Even the word itself seemed wrong to her. It was what it was. It was the reason her mother had so vehemently disagreed with her choice. But Lori had made up her mind, and at fourteen years old, she had entered womanhood and had every right to make this decision. And thankfully, their family had welcomed a third daughter, so their line and titles were secured, more so than ever before.

Five children. Who in the bloody-damned pit would want to birth one child, let alone five?

"Eyes up!" roared Lady Freybjron just Helatha's spear-tip flashed passed Lori's face, narrowly missing her cheek. "It will be to the Pit with me if she take's y'er head off, Lori!"

No! Lori's heart skipped a beat as shame and frustration raged within her. She could not be seen having help. No favoritism. No protection. She had to earn this on her own or she would never be chosen for the Berzerk. She could not fail... not again. Not at this.

"Erk and Krun might be pinned gold this year, but y'er nothing," Helatha spat. She looked as furious as Lori felt, surely upset with Lady Freybjron's interjection.

"What is y'er fascination with then of my house," Lori snarled. "Y'er that needy for a bedding?"

Red flushed the other's face and Lori seized the moment to strike. She darted across the distance between them, her boots squelching in the mud, sending splatters up her bare shins where kilt did not meet boot. With a wild swing of her shield, she caught the haft of Helatha's spear, knocking it wide. Fear replaced anger in Helatha's eyes as Lori drove a crescent pummel into her face with bone-crunch *thud!*

Blood sprayed from Helatha's nose as her head whipped back and her eyes rolled toward her scalp. Like a puppet whose strings had been cut, Lori's opposition crumpled into the mud in a twitching heap.

"Victory to Lori!" Lady Freybjron called out.

A clammer of applause and cheering broke out from amongst the other nine who had already earned their spot, along with two or three true Berzerkers who had come to witness the training.

Despite this, the whole world seemed to close in on Lori's mind. Silence stifled her ears as the rain feel over her body. Nothing seemed real in that moment. Everything was so...right. And yet, so very wrong.

Had she really done it? Had she finally succeeded?

"Lori Ruthvin," Lady Freybjron was speaking, but she sounded an eternity away. "You have been found worthy of servitude in the ranks of the Berzerk. As is accustom, who is it that would give you to us?"

Lori went to step forward. This was it. The moment she had -

"I do!"

Lori whipped her head about, her mind not believing what her ears were hearing.

There, standing in the rain, was her mother.

"As Lady of Talahmnas, I give up my daughter." Her mother's eyes fell upon her for a moment. And was that, pride? No... "She is forfeit of title, clan, and house, and is free to take the Oath of the Berzerk."

Lori felt as if her heart would burst asunder. Never in her life could she have believed that her mother would allow this, much less support it. That feeling blossomed even further as her mother guided Little Ery from behind her back. The shy little lamb was holding her little doll so close to her chest, her big green eyes wide.

"That is y'er sister there, Ery, take note of what a strong woman can do if she sets her mind to it," Lady Sophie said, as if she were really speaking to her youngest daughter, but loud enough that Lori knew those words were more for her than for her sister.

"Then stand forth, Daughter of Daneland," Lady Freybjron proclaimed as she took up a colossal axe, whose head was of ornate design and haft whittled with runic knots and beasts.

Lori stepped forward, rising onto the small platform where Lady Freybjron stood. The Master of Ceremonies hefted the great axe over her head and swung it down with all her might. The axe bit deep into a log, and as it did so, the wood burst apart in a spray of chips and water.

"So as this long was cleaved in twine, so shall y'er be cleaved from y'er family, y'er house, and y'er kin! Now, take up the grey."

Two of the Berzerker women brought forth a grey cloak that matched each of the other nine young women who stood in a line. The third Berzerker hefted off Lori's helm and chainmail. The cloak was then wrapped about her and pinned around her neck.

"Ash to ash, and blood for blood," Lady Freybjron said as she dipped her thumb into a mixture of both ash and blood that was house in a porous stone basin. She then stroked her thumb across brow and cheeks, repeating the phrase thrice over.

"Ash to ash, and blood for blood!" called out all the Berzerkers and the newly indentured young women in unison, Lori included.

Part 2

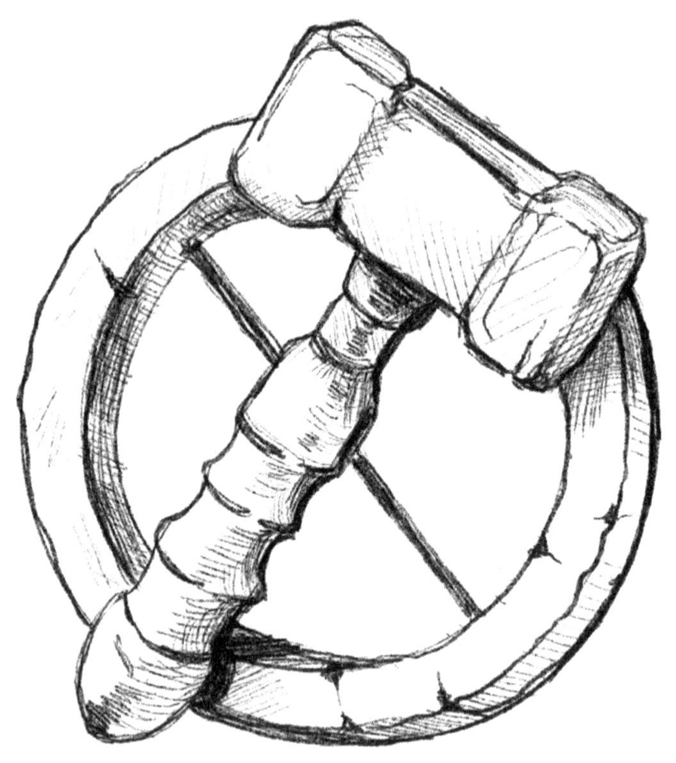

CHAPTER 20: REDEYES
DARIUS

Darius sat in what Lord Erik Ruthvin had so eloquently called his War Room. It was situated somewhere in the High Hill, the lift having taken them down several levels into the core of the structure in just a matter of moments. The room was guarded by Erik's silent guards and his two hounds of egregious size. Darius had always had a fondness for animals, but these two sent the hairs on the nape of his neck standing. Other than Erik, to Darius's absolute surprise, Lori was the only other person there. She wore leather and fur, fitted with scale-plate and iron rings. Two saexs crossed at her hips and a circular shield with a steel spike was slung over her back. She stood silently with her arms crossed and ice-colored eyes fixed on Darius. Erik, too, was in the same garb he had first worn when Darius had met him in Tyree's shop.

"A moment more," Erik said, catching Darius's confused expression. Erik did not stand, but sat in a chair cut out of the side of a massive log with axes affixed by the base of their hafts forming the armrests. His mighty war spear was stationed over his head, the head of which was naked to the eye and shone with a faint glow of moonlight. "Take the hounds, they don't be needing to see this."

Darius could feel the power crackling through the room of hewn stone, all sharp edges and cold. His own ring surged with unrelenting power. The meteor's power continued to affect it and him. During the night, it made his thoughts turn feral, his instincts wild. He felt the urge to say the words, to slip into his Fero form.

Restraint. I must show restraint. Darius repeated the mantra in his head over and over again as he waited for whatever was coming. So caught up in his thoughts, he did not notice the silent sentinels walk past him, nor did he smell the hounds as they stalked by.

Suddenly, the lift mechanism whirled to life as great cogs ground against each other and cables the width of Darius's arms twisted upon colossal spools. Up it rose, leaving the three of them alone in the vast, cold room. No one spoke.

After a long and rather awkward silence, the cogs began to turn once more, sending all three looking toward the shaft where a black-steel basket was lowered. It carried two massive young men with hair so wild and frizzed that they looked as if they had never seen a brush in their life, and so red it could have been fire dancing around their thick skulls. Vibrant green eyes ringed by a mask of freckles peered down from the lowered basket, filled with caution and fire. Between the two, someone———or something———was being restrained, wrapped with heavy chains and a sack of animal hide thrust over its head and bound with strong cords.

"What in Ordan's name?" Darius uttered the words aloud before he could stop himself. The bear in the back of his mind raged against his will. The all-consuming need to rip into whatever that thing behind the chains was tore at every fiber of his being.

"Silence!" hissed Erik. There was no mirth in the big man's voice, and if Darius was not mistaken, a tinge of fear crept along the edge of the command.

Anger surged through Darius's body at the order. How dare this man speak to him this way? Hadn't he shown them what he was? Was he not also by right a leader of men? Who was this painted northerner to tell him to be silent? Lines of red seeped into his vision and his head began to pound.

When the lift stopped and the basket door opened, Darius felt as if fire blossomed up from the cold floor. Sweat beaded at his brow and soaked the small of his back. He reached for... he had no weapon, no tool with which to attack. His fingers tightened into the most reliable weapon he had ever had, joints cracking as the flesh whitened under the strain.

"Hail, father!" called out the leaner of the two men, the one that didn't have a stupid mustache plastered to his face, but a thin shadow of whiskers.

"Erkan," Erik answered slowly.

Lori stood straight now, no longer leaning against a shelf, but gazing with hatred and contempt at the hooded thing. A single hand rested on the handle of one of twin saexs; the other took out a silver vial that hung at her neck. She huffed the contents. A tremor ran through her body, followed by an almost imperceptible loosening of her muscle and relaxing of her face. She still stood firm, but an air of control seemed to pass over her.

Erik, too, had huffed something and had regained his poise. "Not dead, then?"

"Alive and bitin', da," said the other behemoth, and he truly was one. Mustaches braided with iron studs, a nasty scar across his forehead, and a lion's mane of red hair tied at the base of his head and exploding outward like a canon's blast. His arms were so thick, Darius had to take a double glance to realize they were not some kind of false armor. He looked almost exactly like Krarraek, save for the wide mouth and tilted nose his father and he shared.

"Good," sneered Erik. He then turned to face Darius. "I'd like y'er to meet me boys, Erkan and Krunlan, pride and joy of Talahmnas. But don't ask them which is pride, and which is joy. They'll never shut up about it."

Darius felt his eye twitch. Was he...sharing pleasantries? Fury flared within his chest, a proverbial swarm of hornets stinging at every nerve and strand of patience he had.

"Oye, Lori, be a good lass and give 'im some clarity, would ya?" Erik said, motioning towards his daughter with the wave of a hand.

"Father," she replied, pushing herself forward as if it were the last thing she wanted to do.

She walked like a feral cat, every step measured and poised. She stepped right up to Darius and looked him hard in the eyes. "It stings like a bitch." She popped the cork with a movement of her thumb and thrust the silver vial under Darius's nose.

A scent like saltpeter mixed with lightning and a dying goat's arsehole assaulted Darius's nostrils with all the force of a raging typhoon. The room exploded with light as flecks of gold and silver threatened to sear his vision away.

"Agh!" Darius cried out as he jerked his head away from the vial, cracking his skull into a bookshelf, sending its contents across the stone floor.

A cold, chilling laugh stole all the pain, humor, and warmth from the room. Darius felt his whole body go ridged.

"Ghaz-kant jbron." The sound was like locusts, dry grass fire, and death. It came from under the hood and sent the Ruthvins as rigid as Darius.

Eyes still watery, Darius looked at the beast. He had fought Morreans before, but this one, it was different, evolved. He could see the blackened veins under its paled hands; he could sense the corrupting Touch of Iodaba. But there was something wrong with this...thing.

"Ghaz-kant jbron," it hissed again.

Something under the hood rattled like a mount snake, sending involuntary pricks up Darius's neck. Darius's thumb slid over his ring. Power coursed through his veins as anger boiled his blood. He needed to kill this thing. Destroy it. All thought fled his mind as rage pressed itself against his will.

"Smoke it!" called Erik from somewhere very far away.

One of the boys cracked a stick of sorts in front of the hood figure. Orange smoke bloomed, forming into what looked like a mushroom of twisting fumes that rose swiftly, penetrating the hood on the creature. It coughed and hacked. It hissed and screamed as if its very flesh had been set alight. And then it went utterly limp.

Clarity washed over Darius's mind. It hit swiftly, as if his head had been plunged into icy water. He gasped for air as the room reformed around his eyes. He was back. Back in the War Room. Back in reality. He was back, and he had control of himself once more.

"What the bloody pit was that?" Darius asked as he whirled about to face Erik, who was leaning leisurely against the table. Leisurely, though his spear was in his hand and his blue eyes were fixed on the demon.

"That—" Erik twisted the haft his great spear, pointing the tip at the chest of the creature. "—is what we call a Redeye."

With a flick of his wrist, the head of the spear rose in a flash, slicing its way up the front of the hood. An odor so vile, so repugnant that it nearly caused Darius to lose his dinner, filled the room as orange smoke fell to the floor like liquid poured from a vase. From the slit in the sack, Darius saw an eye. A singular red eye. It looked like burning coal, stoked by forger's fire. It blazed with hatred, its two slitted pupils dazed and lacking focus.

"High Father above!" Darius swore as he took an involuntary step back and clutched his fists in a fighter's stance.

"Don't go get'n soft on me now, laddie," said Erik. The lord's eyes did not leave the demon's as he lowered his spear. "Redeye. Bloody damned chutlings, the lot."

"I've never," Darius began, but his words fell silent, his whole focus on the creature's disconcerting double-pupil. Despite himself, he could not look away.

"No one had," Erik said, finishing Darius's thoughts. "Not until about two or three years ago. Took my da, Ordan keep his soul. We were on a hunt, chutlings came out of nowhere. Dozen or so goblins, not a real threat. But then we seen their eyes, void and blood-red. Even as we hacked them to naught but bloody pelts, they fought. That's when we knew something was wrong, very wrong."

Something caught in Erik's voice, a hurt of loss that Darius knew all too well. Darius hadn't even considered the fact that Erik had a father who couldn't have been that old. Halfak's pit, Erik couldn't have been older than his early fifties.

"Draugr came next, riding undead wylven, eyes like hellfire," Erik continued as he regained his composure. "They came over the hills and descended upon us without mercy. Two dozen Danelanders lost their lives. We only had half a dozen Moonstone swords, my

father's spear, and Tyree's magic. To be honest, had it not been for that old mage, I'd be asleep in the mud, resting with the ancestors. But none of that held a candle to our first glimpse of a Redeye."

"Da," Lori started, stepping between Darius and her father. "He is an Outlander."

"He bloody-well might be," Erik said, placing his left hand on Lori's shoulder in answer. "But we're out of our depths here, Lori. I have to trust he came to us by more than chance."

Darius looked into the high lord's eyes. The damp chill was all but gone and the putrid stench of that strange, orange smoke had mostly dissipated, making the room seem almost welcoming. He also felt much more in control, his rage and fury somehow abated.

That realization, the understanding that his emotions had swung so wildly, made Darius felt disquieted to the core. It was not helped that the only reasonable explanation was the creature in front of them, chained and drugged, yet somehow all the more terrifying for it. Its chest rattled as it breathed in and out lethargically.

"By the gods, what is that?" Darius gasped; eyes locked on the hideous fiend.

"What's what?" asked the tall of the two boys.

"Its face, its..." Darius stuttered, stepping closer, drawn in by what he was seeing, as if he had lost all control of his body. No. Not like that, not exactly. It was more like he was in a dream, watching himself from above, but also being in the moment.

"Buggered? Chutting little shite," the mustached one laughed. "Well, bugs for short. Redeye don't catch on to my liking."

Krunlan, that was his name, ripped the bag off of the thing's head. Two sets of bi-slitted eyes blinked asynchronously, lids sliding side to side. Its mouth hung open, revealing a horrendous set of drool-soaked mandibles of both human form and insectoid function. Teeth ranging from molars to jagged and chipped incisors lined the protruding, bony jaws whose putrid flesh looked as if it was sloughing off. On its neck, a series of gill-like fins shuttered with every breath.

"Nasty chuts, ain't they?" Krunlan grunted with a disdainful smile as he dropped the hood to the ground.

"Tahlbjrin root, dried and charred, it's about all that'll knock these things out," Erik said as he lifted the Redeye's face to peer into it with a rough hand. A hand that had just been so gentle now appeared to be strong enough to tear the creature's head from its shoulders.

"Why?" asked Darius, his mind beginning to work once more. "Why keep it alive? Why capture it? Why not kill it when you had the chance?"

"Ah," Erik sighed, dropping the creature's head, which flopped onto his bony chest. "Why, why, why. So many questions, laddie. All with the same answer: information."

It was Lori's turn to step forward. Her saex slid with practiced ease from the scabbard at her back. Her eyes were locked on the Redeye, no emotion on her face other than determination. Erkan and Krunlan hauled the bug over to an iron chair and latched its chains to a set of rings on the floor. The dogs' hackles lowered as they laid next to Erik's feet. They had all done this before. They were accustomed to it.

Lori slashed across the Redeye's chest, the blade's edge biting deep into flesh, grinding as it struck bone, and splattering the walls with black ichor. The bug hissed in pain, though its eyes did not register any emotion at all, drifting in emptiness.

Torture. They would torture it. Grim understanding warred within Darius's psyche. Could he do this? Could he torture something? Kill in a fight for life and death, obviously. But to inflict pain at the highest degree to something bound and defenseless? His stomach turned and his eyes fluttered.

"Look at it, laddie," Erik growled. "This thing ain't human, not anymore, if it ever were. Rot and death is all it is, a plague upon my lands and kin."

"But torture?" The words slid out of Darius's drawn mouth as the blade slid back across the bug's check, forming an 'x' in its ashen flesh. He winced, wishing it would stop. The creature's gills fluttered, the sound like that of dried leaves being crunched under foot.

"Lori here understands," Erik said as his daughter wiped her blade across the bug's tattered clothes. "She knows what it takes. So do me boys. Y'er gonna be in this world, this land, y'er gotta harden y'erself. A darkness is upon us, one that hasn't been known for generations. You y'erself said it. Our only hope is information. We must know what they're after, why they're here. Why they took me daughter."

A fire burned behind Erik's eyes now, and Darius understood. This was about more than information. This wasn't just law and justice, this was retribution. Darius couldn't believe himself. Was he siding with the Morreans? Those that killed his own father and brother. Those that took everything from him. Worshippers of the Fallen Ones, followers of the Blood Queen.

The sickness in his guts worsened because he knew he would not stop them, despite knowing it was wrong. He would not raise his own hand, not in punishment or defense. He would let this happen. His own hands were not clean, that was true. But this was something altogether worse.

"Again," Erik hissed.

Lori's knife drew downward, eliciting the first true cry of pain.

"There he is," said Erik as a dark smile split his harrowed face.

"Ghaz-kant jbron." The words sounded as if they were gurgling up from a mire, thick with pain and inebriation.

Erik nodded to Krunlan, who swung a meaty fist into the side of the Redeye's head. A sickening crunch echoed throughout the War Room as more blood, both black and red, splattered the floor.

"Blood and stone," swore Krunlan as he shook out his hand, his knuckles split and bleeding.

One of the mandibles of the Redeye hung at an awkward angle, bits of Krunlan's flesh caught in its mangled teeth. It rolled its head so that its bifurcated pupils could look into the massive young man's face, and it laughed. A horrid, raspy laugh that sent the dogs to their feet with hackles rising. Low growls rumbled through their throats, their drooling maws clenched and ready.

"Watch where y'er swinging, Krun!" shot Erkan, who was wiping blackened blood from his face.

"That's disgusting," Krunlan laughed as he took a rough towel from a table and wrapped it around his hand.

"Again." Erik's command held no trace of anything other than pure malice. This was personal. Deeply, disturbingly, personal.

Krunlan shrugged and Erkan lifted the bug's head. With a thunderous boom, Krunlan's mighty fist struck the Redeye, this time right in its temple. Its eyes rolled backward and its body went limp.

"Water, Lori," Erik commanded.

Lori, without a word, slid her saex back into its scabbard and walked over to a small pump and began to draw water into an old tin bucket.

Splash
Splash
Splash

The water hit the bucket, over and over and over again. Every time Darius felt a chill. This was not right. This was not right. This was not right. And still, he did nothing.

Cold water was sloshed over the Redeye. It gasped and hacked, struggling for breath, body thrashing against its bonds.

"Better chose real words, bug," Erik seethed. "Why are y'er lot in Daneland? Why were ye taking our children?"

"Blood," the creature's voice was dissonant, slurred by its broken jaw, and distorted from pain. "Blood. Blood shall rain!"

Darius felt a pit open in his stomach. What did it just say?

"That don't make sense," Erik said with a shake of his head, the iron rings in his braided beard clacking together. "Krun, make it make sense."

"Aye, father," Krunlan said. He placed a hand on the Redeye's shoulder, as if he were giving it comforting council. He looked into the thing's eyes and said, "Last chance before things get real nasty."

"Hail the Lord of Blood! Hail the Lord of Blood! Hail—"
Crack!
Erkan struck the Redeye across the left side of its face.
Crack!
Krunlan followed up with a viscous strike to the right.

The fire went out of the bug's red eyes.

"Is it dead?" Erik asked, a hint of disappointment on his tongue.

Lori placed two fingers under its chin, up against its gilled neck. She pulled them back quickly and turned to her father. "Still breathing. But weak. Send him to Tyree?"

"To Tyree," Erik answered solemnly. "And tell him not to stick any trinkets in this one. We need it to talk."

Darius blinked. It was over. It was just... over. He had never witnessed torture before. It hadn't been long. There hadn't been cruel tools and wicked instruments. But it had been torture all the same. Darius felt a bit of his humanity slip away in the moment, and he feared he would never see it back again.

"Darius, ye need to come with me now," Erik said with a deep heaviness to his voice. "There is something I need to show ye."

The War Room cleared, the steady sound of cogs and cranks turning as the metal basket was hoisted upwards through the stone

shaft. Erik did not speak for a long moment, his consternating gaze lingering upon the place where the Redeye had been chained and beaten.

"Darius, y'er have a right not to trust us, but trust me when I say what we do must be done." His words were an echo in Darius's ears. There was a pleading in them, but more than that, a finality that would not be besieged.

"What you do in the shadows is no concern of mine," Darius answered. "These are your people, your war."

"Ah, but that's just it, laddie," Erik sighed out, turning to face Darius with a bone-deep weariness etched across his face. Age showed there, age that Darius had not noticed before. Deep lines and the ever so faint glint of grey in his golden hair, just above the ears. "It's not just me and my kinfolk. It's not my war. And now I am going to ask y'er to do something I never thought I would of an Outlander. Darius, I want y'er to stand with us, to fight this. Call it fate, call it fortune, call it a bloody damn curse for all I care, but ye came to us in a dark time unlike any my forefathers knew before me. Ye came to us as light in the shadow. Ye have knowledge and abilities forgotten to this world, and I'd be a bloody damned fool to let ye just walk away without care or thought."

"What are you asking?" Darius asked as he pressed down the rising churn of unease and trepidation. Elcon wanted him for the Church, to be a symbol of righteous retribution for a faith he did not follow. Now Erik wanted him to stand and fight to defend the borders of a kingdom to which he owed no allegiance. And despite these truths, these obvious reservations he held, could he stand by idly as innocents were harmed?

No. He had sworn his oaths. He would stand for the defenseless, fight for the weak and helpless. He walked in honor and strive for the right, even if—

Find them!

Darius stumbled backward, the Voice ringing mercilessly in his ears.

Find them!

"Is everything alright?" Erik asked, stepping forward and offering a steadying hand.

Darius's back slammed into a wall, the Voice reverberating through the whole of his body, rattling his brains with thunderous proclamation.

Find them, or blood shall rain!

The Redeye. The girl from Tur'Mor. All of this it was connected. And there were others. The question now was whether the Voice was urging him to accept Erik's request or demanding that he leave?

Darius steadied himself, looked into Erik's eyes, and answered, "What would you have me do?"

If this was the wrong choice, surely a god could tell him otherwise. Right?

Concern drained from Erik's face, replaced by a smile both warm and cruel. "First, y'er gonna need a weapon worthy of war. Then, well, the war drums do be a thrum'n."

CHAPTER 21: A BEGINNING
AELLIA

Aellia ran and ran, her mind filled with doubt and confusion... and hope. She ran back to where she had been held captive these past days. She ran back to the place where she believed she could find answers. She ran back to Elcon's manse.

The escape from the Asterivae was not one of particular challenge. Drafting was fast becoming Aellia's favored ability. That and flight. She could do neither now. She was depleted, and the fall from the tower had strained her healing factor as well, leaving her with a scepter that did not shine with Everlight, a wretched headache, and a heart foolishly filled with hope.

It would have been easy to run straight to Elcon's manse, but there were surely Asterivians behind her. Years on the street in Felik's Crew had taught her that it was never wise to run straight home but to backtrack and mislead at every possible opportunity. Twice Aellia saw shadows of people in robes and masks, lurking, searching. Once more, she had almost run headlong into a tall, mustachioed man wearing a top hat and a black overcoat pinned with a silver crest, that of an Inspector.

That would have been bad. Aellia said in her mind as she wound down a back alleyway.

I do not see why? Are not these who are beholden to the laws and ordinances of this place? Should they not provide aid? Why do you fear them so?

You have my memories now. Not such a pretty painting if you've spent your whole life on the wrong side of the law.

But you've changed. You've accepted an Oath from the High Father. Surely, in a place such as this, where there are believers in the ways of our gods, you would be held in great esteem.

Not how it works, grunted Aellia as she flipped up onto an awning and began to race across red tile rooftops, dodging chimneys and flue pipes.

But we go back to the High Priest? This is good, Aellia. I truly believe that we shall fare far better once we set aside our differences and become united with the followers of Ordan.

Aellia pulled up shot, her heels kicking up dust and sending a flock of orange-and-red pigeons darting into the air. "Listen, Iaenora. I am not doing this to build bridges. You heard that voice, same as I. You're looking for your sisters. I am looking for something else. You help me with this, and I promise to do whatever I can to help you with your sisters. But I will not put a single gram of trust in Uppers or their ilk, you hear me?"

What of the Blessed? Surely you cannot mistrust such as pure as they.

Aellia's mind was filled with an image of the twin women who had nursed her back to health, provided comfort and kindness. They were beautiful, angelic beings, far too pure for this world, this city, this place. A pit formed in her stomach, one of shame and hurt. Hurt that her own life had been so devoid of anything pure such as they. And shame for the anger that burned within her soul toward them. They had done nothing but help, and she could not help but hate them for their association.

You must learn to trust someone, Aellia.

I trust you, isn't that enough? said Aellia without even realizing what she said.

A stillness, followed by a rush of warmth.

"No..." Aellia muttered. "No, no, no. don't..."

I knew it!

Gods damn it. Aellia swore. And so what? You're me, aren't you? Shouldn't I trust myself?

Yes. Yes you should.

Those words tore at Aellia's core. She hadn't trusted herself. Not since the incident at the Masquerade. The very event she had planned had led to the loss of everyone she held dear and placed an ancient Sage in her own head.

It is the first step in the healing process, to accept. Then, we shall move on, together.

Aellia started running. If she ran, she could not think. If she did not think, she would not remember. And if she didn't remember, she could not hurt anymore. Pain on the outside was so much sweeter than the darkness that burrowed within her soul.

As Elcon's manse drew closer, Aellia felt her heart begin to thunder. This was it. This was the choice she was making. She was going to have to trust that old codger in his silks and gold. The mere thought of it made her stomach sick. But what else was she to do? Who else could she turn to?

Aellia's attention was torn away from her thoughts as she saw a small party strewn out on the steps of Elcon's manse. A dozen or so Uppers—men in layered suits of stripes and colorful patterns, cuffs frilled and collars high, and women with hair done up like spun sugar fluff and dyed eccentric shades of pinks, blues, and teals in gowns of ostentatious design—stood about chatting under parasols with members of the Cloth. The high priests and priestesses did not wear deep-green hooded cloaks and tunics of the monks and nuns, but stoles and jackets most fashionable, but none so much as Elcon. He wore an emerald coat with rich, golden embroidery up the sleeves, tight britches of matching fabric, and shoes polished so bright one could see their reflection in them.

This was the man she was going to put her trust in?

And who else was Elcon speaking to other than Xander Adelmo, Mayor of Tur'Mor and head of the noble born families. How Aellia loathed that man. It had been he who had held the Masquerade that had led to the loss of all of Aellia's friends. He had probably even been the one who had set that fat Midcouncilor upon them, ruining everything.

At least he was not there.

Aellia hid behind a stack, waiting for the party to disperse into their gilded carriages, drawn by beautiful stallions, brushed and glistening. It was in her secluded position that Aellia felt something creep up her spine. A sudden chill. A moment of alarm before a gnat bit her neck.

Aellia slapped at the bug, but when she pulled a hand away, there were no remains. Confusion flooded her mind as the world became suddenly very grey and still. Her last sight was that of three Aluth dressed in white, rushing silently to catch her before she toppled over the edge of the roof.

***

"Here she comes."

Aellia blinked as she heard the words flowing into her as her consciousness wrestled with the darkness of the drug-induced sleep. Her mind was dull and her head throbbed as if she had been struck, but she did recall perfectly that moment before the poison dart.

"You drugged me," Aellia had meant to sound angry, bold and filled with venom. She, however, slurred her words and barely formed a coherent phrase.

"Well, daughter, I technically had you drugged," Elcon said, not facing her, but standing with his hands fold behind his back so that she could see his various rings. "And what fortuitous wisdom that was."

Aellia felt as if she had been slapped by his words. How dare he. How dare he say that. How dare he try and justify his abhorrent actions against her.

"Brei, Alyn, leave us," Elcon said sharply.

Aellia had not noticed the two Blessed in the room but felt their presence ebb as they exited the opulent room in where she had awakened. It was all gold and green, like so much of this bloody manse, covered in religious symbols and artifacts. Walls of shelves rose about, filled with books both ancient and new, cracked and gleaming. The scent of ivory and clean linen hung in the air. And the steady, near-imperceptible breathing, of another person.

"Avjan," Elcon said far more respectfully, "You may stay."

A woman with steel-grey hair in a militant jacket of white and purple with long epaulets on the shoulders, stood stock-still, having just reached for the door Brei and Alyn had vanished through.

"Your Eminence," she said with a curt nod of her proud head, dropping a gloved hand to the hilt of a glistening saber fixed to her belt.

"You—" Aellia tried to take control, to speak. But her words were stunted and clumsy.

"No," Elcon snapped, whirling about and facing her with a stern but tired expression. "You do not get to speak now. Do you have any idea the situation you've placed me in? Do you know why the Mayor—the Mayor—has come to my manse this day? Do you know what is whispered in the streets? Do you understand, even in the slightest, the outcomes of the errant actions you have so foolishly partaken in have caused?"

The veins of Elcon's neck bulged, but his credit, he did not yell. His voice quivered with rage, but he did not yell. Nor did he physically lash out or touch her, but maintained distance in a perfectly poised stance. A fighter's stance.

"I—"

"No. Now is not the time for you to talk, but to listen, to understand." Elcon removed the spectacles from his face, withdrawing a handkerchief and wiping at them, all while keeping his eyes locked on Aellia. "I have taken you in. Provided you with care befitting a noble born heir. Brei and Alyn, daughters of the greatest Blessed in generations, have ministered to you. I have offered you my own services, laying my wisdom before your feet. Only for you to tramp upon it, upon my dignity, my station. Upon the very Order of Ordan. And for what? For you to take off, running amok, threatening your safety and the veneration of my house?"

Aellia blinked, dumbfounded by Elcon's words, and the truth within them. She had been ungrateful, hateful, and filled with rage. She had wanted to see the Uppers burn for their pride and arrogance. She had wanted all that was bad and wrong with the world to be poured down upon those at the top, not cascaded further upon the heads of the lower class.

But at what cost?

What else was she willing to pay? She had lost all those she knew and cared for. What else was left to bargain, other than her soul?

Aellia. Iaenora's voice was calm and cool, like shade in the summer's sun or a dip in a cool pool of crystal water. Aellia fell into that voice, disassociating herself for the briefest moment. *You can mend this. You do not always have to break.*

Tears burned in Aellia's eyes. She hated it. She hated appearing weak, emotional. But she was. She was weak, and tired, and alone.

Elcon's face softened, and Aellia hated that too. She hated how it comforted her that he saw her, that he observed her state and backed down. That he, even now, was showing undue kindness.

"Daughter," he said with an exhalation. "I only speak out so that I might span the distance between us. I only speak out because I burn with the grace of Gallae and the care of Ordan. As their ordained high priest, it is my responsibility to bring light and truth. And you, Daughter, are filled with much light, so much light."

Aellia looked up into the old man's eyes, seeing past the age, past the station, the wealth and the class, and allowed herself to see a man, a human person. It was hard, so damn hard, but she forced herself to do it. She could feel Iaenora inside her, bolstering her will, urging her forward.

"I—" the words caught in Aellia's throat, which felt as if she had something lodged within it, and she could not swallow. "I need help."

Slowly, cautiously, Elcon moved. He walked next to where Aellia sat propped up on the raised side of velvet lounging sofa and took a seat upon a wingback chair. He crossed a leg over the other and steepled his fingers. His face filled with wrinkles as he delved into deep thought.

Aellia was about to say something else, mutter something to break the awkward silence that hung between them. When Elcon at long last cleared his throat, Aellia let out a faint sigh of relief.

"And what, pray tell, would you have me help you with, Daughter?"

This was it. This was the ledge, and she had to commit to it now or never. She would either dive in headlong or fall backward into uncertainty and darkness. She looked back the old priest; all of the indignation was gone from him, his tired face showing only earnest openness, a willingness, despite all she had done, to listen. Yet that ledge, that leap of faith, it terrified her. Aellia understood darkness, she knew loneliness and abandonment. What if this path, this way forward, was worse? What if it changed her to be something other than the woman she had forged herself into? Was she even capable of change?

"I... I don't know where to start," Aellia muttered out, her eyes dropping to her own hands. Hands that trembled and shook. Why was this so bloody-damned hard?

"Then let me start anew," Elcon said with a soft smile. "For the both of us. I am Elcon von'Harr, High Priest of the Church of Ordan."

Aellia waited for him to say more. He did not. He just looked at her, eyes open, waiting. She knew what he wanted. She knew what she needed to do. And if she wanted to get answers, then this was the pathway forward. But would she think her mad? Crazed? Would she have her executed on the spot for blasphemy?

"I am Aellia of Livitha," she said firmly, raising her chin and staring the high priest in his eyes with newfound resolution. If she was going to do this, she would do it wholly, without guile or shame. She slid the silver scepter from her belt, clinging to it for strength. "I am the Sage of the Winds and Storms, come to answer Ordan's call, and I seek my sisters, so that we might rid this realm of the stain of Iodaba and those whose hearts are corrupted."

It was hard at first, opening up to this stranger. But Aellia did open. She cried as she told of how her father had been taken and the fate of her mother and brother. She laughed as she recalled her time with Felik's Crew, and how they had so often ragged and goaded each other. Tears came back to her eyes as she told him of how she and her friends had been betrayed and lost, and their fates at the hands of strangers with stranger's powers.

After she had finished, Elcon began his own tale. He spoke his in the military and campaigns. He told of his love and their son, the life they had shared, though he had been so absent through most of. He spoke on the loss of youth and the pains of aging. He told her of his journey into the Cloth with his dearest friend, Ranun. Aellia recalled the portly old man who had served bread to those in Southend. One of the few Uppers she hadn't hated with a dark passion.

When he finished, despite everything, she felt a bond of understanding begin to form between them. It was not strong, nor did she wholly welcome it, but she could not deny that they had crossed some unseen threshold.

"Ah, it was a time," Elcon said wistfully. "It was all a time. Youth has far fled my old bones, but my memories are brighter for the years."

"How do you do it?" Aellia asked after a moment's contemplation.

"What do you mean?"

"How do you go on? With the hurt. The loss. How do you just... keep going?"

"Ah," Elcon said with a sigh, taking hold of a saucer and teacup. He raised the elegant brim to his lips and drank smoothly. When he

finished, placing the cup back upon the saucer and resting it upon the table, he said, "I go on, because life is only worth living if one lives. I am not so old that I wish to cease. I have so much left to learn, to observe. Even now, here in this room, I have come to know a new person in yourself. A bright and beautiful young woman, a daughter of Ordan and Gallae, whose face is that of paned glass, many hued, but beautiful none the less."

"I miss them," Aellia said, shying away from his piercing grey eyes. She could not look at him. She wanted to despise him still, but those words had pierced her own armor, sinking into her fragile heart.

"As do I," Elcon answered, though surely speaking of his own lost loved ones.

"What if..." Aellia said slowly. "What if... what if I—? I am going to sound ridiculous, but please, hear me."

"There is no shame here, Daughter," said Elcon in a comforting manner.

"I had a vision of sorts. Ugh." Aellia choked on the words. "When Tomo died, I saw her, but not in her physical body. She spoke to me. Said she had moved on. But what, what if she hadn't, not wholly? Not because she didn't want to, but because something was holding her back."

"I am afraid I don't quite understand what you're asking, Aellia," Elcon said, leaning forward, focus sharping.

"You found me, you know what I am," Aellia, trying to piece together everything in her mind, the many fragment of these past days. "I am, well, I should be dead, but I am not. I bonded to some being greater than I. Well, what if—"

"But you didn't die," Elcon said with sorrow, his face softening and his features relaxing. He leaned back into his chair and steepled his fingers. "Aellia, you were saved, chosen. I do believe our mutual friend had something to do with that."

"Not something, everything," said Aellia, her eye flashing with hope. She pulled at the pouch at her waist, retrieving that hammer left to her, carved with what she knew now were words saying, 'Find Me'. "This was his. He can awaken us, the Sages. And I must find him."

Elcon's face looked puzzled, and he did not speak or move for several long moments. When he did at long last, his words were slow and careful. "Aellia, that man was sent to the capital of Dane, he is probably already there, to meet with another who I had hoped could help him on his own journey of discovery. Had I known, well, I never would have had him leave."

"Had him leave? What man could help him? He is needed to help us." Excitement and frustration began to swell within Aellia. "If I could go to him, find him, I could help. I just—"

"Aellia, listen to me," Elcon said consolingly. "I am no expert in the matters with which you are called to face, but I have spent a good many years studying histories and prophecies. That being said, nothing good ever comes from acting out in haste and impatience. Allow me the time to go and seek council from the Patriarch. I do believe he alone holds the keys of understanding here."

Yes! I had felt that man. He is one called of Ordan. He can help us.

"When can we leave?" asked Aellia.

"We? No, Daughter, not we. You must still recover your strength and lie low. What you have done, going into the Asterivae, that was... unwise. Allow me to take time to smooth things over. It won't take long, I promise."

"Smooth things over?" Aellia was aghast. "What are you talking about? They tried to kill me!"

"You broke into their chambers," Elcon said with a sigh, rising to his feet. "Listen, the Asterivians and the Church, well, we do not see eye to eye, Daughter. And they take great offense when their premises are crossed without invitation. As a member of the High Priesthood of the Church of Ordan, I am afforded, if I so wish, council at the very feet of the Rising Star of Ordiatea. But, behind closed doors, do not misunderstand the powers at play within that secret organization. Deep are their pockets and wide the nets that are cast."

"So you want me to just sit this house while you go off to speak with your superior?" Aellia felt some of the fire return, that disdain of how Uppers always thought, always treated those they felt inferior to their greatness.

"Firstly, this is a manse, not some Southend hovel, there is plenty to do and see. And I am not suggesting you do not sit on your hands. Avjan-Aluth has stated you can train with her green-bands and my libraries are at your discretion. I only ask for a few meager days, so that I may seek counsel. Is that too much to ask?"

Aellia looked about herself. She could see no alternative here. She either waited and got answers or took the risk of being captured. Surely the Asterverians would not come into Elcon's mansion, or manse, or whatever it was he called this place. Self-righteous prick.

"Fine," she answered with petulance.

"Three or four days," Elcon said. "I'll leave first thing in the morning. Besides, I'll return on the holy day of Ordan. I would much enjoy your company in the Sanctuary upon my arrival."

"Depends on what you bring me," said Aellia without trying to mask her displeasure at the situation.

"Well then, it is settled. I shall be off in the morning," Elcon said happily. "I look forward to diving deeper upon my return."

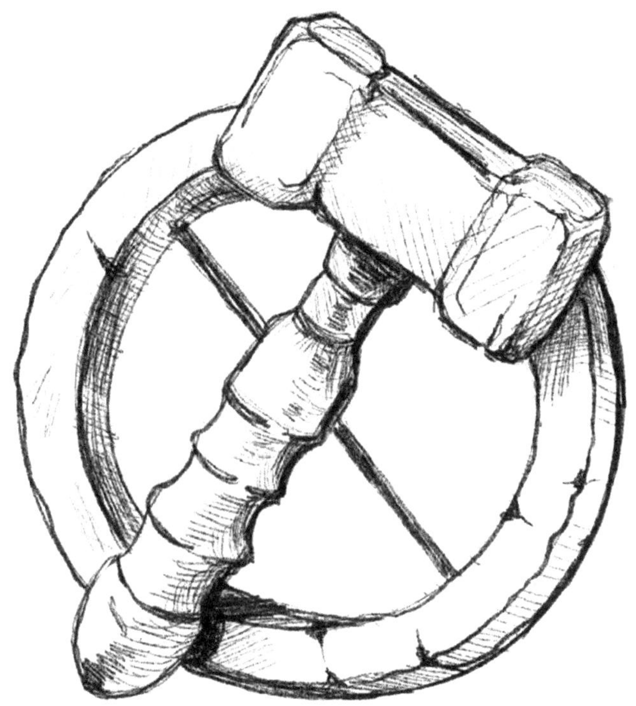

CHAPTER 22: THE ART OF VIOLENCE
DARIUS

Darius ran. He ran and ran and ran. And as he ran, he thought upon the words of Erik within that War Room. A plan. A plan to strike out against the rising darkness. Three days was all he had. Three days until Ulkeniheim. Three days until he would be put in front of Daneland to prove himself, so that when he was stationed next to Erik, none would question his strength of character or his loyalty to Daneland.

A grim smile spread across his lips as he breathed in and out, nostrils flaring. Erik had planned this from the beginning. That man, he was a clever one. Elcon had been wise and learned, but Erik, he was different. He had a magnitude to him, a way that just drew you in, made you want to like him, respect him. How swiftly

had he turned his opinion on Izebal, from Diju witch to welcome guest. How swiftly had he turned the hearts of his court, or at least most of them. Where Elcon had wisdom, Erik had honor. And honor spoke volumes to Darius's soul.

"Pull the lead out of y'er arse and run!" Tyree cried out from the distance, his already alarming loud voice amplified by a conical, flared tube of brass.

Darius winced in chagrin as several other trainees pointed and laughed at him. Children. They were children. Darius was, not counting his cursed slumber, anywhere from ten to twelve years older than those around him.

Let's see them run like this in a decade or two. Judging by their fathers, they'll have guts like ale barrels and legs like tree trunks. Still formidable in a fight, but made for sparring, not running. Danelanders were a hearty lot, and only a select few maintained a lean physique. Strength and honor were apparently fed by red meat and cheese, and required little maintenance outside of tossing massive logs, hefting heavy stones, and drinking. An exorbitant amount of drinking.

After the discussion in the War Room, Erik had invited Darius up to the main hall and there they ate and talked further. Krunlan and Erkan joined them eventually, and they swapped stories and pleasantries as if they had not just beaten a creature half to death in front of him. Krunlan was so much like his uncle, and practically worshipped him, that it was hard for Darius to build a bridge between him and Krunlan. Erkan, on the other hand, was quiet and calm. He sat in silence most of the night, only speaking when directly asked a question. The lad was, in Darius's mind, a picture of his mother's tutelage. Strong and proud, but in a reserved manner, leaning on poise and control, not loud, boisterous flaunting. Despite this, they all drank. Everyone drank and ate, and drank some more. Darius tried to join in, but as always, the alcohol burned through him, and he didn't even feel a tingle for it. The food, on the other hand, he was feeling that now.

"Oye, Outlander," called out a young man with a mustache that looked worse than swamp weed. "Y'er gonna just let that old kook yell at ye like y'er a dog?"

The three boys around him laughed, nudging and slapping him on the back as if he had said some great insult. They all wore the titular plaid and sleeveless shirts, but there was an air of superiority about them that the other trainees on Dwallen Field lacked. Darius had noticed them yesterday, but paid them little heed. They had pointed and sniggered as Talon had instructed him in the art of getting his ass handed to him time and time again. He had a feeling that they were of lesser stock. Why else would they not respect Tyree? Did they even know what he was, what he was capable of doing? Surely not, or else they wouldn't speak about him in such an obtuse manner.

Obtuse manner? Elcon's words, not his. Darius shook his head and tried to keep running. He did not have time for this. Was he not just thinking how much older he was than them? But he still had his pride, and there was a fire in his belly from this running and sparing.

"Pick it up, old man," another called. "Got gray in y'er beard and still ain't proved y'erself?"

"My da says he's an Outlander."

A big lad with shoulders the size of an ox, stood. "Run on, Outlander. Best be thankful. Y'er disrespected me ma and our clan."

Darius stopped dead in his tracks and eyed the hulking boy. His eyes, the way his face came to a point. Halfak burn it. He recognized those features.

"You're Nee'av's boy, aren't you?" Darius asked.

The young man stiffened.

Darius drew in a deep breath. Nee'av had wanted Izebal strung up for witchcraft and had been subsequently humiliated and cast out of Erik's council. This boy was going to be trouble if Darius didn't nip this in the bud. He winced. Another phrase of Elcon's.

"I asked you a question," said Darius, his voice filling with steel.

The three young men bristled, their eyes widening and nostrils flaring. The big one pushed past the other two, moving them as if they were rag dolls.

"Ulkeniheim ain't for three days, Outlander," he said, his voice low and gravely. "But it'll be over my dead body before the likes of y'er gets pinned."

"Listen, boy," Darius snarled as his hands balled into fists. He drew up short. Took a breath. And dropped his hands. "I didn't do anything to you or your mother. I get she was doing her job, and that is all there was."

"Y'er humiliated my ma in front of her commanding officer, in front of the high lord," the big lad countered. He did not loosen his fists and stepped closer as he spoke, his voice dropping lower and lower. "If I had my way, I'd break y'er here and now."

"Bjorne," one of the other two boys called out. "Y'er placed. Don't do nothing stupid now."

The veins in Bjorne's neck pressed against reddening flesh. His eyes were pits of fire. But, to the lad's credit, he stepped back, gaining control of his rage in an impressive manner.

"Ain't worth it," Bjorne agreed with his friend. "I'll have the gold, and I'll get my right. Best believe that, Outlander. Best believe that. Were the Red Dread there, they'd tear ye limb from limb."

"What does being placed mean?" Darius asked Tyree after a much needed drink of lukewarm water from an animal skin.

"Eh?" Tyree said, turning his attention from some distant thought toward Darius.

"Being placed. One of the others said he had a place. What does that mean?"

"Oh, right," Tyree said as he dragged gnarled fingers through his beard. "Those who have placement get t'er chose a name of worth in the last fight, and if they can score a strike against them, they are given a golden pin, like Talon has. It's the highest honor of the Ulkeniheim to do so."

"That's it? Just a golden pin?" Darius asked, slightly taken aback.

"What'er y'er mean, just a golden pin? Are y'er out of y'er bloody mind?" Tyree seemed flabbergasted. For only the second time since knowing the old mage, complete and utter sincerity filled his brutalized face. "It's everything. It's a symbol of strength. Y'er know how many golds there is? No more than twenty that I can think of. And that boy you was talking to, Nee'av's lad. He do be the only one who stands a chance to get one. And if he do, he'll get pinned by High King Sterkamar himself, lord all Daneland. I know folks who'd hack off their left hand for that honor."

"So, what is their problem?" Darius huffed, unable to find the reasoning behind their disdain.

"Their problem? Y'er gotta be denser than molasses in the winter! Lad, ye ate at the High Hall, y'er a decade older than them, ye got real experience. And, as much as it pains me to say it, y'er built of steel. If ye win a gold, ye'd be the first ever Outlander to do so."

And that would be a blow to the pride of every single silver and bronze. Halfak, it would be a blow to the ego of the golds, for they would be no better than him, an Outlander, a stranger to their ways and customs. Chagrin filled Darius's gut. He needed that gold. He needed to be able to go to the Court of the High King, he needed unfettered access to traverse Daneland. He had a purpose, and that was becoming clearer and clearer every day. He needed to find the next Sage, and he was growing more and more suspicious of who that might be. And that thought terrified him.

"Ye see, it's more than them winning, its pride, laddie, and no matter what ye do now, ye've muddied theirs." Tyree shook his head as he ran his gnarled fingers through his beard in contemplation.

Darius looked over at the trio, now several yards away, training together on the heavy stones. An idea formed in his mind, a way forward.

"What's that on y'er face?" Tyree sounded aghast.

Darius lowered his brows, turning his attention back to the old man.

"If I didn't know any better, I would've thought I'd done seen a smile! Bahaha!" Tyree let out a wild cackle.

Darius shrugged his shoulders, allowing the smile to return to his lips. "Maybe you did. Maybe."

***

"In Daneland, those of the Blood are bequeathed weapons of Moonstone, crafted by the moon's fallen tear, to fight against those of darkness," Erik said as he hefted the great spear with both hands. His two hounds pulled at a thigh bone of some great beast; they were never far from their master. "Aithne Lykos, Flame of the Wolf, she do be called. Given to the second son of Dane, my ancestor. Named guardian of the wall and protector of the realm. Undraff, called Darkness Crashing, was given to the youngest son. And then there was Kantuund, the mighty hammer, forged by the hands of the last Iarathor as a gift for our forefather's aid in the Weeping. These three alone are of pure Moonstone. Every other weapon is forged around a shard of the precious ore. But none can smelt the stuff. That knowledge is lost."

Darius's full attention was on the glistening spear head whose pattern reminded him of waves washing over the black sand shores of Morr, not the words which the Lord of Talahmnas spoke. So it came as a bit of surprise when Erik cleared his throat loudly. An action which sent the hounds to their feet and the bone they had wrestled with clattering noisily across the floor of the War Room.

"Laddie," Erik said with a sigh. "Are ye alright? Ye seem to not be focusing."

Darius blanched. It was true. The last two days felt like a haze to him. Between the encounter with the Redeye, Izebal's departure, and exhausting training, Darius hadn't had two moments of reprieve to gather his thoughts.

Erik studied him, his piercing blue eyes boring deep into Darius's. It felt as the man could see straight through him, cutting him to the quick with his gaze. A sensation that felt all the more uncomfortable as a slow smile spread across the man's wide face.

"Ye miss her, don't ye?" Erik asked, thought it felt more a statement than a question.

Darius felt as if his heart had skipped a beat.

"There it is," Erik's slow smile burst into a radiant, thunderous bout of laughter. "Let an old man give a young one some advice. Love is not a fickle thing, and if ye really care for her, just tell her. When I first met my Sophie, I thought the stars had fallen from the sky and formed an angel of light. Those green eyes and that fiery red hair, enough to make a man go weak in the knees and hard as a stone. By Ordan's beard, she did take me then and there. And look at us now, twenty-six years and five piggies later, we're happier than a hog in holler."

Darius couldn't help but smile, seeing the joy and memories in Erik's beaming face. His father had been that way too. He had been so proud of his wife and family. He had loved them fiercely, and died to insure their safety. What Darius would give now to talk to him one more time, to ask him how he knew mother was the right one. To seek his guidance in matters of the heart.

"She's a pretty one, laddie," Erik said as he placed a hand on Darius's shoulder. "Strong and bold. Don't let that pass ye by. It'll eat y'er heart out and poison y'er mind."

Darius, unsure of what to do or say in this situation, nodded. He felt like a fool. It was as if he should say some wise or profound thing, proclaim his feelings or … anything. But words, yet again, failed him.

"Enough of love," Erik said, returning his hand to his spear, lifting it and placing it gently on the stand over his chair. He turned back and faced Darius, face serious once more. "Ye have Moonstone, or Ellitheor Silver as ye do call it, and I've got an idea percolating in my brain that ye do have some knowledge of how to make a weapon worthy of the fight we near."

Right. Weapons, war, and death. That was what Darius was here for, wasn't it? It was what he was born for. Forged and beaten into it. A tool. A weapon of the great Ellitheor. The god's hammer that strikes the hardest.

"Our rings were forged before my people wrote their histories. But it was told they were crafted by the combined power of the Kelpie and Daulkaefar, along with the blood of the Ellitheor. I have no more knowledge or skill in this matter than you do. I am sorry."

"Kelpie?" Erik asked, as if he hadn't heard anything else Darius had just said. "What in the pit is a Kelpie?"

Darius blinked in confusion. How could they not know what a Kelpie was? It was one thing for the people of Tur'Mor with their Church and industry, their forges and factories, to be ignorant of such things. But these who lived on the fringes of the wyld? These who fought against the creatures of darkness and legends? How could they not know?

"Well, out with it, laddie!" Erik said, his thick eyebrows knitting together.

"Kelpie are..." Darius started. How would one describe a Kelpie? He had never thought about that before. His mother had told him of them. The village elder had spoken of the divine creatures with hallowed reverence, her words filled with mysticism and wonder. Yet none of them had truly described the creature. And his own experience, when he had sworn the Oaths beneath the surface of the highest pool of the Iron Mountains, was as a dream in his memories.

"Are what?" Erik blurted out. "I got draugr, goblin, wylven and now Redeyes and bloody-damned Soulless marching on my boarders. Spit out what's stuck behind them gums of y'ers, or I might have to knock it out of the back of y'er head."

Darius actually let out a laugh at the man's words, surprising both himself and Erik, who in turn burst into ruckus laughter.

"Kelpie are guides between the realms, keepers of oaths and pacts between mortals and the divine," Darius started once more. "They are older than the mountains, and more prideful than the

rivers whose patience and tenacity can carve their will through the heart of the earth. They are the elders of this world, having walked across the valleys before men, beasts, and gods."

"Well," Erik said with wrapped mysticism in his voice. "That truly was a loud of flowery horse-shite that didn't tell me a damn thing. How did they make that ring of y'ers and can we use whatever it is ye do when ye go all glowy to make Moonstone into blades or heads?"

"I've told you and your mage this before: I cannot conduct or store my abilities." Darius tried to hold back the frustration that had begun to well up within him. "As far as using it to smelt the ore, I'd burn out far before I could even come close to that level of heat."

"But what if ye weren't holding the power? What if we could channel y'er abilities into something else?" Erik asked as a mischievous grin split across his face.

"I don't know how you could?" Darius began.

"Don't ye worry about the how part." Erik cut Darius off mid-thought, barreling over his words in a tirade of excitement. "Answer the could part. If we were able to do it, could ye teach us how to make such a thing as y'er ring? As this spear?"

"I—" Darius started. His words failed him as a myriad of thoughts crashed over him. Could he? He had been told stories of how the First Oaths had been sworn and the forging of the twelve sacred rings. Myths perhaps, but in every tale, there is a modicum of truth. And if there was a truth he could exploit, then perhaps he could do some real good. Provide some semblance of hope. Even the thought of doing so filled a void in Darius's heart, gave him some measure of light where so much darkness and despair had welled. "Ellitheor Silver is formed of three elements. Ore from Vanherran, of which you have. Blood of the ancestors, which flows through my veins. And the blood of the Ellitheor."

Darius watched as Erik put two and two together, and as the hope subsequently drained from the man's proud face. Ore they had a plenty, and blood of the ancestors could be freely given. But how did one go about obtaining blood from a god? Darius wracked his brain, thinking over every possible scenario. It was for that reason that the warriors of his tribe had used Moonstone as crude, chipped weapons, tethered and bound to hilts of antler and wood. They had experimented, just as these Danelanders had, with foreign weapons of iron around chunks of Moonstone. It was not ideal, but it did the job.

"But the ore still harnesses the power of the sun," Erik said, hope reforming in his words. "If we could smelt it, we could form weapons of quality that didn't crack and warp. We could cast bullets, forge swords longer than my hand. Darius, think on it. An army with weapons made for slaying demons and creatures of corruption."

Darius did think on it. Erik was right. Perhaps they would not harness the full power that items forged of pure Ellitheor Silver did. Perhaps it would not work, and the process might fail. But that would not put them anywhere but where they were now.

Hope. Darius could offer hope. All he had to do was something he had been told his whole life was impossible.

"What would you have me do?"

"Come with me, laddie," said Erik as he grabbed a heavy cloak from the rack near the door and wrapped it around his broad shoulders. He then took up Darius's trench coat and handed it to him. "I have one more thing to show ye."

***

The bell of Tyree's shop rang out as Erik pushed open the door. A rush of warm air and stifling fumes filled the void between shop and the small porch, cascading over Darius and assaulting his senses once more. His eyes watered and the back of his throat burned as he pushed forward behind Erik into a haze of steam, stink, and humidity.

"Gallae's breath! What in the pit are ye do'n in here, ye old badger?" Erik croaked out. This was followed by an uncontrollable bought of coughing.

Tyree, who was behind what looked to be a bronze chalice that was large enough to bathe in and thick enough so that not even Erik's hands could grasp around the lip of it, glanced up with wild glee in his eyes. Boiling purplish-grey liquid fogged the many-lensed goggles on the mage, all of which were turned away from his naked, gleaming eyes.

"I've did it!" Tyree exclaimed in triumph. "I done it? I've doing it? Whatever the Halfak it is, it is boiling!"

"We can see that," Erik said, raising the cloak he wore over his mouth. "But what is boiling?"

"What is boiling, that do be..."

Tyree's voice seemed to fade away into nothingness. Pressure filled Darius's ears, as if he had both suddenly ascended the highest peak of Ethrea and been plunged to the depths of the Western Sea. A throbbing pain pulsated down his spine, burning throughout his body and locking his muscles.

Thump thump!

Thump thump!

Darius's eyes flew wide.

"What is that?" The question burst out of him, as if he had no control over his body, the words raspy and raw.

Erik and Tyree turned to face him with furrowed brows and confusion etched into their faces.

"What was what?" Tyree asked.

"Y'er alright?" Asked Erik simultaneously.

Darius pressed his hand to his forehead. It felt like drums beating behind his ears. The ring on his finger burned with an icy chill, sending a tremor through his sweating hand.

Keyholder! A voice called out in the back of his mind, ephemeral, feminine, and chilling.

Find them!

"Ack!" Darius nearly toppled over as the room swam before his eyes.

Find them!

Keyholder!

Darius covered his ears with his hands. Darkness ate at the sides of his vision. Something toppled as his back slammed into a hard surface, falling and shattering upon the floor. Agony exploded from within his chest, as if a fire were blazing from within his bosom. This was followed by a lance of pain in his abdomen that sent him to his knees, his body crumpling around the hurt.

"Blood and stones!" Erik called out in alarm as he rushed forward toward where Darius had fallen, the mage whirling behind him.

Erik placed a hand on Darius's brow, but jerked it back, letting out a hiss of pain as he did so. "He's burning up!"

Thump thump!

"Can't you hear it?" whimpered Darius. "Can't you hear it?"

"Hear what?" asked Erik. The lord's voice was filled with concern and fear. "What is going on, laddie?"

Darius saw the god from his dreams, chained to the floor. There were six chains, though one had been broken. Another two had weakened. The girl from Tur'Mor. She had held something, a living thing that was not alive. It had a soul, a heartbeat. The chains were breaking. He was the Keyholder. But what did that mean? What was he to do?

More pain, each wave more exquisite than the last, washed over him. His mouth was dry. His throat burned. His ring was so cold it felt as if it would slice clean through his finger.

It was night. He needed to free the beast.

No! Not here. What would it fight?

Find them, or blood shall rain!

Keyholder!

"Ghaz-kant jbron!" cried out a voice from behind closed doors, piteous, yet gleeful. "Ghaz-kant jbron! The Mistress is with us!"

"I. Need. Out." Each word tore out of Darius' throat, the next more painful than the last. Something was warring within Darius's body, and that Redeye was turning his emotions into a cesspit of rage. He needed air. Now.

Erik stood as if he had been struck by lightning. "Master Tyree, clear a path!"

The mage wheeled about, pushing a path clear as Erik hoisted Darius over his shoulder. The man let out a grunt of exertion but lifted him with shocking ease. "We'll get ye outside, laddie, just hang on."

"Moonlight. Then run." Darius's words were disjointed.

"Just stay with me, laddie." Erik's voice was strained as he shoved past the toppled shelves and strewn mess that Darius had caused without realizing.

A chilling breeze turned the hot sweat that soaked Darius body icy cold. They were outside. He could feel the rays of moonlight stretching down toward him, beckoning him to release and become one with his inner beast. He could be free of the pain, the anguish, if he just let go.

Erik lowered him to the ground. They were behind Tyree's shop, atop a small hill in a field surrounded by an old-stone wall that was covered with moss. Fog rose from the night ground, casting the yard into an eerie scene.

"Go!" Darius growled the command, using all his strength to fight down the beast. "Get that thing away from me or there will be nothing left!"

"What are you—" Erik began.

"The Redeye," Darius snarled. He could feel the ache, the need taking him. The words were there, just at the back of his mind. "It's in there!"

"How did ye—?" Tyree stammered as lines of worry creased his already confused face.

"He was with us in the War Room," Erik answered, his eyes not leaving Darius, though he had taken one or two steps away from him.

"But how did he know?"

"Didn't you hear him?" Darius was on all fours, clenching at the dirt and grass for support that would not be given. "Didn't you hear him taunting me?"

"Darius," Tyree said with narrowed. "That thing do be under two tons of stone and steel. It's chained and huffing aethyic herb, higher than a Zau'fi kite!"

No... no, no, no. Something was wrong. Very, very wrong.

A long, hollow thud reverberated throughout valley of Talahmnas, emanating from the raised gatehouse's tower bell. It was followed by two more spaced out notes, each strike causing Erik's eyes to widen more and more.

"That's..." Erik muttered, as if more to himself than either Darius or Tyree. "From Ranok?"

"Lord Ruthvin," Tyree sat fully erect in his chair, his wild features filled with intense concern. "That do be—"

"I know what it means!" Erik cut off the other.

Horns began to sound around the city, pealing note after note of urgency. Darius wanted to tear his ears off his head. The sound hurt him in ways he could not comprehend.

"Ghaz-kant jbron!"

Understanding. *She who walks with us.* Darius was not sure how he understood the words, but he did. Perfectly.

"They're coming," he croaked. "They're coming."

Erik reached a hand behind his back and slid his great spear from over his shoulder. He didn't wear armor or helm, but he looked like a fierce warrior if Darius had ever seen one.

"Erik," Darius's voice was so harsh and raspy he barely recognized it himself. "Whatever is coming, only fire or Moonstone can kill it."

CHAPTER 23: DEATH UPON US COMES
ERIK

The bell tolled low, her melancholy cry reverberating through the walled city he called home. White hot anger coursed through his veins at each hollow strike, every ringing note a mockery of his way of life, his people, his family.

"Laddie," Erik called out to the Outlander. The poor lad was bent over, clawing at his ears and carrying on about something or other to do with the Redeye under Tyree's shop. Erik was certain that one was the least of their worries. If the bells tolled atop the gatehouse of Talahmnas, they had much bigger stones to toss. "Get up off y'er arse! Ye said y'er made for fight'n these black devils. We'll time to put hands on words and get to get'n!"

The lad looked up, no more than a few years older than his own two sons. But he had a harrowing in his yellow eyes, a depth that came from seeing things ye can't unsee. Erik had that same harrowed expression, but by the gods, hopefully he hid it better than this one. Life was like that, filled with moments of golden goodness, but ever marred by streaks of darkness.

"It's calling them," said Darius, his fingertips bloodied from his insistent clawing. "It's calling them!"

Erik, not sure what else to do, did the only thing that made sense in the moment. With all the firmness of a loving father, he drove the butt of his spear into the earth, took two strides, grabbed Darius by the shoulders, lifted him to his feet, and struck him across the face as hard as he could with an open-handed slap.

The strike rang out nearly as loud as the bell tower, and to the lad's credit, he maintained his consciousness, though his eyes rolled around a good many times.

"Get y'erself together, laddie! A hoard of Draugr do be marchin' on the gates and we ain't got the luxury of time on our hands to piddle with."

Darius's eyes snapped into focus. And though Erik still propped the lad up by the shoulders, he could see a manic rage narrowed into icy focus. A glint of something wild flashed behind the young man's eyes, something more than emotion. Actual power, an arc of something white-gold, shining bright as the moonlight.

"The Redeye calls them, laddie, we know that," Erik said as the lad's focus honed in on him. He took out a small tin from his sporran. He twisted open the lid and took a long draw on the acrid fumes. Clarity filled his own mind before he extended it to Darius. "They affect our mood and minds, they control the hordes. But we ain't got time to worry about the one under Tyree's shop. I need it alive. We do have to halt whatever be pushing upon my gates."

Darius eyed the extended tin, looking warily at its contents. Something flashed behind the lad's eyes once more, this time Erik was certain of it. The boy then put out a hand and pressed away the tin, saying, "I have an answer for these, but I need to get outside the walls."

The lad's voice trembled, as if he were suppressing something. And why had he not taken the salts? They would break the hold the bloody Redeye had on him. Magic ring or not, there was no way this lad could do much against a horde of Draugr.

"Laddie, the Skogotuers are called, it takes no less than ten minutes for them to muster," Erik said as he took back up his great spear. "We'll meet them at the gatehouse and defend it together."

"Erik, I need to get to that gatehouse." The boy's voice was nearing pleading, a desperate craze filling every word. "I need it!"

"I told y'er, laddie, until ye complete the Ulkeniheim, ye ain't permitted out of these walls without escort."

"You asked what else I can do," Darius said, his voice turned low and dark. "Let me show you. I need to. It's more than the Redeye. Something is burning me from the inside out. I need to release it. I need it!"

Erik stared at the boy, studying him. It went against everything, every law and ordinance. It was his responsibility, his duty, to protect and secure the Borderlands. To watch over Daneland and her people. To ensure that no Outlanders stepped awry under his watch, so that they could exist in peace and seclusion. This was the pact made when they had joined the Republic generations ago. Would he be the one to break that pact? This was not just a road-weary traveler. He bore the golden hammer of the Church of Ordan. He carried letters sealed by the Patriarch's own hand. This was more than he had a right to choose. He had a duty to stop the lad if anything.

But that fire in the boy's eyes, it struck him to the center. There was something about the lad that made Erik trust him. A certain goodness and honor than was deeper than blood and bone, tougher than steel and sinew. This was a boy of good stock, of whom any father would be proud.

"Tyree!" Erik barked, not breaking his gaze with Darius.

The old mage hurried over to their side, his wheeled chair whirling into life, casting a faint glow of blue and green. Erik had never really taken the time to understand exactly how it all worked, the manipulation and distribution of Everlight and Lifelight, and tonight was not the time for learning but for action.

"I need a charge," Erik said with a dark smile. "And then show our guest out the back door. I do believe he has something up that there sleeve of his."

Upon uttering the words, the young man's face flooded with relief. This was followed by an immediate regaining of composure. "Thank you," Darius said, his words heavy with resolution and resolve.

"Laddie," Erik said as he rolled up a sleeve to reveal a triple-woven knot of pale blue ink. "I'm trusting ye with this. Please, don't disappoint me."

Tyree's gnarled hand took hold of the meat of Erik's bare arm. A surge of power rushed through his very flesh as the head of Tyree's scepter pressed Everlight into the tattoo. The boy's eyebrows lifted at this, and Erik couldn't hold back a smile.

"Protection rune," Erik said as he rolled his sleeve down, the tattoo shining with faint light, winding all the way down to his wrist. "Imbued with Everlight. Keeps the Draugr's bite from rot'n me arm off. The next will be a little more painful," he said as he rolled up his other sleeve.

The cold press of the scepter's head and the subsequent jolt of power made Erik grit his teeth. As the Everlight scorched the surface of his skin, weaving its path down the blue lines of a rage wolf's head howling, he could feel his muscles fill with strength.

"And this'll take the edge off," Erik barked out with a laugh. "The edge being the whole of their bloody-damned heads!"

Tyree, uncharacteristically, did not join in the laughter, but eyed Darius with consternation etched heavily into his ancient face. Did he always look so old and weary?

"Master Mage," Erik said as he hefted his spear from the ground. "Take 'im through the back tunnel. He said he has something to help us. Let's see what the lad is truly made of."

"Ye think that wise, Erik?" Tyree asked.

Erik inhaled sharply, but let it out with a long, low breath. "Draugr at the gates, Soulless in the trees. I don't have time to worry about one lad who ain't done naught but help since he arrived. Take him to the back and then get that engine of y'ers a burn'n. We're gonna need it if the bells already do be a toll'n."

"It ain't ready yet, Erik," Tyree argued.

"You won't need it."

Both men turned once more to face the Outlander. Grim determination was plastered across his face. His right hand opened and closed again and again, and his thumb slid over that Moonstone ring. After tonight, Erik swore he would understand how that was made. And more importantly, how he could make better weapons for occasions just as this one. But there wasn't time. Not now.

"Off with ye both!" commanded Erik. "I go to the gate. If the Skogotuers have failed us, it will be me and the guards who will hold them."

"And what of the Berzerk?" Tyree asked. "Shall I call for them?"

Erik's heart faltered at the question. It was the right thing. But thought would mean putting his Lori in danger. If he failed to secure the gate, they would be in danger all the same.

"Yes," he said coldly. "Call forth the Berzerk, and let's send these black demons back to Halfak's gates in pieces."

***

Erik stood atop the gatehouse of the Spanning Wall. He had ridden hard from Talahmnas with two dozen of his men-at-arms and was now scanning the killing ground between Ranok's distant trees and the tower upon which he stood. The low, rolling hills provided little cover for any who would approach. Beside him stood hulking Krarraek and his two silent sentinels. His two hounds, whom he had fondly named Trip and Nip, stood in their battle-leathers, drool dripping from massive maws.

"Where's the little lad?" Krarraek asked, his green eyes focused forward. Erik did not miss the disdain in his brother-in-law's deep voice. His veins bulged behind corded muscle as he squeezed the haft of his halberd whose spike was formed from a shard of moonstone. "Scared of a little tussle, is he?"

"He has his reasons," Erik countered, his focus ahead of him. The boy had his secrets, and it weren't his right to tell them to no one, not even his brother.

"I don't know why y'er keep 'im around," Krarraek said. "And he came with the Diju. Where is she now?"

"Krak," Erik said with a sigh. He turned to face his brother. "We settled this. We all agreed upon it. They saved Little Ery, when y'er and I couldn't."

Krarraek swallowed hard at that. Little Ery was his brother-in-law's favorite niece, and seeing as he didn't have children of his own, Krarraek had taken Ery's loss especially hard. Even when she had returned, Krarraek kept coming by the High Hall every morning before sunrise to check on Erik and his family. He was a good man, and Erik loved him for his tenacity and strength, but sometimes the brute couldn't see past others' differences. Halifax burn it, sometimes Erik couldn't either. But he was at least trying.

"Maybe," Krarraek said. "That's what they said. But look here now. Draugr and Redeye on the borders. Weren't none before they arrived. None dared come this close, Beyorne being all they'd risk their lifeless necks for."

Erik saw the faintest motion far off in the distance. Riders. The Skogotuers were coming back, which meant the forest line was lost. As they drew closer, Erik realized it was only a dozen or so. Death had come upon them, else they would not have fled. There had been over fifty hardened warriors at the front. What in the pit could have taken out a whole squadron of Skogotuers?

"Y'er seeing what I'm seeing?" Krarraek's question was filled with anger and sadness. Those where his people. As Captain Commander, he was over the Skogotuers and had taken it upon himself to get to know each one of his charges on a personal level.

"Blood and bloody stones," Erik hissed.

Krarraek lifted a bronze looking-tube to his eye. "Nee'av and Orhund ride. That do be Kal, Redick, and Freyjan. Blood and stone, I don't see Helath or Tiny, nor Stern or Ferja. I swear. I'll rip the heads off of every bone-walker that crosses that field."

Krarraek's knuckles whitened around the haft of his halberd. Unlike Erik, who did not wear his official armor and had draped a mail shirt and coif over himself, Krarraek was in full plate and had donned a war-kilt of leather and mail. His greaves shone in the moonlight, which was bright and silver in a cloudless sky. Hundreds of stars glistened, casting light upon the killing field before them.

The Skogotuers rode hard, their horses flying across the sea of grass. A cold breeze reminded Erik that spring had not quite made it to Daneland. He shivered at the touch of the icy wind as it caressed his face. That shiver turned into a bone-chilling fear, for upon the wind rode the scent of death. A smell Erik knew all too well.

"Open the gates!" roared Krarraek, the Skogotuers close enough now that Erik could see their forms without aid of looking glass.

A low note was struck upon the massive gong that hung atop the tower's crenelated peak, reverberating through the very stone upon which they stood. Both portcullises rose to the crank of chain and the grinding of gears. Hoofbeats thundered as they passed under the archway. Erik looked down between the murder holes, watching the remaining of his elite warriors as they trailed into Daneland proper, his heart heavy with the loss.

"Sure'em up, now!" barked Krarraek. He turned and whispered into Erik's ear, his voice low and serious. "We don't have enough here now. Maybe eighty strong. Where are the Berzerk? We need horse and shot."

"I set them to defend Talahmnas's gate," Erik said, eyes steadily forward, watching as shadows began to writhe along the tree line.

"Y'er did what?" Krarraek looked as if he had been struck across the face.

"I left Erkan in charge of the High Hall and the Berzerk to guard the city walls."

"Blood and bloody-stones! Erik…" Krarraek's voice filled with concern and doubt. And the way he looked at Erik, disappointment riddling his face. It shook Erik to the core.

"I have a duty to defend my people as I see fit. I cannot risk them here." Erik spoke with more surety than he felt.

"Erik, you've doomed us to die here," Krarraek stepped back away from him as he spoke. "What have y'er done?"

"Brother," Erik felt the word catch in his throat. He swallowed back hard, meeting Krarraek's disappointed eyes. "I have to protect my family, our families."

"If the Wall falls, how is that gonna protect anyone?" Krarraek's voice was rising.

Trip and Nip stood, their hackles rising as they began to pace around their master's feet.

"Easy boys," Erik said, placing a hand on the droopy ears of Nip's head, giving them a rub. "Easy."

"I asked ye a bloody question," Krarraek pressed.

"We have cannon, gun, pike and spear," Erik said, finding resolve once more. He bolstered himself, filling his mind with that indomitable spirit his father had left him with. "The Wall won't fall. Not tonight."

"They took out a whole squadron of Skogotuers. They don't run lightly, Erik. Do ye even know what's coming?"

Erik slid this spear through his hands, running his fingers across the familiar, smooth surface. He looked at the head, the pattern-forged work of ancient artistry that seemed more magic than mastery. Hope filled his chest. This spear had seen him through fight after fight. It would not fail him tonight.

"Doesn't matter what comes or goes, Krak," Erik said firmly. "We meet it and do what we do best."

Krarraek drew in a deep breath through his nose and nodded his head. "I ain't never been out done by a soft-footed royal type. Ain't gonna start tonight. Ye think we can hold the Wall, then blood and stone, we'll hold the Wall."

"That's the spirit. Now, get down there and get y'er caps straightened out," Erik said, calling the Skogotuers by their nickname in a hope to continue to raise the spirits of his brother-in-law and show that the impending foe was of no worry to him. "We need guns up here, and someone get the pyre's burning. We're gonna have a good ole shoot'n tonight!"

"Aye!" Krarraek spread a toothy smile from behind that mop of a red, curly beard. "A shoot'n we'll have indeed!"

Not more than five minutes had passed when the first cries of torment filled the night. What had once been writhing shadows slowly morphed into the forms of disturbing creatures of the pit. Some had bodies of bone, their black eye sockets misting maroon light. Those would be the Draugr. Other were impish little devils with rows of razor-sharp teeth and putrid-yellow eyes the size of Erik's fists. Bloody goblins. And then there were four figures cloaked in patchwork robes of flesh who rode atop massive grey wylven whose fur hung like icicles and whose dead eyes were sightless balls of jelly. Redeyes.

"Ready the cannon!" roared Erik.

Half a dozen cannons swiveled on platforms.

"Send these little chutlings back to the pit!"

Boom! Six cannon's blasted in perfect harmony. The song of death had begun, ushered in by cannon fire. The accompanying *crack* of Skogortuer long-rifles filled the night with lead and smoke, adding their tune to the deadly melody.

"Somebody give us a beat to sing too!" Erik shouted, his voice filled with dark glee as he watched the swarm of fiends blasting apart.

Two drummers snapped their snares, their tempo fast and sharp. Roll upon roll they played, their beat carrying the feet of those behind Erik as they moved powder and shot to the cannons, priming wicks and loading barrels. Atop the tower, near where the massive gong hung, a piper picked up his sheepskin sack and blared a tune that would raise the hair on any Ordan-fearing man's neck, filling their hearts with vigor and vim.

Pride welled in Erik's chest as he watched the onslaught of death that fell upon his foe. There was no quarter allotted to these fiends. They weren't men, but demons. They had no hope or life in them. And he would personally see to their swift eradication.

His smile faded though as the tide of undead and goblins did not wane. More and more came forth. To make matters worse, those Draugr that had been struck down hefted their mutilated bodies up from the dirt, crawling, dragging, or limping their way forward. Erik snarled in frustration.

"Why don't these bloody chutlings just die already?" he roared into the night. "Get the canisters! We'll send these pit-lickers back to Halfak's gates in pieces!"

Large, brass canisters were hauled up to the cannons. They were placed with powder behind them and driven down the barrel. Erik's grim smile widened as he looked upon Tyree's latest scheme, this one making instantaneous sense to Erik's warring mind. Crushed moonstone was packed into those tubes with a charge of Everlight-infused crystal. The result: one hell of an explosion that could rend demon and beast alike. A blast that not even a Draugr could rise from.

"Fire!" Krarraek shouted.

A hum filled the air as six canisters struck the ground. This was followed by a blinding flash of azure light, as if lightning had sprung up from the very earth itself. There is a unique phenomenon, Erik then learned, when moonstone is super-heated with Everlight. It bursts into the most brilliantly dazzling flash of light imaginable.

White spots filled his vision for long moments after the concussive blast sounded. When they faded, Erik looked upon a field of mangled corpses, shattered bones, and smoldering flesh.

"That was a big damn explosion," Krarraek said as he slapped Erik on the back. "I feel like a bloody fool for doubting ye."

Not even the Redeyes stood. Nothing stood. Nothing moved. Nothing cried out. There was only death and silence under a watching moon. Erik had won an astounding victory without losing one soul at the Wall. He couldn't believe his eyes.

"Someone better tell Tyree they didn't work," Erik said after a few more blinks to clear his vision. Despite himself, he could not hold back the bursting fit of laughter. "The old mage's head'll explode with pride if he finds out about this!"

"By hammer and stone, Erik! The whole world is gonna find out about this," Krarraek's mouth was wide, all smiles and laughter. His eyes then went as wide as his smile, "Wait until Lord Sterkamar hears of this! Erik, by Ordan's stones, this changes everything!"

A low, keening cry rang out from the trees, far in the distance.

Both men turned back to the killing field and stared at something beyond words, beyond terror, beyond imagination. A hulking thing, more bestial than man, larger than an ox and coated in what looked like boiling tar, trudged forward on cloven hooves.

"What in Halfak's pit is that?" Krarraek gasped, his smile devolving into a grim snarl.

"Don't matter," Erik spat. "Canister!"

"Me Lord, only one left!" cried a gunner, whose face was darkened with powder blasts.

The Soulless—for what else could it be—ran forward at breakneck speeds. It used its abnormally long arms to propel itself, its hooves kicking up clods of dirt and grass as it let out a two-tone bleating call.

All atop the wall fell silent at the cry, a terrible stillness taking hold of all that stood in defense of Daneland. Erik, too, stood motionless, his bones filled with lead and fear, his muscles constricted with dread.

Closer and closer came the beast, not breaking in speed to look left or right as it crunched the bones of Draugr and goblin alike. Again it bleated, the horrid sound filling every fiber of Erik's being with fear.

This was it, Erik could feel it. There was no hope, no stopping a creature such as this. What could he do? What could any mortal man do in the face of such dark magic, such death and evil. Yet, even as he stared down in, shackled in unrelenting terror, a memory flashed before his eyes. He saw his daughter, little Ery, her skin pale and lifeless, her eyes dim.

Rage replaced fear. And though the fiend continued its morose bleating, the spell that had bound his body in place was shattered. Strength filled his arms and legs. Agony tore at him as he forced his body to move, his legs to pump and his arms to grab at the bronze canister that had toppled to the ground. Pain seared his sinew, his

ligaments protesting every motion, as he hoisted the shot up and into the cannon's barrel.

"Krak!" Erik cried out, his throat burning with exertion. "Help!"

Krarraek, who up until this point had stood stock-still like every other woman and man atop the wall, turned his head in Erik's pleading direction. Erik gasped as he saw Krarraek hollow, glassy eyes, just like Ery's had been. More anger, more hatred, more animosity boiled within Erik's veins, driving the fear the Soulless cast further and further out of his system.

"Help me turn the gun," Erik called out, his throat finding new strength in his rage.

As if his whole body had been encased in ice, Krarraek flexed his overly-muscular body, shattering the spell all at once. Fire filled the big man's eyes, turning them to a blazing green once more. Heat flushed through his skin, reddening his cheeks and flushing veiny neck. "I. Will. Break. That. Bloody—"

Krarraek's words failed him as he stumbled forward. With a mighty heave, both men pushed the cannon so that the barrel faced the Soulless head on. Krarraek lifted as Erik used a set of iron sights to mark the creature's trajectory.

"Rot in Halfak's pit!" Erik snarled as he brought a smoldering torch to the fuse.

The cannon roared flames and thunder. The canister soared through the air, hurtling toward the Soulless One at a near imperceptible speed. Erik watched in grim satisfaction, knowing the destination would blast the creature into oblivion.

With uncanny speed, the Soulless One twisted about, extending one of its gangly arms and catching hold of the canister. It used the projectile's speed and force to flip itself about and, to Erik's horror, hurl the thing back at them.

The bronze cylinder struck the wall just beneath Erik and Krarraek's feet. Whether it was divine wisdom or supernatural reflexes, Erik's body moved without thought or command. He hurled himself into Krarraek, tackling the bigger man at his waist and driving him over the edge of the wall.

The two plummeted downward as a deafening explosion shook the wall upon which they had stood only a second before. Stone and sparks flew through the air, along with parts and pieces of those warriors who had been rooted in fear upon the wall.

Erik struck the ground, the impact driving the air from his lungs as the full weight Krarraek's body landed atop his own. The tattoos upon his body shone with a bright flash of blue, then faded back unto their dull ink coloration.

The warding rune was expired, but Erik lived. His ears rang and his body ached, but he lived. With shaking hands, he touched Krarraek's neck. There was a pulse, but the fall had knocked the big man senseless and he lay limp atop Erik's own prone body.

"Lord Ruthvin!" cried out a man whom he swore he knew, though he could not focus his thoughts in any one direction so as to place the man's name.

"I'm fine," Erik groaned, rolling Krarraek off of himself with the other's help.

"The wall, it's breached," the man said as he stared down in concern at Erik. "What happened? What are we to do?"

Erik's focus snapped into place. He saw clearly in an instant. There was no time. Their one hope had just become the tool of the enemy, to not only breach the wall but to massacre half of her defenders. Frantically, Erik looked about him, searching for anything or anything to stop the rampaging demon.

Aithne Lykos lay several measures away, the head of the spear buried to the shaft in the earth. Grim determination filled Erik's soul. He would not allow this beast to tear through his homeland, befoul his people, nor harm his family.

"My spear," Erik pointed as he rose to his feet. "I just need—"

Erik's words were cut short as the Soulless leapt through the gaping hole it had formed in the wall. Its eyes leaked a terrible maroon light, its teeth dripping ichor. Antlers like that of a magnificent stag protruded out of oily flesh that seemed to be sloshed over a bony head. Between the antlers, a singular, spiraling silver horn protruded, covered in burning red runes. The beast bleated out, and as it did so, its flesh rippled, and Erik swore he saw the harrowing faces of screaming men within.

Fear lanced Erik's heart, plummeting his mind into despair. There was no hope. How could he stand against this?

No! Not again! He just needed to...

A roar split the night. It was a deep, bestial thing that reverberated across the whole of the courtyard. The Soulless looked up, its bleeding eyes widening with confusion. Then filling with fear.

Erik watched in stunned awe as if from nowhere, a gigantic black bear, far larger than any he had ever seen before, raced toward the Soulless. The bear's eyes seemed to blaze with golden light, twin flames burning with all the fury of a raging inferno. The Soulless, whose fear-filled face had swiftly turned into one set on a fight, reared up on its cloven hooves and bleated out a bone-chilling cry.

The bear bounded forward, leaping off its hind legs, and crashed into the Soulless, sending them both toppling back over the Spanning Wall and into the killing field on the other side.

Erik, unsure what he had just seen, found the strength and courage to rise once more. As he did so, he noticed that all about him were scrambling to their feet, shaking their heads as if they were roused from a deep slumber. Confusion and concern marred their faces. But upon meeting his eyes, each Danelander's face hardened into understanding. There was still a fight to be had.

"To the gate!" Erik roared, breaking the final vestiges of the spell.

Orhund, the man who had spoken to Erik earlier, thrust the haft of Aithne Lykos to him. Erik caught it with deft hands, and as his fingers wound their way around the familiar wooden haft, strength filled his body once more.

"To the gate!" He cried once more. "Open the gate!"

Huge gears turned as the double portcullises were lifted. There would be no army to face, but a singular demon. Erik would show the fiend the true strength of Danelander pride.

With nearly two dozen men, his hounds, who had made it off the wall unscathed thanks to his iron sentinels guard them from the blast, Erik stood steady as the rising iron and wooden bars showed the devastation before them.

Erik was just about to call out a final rallying cry, but words died on his woolen tongue. Awe-struck once more as he beheld two titans of myth and legend clashing before his very eyes.

The Soulless slashed out with its bony hands, tearing strips of flesh and fur from the enormous bear's flank. The bear roared in agony, but brought its own paws, whose claws looked like glistening, curved swords, down upon the fiend. There was a terrible crunch that filled Erik's soul with righteous indignation. The Soulless stumbled backwards, its hands fumbling with its own entrails as it bleated in agony, ichor pouring upon the killing field. The bear bit into the neck of the creature, tossing its head back and forth, showering itself with black blood that hissed and steamed off of the bear's fur.

Even from this distance, Erik could smell the stench of it all, the death and decay. It was sickening. But he did not turn away, nor did he move forward, but watched with riveted anticipation of what would come next.

Battered, bleeding, and mostly dismembered, the Soulless stumbled to the ground. It cried a crooning cry that sent shivers down Erik's spine. The bear did not heed the cry, but roared over it. So loud and thunderous was the roar that the very ground shook beneath Erik's feet. Then, in the pale light of the moon, the bear bit down once more on the Soulless's neck and wrenched its head free from its body in one final motion.

A cheer went up amongst the Danelanders, a rallying cry that could have awoken the dead. Though Erik sincerely hoped the field would not come alive, he could not help but add his voice to the exclamation. Despite all odds, they stood and so did the Wall and Talahmnas.

The bear turned to face them, the wildfire in its eyes still burning. The cheers instantly died as a hush washed over the crowd. Erik tightened his grip upon Aithne Lykos, but did not move into a defensive position. It took one step toward them; the silver streak under its maw was drenched in black ichor. Rising upon its hind legs, the bear released a roar that sent the hairs on the back of Erik's neck erect. And in that instant, Erik knew exactly what, or more importantly, who, that bear truly was. Perhaps the people of Danelander were truly no longer alone in this war against the darkness.

CHAPTER 24: THE STOOL AND THE TWIST
AELLIA

Aellia walked the dark, cobbled streets of Southend. She wore a hood and strip of white cloth over her left eye, hiding the scar from the world, from herself. It still hurt, not badly, but a constant aching sensation accompanied by a relentless itch. Flickering lights from brass lamps lining the streets cast shifting shadows, but Aellia walked in the open, unafraid for her wellbeing.

Women and men ambled about, some swaying from liquor, others with heads down and hands pressed into pockets. They all wore drab greys, browns, and blues. There were patches on their shoulders, denoting their professions. A hammer striking an avail on a square patch denoting the Steel Millers. A golden needle with a length winding golden thread for the Seamsters. Duel cogs set over one another for the Engineering Corps. Two logs crossed and ablaze with a blue flame for the Forgers. And lastly, a lantern alight for the Lampers Guild. Such were the responsibilities of the lower class: labor and grind, soulless work forced upon them to promote industry and keep the masses down. Aellia despised it all.

Yet, there was another profession left to the lower class. One that did not wear badge nor frock of heavy fabric. Yes, one other which

Aellia had used time and time again. It was where her thoughtless feet carried her even now.

Two days had passed since Aellia had opened up to Elcon. Two days of endless questioning, back and forth. Elcon wanted to understand everything about the experience. How it felt. What the catalyst was. Where she had found the Oathrod.

His words washed over her like a tide, inescapable and all-consuming. But she weathered it all, opening up where she could, trying for honesty for perhaps the first time in her life with someone other than Tomo.

When it had been her turn to question him, much to her surprise, the old man opened up as well. Sharing tales of duels and contests, of war and loss. He spoke of his wife and son, how he lost them and how that hurt led him to the Cloth. He shared of his love of Ordan and this people, and what he hoped and dreamed for Tur'Mor. They talked of books and histories, of myth and legend. And despite how much she wanted to hate the man, part of her soft to his wizened ways, his gentle voice, his eccentric mannerisms. He had all the worldly wealth anyone could ever want or need, and she witnessed him giving freely, offering alms, and caring for the members of his Monastery.

It was with these thoughts heavy upon her head that Aellia made her way to the Twisted Stool. She almost journeyed to the place where it had once stood but remembered when walking that it had been burned to ash. Guilt tugged at her heart. That had been her fault. Felik's Crew had been tied to that location, and the Kh'ar had torched it in retribution or in an attempt to drag them out. Little did they know that the Crew was already dead by then.

Fire pricked Aellia's heart. They would suffer for that. They all would. That beaked-nosed brother of Xander. The stranger with the mismatched eyes and disheveled hair of red and gold. And the man whose face was hidden in a haze of darkness that seemed to burn like a fire. They would all pay, for Tomo, for Felik, for everything they had done.

The door to the Twisted Stool opened without creak or strain, it hinges well oiled. Warm light washed over the dark steps and the soft sounds of a listless lullaby played upon a harpsichord filled the alley. Women and men in dainty attire walked about with pleasing smiles on their faces and drinks in their hands, all for their guests, to ease their struggles and calm their strife. It was a place of respite, and it burned Aellia that someone had tried to snuff out a place such as this.

"Welcome, my dear," said Lady Phaedra, her voice throaty and kind. "What can we get you? Wine? A warm meal? Or maybe some companionship on this chill spring evening?"

Aellia did not turn her face to the woman directly and pitched her voice down while taking on the speak of the Uppers. "Wine and corner table," she snapped while sliding two hexagonal silver grams onto the counter.

"As you will, my lady," said Lady Phaedra, flashing a smile. "Henric, please show our esteemed guest to table thirty-two, and bring our vintage bottle, dark."

"Dry," Aellia added as nonchalantly as possible.

"We have a Telnorian Red, full of flavored, tastes of dark berries and plums," answered Lady Phaedra.

Aellia almost coughed. That was a very impressive bottle, probably worth at least nine or ten golden bars. Elcon had only given her two. Luckily, she had appropriated several more.

"What?" Aellia had said to Iaenora as she swiped a bag from one of the high priest's many hidden strongboxes. "I said I was going to be honest with him about me. How much more honest can I get? I am a thief, remember?"

Iaenora had not let her sleep for it, plaguing her mind with unneeded guilt. Hence the trip to the Twisted Stool and the dower mood she was in.

When Aellia looked up and met this Henric, she couldn't help but flash a sly smile. Lady Phaedra was good at her job. He was tall and tan, his long black hair pulled back into a ponytail. His shirt and trousers were tight, not allowing much need for imagining of what lay beneath the stretched fabric. Too bad he was as desirable to her as spoiled milk on a summer afternoon. Any other moody young woman would have opened her purse along with skirts for a man like that, his heavy eyes filled with dark mischief.

So, Madam Phaedra hadn't recognized her. Good. That was good. Besides, she probably should avoid anything that might cause complications. And there were plenty of complications here from all over the Mainland and across the various seas.

The scent of alcohol was already muddying her mind. Cursed Everlight. Why did it have to have this effect on her? She wanted to get lost in the wine and forget, if only for a night. She did not, however, want to be a stumbling buffoon after only one drink.

"This way," said Henric, and gods be damned, but his voice almost lit something in her. "Allow me to take your cloak."

"No!" snapped Aellia, far too harshly. The big man raised a pluck brow, his eyeline sharpening every feature of his face. Aellia almost apologized, but that was unbecoming of an Upper. "I have chill. I shall keep it."

"As you wish, my lady," Henric answered with a warm smile and ushered her to her seat, not even attempting to place a hand on her back as so many others might.

Aellia slid onto the bench, the back of which partitioned her off from whoever was sitting behind her. Whoever it was, they smelled of soured beer and depression. She almost asked to be moved but thought better of it. He would do well to mask her, if she lost her wits in the wine.

"Would you like a tasting board? Cheese or grapes?"

Henric's question pulled her back into the moment, away from the sorry stench of the man behind her. "Be a dear and bring me a small sample of whatever is the finest you have." she said with a wink and tossed him a siglat.

He caught it was a deft hand, snatching it from the air and rolling it over his fingers dexterously before sliding it into a small pouch at his hip. "As the lady wishes." He flashed her another smile and turned away to retrieve her wine and meal.

A warm flash of jealousy pricked her as he swayed away. Why did men have a bigger ass than her? It just was not fair. And now she knew there were gods, and they were all to blame for this. Aellia looked down at her hands, cocking the slightest smile, remember how she and Tomo would go back and forth. She had said it was endearing and that Aellia should be thankful because of how much trouble larger endowments got one into.

She missed her, so much. But those moments, after Tomo had left her physical body, they stayed with Aellia. Skies of purple, rising peaks of pillar-like mountains. And Tomo, sitting there, her body not of flesh. And those words she had spoken to her. *I am here, when you need to find me.*

"Lady," the drunkard behind Aellia shout toward Madam Phaedra in slurred voice. "I'll mine for the night. Same as last time."

Aellia could not help but lift her head and stare across the room at Madam Phaedra. She was good to her staff, never putting them in danger. Which is why surprise took her when a young woman, petite of build, dressed in a tight, white outfit and her hair chopped and dyed white, came up with an easy smile. She did not look scared or nervous, but sent a sensuous smile toward whoever sat behind Aellia.

Aellia's heart went still as stone. That woman looked just like her, as if she had been picked to play her double in one of those stage dramas the Uppers were so fond of. Bile rose in Aellia's throat as rage began to burn. The woman had irises dyed blue, a painful procedure used to turn painted works like this to look Blessed for the more perverse members of Ordiatian society. But this woman were not made to look like any Blessed. No. They looked like hers.

"This way, Regent," the young woman said in a soft, Livithian ascent, mirroring Aellia's own.

Regent? No...

The man who rose was tall but diminished. His fanciful tailcoat hung off of his shoulders ever so slightly and was baggy around the midsection. He was no longer fat like a toad bursting out of too-small clothing, but had the look of a confectioner's prized chocolate sculpture that had been left in the summer's sun. Yet, when she saw the side profile, there was no mistaking the bulbous nose or the thinning hair of the man. This was Aldorian, no doubt about it.

The young lady took him by his arm and led him toward the staircase up to where money was interchanged for private practices. Aellia watched in stunned horror as they walked away, her tinkering like a silver bell, him looking dead headed with hollowed eyes.

"Telnorian Red and Brewmaster cheese, imported from far Talahmnas."

Aellia nearly jumped out of her skin, banging her knee upon the table with a loud crash, at the sound of Henric's voice. Henric, in a fit of surprise, stepped back on one foot, dropping the bottle of wine as he fumble to hold a wooden board of arranged cheeses and cured meats.

With her enhanced reflexes, Aellia's hand shot out and caught the long neck of the olive-colored bottle before it crashed to the ground. The movement had been swift enough that her hood had been thrown back, a gust of wind whipping loose napkins and stray dust up, bursting from her very core.

"By Ordan's beard!" Henric gasped, his chiseled, painted face aghast.

"Shhhh!" hissed Aellia, pleading in her one good eye.

"Of course," Henric said clearing his throat.

Fortunately, the disruption had been minor. The harpsichord was loud for both privacy of conversation and privacy or intimacy upstairs. A few others looked her direction, noting her swift catch of the bottle, but seemed to not notice, or at least did not care in the slightest, about the abnormal gust of wind.

"A Blessed?" asked Henric as he set down the tray of cheeses and slid into the booth upon the other side of Aellia. His eyes were now wide with excitement and questioning. "I've never served a Blessed before."

Aellia flipped up her hood, covering her face from view of prying eyes. "I am not Blessed."

"But surely—"

"I can't heal others. I don't see the future. I am not a damn priestess for that cultish church," sneered Aellia as she popped the cork from the wine bottle. Anything to keep her hands busy and free of shaking.

Henric guffawed, bringing lacquered nails to touch his chest. Aellia rolled her eye as she looked at him, but noticed with a chagrin the small golden hammer hanging about his neck.

"I didn't mean," Aellia started.

Henric, to her surprise, laughed and patted Aellia's hand with a touch so soft and smooth it made her self-conscious of her own, weather-worn and calloused flesh. "My lady, there is no harm. Think that the high priest favors my line of occupation? Here, let me."

Henric took the bottle from Aellia's other hand and poured it into a wide bowled glass with a long, narrow stem and frosted foot. He swirled it thrice over and then sniffed at the aromatics. He smiled to himself pleasantly and then handed the glass to Aellia. "A fine wine, my lady."

Aellia, with all the grass and dignity of a slopping hog, took the stem with her full fist, snatched the bottle and poured a liberal amount into the goblet, some of which sloshed onto the table, and threw it back in one drink.

"Ah," Henric said, leaning back against the bench's rest. "It is one of those nights, I take it?"

"Listen, Henric," Aellia said with a slur. The damned wine was already impairing her thought. "You seem like a nice enough fellow, honest. But you're not my type."

Hernic's smile suddenly became far more genuine and relaxed. "Bummer, I was looking forward to a tussle with one as, how should I say, spirited as you, my lady."

Aellia rolled her eye again, but felt a flush heat rush up her cheek. "Do you ever crack?"

"Whatever do you mean," answered Henric as he leaned forward, resting his elbows upon the table and steepling his fingers.

Aellia didn't like that. Reminded her too much of Elcon. She did not want to think about Elcon right now. She was mad. Mad about something? But her brain seemed sluggish. Iaenora had warned her against drinking, and now, try as she might, she could not hear her inner conscience. It was all swirling oceans and crashing waves in her mind.

"Our mistress has a fine assortment of wines, beverages, and treats. They come in all sorts and flavors," Henric said with a wink. "Does my lady wish me bring her something a little less bold? Perhaps a—"

"I am not here for sex," Aellia snapped. She tried to focus on the man, but he keep swaying around for some reason. "I am just need a few moments and a drink is all."

"I see," Henric said, continuing to be the perfect gentleman. "And does my lady find the wine to her liking?"

"Did you that know the Midcouncilor is now a Regent?"

"Excuse me?" Henric's perfect facade shifted for a moment as lines of confusion creased his eyes.

He is probably wondering how a glass of wine could make one lose their inhibitions so fast, Aellia grumbled in her own head.

One should not drink if one knows the consequences.

It was the first time Iaenora had broken through the haze and it nearly caused Aellia to knock the table again. She could not think of a decent reply, so she grabbed the bottle and poured another glass.

"I do not think that is necessary, my lady. Would you have me call for a coach?" Henric said sweetly, placing a hand on Aellia's.

Faster than a lightning strike, Aellia produced a short knife and slammed it into the table right by Henric's outstretched hand. "I don't need no carriage for me, you hear? I just need a few drinks to make me think again."

Henric's eyes softened. "I understand. Let me fetch you some warm bread and some water as well. I'll be right back, okay, my lady?"

Even the naming of warm bread made Aellia's mouth salivate. But, before she could answer the man, he slid from the booth and hurried to the back kitchen.

"Bloody damned Regent." Aellia said the words, but had no idea why or what they meant. "Midcouncilor. That fat prick!"

Memories came back sluggishly. He was the reason for all of it. But that wasn't all. He was in coercion *...hiccup...* with those two demons. *Hiccup.* Aellia needed to get to them. They had been after her for some reason or another. *Hiccup.*

You're not in the right mind for this.

Iaenora's voice sounded a million leagues away and stupid.

Why not? Why wouldn't I be in the right reason for that?

Aellia stumbled out of her seat and, to the best of her abilities, walked toward the staircase in a discrete manner. Much to her own personal satisfaction, she made it to the stairs, and up them, without tripping up too badly. Even more surprising, no one stopped her.

She made her way down a corridor with a series of thick doors lining either wall with numbers of bronze hanging upon them. She walked and walked, swaying this way and that, a bottle of wine in one hand. Why had she taken the wine and not her knife? Halfak burn it, she really liked that knife.

And then she heard them, or smelled them, she was not certain which. But she was certain who was on the other side of room 17. Aellia lifted the bottle to her lips and drank a long, deep swig of the wine and then rammed her booted heel into the door just about the circular knob, sending it crashing inwardly. What she saw disturbed her greatly.

The room itself was fine enough and the bed within was larger than expected. This must have been a deluxe suite, walls papered with ornate designs and runners made from molded and lacquered wood. The bed in the room was a four-poster bed, dark pillars of carved wood and thick, lush sheets. No, the room itself was not the problem, but the occupants and what they were doing.

Aldorian, who looked even worse with his coat and shirt discarded over the back of a velvet upholstered chair, lay upon his back with his hands tied with white silk to two of the four posters. The young woman was straddling his hips, her chest bare, and was dragging a thin blade down his torso, barely breaking the surface of his flesh, allowing for the faintest lines of blood to trickle off of him.

"What in the name of—" Aldorian yelped as the door came crashing inward upon his private moment.

The young woman turned about, her eyes flashing with surprise and frustration. A hint of shame bit at Aellia. This young woman had only been doing her job, and Aellia was about to take away her most notable patrons.

Oh well, she'd leave her a sack of gold and silver that would cover a year's work. Because that man right across from her, well, he was not getting the ending he had expected to receive this night.

"Shut it, prick!" Aellia barked drunkenly. "Out, ma'am, you don't want to be here for this."

"You... you... you can't be here," the young woman hissed under her breath, eyebrows rising in alarm and frustration. "Get out!"

"You have two seconds to dismount this pig and leave or you'll sorely regret it," Aellia slammed the wine bottle against the doorframe, shattering the bottle into a jagged weapon.

"You!" gasped Aldorian, and he made a noise that Aellia wished she had not heard.

The young woman who had been straddling the man, let out a scream as she dismounted him. "Help! Help!"

Aellia felt a rush. What would they do to her? She was untouchable by these petty humans. She was practically a god now.

"Untie me!" damned Aldorian said in a nasally, pathetic whine. But the young woman had already tossed a robe over herself and was rushing out the door, carefully avoiding the place where shards of glass littered the floor.

Aellia stepped into the room and grabbed the foot of the bed as she kicked the broken door shut. It started to bounce back, but with a grunt of strain, Aellia pulled the bed across the floor, sealing them into the small room.

"You and I are going to have a little talk, Midcouncilor," Aellia said with all of the ominous intensity she could muster.

"It Regent, you insignificant worm! Regent!" Aldorian sniveled.

"It'll be rodless if you don't answer my questions," snarled Aellia as she shoved the jagged end of the bottle to the bulge in Aldorian's britches.

Aldorian's face went pale. "They'll kill you. They'll hang you. I'll make sure you're made a spectacle. You. You did this to me you bloody damned whore!"

Aellia struck the man across the face hard enough to break the skin of his lips and bloody his tongue. "In a place of business, it is uncouth to use such crude terminology, you sniveling piece of goat dung."

"It's your fault," sobbed Aldorian. "It was all going well, and you, you ruined it. You ruined me!"

Aellia blinked.

She ruined him?

What in the pits of Halfak was he talking about?

"He came because of you! He tortured me! He slew my wife, my wife! My sweet Analice! Because of you. He killed Remus and Tiberius because of you! That crazed Hawk, Betrugyn! It was all because of you!"

Aellia's heart was doused with icy water. Betrugyn. The demon. His wicked facade filled her mind's eye, causing a quaver to run down her spine.

"You were the one who was kidnaping those girls for him!" Aellia's senses were muddled, but anger fought to burn away the fog of alcohol. "You let him do that, not me!"

"Peasants! They were peasants!" cried Aldorian, his face wracked with fear and desperation. What had happened to this man? He had once been so proud and pompous, but he was broken now. "He haunts me! He haunts my dreams, whispers in the dark places! I cannot eat. I cannot sleep! You! You did this to me!"

Footsteps clambered about outside now. People were shouting. Someone had been sent to get the guard. Aellia had to act. There were windows, but they were high up and small, not an issue for her. But she needed answers, answers from this man. And how it gutted her to know that.

"Listen here, you fat pig," snarled Aellia, pushing the glass not-so-gingerly downward. "We're getting out of here, together. And if you fight me, Ordan as my witness, I'll drop you onto the cobbles from the top of the Valamour. Do you understand me?"

"You little—"

"Uh uh uh!" hissed Aellia, taking her free hand and pulling back her hood. She then wrenched the bandages from her left eye, revealing the scar left by the same demon who scared the man which she now threatened. "You see this? This is your doing, by siding with the man you now fear."

Aellia reached to the inside of her cloak and pulled out the Oathrod. She allowed the power to flow from it into her body. She knew what that would cause. She knew the fear it would strike into Aldorian's soul also.

Her vision cleared as her left eye was infused with Aetora's Touch. She could see not just the physical, but also streams of air and power around her. She could sense the current and the weight of the much-diminished man before her. It would take effort to steady herself enough to soar through that window with him, but she could do it.

Aldorian let out a gasp. "What in Ordan's name?"

"I am come to cleanse this land of filth like you, Aldorian," Aellia snarled, trying her best to impersonate the sound of the Sage. Of course Iaenora did not condone this behavior, so she sounded little more than a petulant child playing at power. But it did the trick. Aldorian slunk into himself, giving up the last vestiges of resistance.

With a swift motion, Aellia cut the silk that bound his hands. He sat up quickly and awkwardly, reaching for his shirt and coat.

"Hurry, we're about to take flight."

Aellia relished the fear in Aldorian's eyes that darted from her to the window high above them as he realized what she was saying. "You can't be serious."

"Open in the name of the law!" shouted a gruff man on the other side of the door.

"Time's up, swine," Aellia said with a wicked grin. "Who said pigs couldn't fly?"

With that, she wrapped an arm around the man and pushed off into the air. She used his back to break the glass—he let out a grunt of pain in the process—and soared out over the streets of Tur'Mor with a prize in hand that she had wanted for a very, very long time. And when she landed, she would get answers. Answers about Felik, about the Kh'ar, and about Betrugyn and his vanishing companion.

CHAPTER 25: ONE LAST THING
DARIUS

Darius arose to subtle knocking at his door. Groggily, he cracked his eyes open. Pain lanced through his sockets, battering at his forehead in ceaseless waves. The room, which had started out as little more than a swirling mess of light and color, began to take shape.

Blankets were half-strewn over his body, his legs tangled in the white linens. Next to his bed was a toppled vase, its dark contents spilled across the floor, staining the rug with burgundy, and a turned tray of various dried meats and cheeses. He tried to focus on what he was seeing, but the warm light that flowed in from his window made his head ring with pain.

"What?" he croaked out. Upon doing so his stomach turned. What was that godawful smell?

It was his breath.

"Sir," a young maid said from behind the door. "Lord Ruthvin has invited ye to dine with the high family for lunch."

For lunch? Darius squinted at the window, whose light assaulted his eyes in torturous ways. What time was it? It was so bright outside.

"Sir?" the maid's voice rang out a bit louder, filled with questioning and a strange timidness that none of the other maids had ever possessed.

Darius tried to sit up. That was the wrong decision. His guts cramped, along with his left leg, which shot out awkwardly, eliciting a bestial roar as his muscle writhed up and down his bare thigh.

"Help!" cried the maid. "He is having another episode!"

Darius clenched his teeth, tears welling in his eyes. Cramps, how he hated cramps. Yet, when he tried to straighten his thigh, his calf turned to knots and his toes twisted.

"Vinegar!" he groaned as loud as he could. "I need pickles or vinegar!"

The room door burst open a moment later and three women in green skits and white aprons whirled about him. One of them carried a steaming kettle and another a clay cup. They worked in tandem to pour the hot liquid, which shone with a strange, iridescent hue, into the clay cup and then take hold of Darius's sweating shoulders.

"This will be a wee bit hot," said one of the three, an elderly woman with a pair half-moon spectacle sitting on a bulbous nose that was as ruddy as her cheeks. "So, sip careful and don't mind the taste."

Don't mind the taste? As the boiling excrement flowed past his lips and scorched his tongue, pain from heat was the only reprieve from the most horrid taste he could have imagined. And he had just tore out an Itheanam's throat with his mouth last night.

He tried to cough and spit at the same time, but the third maid, who was not holding a cup or kettle, forced his jaw closed with rather strong fingers. She pinched the bridge of Darius's nose, cutting off his air flow.

Panicked, Darius swallowed the swill and then took a gasping breath of air.

"Are you all out of your mind?" he roared, sitting upright and glaring at the three women. Every muscle in his body was tight with suppressed rage, ready to strike out.

Tight. But not cramping.

A smile fluttered across the spectacle wearing maid's thick face. "There's a good laddie. Takes his medicine as well as an ass in the stable. Be thankful the lord didn't ask us to brand y'er rear. Though I wouldn't mind a look at it again."

Heat flushed Darius's face.

Again? When had? How had he gotten into these undergarments? He had no memories of getting into this bed. And what had they meant about another episode? Had it been a cramp? A vision? He didn't remember a vision, and he always recalled them, if only in fleeting bits and strands.

Thankfully, the rest of the bath and dressing went by in a blur. Darius's head continued to ache, but thankfully that was the extent of his morning problems. Or so he thought.

When the maids finished, they urged him follow them to where Erik and his family were seated and eating breakfast. It was almost as if they had not just been fighting for their very lives the night before. Erik was drinking and laughing with Krarraek, who, to Darius's surprise, nodded in his direction as he entered. Lady Sophie, who was always a picturesque form of regal propriety, laughed alongside her brother and spouse, her own cheeks slightly reddened by drink. Erkan and Krunlan had taken their place to the left of Krarraek, both making merry. Lori, who was stationed by her mother's right side, was the only one seated who was not laughing or drinking.

The absence of drink and merriment was not the only thing that separated her from her family. While they all wore casual, albeit fanciful, outfits of cotton and wool, Lori was dressed in battle gear. A chainmail haubergeon was draped over a blue tunic with silver stitching with a quilted vest with a white fur collar buttoned over that. Her legs were wrapped with leathers and boots made for riding.

When Darius caught her eye, it was met with a fierce glare for which he could not find reason. Had he done something offensive?

Other than the family, Tyree and the silent sentinels were present, along with the Talon, Orhund, Nee'av, and a few others whom Darius had seen about but couldn't recall by name.

"Ah! There he be!" Erik shouted, slurring his words as he heaved himself up from his star-carved throne. "Hero of the wall. A great, blood-damned bear!"

Darius blinked at the accolade, but the others raised goblets and glasses in toast, save for Lori.

"Come! Sit," Erik thundered as he pointed a finger to the only open chair at the table. The one right next to Lori. "Eat and drink! Ye've earned it!"

The maid next to Darius ushered him forward, pulling out the chair and helping him down. She placed a napkin across his kilted thighs and then asked what he would have to drink.

"Water," he croaked. "And something dark and hot. Please." Darius added the last part after a moment of hesitancy. He had all but lost his manner in this place, manners that Elcon had nearly beaten into him in his time in Tur'Mor.

The maid made quick work of his request, giving a warm smile to his added courtesy.

Much to Darius's relief, the table seemed to take a collective breath as he settled in. He could feel their eyes on him, watching him as he slowly sipped a cup of hot brew, steadying himself for the impending wave that was most assuredly coming.

Steadily, he set the cup upon the table and raised his eyes. Gradually, purposefully, he looked across the table, meeting every gaze that had fallen upon him until his eyes fixed upon Erik's.

"So," he said with a sigh. He really did not want to have this conversation. "I take it you saw me?"

A moment of silence passed.

"Out with them." Darius grit his teeth, flexing his fingers in agitation. "I know you have questions."

"When in Halfak's bloody pit were ye gonna tell us ye could turn y'erself into a gigantic, damned bear?"

So Erik would cut right to it? Good. It was better that way.

"Never," Darius answered flatly.

"What?" Erik looked as if he had been slapped. The smile that had been plastered upon his face fell in an instant, and Darius could not help but crock a smile at him.

"I told you I was Feromage. I told you I had certain abilities. I said I had a purpose to fulfill. Despite these things, you said that I must earn your trust through your games." Darius's grim smile turned into a hard stare. This was not how he had wanted to start this morning, but he was about sick of the games, the show, the waiting. "Why would I have divulged more?"

"Well, for starters, don't ye think it pertinent information for a lord of a house to know if one of his guests could rip his entire court to shreds if he got a wee bit moody?" said Erik in a cold tone.

Darius could see the veins rise on the man's neck as he spoke. He could feel the icy chill of the room around him. And he could see Krunlan striking that Redeye, over, and over, and over again.

"Did I hurt you?" Darius asked flatly. "Anyone in this house? Did you not just welcome me in as the hero of the wall?"

Erik took in a deep breath. He let it out with a long exhalation as he laid his palms on the table before him. "Listen, laddie, I am not saying we don't appreciate what ye've done for us. But, that's a bit of secret to keep from those y'er sharing a roof with."

"You could send me and Izebal to Dane," Darius answered. "We could have been gone days ago."

A pang lanced Darius's heart as he said her name. He wondered where she was, if she was okay or she had met a similar ill fortune as Talahmnas had. The pain fell into a pit, a deep, dark thing that filled his soul with dread and uncertainty.

"We have protocol." Erik sighed in exasperation.

"And I have secrets." Darius tried to maintain his firmness, but his concern for Izebal was softening his resolve. He needed to know she was okay.

"Alright, Alright," Erik said, lifting his hands. "This was not how I pictured this morning going, if'n I were being honest. Ye have y'er secrets, as do we all. Just, it's not every day ye meet a man who can turn into a bear is all I am saying. Takes a lot to settle in the ole kettle, if ye get my meaning."

Darius looked down at his hands. His mind was elsewhere now, not in this hall having this conversation. It was seeking out, questing for reassurance that everything was well with her, with the woman he was certain he had fallen in love with.

"Well, as long as ye don't spontaneously combust or nothing, I guess we do be straight," said Erik, and with that, the whole room seemed to let out a collective sigh of relief as the tension melted away.

"I want to say," Krunlan said as he hoisted a flagon that sloshed frothing ale over his hand. "A cheer to y'er, lad—sir! I had my qualms, no doubt about it, what with y bein' a soft-handed Outlander and all, but ye proved y'erself true last night. Cheers!"

"Cheers!" exclaimed the table as each raised their drink into the air, slurped them down whole, and slammed their bases onto the tabletop. All save Lori. She stared at her mug, white knuckles around the wooden tankard. Darius could feel the fury seething off of her like waves of heat from a broiling stewpot over a blazing fire.

"Don't mind her, now," Erik said with a halfhearted chuckle. "Lori is a wee mad she weren't invited to the dance last night."

Lori's eyes shot up from their unwavering glare toward her drink, fixing on her father's matching eyes.

"You had no right." Her voice was ice cold, barely more than a whisper.

Erik cocked an eyebrow. He raised a meaty finger to the circlet on his brow, tapping it in exaggerated thumps. "This do say otherwise."

"I am Hal of the Berzerk." The chair beneath Lori screamed across the floor as she thrust herself out of it. "How dare you command y'er personal guard to stay in the city? How dare you insult me?"

"I had Nip and Trip, plus me two sentinels and over two dozen Skogotuers," Erik said placatingly, as if he had already hashed out this argument a dozen times.

Lori's eyes darkened. She was hurt, not just angry. She was seething with an anger Darius knew all too well. Memories of his father being carried into their little village atop the Iron Mountains filled his mind. His cold, stiff body on a bed of shields, skin pale as the snow, his once lively eyes vacant. Darius knew how she felt and more. She was angry, and she had every right to be so.

"Lori," Lady Sophie spoke in low, measured tones. "Still your tongue. That is y'er father y'er speaking to."

Lori turned her attention to her mother, a tremble of rage rippling through her muscles. The veins on her neck were engorged, and Darius could see the blood pumping beneath her flushed skin.

"My duty is to lord and country," Lori's icy voice was no more than a whisper. "That is my lord, this is my country. Do you of all people mean to tell me what is what in the line of duty?"

"Enough." A single word, but it was enough to freeze the ocean in its ebbing. Erik spoke with a harsh finality, his jovial demeanor far from him. He drew in a long breath through the nose, a motion that stilled all around him.

"Father." It was Erkan who spoke next, his voice calm and collected, sounding so much like his dad it made Darius blink. "We must look to the North. Krun and I took that bloody Redeye, but it weren't the only foul chut afoot."

"Aye," Krunlan added with a nod to his twin, his right hand still wrapped from where he had struck said Redeye. "Bloody chuts are crawling through the hills. I don't know if they're connected to the attack on the Wall, but we ain't got the luxuries to sit around and talk pretty to one another."

"We have yet to hear from Tark or MacLystar," Erkan continued his brother's words. "I fear for our northern border and think that the attack on the Wall was more a distraction than anything else."

"What of High King Sterkamar?" Erik asked, turning his attention to Tyree, who had been uncharacteristically quiet this morning. "Have you heard from that magus of his, Tyree?"

"Brainus Brightbeard?" Tyree asked with a half-hearted laugh that sounded more nervous than his usual self. "Not a peep from the kook!"

Erik's brows knit together at the off-handed remark. The rest of the hall, too, seemed to pickup on the unusual tone of the old mage. Darius looked over at the master mage and saw for the first time deep circles under his eyes, dark and weary. His hair, though always disheveled, was especially unkempt, and his beard looked as though he had fallen asleep atop one of his books with the way it was plastered askew on his withered cheek.

"By Gallae's breath," Lori muttered. "Even Tyree is cracked."

"Cracked?" Tyree's blue eyes ignited. He took hold of his bone-white scepter and as he did so, the crystal that was set into its head lit with vibrant azure light. "I'll show y'er cracked!"

He whirled the staff over his head and began to speak in a language Darius could not quite make out, though some of the words sounded eerily like that of the ancients. All the lights in the room dimmed, as if they were being drawn into the head of the strange scepter Tyree wielded. Then, at a thunderous utterance of some foreign word, a burst of sapphire light sent specks of blue hovering over the table.

Images began to form from those dancing blue orbs, forms of men and women, of beast and fiend. Darius stared in awe as he saw many hundreds of trees created from pure light. And then, Tyree spoke as with a voice of thunder.

"Dark have been my dreams, filled with the agony of the broken. Late have my eyes wandered the stars when upon my mind a vision was granted. As Aetora's light flows through me, so does the will of Ordan, High Father of All! A vision I was given last night, and a vision I do share now:

"As fire forges fate, so shall perseverance establish the great. Seven stars shall light the sky, and all mourn. Ancient secrets, sealed in blood, emerge once more. Mist and shadow, lurk and creep. Death takes form and heroes weep.

Seek out the truth. Seek out the hopes.

Find them.

Find them.

Find them each; bound to none.

Take your flight. But mind the night. Forsaken shadows watch and wait.

Mountains high and snows so bleak. Caverns vast and chasms deep.

Ash and fire, pain and heat. Scorch the lands, cut off the deceit.

Oceans vast and jungles old, sorrow spreads from lands untold.

Beast and claw, mind and spirit, so shall an ancient secret soon be told.

A choice to be made, a choice to keep.

Pain and sorrow, together meet. One lies captive, another weeps.

A path you'll cross, to forge your fate. A path you'll take and falter.

A path must be chosen, once more to take. Another you must abandon.

Guard the light, but mind the night, for desolations gather.

Find them!

Find them

Find them, or blood shall rain!"

Tyree whirled his scepter one final time. All the orbs of blue coalesced into a singular image. A massive mountain with a jagged peak whose precipice looked as if it has been burst asunder by a strike of lightning. And in the face of that mountain, a horrid scar was formed, a gash of rock and stone that was without light and devoid of hope.

Just as it had all formed, all the lights flittered away. Warm sunlight soaked the room, released from its bonds within the scepter's gemstone.

All the room was utterly silent.

"Every night," Tyree's voice trembled. "For three nights, and three more, ever since ye walked into me shop, laddie, I've dreamed this dream. But it weren't until last night I could see the vision for what it was. What in the name of all the holy Ellitheor are ye?"

All eyes fell on Darius once more.

Those words, this vision. He had felt them before. Seen them before. The same but different. Deep in the Temple of Ordan, before his journey to the north. There it had been Brei, whose body had shone with Everlight as she had been filled with a vision from the High Father. So too had Tyree shone, his skin bright with the same Everlight, the same vision, but different.

Darius felt those stares, each and every one of them. All the weight of all the eyes in the room bearing down on him. He had not wanted this. He had not wanted to be known, to be scrutinized. All he had wanted was to pass through this place unknown, unhindered.

"In my satchel is a sealed envelope," Darius spoke with a shaking dread. Despite this, despite the fear and uncertainty, he could no more stanch the flow of words than he could turn back the tide. "I have said from the moment I entered this city I was on a quest to Dane, to deliver that envelope to one called the Apostle of Ordan. It contains the words of a vision, a vision almost identical to the one you all just bore witness too. As for what I am, I am just a man. Someone who has a burden that must be born or else others will suffer for it. All I have tried to do is fulfill that purpose. And yet, where I go, darkness follows."

"Why though?" Erik spoke in earnest, his brows furling. "Ye said from the time ye got here ye have to go to Dane, to deliver that letter and whatnot. But why? Why is it so bloody important? We could use ye here! Ye could do real good!"

So there it was. That was the reason. Darius felt as if his heart was an anvil being beaten by a hammer, every pulse of blood a surge of both frustration and reason. Of course they would want him here, to use him. Of course they would do all they could to keep him here. Did he even need to compete?

Erik, seeing the cogs churning into Darius's mind spoke, perhaps a little too quickly, "Listen, laddie, its not like that, what y'er thinking. We didn't know, not truly, until last night."

"How is it then?" said Darius. He felt his thumb sliding across his ring. He felt his left hand reflexively open and close, time and time again. He was getting angry despite himself. Pulses of that strange power seeped through his veins, drawing light from the moonstone-infused meteor before him.

Lori turned on him. "Careful how you speak to the Lord of the High Hall. Guest of my father or not, I'll have y'er tongue." Her right hand drifted to the small of her back, resting upon one of the twin hilts of her saexs.

A grim smile played at Darius's lips. She hadn't been there last night. Heard stories he was sure. But hadn't been there. She had no idea what he could do. However, as he stared back at her, Darius saw something flit behind her irises. It was only for the briefest of moments, but he could have sworn he saw...

"Oye, settle y'er two," Lady Sophie snapped. "Sit! The both of y'er."

Darius found himself plopping into his seat, as if his body refused to deny Lady Sophie's command of its own free will. Lori, too, found her seat, though the daggers she was staring at him remained unsheathed.

"Alright, alright," Erik said placatingly. "We all just need to take a deep breath in through the nose. Now, Orhund, report from last night. Where do the Skogotuers stand? Any news from the North?"

Orhund, who had remained still through the morning's disagreement moved with calculated grace. He was a warrior through and through. Not a hack and slash brute, but a man of discipline and character, Darius could see that now. It was in the way he stood, the way his shoulders squared, not in agitation, but poise. It was the way he drew his hand to his chest and the slight bow he gave, true respect in the salute, not a practiced and meaningless motion.

"We took heavy losses last night, both in Ranok and upon the Spanning Wall. Two dozen good souls sent back to the dirt and on to the endless sleep." Orhund spoke firm, but Darius did not miss the quiver in his voice, the pain in his eyes. He carried deeply for his soldiers, a feeling that thrummed in resonance with Darius's own soul. And with that resonance, a little of the heat, the anger and frustration, ebbed away from him. "Nee'av's squad was lost; she barely made it out alive. They had taken a Redeye, but it was lost in the battle."

"Don't fret the loss of bloody Redeye, Commander." Erik's voice was hard as stone, but filled with empathy. "We do have one that I am sure ye'd like the have a few quaint words with today while our guest here trains."

Darius's eyes moved back and forth between the two men. He saw the fire burst to light behind Orhund's weary eyes. He felt the tension mounting, building like a storm. He knew hate and anger, he was no stranger there. Images of Krunlan beating the chained fiend plagued his mind, unsettled him. He had let that happen. It was cruel and vile. But he had not stopped them. At that very moment, he realized he would not stop Orhund either.

A part of him felt dirty at that realization. However, the throbbing pain in his abdomen, where his body had been pierced by the Itheanam's horn and the searing heat of Mireya's bloodcurse on his chest, reminded him that some hurts went deeper than others. He was dirty, tainted by Iodaba's touch. Contained, true, but he was not clean. Who was he to judge these for their actions? Had he not done terrible things himself?

"No objection?"

Darius blinked in confusion, then realized that all eyes were on him.

"What?" he grunted.

"I'd have thought ye'd be all up in arms about training today," Erik smirked. "Ye've fought it every other day."

"What's the point?" asked Darius as he shrugged. "It's only one more day, right?"

"That is the spirit of a true warrior," cackled Tyree in his obnoxiously whimsical and raspy voice. "Might as well do it, eh? Blood and bloody stones, laddie. Where is the fire? The beast?"

Darius looked up at the old Mage, whose eyes had returned to their normal blue hue, but had not lost their wild sheen. "What is it you want from me? Train or not, stay or leave, it doesn't seem to matter what I chose here, it is the wrong thing."

"Laddie, it ain't the choice, but the choosing," Tyree said with a shake of his withered head as he stroked the top of his scepter with a gnarled hand. "Be proud of y'er decisions. Be bold in them. Ye saved us, twice. Don't take that light. And don't take the Ulkeniheim light neither. It'll be for y'er own good and understanding."

"I said I'd do it," said Darius, his tone going quieter, harder.

"Then, with y'er leave me lord, may I take Talon and the lad to Dwallen?" Tyree asked, turning his attention to Erik.

"Yes," Erik answered nonchalantly. "But, I do have one ask."

Erik's eyes went from Tyree, to Darius, to Lori and then to his wife. A small smile spread across the High Lord's bearded face. "Take me Lori with y'er. She seems to need a tussle. Work out some of that angst she do have pent up."

"Father!" Lori's eyebrows rose nearly as high as her voice, which was steeped in incredulity.

"Krarraek and Orhund will be with me, Nip and Trip and me sentinels too. Ain't no worry y'er mind, lassie," Erik said with a wink. "Y'er may be me Berzerker, but ye be me daughter too. Go. Teach our guest how a Ruthvin fights. Take Erkan and Krun with y'er too, they'd love a go, of that I am sure."

"Father."

"It weren't a question," Erik said firmly, his smile straining. "Off with ye. Daylight be burning and we have... questions that do need answering."

Lori looked a wolf herself, the blue ink on her body pulsing with every heartbeat. Just like her father and brothers. Darius realized that that was no ordinary tattooing, but ink infused with Everlight. And he wondered just what Lori's afforded her.

The meteor seemed to resonate with the pulsing tattoos across her flesh, a strange sensation that Darius could feel thrumming in the metal of his ring. A twitch made his body jerk, his thumb pressing hard into the raised paw of Ellitheor Silver. A single ray of sunlight seemed to find its way to the ring, heating Darius's blood and sending a sensation of ecstasy through his veins. It took all his willpower to hold back the smile, the sigh of pleasure as he felt goosepimples rise across his arms and neck.

"Let's go now," Tyree said, unnoticing of Darius's blissful state, that feeling of small aches vanishing and strength fusing to his sinew and bones. "Ain't got all day. I do have the MAC upfront and ready to ride."

The connection, the Bonding, snapped like a twig being broken between to fingers. The light fled Darius's body, dread replacing it with a disturbing speed.

"What, laddie?" Tyree mused. "Scared of a little ride down the Hill?"

Darius felt his stomach turn, as a word filled his mouth, slithering between his lips before he could stop it, and it was most assuredly not 'dread'.

The whole court burst into laughter at it. All save Darius.

***

Darius wanted to kiss the earth as he stepped out of Tyree's wheeled deathtrap. His hands trembled as he withdrew a cloth from the inner pocket of his trench coat and wiped at his sweat-soaked brow. Erkan and Krunlan were both laughing, their poise finally shattering like a thinly frozen lake when a heavy rock was tossed upon it. Lori did not share in their banter, though her eyes betrayed subtle signs of amusement at Darius's discomfort.

"Alright ye'uns, off to the pitch with ye," Tyree scolded as he too tried to swallow bouts of cackling laughter. "It will be a busy day."

Only Talon seemed to retain true composure. She did not enjoy riding in the motorized wagon anymore than Darius had. Her dark complexion paled significantly and was further marred by a subtle green hue. This had been amplified by a slew of harsh, guttural words as the carriage had struck a rock, jostling all those within in a most unnerving manner.

"I'd face a pack of wylven before riding in that thing again," she hissed under her breath as she shoved past Tyree. She walked with heavy footfalls and used her spear as a support.

"It weren't that bad," said Tyree. His words were hollow and lacked conviction, a fact that was only magnified by his scratching at the nape of his neck. "We made it in one piece."

"If the Ellitheor had wanted us to travel that fast, he would have given us four legs instead of two!" Talon shot back, whirling about and pointing the spear's tip toward Tyree. "Uuradan's flames consume us all!"

Darius could not take the back-and-forth right now. He needed to clear his head, find his center, if he were to perform today. One more day. He could make it one more day. Hopefully, Izebal would be back tomorrow and they could leave this place a memory, a proverbial bump in the road, as it were.

He shirked his trench coat and began to wrap his hands and fingers, all the while thinking of the past few days. They had been a blur, a series of events that had happened so fast, so disjointedly, that he hadn't taken the time to process them. And then there was the vision Tyree had spouted off this morning. Those words were far too similar to the ones of Brei.

The mountain. He had dreamed of a mountain chamber with a table of stone. He dreamed of a woman robed in white and masked with silver, and about her neck, a cloth that bound her, stitched with a flaming eye.

His ring went cold as ice, sending a chill throughout his body.

"Oy, ye alright?"

Darius couldn't move. He stared down at his hands, hands that held white linen wrappings, frozen.

"Darius?"

They all sounded so distant, as if they were in a cave calling out to him. He could not move.

"Is something wrong, laddie?"

The muscles in Darius's neck flared. His heart thundered in his chest. The weight of it all paralyzed him. Cold sweat began to run down his back, soaking his shirt. He couldn't do it. He couldn't do it. His father, his brother. They had died. He couldn't save them. How could he serve Ordan? How could he do this? He had failed. He failed.

A hand rested on his shoulder, a gentle touch. Which was immediately preceded by a jolt of power that nearly knocked him to the ground.

Someone screamed.

Light filled Darius's eyes, a blinding flash of white.

Blue, then green, and then the hard embrace of the earth rushed up to meet him.

Motion.

People running.

His ring. All that power. All that energy, gone.

Tired. So tired.

"Lori." Cried... someone.

"Blood and stone!"

"Is she breathing?"

"She's convulsing, what the pit is wrong?"

"Krun, a hand, get her to the carriage. We do got to get her to me shop, now!"

"What about him? He did this."

"Toss 'em in, we ain't got time for nothing else."

"Ordan, save and strengthen her, ma will kill me if something happens to her. Gallae full of grace, watch over her."

Darius felt two sets of hands wrestle him from the earth. He did not protest. It was too much. Too heavy. Darkness filled his eyes.

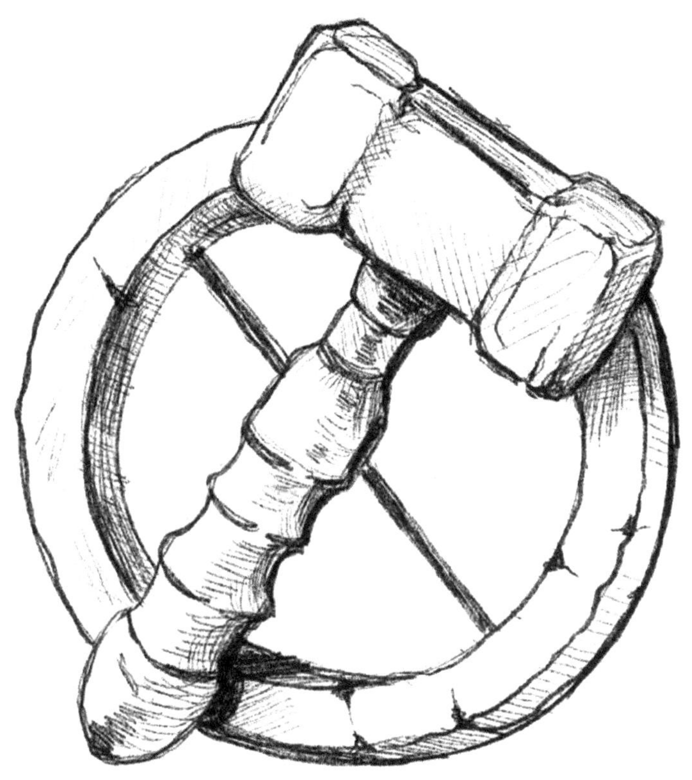

CHAPTER 26: AXE AND HOUND
DARIUS

Darius awoke in a chair. His back and shoulders ached with dull stiffens of confinement. He blinked, but no light came to his eyes, only darkness. He tried to lift his hands but found that they were bound to the arms of a chair with heavy chains. Panic gripped his chest.

No. No, no, no, no!

He slid his thumb over the surface—

His ring. It was gone.

Darius tried to look down at his hand, but he could not see anything, there was no light.

What the pit happened?

Voices.

Slowly, surely, voices began to fill his ears.

Talking. No, shouting. Anger.

Lots of anger and threats. He couldn't make out what exactly.

The sound of metal turning against metal followed by a sharp click across the room drew the whole of Darius's attention. Light cascaded into the room, burning his eyes. And amid that blaze of white light, a figure of sapphire stood whose incandescent eyes pierced Darius to his very soul.

"Keyholder," the figure said in a voice that sounded like brass trumpets blaring in his ears. "We have much to discuss."

The chains were loosed from Darius's wrists in silence. Eyes darted between where Darius sat and Lori stood with eyes blazing with resplendent light.

Shock stole the anger from Darius's heart, shock and confusion. He had been enraged at his confinement, but hadn't had the time to form that fury into coherent thought before Lori had entered, calling him Keyholder.

Keyholder.

A simple title. A terrifying thing.

Darius's mind rushed away for a moment, back to the streets of Tur'Mor. Back to the market. Back to a set of steps where a young woman had lain, run down by Kh'ar Robbers. He had felt that spark, that jolt of light passing from himself to her. He had not understood it then but did so with clarity now.

"I am called Auyxus." Lori's voice resonated with the tones of another. Wisps of blue light misted from between her teeth as she spoke, staining the air about her mouth with iridescent lines of azure. "I am the Sage of Mind, Seal of the Cognitive Realm, Truthspeaker of the Ellitheor."

Darius blinked up at her, his limbs refusing to find their strength.

"Do not be alarmed nor afraid. You have done well, Keyholder," Lori said with a radiant smile that filled Darius's chest with warmth. "Take my hand and walk with me for there is much to see."

Darius, whether in shock or stunned confusion, stared dumbly at Lori's extended hand. As he did so, awe-struck him once more as he studied the runic symbols on her flesh Those that had been pale blue, now shown with brilliance and seemed to move across her arms and hands as if they were living things.

"Come, do not delay. The time is short, there is little remaining. Where we must walk, the body need not travel. Come now. Let us go beyond that place where flesh dies and rots."

Lori grabbed hold of Darius's hand. Her grip was tight, the callouses of her fingers and palm pressing firm into the back of his own much larger hand. With a firm pull, Lori hoisted Darius from his seat though his body did not move from its seated position.

In a blur of motion, Darius felt himself turn inside out and twist about as light and sound rushed through his now crystalline flesh. The room in which they stood fell away from his vision, replaced by a field of black sand and a sky of royal purple. And where there had been pain and confusion, peace and clarity fell over Darius's mind for the first time in a very, very long time.

"Here is the place of Creation, where life and death coexist in perfect euphony," Lori said with a sigh of pleasure. Her clothes of battle had been replaced by a tunic of white and gold whose threadwork was fine and showed off her warrior's physique. The tattoos that had covered her flesh were gone, her skin as crystal as Darius's was. Her eyes though, her eyes were deep pools of starry night, infinite galaxies of unknowable depths. And at her side stood an enormous wolf of azure light, tail bobbing calmly and piercing eyes fixed upon Darius.

"You are not as we intended," Lori said with a hint of sadness. "You have suffered much pain and have carried the touch of Iodaba's corruption."

Darius looked down at his chest where the shimmering print of Mireya's hand marked him. Embarrassment struck him, for he wore only a toga about his torso, draping him from shoulder to waist and then wrapping about his hips to mid-thigh. Despite his embarrassment, the sudden realization that the curse upon his chest, nor rune-marked scare at his abdomen, did not hurt forced his eyebrows upward in astonishment.

"While I am here, the corruption is ebbed. Be at peace, if only for a moment," said Lori in that melancholy, harmonic tone.

"How do we walk here now? How did you bring me to this place?"

"This is the realm of the mind, the place where He is bound."

"I have come here in my dreams," said Darius. "But not here. Where I go is a mountainous place, scarred by lightning strikes and in whose skies is filled with a never-ending expanse."

"So shall he walk between two worlds, but in neither shall he find comfort," Lori spoke, though not to Darius, but of him.

"What do you say? Why did you bring me here?"

"We are Sage of the Cognitive Realm, it was our Binding that that tethered the Fallen Ones."

"Speak clearly," growled Darius, feeling that old familiar rage welling up once again.

"My sisters gave of ourselves to seal away the Fallen Ones so that their evil could not corrupt the physical realm, the plane of mortal life," said Lori as she raised a finger. She drew in the open air, leaving a trail of light as she spoke. "Aetora, Ria'Elahm, and Iodaba. Three sources, three eternal wells of power. Aetora, the Well of Spirit and Mind—" A loop was formed of azure light. "Ria'Elahm, the Well of Life and Matter—" A second loop was formed in the air between Lori and Darius, this of shimmering emerald. "And Iodaba, the Well of Death, Decay, and Corruption." A final loop of maroon that intertwined with the others into a symbol of interconnection, which had no beginning and no end, but flowed endlessness and eternal.

"For countless millennia, all three coexisted in harmony, in perfect balance. Ordan, High Father, and Gallae, Mother of Life, dwelled upon Vanherran as king and queen, where the light of the Three shone brightest. There they had many children, the eldest called Fenron, who was born of perfect order and righteous exactness. Then came their twins, who were Fate and Destiny incarnate, wielders of dreams and visions. There was also Thaellan, shepherd of the fields and steward of the seas, who was most loved by the Daulkaefar. Others too, whose names and stewardships I could recant for ages. But it was Gae'el, who was born last, Daughter of Gold, whose name was given for her likeness to her mother, whose heart was pure and whose intentions were most benevolent. It was her death at the hands of her sisters, who had fallen prey to Iodaba's corruption, that drove Gallae into seclusion and caused Ordan to Seal them away, using Ethra to create Dimdreal.

"Yet, for Ordan's love of his daughters, he could not bear the weight of destroying them, for in his heart was the true light of Aetora. Therefore, he created the Oathbond, forging with Ethra chains of Aetora and Ria'Elahm, each of which was fastened with the souls of my sisters and I, willing sacrifices for the greater good. With chains forged of light and soul, he tethered himself as the barrier between his daughters and the three realms. But he knew it would not be enough, that one day, his power would weaken, that darkness and corruption would overcome his strength. For this cause were your kind created. Endowed with light not from Aetora or Ria'Elahm, but given the ability to harness the power of the sun, and with that power, the ability to awaken my sisters and I from our slumber when our chains broke and darkness was unleashed once more."

Darius stood in silence, the words of Auyxus replaying in his weary mind. He pondered deeply upon what they meant, the clarity they brought to him, and the profound unease that suffused his waking mind.

Long moments passed, neither he nor Auyxus speaking, for in this place, Lori was not herself, the wolf being more her than Sage, until at last he drew in a deep breath and spoke.

"So, this was all known from the beginning, then?"

"Yes."

"Tell me then, did you know the cost when you swore that oath? What would it do? What would it entail?" Darius asked with a trembling voice.

"Each of my sisters knew the cost," Auyxus answered resolutely. "We bore that cost willingly."

"I did not." The words fell like a hammer blow, and as they escaped his lips, Darius wished he could take them back. But they were true, perhaps the truest words he had ever spoken.

"No." Auyxus stepped closer and place a finger on Darius's forehead. A ripple of cold emanated from her touch, drenching Darius with a sensation of being soaked to the bone in icy water. "You knew. You have always known."

Darius felt ill, his joints too loose, his muscles too tight. The icy touch of Auyxus warred with the raging fires of anger in the pit of his stomach. He was a warrior, a guardian of the realm. It was his duty to fight, fight for the gods that had created all. Gods who had turned their backs on mankind and chosen their own over their creations. Gallae had fled. Ordan had sealed himself away rather than destroy the greatest threat to humanity. It made sense now, all of it. The visions, the dreams, the purpose he had thought he had found. He was a pawn, a puppet whose strings were being pulled this way and that.

"Darius." Auyxus's voice was unyielding, battering away the thoughts that plagued his mind. "You must listen to me now. You are, and have always been, a guardian. I know your mind. You know who you are, what you are meant to become. Keyholder. The one who can not only unlock, but bind once more."

"So that is it, then? Am I fated to reforge the chains and seal away my god, so that he can seal away his own daughters?" Darius asked.

"We all have a purpose," Auyxus said. "Yours is to find my sisters, awaken them as you have me and Iaenora. Four others remain. Lamdrean, Telanahr, Auedur, and Zaevot. You must find them and wake them up. Only together can we staunch the rising tide of Iodaba's corruption. We did not see; we could not know. It was never supposed to have ended this way. The Sealing was supposed to cut off Iodaba's Touch from Ethrea, damming its ceaseless tide of corruption."

Darius pondered the words of Auyxus, searching his heart and soul. He felt a strange sense of rightness to what the Sage of Mind had told him. It did not, he considered, change anything on the path he had started.

Darius had wanted purpose, meaning in his hollow life. When he had unwittingly awakened the girl in Tur'Mor—Iaenora he supposed—something in his heart had felt right: a true clarity, a direction. He had seen Ordan chained beneath that mountain, and he had seen the weakening of those bonds of Aetora and Ria'Elahm.

"Tell me," Darius said slowly, fixing his eyes upon Auyxus. "Why was this kept from me? Why not just show me this in the beginning?"

"Ordan weakens, and I fear his last manifestation pushed him to the ends of his abilities, for where he lies, there is no Everlight nor Lifelight. His body decays under the strain of his sins, his imprisonment." Auyxus's voice dropped with sorrow. "It was never his intention to cast this burden upon another. But he had foreseen the folly of his affection and set a plan in motion. A secret plan that we must see to finality if the world is to find harmony once more."

"And what is my part in this? You call me Keyholder, you say I am to find your sisters, to awaken them. But to what end?"

"Only one has that answer, seventh of six. It is he who holds the full truth of Ordan's secret plan, he and the first son," said Auyxus. Suddenly, her body rippled, as if a stone were cast into a pond. "We are being called back to the physical realm. Darius, you hold the key to our salvation. You must seek out the Apostle. My bond with the girl is tenuous. I am not as the other Sages, nor my sister Zaevot. We cannot exist in the physical realm. Heed this last word: go to the mountain of the north, seek out seventh of six. Beware the night, beware she who walks in shadows. Dreams. Beware your dreams, for not all are of light."

Darius felt as if the whole world was torn out from underneath him. Lights and sounds coalesced into a blur. A freezing wind tore at Darius's eyes, momentarily blinding him.

Voices filled the room in which Darius sat upon a chair. Lori was there, her skin pale and lacking any of the luster it had just held. Nausea struck, but Darius forced it down as he rose. Hands grasped him, and to his surprise, they were gentle and helping. Lori was being helped up by Erkan and Krunlan. Erik stepped between his daughter and Darius, placing a hand under her chin and raising her face to look into her eyes. Tyree wheeled to Darius's side, pushing Orhund out of the way.

"Laddie," Tyree's voice was little more than a whisper, but it cut sharp to Darius's ears. "Where did ye go? What happened?"

Darius looked over at Lori. She swayed slightly, but when their eyes met, her's were filled with confusion. Darius shook his head as his thumb slid over the icy metal of his ring.

"I am not sure."

It was not a lie, nor was it the truth. Darius knew the place, but it had never felt so foreign. He had heard the words 'Find them' so many times, they had nearly driven him mad. But now, now he knew exactly what was asked of him. He was the key—or the Keyholder, to be exact—and it was his duty to find and awaken the Sages that held sealed the Dimdreal. Though it was not explicitly stated, the solemn understanding was that if he failed, so too would those chains. And with that failure, the Fallen Ones would be released once more. The very gods of the Blood Queen Mireya, whom the High Priest Diabhail served. They were coming back, and it was up to him to stop them.

"What do ye mean?" Tyree pressed.

"Erik," Darius said loudly. "You were right about one thing."

Lord Ruthvin turned his whole body, facing Darius with piercing blue eyes. "And what is that?"

"I need a weapon," Darius answered resolutely, bearing the full burden of his purpose now.

A wicked smile slid across Erik's face. "Funny ye should say that. I had hoped to keep it a surprise, a token of merit for y'er completion of the Ulkeniheim."

Erik made a motion with his hand, to which Orhund responded with a sharp nod before exiting the smaller room.

"Ye see," Erik continued. "What ye did for us at the Wall, that were the most spectacular thing I'd ever seen. But it got me to thinking about our conversation in the War Room, and how y'er always a fidgeting with y'er hands. I had thought a sword would nice, but from what Tyree and Talon here have said, ye fight with a brute strength, graceful enough and not unskilled. But a sword is a dancer's weapon, something for one who seeks fame. Y'er bigger than that, more than that. So, hope'n ye don't mind, but before the lady Izebal left, she had said she had given ye a stick for thumping about. A stick, bah! Well, that there stick wouldn't break for nothing, so I said to meself, what about a mace head, but that didn't seem right."

Orhund walked through the door once more, and in his hand was gripped the hickory rod Izebal had enchanted, and at the top was a bearded axe head of pattern-forged steel. Darius's eyes widened at the sight of it, studying the runes carved into the head, runes that wound themselves about a singular hole the size of his thumb, with three slits flared out like the sun's rays.

"A weapon made for a man with a purpose, I'd say," Erik said proudly, hefting the axe from Orhund's gifting hands. "Only thing it needs is a bit of moonstone, here." Erik placed a finger on the hole in the steel. "It's a bit of a tricky thing to do; ain't no flame hot enough to melt the stuff. But we can fix a piece in here, and we just so happen to have one that'll fit this slot perfectly."

Darius did not know what to say. Izebal had told them of the rod she had given him. Erik had taken it and forged a weapon for him out of it. And an axe head at that, one that looked strikingly similar to the one his father had carried with him.

A thrum of rightness washed through Darius's chest, igniting a long stilled flame in his heart. He was a warrior, as was his father before him. He could do this, he could be what he was called to be. even if he had not fully understood the depth of the oath he had sworn, he had sworn it, and he would not back down now.

"I accept your gift," Darius said with what he was sure was a daft smile, but he couldn't help himself.

Lori, who now seemed to have regained full composure, nodded in approval.

"So, what do we need to do to get that moonstone set?" Darius asked.

"Simple enough," Erik said with a sly smile. "Every Danelander is given the right to carry a weapon as they pass the trial of the Ulkeniheim. Two evenings hence, once the games are done, we will finish this together and y'er journey to becoming a Northern will be complete. I don't say this lightly, Darius of the Iron Mountains, but ye have made y'erself a Northman in my eyes, if ye prove to Daneland tomorrow the same, I'll grant ye passage straight to the very throne of High King Sterkamar on the fastest rail engine we have."

Darius looked passed Erik, searching out Lori's face. She looked as if she had run some great distance. Her eyes no longer shone with brightness, but gazed in unfocused confusion. Erkan and Krunlan still supported her frame, which trembled slightly in their hands.

"Your daughter, she—"

"We understand what has happened," Erik said bitterly. "Long has it been foretold. We just—we thought this burden had passed her by."

"She will need to come with me," said Darius in a gentle but firm tone.

Erik's features hardened as he drew in a reluctant breath. Pain filled his eyes, not of physical hurt, but that of a father losing a child. As his breath left his lungs, his shoulders fell, though he did not lose his poise.

"Lori is strong and true, she has made the name Ruthvin proud. She will go as she goes, that is no longer my place to say one way or the other, as her father or her lord."

"Da," Lori spoke up, her voice quivering with emotion. "Da, I didn't know."

"Ye've always been headstrong and proud, Lori," Erik said as he turned to face his daughter once more. He stepped close and placed hands on her shoulders, Erkan and Krunlan stepping back as he did so. "Ye've made y'er mother and I very proud, Lori Wolfspirit. Though it is not warranted nor required, I give you my blessing. Go and show the world the true strength of Daneland. And may the Fallen Ones tremble in their graves."

If only they were buried, thought Darius as he watched the tender moment between father and daughter.

CHAPTER 27: PROMISES, OLD AND NEW
AELLIA

Aellia stretched her sore muscles, stiff from the training the night before. The Avajan'Aluth had not taken it gently with her, nor had those training to become full Aluth.

Growing up in the underbelly of Tur'Mor, as a Southender, Aellia had not been privy to many of the customs and traditions of Ordiatian society, and those which she was aware of, she raged against with the utmost disdain. However, these Aluth, they were good with the blade. Damn good. She lost time and time again to children no older than their early teens. In her mind, she knew that if she drew upon her abilities as a Sage, she could mop the floor with them, but as a matter of principle, she withheld her talent. This afforded her the lessons of life that only pain and discipline could bring, and she was sharper for it.

Now that it was early morning, Aellia found that her unusual sense of honor was wasted. So, instead of a hot shower and floor work, she grabbed her silver scepter and allowed the light of Aetora to bathe her body, cleansing herself of pain and fatigue.

"One should be careful of that," came a voice from her open door.

Aellia whirled about, eyes going wide. Not that she cared for other's sense of propriety, but she was only in her small clothes and did not care to give some creeping degenerate a show. When she caught sight of one of the Candius twins—she struggled to tell them apart if she was being honest with herself—Aellia failed to keep heat from rising into her face.

"Careful of what?" Aellia snapped, trying to regain her composure. *How did she sneak up on me so easily?*

She moves with a grace befitting her station.

Oh, now you speak to me? I thought you were done with me?

I did not appreciate your methods with the Regent. As far as this Blessed, she has done nothing but show kindness, and I think it would be wise for you to learn from her.

"Everlight is a powerful gift from the High Father, as is Lifelight from the Holy Mother. We must treat Their gifts with the respect and nurturing they require, elsewise we risk contaminating ourselves and abusing that power."

"Listen, and I mean no disrespect, but I don't really give a damn," Aellia said as she fold her arms and leaned back against a wall, clutching her glowing scepter tight. "Really, no disrespect, but I don't trust any of you as far as I can spit."

"From what I have seen of you, Aellia, I trust you can spit quite far," the Blessed answered with a sly smile.

Aellia felt something rush through her. Was that... was that humor? Did she almost laugh?

"Come now, Aellia, we are Blessed, not statues. Brei and I do have a sense of humor," Ayln tutted sweetly. "Or did you think we secluded ourselves in sackcloth and ash, praying always in seclusion, and groveling in squalor?"

Aellia stared at the young woman, seeing a fire behind those crystal eyes for the first time. Eyes that matched her own now. Or at least her good eye. There was a ferocity and strength in the softness, an iron will to her velvet touch. She was beautiful and kind, but unyielding in her beliefs. Aellia had never had that. A belief in herself, something more, something else out there. She was as a ship lost at sea, driven by the waves. Alyn and her sister Brie were like a lighthouse on the shore. A bastion of truth and light.

"Pff," Aellia made the noise with all the snark she could muster. "I've never seen you in a gown that cost less than six gold bars. Don't talk to me of squalor."

Alyn raised her chin, taking the verbal blow with poise. "Ah, resorting to insulting what was gifted me. How very rich coming from someone who stole money from the very proprietor of this Manse."

Aellia went to say something, a quip she had prepared to launch at the Blessed, the arrow already drawn, barb bare. But the words, the acknowledgement that someone knew she had been stealing, clipped the proverbial bowstring, her insult clattering to the floor of her mouth dumbly.

"Aellia, I did not come her to contend. I apologize," Alyn said in earnest, her face softening as she looked on Aellia with pity.

Aellia hated that. She hated that feeling, that look, more than any thrown insult. But how did Alyn know that she had stolen Elcon's purse? He had hundreds of stashes around this place. Aellia had only found a few of them behind paintings and beneath sculptures. Strongboxes were littered throughout this massive estate, hidden with expertise and protected by thick iron.

"Don't look so shocked, Aellia," Alyn said with a wink. "Brei is a Seer. That is what she does. Imagine being girls together. I never got away with anything."

"Why did you come then?" Aellia asked, trying her best to regain some semblance of control of the conversation.

The soft smile on Alyn's face did not fade as she stepped through the threshold of the room, lighting upon a wingbacked chair with perfect poise. "You are healing far faster than expected, even with your unique gift and my talents. Other than my mother, Gallae watch her soul, I have never met one who could heal as you do. Not even our mutual bearded friend."

Aellia's eyes darted to a small table where the carved hammer that stranger had left her rested. Had he known then what he was doing? Had known who she was and what he was leaving her to face? And how would she get Iaenora's sisters to him if she didn't even know where he was?

"What about him?" Aellia wasn't listening to the Blessed; her brain was doing acrobatics, her thoughts bouncing off the walls of her mind.

"Nothing," Alyn said, tilting her head. "I speak about you, Aellia. You are perhaps the most vital link in the chain of our god's physical absence in all history. I know you are not a religious person, as much as it baffles my mind to say so, but honestly, do you know nothing of our history? Our prophecies? Our legacy?”

Aellia felt discomfort creeping up her spine. This was not the first time she had been preached to in this manse, not by a long shot. But this was the first time it had been by Alyn, and so bluntly placed.

“I know you harbor disdain for our religion, but you must admit, there is truth. You can see it, feel it. It is a part of you, and you a part of the great whole now. And with that understanding, there comes purpose and duty.”

“I have purpose enough,” countered Aellia. She felt as if she were being driven into a corner, her options cut away, leaving only the path chosen by someone else for her to follow.

“Do you?” Alyn asked without guile. She leaned forward, staring into Aellia’s eyes as if she could see into her very soul. “Do you feel fulfilled? Valued? Can you even begin to comprehend the level of trust the Ellitheor have placed in you, Aellia?”

“Trust?” All of the that overwhelming pressure, that rising tide of expectation, was washed away in an instant. “Trust? How can you speak to me of trust? I did not ask for this. For any of it. It was thrust upon me, just like everything else in your world. You take no thought or heed of those around you, beneath you, but only press forward with your own vision of how the world should be.”

“That is an unfair observation, made from a place of animosity not from a position of understanding.”

“Unfair observation?” Aellia felt as if she had been struck in the face.

“Yes,” Ayln answered with a subtle raise of her chin.

By the gods, Alyn was not relenting on this. She honestly felt that she was in a morally superior position here. Aellia was dumbstruck. How in the blazing pit of Halfak could anyone, who lived in this city especially, look about them and believe that the Church, the government, the Uppers were in the right? Were they so blind that they could not see the rampant injustices of the world? Were they so callous they could not feel the hurt and suffering of their lessers?

“We spend our days toiling for the betterment of this people, for society. What we do, what we give, is invaluable. You speak from a place of destitution, where decisions made by yourself and your parents, placed you in a disadvantage. That is unfortunate, a horrid thing that there is pain and suffering. But what have you done to crawl out of that place?”

This argument again? Aellia shut down her mind, tuning out the Blessed, whom, up until this moment, she had held in such high regard. No longer.

Ayln, noting Aellia's disconnection, paused and let out a sigh. "Aellia, please, I meant no offense."

"Your kind never do, do they?" Aellia answered bitterly.

"When Ordan and Gallae created this realm, it was a fractured place, sown with chaos and mingled with decay. Our world, the place we call Ethrea, is only but a portion of this planet. And our planet is but one of countless celestial bodies moving in an elliptical orbit around our shining son. Who is to know the number of suns in the endless sea of darkness that spans out past the eternities? How vain must we be to think our meager existence is anything but a speck of dust driven by a silent wind through the darkening void?"

Aellia looked up into the soft-featured young woman's eyes. They were not filled with distress or fear, but burned with a fervor of something internal that Aellia could not comprehend. It unsettled her, to see that expression on one who spoke of such vast concepts as if they were facts.

"What are you saying?" Aellia asked, her own curiosity ebbing past her seething frustration toward the beautiful Blessed.

"That the glory of the Ellitheor is not contained to this rock, nor this plane of existence. They supersede all things, all time and all space. Worlds without end are there, and endless are they who govern over them."

Aellia had been taught in her youth, as every child had been instructed at the hands of either the most meager of educators in single-room hovels to great scholastic entities that Ethrea was ordained by the Ellitheor. It was crafted by the hand of Ordan and the grace of Gallea into a place for their creations, humankind being the chief of their devising. Other than that, Aellia only knew of the two great stars, whose names escaped her, that represented Aetora and Ria'Elahm. But what Ayln was saying, that was borderline if not outright heresy.

"Our holy order, the Church of Ordan, was made to ensure light and truth were brought upon the minds of the Ellitheor's greatest creations, to ensure they were instructed and kept in the ways of our gods. Through time, prudence has trimmed the further truths down to the essentials. Believe in the Ellitheor, give to those in need, build up oneself, improve and prevail. These are the tenets of eternity.

These are the laws that we prescribe to. But they are the milk, not the meat. To seek a higher station, we must seek further light and knowledge. Our very own High Priest has ushered forth truths that have shaken the very foundations of our faith, uncovered lost knowledge from times when the Ellitheor and their archangels—called the Daulkaefar in the old tongue—walked Ethrea's breadth. Great monuments were built, vast tomes filled, and deep secrets laid bare during those days, now known only as the Lost Era. But lost no longer. And here, in our very courts, in our very streets, a remnant of that time has come forth. And she thinks it prudent to spend her days visiting brothels and fighting street-thugs."

Alyn's words, though sweet, stung like a barbed whip as they caught Aellia in surprise. So enamored had she become, so drawn in by the words of the Blessed, that she had not seen the underhanded blow forming. It burned, searing through pride and animosity, striking at her very core.

"His Eminence, our Shepherd Elcon von'Harr, has seen in his wisdom your great potential, but also your folly. He has asked that my sister and I help you understand the gravity of your situation, to instruct you in the rights and rituals of our faith, so that you might be prepared to face the darkness that comes upon us. Weeks now it has been that we have watched over and cared for you, nursing you back to health and providing the comforts of Gallae's grace upon you. Now, it is time for you to feel the might of Ordan's words and the righteous fury of Fenron's indignation. Too long has the Church of Ordan stood only as a bastion for the weak and the meager. Too long have we focused our blessings upon the sick and afflicted and neglected our duties to the Ellitheor. We were not founded in peace, but as a sword turned toward the darkness, made to cleave asunder that which would corrupt and destroy this place we hold dear. A speck of dust. A meaningless mote in the vastness of eternity. But a speck ordained by the Ellitheor, a people made after their image, endowed with power from on high. We will not go idly into that darkness, but rise as the dawn and bring light unto the eternities. And when we pass, so shall we pass into the endless valley of Vanherran, where we shall inherit our reward."

A righteous zeal burned in Alyn's eyes, a fervor that blossomed with her words, rising, rising into a crescendo. Cascading. Falling over Aellia, crashing down onto her. She was confused. Wary. Wonder filled her heart as Iaenora sang within her mind to the sounds of the Blessed's voice. There was truth to these words, as much as she wanted to dispute that. However, she had felt the power firsthand. She had bonded with one of those Daulkaefar and had become a Sage for this very purpose.

Despite all of this, the feelings and the facts, it did not change what she had experienced. The life she had lived in the hands of these zealots. And what now? Was she to join them? Cast aside everything she had been and was? How could she reconcile that in her mind or her heart?

"This is… it is too much," Aellia muttered, stumbling upon her words as her mind raced in a thousand directions.

"It is the burden we must bear who know the truth. Simple thoughts for simple lives," Alyn answered in consoling tones. "But you are not simple. And it is my responsibility to bring you out of your simple nature, enlighten your mind, and prepare you for what is coming."

"What is coming?" Aellia asked, cocking an eyebrow. "Little ominous, don't you think?

"Aellia," sighed Ayln. "War is coming. Not one of steel and blood, but of light and dark. Long have we held at bay that tide of corruption, the powers of Iodaba's stain. But there has been a shift. Can you not feel it? Have you not seen it in your very own life? When we found you, your body was broken and bloodied, so tainted with darkness it is a miracle you can even draw breath. Yet, you would mock us, simply because of our nature."

"Nature that has allowed countless to suffer and die in poverty and pain. Sorry if I do not feel this burning remorse for your failures."

"Failures? That is very subjective," Alyn said with a smile. "We have progressed, and in progression, some choose to be left behind. Roads are built by the hands of the many, but designed by the understanding of the few. We few understand what must be done and will use whatever tools we have to accomplish that task."

"See! Do you not see what you are saying? Even now, you only see tools and goals, not lives and people."

"We are all tools in the hands of the Master Craftsman. We are all threads for She Who Weaves the Fates. Think not so highly of yourself, even in your station as one called, that you are above the command of the Ellitheor."

"A tool struck to hard will only break."

"But you did not break, did you?" Ayln bore down on Aellia now, and whether it was her blessing or her mere fortitude, Aellia felt waves of pressure emanating from her. "You do not break. You rise. You must rise, above your past, our grievances. All of it is beneath you. You must become more, be more."

"And what if I am not what you think I am? What if I cannot rise to your lofty expectations?" Aellia asked, doing all she could to fight down that silent thrill at the Blessed words. Could she matter? Could she make a difference? She then did the only thing she knew and dug into the last vestiges of bitterness she so desperately clung to. "Or worse, what if I do? Then what will become of me?"

"You would ascend to heights none of risen to in an age," Alyn said with all of the pride and promise the Blessed could muster. "You would become a legend, a hero."

A hero.

Aellia stared into Alyn's eyes but saw nothing. Her mind was far from this place. This room and its vaulted ceilings and papered walls. Far from gilt and glamor. Far it fled, to a distant mountain range of rising peaks, purples skies, and blossoming cherry trees. She could smell the sweet flavor of nature and light. She could almost see Tomo sitting next to her, not the cracked, crystalline facade she had seen in the vision she was recalling, but her smooth, soft skin, her liquid eyes and shimmering hair. She could smell her scent, the roses and silk, honey and wine. She could feel her breath drifting down her neck and onto her shoulders. And she could hear her voice, gentle as a meadow, strong as steel, as she said, "Ethrea needs you, Aellia."

Was this what it meant to be a hero? To forsake everything you had stood for. If there were truly gods, and if they were truly good, how could they allow so much pain and hurt? How could they allow so much contention and division? And how could Aellia, having seen and felt firsthand so much of that pain, that heartache and depravity, be made into a symbol for such?

We are not what was, but the good that could be. Ordan and Gallae saw the good that could be, despite the evil, and they clung to that, sacrificed themselves for that hope, that promise of a brighter tomorrow. We can do this, Aellia. We can become together what neither of us could do alone.

We, in our pride, thought we could contain the evils of this world. We followed Ordan to that place and bound our souls in

Aellia felt as if the world were shifting underneath her. Emotions warred in her head as Iaenora's voice, her admission of her own failures, of a god's own failure, cascade over her weary mind. It was all too much. The weight of it threatened to bury her. Yet there was a light kindled somewhere in her soul. A fire of truth that flickered into existence. And whether it was Iaenora's admission, Alyn's plea, or Tomo's purpose, Aellia felt it burst into being. She felt it warm her, suffuse her body with light and truth, burning brighter and brighter.

Overtaken by this feeling, Aellia rose to her feet and extended a hand. The Oathrod that had been tucked in her belt shot upwards, and Aellia snatched it from the air mid-ascent.

"I don't give a damn about your church or your philosophies, Ayln," Aellia said firmly. "But I am not going to sit around and let those Corrupted off for what they took from me." She raised the rod and tapped at her cold, dead eye, tracing the silver down the scar etched into her face. "I am going to kill them. Every last one of them, starting with the pervert that gave me this scar."

Alyn's smile grew all the wider at Aellia's vulgarity and veneration. She rose up, standing a few fingers' breadth taller than Aellia, and smiled down at her. "Pray tell, Daughter, what can the Church do to support thee?"

"I need answers, Ayln, not half-baked, vague, religious dogma. I need to know what I can do, and I need to know where I can go, if I am to become whatever it is I must."

"Sweet sings the song of salvation, and with each dawn arise with new light," recited Ayln from some script or prayer Aellia was unfamiliar with.

"I am serious, Ayln," said Aellia. "If I am going to do this, I am doing it my way. I won't be a pawn. I won't be taken again."

"Then let us begin with the beginning," answered Ayln, her smile turning into an introspective, distant line as her browns furrowed. "To understand what you are, we must unravel why you are. And to do that, I need to speak to the one within you."

Oooh, I like her. She has great wisdom.

"I am her, talk and I'll answer."

"No, Daughter. I have spoken to the one within, heard her voice. Please, let her come forth so that we may grow together toward that holy purpose."

Are you okay with this? Aellia asked Iaenora.

Am I? Aellia, it was for this reason I awoke. The question is, are you? Once this starts, there is no turn back.

What does that mean?

It means, that more you and I shift control, the less there is you and I, and the more there is only us.

So, you're saying I'll lose control?

No, I am saying we will share control. Our wills, our thoughts and our feelings, our hurts and our memories, they will become one. It has already started. Already I can feel love for those you lost, and you likewise. I felt it in the tower. You felt my hurt when we saw that place of ash, where my sisters and I fought. Where our brother gave of himself.

I... I don't want to lose who I am.

Then don't. Hold firm to those things that make you who you are, just as I have. Some things, not even death can erase.

I am going to trust you.

Iaenora pulsed with a joy so sweet, and a love so deep, within Aellia's heart and mind it almost made her eyes mist. She blinked rapidly to clear her eyes and fortify her mind. She grasped onto her memories of Tomo and the Crew, of her childhood, those bitter, dark moments that made her into her, and leapt into the void of her soul, allowing Iaenora control once more.

"Aellia, are you alright?" Ayln asked. Concern was beginning to fracture the resolve that had been so prominently plastered across her face, making the slightest cracks of worry.

"We are well, Blessed," answered Iaenora, her voice sweeter than Aellia's but still the same. "And we have agreed upon this, together."

Alyn quickly made the sign of the hammer, drawing two fingers from her brow down to her bosom and then side to side. "Blessed be the High Father." She then pressed steepled fingers to her lips and

made a circle motion, closing her fingers once more at her brow, intoning, "Blessed be the Holy Mother. Be upon me thy grace and will."

"I am still the same who was standing here only moments before," said Iaenora with a smile. She then, in a gesture of good faith, raised two fingers to her own lips and then brow. "What then, Blessed, do we do now?"

"We must start, as I said, at the beginning," Ayln said eagerly. She moved as she spoke, making her way over to a desk and taking a seat, hastily opening a large book filled with blank pages. With a click, she prepared one of Elcon's mechanical pens and said, "Please, holy one, tell me your tale, so that I might help divine what must be."

Don't let it go to your head. Aellia said, proverbially rolling her eyes.

I shall not, for I am called and chosen. I do not fall prey to flattery.

You know I can still feel everything that is going on, right? Oh, damn. Does that mean—

Why yes, yes it does. I could feel everything, every time, every moment. We are, as I had said time and again, bonded.

"Let me begin then with our coming to this place, to the time that the House of Or first ventured from Vanherran of my father's silver ships, to cultivate this realm from a barren waste of dragon fire and darkness into a world of beauty beyond compare. Let me tell you the tale of the creation of Ethrea, and of the Fallen Ones, whose dark oaths still ravage this place that would be paradise."

Alyn's pen fell to the paper, moving in beautiful, flowing script, as Iaenora spoke of all the things she had ever known.

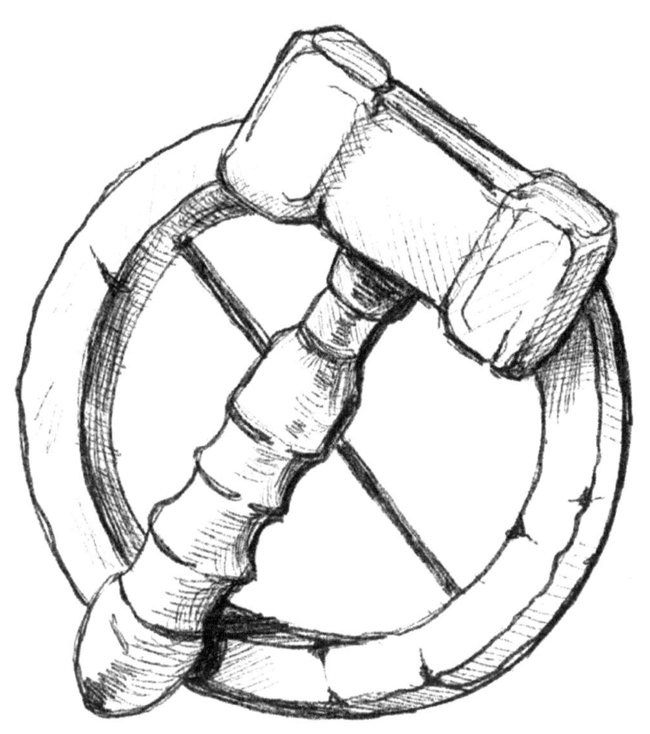

CHAPTER 28: BAGGAGE
DARIUS

Despite the events of the prior night and hectic morning, Darius had still been expected to train under the watchful eyes of Talon and the not-so-gentle hands of the Ruthvin twins, all the while listening to Tyree cackle on about this and that. Erkan had taken especial delight in working Darius on the fine gravel, and to Darius's surprise, Krunlan had opted not to fight, but to oversee the training of carrying heavy stones back and forth across the trodden grass of Dwallen Field. Dozens of other young men and women were training, and today, the stadium was littered with onlookers who pointed and laughed, reminisced about older days, and gawked at the various feats of strength shown.

"Eyes up," hissed Talon as she whipped her spear at him.

Darius barely had time to raise his circular shield, the thin haft of the spear making a loud *thwack* as it glanced just over Darius's head. He countered with a swing of a bearded training ax whose head was wrapped in leather. It had been Erik's idea, to get Darius acclimated to fighting with the axe.

Despite his innate desire to own a sword since seeing the way they were forged and crafted in this new era, Darius could not argue that his hands seemed to know the axe in a way they never did the blade.

Talon dodged the swing of Darius's axe, his muscles worn from countless hours of training. His ring, which was still laced to his shoe as he was prone to do every session, seemed to call to him. How he wished he could feel the thrum of power from the sun's rays. He had even come to realize that he missed the electric sensation from the Talah'El, Ancestral Stone. He had not had the time to think too deeply on how the ancient moonstone was able to harness the light within. But the strange effect it had on him was undeniable.

Something hard struck the side of Darius's shoulder, sending a ripple of pain down his right arm.

"Point! Match!" Erkan barked out. "Talon takes the win."

"Ye fight with passion, but rely too much on y'er strength here and here," Talon said, tapping at his arm and chest. "Ye got tree trucks for legs, use them. Ye could drive a bull off a cliff. Find y'er footing and don't flinch."

"She right, ye know," Krunlan said as he scratched at his stubbled chin; the lad hadn't shaved since arriving back at Talahmnas and red stubble was growing in thickly. "Ye got legs like me old uncle, but ye try to dance about."

"Last time, you said I need to be more nimble," huffed Darius in frustration.

"Last time ye did. Ye were acting like ye were stuck in the mud," Talon said with a feigned nod, as if she were offering some sage wisdom. "Today, y'er dance'n about like a damned fairy in a woodland meadow!"

Darius was about to say there was no such thing as fairies, but he bit his tongue, not willing to get into another argument. His brow furrowed. What if there were fairies? He pictured tiny sprites of

autumn and spring coloration, buzzing about on hummingbird wings.

"What'er thinking?" Erkan asked, stooping down and meeting Darius's eyes as he stood in the pit.

"Nothing," Darius answered, shaking the silly thought aside. It was nice, now that the Redeye was held under Tyree's shop, to have his facilities back to himself. A shiver ran down his spine at the thought of the strange creature, despite the calm clarity he had just been feeling. There was just too much newness: new information, new creatures, new alliances and biases. He felt as if he could barely hold his head above water.

"Best be think'n about how y'er gonna be toss them there bags of sand over them posts faster than me," said Krun with smile as he pulled his shirt over his head, revealing massive muscles covered in pale skin and thick red hair.

"I thought you were observing today," Darius said with a raise of an eyebrow.

Krunlan reached a hand down to his kilt and tapped a golden circlet pinned into the fabric, a tower with a boar's head in front of it. "Ain't no way I'd be letting ye off easy. I was just about learn if ye was actually strong 'er not."

"It's getting late, Krun," Erkan said with a wry bit of amusement. "Twenty bags and then it's off for dinner. I don't fancy miss'n a meal for y'er pride. Plus, Da said we're to have another conversation tonight with our guest."

A conversation. Darius knew what that was, and he wasn't the guest they meant. Memories of Krunlan brutalizing that Redeye filled Darius's mind.

"If I win, I get to come tonight," Darius said it more of a statement than a question.

"Is that a fact, little man?" asked Krun with a feigned look of surprise, barely able to hold back the smile of challenge welling in those brilliant green eyes.

"Afraid of a challenge?" Darius asked, poking at the man's ego. Who was he to call him little man? Darius was at least eight to ten years his senior and was no small person.

"Krun, that's Father's call," Erkan said flatly.

"I don't have my ring on," Darius as he climbed up out of the pit, eyeing the brothers, the metal. "What's the harm?"

"No harm," Krun said with a shrug of his massive shoulders.

"Fine," Erkan said with a huff.

"Let's make it a little more interesting," Darius said, the wheels of his mind turning fast now. This was his chance. He needed to act while their blood was hot and a bet was on.

"Oye?" the twins said in tandem.

"If I win, I want the right to call out my challenger," Darius said. "And if I win, I want a Danelander's reward. I will have earned it."

The two went stock-still. Darius saw it. A perfect way forward, despite all the convolution of his time spent in Talahmnas. He needed to get to the Apostle, to deliver the contents of that sealed envelope, he owed that much to Elcon. But in the north there was that great mountain from his dreams and visions. With Lori's awakening as the Sage of Mind, and her subsequent affirmation of his purpose to find the other four Sages and bring them together to re-forge the chains that held the Fallen Ones imprisoned, Darius was certain of his direction. His purpose. He just needed to get to that mountain.

A smile spread slowly across Erkan's lips. Krunlan cocked an eyebrow before realization seemed to strike him. The two then turned in unison to face Darius.

"Deal," said Erkan. "However, only the Gamemaster can permit a participant to call out a challenge. I will personally ask for this boon if ye beat my brother. Do ye accept on those terms?"

It wasn't perfect, but it was as good as Darius thought he would get. He had a plan. Complete the Ulkeniheim, challenge Erik for the right for an audience with King Dane, use that along with Lori's abilities to show his intent, and at long last, find the others and complete his purpose.

Darius extended a hand and said, "Deal."

Both Krun and Erkan tapped their fists to their brows before taking Darius's hand in turn, saying, "On my head, so be my honor."

When Darius turned about, he saw Talon and Tyree watching, both with amused expressions, whispering and chortling with each other. Let them laugh. Darius did not care. He would show these Danelanders what true strength looked like.

Tyree wheeled away suddenly, leaving the four of them to get prepped for the tossing. Talon helped Darius with his wrappings while Erkan helped Krunlan. She moved with expert swiftness, all the while providing little tips and tricks on how best to hoist and toss the sandbags. Each one weighed between two and three stone, which in and of itself was not that much. But a line of twenty such bags, spaced two measures apart on incremental scaling bars, well, that all added up to make the challenge far more than what met the eye.

"Welcome all!"

The thunderous sound of Tyree's voicing being amplified over the whole of Dwallen Field sent all eyes toward the announcer's box, where a massive, flaring bronze tube was stationed.

"We do have a bit of a challenge here today," Tyree continued on as those who had just been practicing began to make their way off of the field.

Darius looked over at the twins who stood in smug satisfaction at his concerned expression. He had no idea all the attention would be turned onto him. But, upon taking two whole seconds to think about it, this was exactly the sort of thing a people whose whole existence was based around showing off how strong they were would do. Of course any challenge of such would be met, especially when it was between such of the blood of the Ruthvin clan.

"Our very own Krunlan, Red Boar of the High Tower, has been challenged to a feat of strength," Tyree proclaimed with all the magnetism of a great showman. "By the very guest of the High Hall, defender of the Spanning Wall. Ye've heard his name, what he's done. Darius, the Ironbolt!"

"What?" Darius asked under his breath to Talon.

"Didn't think they wouldn't give ye a name?" Talon scoffed. "Everyone's heard about what ye did at the Wall. Though I don't think they actually believed ye turned into a bear. But they done gone and think that patch of silver in y'er beard is right nice. Started calling ye Ironbolt. I kind of like it, meself."

Darius still found the way Talon spoke slightly jarring, despite having spent several days with her. Every time the spear woman spoke, he expected to see pale flesh and red hair, not tan skin and dark eyes. The sash of plaid about her pinned with a golden circlet was the only thing marking her Danelander, but she was Danelander, through and through.

"Ironbolt, is it?" Krunlan said with a laugh, a laugh which Darius was not sure was filled with good humor or hidden spite. He chose to believe the former. "Let's test y'er metal then."

Darius's ears burned as all eyes fell on him. Well, they fell on Krunlan as well, but he hated the attention, the focus. He wanted to shrink away into a cave and hide himself. His thumb slid across bare flesh as an itch of annoyance crept its way up his spine.

Half a dozen lads in dull kilts rushed to and fro, casting heavy bags of sand in a straight line, two by two. Darius and Krun watched, neither looking at the other, though Darius did not miss the stupor of focus that fell across Krun's face. He went blank, as if the whole of existence fell onto this one moment. Darius, however, allowed his mind to race through a dozen means of getting ahead of the colossal Danelander.

"Lifters ready?" Tyree cried into the amplifying device.

"Halfak break the weak," Krunlan shouted in reply.

Darius turned his neck left and then right, cracking it loudly. A grim smile spread across his lips. This would, if nothing else, be fun.

A cannon fired a blank, its report rumbling the ground beneath Darius's feet. Before he even had time to register what had happened, the red-headed Danelander was sprinting toward the first sack of packed sand as a jubilant cry escaped his mouth. Darius tore after him, his arms and legs pumping with everything he had.

Krunlan was, to Darius's surprise, very fast. Absurdly fast actually. The young man moved with a speed that should not have been possible, not for someone of his build. Darius reached the first sandbag and threw it without taking the appropriate time to plant his feet properly. It didn't matter, it was over the bar and he was on to the next, his eyes never leaving Krun's hulking form.

How was he doing that?

The lad was already two bags ahead of him.

Darius saw it. It was faint, but there. The man's bloody tattoos shone with a pale light that was so faint, Darius was sure no one else could possibly see it. So, that was how it was going to be?

Darius dropped to a knee, tearing at his laces. Krunlan moved onto bag five, tossing swiftly over the high bars of the scoring posts. So much for strength and honor. Darius heard someone yelling at him to get up. He was certain it was Talon. He did not care.

Cool, heavy metal slid over his finger. The whole world seemed to slow to a single moment, an exact heartbeat of thrill. Bright, burning beams of sunlight extended themselves from on high. It was almost as if they were calling out to him. And so, Darius answered, Binding those reaching rays of pure power to his very essence.

In hindsight, it was really a careless thing to do. But Darius did not give a damn. Power rushed through him, scorching away every

bit of weariness and soreness that had clung to him from the day's training. Ecstasy danced along his fingertips and acid stung his tongue and eyes. It was a beautiful, terrible cacophony, and he reveled in it.

"Oy!" Erkan cried out from the sidelines. "No ring!"

But it was too late. Darius burst forward. He ran so fast that even he couldn't believe it. The harnessed light from the Talah'El made each step feel as if tiny pins were pricking at his flesh, but he heeded it not. For he was beyond those petulant feelings. Golden tears stung the sides of his face as he threw bag after heavy bag over the posts with alacrity unbound.

Krunlan was only two bags from the finish line. Darius had four. He pulled upon his Bindings, more and more he drew into himself. His blood felt like molten metal. His skin like shattered glass. He was a pressure pot that could not be contained. He was headed toward Burn Out and he could not find it in him to stop. The bliss was far too much, the pain too exquisite. He had never felt so alive.

"It's down to the line!" It was Tyree's voice, amplified by that strange bronze speaker. It felt like nails dragged down glass plates. It made Darius's skin crawl and teeth ache. But it would not stop him now.

Darius reached for his final bag, wrenching it up from the ground with fingers that blistered and oozed. The bag flew far above the needed height required to clear the pole, and crashed down with such force that its seams burst asunder, spewing sand across the grassy field.

"Bloody cheat!" Someone was running toward them.

Darius whirled about, his vision tunneling as the blurred images of two people closing in at an alarming speed filled his focus. Pain struck, like needles jabbing into his eyes. He fell to his knees as wild spasms caused his muscles to tense and twitch.

"That was downright incredible!" Yelled another as a massive hand clapped him on the back, breaking his focus.

Lights whirled around him, everything melting into hues of gold and black.

"Stand back," a female voice called out in clear command. "He is burning up."

"Haz'draff kleven!"

A bout of icy water splashed over Darius's face, breaking his concentration and the Binding he was clinging to with every fiber of

his being. He heard as much as felt the hissing and splatting of the water as it turned to steam upon his burning flesh. He could smell the acrid scent of cooked meat and charred hair. But he could smell something else too. The sweet scent of spiced honey and lilac.

"You're alive." That was it. That was the best Darius's half-fried brain could come up with? Embarrassment cascaded over him as he slowly blinked his eyes open.

There she stood, sunlight blazing around her silhouette, casting a shadow over him. Her hair was loose, long waves of onyx that fell on to bare shoulders. His eyes drifted down from her hair onto her slender neck, which was wrapped in a high collar of her green dress. It had a window over the top over her cleavage—a feature Darius's eyes were hung up on for a second too long—and frilled sleeves that attached to the dress at the bust. She had fingerless black gloves of lace, which were gripped tight around her ivy-twisted wand. Which was pointing directly at him; the remnants of an emerald rune fading into motes of light still hung around the tip.

"What in Ethenealal's name are you doing, messenger boy?" Izebal's voice was filled with scorn and reproval. "Are you trying to get yourself killed?"

Darius could hear the whispers, even now, rising up. Murmurs of 'Diju' and 'witch'. It seemed that even though their Lord had commanded that Izebal be treated with respect, not every Danelander was on board with such a notion. Izebal, to her credit, did not seem to notice them in the slightest. Perhaps she couldn't even hear them. Darius's ears were still enhanced from his Binding, though that power was rapidly ebbing away.

"No," Darius croaked, his throat feeling as though he had drunk molten glass.

"Save your strength," Izebal said as she slid her wand into a holster at her hip, the split fronts of her skirts whipped aside to reveal the skin-tight trousers and thigh-high riding boots she wore.

"How…" Darius started, but it felt as if a thousand drummers were beating a war song between his ears. He winced and rubbed at the bridge of his nose.

"Krun, you great oaf! How dare you use your sigils here?"

"What?" Krunlan answered with wheezing breaths. "No one said it weren't allowed!"

"Blood and stone, Krun! At least ye could've won?"

"What?" Krun thundered. "I did win!"

Darius couldn't stop staring at Izebal. She looked like an angel. He wanted to reach out and touch her face. It looked so smooth and soft. He wanted to touch more than her face, he wanted to run his hands down her back, to tangle his fingers in her hair. His thoughts drifted as his head dropped on his shoulders. His body was soaked with once-frigid water now turned to steam, but he couldn't feel any of it. His nerves were burnt away. He couldn't have even felt her if he tried.

That dark thought turned his guts into knots, a mingling of unexpected shame for thinking such crass things about Izebal and a morose reality of just how different they were. She was a beautiful woman, a high-ranking member of the Diju troupe and powerful mage. Darius was a lost and forgotten warrior. True, he had a purpose now, but was there room for anything other than that in his life now? Sharp bitterness stung his heart and soul.

"By my beard," cackled in an unmistakable voice. "Y'er a sight for sore eyes, I do say! Blood and bloody stone, don't that be the truth!"

Tyree's voice broke Darius's melancholy spiral of self-loathing. Was he really that pitiful? Or was it the aftermath of Binding and his nearing the burning point? Did it matter? Was any of it a lie?

"Tyree, surely there must be a rule against this?" Erkan said in a huffing, condescending voice. "It broke the terms of the engagement."

"Broke what terms?" Tyree quipped. "As I do recall, ol' Ironbolt here didn't say he wouldn't use his ring, only that he weren't wearing it at the time. And besides, Krun used his sigil plain as day. These non-sighted folks might not be able to seen it, but y'er brother here tapped into his wells way before Darius ever touched his ring. So, who's playin' fair or not?"

Erkan went beet red, but Krunlan just let out a thunderous laugh that sounded almost exactly like his father's. "Ye got me there. Both played on a technicality, that do be the facts."

"Ye stone-for-brains chut!" Erkan shouted as he slapped Krunlan across the back of his head. "It's gonna take days to replenish y'er sigils. I told ye we have an appointment tonight."

Darius's brain seemed to be catching up, for that bit finally made sense to his addled mind. Tonight. The Redeye. He needed to be there. Questions. He had—

Something soft and smooth touched the side of his face. Again the soothing scent of spiced honey and blossoming lilacs wafted over Darius.

"Re'en brenael, al'kuz tra'nal."

Three green runes formed around Izebal's hand, swirling forms of light. Her eyes shone, as did her amulet, in a manner he had not seen for some time. She had recovered her full strength. It seemed her journey to Beyorne was a success. Darius would need to ask about that later.

A shock of vitality, unlike anything he had ever felt before in his life, coursed its way through his body and made every muscle in Darius's body constrict in painful cramps. When the healer Ayln had helped him in the Temple of Ordan, it had been like water washing away his pain, cool and refreshing. This was like an avalanche tumbling through his flesh, tearing away his maladies in a ferocious rumble. However, that was nothing compared to the sensation when the spell touched the wound in his abdomen. Pain, sickening and sudden, lanced through that rune-scrawled marking.

"Be still, messenger boy," Izebal chided in her musical voice, as if she had not a care in the world. "I am trying to restore you to the best of my abilities, and you are making it very difficult."

"Ain't never seen Lifelight used in such a way," came Tyree's voice from seemingly nowhere. "Makes sense though. It do be called Lifelight after all."

Izebal gave a snort and a roll of her beautiful green eyes at the old mage's remark, an action only Darius could see. Then she winked at him. All of the pain seemed to dissipate at once, replaced by a numbness he had never before experienced. It felt as his heart had stopped beating. This was only amplified by the sudden and overwhelming need to swallow. The only problem was, his mouth had gone dry as a desert.

"It is the way of the Tapestry," Izebal said, rising up once more and turning away from Darius to face Tyree.

Darius felt a jolt of jealousy that she would turn from him, leaving him on the ground. This jealousy immediately turned to embarrassment, burning his ears nearly as badly as if he had drawn upon his Binding once more.

"Y'er quite the impressive study, lassie," said Tyree without a small amount of adoration. "Never would I have thought to use a repelling incantation on an injury like that."

"Darius is strong," said Izebal. A statement that seemed to kick start Darius's heart back into beating. "I did not need to heal him, only purge out the effects of his overconsumption. His body will do the rest for him. Besides, I think it will do him well to learn this lesson. It is not the first time he has almost died due to his stubbornness."

Darius took that as his cue to rise up. Carefully, he drew on a single ray of light, binding it ever so gently to his essence. He could feel the very hairs on his arms sprout as the blisters of his flesh seemed to melt away into whole skin.

"I am fine," he grunted. "Thank you for asking."

"More than fine," Izebal said, turning her attention back on him. "Though you do seem to have a nasty habit of losing your shirt."

Darius blinked in confusion before a secondary wave of mortification washed over him. It had not seemed uncouth to remove his shirt for training. It had not bothered him to be bare chested around the twins or even Talon. But he suddenly wished he could crawl into a cave and die now under Izebal's discerning eyes.

"This is all fine and dandy talkin', but who won, Master Tyree?" interjected Krunlan in a merciful display of his utter lack of decorum.

"Won?" Tyree said, whipping his head up from Darius and focusing on the younger, but broader of the two brothers. "O, yes, that do be right. Won is an interestin' word, ain't it?"

"It ain't interestin', it's a simple one. Who tossed their last bag first?"

"Tossed? Oh, that do be ye, Krun. No doubt there," Tyree said with a smile that spoke of too many other thoughts.

"What does that supposed to mean, ye kooked up old codger?" asked Krunlan, the back of his neck turning bright red.

"Well, ye tossed y'ers first. Plain and simple. But his did clear the post first, flew faster than a sinner out'er service. By blood and stone it did."

"So, I won," Krunlan stated, not as a question but an immutable fact. "Rules is rules, and they state the first who tosses their last bag wins."

"Ah, but don't it say something for the little man who did get all the way caught up and tossed his past y'ers?"

"I don't give a bloody piss what ye've got to say for it, the chut didn't win, I did."

"If that is what you need, then I concede," said Darius, not wanting this to sour anything. He had what needed. He could still win the Ulkeniheim. He would still get to Dane. He'd just have to figure out the best way to gain access to the Apostle and then convince this High King of his need to find a random young woman who could potentially be a long-lost sage. Come to think of it, this was not nearly as clear and clean cut as he had felt it was at the conclusion of his vision.

"Don't ye do that!" Krunlan said. "Y'er concedin' nothin'! I won! And as part of me win'n, as is my right, I'll allow ye a boon. Ye can come with us tonight to see the Redeye."

"The what?"

All eyes whipped to Izebal. Any humor or levity that had been in her face prior to that moment was gone, replaced by an intense expression of confusion and anger.

"We captured us a Redeye," Krunlan said awkwardly, trying to regain some of his lost momentum. "Got 'im chained up under Tyree's in a Moonstone cell with a kroichae about the chut's neck so it can't do no harm."

Izebal's eyes flashed between those around her, landing on Darius's. Something passed between them. It was subtle, but he felt it. He felt her concern, her anxiety about this new found fact. He hadn't liked the idea of keeping the Morrean-spawn around. In all honesty, he wasn't even sure of how the thing had come into existence. But there was something dark in Izebal's expression that sent a cold spike of dread deep into his core, right under the handprint seared into his chest.

"It's in my house, and y'er me guest," said Tyree, his voice as aloof from the mounting tension as it could possibly be. Seemingly unaware of all the glaring eyes that fell upon him. "Tell ye what, lassie. Ye tell me how ye did that little trick with Darius there and I'll introduce ye to the chut meself."

Izebal did not move for a long moment. Darius could see the thoughts whirling behind her emerald eyes. There was pain there, deep, ugly pain, but also concern. Darius had witnessed firsthand what those Huntsmen had done to her troupe. Had she also encountered these Redeyes? He was certain now that she had. It was written all over her stoney facade.

"Tyree..." Erkan started.

"Pipe down, laddie," Tyree snapped. "It's up ter' ye, lassie. If'n ye want, ye can come."

"There are things I need to discuss with Darius," Izebal finally said after another few moments of silence, the offering dangling over her head like sword. "I accept your offer, Master Mage, but if I decline later, please understand I mean no offense by it."

Tyree looked between Darius and Izebal, a slow smile growing upon his wrinkled and scared face. "Of course, lassie. Of course."

"I need to talk with Father," said Erkan as he gripped his brother's arm. "Let's be off before ye spill anything else across the table, eh, brother?"

"Bah!" Krunlan said, "I told ye I'd beat 'im. Ye be overthinkin'!"

Erkan turned his brother about, something Darius was a little surprised he was able to do due to the size difference. But Erkan was no small man. If Krunlan was a stone wall, Erkan was a tower, looming and imposing, containing all his mother's poise and regality. Darius even found himself smiling as he watched the two saunter off, sending biting comments back and forth in low tones. Talon had chosen to follow them and soon joined in the fray of loose insults and peeling laughter.

"They do mean well, they do," said Tyree, who had taken note of Darius's watching. "Lady Sophie raised 'em good'n right, that she did, Gallae grace her soul. A little bull-headed, but that's needed these days."

The stands of people seemed to drain, most of them pressing themselves toward the two brothers, crying out words of praise for Krunlan's strength and the honor he brought to the House of Ruthvin. A few looked as if they wanted to come and talk to Darius. That was the last thing he wanted right now. He had almost forgotten that his whole event had taken place before an audience, and he kicked himself now for allowing it to even happen. What was he doing? He was a Guardian, and he was playing games?

As if he could read Darius's mind, Tyree wheeled about on his chair and shouted at the press of onlookers. "Of with ye. Ye had y'er show. If ye want to see something truly spectacular, come back tomorrow for the Ulkeniheim. Now, off I said, off or I'll turn the whole lot of ye into swine!"

The crowd seemed to get the picture for they turned away with a singular sigh of both disappointment and reluctance, but the concern of Tyree's retribution seemed to keep them in check. Darius

could not help but wonder if the old man could turn someone into a pig.

No. Of course not. That was impossible.

And yet, Darius had seen too many impossibilities these past days here in Talahmnas for him to mark it off as verbal bantering. If there was someone who could, and more importantly would, turn someone into a pig, it would be Tyree McDoogle. Of that, Darius was certain.

Tyree turned his attention back on Darius and Izebal. "Y'er both welcome at me home tonight, I do hope to see ye. I'm sure ye two have much to discuss. And don't worry about the crowds. Follow me and I'll show ye a hidden way out. Made it just for folk like me who have brains that work better'n our feet. Oh, and the lassie is right: won't ye try coverin' up?"

Tyree turned a bronze knob on the side of his chair, which activated a series of loud clicks and a whirl of turning tumblers. A spring-release opened a small compartment from which Tyree retrieved a glossy blue tunic of sorts with a silver collar with moons embroidered upon it.

"It might be a bit snug but looks like y'er shirt was hauled off with the rest o' the gear back there," Tyree said as he tossed the glistening shirt to Darius.

Darius caught the silky shirt, which felt like liquid in his gruff hands. He had a sudden fear the threads would catch on his calluses and tear, but it was not so. Nor did the grime and dirt on his fingers stain the pale blue cloth. Darius tugged the tunic over his shoulders, covering himself and hiding away the only two scars that seemed to stay on his body now.

"Blue is not your color," said Izebal with a snort. "And it does not go well with your skirt."

"It's a kilt," rebutted Darius before he could stop himself.

"Ah. So you have assimilated yourself well then, my messenger boy?" Her voice was sweet as honey, filled with a levity he had not heard from her before.

"I take it your journey to Beyorne went well enough then?"

"You could say that," Izebal said with a shrug of her shoulders. She seemed brighter, as if freed from some darkness that had held her. "It feels good to have meditated in such a sacred place."

Darius almost said that he had missed her, but then thought better of it. Instead, he chose to point at Tyree's shrinking form and

said, "We should follow. I don't really want to be stuck around anymore Danelanders right now."

Izebal let out a soft laugh as she shook her head. "You are beyond me, Darius. All this power, so much fear of others."

"I don't like the stares people give," Darius grunted as he began walking. "It's like they can see right through me."

"And what is there to hide? I have never met a man so good as you, who fears so deeply the premonitions of others. I dare say that I, a Diju, am more comfortable walking amongst these than you."

How did she do that? How did she make light of a centuries-long prejudice fueled by hate and misconception? She had feared stepping foot into this place so deeply in what seemed like only a few days ago, and now? Now she walked about with a smile so bright it could cause the flowers to grow.

"Take a breath," Izebal said. "I will protect you if needs be. There is no need to fear now that I have replenished my wells."

Darius wanted to retort, to say he didn't need protection. But that would have only made him seem more petulant, more weak and cowardly. He, once again, chose a grunt and silence as his conversational tool.

The two followed Tyree in silence, winding their way toward a hidden gate in the oval stadium. Tyree hefted his strange scepter, something Izebal stared at through the corners of her eyes, and waved it about. Blue light cut a doorframe out of the wood which swung inwardly, revealing a path away from the field.

"Keep close, it's a wee bit tight, mind ye," said Tyree over the back of his chair as all three stepped into darkness beneath the rafters. With a word, the head of his staff turned into an overly complex Fragtorch, drowning the wooden supports and a narrow path in pale blue light. "This'll wind about to where me MAC is at, if'n ye want to ride with me. If not, ye can make y'er way to the bottom of the High Hill, and take a pony or two up t'er the top from there."

"We'll take the pony," Darius said a little too quickly for his pride, but not fast enough if it meant staying out of that deathtrap.

"Suit y'erselves," Tyree answered. "I'll be off then. Up ahead the path will end. At the wall, just say, 'jrot'kaj' and pour a little light on it. It's made for Everlight, but I don't see why Lifelight wouldn't do the same. Words is words, ain't they, lassie?"

"Jrot is to open," Izebal said slowly. "What is kaj?"

"Ha! And they say Danelanders ain't got no manners!" Tyree laughed out in rolling bouts of manic laughter. "Please! Ain't ye ever heard of it? By my beard and stones, Diju indeed. Ain't nothing wrong with that, I knew me a nice Diju lady 'bout sixty years or so ago. Nice woman, tall and sweet as honey and Spring flowers. Them were the summer nights, they were."

"Respectfully, I don't think any Diju would lay with a Danelander, even if it was decades past," Izebal said, trying her best to cover the scorn in her words with a laugh. She seemed to notice the turn of her tone, and added lightly, "That was rude of me, I am sorry."

"Bah, think nothin' of it, lassie. I wasn't always a mangled old codger," Tyree said with a twinkle in his eye. "I used to be quite handsome, mind ye. And she was a beauty beyond compare. That why I never settled down with her. I mean that and the fact the wylven took a stone with 'em with they tore into me leg!"

Izebal's face burst into scarlet at Tyree's crude joke. Darius had to choke back a laugh, which turned into actual choking. Tyree joined in with another peel of laughter as he wheeled his chair about and began to drive off in the opposite direction, humming a merry tune.

Darius, without thinking, raised a hand and placed it on Izebal's shoulder as he fought to regain his composure in the dark. He froze instantly, going stiff as a board.

"I am so sorry," he muttered, dropping his head to his side in utter humiliation.

"Don't be, messenger boy," answered Izebal.

And there, in the darkness, he felt her hand grab hold of his. Long, slender fingers found their way through his. Cool flesh and the soft cloth of her glove was all that there was in the world in that moment. Darius's heart simultaneously froze in his chest and beat wilder than a feral hound chasing down its prey. She drew closer, her body pressing against his arm, her other hand wrapping around his bicep.

"I was worried," she said softly, her voice barely more than a whisper. "I did not want to leave you like that. I—"

Her words fell into the darkness.

What did he say? What should he say?

Darius tried to think back at all the words of adoration his father had bestowed up his own mother. But none of them were his words for Izebal. How could he tell her the hurt and fear he felt at night when she was gone? How could he tell her how much his missed seeing her face, how her eyes would light up the entire room when she entered? He had to say something. Anything.

She let out a soft laugh. "I am just glad you are alright, Darius." She moved quickly, rising up and placing the softest kiss on his cheek.

Izebal let go of his arm, stepping away quickly. "I am so sorry, Darius. I—my—I did not mean to overstep."

Darius stepped forward, reaching into the darkness until his hands found hers. He grabbed them, holding them as gently as he could, knowing that his own hands trembled and shook. "Don't go."

Izebal fell into his body, casting his arms to the side as she drove her head into his chest, just as she had done that dreadful night. She clung to his body, wrapping her arms about him. This time, Darius did not struggle to know where to place his hands, he did not second guess every motion. He acted on instinct, wrapping his own arms about her waist. Izebal was larger than life in his eyes, but in the dark, she was lean of frame and fit so perfectly into his arms that it seemed they were made to hold her.

Neither said a word, they just stood there for long moments of silence, each clinging on to the other. They were all they had left in this world. She was not a sage; he did not have to find her. She had chosen to be here with him. She had lost her family, so had he. She had been hurt, was hurting. And yet, she strengthened him, poured into him, cared for him. She had chosen to come with him to this place, to enter the realm of her adversaries just to save little Ery. And maybe that, more than anything, was the truest reason he had fallen for her.

"Izebal," Darius's voice was strained and, much to his chagrin, a little high and cracked. He cleared his throat.

Izebal lifted her head, and thanks to his enhanced eyes, he could just make out those beautiful green eyes. He stared into them, losing himself for the briefest moment before regaining his composure. "I have never done this before."

"Shh," Izebal whispered up at him. She rose on her toes once more and kissed him softly on the lips before nestling in close once more. "Not here. Just, thank you, Darius. Thank you for being you."

CHAPTER 29: LIE UPON LIE
AELLIA

Aellia sat in the ashen remains of her old room. The mostly dilapidated tower, being one of the only remaining structures of the Loft, loomed over the charred remains of the Crew's fortress. The Loft, the place she had learned to call home, was gone. But the memories burned hot behind her watering eyes. In the center of what had once been the common area, where Felohme and Belthazer would banter about their shared-but-differing heritage, where Felik would stoke an open flame, saying it was what brought people together, where she and Tomo would antagonize Tornak, thankful to no longer be the youngest, Aldorian was now tied to a chair. He who had caused the loss of all of this, who had extorted Felik into taking the job and subsequently ratting them out to the Mayor. He who had relished in their demise and profited for it. He who was in league with those who took away her love.

Two days had passed since she had broken him free of the Twisted Stool. For two days she had come and visited him, ungagging him and forcing soured water down his throat. She hated him, but she needed him alive.

Today, she would start to ask questions.

Today, he would answer.

Aellia dropped down from her perch. The wilting, sniveling cur winced as she did so, nearly toppling over in his chair. He smelled of excrement and sweat. His fancy trousers were stained and the place below his seat where she had carved a hole with a knife was a picturesque image of true depravity. Aldorian's eyes were sunken and his skin pallid. Sores were beginning to form around his wrists where she had bound him, and not even the steady rain could cleanse him of the grime and suit that covered his bare torso.

"Pathetic, in'it?" Aellia said as she drew not Tomo's Di'kha, but a ladle, dipping the cold, metal spoon into a bucket of rainwater. "Drink, Regent?"

Aldorian no longer swore at her, no more threatening or masquerading. No, the pig squealed for mercy, eyes weeping gruesome tears. It was pathetic. Aellia sloshed the ladle's contents over his face, causing him to flinch back.

"You seemed so eager to see me before," Aellia snarled, recalling the young woman who had been bought and paid for to look like her, to do things to him that no woman should have to. Not to a man like this. She slid out a pair of white gloves, causing Aldorian to shrink further inward.

"Please," Aldorian choked out. "Please, spare me. I... it wasn't... he killed my father. I didn't..."

"Shut your whore mouth," Aellia spat. "You speak only when spoken too, Regent."

Aldorian seemed perplexed by that. She saw color rise in his neck, though it did not make it to his face. So there was still a little fight in the fat pup after all. Good. He would need it.

"We're going to play a little game, you and I," Aellia said, sweetening her voice as she leaned close to him, placing her hands on his thighs. Even that meager touch made her stomach turn. "As you can clearly surmise, you are in deep shit. I didn't want this, any of it. But you, you're going to help me get to the bottom of it."

"But... but... I don't," Aldorian stuttered.

"Shh shh shh!" tutted Aellia as she rose back to her full height, which was barely taller than the seated man. She rubbed the bottom of her chin with a gloved finger. "This is the point of the game where I ask a question, and then you answer. Plain and simple."

"Anything, please, please, just, don't hurt me."

"And why would I hurt you? What could such a noble and good man as you, Regent of Southend, have done to harbor scorn from one so lowly as I?"

"Stop! Please!" Aldorian was crying openly now, weeping great tears and trembling.

"You're pathetic," Aellia huffed, crossing her arms. "Uppers, the lot of you. Pathetic."

Calmly, Aellia, we need answers. Honey coaxes the bear, not thorns.

Bees sting bears.

And what does that accomplish in the end?

You had your turn at the helm, speaking sweet words and fanciful histories. If I didn't know better, I'd say you had a soft spot for that Blessed.

Fine. Get your answers, but remember, you chose to be more, to be better.

Aellia let out a frustrated huff. "Okay, before we play our little game, let us introduce ourselves clearly. Why don't you go first?" Aellia flashed the man a wicked grin.

"You know me! You know who I am! I didn't do anything! He tricked me! Used me!"

"Well, that is an interesting name indeed," said Aellia as she began to walk around the man, dragging a fingertip across his shoulder as she did so. "I had thought it Aldorian. Perhaps we can try again." Aellia stopped, slapping both hands down hard on either side of him, causing him to flinch violently.

"Arrius! Arrius Aldorian! I am your, erm, Regent of Southend! I was trying to make it a better place, safer place!"

Aellia struck him across the back of the head, holding back so as to not crack his skull, but hitting him hard enough to send a message. "I said your name. Is that such a hard question to answer? Come now, Arrius, let us be eager in our listening, so we do not cause unnecessary pain."

Aellia!

He knows who those demons are! He knows where to find them, and if he knows about them, he can help us find your sisters. That's who they were after. Besides, Elcon is gone to Templetown right now. What else am I to do? Twiddle my thumbs?

Kindness is free.

Was it freely given to those Morreans the night of the Plight? You sure went into great detail of the slaughter that day. The way in which you had spoken of the beautiful dance of death your brother danced. The way your sisters crushed and burned and drowned hundreds. Do you not recall that?

Iaenora went still in Aellia's mind. That hadn't been fair. They shared openly their memories, and that was a low blow, even for Aellia. She had seen how Iaenora and her sisters had slaughtered thousands alongside the armies of the Daulkaefar. She had felt the pangs of each life Iaenora had taken, and despite the depravity, she had also felt the seething hatred Iaenora had harbored against those corrupted beings.

I need him to talk, Aellia echoed in her head. *I need this for both of us. If we're going to work together, we're going to have give and take. And tonight, we take the answers.*

I understand. I will strive to not intervene again this night. But I do not approve. This one is not corrupted by Iodaba's Touch.

No, and that is what makes him worse. He had no reason, not external factor driving him to evil. He chose it. Every step along the path he chose himself. Well, I am the end of that path, and he will reap what he sowed.

Aellia cleared her throat, returning her attention to the quaking man. "Sorry, I had a minor distraction. Can't say it won't happen again. You see, in your pathetic attempts to make Southend a 'safer place', you catapulted me into a world that shouldn't be. You see, my whole life I was taught, by schoolhouses and churches alike, that there was no magic. That Ordan and Gallae reigned supreme. That fairytales weren't real and demons were locked away behind Halfak's fiery gates, sealed by Ordan's might and Gallae's grace. Imagine my surprise when I found myself surrounded by men who walk through flames and fly through the sky? Imagine my stupefaction when little old me found out that I could control the very winds."

Aellia walked in front of Aldorian and raised a hand to his face. She created a small sphere of condensed wind, a tiny thunderhead held in the palm of her hand. His eyes widened with shock and awe.

"You see, I am beginning to think that I am not alone in my discoveries, that people like you have known about this all along and, despite my better judgement for thinking this way, used it as a means to push us down."

"I didn't know! I didn't know!" Aldorian cried out, his body convulsing as Aellia pushed the orb of storms closer to his face.

"Of course you didn't! You're a piss-ant!" shouted Aellia as she crushed the storm in a fist. "But you found out! You found something, and you jumped blindly into it, because why? Why did you do it?"

"I didn't know!"

"I asked you a question!" Aellia struck him across the cheek, re-splitting his lip.

"Answer me!"

"He... he promised. He said—" Aldorian tried to speak, but his tongue was swollen and his eyes unfocused.

Aellia threw up her hands into the air in frustration.

You hit him too hard.

Obviously.

He is not going to speak if you keep breaking his jaw.

Aellia wanted to slap Iaenora.

That is impossible, as I am only Aethereal now; your soul and mine mingled together.

I'd step off a bridge if it meant getting you to be quiet every once in a while.

That would be most unbecoming and unnecessary. Not only would the impact hurt yourself and not I, but your body would heal itself in time, as long as there was Everlight near.

So I'll dive off of a bridge far away from any Source.

There are over thirty wells in this region alone. Though many have grown significantly stagnant in my long slumber. That being said, I think I could still mend you with even the most meager amount Everlight.

What did I do to deserve this?

You chose to stand against those emboldened by the darkness of Iodaba, to stand for the Light and protect those who live in innocence.

I don't remember doing any of that.

Funny how the heart refuses to lie even when the mind does.

"I wanted revenge."

Aldorian's words startled Aellia; she had fully turned her attention away from the incoherent man. Incoherent no longer.

"The man you called Felik. He was a lie. His name was a lie. He killed my father. He deserved what happened to him." A lingering smile spread across Aldorian's bloodied lips as he spoke. "He was a failure. And his failure cost lives. Lives of pureblooded men. Honorable men. Had our government not gone soft, never would we have allowed tainted blood into positions of authority and power."

"What are you going on about now, you fat pig?" asked Aellia as she stomped toward the man.

He did not flinch, not this time, but raised his hollow eyes to meet hers. A fire burned behind them, cold embers igniting into hot flames of hatred. "He was piss. And because of his cousin, he was given a command. My father was a gods-damned war hero, and that buffoon led them to their deaths. Do you know of the Folly of the Fourth? Have you not heard of that? A shame hidden. But carried by each living family member of those lost. And imagine my unwelcome surprise to learn that their annihilator walked free, in my own city. I did what was just!"

"You made a deal with the Fallen, sold your blood for vengeance. Now look at where we are! What you've done!"

"What I've done? Me? You pretentious little prick! I was trying to save our people! Wash away the stain left by your kind."

"My kind?" Aellia blinked. "What are you going on about?"

"You filthy little low-blooded swill," Aldorian sneered, raising his chin. "Look at what you have done to my country, my world. Danelanders and Galacians acting as if they are better than us, raising their noses at the taxes we request to ensure their safety. Voting, voting for women and men to be in positions of authority? My grandfather is rolling in his grave, rest easy his soul. Voting, as if the divine call and appointment of the Ellitheor means nothing. Calun is right in one thing: a king is needed, not mixed opinions and filthy democracy. How can one as low as you rabble know what is best for a city, much less a nation? We were great. I wish only for greatness again."

Aellia stared down at the man, well, not really down. Him sitting put them at eye level. But, that did not stop her for glaring at him with shocked stupefaction. "Are you joking right now?"

Appearing affronted, Aldorian sneered up and said, "Even now, a low-born such as you can't comprehend the necessity of society, of kings and leadership. What? Do you think this whole world just happened without guidance and control? You dimwitted vagrant, kings did this, queens made this. All of it. None of it just simply happened into being. And now it is being stripped from the hands who crafted it and given to swine!"

"My friends died because... because..." Aellia could not speak due to the rising lump in her throat and burning heat behind her eyes. They had died, each and every one of them, for what?

"My father died because lessers thought they could be more. No pure blooded Ordiatian would have failed that charge. Look at Southend, the filth that oozes from the streets, all because lessers were allowed control."

Aellia stood there, body trembling with rage, unable to move, much less speak. She could hear blood pounding in her ears, and not even Iaenora was whispering sense into her mind. There was only a pulse, a pulse of loathing and enmity.

"What, what are you doing?" Aldorian's voice sounded strained, scared. "Put that down. I am talking! Gods, no! Please! Please!"

Aellia stared at him. What was he saying? She could not hear him.

"Please!" He screamed out in abject terror.

Aellia looked at a knife's edge, so sharp and clean. It reflected her own eyes in it, dead and broken. It reflected Aldorian's eyes, filled with tears and bloodshot. Where had that come from? How had it found its way into her hands? Why was it moving toward Aldorian?

So many questions, but Aellia could not think straight right now. Her mind was a blank slate. Her heart was ice. And when that sank deep into Aldorian's leg, and the man screamed and wailed, Aellia felt... nothing.

When blood that she knew should have began to stain her hand, Aellia could not feel it. When muscle and sinew should have caught and resisted as she tore out the blade gave no protest, she thought nothing of it, for she felt nothing.

"It was the Kh'ar, they forced me to have the King's Jewel stolen! Please!"

Aldorian was screaming, vomiting words out of his mouth. Anything to get her to stop.

She drove the knife in again, confused how it came to be removed in the first place. Aldorian wailed. He swore and he spat.

"I didn't want to! Why would I?" Aldorian was pleading as the blade dropped down for a third time. "Stop!"

Aellia stepped back and looked down at the author of her pain. This man, who had done so many vial and heinous actions that Halfak itself would turn his damned soul away. She looked at him and felt no remorse in her heart. She looked at him and could not even muster up a siglat's worth of compassion.

"Did you stop?" Aellia asked, her own voicing sound dead in her ears. "Did you stop when they died? Did you care? Did you even know their names?"

Aldorian shook, hands bound behind him, leg bleed profusely. "I... I..." his eyes began to roll up into his head.

"No you don't!" Aellia hissed. She had come here for answers. He was not going to get out of this easily. Drawing upon only the faintest portion of her power, she summoned lightning across her fingertips and pressed them into Aldorian's chest.

"Agh!" The man screamed out, eyes flashing wide with shock and pain.

"How did they find you?" Aellia was close, so close. She could smell his stench, his sweat, feel his breaths as they heaved in and out.

"Who?" he whimpered through gasps.

"The demons you sold your soul to," Aellia snarled. "I want them, and you're going to give them to me. Or better yet, I'll use your corpse as bait."

Aldorian's face went blank, eyes widening, pupils dilating. "No."

The word was hollow, barely more than a whisper. His body stopped shaking and went rigid.

"No?" Aellia ran the tip of the blade up the Regent's belly. "You'll sing willingly, bird, or I'll open you up and make you."

Aldorian did not speak again. He just stared.

Aellia felt a chill crawl up her spine, breaking the pseudo-trance she had fallen into. Something was happening to the man. He didn't look right. The veins about his neck and face suddenly started to turn dark, bulging against his flesh.

Get away!

Aellia Drafted.

Wind took Aellia from that place just as a rush of searing heat filled the air, so hot it melted the stone about where the Regent was chained. And when Aellia returned to her physical form, smoke rose from the charred ends of her clothes.

"What in Halfak's pit?" Aellia swore, eyes wide with terror and shock.

Bloodflame!

Aellia slowly made her way back to the remains of the Loft, to the place where Aldorian had been chained, and found only slag. The whole of what had once been the Crew's central meeting place looked as if a smelting pot had poured its contents over a crater. And in the center of the crater, something dark glinted.

Watch your step. Iodaba's corruption is near.

Aellia, noting Iaenora's words, descended into the shallow crater and found the only remains of the Regent. A blackened ring with an onyx gemstone set into it. And in the surface of that stone, stick crackling with maroon anti-light, was the symbol of an upside down eye wreathed in flames. Aellia used the knife she held to lift the ring.

The mark of the Fallen Ones.

"I've seen this symbol before."

It is a dark tiding, one that does not bear hope. We must hurry to find my sisters. The time is not far if such evils are once again upon the face of Ethrea.

"He was supposed to be our source. What now?" Aellia asked as much to Iaenora as to herself.

I think we pay these Kh'ar a visit.

"I don't know if I like that we agree on things more and more," said Aellia with a dark laugh. "But one thing is for certain, Aldorian wasn't bright enough to orchestrate any of this. And if he was in league with the Kh'ar, how deep does this go? Why did they want the King's Jewel?"

I am more worried about why they were after my Oathrod.

Aellia froze. She had not even thought of that. They had been there, the day she had stolen it from the Mayoral Residence, hadn't they?

But such realizations only begged further questions. How did the Mayor end up with the Oathrod? Did he know what it was? Elcon had spoken so openly about it as well. Where had he learned of such things? And could he know how they could find the rest?

Wrap that thing up. I do not trust it. And let us go. I believe the High Priest should be returning soon. Let's start there.

"We'll start there, in the light of day. But when night falls tomorrow, we hunt Kh'ar."

CHAPTER 30: A FEAST
DARIUS

Darius sat on the wicker chair if his room, staring blankly at the dull tapestry hanging from the wall. He could not see it, for his eyes and mind were not focused upon the here and now, but cast ever back toward that stolen kiss under the stadiums of Dwallen Field. It was almost as if it had all been a dream, and Darius fought fervently to keep telling his mind it was not so.

Frustration warred with elation inside him, both fighting for dominance of mind and body. He was being foolish, but he couldn't help himself. He could feel the constant pull of a smile upon his lips, just where Izebal's had touched his. He could still smell her; the sweet scent of honey and warm aroma of lilac was near intoxicating. And at the same time, he knew this was all frivolous. He had a purpose to fulfill. He had just awakened another sage, seen where he was meant to go, needed to go. Yet, here he was, sitting and reminiscing over a kiss like a boy.

The now all-to-familiar *tap tap* at his door, accompanied by the proper tones of a maid calling, "Dinner, sir," shook Darius out of his wistful stupor.

"A moment," he answered, jumping up from his seat in a semi-startled manner, knocking over a pitcher of water from his nightstand. "Halfak burn it!"

"Is everything alright, sir?"

"Fine. Just, spilt my drink is all."

"Leave it," answered the maid brightly. "We'll have it tidied up this evening. Come then, the Lord of the High Hall is expecting you."

Darius did as asked, having learned that these were not ones to question or argue with, that humiliating bath ringing clearly in his mind. Never before had he had his personal space so invaded, and he had vowed to himself afterward he would never go through that again.

The maid led Darius down the hall way to where the other intersected into a T. As they walked, Darius picked up the subtle sounds of another two sets of footfalls. When they reached the crossing Darius's heart nearly leapt out of his chest.

Another maid in grey with white apron and bonnet was walking and talking softly, giggling about something Darius had not heard. When he looked to see with whom she was laughing with, his eyes fell upon Izebal, whose radiance shone like the moon and stars glistening over a still lake. Her hair was curled and done up, wrapped with slender golden chains and coins. Her eyes were powdered with dusk and emerald, the light of the lamps sparkling off of them in a mystic manner. Her dress was fashioned after the Danelander style, long and silken, a soft green with pale yellow panels that made her appear as a faerie of Spring. She wore the sash and crest that Lord Ruthvin had gifted her, draped over her left shoulder. Most surprising was the golden amulet about her neck, the reason being the manner of which the gemstone set in it shone, far brighter than Darius had ever seen before. There was no sign of her wand or dagger, no signs of the hard edges Izebal had shown before. She was beautiful. An angel of light and nature, a perfect portrayal of all things living and warm.

"You look..." Darius stumbled on his words. The maids noticed and tried their best to hide their delight. Darius let out a stilted, breathy laugh. "You look amazing."

The smile that spread across Izebal's ruby-painted lips rivaled the sun for all its glory and splendor. "You don't look half bad, messenger boy. I almost regret them putting the shirt back on you. Though that coat does you justice."

The two stared at each other in blissful silence for a moment or two, until the maid that was leading Darius said, "It is custom, in Daneland, for the woman of the house to lead her son into the Feast of Sons before the Ulkeniheim. Our Lady thought it prudent that, given the circumstances, that Lady Izebal lead Darius in tonight, to give him to the Lord of the High Hall in competition."

Darius had forgotten about the Feasts of Sons; his mind had been elsewhere this day, especially this evening. He had recalled Erik talking about it, the priority of it. But had not remembered that it was tonight and that he would be expected to join in.

"Be my guest," said Darius with a shrug. He did not care who led whom. His mind was elsewhere. His chest felt like it was on fire, and for the first time not from the handprint blazoned there. Darius wanted her, here and now. Perhaps not in front of the two maids, but every move Izebal made sent jolts of desire to the pit of his stomach, burning all the way down.

"So docile," smirked Izebal. "I would not have thought that of you, my messenger boy."

Her words did to him what no amount of alcohol could. His head swam and his ears felt stuffed. He wanted to turn about away from the double doors before them, to sweep Izebal up in his arms and carry her back to his room.

Wait... What was he thinking? Not this again, not now.

The two maid rushed before them, their skirts refusing to crease with every step they took. Darius latched onto this oddity. It had piqued his interest before. Now he filled the entirety of his mind with how it could be possible. He needed to think about anything other than—

Izebal's hand slid across his own, soft and gentle.

Halfak take me. How was he to focus on anything other than her? To think about anything more than her? His heart burned for her, his soul yearned for her. He would have stood before the very gates of flame for her.

Blessedly, the heavy doors opened, letting free a chorus of sounds and scents that filled the hallway. Darius drew in a deep, calming breath. As much as he despised the constant noise of pipe and drum and the ceaseless boisterous laughter, it was a reprieve to his carnal desire, for those things forced himself inward, shutting out all else.

"Don't be so tense, messenger boy," whispered Izebal into his ear, allowing her lips to just graze the lobe. "I will protect you from the scary pipers and skirt-men."

Darius let out a chortle, a half-choked laugh. That was before he realized that he too was wearing a kilt. Flames of embarrassment liked at his ear, just where Izebal's lip had brushed it.

He could feel her silently laughing as she led him forward, up the fanning steps, and into the High Hall.

Darius blinked in surprise as he took in the sight. The great table that traditionally ran the length of the room was now turned so that it divided the room width wise. From once bare banisters, dozens of flags hung, each bearing the crest of a different clan, some of which Darius recognized, most of which he did not. Over the high table, draped from the bannisters, and at least three times as large as the others, five black banners were unfurled, each bearing a silver wolf howling with its eyes blue as lightning.

As they walked forward, Tyree, who was stationed alone at a raised table that was draped in blue and silver cloth to match the old mage, loudly proclaimed, "Here enters Darius, the Ironbolt. Defender of the Spanning Wall and Friend of Clan Ruthvin. Hail the Lord of the High Hall!"

"Hail the Lord of the High Hall!" The whole of the congregation cheered with raised mugs and tankards as boots were stopped and hands clapped.

"Come forth, son of the Iron Mountains and take up your seat at this the Feast of Sons!" shouted Tyree over the noise of the High Hall, a feat in and of itself that was most impressive.

Izebal paused for a moment, scanning where to go, looking as confused and nervous as Darius felt. Two seats were left open at the turned high table, in between Lori and Ella Ruthvin. It was obvious, at least it seemed to be, that this was to be their placing. Darius did not miss the placement of Lori, a seat closer to her father, now by her mother directly, her brothers seated on the other side of their father.

Darius nodded, squeezing Izebal's hand ever so slightly. All eyes turned on the two of them as they made their way to their seats. Not for the first time, Darius became acutely aware of the average

Danelander's thoughts toward the Diju. His stomach clenched and his veins constricted with senseless anger toward them for this. And yet, he knew he was no better than they in his snap judgement of them.

Izebal led him forward as if she had been told exactly what to do. Lady Sophie had requested her attention that first day after she had gifted her the bolt of patterned fabric that was now draped over her shoulder.

"May I present," Izebal called out, "he who would stand as one ready to be made an example of, he who I deem worthy to contest for the right of the blood."

"Well met, Izebal," Lord Ruthvin said as he stood. He was adorned in a coat not too dissimilar to the one Darius wore, blue and well cut, with silver buttons down the left side of the breast. His differed in the fact that he wore a cape of sorts of brilliant blue that was clasped upon his chest with silver circlet bearing the image of the howling wolf that must have weighed half a stone. "Sit and let us begin."

Maids pulled out the two chairs and ushered Izebal and Darius into their places, Darius next to Lori and Izebal next to Ella and Ery, both of whom were in dresses of pure white with a crown of heather upon braided hair. Ery smiled shyly at Izebal, her bright face so filled with warmth and life. Darius felt a tug at his heart at the vitality that filled the young girl. Ella was the picture of poise this evening, eyes straight forward, directed at a young man who, like Darius, wore a blue coat. The lad, on the other hand, wore the most ridiculous haircut, that of a inverted bowl. So, he was to be tested tomorrow, too. Darius wanted to reach up and touch his own hair, run his fingers through his beard in thanksgiving that Erik had not asked him to shave them in such a ridiculous manner. He was not certain he would have gone along with all of this had that been the final ask.

"Keyholder."

The statement from Lori nearly caused Darius to jump out of his skin, and when he looked upon her it took all his willpower to not let his mouth fall open. Upon her head was the pelt of what he could only assume of that of the mystic wylven, whose ice-white hair looked more like that of a porcupine's spines than a wolf's mane. Her tunic was no less ostentatious, bright blue with silver brocade work. Her face shone with a pale light cast by her tattoos, charged by the light of Aetora which coursed through her veins. At her hip was the silver Oathrod, her left hand resting atop the shining sapphire.

"Lori," Darius managed to answer after a moment of taking it all in.

"I look of the Five Fools," Lori his under her breath. Which she followed with a sharp laugh and a long drink.

"You sure that is wise?" Darius asked in a low voice. "From what I've heard, being able to Touch makes one more susceptible to alcohol."

"Then may Ordan grant my mother strength," she scoffed and raised the tankard once more, draining it with a long pull. Blue lightning cracked behind her eyes as she set the iron-rimmed mug down with a hollow thud.

"Glad to know I am not the only one who doesn't want to be here," Darius said with a commiserating laugh, taking his own mug from the table as Tyree began to spout off something about the first Danelanders and how strong and important they were. "Only thing is, alcohol does nothing for me." He tossed his head back and drained the honey mead with ease and called for a second.

"Making friends?" Izebal crooned into Darius's ear as she slid her right hand up his left leg, causing him to nearly choke on his drink. Izebal then leaned over the table, so that she could see Lori. "I see congratulations are in order... do we still call you Lori?"

"I am what I am. Lori will always be my name," Lori answered a bit coldly.

Darius looked between the two and could not understand the hostility. Izebal's hand tightened on him and he realization struck like a gong. He turned himself, leaning more into Izebal. He had never really been able to court a woman properly before. He would not mess this up, not when it had only just begun.

"A Sage, is it? Such a powerful thing," Izebal said with no small amount of wonder in her words.

The room burst into laughter and applause. Tyree must have said something funny. Darius had not heard it. Lady Sophie seemed to be taking note of their side conversation, for she placed a well-timed elbow into Lori's side, which earned a scowl from the young woman. Sage or not, apparently no one was over their own mother.

"It is said in the Valean way, the Way of the Diju, Nkuaue was bound in a prison of seven by those who vowed after the great

mother, Ethenealal. Perhaps our faiths have more in common than we would care to admit, eh?"

"Perhaps," Lori answered as she reached for another cup from a passing maiden who carried a tray of such.

"And may Halfak's gates shake at the presence of our sons!" Tyree thundered, this time capturing Darius's attention. "Let the feast, begin!"

The thunderous pounding of hands on sheep-skin strung drums reverberated through the hall and a squad pipers joined in with a bright song as the doors were flung open. Dozens of maids in grey and white floated into the room, each bearing trays of food and drink upon their shoulders. They weaved in and out amongst the dozens of smaller tables where the families sat, each with a son or daughter in a blue coat and ridiculous haircut.

Darius watched the procession with an admitted air of wonderment, unable to hold back a slight grin when six maidens carried in a full cooked pig upon a platter and set it before the high table then began to carve it into huge slabs. Steam rose from the slow-roasted beast as knives worked, filling the room with the pungent aroma of spiced apples and roasted pork. Darius's mouth began to water and all thoughts melted away from his mind.

Plates clattered as forks and knives scraped. Men and women laughed and drank. The cacophonous sounds ebbed to and fro like the waves of the sea, washing over Darius as he sank into the juiciest hunk of pork he had ever tasted. The pipers' song slowly faded away, replaced with calming strums upon a great harp by a young woman in a pale dress. It all was suddenly very enchanting, and whether it was the food or the proximity to Izebal, Darius found himself relaxing for the first time in an exceedingly long time.

Time seemed to pass in a blur, but the sensation of levity eventually ended as Tyree's voice cut through the music and chatter once more. "Mothers and fathers, sons and daughters, indulge me once again this fine feast, in which we celebrate the rites and rituals of our forbearers long past in honoring the strength of our youth!"

A thunderous cheer accompanied by heavy drinking and slamming of mugs and tankards reverberated through the hall.

"Remember well the prophecy of old, that of the blood of Dane First Father, a child would be born to take up the duties of the one who came before. A daughter would be brought into this world, upon whose shoulders would be placed the mantle of old. Every son since that night has performed the rights known as the Ulkeniheim, to prove their honor and strength, to defend that one who would be called. For over three hundred years, our blood has performed this rite. And tonight, Ordan and Gallae smile down on us, for that daughter was born.”

This time, the cheers burst through the hall, loud enough to wake the dead. Boots were stomped and hands clapped as all attention was cast upon Lori, seated next to Darius. This was only amplified by a spell formed by the Master Mage, to illuminate Lori, casting her in brilliant blue light that danced off the white pelt over her body.

“A prophecy foretold! A prophecy fulfilled!” Tyree strained, raising his raspy voice as if to shatter the ruckus he himself inspired.

Darius wished he could shove cotton in his ears. Anything to drown out the noise. Worse than that was the attention. He was seated directly next to Lori, her body’s light cascading over himself. The spoon in his hand warped as his fingers tightened and his breathing faltered.

“Silence!” boomed Lord Ruthvin as he rose to full height once more.

The whole of the room hushed in an instant.

“Me own daughter, me own flesh and blood, has been graced by the Great Mother,” continued Erik as he drew his eyes slowly across the room. “Now each of ye will show her the respect and dignity of this moment.” Erik’s stern expression blossomed into a brilliant smile. “Me own daughter! Ha! What more could a father want? Anyhow, continue on Master Tyree, I am sure these good folk would love another drink or two, eh?”

The room was enfolded in a warm bout of merry laughter, much muted compared to before. The light, however, did not fall from Lori, and subsequently, Darius. Grateful for the lessening of the noise, he chose to focus on that, turning his attention toward Izebal. He nearly jumped out of his skin when he saw her expression, which was unlike any he had seen her wear before.

“Enjoying the view, Darius?” she whispered under her breath as she raised a chalice of wine to her lips.

“What?” he grunted back to her, unsure of what he had done wrong, but the look she gave him left little room for misinterpretation.

“It’s nothing,” Izebal scoffed with a roll of her eyes.

Tyree was going on and on now about the heaping magnitudes of honor Lori was bringing to her family and clan, about the feast and more Danelander history that Darius simply could not follow in the moment. No. His attention was completely fixed upon Izebal's face.

Where he had only seen radiant beauty moments ago, now he saw lines of weariness, signs of exhaustion and fatigue. Her cheeks were hollow and her collarbone protruded a little more than normal. While he had been eating and exercising these past days, Izebal had been sequestered in the forest in the gods-know what kind of condition. In truth, it had probably been since before they had met that she had slept well, truly and actually slept.

"I didn't mean to offend," he said under his breath as clan upon clan was being called upon to show off their sons and daughters yet again, this time in announcing some arbitrary talent they had collected over their short years of mouth breathing. "I am sorry."

Izebal scoffed again, a little huff of a laugh. And in that laugh there was a sadness deep as the sea and heavier than all the stones of Daneland. Her hand fell on his, her long fingers wrapping around his own, and though she did not say anything, Darius could hear her words in that touch he had found he had longed for.

Neither spoke again for the rest of the meal. Darius stood when Erik announced him and recanted their journey through Ranok with Little Ery, who beamed up at him with the brightest smile. He applauded the Skogotuers on their vigilance in protecting their city and countrymen. His tale lacked much of what had truly happened, and the way in which Izebal was handled was painted in a far more peaceful shade of truth. She did not seem to mind, nodding her head in kind as Erik told of her many virtues and recanted some witty banter they had shared before Darius had awoken one morning.

After that, everyone ate in relative—or at least huddled—peace, the noise of slow talking and gentle harping and piping replacing the chaos from earlier. All seemed to be going according to whatever customs and dictates the Danelanders held to. The young men who had harassed Darius the day before seemed to do all they could to avoid eye contact with him during the meal, and he was ashamedly smug about it. How must it feel to see him sitting at the High Table and they there with all their pride and pomp getting them nothing more than the next Danelander?

The evening ended with a final speech from Lady Sophie. She spoke pointedly about the need for mothers to raise strong sons for

Daneland and wise daughters for their clans. Again Darius could not help but feel a connection between the Ruthvins and himself, leastwise the tribe in which he was raised. They shared so many of the same values and traits, so many of the same things did they hold dear that he could not help but feel kin to them in some deeper way than he had cared to admit earlier.

"Is that a tear?" asked Izebal playfully. They were the first words she had uttered since her untoward comment earlier.

Darius stiffened like a board. What was coming over him? It was as if ever since he had come to this place, every part of him was off-kilter. A flash of heat burned at his memories as he saw the Redeyes's duel irises blazing in the back of his mind. He jolted upright, clutching at his chest.

He needed air. The wound in his abdomen pulsed with pain.

No! No! He swore in his mind. Not now, not tonight.

He felt as if he were in the cave once more, the Itheanam's horn plunging into him, rending flesh and sinew. He wanted to cry out, to scream.

"Ex-excuse me," he muttered, clutching at his head with one hand and his side with the other.

Izebal was on her feet in an instant, as was the whole of the Ruthvin family. She placed a hand on his back and ushered him toward the doorway from which they had entered at the beginning of the night.

Every step came to a colossal amount of effort. His heart was on fire. The handprint seared into his chest was ablaze. The wound in his side felt as if it were ripping open. He did not want to die. The fear of falling into that black nothingness tore its terrible talons through every shred of will he had, rendering his legs useless.

He was falling. He was falling.

"Stay." A voice broke through the fog, warm and strong. A female's voice one Darius had heard before. *"Stay with us, Keyholder."*

Auyxus.

Soft blue light cut through the haze of his mind. However, when Darius opened his eyes, he was not in the High Hall, nor was he surrounded by those who had only just been there.

"Denathurias, son of the mountains, can you hear me?"

Darius struggled to bring air into his nostrils, unsure if he even needed to breathe in this place of purple skies. However, every breath sent a jolt of panic through him, causing his body to quake.

"It is alright, Denathurias, you are safe now."

"Why? Why does this happen to me?" Darius felt the quiver in his own voice, and he was ashamed.

"You who have endured so much, lost so much, hurt so much. Is it a mystery that your physical body is not the only casualty in this war you wage against demons and monsters alike? You need time. Time which I am afraid we do not have."

"It's the Redeye," Darius grunted, trying his best to put on a strong face. "It's been messing with my mind these past days."

"I don't recall you mentioning a Redeye when you fought the Itheanam in Ranok. And yet, I sense that dread there, in that dark place in your mind."

"Stop that!" Darius latched onto the anger that bled from this breech of privacy. "Don't pry through my memories."

"We are the Sage of the Cognitive, Masters of the Mind. Your thoughts are laid before me like a feast. I do not pry."

"There is a young woman in there, too," Darius said, rising slowly, gripping his left arm with his right hand as he did so. "It's not just some ageless Sage from some godsbedamned story. Lori is in there too!"

"Yes, I am here as well," came a younger voice from the glowing personage that hovered over Darius. *"We're not trying to hurt you, we're trying to help you. We cannot stay here long. We must return back to the Terral Realm. But Darius, you must keep control of your mind. Far too much rides upon your ability to do so."*

"Maybe you should find another Keyholder," Darius scoffed.

"Don't be daft. There is no other, and still four slumber, though now they are nearing their awakening. We must find them, awaken them so that we can mend what is unraveling. Do this, and we will find you peace."

The world twisted about itself as Darius blinked. He was about to throw another retort, but found the polished floor of the High Hall coming up to meet his face with alacrity.

Two sets of hands caught his fall. His head was in Lori's hands, her eyes blazing with sapphire light. Behind her, Izebal peered down at them, barely managing to maintain her composure.

It was that, seeing true concern in her eyes, which brought the room back into focus and stilled the wild racing of his fever-sick heart. He felt as he could breathe once more, as if he had not just been spiraling into certain doom and destruction. Embarrassment at his behavior heated his ears and the back of his neck. Izebal was having none of it.

"Is he okay?" Her voice was strife with impatience and worry, and her hands were trembling ever so slightly.

"I just had an episode." Darius tried sound nonchalant, but realized all too late that that was very hard to do, kneeling on the floor while being held upright by a set of very inebriated twins.

"Nkuaue in all his greed did not cause Ethenealal the grief you cause me, messenger boy," hissed Izebal as she wrenched him to his feet. "Tell them he had too much to drink. I will take him to his room. Good night."

The next thing Darius knew, he was being forcefully led down out of the High Hall and down the carpeted halls like a scolded child. He meant to protest, but he could not find a means to get one single word out of his worthless mouth at the moment.

A maid, who looked shocked beyond comprehension at the state in which Izebal was forcing Darius forward, rushed past them, stuttering, "My lady, where would we had, we... I do mean to say, what is the matter?"

"Our friend here has had one too many to drink," said Izebal. "I am taking him to his room. Do not disturb us for anything less than a fire or an all-out assault on the High Hill itself. Is that clear?"

The little maid pulled up short, as if she had just been struck. "Begging y'er pardon, my lady—"

"I said to not disturb us. Is that clear?" Izebal fumbled behind her back to turn the knob of her room. "Go and ask your master, I am sure he will oblige me. Good evening."

The door slammed shut, pushed there with the flat of Izebal's heeled foot. Darius stumbled forward in the dark of the room, his eyes trying their best to adjust to pitch dark.

"Take your shirt off."

Darius felt his heart skip a beat.

"The runes I inked into your abdomen, I felt them break. Take your shirt off, I must reapply them," said Izebal with a shake of her head.

"How... how do you know they broke?" Darius muttered dumbly.

"I can feel every rune I carve. Such are the Words of the Tapestry. I give them Lifelight, so they are ever part of me," answered Izebal from a kneeling position. She was pulling out a series of veils held together with leather straps from her satchel, a sight which forced Darius to rub his eyes as the veils kept coming and coming like a stage act.

Darius dropped onto the bed catching his face in his hands as his elbows drove into his thighs. This turned out to be the wrong move, for the pain that blossomed from the puncture caused him to let out a string of profanity so loud it could have woken the dead.

"Is everything alright in there, my lady?" came the sheepish maid from the other side of the door.

"I said do not disturb us any further," Izebal said in a tone that was perhaps the worst attempt of feigned politeness Darius had ever heard in his life.

There was no corresponding response.

"Is your shirt off yet? I am not inking through your linens."

"I, um, I..."

"I've seen you naked before," Izebal said over her shoulder. "And I was the one who put those the current runes into your flesh."

"We weren't in your chambers with no lights and no company," Darius said as he begrudgingly pulled off his coat and began unbuttoning his shirt, his fingers fumbling almost as bad as they had at Ranun's bread house.

"If you're worried about me taking advantage of you, let me put those concerns to rest," Izebal said flatly.

"Advantage of me?" Darius scoffed.

"Kee'b jhat yun," intoned Izebal.

The uttered spell was followed by a quick flash of green light from her necklace and a strange sensation that covered Darius's feet. When he tried to lift his legs, he found that he could not move them at all.

"Men. All the same." Izebal scoffed as she rose to her feet and sauntered toward him, swaying her hips this way and that as she walked. "You all think because you are big here—" She pressed him on his chest, sending him sprawling onto his back onto her bed. "And here—" She ran a hand along his torso, "—that we can do nothing." She moved her head up the side of his body, breathing slowly so that warm breath drifted over his bare flesh. She then placed her lips so close to his ear that he could feel them, her hand still on his arm, and whispered, *"kee'b jhat yun."*

There was another flash of green light from the amulet that hung just over Darius's face, followed by what he could only best describe as warm mud pouring over his arm, latching him to the bed where her hand had been only a moment before.

"That was dirty," grunted Darius, trying to sound more annoyed than aroused. In fact, he realized for the first time that Izebal was not only a beautiful woman but also a very sensual one too when she wanted to be.

"Don't worry, this will remove all those feelings you have." Izebal traced a finger down his chest and stomach, stopping just above the wound in his abdomen. "Tsk! You've not been too careful, messenger boy."

"I've been training for this good-for-nothing game, and the Redeye, and then Lori's—"

"Just stop talking," Izebal said as she walked to where she had been rummaging through her satchel. She snapped her finger and all the candles in the room flashed brightly, echoed by a strange sound that filled the room, sending a chill down Darius's spine. Izebal stopped suddenly, turning to look back at Darius. "That Redeye, is it still under the Mage's shop?"

"As far as I know," answered Darius.

"Are the twins still planning on going back there tonight?" Izebal's words were stilted, every word drawn out as if they physically pained her.

"I don't see why they wouldn't," Darius grunted. "I don't like it. Don't get me wrong, I have no love of Morrean witchcraft. But..."

"They are demon's of Nkuaue's perversion," Izebal spat. A dark fire burned behind Izebal's eyes, one he had not seen since the night of the huntsmen. It chilled his own blood, but understanding resonated deep within him as he looked into her eyes. "It is blood magic, the mingling of the flesh of man and deathspawn."

"I am still going," Darius grunted. "I need answers more than I hate torture. Gods above. I need to understand what is going on in this place."

A long silence spread between them; only the sounds of their breathing and steady crackling of a hearth fire that Izebal had lit with a snap could be heard. Izebal stepped forward, her quill in hand, along with two vials of green ink.

"We will go then," she murmured as she sat beside him.

She rested a hand on his chest. Her hand was cool, her skin soft despite the calluses on her fingers and palm. She was gentle and strong, and very, very beautiful. Darius, not for the first time, caught himself wondering how they had come to this moment. He knew how she had stolen his heart, captured his attentions and won his affections. She was kind yet fierce, hopeful and helpful, willing to see past differences and give when others would not. She was strikingly gorgeous, every part of her affirming his belief that Gallae's grace extended well to her daughters. Yet, there was something else there, a tantalizing something that he could not put to words. But it drew him deeper and deeper in.

"Izebal," he grunted as she lifted the quill to begin working her magic upon him. "I want you to know, I... I am grateful for you. You...you mean a great deal to me."

Izebal blinked, then quickly averted her gaze from him. A tension welled between them, like a bow being drawn back and left unreleased. Darius immediately regretted speaking. They had been talking. They had been doing well. Fear that he had ruined it all crept through his mind, leaving him feeling foolish and desperate to go back and snatch those words from time's clutches.

When Izebal looked back, her eyes glistened and her expression radiated with a soft smile. "Sometimes, messenger boy, you say the right things—Ethenealal take you—when it is not the right time."

Darius felt as if his guts had been plunged into the depths of the northern ice seas and his heart kicked by a mule. He wanted to both vomit and disappear at the same time.

"I... I did not mean too—"

Izebal slid her hand up to his face, stroking his cheek with her thumb. "Darius. You are a good man. Too good. Don't lose that, please." She smiled softly once more before drawing a deep breath and clearing her throat. "Now, as I said before. This will hurt a tremendous amount. Would you like something to bite on?"

Darius, confused as ever, his heart feeling as if it had been cut out and attached to one of Tyree's wheels, then driven over a rocky knoll, only to be reattached and bolstered with vigor and warmth, grunted per usual. Izebal chuckled as she retrieved a strip of leather and put it between his teeth. She then patted him on face and went to work rewriting the runes in his flesh in painstakingly slow and forceful strokes.

When the work was finished, both Darius and Izebal were breathing hard, covered in sweat, and shook from effort. Izebal, despite her exhaustion, moved with graceful motion as she wiped the newly inked runes down with a clean cloth. Darius grunted as the coarse fabric slid over the puckered scar of the Itheanam's horn.

"Of all the scars to not heal," Darius said with a faint and soulless laugh. "That had to be the one that stayed."

"You still have that handprint, too," Izebal jibed as she tossed the towel onto his chest. "Clean the rest of yourself. I am quite done bending of over you... for now."

Darius felt his checks flush with heat, and suddenly all of that pain that had consumed him as Izebal had worked vanished into thin air.

"El'al eska."

A bright pulse of light radiated from Izebal's amulet as she spoke the word. The sensation of force that bound Darius's hand and feet vanished in an instant.

"Hurry and get dressed," said Izebal as she gathered up her tools and began to return them to her bottomless satchel. "If we plan on meeting up with the twins to see the Redeye, we must get ready soon. It is almost high moon."

Midnight already? Darius blinked. How had the time flown so fast? And without sleep, how much worth would he be for tomorrow's games without his ring's help?

"Stop roaming with your eyes, messenger boy," tutted Izebal without looking over her shoulder at him.

Had he been staring? Maybe he had. How would she have known? Magic. It was always magic.

Clearing his head as rapidly as he could with a firm shaking, Darius rose to his feet and retrieved his shirt. His fingers were less than steady, but they worked the buttons with an efficiency that belied his internal turmoil. Darius pushed it down the best he could, trying to focus on the task at hand: the Redeye.

Darius and Izebal met Erkan and Krunlan in the stables at the back of the High Hall. There were four beautiful horses saddled and ready for departure. Each was a large beast with muscular shanks, braided manes, and long feathered hair that draped over shod hooves, polished and glistening.

Darius let out a sigh of relief as he mounted his bay gelding, thankful to the Ellitheor on high for not having to enter Tyree's

death trap again. Izebal nearly leapt into the saddle of her black stallion, in whose mane were braided strips of blue and silver fabric. Darius's own bay had iron beads woven throughout that jingled softly as they road down the High Hill in silence, echoed by the *clop clop* of horse hooves striking stone.

By the time they reached Tyree's house, the moon had waxed full and heavy, a great silver orb that filled the night sky. Only the two Great Stars, one sapphire and the other emerald in coloration, could stand against the countenance of the moon. Away from Talah'El, Darius basked in the calm, pale moonlight whose rays rested easy upon the ring he wore. There was still that foreign sensation, but since the fight at the wall it had lessened, leaving him feeling more himself once again.

The bell of Tyree's shop rang out as Erkan pushed the door open. It was not locked, for Tyree had been expecting them. Darius smirked as he allowed his mind to consider some poor, uninformed soul attempting to rob the old mage. Images of a man being transformed into a pig or rat danced in his mind for the briefest of moments until he remembered why they were there.

"Down this way, laddies," called Tyree from the back of his shop.

The group made their way past shelves and stands, through a maze of bones and boilers, books and scrolls, and countless other arbitrary knick-knacks and collectibles. When they reached the place from which the old man's voice had emanated, they were greeted by a hatch that had been concealed under a heavy rug that had been haphazardly thrown aside and lay in a crumpled mess. A spiral of stone steps wound ever downward into the earth deep beneath Tyree's shop.

"Does everyone's house open into the earth?" grunted Darius as he stared down into the darkness.

"It's said that in the ancient times, men and women had to hide themselves beneath the earth just to escape the things of night," Erkan said as he clapped Darius on the shoulder. "But I am sure a big, strong man like y'erself ain't scared of a little dark."

"It's not the dark that bothers me," grunted Darius. "But what lurks within it."

"Well, that little chut ain't lurking nowhere," laughed Krunlan as he drew out a knuckle duster from his pocket and placed it over the fingers on his right hand. "He's bound up nice and tight, even collared. Ye ain't got nothin' to fear. But ye can stay up here if ye like. Save y'er strength for tomorrow."

"Is that really necessary?" asked Darius, eyeing the bronze ringlets.

"This?" Krun asked, raising his hand as if to admire the gruesome tool. "Absolutely. Ye see, I ain't got a pretty face like ye do. So, I gets them talkin' the best way I know how. And there ain't no better way than a little loose'n of the jaw, if ye catch my sayin'."

Darius felt his own fingers curling into fists. But he stilled his hands, drawing in a calming breath and focusing his attention on the winding steps.

"We go down, but we don't beat it unless I can't get it to talk."

"Ye?" Krunlan looked taken aback. "I don't recall ye being the one that bested the fiend and half a dozen draugr, dragged its merry arse across the whole of Beyorne, and chained it up. If ye want to have a cozy talk with tea and crackers, go get y'er own."

"Krun," grunted Erkan. "That'll do. Tyree's waiting. Let's not drive the post before the hole is even dug, alright? Now, we're gonna go down and have a wee chat with that bug, and ain't no one getting ahead of themselves, ye hear?"

"Oy," grunted Krunlan. "Ye take all the fun out'er everything."

The party wound their way down the steps, which were lit by small gemstones that glowed faintly with azure light.

"Is there a well of Aetora's light nearby?" Darius asked. The question had burdened him since Izebal's departure to re-infuse her own gemstones with Ria'Elahm's Lifelight.

"No, not close," answered Erkan over his shoulder. "It's why the Republic still exists. We control the majority of the raw ore, but Ordiatian prudes hold the key to real power, bloody chuts. It's a balance made of necessity. And the lot of them pretend in their little minds that it's Ordan's will that they have it. That church is made of a—" Erkan stopped himself. "Listen, I didn't mean no offense to ye in particular. But ye gotta understand, they do have us by the stones. We send an envoy every month or so and have t'er haul these big damn crystals to be infused. They last long enough, but it is a right pain in the arse."

Darius's mind returned to the Temple of Ordan, to that room where the Oracle had shown him the vision, the very vision that had set him out on this journey. That was the well there, the place that they would sojourn to receive Everlight.

"Do the Danelanders and Ordiatians truly think so little of each other?" Darius asked. "It seems like you each benefit."

"Benefit?" scoffed Erkan, stopping and turning to look directly at Darius with hardened eyes. "It's bloody-well extortion. We sell iron, copper, and silver for two siglats to a gram. We defend the borders so they can live their little lives not worrying about nothing. Ye know what my da says, says they don't even believe that draugr or wylven are real. How in the blazing pits can ye not believe in something like that? They got girls with eyes blue as me sister now healin' folk, and they say there ain't no magic in the world no more? What a load of goat balls! And what do we do? Well we lick their boots, because without 'em, we'd have no Light, save for the Talah'El, me father's spear, and a few shards of moonstone beat into cold steal."

Darius felt his blood heat at the words. Sure, the Church was not perfect, and he had been scoffed and demeaned at the hands of some of Tur'Mor's upper class. But he had been taken in as well, treated with dignity and respect by the priest of the Church. Had it not been for Ranun, who knew where he would have ended up? Had it not been for wise Elcon, he would not have been helped on his journey here. He would not have been able to save Talahmnas from the Itheanam, nor saved little Ery from the other in the cave.

"Oy," came the raspy call of Tyree from a few more turns below. "Ye lot gonna come on down or not?"

"Right there with ye," shouted Krunlan into the void, followed by slow, deliberate steps downward.

"It's the Redeye," Izebal said softly. "I can feel it pulling on my emotions, even now. We must resist it."

"She's right," grunted Erkan. "Ain't no need for no nonsense, we're all friends here, aren't we?"

Darius grunted and followed.

The conical stairwell opened into a small foyer with a lone door welcoming them. The wood of door looked as if it had been salvaged from an ancient ship, pocked and marred with barnacles. The frame of the door was made of heavy stones of granite, each etched with lycan-strewn runes, harsh but fading with age. A smell of still water and rot permeated from the sealed door, and a thick dampness clung to the musty air.

"What is this place?" asked Izebal, raising a hand to cover her mouth and nose.

"Brackenwell," answered Erkan with a laugh, though he too wore a frown of disdain at the odor. "There are hundreds of subterranean wells throughout Lowerdane. Tyree built his shop here for this very reason. The minerals in the water staunch the powers of Light, and too much inhalation can make one weak."

"Great place to lock up the undesirables," chimed Krunlan, echoing his brother's tone in an almost eerie manner.

"Don't ye worry," continued Erkan, his attention wholly on Izebal. "Y'er gonna be fine. It ain't total or permanent, just makes those who Touch a little woozy is all."

Izebal's hand slid from her mouth to the amulet about her neck. She clutched the stone hard, hard enough that Darius noted the raised tendons in the back of her hand. Driven by some unseen force, he stepped forward and placed a comforting hand on her back. When she turned and looked to him, he saw the slightest tell of concern in her eyes. That and a deep anger.

"This thing in there, it is a terrible evil," said Izebal in a cold voice. "It should not be permitted to exist."

"Tyree, despite his frame, is more powerful than ye give him credit for. Don't ye worry about us none, ye hear?"

"I don't worry about you and yours, Danelander," sneered Izebal. "I worry for the world, for the sake of Ethenealal. Nkuaue's ilk should not be permitted existence."

"Something is happening," grunted Erkan over his shoulder as he reached for the bronze doorknob. "And we're gonna get to the bottom of it."

"They're right," said Darius in a calming tone, though he could feel the vile thrum of the Redeye's power coursing through him. "We need clear heads to see the best path forward."

Izebal did not answer, but drew in a steadying breathe. She yanked at her amulet, the clasp clicking as it broke away. She wound the chain around her hand, uttering a low stream of words in Vaelan as she did so. She then looked up into Darius's eyes, her own having dimmed a great deal so that now they were a more natural tone of green.

"You have your path," she spoke softly, barely a whisper. "Do not let these fill your mind with ways that are not your own. Redeyes are vile things, but so are the machinations of man. Resist the draw to be more than you must, for you cannot be everything for all."

Darius let his hand fall as he blinked in confusion. Where had that come from? Even now, as Izebal followed the twins through the doorway, he felt his mind running in circles, pulled in too many directions. Taking a deep breath himself, he pushed those thoughts back the best he could. He had to move. Forward. He had to push forward.

CHAPTER 31: WAYGLASS
AELLIA

Aellia stood still, mind blank and body numb, as water flowed from copper pipe and splashed over her, washing away ash, sweat, and blood. The murk circled about the drain set into the mosaic tile floor. Like every other thing in Elcon's Manse, this shower, which pumped hot water through pipes from a furnace below the building, a fact that still boggled Aellia's mind, was overly ornate and gaudy. A mural of Gallae plastered the wall with her lounging in a meadow as she was so often depicted doing, animals gathering about her feet and her twin ravens on her shoulders. Aellia stared through it, not focusing on anything. Her body and mind were shot.

When she had finally returned to Elcon's Manse, it had taken her nearly two hours to fall asleep. She had not the energy nor the will to peel herself out of her leathers and boots, so when she had awakened this morning, her once-emerald-and-white sheets were a mess of grey and red. Aellia knew the staff would be wroth when they found their linens so disheveled, but she could not muster up a single siglat's worth of worry for that or anything else right now, for her mind was wholly overtaken with the events of the day before.

It had been a lot. A lot, a lot. Aellia and Iaenora had come to an equilibrium, their connection feeling so strong that it took no more

than a thought for the one to slip into control of the body and vice-versa. It had scared her at first, but when it felt as if her mind had cracked under the weight of learning that all of her friends had died for such base reasons, and her subsequent reaction to such knowledge, Iaenora had been the one to take her back to the Manse.

Thankfully, Iaenora had enough Everlight to be able to Draft them across the whole of Tur'Mor in only three sequences. Aellia had to admit, the Daulkaefar spirit was strong, able to do things with ease that boggled Aellia's simple understand of what was physically possible, even with her newly enhanced body.

The world was just so big, and despite everything, Aellia felt so small. Sadness gripped at her chest, memories of the Crew, of Tomo, never leaving her. Anger boiled in her veins, fury at the injustice of it all. Questions rattled her mind, threatening to send her over the edge once more.

Peace, Aellia. We will have answers.

Answers.

So far, every answer came with more hurt and more strife. But there was no going back now. Aellia knew this. She knew it, but she still feared where they would lead her. The past was dark and filled with pain, but she knew it. The future was the void, the endless unknown, a ceaseless chasm of potential hurt and sorrow.

And hope. A hope for a brighter tomorrow instead of this ceaseless night you're living through.

Answers.

Aellia would have answers.

***

A carriage arrived at Elcon's Manse at a quarter past the hour of ten. The sun was high and the sky bright when Aellia stepped out of the mansion and up into the carriage. She had been told via missive, sent on foot by runner boy this morning, that Elcon was at the Monastery and would like to meet with her there. So, with that little bit of knowledge on what the day would hold, Aellia sat upon a padded, velvet bench and crossed her legs as she stared into the eyes of two silent Aluth.

"Morning, boys," she said with a purr in her voice, sizing up the two of them. One was thick as an oak, and tall to boot. The other was lithe and lean, his hard grey eyes poking from behind the Aluth's wrappings bearing down on her with all the weight of the unknown. "You two seem a cheery lot."

They did not answer. She knew they would not, and that was half the fun. Aellia stretched her arms, bare at the shoulder save for a pair of long white gloves. Her joints popped as she did so, and when she tossed her head side to side, her neck let out a loud crack.

"Sorry, it has been a rough couple nights. Your green bands have done quite the number on me."

The carriage began to rumble down the roads, the springs under the wheels absorbing most of the shock, though it was still rather bumpy.

"It is strange though, that you aren't allowed to talk. Who came up with that anyways? I'd say it was a smart woman, but your fraternity seems as much composed as women as men. But then there is your Avajan. She has no problem hissing and spitting. Ah, did I strike a nerve?"

The big one had flinched, his eyes narrowing on Aellia as she spoke even the meagerest of ill remarks toward their leader. The leaner of the two raised a hand to his friend and shook his head ever so slightly at Aellia, as if telling her not to provoke the other.

It was at this motion that Aellia noticed something different about the lean one. About his arm, tied after the Aluth manner of green bands, a blue cord was wound. And though Aellia had no idea what that could possibly mean, a thrill rushed through her, sending the hairs on her arm erect.

"What's that then?" she asked, pointing to the blue cord.

The Aluth, whose face was still concealed, smiled. Aellia could see it in his eyes, in the way the cloth moved.

"Don't get smart with me," Aellia said, trying to push her feelings of frustration to the forefront, not allowing the concern of the unknown to overtake her. "I asked a question."

Both Aluth—apparently the simple act of causing her discomfort brought joy to them—folded their arms in an eerily synchronized manner and leaned back. Their grey eyes seemed to dance with delight at Aellia's frustration, and she wanted nothing more than to reach out slap the thin one.

"Fine, suit yourselves," Aellia huffed after a protracted moment of unbearable silence. "You were lousy company aways."

The rest of the ride was met with silence, none of the three uttering anything more than a cough or snort, all of which came from Aellia.

Did those things even breathe?

When the carriage at long last pulled to a stop, Aellia let out the longest sigh of relief she could possibly muster, craning her neck and arching her back as she rose.

"Watch your step, ma'am." The voice came from outside the carriage, startling Aellia.

The door was opened outwardly, revealing the sandstone-colored Monastery of Tur'Mor. The coachman wore a tight coat with a tall collar and tri-cornered hat. Aellia nodded her thanks to the man, not knowing what else to do, and stepped toward the Monastery.

"The High Priest will be in the courtyard, ma'am," said the debonair driver, raising a gloved hand to tip his hat before stepping up into the carriage and grabbing the reins. At his seat, one of those new wheel-lock guns was placed in a holster.

"You expected trouble?" Aellia asked, eyeing the weapon.

"We always expect trouble," the coachman said with a wink. "Better prepared and not needed, than not prepared and needing to be. Good day."

"And to you," Aellia answered before she could stop herself. What was she doing? She didn't talk to Uppers like this... It must have been aftershock from last night.

A shudder moved through her body as she recalled how Aldorian had burst into nothingness. Her hand drifted to the small pouch at her hip. The ring lay in there. It still felt hot, even through the leather of the pouch. She could feel it burning at her side. Or at least she thought she did.

Focus, Aellia told herself. *Focus on the task at hand.* She was here for answers, and answers she would get.

The Monastery was a large, blocky complex, perched atop a gentle hill with a singular bell tower rising high into the sky. It was not an ornate building, but it held a rugged beauty that Aellia appreciated. There was no wanton waste here, just solid stone, carved and placed by a master's hand. From a few of the windows, green curtains could be seen with embroidery of Ordan's hammer on them, providing the only pop of color outside of the gardens.

There were only a few places like this, in all of Tur'Mor, where the sounds of the massive city seemed to quiet. A haven from the ceaseless noise and endless drone of industry. There was no smoke or ash, no mechanical whirl or cog turning. It was blissful silence. It was far too peaceful for Aellia's liking.

"Lady Aellia," said a man in a dull green habit, his head shrouded by a heavy hood with a golden chain hanging about his neck bearing the emblem of Ordan's hammer. "The Shepherd calls you forth."

Right. Aellia steeled herself, pushing back the unease of following another hooded figure into a strange place. This was a monastery, these were priests, they would not hurt her. They would not hurt her.

The priest turned about unceremoniously and began to walk toward the wrought iron gait without waiting on Aellia to follow. Drawing in a deep breath, Aellia followed after him. The gatehouse, if you could call it that, was occupied by a single Aluth. She was tall, having deep brown eyes and a sun kissed complexion, from what Aellia could see of her wrapped face.

When the priest approached, she silently turned a wheel that opened the gates inward, allowing the two to pass through unhindered. Green grass grew on either side of the cobbled pathway that led up to the main doors of the Monastery, exceptionally manicured. Aellia noted that everything was clean, tidy, and exact.

"Don't have much of a life outside of manicuring, do you all?" Aellia scoffed as her eyes fell upon a row of vines with purple blossoms opening to drink in the Spring sunlight.

"The House of Or is a house of Order, thus stems the name," the priest answered with a flat voice. "As we strive closer to godliness, we feel their presence evermore in our lives. As it was written, so it shall be."

A long, heavy chime rang out from the bell tower, causing Aellia to flinch. Her hand had already gone to her back, where Tomo's Di'kha should have been strapped, but it found only empty air. She had been asked not to wear it around the city, so as to not cause a spectacle. No sooner had that bell tolled then dozens, if not hundreds of bells throughout Tur'Mor began to echo its solemn refrain, ushering in the noon hour.

It was strange, how many things become so commonplace in a city like this when you lived in it every day. Aellia could not honestly recall the last time she had actually noticed the bells of the Sanctuary tolling, much less any of the minor churches or houses of worship. But here, standing under the belfry, it was hard to miss that calling tone.

"Peace be unto your soul, Lady Aellia," said the priest, and Aellia was almost certain she could hear him holding back a fit of laughter. "The bells bring peace unto the nation, warding off the evils that would threaten our homes. As it was written, so it shall be."

Aellia rolled her eye. These people.

The Monastery, much like the outside, was clean and exact on the inside. Paintings hung down the entryway of the priory, each depicting who Aellia assumed were the High Priests and Priestesses who had overseen Tur'Mor since the foundation of the city, the last of which depicted Elcon von'Harr in all his religious frill and gaudery. At the end of the entryway was another set of double doors, these however were carved through with exquisite craftsmanship, a juxtaposition to the rest of the prosaic holy house.

"There you are, daughter Aellia."

Aellia's eyes were drawn away from the rows of prayer benches to the front of the main worship room of the Monastery. At the foot of two marble statues, one of Gallae and the other Ordan, stood Elcon. He wore some hybrid form of robes, elaborate stoles, and a headpiece that looked utterly ridiculous upon his head. Aside from those, his prayer chains were thick and glistened with the shine of real gold, not just dipped iron rings. And the hammer that hung from it had a tiny gemstone that shone with emerald light set in its head.

"Come, come, I am just finishing my benediction," Elcon said with a gesture of welcome.

Aellia, feeling very out of place around the several kneeling monks and nuns of the Monastery, made her way to where Elcon stood. She had not noticed at first, but in his left hand he held a book of eminent size, whose yellowed pages looked brittle and worn.

"What is that?" Aellia asked, nodding to the book.

"Walk with me, Daughter." Elcon turned as he spoke, a slight limp in his left leg. "Let us talk in the light of the sun."

Elcon led them from the worship room through a maze of halls and rooms. He did not speak, though he nodded and gave signs of the hammer to those whom he passed. A few small children that were scurrying past stopped in awe at his passing and he gave them each an encouraging word, which to Aellia's ears sounded recanted and spoken many a times.

The lawn to which they walked onto was surrounded by high shrubbery and in the middle of a manicured walk, a large sundial rose, like the bow of a ship cresting a wave.

Magnificent, is it?

It's a rock with a shadow on it. Aellia huffed back in her mind, though she could not help but feel a small bit of awe at the simple beauty of the Monastery's gardens. The trees were in blossom and rows upon rows of flowers bloomed in various shades of green, blue, and yellow.

"My Blessed informed me you have had a rough time of my absence," Elcon said as he set the old book on a stone bench. He then walked to one of the rows of rising sun flowers, gazing up at their towering stocks.

"Did they?" Aellia answered, unsure of how much or of what they could have told him. She did not feel guilt for her actions. She did, however, hope that somewhere in that old brain, she could gain answers. So, she let out an exhale and tried again, just as Elcon turned and met her icy glare with a knowing smile. "I am trying, you know, to find answers to what I am. That is the point of all of this, isn't it?"

"Of course, Daughter," Elcon answered calmly.

"Well, turns out, I've got a bit of rotten luck with finding answers," Aellia continued, determined to be a better person and get through this conversation. "My one lead up and burst into flames."

"That is most unfortunate," Elcon said with a little laugh. "I never cared much for the lard bucket. His father was a good man, as was his grandfather. Arrius was...a jealous type. Never spent much time in worship and less in the service, getting out on a cracked-up excuse of a hand injury. It was a shame when I learned of his father's passing. The Folly of the Fifth, such a bitter thing. I lost many a good friend that day."

"As much as I enjoy learning about old men's wars, I am far most interested in what is happening here and now," Aellia said with a bit of impatience bleeding through.

"Old men's wars, you say?" Elcon said with a wry smile. "You'd be amazed just how many ripples spread across the spans of time due to 'old men's wars'."

"Don't," Aellia groaned.

"Don't what?"

"Go all philosophical on me now," said Aellia.

"Is that not why you came? To seek answers and further understanding?"

"Facts. I want facts. Not fantasies and weaponized theology. It is hard enough for me to admit that the Ellitheor are even real, okay? I don't need to be badgered by your cultish practices. I just want facts."

"Well, let us talk facts then, Daughter," said Elcon. "Let us begin, with your approval, with my trip to Templetown and the reasons for my leavings."

Aellia listened as Elcon began his tale. He went into long droning backstory of his and the Patriarchs history and tenuous relationship, and how, in time, it had blossomed into a friendship of true note. Aellia could not possibly have cared any less for this blathering, and was about to cut off the old priest, when Elcon said, "—and with your subsequent awakening and those temporal rifts we found torn in our mutual...acquaintance's estate, Patriarch Orrum was most intrigued to have me come to Temple and meet with the High Council. Is everything alright?"

"The Patriarch, he was in your house not long ago, wasn't he?" Aellia asked, a memory coming back to her between bouts of sleep and healing.

"Ah yes, that actually was where we had come to the conclusion to convene said Council," Elcon said with a raised brow. "I was unaware you were lucid during his visit to the manse. Though, his prayer surely aided in your recovery, as you have seemed to come far from those early days in our care."

"So why the Council?" Aellia did not have any patience for more side stories. She could feel a pressure growing inside of her. An urgent need to act. To go. And it was pulling her westward, though she knew not why.

"Well, the Church does not act in matter of such gravitas without convening," Elcon said, taking out a handkerchief and wiping the lens of his spectacles in an infuriating manner. "And seeing as the last time we gathered together, it was with the purpose initially of sequestering a rather unorthodox individual."

"The Keyholder?"

"At the time I was unsure of his origins and his purpose," Elcon said with chagrin. "He had been so desperate to help, to make sure you got that engraved hammer, to be something to someone. Had I known just how important he truly was…"

"You sent him away?"

"Ha," Elcon scoffed as he shook his head. "We did not just send him away, but onward. And we did not know the full extent of what he was capable, who he truly was."

"So, because you deemed him worthless, you cast him out?"

"Daughter," Elcon's voice lowered to barely over a whisper, turning hard as stone and sharp knives. "You speak flippantly of matters you know nothing about. For over seven hundred years, we, this church, have stood a bastion against the storm, weathering countless would-be-tyrants, corrupted politicians, zealous false priests, and endless tides of unbelievers. The sanctity of our homes, of our very lives, is built upon a foundation unshakable in its perception. And if that facade is cracked, what do you surmise would happen? Do you believe, truly in your heart, this world would be a better place without the guiding hand of the Church?"

Aellia felt her mouth fall open as the open admission crashed upon her. Could Elcon truly have just said what she had heard him say? Was that an open admission that the Church, the so-called infallible thorn in her side, that great black scar in her past, was actually broken? That it was not without its own faults by admission of one of its chief members of clergy?

"Surprised, Daughter?" Elcon mused. "The faith of the many is more powerful than the faults of the few. You yourself cannot deny the existence of the Ellitheor. You yourself cannot deny the reality of evil, and more than the machinations of mankind. Who then can stand against such malevolent corruption? Bloody is the hand that swings the executioner's blade. That truth, however, does not make the work any less necessary, nor the hand less pure for it. The blood of the damned does not stain the garments of the holy, but is washed clean in the eyes of our gods."

"That is a very contrived way of saying the ends justify the means."

"Do they not? What would you not do to seek retribution for your fallen lover? For you friends?"

"I don't claim to be holy." Aellia did not let her eyes fall from the old priest's as she answered him.

"Touché, daughter. However, I think you misjudge the Church in its whole due to your lack of understanding. I mean this in every amount of offense I can offer to one who has had countless opportunities to learn, to better themselves, but has chosen neglect and self-pity every time. You condemn what you do not understand, but now that your part is to be played, you seek veneration," said Elcon in words that somehow cracked like a whip, and yet were gentle and smooth. "My faith, the faith of Might Ordan and Gracious Gallae, is not one of gentleness only. Our gods fought by our sides, warring with us against the darkness. Think you that we worship silent entities who care only for alms and prayers in ash and sackcloth? No, no, daughter. It is not so. We worship powerful gods who would shook the foundations of the world, forging them into a place of beauty, and then entrusted us with its keeping. So, think it not strange that a Church after that holy order would turn and tuck tail at the slightest provocation. To command such authority, measures must be taken. And in so doing, we enact the will of the holy Ellitheor. I told you, no lies between us, Daughter. But I cannot have every word I speak measured by one who has no understanding of either doctrine or intricacies of both national and international policies."

Aellia fumbled for her words. Any retort or biting remark would do, but nothing came out. She had never been so thoroughly and blatantly criticized in her life. Not like this. And it stung.

"So, can we cross over this murky water and settle on clean grounds of understanding?" Elcon asked after giving a moment of silence for contemplation.

With every ounce of self-respect Aellia could muster, drawing upon those last words Tomo had spoken to her, she answered. "I'll cross. But this, it does not change the past."

"The past is stone, the future clay," Elcon said with soft smile. "Let us continue then to the matter at hand."

"Fine."

"That scepter you hold, Oathrod you called it," Elcon said, pointing to the sinuous rod at Aellia's waist. "There were six forged in the night that ended the Plight. Six angels fell, sacrificing themselves to guard this world. This part of the story relatively well known, if not talked about oft. However, the seclusion of the six scepters that were found in their place, that part of the story has all but completely been emitted from the annals of history. But in searching for our mutual friend's heritage, I stumbled upon a rather interesting find. A tome that made mention of the Covenant Oath, or the Binding Promise, depending which of the two late theologians who deliberated the account. Either way, one thing was certain, that there were remnants of the angles' glory, six silver scepters, in whose tip was a Heartstone of either Ria'Elahm or Aetora. Now, I did not spend time on this finding with young Darius, as his focus was whole upon some rivalry with bloodmages or some sort. But it stayed in my mind, nestled there until that fateful night we found you. Had I known then what I know now, Darius would have never left our city."

"So, wait, give me a moment," said Aellia, trying to piece together everything Elcon had just stated. "I get that there are six Oathrods, I could have told you that. I understand that Darius is this Keyholder, right? He can awaken the spirits of those bound. But why do you wish he could have stayed? Surely he is out finding others, as I should be."

"Well that is just it, Daughter," Elcon answered patiently. "I think I know where another is, if my sources are to be correct. And they most certainly are."

"Wait?" Aellia gasped eyes flashing with excitement. "You know where one of my sisters lies?"

Sister?

Sister. We are bonded. They are ours.

Right.

"Almost certainly," continued Elcon, relishing in Aellia's surprise. "A voyage was taken, near the head winter, from Tur'Mor's harbor to Gal, and from there, Westward into the unknown seas. A member of our priesthood was upon the vessel, providing regular updates, even stating the peculiar nature of a particular Galacian noble born."

"I don't really care about princes and nobles." Aellia said with a roll of her eyes. "I want to know about the scepter, did your informant find one or not?"

"Firstly, Daughter, patience is a virtue. Secondly, the individual I am speaking of is more than a mere informant, but a holy member of cloth. Thirdly, Galacians are a matriarchal society and only the female members can be considered noble born."

"So what? Who cares who pulls the strings, it's still Uppers having their way with those who have no say," huffed Aellia.

"If you would just open your mind and seal your mouth, you might learn something," scolded Elcon.

Alright this is too far. I have had enough of this old prick.

Aellia, perhaps you should listen. He knows about that final night. I cannot... I cannot remember but there is truth in his words. I feel it to be so.

"You're lucky she likes you, priest," said Aellia, not able to wholly swallow her pride and anger. "Because you're getting on my last nerve."

"Perhaps you should let her out so we can have a more amicable conversation," countered Elcon.

Aellia's eyes flashed blue, her left remaining bright.

"Let us continue, then, high priest."

Elcon blinked in surprise. "By the holy Ellitheor's' throne, how...when did you learn to do that?"

"Aellia and I have come to a certain...understanding now," Iaenora said with a smile that felt foreign on her pained lips.

"Well then, I shall continue. The young Galacian woman was seen with a Tel'un Aund."

It was Iaenora's turn to look surprised. "How did you come to know of the language of my people?"

"Well, we did worship the Daulkaefar, in a sense, calling them angles. How else were we to denote them, our frail and meager minds just only beginning to take root in the soil of understanding. We saw things beyond comprehension. Thunder and lightning, fire on the very seas, all called upon by those who, while after our own appearance, shone in glory and resplendent beauty."

"One might think you are trying flattery," Iaenora answered. "But we digress. You say that another Oathrod was seen?"

"Yes," Elcon said with excitement. "The only thing is, I have not been able to contact my source. Their messages have stopped, and their receptor has failed. I fear dark tidings have come upon them. And, for this cause, I called you to me."

"You want us to retrieve your source?"

"I want to a life saved. For all we know, this person could be in grave danger. Everyone aboard could be in grave danger. Just think, for a moment, upon the days since your awakening. Two different servants of the Fallen Ones have threatened your life. I think it safe to assume that this young woman with whom my associate sails with

is in mortal danger. A young woman who carries a Tel'un Aund as you do."

"You said that they had set sail westward?" Iaenora asked a spark of excitement blossoming in her bosom.

"Yes, and I have already sent to have arrangements made for you and a small party to set sail, as early as tomorrow morning," Elcon said with a smile, but then quickly added, "If you agree to it, of course.

"How did you communicate with your source? Birds would be too slow and messages would not travel across the oceans fast."

"Ah!" Elcon said, eyes growing bright with excitement. "With this!"

Elcon pulled from an inner coat pocket, a silver mirror, not much larger than his palm. In the bottom of the mirror, two gemstones were set, one emerald and the other sapphire.

"Sy'ey Aund kae notrae," Iaenora said in awe. "How did you come upon this thing?"

"You of this?"

"Know of it? Priest, my brother created these," Iaenora said with fondness. "So misunderstood, my brother. All he wanted was to help heal the world, but of Talents he had none, save for the art of death, for he was the master of the blade."

"Can you fix it?" Elcon asked, extending the device to her.

"Fix? There is nothing wrong with this device," answered Iaenora as she ran a fingertip across the cool silver, studying the near-imperceptible grooves of her native tongue.

How long had it been? How many eons had passed since the last time she had walked the ancient costal forests of Ruenval flowing from the Ellin Mountain of Vanherran? When was the last time she recalled the sweet scent of Yventhal blossoms or robust citrus taste of zakrine berries? A lifetime ago. A lifetime lost. How her heart ached for the emerald walls of Ilvima under the canopies of the deathless trees.

"It is a funny thing, you know, that your people speak of Vanherran," Iaenora said, still looking into the glassy surface of the Wayglass. "I've heard it called the heavens, the final resting place, and such. But to me, it was home."

With those words, Iaenora pushed a measure of her power into the Wayglass, causing the sapphire to burst into light. Elcon let out a gasp as the surface of silver began to ripple like a pond whose

surface had been broken by the toss of a pebble. Slowly, the ripple coalesced into a solid image once more. That of an eye staring back at them, wreathed in flame, consumed with fury.

Iaenora dropped the Wayglass, stepping back and holding at her hand.

"What was that? What happened?" asked Elcon, stepping over the Wayglass and reaching for Iaenora's hand.

Whether her own instinct or that of Aellia, whose body she inhabited, Iaenora jerked her hand back from the old priest, shooting him a hard glare.

"I meant no offense," the high priest said as he raised his hands up in self-defense. "Only making sure you were okay. You are okay, aren't you?"

"It was more surprise than anything," Iaenora answered sheepishly, walking back to the Wayglass and plucking it from the manicured grass. "I was only trying to see the last transmission, to see if I could surmise where your companion was when they sent it."

"It is strange, Daughter," Elcon said with a half laugh. "To hear her voice and your words, your mannerisms."

"She is a good soul, as much as she'd want you to think otherwise," Iaenora said with a smile.

No! No, no, no! I didn't agree to this.

Hush now, Aellia.

I will take back over! This is my body!

Our.

"Might I ask, what is it like, to have another voice in your mind at all times?" Elcon asked, breaking up Aellia and Iaenora's argument.

"Most of the time, it is just fine," Iaenora said with a sigh, tinkering with the Wayglass. "Yet at others, well, it can be rather complicated. It is like this Wayglass, in a way. You see, there are two sides to it. The one we hold here, the other wherever you counterpart is. They both see differently, but they share the same view. It is a strange dichotomy to be certain, but I think the allegory works. For you, just as this glass here is vital, without the other, it is worthless. Just a husk."

"Fascinating. Would that I could spend a lifetime learning at your feet, Daughter," Elcon said with adoration. "So many secrets, just boundless knowledge."

"A moment." Iaenora needed to focus now, and while she appreciated the priest's sentiment, what she did next was rather complex. The operation of a Wayglass required three things. Everlight, Lifelight, and the will to push a message through. With enough Lifelight and Everlight, one could send an image. Iaenora had expected to see a human face on the other side of that Wayglass. What she had seen made little sense, and shook her to the core. It had been an eye, slitted and burning with ancient fire.

A dragon's eye.

But that could not be right. Fernon had led a righteous campaign against the Motherhorde, demolishing dozens of the winged demons, those worshippers of Iodaba's blackflame. They were vile, twisted things, with minds like that of a mortal, and bodies infused with the very nature of their surroundings. But they were dead. Gone. Eradicated from this world. Their siding with Moranna and Morganna had sealed their fates, their doom.

"Is everything alright?" Elcon asked, stepping a little closer, bringing Iaenora back to the present.

"Yes, sorry," Iaenora answer, rubbing at her forehead. Aellia's forehead. It was still strange to feel a human's flesh. So coarse and oily, filled with so many imperfections, it made her skin crawl.

Oh, come off it. It's not like I don't bathe.

"Everything is fine, I am just going to try and ope—"

The Wayglass burst into light. Iaenora tried to drop it, to do anything to get away from that all-consuming brilliance. And then she was whisked away, drawn into the silver light, body, soul, and mind.

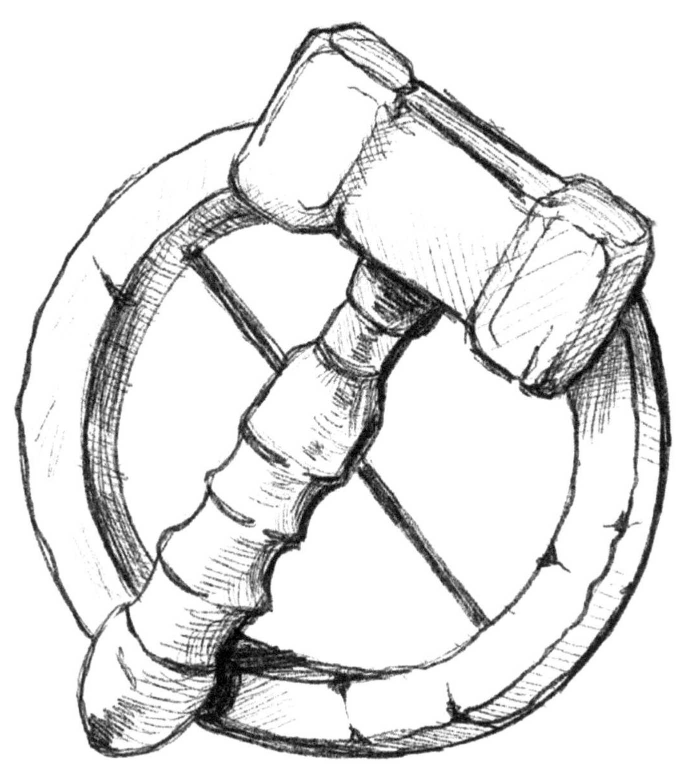

CHAPTER 32: AN OATH
DARIUS

The cavern—for the room was neither touched by carpentry or masonry—that opened before Darius's eyes was nothing like what he pictured. Large, coarse ferns, nearly as tall as himself, covered the vast space. Pools of murky water reflected the light of dozens of hanging lanterns and reflective mirrors, their chains bolted into the rock above. A path of smooth stones cut straight through the greenery, guarded by a low chain fastened to iron spikes on either side. At the end of the path, there was a large pool of grey-green water that was cut through with a wooden dock, upon which sat Tyree and the Redeye, neither of which looked to be in good shape.

"Master Tyree, is it safe to come across?" shouted Erkan.

"Aye, it do be, but hurry," grunted Tyree in response. "This little chut here is strong-willed."

The group four made their way across the floating dock, which ebbed and bobbed with each step. Darius looked over the edge and saw his reflection staring back at him. Despite having seen it time and again, it still took him by surprise to see a scarless face with a straight nose. But that was not all: his features were filled out once more, thanks to days of feasting and nights of sleeping out of the dark of Ranok.

"Stop y'er dawdle'n and get on with it," called Tyree. "Ain't got all night here."

Darius tore himself away from his reflection and tried his best to focus his mind on the task at head. He suddenly felt very anxious and tired, as if the weight of the days here in Daneland suddenly fell squarely on his shoulders. However, when he looked up at the creature chained to the iron chair, realization struck his brain like a bell.

"I think I hate Redeyes more than Itheanam."

"You have no idea," hissed Izebal in response. She then took hold of his hand and pulled him along the path toward that creature of corruption and lies.

"Ye get anything out of it?" Krunlan asked Tyree.

"Not a peep," said Tyree as he pulled his fingers through his wild beard. "Just mutterin' about this and that. Damned thing's gone wrong in the head."

"Let me see if I can't knock some sense into it."

Krunlan cracked his knuckles as he turned his attention to the chained demon and away from Tyree.

"Listen here, little chut, ye remember me?" Krunlan placed a hand on the Redeye's chin and lifted it up so he could look it in the eyes. "Ye killed a lot of folk out there. A lot. I'm gonna give ye once more to open that split jaw of y'ers to spill y'er guts proverbial before I actually do."

He then looked over to Erkan with a wink and said, "How's that for diplomatic?"

"Da would be proud," answered Erkan. He had his arms folded across his chest, and though he had laughed at his brother, Darius could see the tension winding tight behind his eyes.

"Good."

A loud crack rang out through the cavern as Krunlan's open palm struck the side of the Redeye's face. Izebal jumped at the sound, her fingers tightening around Darius's.

"Now, that was just to remind ye in case y'e forgot," Krunlan said as he rubbed his hands together with a cruel smile. "Get talk'n."

The Redeye's head lulled on its shoulders, its dual pupils unfocused, and its right mandible hanging loosely. Blood tricked down its emaciated body from where the black collar had bit into its neck and shoulders, and dark bruises spotted its pale flesh. Darius winced as he looked over the creature. That was, until their eyes looked.

At once, focus returned the Redeye's face. It jolted upright, straining against the chains. Wild screeching sounds ruptured from its chest and mouth, like ten thousand locusts screaming as boulders slid down atop them.

"Ghaz-kant jbron! Ghaz-kant jbron!" the thing screeched, time and time again, filling the cavern with the horrendous sounds of its voice.

Crack!

Krunlan bareknuckle walloped the Redeye, sending its head whipping to the left.

"Not that nonsense again, chut!" Krunlan squatted low in front of the Redeye so that he was at eye level with it. "I'm going to give ye one last chance."

The Redeye spat black blood onto Krunlan's face.

"Agh!" Krunlan roared, stepping back and wildly wiping at his face.

"You...are...marked," croaked the Redeye. "You...are...dead."

"Get it off!" Krunlan cried.

Tyree threw a handkerchief from an inner coat pocket to the lad, who caught it with one hand then wiped vigorously at his face with the towel.

"What did you say?"

Darius had not realized that Izebal had let go of his hand. His head snapped from Krunlan—whose face was spattered with blood and ugly red welts—to the Redeye. Izebal was storming towards the creature, her right hand still clutching the amulet. The room began to grow dark, eddies of blackness tinged with maroon swirling about, emanating from the chained fingertips of the Redeye. Izebal pulled upon the Lifelight, every muscle tense, every tendon raised. Still, it did not dissipate the looming darkness.

"Oy!" exclaimed Erkan, shaken awake from his deadlocked gaze with the fiend. "What are ye doin'?"

"Khal ez'fallun!" cried Izebal as she drew and pointed her wand in a fluid, spiteful manner. A spark of emerald light ignited at the tip of her vine-strewn wand. That spark became a blaze as it hurtled toward the Redeye.

The blast took the Redeye in the side of the face, searing flesh and bone, filling the room the distinct odor of cooked meat and burnt blood. That and a revolting undertone of rotten cheese. Darius nearly gagged.

"Ahk." The Redeye coughed and made a wet, gurgling noise, accompanied by an ear-twitch grind of stone on stone. The fiend lifted its bi-pupiled eye to meet Izebal's glare. "Diju. We thought we wiped the last of your ilk from Ranok."

Erkan stepped forward as if to intervene. Krunlan caught him by the arm and whispered, "This ought to be good. Let her cook the bug."

Darius felt a pit open in his stomach, that old sensation of wrongness filling his soul. Torture and murder. They were different from fighting and killing.

But this thing was evil. It had to be exterminated like the pest it was.

"There must be a better way."

All eyes turned on him. He had spoken aloud without even meaning to.

"This is a great evil, it cannot be permitted to exist." It was Izebal who spoke first. And though her tone was softened, her eyes were hard and features stricken.

"The Diju's right," said Erkan. "It ain't uttered a peep that wasn't hogwash since we did bring it here. Better to cook it than feed it more."

Darius stepped passed them, his shoulder knocking against Erkan's as he moved toward the Redeye, pushing the younger man out of his way. Krunlan glared at him for a brief moment but stepped aside with a shrug, as if he too were curious as to what Darius would try.

"Give me a key to the collar." Darius's words were a command, not even the slightest hint of a suggestion to them.

"That kroichae do be keeping that chut from breaking our minds," replied Tyree solemnly. "We don't be taking risks here and now, not with all that has happened these past weeks."

"You said the cave dampens their abilities, didn't you?" asked Darius over his shoulder as he squatted down to look the dazed fiend. "Surely between the four of us, we can handle it."

"That do be a dumb statement, if I ever did hear one! Bah!" Tyree cackled back. "Ain't no reason to. We do need answers, not a bloody Redeye on the loose in the heart of Talahmnas.

"War is coming, more than petty fights in the trees Ranok," Darius grunted. "Already they have come upon your walls, and not just goblins and Wildman, but Itheanam and fiends of Iodaba's corruption. This is more than a border-skirmish. Even one of your own has taken upon herself the Oathrod—"

"Ghant-zak keln!" screamed the Redeye, causing Darius to stumble onto his haunches. "She calls in my dreams! Awake! Awake! She comes to me, my mistress!"

Darius scrambled to his feet, wildly grasping at the tattered rags that hung from the creature's emaciated body. "Who? Who calls?"

"Blood! Blood! Blood shall rain!" The Redeye's eyes rolled back into their sockets as it began to laugh uncontrollably.

Darius shook the creatures, sending its head to and fro. "Who is your mistress? Who?" Terror filled Darius's heart. It could not be her. It could not. He had killed her, driven a knife through her very heart and cast her into the pit.

"She sings a song of blood and death. *Ahk!* She cries a croon that none can resist. She is two, and two is she. Not one, not three, do there be. *Ahk!* My mistress serves and so die, those two that cannot die."

The Redeye lifted its head, lucidity filling its eyes for the first time. Despite the mangling of his jaw, a smile so hideous it cause the pit Darius's gut to turn spread across its cracked lips.

"They come. She knows it. She has seen it. So have you, beastman. Your god is weak. Ours is strong."

"Tell me where your mistress is, or I'll let them break every bone in your worthless body," roared Darius, shaking the Redeye as if it were a rag doll, sending the chains that bound it clattering as he lifted it and the very chair it was chained to into the air. "Tell me!"

"Never far from me, Ahk! Never far," cackled the Redeye. "Ghaz-kant jbron!"

Darius slammed the chair on the dock floor, whirled about, and pointed a finger toward Tyree's chest. "Give me the bloody-damn key. I have felt that collar's touch. I want this thing to be coherent. I want answers."

"You've had my answer, you've seen my dreams. A black dawn, a blood moon, a silver crescent that hovers through the night sky. A cavern with a table of stone. Five chairs, devils' thrones. Rise again. Rise again. Rise again!"

"I'll break the bug's other bloody mandible," Krunlan growled as he stepped forward.

Darius shot a hand out, stopping the burly twin in his tracks.

"What did you say?"

"He is waiting. Blood of blood, bone of stone, and heart of fire. He is there, waiting for you, beast man. Your god has forsaken you. The world is damned."

Something hot began to trickle down Darius's lip. He raised a finger, and when he drew it away, it was coated with blood. A sharp pain began to cut deep in his mind.

"Agh!" cried out Tyree.

Erkan slumped over, falling face first onto the deck. Krunlan double over, his knee striking the wooden planks with a hollow thud as he clutched at his ears.

The Redeye stood, the chains that held it bursting with seeming ease. It raised its hands and took hold of the kroichae. Letting out a terrible scream, it wrenched the black metal collar off of its neck and cast it into the water.

"Darkness feeds darkness," hissed the Redeye as its jaw cracked back into place. "A darkness resides in you. I feel its corruption gnawing away, like spiders over a carcass." Its forked tongue slid out over its lips as it smiled in sickening glee. "My mistress calls to me—"

"Hazbakk kra!" cried out Izebal. Her words were followed by a beam of emerald light that burst from the tip of her wand.

The Redeye's eyes widened for the briefest moment, shock filling them, before the torrent of green evaporated it where it stood. Triumphant one second, gone the next, leaving no more than ash in the air. All at once, a shockwave reverberated through the cavern, hot air whipping at Darius's eyes and beard. This was followed by a deafening silence.

Izebal let out a howl of agony as she dropped her wand and clutched feverishly at her neck, rocking back and forth on her knees in pain.

"What did y'er do?"

Tyree's voice sounded as if it were coming from miles away to Darius's ringing ears, but the question rang true. Never had he seen such a display of power before. Never had he see something simply eviscerated in a single instance like that.

Darius, addled and aching, gathered his composure to the best of his abilities and rushed to Izebal's side. As he fell to his knees beside her, she cast herself into his arms, weeping openly and repeating, "I didn't mean to. I didn't mean to," over and over again.

"Krun, ye big oaf, y'er alright?" called out Erkan from the other side of the dock, the twins having been thrust backwards upon the impact of the blast.

"My head feels like a struck bell, blood and bloody stone it do," groaned Krunlan in response.

"What in the flaming pit is wrong with ye?" Erkan whirled around as he rose to his feet, eyes flashing with rage. "Y'er killed the one bloody thing that could give us answers!"

"It got in my head, in my head, it's in my head," whimpered Izebal into Darius's chest. Her whole body shook. Never before had he seen her in such a manner as this, and it caused his anger to go cold as ice.

"Watch it," grunted Darius as he scooped up Izebal with ease and rose in one fluid motion. "You don't get to point fingers here."

"What are ye on about, outlander?" Erkan had fire in veins, his whole body trembling just as Izebal's was, only not with sadness or grief.

"Your brother would've just beaten the damn thing to death. Halfak take me, I almost did."

"Krun was getting answers. What do we tell Father now? That the bloody Diju blew up our only hope of finding where they're massing?"

Izebal lowered the hand she held against her neck. Thick, dark blood matted her fingers. Her eyes looked vacant, but she mustered some semblance of strength and said, "Place me down."

Darius wanted to argue, but thought better of it. Gently he lowered her to the ground. She took a moment to steady herself before looking over the wreckage she had caused. Slowly, her eyes regained their focus, a focus which she heaved upon Erkan, stopping him in his tracks.

"I saw its mind, just as it tried to ravage my own." Izebal spoke calmly, though she did not totally hide the bite of her words. "They gather to the North, that you already knew. But time is far spent, there is little remaining. They gather for a blood moon to shed her rays upon the night sky. When it does, Halfak's very gates shall be burst. We were a distraction. It was all a distraction."

"A distraction? What do you mean, distraction?"

"It wanted to be dragged here, for if it was here, you would not be there," Izebal said, silencing the elder of the twins. "We miscalculated, and now I fear it is too late. And yet..."

"And yet what?"

"It did not know, and thanks to your cursed collars, it had no way to inform the enemy," Izebal answered, pacing now.

"Spit it out, woman!" thundered Krunlan, who had regained his composure as well and now joined his brother's side.

"Your sister, Sage of the Mind, they do not know. They still believe she is your youngest, laid up in the very depths of the cavern where Darius slew the Itheanam."

"Little Ery? They think she was the Sage? She ain't naught but a wee lassie, how could she swear the oaths?"

"I am afraid I know little more than this, for this is all I have seen in the beast's mind." Izebal shuddered as she spoke.

"That is more than we knew," said Darius as he placed a tender hand on her shoulder for support.

She looked up at him, and though the gleam Lifelight was gone from her eyes, something else blazed there. Something that sent a pang of longing into Darius's core. The moment was broke as her eyes widened.

"My amulet and wand, where are they?"

"Here, me lady," said Tyree as he wheeled forward. The two locked gazes before a nod of understanding passed between them. "That was a bloody show if I've ever seen one. Where'd ye learn Words such as those?"

"My grandmother. She was one of the last Weavers of our Troupe. She kept a record, a record that is never far from my side," answered Izebal as she looped the golden chain of her necklace around her neck. Instantly, emerald light burned within her irises. "I'm quite certain it has saved my life three or four times now in just a matter weeks."

Tyree's face held none of its regular quirk or whimsy. The burn mark—which looked far angrier than only moments before—added a darkness to his demeanor, the likes of which Darius had never seen in the old mage. He stared at Izebal for a long moment, his blue eyes unwavering he seemingly peered into her soul. Then, as if struck by an idea, his expression softened and he barked, "Krun, Erkan, go tell y'er father all that happened. The Ulkeniheim must go on, but we can't be foolish. If the lassie says there do be trouble—and we have seen enough to know she ain't spitting mud—then there do be trouble brew'n. Off with the two of ye, or I'll break me good foot off in y'er arses!"

Krunlan and Erkan snapped to attention, some pre-conceived response to the old mage's sharpness begging no quarter or quarrel. With a nod to the old man, they both rushed down the dock and headed up the spiraling stair.

"You'll have to teach me that trick," said Izebal with a shocked scoff. "I've read many a Word, but never one to get boys to do as they were told so suddenly."

"Tone, lassie, it's all in how y'er say it. Survive a wyvern attack or a goblin horde, and they're bound to listen when they know y'er serious," Tyree said as he watched them depart. He turned his attention full back onto Darius now, looking past Izebal. "Ye've been delayed too long now in what the Lord of the High Hall did say. It's high time we got ye a weapon."

"Erik said it must be after the games were completed," answered Darius, remembering the beautifully crafted axe Orhund had presented him the night before.

"That he did," answered Tyree as he tugged at his beard. "Erik is wise and prudent, but a lot has bloody damned happened in the past day, ain't it? Lori made into a Sage being the most prominent. I ain't one to sit on me laurels while the world burns around me. I ain't no good in a fight no more, but that don't mean I can't get you ready. Even the lassie has that there dagger and wand of hers. Ye had a stick."

Though truthful, the remark bit Darius's pride. He had not done half bad with that hickory rod. As a matter of principle, he wanted to point out that he had taken down an Itheanam—two actually—with only his 'stick' and his ring. But memories of how badly that first fight had gone in the cave made him rethink that retort.

"Bah, don't fuss none now. But if I do have half a brain, and the flames only took half my face, so that checks out, then we won't be havin' much time the next few days for much more than hit'n things." Tyree whirled his chair about with a deft movement of nobs on the arm of his chair. "Up with the two of ye, Ordan knows we're going to need all the help we can get now."

Darius looked to Izebal for questioning and assurance. She shrugged, the weariness washed from her eyes, replaced by cool confidence and resilience. Darius's heart skipped a beat at the smile she flashed him, and when she nodded her head to him, he knew what needed to be done. "Let's go finish an axe."

Tyree's shop was laid out in the most peculiar manner. However, one of the back rooms held perhaps the strangest mechanism Darius had ever seen. A gigantic bronze orb with strange protrusions jutting out of it at odd angles, several coiling tubes attached to valves and release points, and a latch that held the hinged halves together that looked as if it would keep the very pits of Halfak sealed all on its own. Next to the machine, an aperture that looked like an arms' length gauntlet of metal, coils, and springs. It hung from a set of wires, fastened to the ceiling, and had a harness to wrap around the right breast of the wearer.

"Moonstone to be a real pain to work with, but this little thingamajig do make it a little more pliable. I do call it Artificial Regulation Mechanism, or ARM! Bah!" Tyree cackled as he wheeled past the contraption and over to where a long oak chest lay on a haphazardly cluttered table. With two clicks, the chest opened, revealing the axe with Darius's hickory handle laid upon deep blue velvet. "With this machine, we fuse this here chunk of blemished Moonstone to the inside of y'er axe. Then when ye lop of the head of Draugr, it won't get up and hump y'er leg!"

Darius felt his lip curl back at the crude remark. Did everything this old man have to say be a joke or veiled comment? He pushed the thoughts away, focusing on the machinery and the axe which Tyree was now extending toward him.

"Only seems right ye to be the one operating me ARM for this. It'll be a wee bit snug for a big, strong, lad like y'erself. I ain't go much meat left on most of me body." Tyree winked at Darius with that last remark and transferal of the axe.

"Ye just put it in there, place the Moonstone in the cavity, and then seal the orb up. Y'er then gonna use that ARM there to put y'er own hand in through that opening there." Tyree pointed to a circular disc that could be raised and lowered by cracking a small knob. "The ARM has three crystals set, one at the back of the hand, one at elbow, and the last at the shoulder. They do take the heat from inside the orb and store it. We send them to the kilns for making pottery. Ain't' nothing goin' to waste here. And I know what ye do be thinking: what if it do melt me arm off? We'll laddie, I've done this a couple dozen times and ain't never had no problems, and I clearly can't heal too good."

Darius stared at the bronze arm with all its coils and springs. It looked terrifying. As with the MAC, he was putting himself in a tight space that sent his heart racing. Fear of the thing tearing his arm off, or needles being inside of it randomly pressing through his flesh, filled him with dread.

A gentle hand pressed on the inside of his arm. "It will be okay." Izebal's whispered confidence filled Darius with much needed courage. He could do this. It was fine. It would all be alright. What was the worst that could happen?

"So that is all?" grunted Darius, trying to fill his voice with as much confidence as he could muster. "Just stick it in there?"

"Of course not? What in Halfak's pit would I need that whole set up for if all ye needed to do was 'just stick it in there'. Gallae take me, I thought ye were brighter'n that?"

Darius felt his hackles rise, but he pushed it all out, exhaling heavily through his nose.

"Bah! Come on, laddie! Take a joke, won't ye? Light'n up some. Tomorrow we might be overrun with demons and the dead, might as well enjoy the night."

"Just tell me what to do," grunted Darius as he pushed past Tyree with heavy footfalls. The sound of Izebal snickering further spiked his anger and outrage. It felt as if he were always the butt of some joke anymore, a cruel, mean joke.

"Let's get ye hooked up then. Lassie, ye mind strapping him in? I ain't got the height for it. Make sure it is tight. Spin those wheels on the forearm and shoulder. It needs to be tight, no slip'n. We don't want nothing to go wrong, now do we?"

Izebal nodded her assent and made her way back to Darius's side.

"Oh, and take his shirt off, would ye? Metal has to touch flesh, there be probes in there, and they do react with the muscles."

Darius was certain Tyree added this last part only to further humiliate him. But when the old codger did not laugh or call out another bit of wild information, Izebal gave him a helpless shrug of her shoulder and began undoing his buttons. Heat flushed Darius's neck and he prayed to Ordan that it did not touch his checks. Before he could say this or that, he was, yet again, shirtless before Izebal.

"I feel like you're beginning to enjoy this," she said in a whisper in his ear as helped him slide his arm into the aperture.

Despite the cool, smooth texture of the metal armament, he could feel dozens of little creases where plates slid together in perfect harmony. Izebal traced a finger across his back as she pulled the leather straps tight against him. A chill broke out across him and goose bumps covered his flesh. Whether from the helplessness of the contraption latched to him or from her touch, he could not distinguish.

"Get ready laddie, it moves fast from here!" cackled Tyree, who had wasted no time in getting himself ready in the interim. He wore those damnable googles and a heavy leather apron now, along with a set of thick gloves that looked as if they were sewn lizard hide. "I'll work the furnace while ye set the Moonstone. Y'er ready?"

Darius flexed his hand, and as he did so, the three stones set into the metal arm ignited with light. A grim determination spread through his mind, replacing all other thoughts and sensations that had so recently plagued him. He could do this. He would do this.

Tyree yanked on a lever with manic glee. The orb began to rotate this way and that, concentric rings passing over the face of the great sphere. Bouts of white-hot flame spewed from the small spouts on the contraption, hot enough to singe the hairs of Darius's face.

"Put a blaster on 'em, Krun!" roared Tyree as he thrust a tube of glass tube filled with bright green and blue gemstones capped with

bronze into an opening. He slammed a circular barrier shut behind the tube and turned a small locking crank with feverish haste.

Krunlan, spurned to life by Tyree's shouted command, rushed to the wall where a series of different googles, glasses, and face-shields hung. He wrenched a blackened mask that covered the whole face with only a small slit with visor set into it off the wall. He slammed the mask over Darius's face, partially blinding him for a moment to the whirling furnace.

Not for the first time, Darius questioned the old mage, but he thrust those fears and doubts aside as swiftly as they came upon him. He needed to act and act fast. Where there had been utter darkness, when he turned his face toward the gleaming orb, he could see as if it were twilight.

"Open the hatch and set the Moonstone, laddie! It won't get no hotter if a damned wyrm were to vomit great bouts of magma on it!"

An opening appeared in the orb, unlatched by a series of movements from Tyree. Darius stared into the inferno. His axe lay there, the head bright as the sun, the enchanted hickory whole as the night Izebal had bewitched it. Drawing a steadying breath, Darius took up the chunk of Moonstone and made his way forward.

Sweat poured off of the back of his neck, down his arms, and stomach. The Moonstone shone with a brightness that seemed to reverberate with the ring about his finger, sending a sensation like that of strummed harp's chord through his soul. It was then, Moonstone hovering just over the blazing head of the axe, that a memory struck him.

Three things to make Ellitheor Silver. Metal of the heavens, sent down from Vanherran. An Oath of the Faithful, sworn to the Light. And Blood of the Ellitheor, to bind.

Elcon had said that they were blood of the blood, Feromage made by Oathpact. Could Darius's blood carry that of the Gods? Was he not chosen? Could he make once more what once was lost?

Caught up in the moment and spurred forward by some subconscious fury, Darius slammed the Moonstone into the gap made to hold it. He let out a howl of pain as he slid his thumb across the edge of the axe head, the enchanted metal cutting through the apparatus that should have protected his flesh.

Part of him expected the red-hot metal to warp at his touch, to give way to the force with which he had grabbed it. Bright tendrils of sapphire and emerald danced inside the orb, blinding him for the briefest of moments. Icy cold pain rushed along the length of his thumb as his gauntlet gave way to the axe head's edge.

A sharp *ting* reverberated throughout the room, followed by what felt like a great inhalation. This was followed almost instantaneously by a concussive shockwave that threw all those around Darius to the ground. Still he held firm, eyes fixated on what was happening before him.

Blood ran from his thumb, coursing through the head axe toward that bright stone in tiny forking streams. And as blood touched Moonstone, a secondary *ting* rang out.

"The First Oath is to the Binding to the Light, the Second to keep at bay the darkness of the Night. The Third Oath is secret, to which each has sworn. Hear my Oath now High Father, aloud. I swear by this axe and stone to be what I have been called to be, to cast off question and doubt. And with this axe, I will complete what I started a millennium ago on Morr's mountain side in ash and snow. This I swear, lest blood shall rain."

For a moment, Darius was neither in that room nor in the realm beyond, but somewhere in between. His flesh was his own, but his eyes saw what was not there. Heat from the furnace threatened to melt his body, but icy wind tore at his hair. And deep in a sky beyond his mind, he heard the words:

"Your Oath is accepted, Guardian. Mind the night. Darkness comes upon you."

Darius fell backwards as the furnace's light blinked out.

"What in Ordan's beard was that?" roared Tyree as he pulled hard upon a lever, having recovered himself in some small manner.

Darius did not answer the man, his eyes unable to focus on those around him. Something blazed within his chest, something he had not felt since swearing the first two oaths all those years ago. He was not sure if it was pride or some deep existential dread. He did not care. Ordan had answered him, he had accepted his oath despite all of his shortcomings and failures. He had answered him.

"By my beard." Tyree's voice was so ripe with awe it barely held a trace of his ascent.

"What is it?" asked Krunlan as he and his twin hurried over to where the old mage sat in wonderment.

"What's going on?" Erkan echoed, having dropped all pretense of decorum, moving in childish excitement.

Darius cast his eyes about. He had not yet seen Izebal. Fear spread through him in an instant when he saw her huddled against a wall. She had a hand to her eyes and appeared to be wincing in pain.

"Are you alright?" The metallic taste of blood filled his mouth as he formed the question. He must have split his lip for a moment. But that was not all; an acrid scent of something rotten filled his nose. He pushed this aside. Smells and tastes be damned, he needed to make sure Izebal was alright.

"I'm fine," answered Izebal as she fumbled her hand about on the ground. "The fire of the blast burned my eyes. I'll be fine. I just need my amulet to draw upon, but I've dropped it."

The malodor of burnt things—who knew what all was in Tyree's shop—turned Darius's stomach despite his drive to help Izebal locate her mother's amulet. Anger began to boil his blood as he crawled about on hands and knees, casting aside turned articles and charred bits of loose parchment.

Sudden realization struck him. It was the metal contraption about his arm that was frustrating him so much. He wrenched at the shoulder, but could not reach the straps. Panic quickened his heart, but before he succumbed to a fit of rage, a soft hand rested upon him.

"Found it," Izebal said into his ear as she pulled upon the buckles that held the gauntlet to him. "Now let me help get this off of you."

It fell away with a clatter, revealing a sweaty, but whole, arm. A pale white line ran the length of his thumb. And his ring shone bright white.

That strange resonant sensation thrummed through his hand, emanating from his gleaming ring. Perplexed, Darius opened his hand. An animalistic instinct filled his mind, a connection which he could not fully comprehend but somehow intimately understood. Slowly, he outstretched his arm, and with palm still open, he called to his axe.

Tyree let out a yelp of alarm as Krunlan and Erkan hurled themselves aside. A low *whoosh* filled the air, followed by the solid—and deeply satisfying—metal slap of wood on flesh.

Darius rose from his knees in a fluid motion, eyes locked upon the axe in his hand. Where his blood had flowed from thumb to stone, rivulets of both emerald and sapphire light shone like lightning strikes frozen in time. The Moonstone was pale white, just as his ring had been, though the rough-hewn circlet was already dimming to his natural tone.

"Stahlbak Hi'el," Darius spoke the words in the language of his peoples in absolute reverence. It felt strange to his lips to utter such things, for it had been long since uttering any save for the Second Oath. But these words felt right. An Oath of Vengeance. This is what this was, so it would be as it was spoken.

Izebal rose up beside him, her eyes fixated on the bearded axe's mesmerizing gleam. He looked from the axe to her, and for the first time, felt a deep and abiding sense of wholeness, or completion.

"Well by blood and stone," gawked Tyree. "I never thought I'd see another. Like Aithne Lykos it gleams. Ye've done it, laddie. Ye've done it."

Darius took in a deep breath. He had done it. Now, he would find those Sages, awaken them to their duty. He would fulfill his oath. Then, he would hunt down the man who was responsible for all of this. The one who showed himself in a mask of flames beneath the dark of Ranok. And he would end him as he should have atop that mountain when he had the chance.

Interim 3

Henri and the Dragon

Ranella

The High King of Calun

Henri walked behind Una'pahu and Seamus, or the thing that used to be Seamus. He had seen with his own two eyes the wings of smoke flame, the horns of curling fire, and those eyes... that image was seared into his memory, irrefutable. His heart tensed in his chest when Seamus turned his head, gazing down the tunnels of molten rock, down where all had changed for them. Scars covered his friend's face, melted flesh that looked like the scales of a serpent extending from his brow down his neck, over his bare shoulder and down the length of his arm.

Pity.

Henri was feeling pity, and why wouldn't he?

And yet, Seamus was as a god now. And if what his friend had said was true, that sword strapped to his back, that was Fenron's own blade. Seamus's blade. For he was not only man now, but was somehow fused with both dragon and Ellitheor alike.

Then there was Una'pahu. She had commanded the very waters to do her bidding. She had slain one of those infernal demons by her very will. Her eyes were bright with the emerald light of Ria'Elahm. She was Ta'ala Gau, Wave Guider.

Henri walked behind giants, and the wrappings about his brow only served as a reminder of just how insignificant he truly was. Even the Specter had harnessed strange abilities, allowing him to appear out of seemingly thin air, and then slunk away into the shadows.

"I do not know what you hope to find down here, Seamus," said Una'pahu, breaking the perpetual silence.

It was strange, to hear her call him by his name. Not Quickie, not Msa'oo. But Seamus. It sounded too foreign, too lifeless.

"Answers," answered Seamus, his voice raspy and low, like stones rolling and fires burning.

When they at long last entered that chamber where their lives had forever changed, a hallowed silence fell upon them. The bridgehouse was easily visible now, knowing what to look for. The bridge itself was deep under the magma. Corpses littered the floor, skeletons whose flesh had turned to ash, mouths open in endless screams of agony. It was harrowing to behold. Yet it was the memories that came crashing down upon Henri that struck him the hardest.

He had been so scared. Scared for himself, true, but more so for his friends. He had to watch from that narrow window as Seamus ran the length of that blazing drawbridge. Memories. They came upon him, nearly taking his feet from under him, turning his mind to blackness and his knees to water.

"Henri!" scream Una'pahu, barely managing to catch him before he struck the cavern floor.

"I am fine," he grunted in response, feeling shame wash over him. Not only was he without any newfound abilities, but he was an absolute liability. He was only slowing them down.

"We cannot stop." Seamus's words struck a gong. No emotion, no empathy. Only unrelenting drive and purpose."

"Your friend is hurting, Seamus," Una'pahu said, rising to the full measure of her height. Which, against Seamus's new physique, was barely chest high. "You will stop, now!"

Seamus's eyes flickered between Una'pahu and the silver scepter tucked into her havu'havu. Surely he had seen it a thousand times, just like the ink that covered her body. Ever since his transformation, when he would look at her, her scepter, he would go distant, cold. Always, though, Seamus would come through, fighting down whatever had changed inside him.

"Can you heal him?" Seamus asked, his voice no softer than before.

"Not that kind of hurt," Una'pahu sounded exasperated. "I am trying, Quickie. I am trying. But I need you to let me in. See me. See us! We are your friends. We love you."

Seamus paused for a very long moment, staring between them. Henri could see the war behind those shifting eyes. Not for the first time, his heart went out to his friend. He wished he could do something, anything, to help Seamus. But what could he do? He was just as worthless as a rag.

"In the chamber below, there is a chart, something unlike anything I have ever seen," Seamus finally spoke, his voice more his own than that of whatever inhabited his body. "One thing is certain, I cannot read it. I was hoping that, between the two of you, we could decipher it."

Henri felt a surge of hope. Seamus was reaching out, offering something other than brooding silence and angry glares. He would take it. Anything at all, he would take, if it meant he could get his friend back.

"But how will we cross? The bridge is broken?" Henri asked, rising up to his feet.

Seamus smirked.

The air seemed to burst into flames around Seamus's back, dancing fire of black and ruby red licking upwards, forming into horrible wings like that of a great bat. As they unfurled, sinuous tendrils of flame danced along their span.

Una'pahu had the right of it, jumping back and sliding her scepter out, holding it like a sword ready to guard. Henri just stood there, dumbfounded at the dark magnificence of the wings.

"I can take you, one at a time. Fly you across the lake of fire and into the cavern below."

"You must think us crazy, Quickie!" Una'pahu lashed out, her hands shaking but stance firm. "You go shifting from one guy to the next up there, and you think we're just going to trust you flying us over that, with those? How would they even hold us up?"

With one, two, three mighty beats of his wings of flame, Seamus lifted himself up into the air, hot gusts of wind blowing dust and debris about, stinging at Henri's eyes. That being said, Henri would not lose this moment, the momentum.

"Take me first," said Henri. "I trust you."

A smile, wicked and fierce, flashed across Seamus's scarred face. "Even after the cheese incident?"

And there he was. If only for that moment, Seamus was back. "Think you can lift me with those dainty hands of yours? They were always better suited for picking locks and swiping valuables."

"Strong enough for you, Lightfoot. I'm not the only one who has changed," Seamus said, dropping down to meet Henri in the eyes. He placed hands on either of Henri's shoulders, and his smile faded. "I never meant to hurt you, Henri. You were always a better friend than I deserved."

"Bah, I was a fat boy with a dream to become a cartographer. You helped me become one and overcome the other," Henri answered, feeling as if his heart would beat out of his chest.

"One day, you will make some young lady very happy," said Seamus. "I promise, I will get us out of here and you will sail the

seas and chart all the stars of sky, honor be upon my holy blade, thus I do swear it."

The next thing Henri knew was open air and infernal heat. He tried to get his hands over his face, fearing his beard and hair would burst into flames. Then, to his embarrassment, he thought of how Seamus now looked, the way his skin appeared to have melted part of his face then formed like a lizard's scales. He feared that it would now happen to him if he had to endure the heat any longer.

However, just as he was about to cry out in pain, his feet found solid ground. Blissful coolness—an odd experience in the bottom of an active volcano—kissed his flesh. Before he could say anything else, there were several powerful wingbeats, and Seamus was gone, leaving Henri alone.

Henri's first instinct was to yelp, to cry out to not be left alone. However, his cry died in his throat as his eyes took in the scenery around him. He was deep, deep in the heart of the earth. And how did he know this? Well, pillars so tall and so broad that it made him feel like an ant gazing upon a palm tree rose row by row as far as his eyes could see. The floors were not that of a cave, but masterfully worked stone, though they were scarred with gashes deep and terrible. Char clung to the air, the scent of a flame that could never be sated. And there were bodies. Bodies everywhere.

Henri stumbled backward, eyes trying to focus in the dim light. Dim light that came from where? Henri tore his eyes away from the floor and up to the ceiling. Broken mirrors hung throughout the hall. Grandiose chandeliers that housed dozens of colossal gemstones apiece dangled from thick chains that were red with rust. Across the far side of the room, the pale source of the light was made manifest. A singular beam of light, faint but true, cascaded down upon the floor.

"Wow." The word slipped out of Henri's mouth, unbidden. His eyes could go no wider, though they drank in the sights like a water-deprived horse at a desert oasis.

Many of the bodies that littered the floor wore plated armor with the heads of spears laying beside them, though not a single haft remained. Nothing of wood had survived this hall, nor cloth or hair. A fearsome blaze had consumed all in its path.

And Henri was rapidly putting two and two together.

But that was impossible. It could not be so.

Dragons were a thing of myth, of legends. They weren't real.

Consumed by his warring thoughts, Henri walked the length of the floor, drawing ever closer to the singular point of light in the distance. Only a few weeks ago, there had been no such thing as demons either, and he had come face to face with an immortal sea witch, a blood-sucking demon, and a Biter. So why not dragons?

If the legends were true, the first Biters were descendants of the ancient wyrms. Humans who turned to dark practices, consuming the blood of a winged serpent freely given in a rite that was more perverse than anything else under the Great Goddess Gallae's holy heaven.

But those were children's tales. Not real. Not real.

Henri trip, stumbling as his foot fell into one of those wicked gashes that covered the otherwise beautiful floor. He caught himself, his hands narrowly finding purchase between another two slits.

"Claw marks!" Henri gasped, realizing what they were in a horrific moment of clarity. "By the Grace of Gallae, there was a dragon here!"

With strength renewed, Henri rushed forward. He had to get out of the darkness and into the light. He felt as if hundreds, no, thousands, of eyes were upon him. He could feel the heat in the air, the malice, the fury. He had to run! Run! Reylelan was coming. The Biters were there, in the shadows. He could feel them. Hear them. Smell their putrid stench. He had to escape!

Henri broke into an all-out run, leaping over the fissures caused by dragon's claws. He hurdled bodies, whose contorted shapes and strange armor took no purchase in his mind in his current state. He had to get to the light. Why on Gallae's green earth had Seamus not dropped him in the light?

The closer he got to the light, the more the room came into focus around him. No longer were they ominous, bleak pillars, but glorious works of ornate craftsmanship every one. Henri's feet slowed, the fear falling back into the darkness behind him as his heart continued to hammer in his chest, whether from fear or from running, he could no longer tell.

"Impressive, aren't they?"

Henri wheeled around, blindly throwing a first as hard as he could in the direction of the voice. It struck nothing but open air.

One, two, three great wingbeats later, Seamus was standing before him, Una'pahu held tightly in his arms. She seemed so small there, and yet Henri did not miss the look in her eyes, that ferocity that would come over her when she was determined not to show fear.

"Stuff it, Lightfoot," she said as she dropped to the ground, noting Henri's smirk.

"I just need to catch my breath," Henri said, leaning into the heavy breathing and away from the desire to raise an eyebrow at his friend. She still clearly had feelings for Seamus. How complicated must that be?

"This is a lost hall of the Iarathor, Dhalnalk'Ra it was call in their time." Seamus spoke as he drew that massive white-gold blade from his back. "Tunnels spanning further than we had ever dared dream possible. Each connecting islands far and wide, acting as ventilation shafts to supply fresh air and light. Long had the lay silent under the waves of the sea, far from the thoughts and minds of those of the surface. And then the wyrms came. Foul beasts of earth, fire, water, and ice. Some flew, some burrowed, and other slithered, yet where then went, destruction followed. My father charged me with the duty of seeing an end to this destruction, this wanton death and decay. And it was here, in this cave, my own fate was sealed."

"What are you talking about, Quickfingers?" Henri asked, worried about how his friend might answer, but desperate for the truth.

"I am not him any more, not wholly," Seamus answered. "He is here, in me, and I am he, and another. It is...painful. Know that he cares for you; that he holds you both in the highest regards. Yet I have a duty to fulfill that outstrips all other need, all other desire or purpose. I must cleanse this land of the corruption that—" Seamus winced, his face contorting as gouts of flame burst from pressed eyelids.

"No! We must hurry, to the Stargazers Sanctum. Now!"

Seamus pushed past Henri, a ferocity on his stricken face that pulled at the very bottom of Henri's heart. His friend, he was in there, fighting for his very existence. And Henri swore to himself then and there that he would do whatever it took to get him back. All of him.

The Stargazers Sanctum was aptly named. A massive, domed corridor opened before Henri's eyes as he stepped through ruined doors, blasted away by a ferocious strike of dragon's claw. The room itself held a pool of water, no deeper than the top of Henri's feet, circled about by chairs of an ornate design unfamiliar to his eyes. They were also, to his surprise, very low to the ground and wide of seat, as if they were made for very portly children. However, Henri's focus did not remain upon the squat chairs, for how could it, with what met his eyes upon the ceiling?

Vast as the eternities it represented, the domed ceiling of the Stargazers Sanctum dwarfed any other structure Henri had ever seen. More than the size was what was etched into its liquid black surface: thousands upon thousands of gemstones, varying from what looked like pinpricks to jewels that must have been larger than a person. And not one was set without purpose.

"By the gods in heaven, it's the heavens!" Henri breathed out the words as he took it all that he could. Would that his eyes were endless, so that he could see all at once. But he could not. So his eyes darted back and forth, to and fro, until his head began to ache.

"The Iarathor worshipped the stars and the moon, saying that it was from her bosom they were born. My gods tried to teach them otherwise, but their hearts would not turn, nor would their minds be moved. Like the stone from whence they came, so were their spirits immovable and unbreakable, until they were broken. Bodies destroyed in black flame and talon fall. An entire race, extinct. Eradicated for greed."

"Seamus, I...I could spend a lifetime here, honest and true," said Henri, peeling his eyes from above with all the strength of will he could muster. "But why? Why bring us here?"

"There is a riddle in these stars," Seamus said coldly. "And though I have stared into the cosmos for eons uncounted, it was never pertinent for me to learn the constellations. There is a secret here, and this—" Seamus reached into his britches' pocket and retrieved that broken silver mirror, "—and these devices needs that secret unlocked, sure as I draw breath. The Iaranor spoke of a ritual of lights, a convergence. Here, they were said to have recreated that very moment in time. But it looks like no convergence I have ever seen."

Henri's eyes darted between the mirror and the ceiling over and over again. Questions, so many questions. What was that device? He had seen the Specter talking into it with someone, but how? Why did Seamus need it? Was he hoping to contact someone to come rescue them? Who? They were leagues away from anyone or any place that would risk their necks to come here. And most importantly, what was he going to do?

His thoughts stood still. And whether it was divine intervention or pure, unadulterated luck, something strange caught his attention. In one of the minor constellations, the stars were not aligned appropriately for the rest of the stars in the sky.

Confusion settled upon his mind.

Why would a people who were so persnickety about every detail—

"What does this do?" Una'pahu spoke the words, breaking the trance Henri had fallen into. She pulled something on the wall, a leaver of sorts. A grinding sound filled the empty chamber, a low grumbling noise that caused the pool of water to dance about wildly. The chairs did not move; they had been bolted to the floor. But the rest of the room did. The stars moved across the sky, the ceiling shifting and turning, causing the whole stratosphere to realign.

"What did you do?" Henri asked frantically, his mind trying to trace where each new star was. For there were new stars now, and others gone dim. How where they being lit?

"Look!" exclaimed Seamus, pointing a finger north, northwestwardly. A green gemstone began to shine, a massive chunk of emerald set to represent one of two great stars.

"Summer solstice," whispered Henri. "This is the summer solstice!"

"It is?" Una'pahu asked. "Well does that mean then?"

"Why are you asking me? Dragon boy here seems to be the one chock-full of useless ancient knowledge."

"I am not a dragon!" Seamus growled, and Henri thought he could see the faintest plume of smoke escaping his friend's maw.

"Of course you aren't," said Henri, turning his full attention to his friend, or what was left of his friend. "But let me make one thing clear, whoever you are. I want Seamus back, do you hear? I want him back if we get out of this. Not whatever it is you are."

"I am Fenron, Blade of Righteousness. I am—Henri, I am here! I—I am come to cleanse this realm once and for all of Iodaba's stain."

"Do you know when the convergence of Ynazranal and Ephranden take place? Do you know what that even means?" Henri snapped back. His heart was pounding, hands shaking, but he had put it together. He had always been quick with a puzzle and a map. But it had always been Seamus who had put his plans into action. He would not do this without his friend. "So help me, I will die in this cave before I leave without my friend! On Gallae's breath, I swear it."

A long silence fell between the two friends, neither willing to back down. Seamus went rigid. His eyes glazed over, one white-gold and the other slitted and red as fire. He stood there, unmoving, unblinking. Just...standing.

Seamus stepped back, bringing a hand to his head as he winced yet again. His eyes, those blazing, burning orbs of white and red fire, both turned a dull green. Before Henri's very eyes, his friend shrunk down, down until he was the same height as he was before all had gone so terribly wrong. Seamus's hair remained long and his face still bore that horrible burn. But Henri saw him, his friend. And he was still warring with whatever was in his mind.

"We came to an accord," Seamus said as he rolled the silver mirror between his fingers, just as he used to roll his knife or a wooden playing card. "I help you, and when the time comes for fighting, Fenron comes out."

"And what of the dragon? Seamus, what—"

"The dragon cannot be let free!" Seamus snapped. Seeing the impact of his sharpness, Seamus let out a groan. "I am sorry, Lightfoot. I just, they're so loud."

"It is okay," Henri said, placing a hand on Seamus's shoulder. He wanted to jerk back as soon as his hand touched his friend's should due to unbearable heat emanating from it. But he held his hand steady and true. "We'll get through this, we'll get you sorted out. Promise."

"I know so many things," Seamus whispered. "Dark, terrible things. I...I don't think I'll ever go back to the way I was."

"Fine, maybe you won't, maybe none of us will. But I'm not giving up on you, and neither are you."

"Henri's right," Una'pahu said, cutting in, offering support. "You're not alone. We're here."

Seamus looked on his lover, his friend, his companion through so many adventures. Henri could see the love in his eyes, but also, there was hurt. Something dark lingered there, but he hid it quickly, flashing a quirky smile.

"We don't have long. The godling doesn't like giving up the helm," said Seamus. "So, what is this discovery you're willing to die for?"

Henri, feeling that now was not the time to press, pointed to the device in Seamus's hand. He would get answers. They just had to get off this accursed island. There would be time. "That thing, it operates off of Aetora and Ria'Elahm's light. Ynazranal and Ephranden are said to be the mothers of the Lights, having birthed the Sources into existence. Now, I am not chronologian… no, that is not right. Historian. But, every kingdom of note has sprung up around one of these Wells of Light, the Republic of Ordiatea being the most notable, with Wells of both Lifelight and Everlight strewn throughout the Three Country Empire. The stars tell the story of that day, and every year during winter solstice, Galacian's celebrate the birthing of the star's light. Those from the Mainland, whose faith is filled with religious dogma and propaganda, they have erased this from their history, stating it was a pagan belief that should not be written nor remember."

"Get to the point, friend," Seamus said with a bit of annoyance in his voice.

"Does your guest not share my sentiment about faith?" answered Henri with a raise of his eyebrows.

"I think it best we do not press the topic, or our luck, Lightfoot." Seamus tried to add levity when he spoke, but Henri saw the strain. This was no easy task. And how long would they let him remain in control?

Focus. Moment at hand. Focus.

"Alright, long story shortened, I think there is a well here fulling these gemstones," Henri said. "I noticed in the hall, the mirrors and the chandeliers. But, something was missing. A source. A Source."

"Ah! Here, above, you believe a chunk of Lifelight is here," Una'pahu said with excitement. She looked at the dull gemstone in the head of her scepter.

"No, well, maybe. But more likely, Everlight. Look at the walls, the pooling water. This whole sanctum is set up to celebrate the changing of the stars. But see those seats there, the larger ones, they're off center, they do not align with the rest. They are made to look in a very specific direction."

Henri began to walk, his mouth moving faster than his mind could tell him to stop. "And there, where Una'pahu moved that lever. That changed the sky so that it appeared to be the summer solstice, and the main chairs there, they rotated on the floor, separate from the rest."

"But you're not going to the lever," Una'pahu cut in.

"Not that lever, that one is useless," Henri called over his shoulder. He was nearly at a run now, cool water splashing up his calves and soaking his trousers. "There are more—I'd wager at least thirty-two, for each major change of the night sky—but these are not from our world if Seamus is to be believed. There could be over six hundred levers in this room. We only need one!"

"But how will you know which one?" Seamus asked, his breath coming short due to the run.

"It will be in the Orshi Constellation, just over Nar'el. It will be lower to the ground as it is mapped out to match the surface of all of the world. Look, look at this group of raised ground here, this Gal! Heaven above, this is incredible!"

"Henri! Slow down. When did you get fast?"

"When I was locked in a cage and forced to eat swill until I vomited my guts out on a Biter, and then was subsequently marooned on a cursed island where I fought said Biters yet again!" Henri laughed, the high of running taking him by surprise. "By Gallae's grace! Look!"

Exactly where he knew it would be, a pillar rose up from the floor, a bronze lever with a circular handle protruding from its center. Words in a script Henri could not understand wrapped up the sides of the pillar, all pointing to that glorious handle.

"Here it is!" he shouted, not waiting for the others to catch him. Henri heaved with all his might. It was him. He was going to do something. He was going to help save the day. He was not going to be worthless any longer.

The skies above shifted, black matter moving across the hemisphere. Constellations shifted and turned. There, rising in the east, Ynazranal and Ephranden slid into the open, the former blazing with sapphire light.

"What holy name of Ordan!" shouted Seamus, as if something had struck him.

Henri pealed his eyes from above and toward his stumbling friend. A beam of that sapphire light struck the face of the silver mirror, igniting the device with brilliant luster. Then, as if scripted in a stage show, the emerald light of Ephranden shone from above, down, down on the mirror, as if it were drinking in their light.

"What is happening?" cried Una'pahu, who stood with a hand over her eyes as if to block the radiant beams from blinding her.

"Something is opening!" Seamus shouted, the mirror falling from his hands into the shallow water.

"Opening?" Una'pahu called out.

"Get back!" shouted Seamus as he dove for Una'pahu.

Henri raised his hands. He was further away from the other two, so while the air shattered like glass and all the light and sound of the room was sucked into an infinite void, he was not pulled forward into that abyss. "Seamus!"

Darkness overtook the room. Complete and utter darkness, accompanied by deafening silence.

And then, as if an angel had fallen from heaven, a figure emerged from the endless shadows, bringing with her brilliant light.

"What in Halfak's flaming pits was that, Iaenora?"

Ranella, daughter Telda, sat with legs crossed, the pointed tips of her fur-lined boots positioned so all could see the new beads of cut amethyst tethered to them. It was a great honor. These symbolized her journey, not just up the mountain but into her rightful place amongst her tribe. Alma was positioned next to her with a beautifully crafted Hurdy-gurdy in her lap, which she played with an alacrity that warmed Ranella's heart.

Alma's eyes lit as she turned the crank on the hurdy-gurdy, changing the tempo and key of her playing. She cleared her throat and began to sing in low, melancholy tones:

> Over mountain high, through rivers deep.
> So go I now, to find my sleep.
> Mother, shepherd, hear my song.
> Keep me safe, all the night long.
> Watch my door, for that night stalker.
> Protect me from the Duskwalker."

"Tsk tsk!" hissed Ranella, pushing on her Lamplighter's arm, stopping the music. "Look to the children. They do not need such songs before bed."

Alma lifted her gaze from her instrument to look over the other children who sat around the circular, blackened steel furnace where the whole of House Tordak would gather each night outside the circular tents to cook and tell stories. Their eyes were wide, the stain of fear marring their beautiful little faces.

"Shhhh, shh little ones," said Ranella brightly. "Do not fear what is not there. It is just a tale."

"Tsk tsk," Alma replied, her brows furrowing in dismay. "Don't say such things, Ranella. It is our duty to teach the young ones the deep lessons."

"Jin-jin, mu-uhta!"

"Gae pha ya, tun lan."

"Kha mae rya," scoffed Ranella with a roll of her eyes.

The young of Coghda were not schooled in the old tongue, therefore it was common place for those of the Path to speak it when children were in their presence so as to not cause alarm. Telda had taught Ranella in her younger years, despite council from the elders, stating that if she were to take her place one day, she needed to understand the weight of words. All that to be said, Alma had a point. It was not prudent to say that the old lore was false or tales. In fact, many years ago, she had seen the Duskwalker. When Ranella had told her mother, Telda swore her to silence. Yet, on nights like these, when she fell into a deep sleep, she would see those mismatched black-and-green eyes staring at her in the shadows. Hungry. Watching.

"Off to bed, little lambs," Alma said sweetly, a gentle command that was met with a chorus of moans of dissatisfaction. "Great Ranella is tired from the Great Task. Let her sleep well so that her strength will be a beacon for all our sisters and brothers."

Ranella blushed at this comment. She still struggled to hear words of compliment or acclaim, though she was deeply thankful for reprieve. Her body was weary still, despite days still of respite. Not for the first time, she wondered how her mother had done this year after year yet never wavered or complained. She looked down at her hands; the skin was still raw and pink, tiny blisters marring her palms and fingers. She would not complain. She would not break.

"Far cry!" echoed a voice throughout the camp. "Hear all, hear all. A message from Daneland!"

The children, who had already begun to disperse, wheeled around, gathering in a cluster behind Ranella who rose steadily to her feet, her thighs and knees protesting all the while.

"Come and hear, come and hear!" the harbinger shouted from his stallion's back as he thundered into the settlement. "Lord Ruthvin of Talahmnas sends tidings! Come and hear, come and hear!"

The man's face with wind-whipped and his eyes were bleary. His mustaches were frazzled and the braided top knot of golden hair whipped behind him as he pulled his mount to a halt. His vestments were bright and colorful, and the ceremonial sword of office that swung from his hip clattered against his mail vest as he dismounted.

"What word bring you, great harbinger?"

Ranella's attention was torn from the heavily breathing man to the calm and steady face of her mother, Telda. Tall and broad, with silver hair and hard features, Telda was a woman of presence and power. And though strict and firm, Ranella alone knew of the tender heart deep within her bony chest.

"Come and hear, Great Telda!" proclaimed the harbinger as he fell to a knee and raised interlocking fingers over his head in greeting.

"Rise up and speak true."

He did so, taking from a small tube that hung from his sword belt a bit of rolled parchment sealed with silver wax stamped with a howling wolf's head in the process. He unfurled the paper and read load and clearly:

To our kin to the East, hark and hear.

Long has it been told of the blood oath of Dane, our shared kin, whose sister's blood runs in your veins, as his does in our own. Long has it been said that one would be chosen to take upon her the mantle of power and bring us forward into a new day.

We proclaim this day is now.

Lori, Daughter of Erik and Sophie Ruthvin, eldest daughter of their blood, has taken upon her the Oathrod and thus awakened what she says is the Sage of Mind and taken upon herself the name of Auyxus.

This is not all.

As is customary to our people, the Ulkeniheim approaches. We invite you to join us in celebrating this momentous occasion as our honored guests. But this will be no ordinary Ulkeniheim, for one has come from the Outlands whose uniqueness is beyond the written word. We invite you to watch as a champion is born of blood and stone, with eyes of golden fire, and abilities that would shock the mind.

All haste and Ordan's blessing be upon you.

A mechanized carriage awaits you at the border if you so chose to make your presence known and share in this momentous occasion.

There was a stillness that followed the announcement that felt to stretch on for three or four heartbeats too many before Telda cleared her throat to speak.

"Well delivered, great harbinger. May your flocks flourish and your strength never falter."

"Great Telda, this honor is too much for one such as I," snapped the harbinger as he fell to one knee once more.

"This is exceptional news, is it not, Daughter?"

Ranella felt her heart skip a beat and her guts twist. Never once had her mother spoken to her in a such a setting as this, addressing her as an equal and asking her of her own opinion.

"Great mother, I am humbled by your—"

"You have completed the Great Task, you are Ranella, Daughter Telda, not child of Cogadh," cut in Telda with a beaming smile of pride. "No longer shall you speak as one less than I, for we are equal in strength and character. So, what say you? Will you go to Talahmnas? Will you see these things to be true? An Oathrod has been awakened, this is a great wonder."

"Great—" Ranella caught herself, not wanting to shame her mother after such high praise, especially in front of all her tribesmen. "Telda, I will answer this call and go to Talahmnas, to see these things and to make certainty of their claims."

"Go then with the strength of the Great Kalnan at your back and the aid of your Lampholder at your side."

"The Great Telda honors me," said Alma with a deep curtsy.

"Go then, and bring honor to us all," Telda said. "Make haste, for the moon waxes full. The Ulkeniheim is fast upon us. Ride the iron horses through the night and may the Great Kalnan watch over you and keep you from Belaz's treachery. But be warned, the peoples of Daneland are full of pride and secrets. Do not trust far your hearts nor your eyes. Be vigilant and remain true."

"As you command, Mother," answered Ranella, her heart filling with glowing excitement. For she was now a woman in truth, and she would bring honor to her name with this.

Edous pulled silken sheets from his naked body, the small bone protrusions that covered his flesh, jutting out from joints, ribs, shoulders, and back, catching and tearing the red fabric. A snarl pulled at his mouth, anger boiling through his veins. His body had transcended the feeble bounds of mortality -he was stronger, faster, harder than any man could ever dream of being - but he was now hideous to look upon. The transformation from man to godhood had utterly corrupted his former beauty.

He looked across the bed - three this time. All young and supple. Curves stained by their own blood. Limbs twisted into terrible angles, shattered bones jutting from flesh. The smell of death hung heavy on their air. And Edous savored it all. The sweet scent of Iodaba's power swirled about, taunting him once more, urging him to devour even more. But Edous had his fill, he knew that. And too much of a good thing would make it lose its savor.

With ease, Edous slid jewel-encrusted rapier from the body of an olive-skinned Calun woman - mixed-blooded, a distasteful practice, though it made for exotic specimens - no blood spurted as he did so. She, like the other offerings, had been utterly drained of life. And Edous could feel that life surging beneath his flesh, pumping through his crystalline heart, fulling Iodaba's touch upon him.

The snarl faded from his lips, replaced by a malicious smile. He was a god now. His strength, influence, and power knew no end. He was a god, and soon the world over would know his name. He was Edous, Vessel of the Divine Ones, High King of Calun, and soon the god-king of all Ethrea.

Four priestesses of the Divine Ones, each wearing golden veils and sheer, red garments that clung to their bodies, stood silently at each corner of his massive bed. Behind their veils, porcelain masks, each with Eternal Eye engraved upon the forehead, was the only feature that could be seen. Their holy robes were made in mockery of Ordiatian propriety and antithetical to The Church of Ordan. The symbol of the Burning Hand, stitched in red upon a bolt of black silk, hung from their waists - their aprons of authority.

"Was my lord pleased with the offering?" Said the priestess closest to Edous. Her voice was deep and sultry. She had been burning incense and taking in her fair share of the psychedelic vapors, as was commanded of the Priestesses of the Divine before watching over their lord.

"Bring my robes," commanded Edous, not answering her question.

"As my lord commands." as the priestess walked away, hips swaying as she did so, the tinkling of cymbals on her toes and bells at her ankles filled the massive chambers with rhythmic sound.

Edous stared at the priestess as she walked away, a carnal lust burning in his chest. Despite a night of partaking, the urges never truly went away. It was not just the sex, though that was always to his pleasure, it was the thrill of Iodaba's power flowing through his veins. It was the pleasure of life leached from another and absorbed into his own body. It was all of it. The screams, the pain, the pleasure. He yearned for it all, more and more. But now was not the time for frivolities. Edous needed in senses about him, and it could take hours to regain his composure after a feeding.

The priestess returned, the tinkling of bells and cymbals announcing her before she had even re-entered the room. Behind her four women, with heads shaved and wearing nothing more than beads, necklaces, and ringlets followed. Each of them was of southern Calun lineage, which had recently been conquered under the rule of Edous - at that time called Uzermon Thynalan IV - around a hundred and forty years ago. Their noses, eyebrows, ears, breasts, and navels were all pierced by rods of silver, gold, precious stones, and chains. Their eyelids were painted with a shimmering, golden paint, as were various other parts of their bodies in artistic, looping patterns. Each of these women carried parts of Edous's raiment, symbols of his office and authority. Long red robes, sewn of the finest silks, imported from the far shores of Zau'fi.

The four clothed Edous. First, about the waist, they adorned him with a short wrap that was pulled around him three times over. This had a name of importance to them, but Edous could never seem to recall it. It was in their dirty, southern tongue, a language he had all but eradicated from Calun. Next came the vestments, which were draped over his shoulders with practiced hands, careful not to catch on the bones and rend the fabric. These four had been dressing Edous for over two years now, his last batch having been offered up as sacrament to the Divine Ones when they had torn his favorite coat. Lastly, they placed upon his head a mask of ivory, gilded with gold, in a replica of his former face, before the horns and blood markings etched into his flesh.

Another priestess brought forth a mirror, holding it up so that Edous could study himself. Everything was perfect, save for one thing.

"Scabbard!" he roared, his anger burning through his veins, pulsating behind his eyes. Stupid, useless, insolent fools! How could they forget that?

All four of the painted women fell to their knees, pressing their foreheads and hands to the floor in supplication. None spoke, though Edous could see the faintest hints of trembling rippling across their naked flesh.

"My lord," said the priestess that was stationed at the foot of his bed, nearest to where Edous stood, stepped forward. She extended her hands, proffering his scabbard. "You gave this to me to hold as you offered up your sacraments to the Divine Ones last night."

Edous looked from the scabbard to those on the floor. A cold glee rushed from where his heart had once been, quenching the fires of anger within. He loved to see those beneath him scrape and beg, as was their place. He was a god. And today, he would make his godhood known to his people. Today, he would no longer just be the High King of Calun.

Today he would ascend, and all would worship him together.

Edous, god-king of Calun, drawn by Aaron Moschner.

Part 4

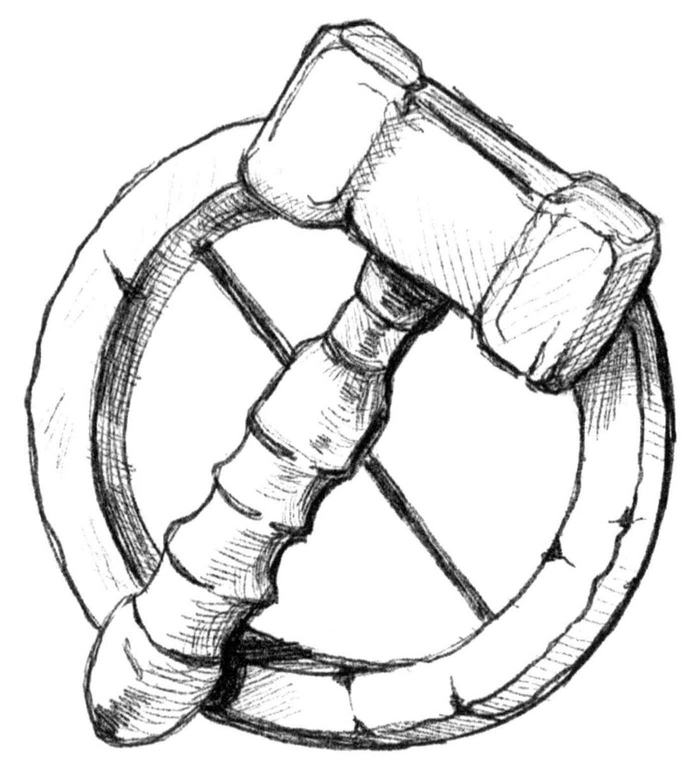

CHAPTER 33: A MOMENT IN TIME
DARIUS

Darius stood alone in his room. Hours had passed in stillness. Dawn would not be far off, perhaps one, maybe two hours more. But how could he sleep? How could he do anything other than try to take everything in all at once.

It was too much.

Stahlbak Hi'el. An Oath of Vengeance. So that is what it would be then? So be it. Vengeance for his father, his mother and brother, for these kin and tribesmen. For the world who wept at the hands of the corrupted. Iodaba had too long plagued this land. This land that, despite its quarrels and qualms, was his land, his home.

Oddly enough, since first arriving in Daneland and coming to Talahmnas, this was the first time his mind was truly at peace. No longer did he feel the strange pull of the Moonstone-rich Talah'El, Stone of the Ancestors, nor was his mind muddled by the powers of the Redeye. He was himself now and all was quiet in his head.

Darius was just about to retire to his bed, to try and force an hour or so of sleep upon himself before the Ulkeniheim, when something drew his attention.

Soft footfalls fell outside his doorway. Darius's heart began to beat rapidly. He extended his hand, instinctively calling his axe to him. It whooshed through the air and thudded into his palm as he slunk toward the door, every step silent as could be. The motion was hesitant outside, as if whoever was nearing was uncertain in their approach. Perhaps an assassin? But who?

Images of huntsmen in black, their strange silver crows' wings spreading over the brims of their hats and long, dark trench coats filled his mind. He saw their eyes, black as night, soulless and evil. The wooden haft seemed to creak under his grip as he prepared himself to strike, his knuckles straining and whitening with every passing moment.

The faint hint of spiced honey wafted under the door, catching Darius utterly off guard. A hand touched the bronze door handle, but then fell away.

Another long pause filled the silence as Darius felt the tension of battle flee from his veins, sending a wavy, unexpected weariness through him, forcing his knees to weaken. His back pressed hard against the wall, and suddenly, he found himself sliding downward to the floor.

To his sudden horror, the feet turned themselves away from the door and began to unsteadily walk away. Darius's heart lurched in his chest. Without thinking, he let his axe fall to the ground and he scrambled to his feet, tripping clumsily over himself while doing so. Hands that held firm against hordes of Morrean and monster alike now were sweat-slicked and shaking as he reached for the doorknob, praying to Gallae that she had not just walked away.

The hallway was dimly lit by iron candelabras casting flickering light down the carpeted path. But it was not the carpet nor the several suits of armor that caught Darius's attention. There, only a

few inches away from him, stood Izebal. Her hair was brushed back, held by an elaborately stitched kerchief of pale green and soft gold. Her lips were painted red and her eyes—by Gallae's grace, her eyes—shone with a hungry fire that spurred something deep within Darius's belly. A robe to match the kerchief was draped over her body, leaving little to Darius's imagination, the silk fabric barely touching the middle of her thighs. Her amulet of bright emerald and gold hung about her neck, drawing once again Darius's attention to places he knew better than to linger.

Izebal looked up at him and blinked as if surprised. That lasted only but a moment as a shy smile formed across her lips and she took a purposeful step toward him. And then another, and one more. Her hand pressed against his chest, forcing him back into his room.

Her eyes, those beautiful, emerald eyes, had lost any semblance of shyness and were totally filled with a hunger and longing that he knew his own were casting back. But this was happening so fast. So suddenly. Darius could not think, could not act. He found himself utterly helpless to her will as she raised a hand and placed it upon his cheek.

A flush of heat burst inside him at the cool touch of her hand while the intoxicating scent of spiced honey and lilac aroused something within Darius he had never known before. Izebal pressed her body closer to his. No words were spoken. He felt as if he would drown in euphoria. His left hand found the back of her thigh, just over her shift, and as he pulled her closer, ever closer, his other slid up the back of her neck and into her hair. She let out a sigh, then pressed her lips against his, soft and moist. Darius was clumsy and slow at first, but he drank her in. Blessedly, after a few awkward moments, his own lips began to find a rhythm with hers.

Izebal pulled back suddenly, and her eyes shone with emerald light. With a whisper, a rune formed around her hand. She thrust it behind her. With a thud, the door suddenly slammed shut, leaving them alone in the darkness. Darius felt a hand touch his chest once more. A blossom of heat rushed through him, sending the hairs on his arms and the back of his neck on end. This was more than flesh on flesh, she had set some kind of spell on him. It had to be.

He gasped.

She laughed. A soft, sensual laugh.

"Easy, messenger boy," she said sensually, the once teasing moniker taking on an edge of lust and desire.

"I..." Darius started but then stopped, heat burning across his neck and face as a flush of embarrassment marred the moment.

Izebal looked at him quizzically at first, but he saw the moment realization dawned on her. "Take a breath, messenger boy. Let me show you." Another glow of green flowed from her fingertips like vines tangling outward. The tendrils of power flowed over the buttons of his shirt, slowly undoing them one by one.

Darius's heart began to hammer in his chest. His ears rang so loudly he could barely hear a thing, and his throat felt as if it was swollen shut. Anticipation and fear wound their way around his brain, fogging his mind, blurring out reason, and leaving nothing but a surging need eating at his will.

Izebal's lips found his once more, moving with more fervency now. It was a feral thing now, civility and restraint be damned. Darius grabbed her. She was shockingly light. Her body melted into his hands, every part of her smooth and soft. He tasted her neck, then her shoulders. Eagerness overtook him. He tore away that flimsy bit of fabric that separated them.

Izebal let out a moan of pleasure as she took his other hand and pulled it around her waist, guiding him through the motions. Her body was warm against his own bare chest.

Where had his shirt gone?

She let out a growl that sent something off in Darius' brain he couldn't control. His eyes grew wide and his heartbeat threatened to deafen him now. He took her to the bed in three strides but nearly tripped over something.

Somehow, Izebal had removed his belt, along with his trousers.

"Magic?" Darius laughed. His voice was low and horse. He hadn't expected that.

And though it was dark, he could see the smirk on his face. Her beautiful, breathtaking, face. His mind went a little fuzzy, and it felt as when he had held his Binding too long. But this time, the burning was so good. Exquisite lust and tantalizing thrill streamed through his veins, pumped harder and hard by his pounding heart. There was no stopping now. Darius gave in to the feeling and leaned into her again, lips touching, first slowly, then increasing in speed and intensity.

Her fingers traced down his back, and as they did so, small jolts of energy flowed from her into him. It was maddening. Every burst of power made him want more and more. She laughed again, throwing her head back as he sank his teeth into her neck. That laugh morphed from joy into pleasure, ending in a longing moan.

But it was not an ending, only the beginning of something that Darius would carry with him the rest of his life.

Darius woke in a tangle of blankets and hair not his own. At first, he could not put two and two together, but all confusion was cast aside as he looked over to see the sleeping form of Izebal next to him. He looked down at her and felt that if he could, he would freeze this moment forever. However, that moment was shattered by a steady knocking at the door.

"The Lord of the High Hall invites you to breakfast, sir," said one of the various maids of Talahmnas. "He asks that you prepare swiftly, as it is the Ulkeniheim today, Ordan be praised."

"Ugh," groaned Izebal as her eyes fluttered open. When they finally focused, she stared daggers at the door, and Darius felt a sudden jolt of fear that Izebal might just blast the door and whoever was behind it to smithereens for waking her.

Despite her groggy frustration, Darius did not think he could picture anything more beautiful than Izebal now, disheveled hair and all.

"A moment," replied Darius, realizing that the maid would not leave until he had replied. They were persistent in their sense of duty and priority.

"Good day then, sir," said the maid in acquiescence. She then paused for a moment, and unsteadily added, "The lady whom y'er traveled with must have went out again. We tried her room and she weren't there. Sorry, sir. I know ye'd like her to be there today at the games."

"I think she'll find her way there," answered Darius as he scratched at the back of his neck.

Izebal drove an elbow into his ribs playfully before rising up to a seated position. Beams of golden sunlight bathed her, pouring in through the panes of glass in the window. She looked like one of those statues carved from marble in the Sanctuary, a figure of perfect beauty.

"By Gallae's grace, you're beautiful," Darius uttered the words without thinking.

Izebal cocked her head, letting her loose curls fall down her shoulders, and raised an eyebrow. Darius felt as if the whole world would burry him; he would accept it, if only to hide from his embarrassment. Why was he so clumsy with these things? He was not a man of words or passions.

"Messenger boy, you are without a doubt the most innocent man I have ever met," laughed Izebal.

Darius felt further embarrassment at her words. She was beautiful, powerful, brilliant. Of course she would have known other men. Why wouldn't she? But the thought of her laying with another right now made his stomach sick and his heart burn in undignified jealousy.

"Don't look at me like that," she tutted as she leaned back and stretched.

Darius was certain that she was antagonizing him now. And so what if she was? This seemed like a much better time spent than breakfast with Erik and his family.

Before he could think or stop himself, he snatched her up in his arms again. She let out a playful laugh and nipped at his ear. He kissed her and she began to kiss him back more and more passionately. They found themselves once again moving together in passion and pleasure, laughing and working, trying their best to understand one another.

The encounter was short-lived, and yet more fun than the night before, something Darius was not sure was possible. Not for the first time, he felt as if his heart would burst at the sight of her. He loved her.

"Alright, messenger boy, we can't keep the Danelanders waiting," sighed Izebal into his chest. His arms were still wrapped about her, the sheets long gone from the bed. "Their pride does not allow for even the smallest of slights."

Darius did not miss the sardonic nature of her words, but did not know if he had to will power to pull away from her and get ready to meet the day.

"You know," Izebal said as she traced lazy circles on his chest. "We could always just leave. Disappear together. Forget all of this."

Darius stared at the ceiling, her words striking an uneasy cord in his mind.

"I mean, what do you owe them? You saved their daughter, their lands, and even awoken another to some great power. Surely you have done enough for them?"

"I am a guardian, last of the Feromage," Darius protested, though weakly. His mind was not ready for a discussion, much less of one of this magnitude. "I have seen what I must do. I am called to find those who will reforge the seal that binds the Fallen Ones."

"The people here speak of one who haunts dreams," said Izebal, her voice taking on an edge of sadness. "These dreams seem so much worse here than before. What if it is another's doing?"

"I have seen the High Father," said Darius, rising up to a seated position, a bit of incredulity bleeding into his voice. "I have told you this. It is why I am on this path."

"But why? If your god is so powerful, why does he need you?"

Izebal's words cut him, even if they had not intended to.

Where was this coming from? Why was she suddenly acting this way?

"Darius, please." Her voice sounded hurt now, hurt and pleading. "Everyone and everything I have ever loved has been taken from me. My mother, my grandmother. My Troupe. All destroyed. I loved them, and they are gone. I can't lose you too."

The hurt in her words, mixed with the baring of her soul, pricked something within Darius's own heart. It was true. Izebal had lost everything, and in the same manner as he had; it was things beyond his power and ability that took them. Her family was lost because of his struggle. Had he chosen another path, perhaps they would still be living happily in Ranok, ever searching for their lost Words.

"I... I don't think that is possible," muttered Darius. "I swore Oaths. Not just hollow promises, but Oaths, upon my blood and the blood of my ancestors."

"So you go north to fight some demon, and what if you win? Then what? Another demon? Or will your god be satisfied?" Tears were beginning to well within Izebal's eyes as she spoke. "Damn it all. I wasn't supposed to... it was not supposed to happen. I tried."

"You tried what? Where is all of this coming from?" Darius asked, dropping any thoughts of himself or his own plight.

"I tried not to love you, damn it. I knew you could not choose me, but I let myself." Izebal practically jumped out of the bed. She reached to the ground where her shift lay crumpled and pulled it over herself in a rush of tears and struggle.

Darius wanted to get up, to stop her, but despite himself, he could not force himself to move. His body felt as if it were made of lead, the only living part being his heart, which felt as if it had been torn from his chest, set ablaze, and kicked mercilessly down a staircase.

"There it is," Izebal said, tears now streaming down her face. "I love you, Darius. But I cannot watch as you go and get yourself killed for your convictions. I saw it last night, with the Redeye. You would have let that thing consume you before you broke."

"I..." Darius tried to mutter.

Izebal drew in a deep breath and forced a smile upon her lips. "It is okay. It is not your fault. I need to go, though. I need to leave."

Darius could not answer. He could not speak, or move, or scream, or do anything. And as she walked through that door, the sound of it shutting nearly broke him into pieces. But she was right. As much as this hurt him, she was right. He knew, in his heart of hearts, that he would get up and face off in the Ulkeniheim, for it was the most reasonable way to get him to Dane. From there, he would find that cave and slay Diabhail, casting that fiend's bones to Dimdreal. After that, he would go where commanded, find whom he should find, and be alone once more.

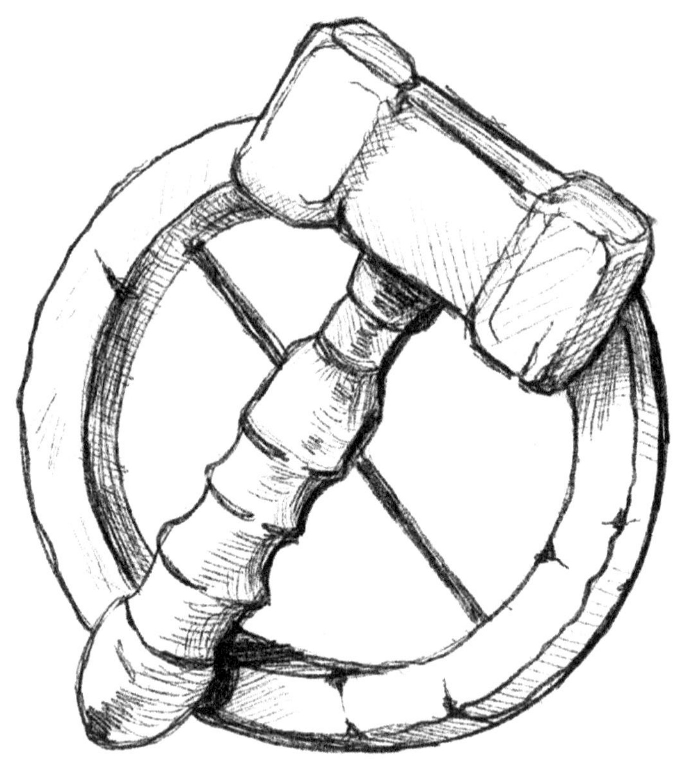

CHAPTER 34: ULKENIHEIM
DARIUS

Breakfast was a solemn affair for Darius, despite Lord Ruthvin's boisterous proclamations, the excessive plucking of the harp, and the sporadic, gruff barks of Nip and Trip as the two hounds fought over bones and scraps. Lady Sophie was in her regular regalia, sitting prim and proper next to Ella and little Ery. Lori was nowhere to be seen, and when Darius begrudgingly asked, Lady Sophie cut the question down with a sharp, "About her duties." Krunlan and Erkan were eating and laughing, both wearing rather ostentatious attire, as if last night had never even happened. Tyree was absent this morning, but Krarraek had taken his place at the high table. Other than that, the hall was rather empty, all the clansmen who had gathered the night before having taken their breakfasts elsewhere, though Darius had no idea where, nor did he care to ask. He just wanted to be done with this day, these games, and this place. Bitterness did not sit easily in his belly.

"Laddie, ye look worse than a tin anvil. What's got y'er beard in a knot?" said Erik, jerking Darius's attention away from his dark thoughts and self-loathing.

Darius looked up at the man with hesitation, certain he could see right through him. He was not sure what it was about Erik, but he had an uncanny ability to just 'know' things about people, it seemed. And what could Darius say?

Oh, you know, Izebal and I spent the night together only to be torn apart by some petty, unfounded argument? Or should he ask advice? *What would you do, Lord of this Hall, if your people needed you, but you really liked a woman? Would you abandon everything and everyone to go chasing your fantasies?* Darius had sworn an oath. An oath, gods damnit. He would be true. He had to be.

"It was the Redeye, weren't it?" Erik's voice turned conciliatory. It galled Darius. He was not a child that needed consolation or comfort. But he was acting like one now. Petulant and moody. "Erkan told me what happened. Nasty business. Would've liked to'ev had a few words with it meself before it were blasted to smithereens, but what's done is done, and ye can't change the past, now can ye?"

"No," grunted Darius as he looked down at his cup of untouched wine.

Izebal had not come to breakfast. He should have gone after her, at least attempt to make matters right.

Why though?

Were things not going well enough?

Sure, he was clumsy and fumbling. But, they had found rhythm and satisfaction with each other, hadn't they?

"Chin up, then, laddie! Ye'll be the spectacle of the ages today. Folk have come from far and wide to see ye. Even heard the tale of a few of our neighbors from Cogadh that've done make the trek over their mountains to see ye perform."

"What?" Darius looked up from his wine.

"The Advise of Cogadh has sent one of their daughters and a small tributary. Arrived late last night—" Erik was cut off as a loud *thump thump thump* rang out across the hall from the double doors at the far side of the room. "Speak it and so it do be. That must be them now."

Erik turned his attention to one of the maids that were never far and always ready to serve. "Go, get the door." He turned his attention to the table and those seated about it. "Be kind. Cogadh ain't Daneland. They do have some strange ways about them."

At this, Erik rose from his seat and pulled his great spear from its resting place over his head and set the butt of it against the ground. Sophie rose as well, her rich ivory and cornflower blue dress mirrored in her daughter's less-intricate ceremonial dresses, though their hair was braided tight and tucked under white caps banded with golden wire. Darius rose slowly, eyeing the door with suspicion. Not only had he never met a soul from Cogadh before, but he was in no mood to entertain.

The double doors swung inward, letting in a gentle flow of warm light. What followed in the wake of said light was unlike anything Darius had ever seen before. A lean woman walked forward adorned in a ceremonial dress—for what else could it be—of royal blue, red, orange, and bright pink. She wore a hat so tall it barely fit through the doorway with a brim as wide as her shoulders, from which hung a waist-length veil of sheer fabric that did not hide her surprising beauty. This was, however, not the oddest thing about the woman. That would be the slender, yet prodigious candelabra of silver, set with countless, tiny gemstones.

The woman walked forward and thumped the towering candlestick squarely in front of her, sending out a resonating *thud*.

"I am Alma, Daughter Ingrid, Lampholder of the Mighty Ranella, Daughter Telda of House Tordak." The woman's voice was captivating and jarring at the same time yet mesmerizing all the same, the words sounding as if she were talking around a stone in her mouth. "We thank the Lord of Talahmnas, Erik son of Ruthvin, descendent of Dane of the First Blood, with whom we share the blood of his sister, Lady Ethlae of Cogadh, Mother of our Hearts."

Darius blinked at the woman, his mind unable to follow the loud proclamation of so many words and titles in one sentence. Thankfully, it was not his place to greet or announce anything. That was Erik's, who tapped the butt of his spear onto the ground twice over and began to speak.

"Lampholder Alma, we greet ye with open arms in our home. Our hearth is y'ers, as our blood is also. Come, dine with us, so that we may be one in all things."

"May Great Kalnan strengthen thy arms and lengthen your beards," Alma answered in kind. "May I introduce, Ranella, She Who Completed the Great Task and has spoken to the winds and skies. She, who upon her shoulders, would carry the weight of our burden and watch for the Return."

At these words, a young woman who made Lady Sophie seem petite, stepped purposefully around the Lampholder and dropped to one knee. She wore no finery as Alma did, but very practical garb of wool and earthen colors. Her forearms were wrapped with leather bracers with fur poking out of the top, matching the soft boots she wore, in which the ends of her trousers were tucked, straining against the bulging muscles of her thighs and calves.

"I am Ranella, Daughter Telda, and I have come at the command of my mother to meet this champion of whom we have heard such strange deeds."

Darius wanted to be sick.

"Rise, rise! Take a seat and drink with us. Come now and let us do away with ceremony, for we will have enough of that during the Ulkeniheim."

A bright smile pulled at Ranella's thin lips and she rose from her kneeling position and stretched her back. Half a dozen other attendants from Coghda hurried into the room, carrying a rather plain looking chair of no beauty or seeming need of ceremony. But they placed it at the table all the same, one of Lord Ruthvin's maids having already cleared as space for it. Ranella took her place there while all others sat in the chairs already provided at the table.

"Great Kalnan be praised for the food and drink, Lord Ruthvin. And may the hands of Lady Sophie be ever strong. My own mother was of noted strength as yourself, High Lady."

"Y'er words are most appreciated," answered Lady Sophie with a subtle nod of her head and flicking her own lips in an upward sibilance of a smile. "But I pale in the shadow of y'er own strength, and I am certain y'er own mother is mighty in word and deed."

Darius's head was starting to spin, and the frustration of this mornings argument was starting to rear its ugly head once more now that the shock of new was wearing thin.

"You must be the great champion who has slain a creature of Belaz's pit." Ranella said with surety as she looked Darius down with measuring eyes. "Great words have reached our boarders of you and your deeds here."

Darius grunted in response, he was in no mood for this.

"I excepted something... more," Ranella said in a confused tone, as if she were offended merely at his presence.

Darius did not care. He just wanted to be alone.

"Come then and eat," Erik said in an attempt to break the chill of the room. "Lots of good eating to be doing. And lads, won't ye two take Darius here down to Dwallen and prep him up good for the Ulkeniheim while y'er mother and I do catch up with our guests."

"Aye, Da, will do," answered Erkan as he rose to his feet, Krunlan following in tow.

Darius rose as well, not caring if it were rude. He was in no mind for any of this. Not games, not for the pomp and showmanship of the Danelanders. He wanted to know what had gone wrong, where he had messed up with Izebal. It had been going all so well... until it wasn't.

As Darius walked past the hulking Ranella, he felt a strange jolt. Her eyes flashed to his, drawing him up in measure once more. Darius, for his part, did not lower his eyes from hers. This was a woman of true grit; he could see it in every feature of her face. Raw power, that was what she was. An immovable foundation, like the stones of the very earth.

"Apologies," he muttered out, as he shouldered his satchel and pulled his trench coat tight. "I meant no offense."

"None taken, little man," answered Ranella with a challenging smile, one that Darius would not have described as warm or welcoming.

Darius bit his tongue and moved on, pushing into the hallway and away from the clamor of another round of breakfast. It was time to prepare for the Ulkeniheim. Then he could leave all of this behind like a bad memory.

***

Dwallen Field's gymnasium was set just below ground level and divided into two by stone partitions. On one side there were blue tiles leading into the women's bathing area and on the other were

silver tiles leading to the men's. Inside, high ceilings were hung with oil lamps, and a series of shelves and benches were hewn into the walls. The baths were heated by underground furnaces. Fresh water pumped through boilers and channeled along copper pipes ran all throughout the rooms. The smell of herbs and soft spices filled the air, along with powders to stifle the stench of preparation. Despite being a more hearty people, Darius had been ever thankful of the cleanliness of the Danelanders, a trait they shared with their neighbors in Ordiatea, even if they would never admit to it being a binding part of their societies.

Erkan and Krunlan showed Darius to his space, a wide shelf and smooth bench with a strongbox chained to the inside. "Here's y'er key," said Erkan, handing Darius a bronze key. "Place y'er ring inside the box, and it'll be here when ye return. Tie the key to y'er laces, as do everyone else, and ye'll have little else to worry about."

"Y'er kilt and shoes are here. Change into these," continued Krunlan without breaking pace of his twin's speaking. "Bracers are here and ready for ye, along with chew if ye need it, to calm the nerves."

"Hurry now and get ready. Ye've got about half an hour or so before everyone starts to show up," said Erkan as he produced a wooden board with a sheaf of paper tacked to it. "Ye list in Gold party, which makes sense. Bronze and Silver will compete first. Ye can stay down here or watch from the boxes if ye like, don't matter me. Ye'll be up against Bjorne, special request."

Darius's memories immediately jumped to the other day when he had been taunted and insulted by the incessant trio, Bjorne being their leader. His guts soured. There was no way to make this look good for himself. He was over ten winters the other's senior and had decades of fighting experience. Even without his ring, he knew the young man did not stand a chance, but where was the glory in beating one so much so your inferior? Had the fates deigned to play one final cruel trick on him this day, and were he to lose, it would be a shame he would not easily shirk.

"Well, looks like ye've got a lot on y'er mind. We'll leave ye to it," Erkan said, tapping the board with his pointer finger. "We'll be up above, so if ye need us, too bad. Get dressed and prepared. The Ulkeniheim tests the metal of all, don't yer forget it."

The twins turned away from Darius, leaving him alone with nothing but his thoughts, and those were a darker foe than any he had fought these last days. Darius found his way to the back of the gymnasium to where a steaming bath lay empty, and plunged himself under the warm water.

Cheers erupted from above, echoing off of the walls and ceiling as the Bronze line up made their way onto Dwallen Field. Darius had noted that most of the Bronze competitors were wiry lads whose rough-spun clothes denoted a much simpler life than those of Talahmnas. He did not, however, go up to watch the procession of young men, but stayed firmly planted in his seat.

It was the same with the Silvers. Like the Bronzes before them, the Silvers were not of the High Blood, yet there was clearly of a higher station. The difference here was the fact that, like the Golds, Silvers were expected to fight in the pit after their three trials of strength. Unlike the Gold, they would be pitted against each other, and not a named opponent. Darius had been told to choose Talon. They had fought many times together, and though he was not sure he could match her in speed or technique, he could put on a show well enough to be given the Golden Pin, and thus make his way across Daneland without escort or harassment.

When the lads from Silver found their way back into the gymnasium—many of whom were battered and bruised, though this did not dampen their spirits in the slightest—— Darius knew that it was time for him to make his way up. He had paid little heed to those who were in the gymnasium up until this point, but his peaceful solitude was broken by the boisterous laughing of Bjorne and his lackeys.

Darius did not know why the little gang bothered him so much, but something about them gnawed at his self-restraint. Perhaps it was their youth, and he knew he was just on the tipping point of no longer considered young. Perhaps it was their arrogance, and how they flaunted family names and titles as if that entitled them to anything. Or, and most likely of all, Darius was just so filled with his own issues that he was pushing his own frustration onto their excitement. This was, after all, the most important day for many of these lads' lives.

"There he is, isn't he?" sneered Bjrone as he tightened his leather bracers about his forearms. "Ma said y'er lady friend, the Diju witch, went out this morning. Ain't even gonna watch ye, is she? Damn shame, old man."

Never mind. These were pricks, and any sense of exoneration he had tried to muster up earlier for them was washed away in an instant. Darius looked up at the trio, all, save for the hulking lad, being a good two or three fingers shorter than him. "Not today."

"See, told ye," scoffed Bjrone. "Ma said he was in too tight with the witch, and she done left him here alone. Shame ain't it, though. She weren't bad looking, for a Diju leastwise."

Darius erupted to his feet, fists tightening into balls. "Watch your tongue, boy."

"Boy? Ye hear that? Thinks I'm a wee laddie, does he?" Bjrone looked over his shoulder to his friends. He then took a step closer and said, in a low whisper. "Best be thankful ye can even compete. Ain't right y'er allowed Gold. But don't y'er worry. We'll show the world what it means to be a true Danelander. Not some weak-blooded outlander with his pet witch."

"Oy!" A shout broke through the gymnasium, cracking like a gunshot. "Ye better calm y'erselves. Save it for the field. Ain't reason to tie y'er kilts in a knot about y'er stones."

Darius did not dare to look away from the trio in front of him, but recognized Krun's voice instantly. He had never been more thankful and at the same time more disappointed. He wanted nothing more than to pound that smug look off of Bjorne's freckled face.

"Aye, cuz, of course," Bjorne said with a roll of his eyes. "Wouldn't dream of no dishonor here." He looked Darius in his eyes and added, "There's already been enough of that."

Darius did not think, his body reacted on its own, and he could not have been more self-satisfied with it. His lips spread into a smile and his head nodded cordially. Much to his added, bitter delight, this gesture made the tips of Bjorne's ears burn red with anger.

"Best watch y'erself out there," the young man spat. "Lots can happen. Lots."

With that, Bjorne and his cronies turned away from Darius and found their own place, only the droopy-faced lad showing any kind of embarrassment for the interaction. Not enough to stop his friend. Darius decided if it came to it, he would not maim him, only give him a good scare. These boys had no idea who they were messing with, and he would show them.

Just like that, all of Darius's attention immediately locked onto the Ulkeniheim. He would not just win. He would dominate this game and show these backwater people just how much he had held back these past days here in Talahmnas.

Thunderous applause greeted Darius, along with blistering rays of golden sun. His thumb immediately slid across his bare finger, hungry for the sensation of Ellitheor Silver. It would have to wait, though he had to admit it would almost be worth it to show these people what he truly could do. But there was no honor in it, and that was the point he was trying to prove. You could be true to yourself and others, and keep your honor, even when everyone and everything around you was telling you otherwise. There was always an easier way, a less burdensome load. But his mother had taught him to be true and just, just like his father, and he would honor them both today.

"Lord and Ladies, honored and esteemed guests of the Hall of the Wolf, welcome, the Golds of Talahmnas!" roared Tyree into a amplifying horn of brass from his high box.

Two dozen drums and eight pipers began to blare a tune as Darius and the other fifteen lads and eight lasses made their way onto Dwallen Field. Banners snapped in the wind and the crowds cheered as they walked up onto the green pitch. Dozens of men and women in armor stood around the base of the high box, their black kilts with silver and blue plaid matching the capes pinned to their ornate breastplates.

It was an overwhelming sensation, if Darius was being honest with himself. He felt his heartbeat quicken at the same time a sudden wash of weariness took him, as if were he to stop moving, he would crumple into a ball and sleep immediately.

Nerves, he told himself as he walked forward, it was nerves.

Despite himself, Darius scanned the crowds. His hopes were dashed to shreds as he searched in vain to spot Izebal. So she had left in truth. The weight of that understanding fell upon him in waves, churning with the roiling feelings of nervousness and animosity that were already coalescing within him.

Lady Sophie rose from her seat next to Erik. Both chairs were high-backed and ornately carved, befitting their station. She walked forward to the edge of the banister and, into a conical bronze amplifier as Tyree used from his position, began to speak.

"We welcome each and every one of ye to this hallowed occasion. Each of ye are of thick blood and hearty stone. Long has our world been protected by the likes of ye. Many thanks we give, and honors grant, upon our beloved Master Mage Tyree McDoogle, who has for three generations aided in the protection of our lands. But his magical might alone does not the land defend. Sons, and daughters—" She proffered a hand to where Lori sat, draped in silver and blue armor, face painted like a fierce warrior, her hair pulled back into double-braids showing the sides of her shorn head, "—have spilt their blood on these stones in defiance of all that is dark and condemnable. We spit in the face of evil, laugh in the presence of the dark. And in the bleakest night, it do be us who raise blades in the pale moonlight."

The whole of Dwallen Field erupted in a shared shout, a single chord of unity and defiance. Darius felt his heart swell with unearned pride, as these were not his people, though this was his fight. He shared that with them, if not their blood and heritage. He shared their mission and resolve.

"Our own two sons do officiate this Ulkeniheim, and our very own daughter is Chosen! Honor to the Ruthvin Clan! Honor to Daneland and every Dane in all of Ethrea and the shores beyond!"

A second thunderous shout rippled throughout the crowd, louder and longer than the first. Darius spotted the coloration of uneasiness on Lori's face. She did not seem to relish in the attention heaped upon her. He could understand that feeling as well. Though he was quite sure no one else could see those faint changes, not from this distance leastwise.

"So, we begin the final display of honor and strength," Lady Sophie said with a raise of her hand. At that, Erik rose from his seat and marched purposefully next to her. He took her hand and kissed her on the check. Lady Sophie allowed this with the slightest hint of a smile.

"Honor," Lord Ruthvin said into the bronze amplifier. His already rich voice reverberated throughout Dwallen like an avalanche. "The trait of the True Blood. Honor is found in strength of character more than strength of arms and legs. But strength is a sign of commitment to said honor. Work begets strength, and that don't come easy. Look at my own lads. Do any dare to ask them if they do lack commitment or strength? Brought a Redeye in chains from Beyorne, they did! Look at me own daughters. The three of them be filled in their own ways with strength, each befitted to their place. And even that crumpled old chutling, Tyree, he do have more fire in his belly than Nip and Trip when they ain't been fed in a day."

At that remark, a rumble of laughter burst throughout the crowd. At the same time, the two hounds that had been lying listless at the foot chairs, perked up, as if they had heard they would not eat and were ready to make their feelings known.

"Each of ye down on the pitch do stand to make a name for y'erself this day. Olfund the Hound; Bendrak Drake of the North; Talon, Viper of the Sands; and even the mighty Red Dread. They were all born in this pit, bathed in the sweat of their lessers, and raised above all who stood before them."

More cheering. This time, those who stood around Darius joined in. Some were wildly beating at their chests while others were crying their family names. Darius just stood there, eyes fixed on Erik, who seemed to have spotted him. The Lord of the High Hall winked before continuing, and Darius was almost certain that was meant for him.

"The first trial will be brute strength. Ten round stones must be carried and placed over that wall. Y'er gonna go two by two, lads with the black stones and lasses with the gray. It ain't the weight of the first that'll do ye in, I'll say that much. Second trial is that of endurance. Two great logs bound with chains will be positioned to either side of ye. The test is simple enough, whoever can hold them upright longest, wins. Lastly, a test of skill, the one we all do want to see. The Spar!"

Another cheer burst throughout the crowd and competitors. Boots were slammed and dozens of fictitious names were hurled out, such as 'The Hound' and 'Stonebreaker' or 'Skullcrasher' and the like. Darius blinked back the building pressure behind his eyes. His head felt as if it were going to split, and that constant, bone-deep weariness came back tenfold upon him. Darius inadvertently reached his hand toward an errant ray of sun, subconsciously attempting to Bind to it to draw strength. A hollow sensation flooded his soul as he was reminded he had no ring here with which to Bind.

"Let the games begin!" roared the Lord and Lady of the High Hall into the amplifier. Their cry was echoed by drummers drumming and pipers piping, all to a wild and fast tempo tune that beat at the very doors of Darius's already fraying nerves.

"Alright ye lot," shouted Erkan over the crowd to the gathered Golds. "Two by two, ye each know who y'er up against. No hitting, spitting, biting, slapping, or otherwise physically interfering with the other."

"Rude words, gestures, or feelings are, of course, absolutely permitted," added Krunlan with a dark smile.

Erkan rolled his eyes as he continued his list of rules of engagement, "If ye break a bone and cannot continue, y'er out. If ye can't complete a task, y'er out. If ye pass out, y'er good an' out. Only in the Spar is it okay to be beaten, broken, or otherwise maimed and knocked cold. That is to be expected, but at least do y'er family proud and take it like a Danelander. Other'n that, it's y'er honor on the line, not mine. Understood?"

"Yes!" echoed the whole of the Golds.

"Right then," said Krunlan as he cracked his fingers. "Ladies first. We're nothin' but proper, ain't we. Angthea and Yera, ye two up first. Let's give 'em a show."

The first task seemed to take ages, and Darius watched in what could have appeared as abject boredom from the outside. But on the inside, his whole focus was razor sharp. He watched each match up, looking for means and ways to find an advantage. It was not lost on him that the Ruthvins had pitted him against the largest of all those competing. It looked simple enough. Squat down, cup your arms under the bottom of the round stone, lift it onto your belly, and then haul yourself across the pitch to roll the stone over a chest-high wall—waist-high for Bjorne and stomach-high for Darius.

What seemed like both forever and no time at all passed as Darius studied every motion intently. Anger welled up in him once more, flashes of wild, savage heat coursing through his soul. These people whom he was playing games with had driven her away. It had been their arrogance, their pride and their bigotry. She had saved one of their own and they had treated her as dross.

Such thoughts consumed Darius's mind when Krunlan and Erkan called him forward to face off against Bjrone. Darius eyed the young man, and for the first time, he caught a glimpse of something familiar in his face, and there was no doubt in his mind as to who his father was. Realization dawned on him, bringing irrefutable clarity.

When the gong struck, Bjrone raced out in front of him, arms and legs pumping wildly as he did so. Another few inches, a few years, and a blazing red beard.

Darius snapped his focus forward. He would win this. He would beat the pride from these brutes and teach them a lesson they would soon not forget.

Wind tugged at Darius's kilt as he rushed forward, his legs pumping as hard as he could push them. The first stone felt as light as a feather, and he hefted it in one swift motion, his elbows digging into the rock as his forearm bracers clamped down on the spherical underbelly. That crackling sensation, that bizarre feeling of lightning and power arcing up his skin, charging through his veins, mixed with anger and frustration.

It had been several days since he had felt that galvanic disruption flowing through him, accompanied by the metallic tinge on the back of his tongue. But he welcomed it, the sweet burst of power that came to him despite not wearing his ring, let it circulate through him. He could feel the beast inside him, always dormant in the light of day, growling within. And he could sense the inky darkness, the putrid tinge of corruption welling in his abdomen. He used it all to propel him forward.

"Pig chut'n Outlander," snorted Bjrone under his breath, hurling the insult at Darius as he heaved the ninth stone over the barrier. "Y'er weak and slow. Go back to y'er church and robes, and leave the fight to real men."

Darius almost let out a laugh, a bark of scornful retribution. Bjrone was mocking him, not because Darius was weak, but because he had been able to keep up with him. Despite not being 'of the blood', he was strong. And above all else, Danelanders valued strength.

So, instead of retorting with words, he dug in deeper, drawing up on that strange sensation, pulling upon whatever that power was that crackled within him, and ran.

"Bjrone, son of Nee'av, leads the way into the last stone," commentated Tyree. "But the Outlander, Darius the Ironbolt, do be on his heals. Bjrone's last rock is up, a whoppin'n twenty-two stones in weight. Almost as much as me own pair!"

A laugh rang out through the crowd, but Darius paid it no heed as he ripped his rock from the ground, only a step behind the red-head. He ran, more like waddled at this point, forward, the weight of the stone pressing into his cheek and back, his legs screaming in weariness. When he reached the pedestal, he heaved the great rock over the edge with a final roar of effort, the cry tearing through his lungs.

"Point: Bjrone! By a goat's hair!" Tyree cried into the amplifier. "We ain't seen a show like that in an age, folks! Let's hear it for the Golds and their first trial!"

The stadium burst into cheers and applause.

"Outlander," hissed Bjorne under labored breaths as he pushed past Darius, knocking him with his shoulder. "That do be a point for me, I think."

Oh, I'll give you a point. The insult almost leapt out of Darius's mouth, but he bit down on it, along with the anger and frustration he felt at losing. He did not lose. He never did. Darius turned his thoughts inward, hearing his own father reprimanding him.

"Deeds done in malice are deeds unworthy of doing. Be better, son."

It had come from the distant past, when he had fought another boy of his tribe over something so foolish Darius could not even recall what. But he remembered the lesson, when his father had made the two of them go into the woods together for three nights, to learn how to get past petty grievances.

"A good man does not need to put another down to rise up."

A sudden realization struck him, manifesting itself from the darkest parts of his mind. *Why be a good man? What has it profited you thus far?*

More of the blackness leaked into him from his wound, he could feel it seeping in. Despite Izebal's runes, he could feel it. Or at least, that is what he told himself it was. Or maybe it was the burn on his chest, that imprint of glass that Mireya had left upon him. He had been a good man that day. He had walked past Diabhail when he wanted to slay him. It would have been easy. And look at the world now, the trial he was up against. It was because of the weakness of a good man.

"The reason, above all else, that I love your father—" It was his mother's voice now, ringing in the back of his mind as clear as a bell. *"—is not for his strength of body, but of character. Be that man, my sons. Be a man like him."*

Shame lurched Darius's stomach. He had lost a game. That was all. He would not stoop low because of it. It was only a game. His purpose lay beyond this field, these petty games.

"...test of strength!" Tyree's final remarks cut through the haze in Darius's mind, returning his attention to the present.

Dozens of men and women were setting up the next event. A large platform stationed in the middle of Dwallen Field with two enormous logs wrapped with chains was being looked over and wiped clean of sweat and tears.

Darius steeled himself as each individual made their way up into the sun and onto that platform. Six massive barrels of sand with small stoppers circled a great scale. As each competitor took hold of the handles at the end of the chains and the logs were released, one of the stoppers would be loosed. Sand would fall freely onto the scale until said barrel neared empty, then the next would be released. This happened until the competitor could no longer hold. When their strength failed, the barrel would be turned up, so that no more sand would spill upon the scales and that measurement would be recorded on Erkan's tablet.

"Darius," called out Tyree into the amplifier.

To his surprise, the audience cheered loudly as he walked across the field to where every other competitor had before him. Heat burned the back of his neck. His arms and legs were sore from the stones, but he bit down on that pain, using it as fuel to stoke the silent flame within him. That weariness, the bone-deep exhaustion, came upon him again as he stationed himself between the two logs.

"Take hold!"

Darius knelt down and grabbed the two handles, one in either hand. They were wrapped with leather that creaked under his grip and smelled of sweat. Droplets of blood and sweat covered the platform. Nosebleeds were a common occurrence during this task.

Darius blinked. He could have fallen asleep at that very moment. Yet, his heart thundered within him. His blood pumping with every beat.

"Bjrone leads with a weight of forty stone. May Ordan grant ye strength!" roared Tyree.

At this remark, the supports were knocked away and the logs fell outward. The chains clinked and his muscles screamed as the two massive trees stopped, his arms extended in a perfect 'T'. The weight pulled at his flesh, threatening to rip every bit of meat from his bones.

Darius closed his eyes in silent struggle, casting himself into the cave where the Itheanam had impaled him. He cast himself onto that beach of black sand, when his brother and kin had died around him, where his chest had been burned by a witch's hand. He cast himself back to his village, where his father had been carried on the back of shields. He cast himself to where he had felt pain so deep that none of this mattered.

And then his grip failed him.

His left hand cramped as his right popped. His shoulders screamed in agony. Warm, sticky blood ran down his mustache and across his lips, dripping steadily down onto the platform between his planted feet. His knees wobbled, then gave out.

A loud *thud thud* echoed out as the two logs struck, followed by a much softer *thud* as his knees struck the platform. That was all he could do. He could not have held it any longer.

The hollow silence abated in a cacophonous roar of applause and manic cheering, echoed by the thunderous voice of Tyree cackling into the amplifier. "Ironbolt indeed! Did ye ever think to see someone hold for five whole barrels? Never in me life did I!"

Darius blinked as he looked in front of him. The sixth barrel was turned away, the stopper having been loosened from it, though he had no idea how much had fallen. But when he looked at the scales, he could not keep the pride from welling in his soul, that carnal bit of triumph that rang out in every labored beat of his heart. The bronze pointer quivered right at the fifty-one mark. Almost a whole rotation.

Darius rose, his eyes finding Erik's. The Lord of Talahmnas bore a look of both surprise and pride. He nodded down at Darius, flashing a smile. In the same box, seated near the Lord of the High Hall, was that mountainous young woman from Cogadh, who, to Darius's surprise, also wore a look of interest, as if he had proven something to her as well. And he did not know why that meant anything to him. But it did. Somewhere deep within him.

Darius walked away from the platform, his spirits elevated for the first time since stepping onto the pitch. However, this was short lived. For as he walked past Bjrone, the brute muttered, "So you can stand there and take it. Big deal. Bet ye did the same with that bloody damned witch."

Darius whirled around, but Erkan was there suddenly between them.

"That's enough!" Krunlan snapped.

"Don't tell me y'er taking sides with this Outlander?" Bjrone looked as if he had been struck. "He brought a Diju to our borders."

"Bjrone, just shut up," Krunlan said as he rubbed his thumb and forefinger into his forehead.

Both Darius and Bjrone looked as if they had been struck by his words. Darius was almost certain that was the first time Krunlan had ever taken his side over another Danelander, and he was positive that it was the first time he had stood on the opposite side of Bjrone. And while Darius did not know their history, he had seen them together many times, especially in the company of Krarraek.

"Darius, y'er nearly ten years his senior, let it go," Krunlan snapped, sensing an awkwardness forming between them. "Bjrone, y'er son of the one of Talahmnas's Skogotuers. Act like it. The both of ye. There do be gold pins up for the take'n. Don't let y'er own problems get in the way." Krunlan tapped at his kilt pin, a golden circlet denoting he had gone through these same trials before and came out successfully.

"Now for the trial of skill!" Tyree's voice cut through the tension between the three.

Darius, for one, was thankful for it. He felt the hot fingers of shame pulling at him. It was hard, at times, for Darius to remember he was not just a boy. At times he felt as if he had lived that thousand years he had slumbered, countless lifetimes of struggle and strife. And yet, he was still a young man. Getting older, but still young and dumb and filled with that fountain of youthful rage that dulled the mind and heightened the senses. It had been that same youthfulness that had filled last night with pleasure that filled this moment with bitter resentfulness. He was, after all, only a man.

"Keep y'er eyes up and guard ready." Krunlan said to neither one of them in particular. "Every true Gold has earned that right. Ye may wear the pins of on to compete for it. But fail to show a good hand today and ye'll never wear gold again. We fight for the good of all Daneland here, remember that."

With that final reprimand, Krunlan turned away from them and made his way to where the sparring would take place. He leaned next to Erkan and, undoubtedly, informed his twin of Darius and Bjrone's squabbling. Which Darius thought was rather unfair, as he had not done any of the said squabbling. If there had been any doubt before of his next actions, it was all gone now. Darius cleared his mind and prepared for the final trial.

Every Gold fight was something of beauty to behold. Some chose broadsword and targe, others axe or spear, and one of Bjrone's lackeys had chosen twin daggers. The one constant, despite weapon, size, or status, was that not a single competitor bested their Gold. Not a single one.

"Last, but not least, come forth, Darius the Ironbolt, Defender of the Wall and Bear of the North!"

Darius stepped onto the sand of the fighting pit. His eyes flashed across those that stood before him. He could not call upon Erik, that had been made clear, nor his two sons. He was supposed to call upon Talon as he had trained with her and he would not embarrass himself more than necessary. All he had to do was—

"I call upon the one called the Red Dread!" Darius roared into the stands, his eyes flashing about, seeking out Krarraek's face. He could not wait to see the gloat, the surprise.

The whole crowd went silent at his proclamation, his challenge of their mightiest Danelander. A stillness settled in, and Darius felt his confidence shift some, but he did not stop his search for Krarraek's proud face.

"I accept."

Darius's eyes shot back to the high stand where Erik sat, his eyes cold and hard now, not a trace of that warm, mirthful smile upon his face. Next to him, Lady Sophie had risen, her hand upon the clasp of her cloak. A golden pin.

"I accept your challenge, Outlander," Lady Sophie answered with all the pride and priority he had come to know from her as she undid her cloak to reveal a warrior's leathers and mail.

Lori, who had been sitting in an unnatural stillness, allowed a thin smile to purse her lips as blue fire ignited in her wolfish eyes. A mental link sprung between the two of them, along which a simple phrase, filled with all the subtlety of a screaming boar, fluttered. *"You chose poorly, Keyholder."*

Darius's gut twisted into knots and his neck broke out into a hot sweat. He had not meant to call out Lady Sophie. He had wanted to crawl in a hole and die as hundreds of eyes stared down at him in shock. Shock which suddenly erupted into applause as their High Lady made her way down the steps and onto the pitch.

Talon was the last face that Darius saw before he turned back to look at Lady Sophie. The half-Tuawtian woman wore a smirk as

wide as the seas, her tanned body shaking with silent laughter as she shot him a look that said, *you should have just chosen me.*

"What'll be?" Lady Sophie's question caught Darius by utter surprise.

"Ma'am, I meant no disrespect. I can choose another…I—"

"Hush boy," she snapped in a hiss. "Do not embarrass y'erself or me. Pick a weapon and prepare y'erself."

"I…"

"Double blades it is then," Lady Sophie said as she drew matching swords from her hips. Darius did not miss the muscle that rippled in her arms as she drew the single-handed swords simultaneously, the metal rasping against the leather. "Grab y'ers and get ready."

Lady Sophie pointed the tip of one of her blades to the weapon rack. Darius, swallowing whatever pride remained within himself, walked to the stand and picked up matching blades. They were light in his hand, their weight mostly contained to the hilt and short guards. The edges were dulled and the tips rounded, but Lady Sophie's were not.

"Don't worry, I won't hurt ye," Lady Sophie said as she caught his stare. "Not too badly, leastwise."

Darius rolled his shoulders and wished, not for the first time, that he would have been able to spend more time training with the Avajan'Aluth. He prayed to Ordan that he would grant him strength and to Gallae that she would be merciful. He did not want to hurt Lady Sophie. She had been nothing but kind and respectful. It had been she that had taken in Izebal, providing her with an outlet and means to move about Talahmnas unhindered. He had not only embarrassed her now, but also Erik. Erik, who had taken him into his home and given him shelter, his only ask? To prove himself worthy of his trust. And this was how he had repaid their kindness.

"Fighters, take y'er stances," Tyree called into the amplifier.

Darius mirrored Lady Sophie's positioning, a blade held low guard and the other mid, poised to strike.

"To incapacitation or death," Tyree cackled loudly, his voice distorted further by the bronze mechanism. "Yielding is two taps on the sand or the other's person, or crying out like a child to his mammy!"

Erkan walked onto the pit, looking over both his mother and then Darius, "No cheap shots, no strikes to the back of the head. If

ye tap out in the first thirty-seconds, Darius, ye don't get Gold. Ye understand? I won't stop the fight for blood or broken bones, only if ye can't go on no further. Understood?"

"Yes," answered Darius.

To his surprise, so too answered Lady Sophie, who had a fire of delight blazing in her eyes. He could see now why she had earned the title Red Dread, with her flame colored hair double braided down her neck and the way she stood, utterly without fear. If the stories had been true, she had not beat one but three champions in the pit. Dread filled his own heart as he looked into her eyes.

"Oh, and Darius," Erkan said as he tapped his pad. "That do be my mother there. Remember that."

With that, Erkan whirled on his heel and marched out of the pit.

"May strength fill y'er arms and solitude y'er soul," said Lady Sophie as she slapped the tip of her low guard blade against Darius's.

He had nothing smart to say, nothing to strike fear or respect into his opponent's heart. The only thing that was filling his mind at the moment was a heaping amount of regret and embarrassment. Though he was painfully aware that that embarrassment might be doubled in only a moment or two, and that regret would turn to agony.

"Ready?" Erkan shouted. The whole stadium seemed to take a collective breath in. "Fight!"

Lady Sophie did not immediately strike out as Darius had expected her to. In fact, her lack of striking put him off foot from the start, having stepped back and ready a guard counter. This motion made him fumble and look weak, to which Lady Sophie tapped the tip of his sword once more and said, "Blade up. Show me what y'er made of."

Darius re-centered himself, doing his best to block out the laughter and jeers of the crowds at his misstep, and raised his swords once more.

Lady Sophie began to circle, Darius followed. They tried each other's stances and positioning, swift jabs here and there, followed by the ringing sounds of metal upon metal. Darius lowered his heart rate, but he could not keep out an annoying sensation that gnawed at the back of his mind. It was as if his mind, without that ring, felt vulnerable and was calling out to something, anything to help him.

Lady Sophie struck like a viper, suddenly and relentless. Blow upon blow descended upon Darius, who did all he could to just keep upright. Sharp strikes bit at his arms and legs, tiny marks letting him know that she could have done much, much worse had she wanted to. Darius parried what he could, using his whole focus on defense. He had no thought of offense against the onslaught of sharp steel.

Suddenly, one of his swords was wrenched from his hands, Lady Sophie having turned it with such speed and grace that Darius was left gawking at his empty hand. She descended upon him once more, no malice in her flaming eyes, only focus and determination. This was a thing of pride for her, and she would show the world what a true lady could do.

Darius parried and parried, bobbed and weaved. He urged his legs to move, but the strain from the stones and log hold had rendered his body utterly useless in this high-speed fight. He had wanted a test of brute strength, to beat and pound against a massive target. He was now faced with his second sword master in his life, and she was even scarier than Ajvan-Aluth, for she had no calculated coldness, but flame and fury.

That worry in the back of his mind sparked something in him. A jolt of power rushed through him, but dissipated as it leapt from the fingertips of his swordless right hand. He blinked, confused at the surge of worthless power.

It was only a moment. But a moment was all Lady Sophie needed. She darted forward, her weak hand distracting Darius's eyes. He raised his left hand to block, but the strike came not from above, instead twisting up from below. The sword was torn from his weakened grip. And then she kicked him in the chest, hard.

Darius rolled across the pit, spots flickering in his eyes as he did so. Blood and sand filled his mouth as the crowds roared their approval.

"You've done well, laddie," Lady Sophie said through measured breaths. "Far better than I do believe anyone gave ye credit for. Ye've earned the Gold."

Darius looked at his hands, raw and red, the tendons raised upon them. Sweat speckled the sand around them, along with a steady trickle of blood. He had failed. He would not be granted an audience for this. He would have to travel across Daneland alone and just try his best to find this so-called Apostle. He would have to

travel alone, because he couldn't give up on this to be with Izebal. And he had failed, all because of his arrogance.

"I do not yield," Darius grunted as he pressed himself upward.

"The fight is done," Lady Sophie said firmly.

Darius did not miss the way she tightened her grip on the hilts of her swords. Good. Let her be ready. If he failed in truth, he would not be awake to know it.

Darius rushed at her, lowering a shoulder as he drove his left hand into Lady Sophie's wrist. She too had chosen to fight. She came down from her seat. She had chosen, too.

***

~Sophie~

Sophie looked down on the young Outlander. Not that young. There was something in his eyes, an age to him that belied his years, a hardness that had been forged through trial and heartache. She had been impressed. Few could hold their own against her, and while she would never admit it to another being, two or three of his blows almost connected with her. It had taken all the strength she could muster to turn his hand over and remove that blade. His grip was like iron. His heart, a furnace. She respected him for it, more than he could know. Which was why when the fool drove his shoulder into her chest she was taken by utter surprise, only her instincts keeping her blade in hand.

Years of training. Countless battles fought and won. Never before had someone gotten inside her guard so quickly, especially not someone as big as he. He moved like lightning. Erik said his ring had given him powers, but she saw no silver on his finger. Still he drove her back, driving the breath from her lungs and sending specks of white and black to her vision.

She roared into the blow, driving the pommel of her sword into his back, over and over again. He did not let up, he did not even flinch. Upon the fourth strike, the pommel caught on his shirt and tore the back away. The ripping noise distracted Darius; he looked down quickly. That was all she needed to put space between them.

Sophie drove a knee into his guts, hard and sharp, while simultaneously striking him across the side of the head with her fist. It was like striking stone. Sophie had been raised with Krarraek as a brother, and she knew how hard his head was. But this man, his head had barely moved with the impact. It was enough though. Darius's grip broke and he stumbled backward, granting her the space to regroup.

Decades of training had honed her into one of the most, if not the finest, swordswoman in the whole of Danelane. Yet, as she had moved through the motions, this Darius had seemed to mimic what she was doing. Sure, he was not as exact or poised as she was, his elbows dropped here and there, the finer points being off, but he was so damned fast and strong. Sophie was finally seeing what Erik had raved about for the last several days. She was seeing the beast within, the wild fire in those yellow eyes of his. And Sophie reveled in it.

She pounced, forgoing form and grace, and began to batter wildly at Darius. He moved in a mind-jarring blur, as if he knew where her blades would land before she had even swung. But she was gaining ground, she could feel it. With every slice and hack, she saw the distance close.

There was no hate or anger in her heart, only challenge. Glorious, beautiful challenge. She would wear him down, and this time, when she gained the upper hand, she would not allow him space to yield. She would drive him into submission, not to kill, but perhaps serious maim. Tyree had a potion for that, or some sort of spell. Besides, Erik had said he could heal once he got his ring back. Let the world see what she was, who she was. She was dread incarnate.

***

~Darius~

Darius faltered, his back foot twisting in the sand. A sharp kick to his thigh brought him to one knee. It was over. It was all over. He could see the victory in Lady Sophie's eyes. And he did not begrudge her for it. She was a master of skill and tenacity. Yet, as she swung down her two blades, turning them so that it would be the flat not edge that would strike his shoulders, the sensation that had leapt from his fingertips returned, and with it came a sound of howling wind and crackling light.

Stahlbak Hi'el, Darius's enchanted axe, slammed into his outstretched hand. Lady Sophie's descending blades crashed on its bearded head, sending a spray of sparks and crackling light. It had come to him. Despite him not wearing the ring, it had come.

Darius did not have time to wonder at the arrival of his axe, the edge it had given him. The opportunity that had presented itself was far too present, yet so slim and fleeting that he knew that if he did not act now, he would never get the chance again.

With a roar, Darius drove the axe forward, knocking the flats of Lady Sophie's blade back into her stunned face. He whirled on his right leg, catching her left foot with his own, and knocked her to the ground in the same way Talon had taken him down time and time again. A final surge of strength sent him forward, his knee landing across her shoulder and the edge of Stahlbak Hi'el gleaming head resting just a hair's breadth away from Lady Sophie's bobbing throat.

"Stop!"

Darius's head snapped upward. His eyes flashed about for the source of the noise, struggling to focus through the pounding of blood and beat of battle that thrummed at back of them. Yet focus they found and when they settled on Erik's reddened face, he knew that he had gone too far.

Darius leapt back from Lady Sophie's body, wrenching the axe away from her exposed throat and holding it as if it were a viper in his hand. Sounds began to fill his ears, beyond the deafening thudding of his heart and the muffled rivers of blood that cascaded through his adrenaline-charged body.

Erkan and Krunlan were there in a flash, rushing to their mother's side. The crowd was silent. Everything was so quiet that it hurt. Darius wanted someone to yell, to scream at him, berate him. Anything to break the expansive silence.

"Shove off, boys."

That was Lady Sophie's voice. Darius latched onto it. He whirled about, expecting to see rage and fury. What he saw was a smile, bloodied, but vibrant as the blazing sun.

"I'd say ye cheated," Lady Sophie continued as she pushed past her sons and drove her swords into their sheaths in a practiced motion that must have taken years to master. "But it was a damned good fight. Best I've had in years. Gold indeed."

Darius could only stare in response, all sense of reality fleeing from him. When she took him by the wrist and thrust his arm into the air, shouting, "Gold!" he still could not comprehend what was happening. Not even the cascading report of applause and cheering, which had started off wary and slow but gathered in fervor and volume, could shake away his stupor.

"Does the champion concede the fight?" Tyree asked into the amplifier, his own voice as unsure as Darius felt.

"A technicality," Lady Sophie answered, her smile broadening even further.

"Mother," Erkan interjected. "The fight is forfeit. Ye know the rules, no enchantments or magic. Such have always been the way of the Ulkeniheim."

"This man went toe to toe with me, even after I struck away his blade. Would any of ye contend that fact? Did ye not see with y'er own eyes?"

Why was she doing this? Why was she helping him? He had embarrassed himself and her in the pit. He had known it was against the rules to use magic. But that was his choice. Despite that, the question still begged being answered, why was she standing for him now?

"That's what I thought," Lady Sophie smirked. She reached into the sporran that hung below her belt and withdrew a golden circlet. She turned to Darius and said, "I had this fashioned for ye. In truth, I had not expected to give it to ye on the pitch, but in a more formal setting. But I guess now is as good as ever."

She extended the golden pin to Darius, and as she did so, Darius felt an understanding pass between them. He knew she was better than him, and he knew that she knew that he knew it. This was a boon.

Lady Sophie leaned in as he took it and said in a low voice, "You returned to me my daughter, saved our city, and exalted Lori. I do not care what anyone else do say, y'er a Danelander through and through, even if ye don't see it. I do."

With those words of unexpected kindness, Lady Sophie turned away from Darius and lifted a hand into the air, shouting, "By my blade, the Red Dread of Talahmnas does not concede the fight, but by my honor I do admit that I was bested in the end. Let it be recorded as our first ever stalemate and let us drink, gods damnit. It's been a long day!"

The crowd answered in kind, cheering with loud hoots and hollers, with feet pounding the wooden planks of the stadium and music erupting from pipe and drum alike. Darius stared down at the golden circlet, in whose center was a bear's paw overlaying a rising sun whose rays furled outwards to the edges of the pin. As he looked down at it, understanding dawned on him, like the sun of the pin itself. He was going to make it to the Capital. He was going to fulfill his purpose.

"Attack! Attack on the Lord Commander's Escort!"

Darius's eyes flashed upwards, meeting the horseman's cry. He was bloodied and battered, fear dripping from every word that his cracking voice screamed into the crowd.

"To arms! For Daneland. We're under attack!"

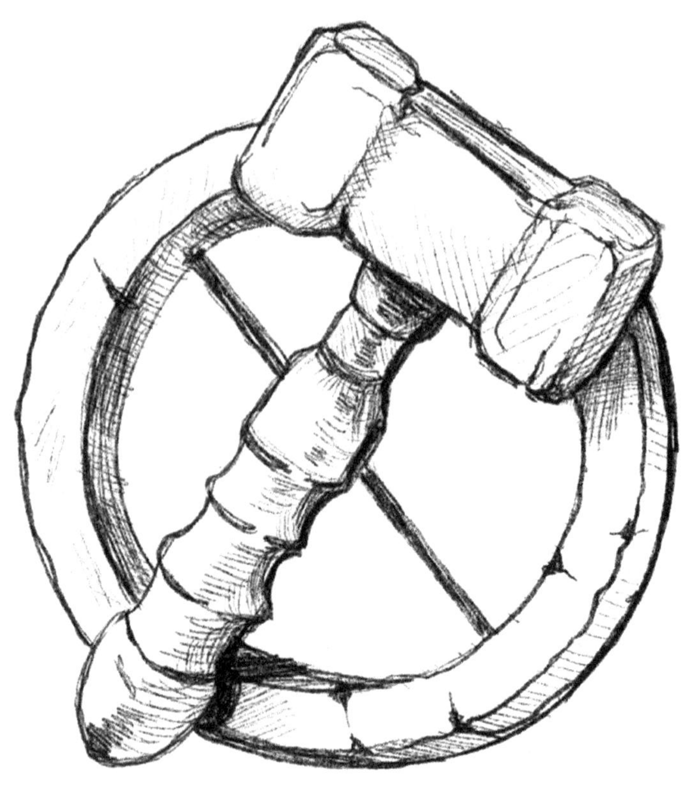

CHAPTER 35: STAHLBAK HI'EL
DARIUS

Darius ran against the tide of Danelanders who were pouring from the stadium of Dwallen Field. It all came together in terrible, perfect clarity. Why Krarraek had not been present. Why Erik had acted aloof this morning around Izebal's absence. Why Darius had felt that distance, the hurt in his soul. Izebal had left in truth, and Krarraek had been asked to guide her out of Talahmnas. And now they were under attack. It made sense, it all made sense. But Darius could make no sense of it.

It had only been a small argument. Why had she chosen to leave? They could have talked things through, couldn't they? He

could have better explained himself. There were just too many things Darius wished he could do differently. But it was too late for that now.

Darius almost tore the locker door from its hinges in his haste. He fumbled in near hysteria at the key tied to his ridiculous little shoes, eventually snapping the laces as he wrenched it free. He shoved the little key into the strongbox and cracked it until the inner mechanisms clicked free, revealing his silver ring lying on velvet.

As the cool metal slid over the second finger of his left hand and nestled into that divot of flesh against bone where it was made to rest, a wash of relief spread through Darius's heart. This afforded him a brief reprieve from the madness and anger that boiled within. He only had moments, and he knew he needed to make the right decision now. He snatched at his trousers and boots; the thin-soled shoes would do him little good in a fight and the kilt he wore would only get in the way.

"Oy," called a familiar voice.

Darius whirled about, his hands still fumbling with the heavy belt buckle that held up his trousers. In the entryway stood Erkan, his expression pained but resolute. And in his hand was Darius's trench coat.

"Da wanted you to take this," continued Erik as he stepped forward, proffering the heavy jacket that had accompanied Darius for so long now that it nearly felt a part of him. "And wanted me to tell ye to hurry. Tyree is taking him, Lori, and Krun in his rig to head straight to the fight."

Thankful for the added protection the heavy coat would afford him, and yet unclear as to the dejection in Erkan's voice, Darius answered, "Thank you, but surely more can fit into that death trap?"

"I am to rally the Skogotuers and bring them forward," said Erkan. "But we don't have time, someone has to get there fast and Da made it clear where my responsibilities are, first born and all."

Darius actually felt sorry for the young man staring at him, all while an outpouring of respect filled his chest. This was a son who knew his place and did not question his father, leastwise not in situations of life and death. Yet, he could not help but empathize with him, remembering every time until the last that his own father would leave out for glorious battle to protect those he led.

"Hurry, Outlander, and keep my family safe."

"On my honor," said Darius as he outstretched his hand once more. Stahlbak Hi'el jumped from where Darius had dropped it into his palm. "I will do what I can."

"May Gallae's grace guide you," Erkan said with a final nod before hurrying back up the steps.

Darius made to follow after Erkan, but as he did so, something golden caught Darius's eye. Atop his kilt lay the golden pin Lady Sophie had given him. He snatched it up headed up out of the gymnasium.

As fast as he could, Darius ran toward where he saw Erik shouting commands. Orhund and Talon were there, eyes locked on their lord, mentally jotting down everything he said. Yet, as Darius approached, the two turned to leave.

"Strike true this night," said Talon as she rushed past him. "Do not let these fiends slink away into the darkness."

Darius grunted in response, but she had already burst into a full sprint in Erkan's direction, and Erik was beckoning Darius forward with haste. As he too began to run, he outstretched his hand, grasping at the finally rays of the setting sun.

Warmth rushed into his veins as he caught hold of beam of golden sunlight. He infused it into his bloodstream, drawing its heat into his very essence. Sparks of life ignited inside him as all the little pains, the scrapes and bruises from today's bout burned away in an instant. However, this act only magnified the pain in his abdomen, the runelight beneath his shirt slowly dimming.

"We'll have to take it from the southern road," said Erik, who was talking now with Lady Sophie, Krunlan, Lori, the Coghda woman, Ranella, and her slender companion. "Ye must return to the High Hall."

"I have ten strong soldiers we could lend to your cause," Ranella answered.

"No," Erik's voice with not sharp, but it was firm and unyielding. "Ye cannot risk y'er blood. Long have our peoples been well. Let's not ruin that this way. Go back to y'er homeland. Let them know what ye've seen. Darkness is upon us. Ye see me daughter, so too is light. The world is awakening once more. We'll need y'er kinfolk in the days to come."

Ranella took a long moment to answer, and by this time Darius had reached them, stopping just shy of the group. All eyes turned on him for the briefest moment before Ranella answered, "I will go to

my mother and tell her of the great deeds I have seen. May the strength of the Great Kalnan go with you this night and keep your people safe."

As Ranella turned to leave, Darius felt something stir within him, a deep, unsettling pulse of power. He turned, outstretching a hand to stop her, but the slender woman who walked along side her, thrust out her ornate candelabra to stop him.

"No one is to touch."

Ranella turned about and looked directly into Darius's eyes. "We will meet again, Darius Ironbolt. Of that I am certain. Come, honored Lampholder, we must return and report to my mother with haste."

Darius felt like he needed to say something, though words failed him yet again. There had been something there, something that had wanted—needed—to be said. But he could not for the life of him think of it. And as she walked away, that impulse vanished and his attention went back to the matter at hand.

"Erkan is gathering the Skogoluers alongside Nee'av. My lady, y'er off to get the Berzerks. We'll rush forward and try to secure the party, and I am sure with Krarraek, my two sentries, and our powerful Diju friend, they're fine." Erik said as he looked around the remaining members of his party, his haggard face belying the confidence in his tone. Nip and Trip, his two black hounds that had been pacing around his feet, let out a small whine. "We'll pull through this. Krarraek is strong as a mountain and hard as stone. And ye two gonna get to try out them new vests we got ye for Winter Solstice." Erik said as he scratched at Nip's ears.

"Be strong, husband," said Lady Sophie, though she too wore a pained expression. She then turned her attention onto Lori. "Ye too, little lady. I expect ye to show these tainted chutlings what a woman can do."

Lori did not even try to contain the smile that flashed across her face, her pale blue eyes igniting with azure flame. "Yes Mother. We shall raise them to ash and cinder." Her voice was not wholly her own, but this only brought an echo of confidence to Lady Sophie's face.

"Chosen indeed," Lady Sophie said proudly as she drew her daughter's forehead to her own. "Go, and be strong."

Erik grabbed his wife and daughter in a massive bearhug from the side, his arms wrapping tight around them. "I love you." He said.

I love you. Words Darius would never hear his father say again.

He had thought it impossible to gain more respect for Erik. A flood of powerful emotions cascaded through his soul, nearly bringing him to tears. Darius rubbed at the burning sensation in his eye, turning away abashedly, fearing what they might think of this moment.

Lady Sophie turned to him next. She placed a hand upon the golden pin she had given him. "Ye've already brought one daughter home to me. Bring back Lori, is all I ask of ye."

"Yes ma'am."

"Good lad. Now, off with the lot ye, ye've got y'er own lass to save along with my bull-headed brother. Go now, be swift."

"I love ye, bonnie lass," said Erik, planting a final kiss on his wife's forehead.

Lady Sophie took a final glace at those remaining, turning lastly to Krunlan. "And I expect ye to break bones and make songs of it, ye hear me?"

"Aye, Ma, that I do," Krunlan answered with pride.

The horrid sound of Tyree's mechanized deathtrap just outside the arena broke the tender moment. Darius felt his heart skip a beat as dread filled his body.

"Ordan protect ye all!" Lady Sophie called out one last time as the four of them, along with Nip and Trip, hurried away.

Tyree's MAC thundered down the road, jostling the silent party as dusk began to fall. Darius clutched Stahlbak Hi'el with whitened knuckles, his face surely as grim as he felt on the inside. No one had dared speak, each preparing themselves for whatever they would face at the end of the road.

There had been too many coincidences these past few days. The attacks could not have been random. And to make matters worse, Darius could not get the words of the Redeye out of his head. It was almost as if it had wanted to be captured, drawn in. Yet it had been surprised by something. But what? Then there was the attack on the Wall. So many powerful creatures, so many conjured up, but how? Darius had not felt the presence of a blood queen. What else could have constructed these dread beasts?

Weariness began to take Darius's mind into dark places, the rattle of the rolling tomb lulling his body to sleep. He had not realized just how tired he was. There had been little sleep the night

before, and he had exerted himself today in the Ulkeniheim. The Binding had healed his wounds and given might to his body, but he needed sleep. Perhaps, if he could just drift off for a moment, he could regain some of his strength. As when he had prepared to compete, his heart rate still thundering, Darius drifted into a state of neither lucidity nor slumber.

Ash fell all around him, the acrid smell of charred flesh and molten metal filling his nostrils. Trees burned and the people screamed in the distance. A sound like shattering glass reverberated through the forest before him, followed by peeling laughter, manic and deranged.

Darius rushed forward, willing his legs to move with everything he could. But it was as if he were in a mire, his body constrained by an unseen force. He was so slow. But the screaming, that terrible, ceaseless screaming, urged him forward.

From a fissure of utter darkness, a being stepped into existence, one which Darius was becoming intimately familiar with. It was demonic man with pale flesh-covered protrusions of bone-like chipped shale jutting out of him and red markings like rivers of blood flowing from the top of his head down his neck and cascading over his torso. And in his hand he held a sword with a jeweled hilt, each gemstone black as sin, leaking tendrils of onyx mist and crackling with bursts of maroon lightning.

The man's eyes burned with black glee as he strolled through the wreckage, oblivious to Darius's presence. Bodies were strewn about, mangled and savaged. Darius saw Krarraek and Krunlan, broken and battered. Erik, impaled by his own great spear, his two hounds lying motionless beside him.

Lori, where was Lori?

Darius cast his eyes about, his body still moving agonizingly slowly.

He spotted her. She was crumpled over a body as if trying to protect it. A body in white robes wearing a mask of silver with a red scarf lashed around its neck.

The Mistress of Dreams raised her covered face, concealed eyes staring directly into Darius's soul, and screamed into his mind. The cry was so sudden, so terrible, that it drove Darius to his knees. He thrust his hands up in vain attempt to block the blood-curdling screech. But it was to no avail.

The swordsman threw back his head at the scream and laughed. He laughed, and laughed, and laughed. It was the most horrific sound Darius had ever heard, filled with hysteria and death. Yet as his laughter died in his throat, he snapped his head in Darius's direction and crooned, "I see you, Keyholder. Blood for blood. My Mistress is calling. Come. Come to me, so that blood may rain. Come to my sanctum so that I might extract that which is owed. I have something you want."

Lori's eyes snapped open. A surge of sapphire light, in the form of a great wolf sprung forward, directly toward the swordsman. And Lori screamed...

"Darius! Wake up."

A hand was shaking him. The world lurched in his mind.

Darius was on a velvet-lined seat. The sounds of crackling fires and dying men faded into nonexistence. He was back. Back in reality.

"Darius?" Lori said. She was staring at his face, eyes filled with concern. "You were talking in your sleep."

Darius tried to focus, but the dream was still burned into the back of his mind. He could still smell smoke. He could still hear that horrific laughter, the malice and hate curdling the blood in his veins.

"Oy, y'er good to fight, laddie?" That was Erik talking, but Darius could not lift his head to meet his gaze. "Y'er friend is depending on ye."

My friend. Izebal. Izebal...she needed him. She was in that forest. He had not seen her. She had not been there. The words came back to him, each one chilling him to the bone. "I have something you want."

Darius began panting, gasping for air. It felt as if he had been struck in the chest by some invisible blow. *No! No, no, no!* The words thrummed throughout his mind, beating listlessly against his lips, though he uttered not a sound.

"Darius?" Lori asked, placing a hand on his face.

A sensation of power flowed from her fingertips into his mind, washing away the fear and anger that roiled within him. Clarity began to form as the ringing quieted. Darius blinked, and when his eyes opened, he saw that Lori's glowed with azure light.

"Keyholder." She spoke not in her voice, but that of Auyxus, Sage of the Mind. "Govern yourself. Allow me to see."

"It is darkness in my mind," Darius answered in a voice that sounded too hoarse and raspy to be his own. "I do not wish my thoughts upon any."

"Open for me so that I may help you," said Auyxus as she placed another hand onto the other side of his head, cupping his ears as if to quiet all the horrible things he could still hear.

Darius wanted to push her away, to guard his thoughts and sorrows. Yet something in him cried out to let her in. It was a familiar voice, the words of Izebal ringing in his soul. He did not have to be alone. So Darius conceded control and let Auyxus in.

It happened so fast Darius did not have time to react. In one instant, Auyxus was cradling his head. The next, she was stumbling backwards into her own seat, Erik and Krunlan catching her as she fell.

"We must hurry," Lori said in a voice that trembled and shook. "Edous, Finger of the Dorr A'Gadah, walks amongst us. He is death and corruption incarnate. And so does another. I felt her presence. The Mistress of Dreams."

"She is trapped by them, chained." Darius answered her, not understanding where the sudden urge to defend the silent mistress was coming from.

"She is a Dorr A'Gadah," said Lori with a more than a hint of guile. "She has sold her soul to the Fallen Ones. She must be destroyed. If she, too, is in this forest... I do not know if I have the strength without my sisters to fight them both."

"Y'er not alone," said Erik, his arm still steadying his daughter. Somehow, that behemoth of a man looked smaller than his daughter, who fit in his arm like a child still. He held Aithne Lykos in his other hand and he slammed the butt of it into the carriage floor, sending a reverberating thud through the space between them. "I'll gut anyone who tries to harm ye."

"You are a good man, Erik Ruthvin," said Lori in voice between her own and Auyxus's. "Take this light to your soul. May it keep your mind clear. You too, brother."

Lori outstretched her hands, placing them on Krunlan and Erik's foreheads. Azure light wound its way into their flesh, carving new tattoos and brightening the others upon their arms and chests.

"These will ward off the Mistress of Dream's touch, but it is not foolproof. If you see her, run. If you see Edous, a man of red-painted flesh, run. You are not strong enough to best them. No man is."

Erik, whose face had lit with a surge of strength and pride at the rush of power imbued into his flesh, could not seem to keep the look of challenge away as he met his daughter's eyes. "I will do what I must to protect my people."

"And I am telling ye, those are fights ye cannot win," said Lori sternly, her voice coming through now heavier than Auyxus's, though still reverberating with ancient wisdom. "Leave them to me and the Keyholder. Ye two should get uncle Krarraek and the Diju woman out."

Darius bristled at the way Lori spoke about Izebal, but he pushed it away. They were going to help them both. They were risking their lives to save them. Let bygones be bygones, he told himself. Let her be alright.

"Save y'er voice and y'er strength," said Erik after a long moment of silence, nothing but the mechanical whirl of the Tyree's horseless death trap and the rumble of wheels over the forest trail filling the void.

Darius, wanting nothing more than to burst out and rush towards that vile darkness he felt building in the distance, bit his tongue. He had said all he would say. Only actions remained.

When Tyree's wagon finally halted, the back door opening to the clinking of chairs and whirling of cogs and spindles, Darius stared into abject darkness. Mist coated the forest floor and a chill hung heavy in the air, mingled with the sharp, odious scent of death. Iodaba's corruption was near.

"Trail ends here," said Tyree over his shoulders, his multi-lensed goggles obscuring most of his face. He held in his hand what looked like a large compass of bronze, but instead of hands, two gemstones swirled around in liquid mercury. They both now pointed to the left of the wagon. "We go on foot."

Darius looked up sharply at the old mage, unable to keep his brows from furrowing.

"Don't ye worry y'erself about little ol' me, laddie," Tyree said with a wink as he unfastened his wheels from the controls. "These will do me fine enough." He then drew out that strange staff of his and patted its head like it was a cat. "And this will do the rest."

Tyree's eyes began to shift into deeper and deeper shades of blue, the whites disappearing in a rising azure tide until all was consumed with light. He swung the short staff over his legs, suffusing the wheeled mechanism upon which he sat with motes of

tendrils of Everlight. Trip and Nip began to whine anxiously, the hairs on the nape of their necks rising. Darius could not help but feel the same way, as if something unnatural was about to take place.

A loud *pop* broke the tension of the group, a sound like a waterskin bursting from too much pressure. Then, the whole of the wheeled chair upon which Tyree sat began to shift and move, bits of metal, tubes, cables, and sprockets crawling about like living, wriggling creatures. The transformation happened so swiftly, Darius had barely had time to register what was going on until Tyree stepped forward, his entire lower half covered in what looked like a living suit of mechanized armor with a pack strapped around his back and chest, gemstones gleaming and cogs grinding as he stepped forward with a heavy *thud!*

"Bah! Don't look at me like that, laddie," Tyree said with a cackle. "Didn't think I'd try to wheel meself around the damned forest, did ye? And I know what y'er think'n, but this do take a lot of power, mental and Aethereal, to construct. I can only hold it for so long, and under much concentration."

Erik did not seem to be bothered in the slightest by the change that had taken place right before his eyes. Neither did Lori. Darius guessed this was not the first time they had seen something like this, but it was most certainly the first he had. Darius was reminded just how much time had changed since he had fallen to Mireya's bloodcurse.

The lord of the High Hall stepped forward, extending his forearm to Tyree, and said, "Give me y'er best."

"Don't ye think she—" Tyree started, only to be cut off by Erik's grim expression. "Alrighty then. Hold fast, me lord, this'll burn."

Tyree pressed the head of his scepter into Erik's forearm. Radiant beams of sapphire light arched from the crystals into Erik's flesh, infusing his tattoos with power, power that Darius knew fortified and strengthened his body. He still was not exactly sure how that worked, and his mind wondered, if only for a moment upon the utility of such a power. Krunlan stepped forward next, and as he did so, Darius was struck again with the aftereffects of his vision in the carriage. Krunlan lying broken and bloody next to his uncle. The hounds motionless. And Erik, impaled by his own spear.

A cold sweat broke out on Darius's back. Lori turned to him, her eyes focusing in, as if she were seeing into his very thoughts, the implication of which shook him to the core. Could she see his thoughts? She had been holding the Mistress of Dreams as if protecting her from the one called Edous. But why would she, if this Mistress of Dreams was just as vile and wretched as Edous? Why would Lori protect her? Unless the witch was trying to get into his head.

"Oy," Erik said sharply. "Ye alright, lad?"

The question jostled Darius from his thoughts.

"We need ye, laddie," Erik said solemnly. "We all need ye. Are ye ready for this?"

Darius looked into Erik's eyes. They had always been so bright and filled with cheer. Now they were hard as steel and colder than ice. The faint glow of his tattoos gave him a ghastly appearance, which made Darius grateful he was on this side of the ensuing fight. Though he was certain there would be plenty of dark and terrible things they would face soon enough.

Darius grunted as he stretched out his hand toward the horseless wagon. Stahlbak Hi'el rushed out to meet his open palm, a satisfy slap of wood on flesh reverberating through him as he snatched it from the air. Crackling tendrils of green and blue imitated from the gemstone embedded in the head of the axe, and Darius could feel the power thrumming through his body. A thrill of battle surged through his veins as a dark smile spread across his lips.

"I am ready," answered Darius in a tone that belied his zeal. He would cleanse this forest, just as he had Ranok and the Wall. For he was Ordan's hand, extended in righteous judgement.

"Ye best be," said Erik with an equally dark smile. He slid the cover from the head of Aithne Lykos, the moonlight glistening upon the pattern-forged metal of the great spear. "For tonight, we do battle."

"Alright, alright," groaned Krunlan with an overly exaggerated tone as he hefted his poleaxe, which only held the smallest chuck of unforged Moonstone in the spike at the top. "We get it. Ye both got fancy weapons. But, I'll tell ye this. I plan on cleave'n me fair share with ol' reliable here. Good Danelander steel and pure, unadulterated strength." Krunlan pounded his chest, which was now covered in a simple breastplate that had been stored in Tyree's weapon box in the carriage.

Erik broke out into a hearty laugh, saying, "By Ordan's beard, son, that ye will. That ye will."

It was Tyree that sobered the group as he stepped forward, holding that strange compass in his hand and looking stricken with concern. "We must hurry. I fear time is short."

Lori, who had been standing silent, sent out a mental projection of a great wolf composed of pure Everlight. "Run fast. Protect my family." Lori commanded in a voice that rang with power.

The Aethereal wolf sprang forward, rushing through the trees, leaving a trail of misty light. With resolution filling their minds, the party took off after the wolf, rushing forward without second thought.

It took nearly an hour of straight running before Darius could smell the acrid scent of Iodaba's Touch. Within fifteen more minutes of running, he could see the telltale signs all about him. Withered trees, animals that had fallen already decaying at an unnatural rate, and pockmarks of ash and char all about the forest floor. On the pressed, and Darius was surprised to find that it was he who was the slowest member of their party. Even Tyree, a man whom he had only known as cripple, ran on forward on mechanized legs, bouts of steam puffing up out of a small exhaust pipe on the back of his pack.

They passed by two bodies which they only stopped at for the briefest of moments to verify their identity. Erik wore a pained expression as he examined their mangled and rotting flesh. As he rose, he let out a cry of agony before rushing on. Neither fallen Danelander had been Krarraek, though Erik must have known them personally for that outburst. But they had not the time to mourn, not now.

As they continued onward, they began to see more and more signs of battle. Blasted trees still smoldering. Great gashes in stone and the earth. Sprays of blood and black ichor. Broken bodies of Danelander and Draugr alike, the skeletal creatures each decapitated and broken to a point where it was hard to make out what they truly were. There had also been a Redeye, its body split nearly asunder. Its mouth still twitched, but there was no life in its dead eyes.

Screams of rage and battle began to fill Darius's ears. The dogs began running faster, pulling ahead of the group. Erik, who had led the war party, shifted the grip on his spear and pulled his targe from his back, the leather covered small shield toting a long, silver spike in its studded center. "To battle!" he screamed as they crested a hill.

As Darius crested that same hill, the scene that unfolded before him filled his soul with anger and despair.

He only had a moment to take it all in, but that moment was seared into his mind with all the horrific shock as the handprint had been seared onto his chest. Dozens of undead creatures pressed upon three remaining Danelanders, their black eyes leaking Iodaba's corruption. Behind the Draugr, two Redeyes stood with hands extending, chanting in a horrific, insectoid language.

Darius tore his focus away from the Redeyes and back to the trio of Danelanders, panic filling his heart as he searched for Izebal. Krarraek stood at the head of the three, a half-moon axe soaked in black ichor in his hands. He was covered in cuts and bruises, his flesh leaking blood like small waterfalls, but he stood firm. Darius did not recognize the two that stood next to him at first, but realization dawned on him when he realized one of the silent sentinels was missing an arm, though no blood flowed from the open wound.

And then he saw her.

Izebal was behind the three, lying against the roots of a large tree. And though he could not be certain from this distance, it looked as if she were holding at her stomach in overwhelming agony. Something broke in Darius's mind at the sight of her. His father. His brother. Ranun. Images of those he had cared for flooded into his mind. Images of those who had died, who he failed to save.

A war cry tore from his chest, a terrible, bestial thing filled with rage and malice. If Erik's cry had not alerted the enemy of their arrival, Darius's certainly had. Dozens of undead heads snapped in their direction, ink-black eyes staring up at them from putrid sockets of corrupted flesh.

A flash of azure light. A scream. One of the Redeyes burst into a spray of black mist as Lori's Aethereal wolf projection leapt upon it and tore its spirit from its body in a single, ravenous strike. The other Redeye struck out at the wolf of light, the fiend holding a twisted scepter set with jagged onyx gemstone. The wolf dissipated into nothingness and Lori staggered in her place, a hand rising to her head as blood trickled from her nose.

"We must strike now," she urged in the voice of Auyxus. "Darkness comes upon us all."

Darius needed no further command. He threw Stahlbak Hi'el in front of him as raced down the hill. The axe flipped end over end

until it struck a draugr in the face, showering the creature in a spray of ichor until it imbedded itself into the chest of another. Darius lowered his shoulder as he barreled into another draugr, bones crunching at the impact, as he extended his hand toward his axe, willing it to him.

"The Lord of the High Hall has come!" cried Krarraek in a cracking voice filled with renewed vigor, raising his own half-moon axe in both hands over his head. He rushed forward, meeting his brother-in-law, cleaving heads as he did so.

Tyree stayed atop the hill, his staff beginning to blaze with an orb of Everlight. He cast a spell of pure light directly at the Redeye, whose own staff—which seemed to suck the light into a negative space of unyielding darkness—shot a beam of black back. The two spells collided with a terrible sound of shattering glass and lightning crashing, sending errant beams of power ripping through the earth and trees about them.

Darius could feel the power of that clash of spells, but he did not have the time to worry about that. He needed to get to Izebal. He needed to make sure she was okay. The only problem was that about two dozen undead draugr standing between he and her.

Stahlbak Hi'el crashed into two, both of which wore tattered chainmail kilts and had braided beards. These had not long been dead, though their pale flesh was already turning green and stank of decay. Understanding filled Darius's mind with horrid truth. Every Danelander that fell was little more than an additional warrior for the Redeye. It needed to be stopped.

Darius looked over his shoulder. Tyree had engaged the Redeye once more, sending what looked like a shower of falling stars upon the fiend. The Redeye, however, had cast some kind of barrier over itself. The azure stars crashed into the orb of black, sending sprays of sparks, but doing little else.

What could he do in a fight like that? Nothing. But he could get to Izebal. He could... he was not sure what he could do if she was badly hurt. But he could do more there than in a battle between mages.

With a ferocity born of desperation, Darius cleaved the two draugr in one blow, taking the head from one and the other through the midsection. The Moonstone seemed to sear their corrupted flesh, for as they fell, their bodies smoldered with silver fire.

That was new.

Darius had not realized this up until this point, but a quick glance showed that not only his axe but every weapon infused with Moonstone burned the flesh of these creatures. Good. Let them burn. Let them all burn for eternity.

Darius had nearly reached Izebal's side when a trumpeting call reverberated through the forest, drawing him up short of his destination. Darius knew the call in an instant, and the implication that came with it. Itheanam.

A hand landed on Darius's shoulder, sending him whirling about, axe rising, posed for a strike. Lori faced him, eyes filled with Everlight, her expression grim. "Do not let my father die. I will see to Izebal."

Darius twisted his head back, looking at where Izebal lay, not twenty measures away. The Itheanam trumpeted once more, much closer this time. Darius looked back at Lori. "Go. I will protect her."

Darius warred with himself. The need to get to Izebal's side, to protect her, conflicted with his need to protect those who were fighting around him. He knew that Lori could protect Izebal, possibly even heal her. She was a Sage, and it had been Everlight that had healed his own wounds when he had not had the strength to do so himself. But could Erik defend himself from an Itheanam? No.

Fury blazed through Darius's mind, filling his vision with red. The beast inside of him clawed at his will, fighting to get out. But he needed control now. He had his axe now, and dark part of his mind wanted to know just what that would look like. Would the Itheanam's flesh burn with silver fire as he cleaved its head from its shoulders? There was only one way to find out.

"I am trusting you," said Darius darkly as he shifted his axe in his grip.

"Likewise, Keyholder," Lori answered.

Darius gave into the fury within his heart and soul as he turned away from the woman he loved and looked upon the towering creature of darkness that broke into the clearing where they fought. The Itheanam let out a cry, a bloodcurdling scream as it rose upon on cloven hooves. This one looked to have the head of deer, though its skull was white bone. Souls of wailing dead wriggled in its inky flesh, like faces under a coating of tar. Hands as wide as a torso and multi-jointed fingers tipped with talons opened wide as it bellowed.

The forest went quiet for a moment upon the end of its deathly call. But Darius answered it in kind. He rose up to his full stature, hefting his axe in one hand over his head, cried out, "At me! Come to me," and rushed toward the beast as golden tears began to stream down his face.

CHAPTER 36: INTO THE DARKNESS

Darius & Lori

Darius crashed into the Itheanam, axe bearing down on the horrid creature with all the strength he could muster. The pungent mix of ichor and sludge that sprayed across Darius's face made his stomach lurch and nearly cost him his eyesight. The Itheanam, for its part, let out a bleat of agony as the bearded head of Stahlbak Hi'el carved

away putrid flesh and broke bones. But the strike did not slay the beast, only enraged it.

"Rhaz-khal!" cried the Itheanam, its voice like boots squelching through a swamp and a bleating deer joined into an unholy cry. It reached one of its unnaturally long arms out to push its cloven flesh back together. Tendrils of inky-black reached out, like hundreds of insectoid limbs grasping for one another as it mended itself before Darius's eyes. "Rhaz-khal. Must. Feed."

"No," Darius growled as he swung his axe back into a ready position. "Rhaz-khal must die."

The Itheanam let out a mournful laugh, a terrible noise filled with clattering bones and soupy squelches. "Rhaz-khal will taste your soul."

Darius had nothing else to say. So he rushed forward again.

To the Itheanam's credit, it dodged his hacking blows this time, not allowing Darius's blade to touch its roiling flesh, all the while making great sweeping motions with its clawed hands. Trees burst as its talons passed through them, sending sprays of splinters and full chunks of wood at Darius. Still he pressed on, fury burning through his veins. He could do this. He *would* do this.

Step by agonizing step, Darius gained on the Itheanam, driving it further away from the remaining Danelanders, affording them the ability to regroup. He could hear Erik behind him, shouting commands. He could feel the blasts of power as spells crashed into one another while Tyree and the Redeye dueled. But he could not feel that light, the power of Ria'Elahm. He had to act fast; Izebal was fading. And it was all his fault.

Why had he chosen others over her? Why couldn't he have just left with her? He was no closer to the Capital now than he would have been had he left. In fact, he was further away and she was hurt.

Rage boiled his blood as these relentless thoughts cascaded into his mind. He was angry, so angry. He was angry at the Danelanders for having delayed him so. He was angry at Izebal for choosing to strike out on her own. But mostly, he was angry with himself. And this Itheanam would feel the repercussions of his anger.

Blow after blow, Darius hacked away at the creature. Still it did not fall. In fact, it managed to land a strike across Darius's chest, tearing away leather, fabric, and flesh in an instant. White-hot pain rippled through Darius, though it only stoked the fire within.

Darius roared as he drove the creature back in the direction it had come from, back and back and back. It dodged and lurched, its body wriggling and writhing as it either moved through or bowled over trees. A sound like glass shattering rippled through the trees, but Darius paid it no heed. His mind was consumed by the foe before him. And despite its uncanny evasions and pure strength, Darius finally drove the Itheanam to the edge of rocky cliff, the sounds of water falling echoing through the hollow night.

"Rhaz-khal win." The creature's voice was gurgled with blood and death, though pride burned in its dark eyes.

"No," Darius grunted. "Now you die."

"No alive. Rhaz-khal win. Hail the lord of blood," cried out Rhaz-khal as it stepped backward over the edge of the cliff, its body crashing against the rocks below.

The night went silent.

Silent.

Darius could not hear the battle he left behind.

Panic cascaded over him in waves. He could not hear the battle. Not a cry of war nor of victory. There was only silence. Darius ran. And as he ran his mind was filled with images of his friends, broken and dying, strewn about the forest floor.

No, no, no! Not again. Never again.

The scene that filled Darius's vision as burst into the clearing, lit by moonlight and smoldering flames, pierced him to his very core. And though his eyes took in all things, he could not comprehend them.

Krunlan lay next to Krarraek's body, blood soaking the earth. The two silent sentries had been utterly decimated, their corpses a smoldering pile of blackened metal. Erik was on his knees, his hands gripped around the haft of Aithne Lykos, the head of which was jutting out of his back, having pierced him through the torso. Across the grove stood Lori, blue fire in her eyes as she faced a demon made flesh.

Diabhail?

It was impossible. But there he was. Only, not exactly how Darius had remembered him. He was bare chested and only wore pair of loose trousers of white, which were stained red with blood. At his hip hung a jewel-encrusted rapier hilt in an elaborate sheath. Black veins covered pale flesh, flesh from which jutted what looked like shards of chipped stone. On his head, a crown of similar stony protrusions formed. And when he turned his red-inked face to stare upon Darius, a rictus grin spread across grey lips.

"Keyholder, is it? Long have I wanted to meet you."

"I should have killed you when I had the chance," snarled Darius as he tightened his grip upon his axe.

"A thousand years have not increased your understanding. A brute you were, and a brute you are."

Darius had nothing else to say. If he wanted a brute, a brute he would have. Darius rushed forward, swinging Stahlbak Hi'el with all the force he could marshal. His blow was knocked aside with the most careless backhand he had ever witnessed, though the reverberations of the strike sent a shockwave of pain through Darius's hands and forearms, almost causing him to drop his axe.

"Weak too. Honestly, I expected more of you."

Darius went to raise his axe, to strike down his foe, but in a blur of motion and a sound like shattering glass, the demon vanished. All that was left where Darius's axe fell was a haze of heat that rippled the air.

Something hard struck Darius in the back, sending his body flying forward into a tree. The impact made a sickening crunching sound as the tree splintered and Darius dropped to the ground.

Dazed, Darius turned his head to the side an attempt to see anything, any angle he could use to aid him. Never before had he felt so outclassed in raw strength and power. It was then that his eyes fell once more on Lori.

She was standing, hands to either side as if nailed to a cross. Her Sage's scepter laid on the ground at her feet and her body trembled silently, as if she were straining against some unseen force.

Behind her lay Izebal. It was clear now that she had been wounded, and grievously at that. Dark red stained her dress and her skin had grown ashen. Her eyes were closed and her hands rested over the wound. She had passed out or had otherwise been incapacitated.

No one else remind. He was it. There was no sight or sound of Tyree, nor the hounds. It was only Darius. Only he stood between his friends and certain death. So he rose.

"Ah, the bear cub rises. Won't you bring the beast out to play?"

"I'll carve your heart out."

"That does not sound very Guardian-like, Denathurias of the Iron Mountains."

Something in Darius's heart lurched when the other said his name. An oily wrongness wriggled through his veins, sending his hairs on end and a shiver running through his flesh.

"Did you not know? My masters have told me all things. For great is their wisdom and glorious shall be their reign."

"Who are you?" Darius asked, raising his axe and pointing it at the other. "You're not Diabhail."

Fury blazed in the other's eyes. The air rippled, echoed by the sounds of shattering glass. Suddenly, he was right before Darius's face, striking out with another backhand. Darius tried to raise his axe to stop it, but he was too slow. It struck thunder and felt like a landslide. Forest and sky blurred together as Darius toppled end over end until he hit the ground once more. He was being played with like child tosses a rag doll.

"I am he! We are him!" cried the demon as he traipsed forward, the grass withering to ash at each footfall. "I am the beginning and the end. I am he that sojourns through death. Dorr A'Gadah, Hand of Khadais. I am Edous! And you are in my path."

Darius grunted as he pulled himself up off the forest floor. He could feel himself swaying under his wounds, but he rose nonetheless. Blood from a gash on his forehead blurred his vision in his right eye, but that did not matter. Nothing mattered now, save for this creature's death.

"In Ordan's name, I will kill you," spat Darius, along with a wad of bloody phlegm.

"You don't get it, boy," sneered Edous. "I am not here for you, not yet. Your people are decimated. You mean nothing. Are nothing. But her..." Edous looked across the clearing to where Lori stood, and behind her, Izebal. "She has been a thorn in my heel for far too long."

A grunt drew Edous attention away from Darius. Erik had risen to his feet. Blood trickled down his mouth and his legs wobbled under the strain of his weight and the grievous wound that still afflicted him, but rise he did.

"I...am not—" Erik coughed, and blood splattered from his mouth. He tried to take a step forward.

In an instant Edous vanished and then reappeared directly in front of Erik. With an unceremonious motion so fast that Darius did not have time to react, Edous wrenched the spear from Erik's body, pushed him bodily with one hand, and tossed the spear without

glancing Darius's direction. He did not, however, miss his mark. Aithne Lykos took Darius in the shoulder, lifting him from his feet and pinning his body to a tree.

"This is taking entirely too long," Edous sighed, though that rictus smile never left his horrid face.

Edous stepped past Lori, whose whole body shook violently as he did so, though it moved not an inch. Though pinned to a tree, Darius could still see everything happening, but just like Lori, he was utterly helpless to stop it. His strength was gone. His body was broken. But it did not stop him from letting out a howl of agony as Edous crouched down next to Izebal and stroked her face with a bony hand.

"Come now," said Edous as he lifted Izebal's limp body with ease. "I have a queen to resurrect."

Darius continued to howl as he pulled at the spear that pinned him to the tree. Edous raised a hand and clawed at the air, ripping it asunder. No, not ripping, shattering it like glass. Tendrils of black that crackled with maroon lightning leaked out from the void as Edous stepped through, vanishing from sight, taking Izebal with him.

The forest fell silent.

~LORI~

Lori screamed as the binding of Iodaba that held her in place shattered. She had watched it all happen and had been utterly useless. Everything felt dead and grey, her perception of reality stunted. Auyxus had tried to warn her, but she had shut her out, trying to focus her attention on healing the Diju woman. And it had all been for naught.

"Da!" cried Lori as she stumbled on hands and knees, snatching up her Oathrod, and scrambling to where her father lay on the forest floor, his lifeblood leaking from him. "Please, Auyxus, there must be something you can do!"

The Oathrod did not glow; the gemstone's light had been utterly vanquished by the one who called himself Edous. But Lori did not have time to think about him now. There had to be something. Anything. Lori cast her eyes about her in a frenzy, and that is when she spotted Darius's body, dangling from a tree.

Torn, but elsewise out of ideas, she rushed toward him. Darius was raving now, his golden eyes streaming tears of brightest yellow. But his wounds, so many wounds, were not healing like they had before. Drawing upon the physical strength she possessed, Lori drove a foot into the tree and wrenched the spear free, leaving Darius to fall in a lump upon the forest floor.

Immediately she crouched beside him, placing a shaking hand upon his shoulder. "Are you alright?"

To the Outlander's credit, he ceased his incoherent rambling and crying, his face shadowed in rage. He rose, and Lori, for perhaps the first time, saw him for the man he was. Ever since his arrival into Talahmnas, Lori had judged him harshly, had seen him as self-righteous and self-centered. He had defied her father, his court, and the laws and traditions of the land she called home. Even after her bonding with Auyxus, Lori had seen him more as a danger than an ally. But after seeing him now, the way he had fought for her family, the way he cast himself at the foe, an ember of respect ignited in her chest.

A grunt of pain turned Lori's attention away from Darius and back to her father. He was bleeding so much. Desperate, she looked back to Darius. Where the spear had pierced his shoulder, only a white scar remained. Hope blossomed and she asked, "Can you save him?"

Darius looked from her to her father, his golden eyes dark. Without speaking, he lifted his hand. There was a rush of power, a pulse of unseen energy. This was followed by a *whoosh* as his axe slammed into his open palm. Power crackled around the head, arcs of emerald and sapphire.

"Draw what you can," he said coldly.

Lori lifted her Oathrod and touched it to the gemstone embedded in the axe's head. Everlight flowed into the scepter, and Lori felt it bring Auyxus back into her mind.

The world instantly became clearer, more vibrant and alive. She could hear, smell, and see with such clarity that the shock of it nearly cost her balance. And when Auyxus spoke to her, it nearly brought tears to her burning eyes.

"We are weak, but we can save your father."

Lori did not think, did not resist, but gave herself wholly over to the Sage of the Mind. Her skin glowed with a faint light and her vision narrowed on her da. She could see his mind dimming, she

could see the lifeforce leaving his body, draining from the wound in his gut. Knowledge came to her as if from afar. Lori stepped forward, drawing upon the meager pulse of Everlight in the Oathrod. She placed a hand on his wound and poured it into him.

Slowly, so slowly, the wound began to knit itself together. Lori felt herself weaken as she did so, and her hand trembled where she touched him. Warm, sticky blood began to fall from her nose, splatting onto the back of her hand and her father's torso as she pushed as much Everlight as she could into him. With Auyxus's sight, she could see that it was working, not only on the outside, but within as well.

Erik gasped, the sound of which made both Darius and Lori jump. His eyes were red, blood vessels having burst, giving him a ghastly appearance. Not only that, but his teeth and tongue were coated in blood, his blood. "Kru—" he tried to say. His voice failed him, but his eyes did not.

Lori followed his father's gaze across the glade, to where Krunlan and Krarrack lay still. Sudden dread lanced Lori's already weary soul. She did not have enough power. She did not—

"Ordan, grant me strength."

Lori, whose mind was about to crack under the strain of everything, turned to see Darius staring into the distance, his axe raised in a fighter's stance. Something was coming. No. Not coming. It was here, and it was many.

~DARIUS~

Darius smelt them first, through the blood and death that surrounded them, that old, familiar stink that could not be hidden. Then he heard them, sounds of bones clacking and leaves crunching as dozens, if not hundreds, of these new Morreans called draugr came rushing through the forest.

"Ordan, grant me strength," he muttered aloud as he glared into the dark of the forest. What was he supposed to do now? How could he stand against so many? Fear gripped at his heart, but he pushed it down. They could not kill him, not yet. He had to make it to Izebal, to save her. He just had to survive one more fight.

"What do we do?"

The voice came from behind him, reminding him he was not alone here in this forest. Lori was there, a Sage. Perhaps she could help. However, when he turned hopeful eyes toward her, said hope was dashed to pieces. He saw not a powerful Sage, but a young woman, blood-soaked and weary. Her hands shook and her eyes wandered far-off, unable to focus on anything in particular. Next to her was her father, Erik. If he had his strength, he would be worth something in a fight, but he was pale as sheep's wool and his once-glowing tattoos were all dim.

"Can you get him out of here?" Darius asked, trying his best to keep the panic from his voice.

"What?" Lori's eyes were darting everywhere. Her heart rate was spiking and her breaths were coming fast and short.

Darius only had a few seconds at most before they were overtaken. He needed Lori to focus. To be present.

"Get your father out of here!" he barked, feeling no guilt for the sharpness of his voice. These were a warrior people, were they not? Well, this was war. It was not pretty or neat. It was a bloody mess, and you either killed or were killed. "Take him and go!"

"But... Krun," Lori protested.

"I am going to hold them off the best I can," said Darius, cutting her off as he reached down and picked up Aithen Lykos, shifting his own weapon to his offhand. "Get out. Get help. Run."

Darius walked past Krarraek and Krunlan's fallen bodies and as he did so a pang of guilt and sadness pulled at him unexpectedly. Neither had been warm or accepting of him, but they hadn't deserved this. No one deserved this. In that moment, Darius resolved to not allow their bodies to be desecrated further.

Darius gave over to the anger, that blazing fury that roiled within his soul. He hardened his heart as he tightened his grip on the weapons he held, all the while the demons drew ever closer. Then he felt it, that horrid sensation gnawing at his will, his focus: Redeyes. Well, let them come. He would rend them limb from limb.

Cries of war, dark and terrible, echoed throughout the trees as bodies began to coalesce from the mists of moonlight. Skeletal bodies draped in rusted mail, tattered clothes, and dented metal loomed forward. They did not run, but marched hauntingly forward. Blackness leaked from their eyes and arcs of wicked maroon lightning jolted from bone and exposed sinew alike. These were the undead and undying. These were no longer human, not even half-lifes. Darius would feel little remorse removing these from existence.

"Death!" Darius roared at the top of his lungs, and then charged into the fray.

Darius moved from draugr to draugr, swinging with a savagery he had held back his whole life. These were not living. These were the damned and undead. He would not ease them back to their slumber, but eradicate them from existence. With every strike of his axe, tendrils of ink-black mist fountained as the hewn draugr cried out wordlessly and died their second death. With every stab of Erik's great spear, another would burst asunder, the stored moonlight vaporizing Iodaba's hold on their bones.

But it was the Redeyes that needed to fall. They were the source of this plight. Three of them stood far back, hands laced together, draped in robes of sewn flesh, chanting in their chittering tongue. Darius had tried to assail them twice now, but both times he had been driven back. Once had been by what he guessed were reanimated wylven, their eyes black and hallow and their fur missing in large clumps, showing bone and no blood. The other had been by a sudden burst of dark thorns, dripping with ichor, that had sprung so suddenly from the earth, that they had torn the flesh along Darius's right thigh. That wound had not healed as had the many cuts inflicted from draugr blades.

Darius stumbled now, the pain in his thigh beginning to worsen with every step and parry. Despite his weariness, he hefted his axe once more, splitting a draugr in half at the shoulder. He was getting tired, and he knew he had little left in him. He could only hope that Lori had escaped.

Drums sounded in the distance. Snares reverberated through the trees. And then pipes began to blare. At first it was one. Then one hundred. A burst of sapphire crested the hill that Darius had descended to meet his foe, falling into a body of draugr, blasting them into fragments in a flash of light.

The Redeyes stopped their chanting, looking up for the first time since the fight had begun. The draugr all stopped, as if they had lost all motivation to push forward. That momentary lapse afforded Darius a glimpse up the hill, where his eyes were filled with a vision of salvation.

"Hit the dirt, Outlander!" roared Erkan. Dozens of Skogotuers lined the hilltop, their octagonal barreled rifles resting upon the heads of crescent moon axes.

Darius only had a moment, but drop he did. The Redeyes seemed to notice what was happening the same moment Darius did, their hands raising another wall of thorns as Darius fell to the forest floor. The crack of gunpowder tore through the trees. Bones burst and draugr howled as lead struck the undead in a relentless volley. However, the wall of thorns stood unmolested, their corrupted vines unyielding to mere metal and powder.

Darius, realizing what was about to happen, began to rush up the hill as fast as his crouching body would allow. He heard the call as he did so.

"For Talahmnas and the Lord of the High Hall!" bellowed Erkan. The Skogotuers, in clockwork timing, laid their guns to the ground, hefted their axes, and began a war song as they marched down the hill.

"Death." They sang to the drums and pipes. "Death and glory. March for victory. Death and glory, as we go. Death and glory, be our witness, as we crush our petty foe!"

They moved as one, marching passed Darius, who suddenly felt the weariness of a hard fought battle. It was Erkan who met him, stopping and offering him a hand up. "You did us proud, Outlander." Darius could see the hurt in his face, hear it in his voice. His eyes were red and wild. He had seen his brother's body. It was the only answer.

"Take your father's spear. Avenge your brother," Darius said coldly as he handed Aithne Lykos, Flame of the Wolf, to Erkan.

The young man took his father's spear as a whirl of emotion crossed his stricken face. "Ye do me a great honor, Ironbolt." The Skogotuers crashed into the draugr's line.

"Don't leave a single one of them standing," Darius said.

"Will ye not go now with me?" Erkan looked confused and his eyes darkened.

"You've got this," Darius answered. "But he took Izebal. I have to save her."

Erkan stared into Darius's face, and Darius could see not only Erik there, but Lori also. Wise and strong, proud and able. Erkan would be a good leader one day, perhaps even great. But only if Darius could stop this Edous. He had to give this people a chance.

"Keep my sister safe," was Erkan's only reply as he turned away from Darius and rushed toward the front lines.

At the top of the hill, Darius found the rest of the high family. They were gathered around two motionless bodies. Erik, to Darius's great relief, was sitting up on his own. He still looked pale and weak, but he was alive. Both his hounds were by his side, bloodied like their master, but guarding him nonetheless. Tyree, still wearing his mechanical legs, was knelt over Krun's body and administering some kind of magic to him, though Darius could not sense any life there. And Lori was weeping openly, howling in agony as her mother held her tight against her.

Fury once again welled in Darius's soul as he heard Lori's cry. It was more than a mournful wailing. It was deeper. Ancient. It was not just Lori, but Auyxus as well. Something in this night had triggered the true Sage herself. Yet, as she wept, Darius felt something deep within himself. A pulse of power, like a bell ringing clearly in a silent night. He could sense something, something had never been able to quantify before this moment.

"Lori!" he yelled, as realization washed over him.

The royal family, who had not noticed his arrival, all looked up at his shout. Darius was met with a myriad of expressions, all of which were dark.

But Lori answered none the less, though it was in that mixed tone voice that was neither her nor Auyxus's, "Keyholder."

"Yes!" Darius exclaimed as he ran to her. "Keyholder. Keys open doors. They unlock. I understand."

"What are you saying?" Lori's grief stricken face turned fully upon Darius, eyes shining with azure light.

"You are the Sage of the Cognitive. The Cognitive Realm is the way of the mind." Darius could not get his words right. He hated trying to explain himself, especially under such pressure and urgency.

"Yes," Lori answered flatly in her two-toned voice.

"When I dream, I leave this place. But only my mind. But my body, it remains. But Edous, he rends the realms and moves between them. I saw into that abyss. I saw the familiar. And he left a scar!" Darius said, pointing his finger to where Edous had vanished with Izebal.

True enough, as slight shimmer remained where Edous had vanished, like a spider's web, a crack hung in open air. Darius could sense it more than see it, though he was certain Lori could see it for what it was.

"When I travel, I am there, physically, but not in this body," Darius continued, not worrying if his words made sense. Maybe, if he could just get them out, she would understand. "You can open a way to that realm, through me."

Lori blinked at Darius, as if she had just been splashed in the face with a bucket of icy water, and he had been the one to do so. However, after just a moment of contemplation, her eyes lit with blue fire.

"What you said, it is not impossible, but without being able to meld both Aetora and Ria'Elahm, it would—" Lori stopped, eyes flashing from Darius to his axe. "Edous would have moved through paths of decay and mind. With your axe, perhaps I can carve a path through life and light. But Darius, there is no guarantee that this will work. You could be lost in the Aethereal forever."

"And if I don't, I damn Izebal and we lose out on our chance to catch this Edous."

"He is too strong. He tossed us both like chaff in the wind," countered Lori, but Darius could already see her mind working.

"We don't have time for this. I feel the way closing."

"Lori," Erik said from where he leaned. "The man has fight in him. If ye can help, help."

Darius looked at the lord of the high hall and could not help but fell a rush of gratitude and respect for the man. He wished had the words to express his thoughts and feelings, but that was just not who he was. So Darius nodded in appreciation as he headed to where the scar of Iodaba's Touch hung.

"I am not sure what you expect—" Lori began as she walked toward his side.

"By my axe and the stone set within, an Oath was forged," said Darius, cutting Lori off without guile. He looked inward, focusing his memories upon that visit to where he conversed face to face with Ordan. That been different. He had been transported to that place, not just mentally. But he had been there, felt it, knew it.

A strange sensation began to well within his mind, his body, and his soul, as if all three were converging into one single point. His ring shone with white light, Ellitheor Silver burning with the blood of the gods. His axe head began to shine, mirroring the light of his ring but suffused with sapphire and emerald power.

Instinctively, Darius grabbed for Lori's hand, the hand which was gripped around her Oathrod. All the power that was within his body surged between them and amplified the light within her own. She let out a cry of pain, of ecstasy and exhalation, and as she did so, the form of a wolf composed of azure light leapt at the scar Edous had left.

The air expanded suddenly and then solidified with a thunderous boom. Darius heard people gasping, and why wouldn't they? A mirror of shimmering light had just exploded into existence before their very eyes. But he paid them no heed. The deed was not yet done. There was still one last thing that needed to happen.

"Where you go, I cannot follow," Lori cried out over the noise of the battle, of the swirling vortex of shimmering light. "I don't have the strength for it."

"I know," Darius answered. "But I must go all the same."

He slammed the head of his axe into the mirror of light, filling the hilltop with the sounds of shattering glass, a noise which sent a chill up his spine. Where there had been a reflective surface, now stood an open gash with a sky of deep purple and stars that swirled in endless, drifting space. Across that opening, a secondary scar hung, showing a pinpoint of darkness. A pinpoint, that was steadily shrinking. Darius rushed through the opening, leaving behind him the world he knew, diving into nowhere.

CHAPTER 37: CAVERNS DEEP

Darius

Darius stepped into silence abounding and felt the weight of the realms crash into him. His body felt as if it were composed of stone, not blood and bone. His joints ached as he pressed forward across emptiness toward that speck of darkness that led to where Edous had fled.

Hatred more than hope spurred him forward, every step agony. Why was it this way? It had never been so in his dreams. But this was not his dream; he was awake and aware, fully lucid. He dared a look at his hand. Flesh. Not crystal. Yet beneath that flesh, his raised veins shone with golden light. In this place, this realm between realms, Darius was neither man nor spirit. And it hurt, so bad.

In the distance, Darius heard a trumpeting. A sound that was so foreign, so unnatural, and yet deeply familiar, as if it was from a memory long since forgotten. The hair on his neck rose as anticipation of the worst filled his aching chest.

A beast, more majestic than words could describe, stepped out from the swirling shadows of mist and ash. Its fur was more like the scales of a rainbow trout, but deep purple and blue. It had eight powerful legs and a swirling horn of purest silver. And its eyes. Its eyes were depthless, filled with such ancient understanding that it shook Darius to the core.

Kelpie!

A voice spoke inside Darius's mind, neither harsh nor loud, saying, "Long has it been since one such as thee has come to my domain."

"Great guardian of the Way," Darius said from fallen knees. "Help me."

"She knows your heart, Son of Denth. She has sent me to bring thee through," said the Kelpie as they bowed their head in acknowledgement of Darius, sending their liquid mane cascading in rainbows of silver, blue, and purple.

Darius could barely hold his head up now, the pressure of this place between places bearing down on him, crushing him. Yet his mind was in utter awe. This was the one that guided every Son, every Feromage, on their journey. It was by their guidance that each Guardian swore their Oaths. Though it was only a pale reflection to this majestic divinity. For divine it must be to stand in such radiant splendor and power in a place such this.

"She weeps for those she has lost. She weeps, and in her solitude, she mourns all. Ever living, never loving. Separated by love, barred by hatred. Ride upon my back, Son of Denth, and I shall carry thee to the end."

The Kelpie lowered them to Darius, allowing him to throw an arm over their glistening coat and pull himself onto their back. The beast's body was lithe and filled with muscle, and as they shook its head and trumpeted, Darius felt awe burn within his soul.

The Kelpie burst into motion, taking the Way by great leaping bounds, carrying Darius as if he weighed nothing more than a hair. Splashes of light flashed at the beast's hoof-crashes, veins of silver light spreading from the collision through the mirrored realm. On and on they ran, and as they did so, they filled Darius's head with memories that were not his own.

In a glade of natural beauty beyond description sat a goddess bathed in golden sunlight. She had hair black as night and eyes of bright emeralds. Upon her shoulder rested two crows, whose eyes were emerald and beaks shining onyx. The goddess wore a crown of living vines that blossomed with flowers of color. Her feet were bare and her arms unadorned. However, around her neck hung a silver chain with perfectly cut sapphire. When she turned her endless eyes upon him, pain so vast that it nearly took his breath away cascaded over him. Then he heard the command.

Save him.

Save him.

Save him, else all shall fail.

The words had not been spoken to Darius, he knew that, but to this Kelpie upon which he rode, though they struck him all the same. He could feel the weight of those words. He then felt the pain that it caused this majestic beast to leave their creator's presence. They left a perfect world, where nothing changed and all was alive and filled with light, to come to this place of passing.

Why?

Why was Darius so important?

What was it about him that the Ellitheor were going to such great lengths to aid him? Surely there were others. Surely he was not the sole person able to do this.

"My goddess does not err in her wisdom. Wouldst that thou should turn from this, but far is the sight of Gallae, and immeasurable her grace. Do not scorn her, for she has chosen thee. Wouldst that thou should awaken those who can save, but darkness paints your heart."

Darius could not open his mouth to answer. The pain was too much. And, to his horror, he was losing the fire in his belly, that burning hatred that he need to fuel himself to meet his.

Another vision filled his mind. It was fragmented and broken, like seeing images in a thunderstorm, only brief flashes that left Darius more confused than informed.

A forest unlike any he had known before. A hunt. Twelve men stalking an occex. Then cries of battle. A woman born of blood birthing a demon of the same: an Itheanam. An angel of death,

covered in pearlescent armor and wielding a curved sword that seemed far too large for any mortal to manage, descending upon a foe. Death followed. So much pain and death, but also hope. An Oath was sworn to stave off evil, so than no other mortals would face such a threat as this alone. Twelve rings were forged. An Oath, born of blood and sorrow, tied the realms together.

Darius blinked as he was returned to his own mind. The Kelpie had shared their memories with him, though he could not understand why. He had known the tale, the history, of his people. But there was something the Kelpie was trying to show him.

The Kelpie stopped suddenly, jolting Darius back to the moment. *"There is always a choice, Son of Denth. Always."*

Darius looked from the Kelpie's endless eyes to the fracture in the realms before him. He could see a jagged peak rising high into the night sky. He could see a scar in that mountain, a gash that he knew led to a place of great evil. Darius knew what was in that cavernous abyss. He recalled the table of stone. The runes of death. Torches that sputtered with bloodflame. And he knew that Izebal had been taken there, captured to draw him in.

Yes. There was always a choice. But what was he to do? Leave her to this Edous's machinations? No. He had made his choice, just like his forefathers, his own father, and his brother before him. He would save those who could not save themselves. That was his oath, his first oath. He was a guardian, he was Feromage.

"Thank you," he muttered through gritted teeth as he lowered himself from the Kelpie.

"A path thou'll cross, to forge thine fate. A path thou'll take and falter. A path must be chosen, once more to take. Another thou must abandon. Guard the light, but mind the night. For desolations gather."

The words seemed to ring in Darius's ears, clear as a bell but as foreign as this place in which he strode. He had heard them before, yet they meant so much more now. He had chosen this path, crossed it by the aid of another, but it was by his own fruition none the less.

"Go with the Grace of the Mother, and do not lose that which is most precious to thine soul." With those last words the Kelpie leapt off, dispersing into fragmented light.

Cold air bit into Darius's exposed face, so suddenly it caused him to stumble. As he placed his foot upon solid ground, he felt the pressure of that way between realms dissipate from him. Breath came suddenly to his burning lungs, and strength to his aching limbs. And with that renewed source of vigor, so sparked anew the embers of malice within his heart. Darius raised his eyes toward that gapping maw of stone and darkness and set his feet in motion.

The closer Darius drew to the jagged maw of the cavern, the more he felt the sensation of wrongness that clung to the bitter air. Sharp pricks of ice nicked him as he climbed, like tiny razors gnawing at his will, annoying more than hampering. Those small cuts healed as fast as they formed, the white light of his charged ring acting as conduit for his healing factor. It was strange. Never before had he thought it possible, but thanks to the long exposure to Talah'El, Stone of the Ancestors in the High Hall, Darius had a portable source of light he could pull upon himself. And though it felt volatile as it crackled under his skin, and itched as it flowed through his veins, he was thankful for its power.

The moon was a high crescent, though dawn was not too far off. Red brushed the starlight sky, soaking the horizon in a crimson tide.

Blood.

The thought sent a chill down Darius's spine, but he did not have the time for superstitions now. He knew what faced him in the caverns before him. Chairs with chains. A table of stone inlaid with runes of death. Darius tried to still his mind, to focus on what he could do.

Edous was powerful beyond what Darius could have imagined. The fiend had carved through Krarraek, Krunlan, Erik, and the two sentries as if they were nothing. He had broken Lori's mind, holding her in place with his very will. And he had tossed Darius as if he were chaff in the wind. Darius needed a plan, and fast.

With haste, Darius patted down his trench coat, searching for anything of use. To his dismay, the only thing contained within was the sealed parcel for the one called Apostle.

An urge to turn away from this path, to go and find the others, surged through Darius's mind. He forced that thought away, silencing them. He would not abandon Izebal to this demon.

Stahlbak Hi'el shone faintly with twin-tendrils of light, sapphire and emerald intertwining in mesmeric twists of power. As he looked on it, an idea sprang into his head. Iodaba was the antithesis of

Aetora and Ria'Elahm, that much he had remembered from Tyree's rambling and Elcon's holy talk. It was strange how different those two men were, yet how similar their conclusions came out to be, despite the utter lack of religion on one side and the over abundance on the other.

Darius pressed at the bridge of his nose. What was he doing? He needed to focus.

If he could reach Edous with Stahlbak Hi'el, he could force a pulse of power that could disrupt the demon's power, if only for a moment. It would leave the axe without any of its light, but it would give him a window, if only for a second. He only needed a second. Darius had not had a magic axe or Everlight and Lifelight when he had fought Diabhail and Mireya. He could win. And now he knew how to pull it off. He just needed the perfect moment to strike.

Down Darius descended, winding further and further into the cavern. Down Darius pressed, and all the while he allowed the power of his ring to cycle into to Stahlbak Hi'el. He felt the strange sensation winding through his flesh and into the axe. He saw the light of his ring dim as the twinned stone shone brighter and brighter, leaving trails of wisping light as he rushed ever onward.

As Darius descended, two things struck his attention. Firstly, this cavern was no longer wholly natural. Steps had been hewn into the floor, jagged, sharp things that caused him a small measure of stress, the stoneworker in his heart raging at their design. The other was that it was no longer utterly dark. Iron sconces burning with red fire were bracketed to the walls, lighting the path forward. A chill ran up his spine at this, for there was no kindling of fuel for said flames, only burning orbs of crimson. Blood magic.

At long last, Darius found himself in a large corridor where stalagmites and stalactites met in warped fashion. A cursory glance showed walls etched with cruel carvings depicting horrific scenes of sacrifices and rituals undertaken under the direction of the Morrean's occult leader, the Blood Queen. Everywhere Darius looked, he saw death and decay, and alongside it, a symbol much like a triangle with an upside-down eye with two pupils burning with fire.

A chill ran down Darius's spine, though he knew not why. All of this, the death, the corrupting power of Iodaba intertwined with the dark practice of blood magic, it was all something Darius had seen before. Yet it struck somewhere deeper now.

All of Darius's life, he had been raised to be a warrior, to fight against the rising darkness. 'The Light Must Return'. It was a phrase embedded into his mind, suffused into his very soul. It meant he was to rise. He was to stand, even if it meant he stood alone.

Yet, since his awakening, he had found friends, people who had helped and trusted him. They had given him a home as a stranger, food and shelter when he had nothing. They had taken him in and helped him, both in Tur'Mor and Talahmnas, each with their own set of stipulations, though they helped him nonetheless.

If he failed, these would suffer further. Ranun had died because he had interfered with fate. Krarraek and Krunlan too had fallen because of his decisions, along with countless other Danelanders. But if he did nothing, Izebal would—

Darius stopped himself. He needed to act, now.

While drawing in a breath, Darius cast his eyes over the cavern once more, searching for what he knew he would find. And there it was. A door of bronze with an upside down eye embossed into its face. He knew what was on the other side of that door, waiting for him.

As Darius approached the bronze door, sounds of chains clinking and machinery whirling filled the cavern. Darius tightened his grip on Stahlbak Hi'el, raising the axe into a defensive position.

With a sharp *clang!* the bronze door dropped down into a fissure and a stream of black fire jetted toward Darius's face. On instinct, Darius struck at the bar of onyx flame with Stahlbak Hi'el, cleaving the spell from the very air. Trenches of molten stone formed on either side of him as he stared into the black eyes of Edous.

It was a surreal experience, seeing the crazed man before him. The horns, the tattoos on his face and chest. He looked just like Diabhail. And when the man spoke, it was with that high priest's voice.

"Denathurias, Last of the Feromage, comes to me in my own abode to die, so that in her glory, my queen might rise once more."

"I am going to carve you from existence," snarled Darius in reply as he began to run.

Edous's smile was wicked, filled with mirth and contempt. Darius wanted nothing more than to cleave his head from his neck, if only so that he never had to look at that face again.

However, Edous was fast. Very fast.

Darius swung and open air, time and time again. Edous's blade hung at his side and his hands remained crossed behind his back. With every motion, the air seemed to crack and the sound of shattering glass reverberated through the cavern over and over again. It was deafening. It was infuriating.

"Come now, boy," said Edous in mocking tones. "Did you really think you could touch me?"

"Where is she?" roared Darius, stoking the fires of rage within his chest.

Edous cocked his head as his smile grew wider and wider, revealing teeth so white and sharp that they did not appear natural.

"Our guest is sleeping now, curtesy of the Mistress." Edous laughed as he said, appearing suddenly at Darius's side. The madman raised his bare foot and kicked Darius with his heel directly in his chest, sending him toppling across the cavern and through the doorway from whence Edous had appeared.

Darius crashed into a high-backed chair, then a table of stone, and then the wall on the other side of the room. His body screamed in agony as he felt his ribs crunch on impact.

Before Darius had even a chance to gain his bearings, a hand grabbed him by his hair and lifted him from the floor.

"Do you see her now?" Edous whispered, then dragged the length of his tongue across Darius's ear. It was warm and wet and made him want convulse. But he did see. Izebal was laid upon the table. Her green dress was gone, replaced by one of sheer black fabric. She had been stripped of her amulet, dagger, and wand, along with her satchel she wore at her hip.

The hot rage that boiled in Darius's veins went out in an instance, replaced by a fury so cold Darius could feel it was over his flesh. The room became silent, though Edous crooned something else in his ear. He could hear none of it. He could not see anything. He was utterly numb.

"—stone of fire, a heart of death, a living gemstone from one on high. Cryptic, don't you think?"

Darius had not heard what Edous had said. He did not care. But he was holding Darius now, rambling on about something. So Darius seized the opportunity. With a twitch of his wrist, Darius summoned Stahlbak Hi'el. The air seemed to warp as the axe rushed toward his hand. Time seemed to stop as Edous's eyes widened with surprise. And all of the hate and anger, all of the hurt and loss and pain that Darius could muster filled his body with strength as he drove the head of the axe at Edous's face.

A burst of light preceded an earsplitting *boom* that shook the mountain. Darius found himself flung through open space, having no understanding of up nor down, left nor right, until he slammed into something solid, taking away his consciousness.

A scream sent Darius jolting upright. Pain sent him falling back onto the ground. Darius looked at his hand, to where his ring rested on a blooded finger. It was almost utterly dull now. He could feel the last vestiges of power healing those most vital parts, but he was without the ability to fully recover, and he knew it.

"That axe of yours, now that is a real downer," Edous said as he walked through the doorway.

On the demon's face, a single line of blood ran from a slash on his cheekbone. Edous raised a long, pale finger to the shallow wound and pressed it. His eyes filled with black flames as he did so, and when he drew away his fingertip, the wound was whole.

"Do you have any idea what you did?" snarled Edous, his voice rising in hysteria. "Do you know what you've cost me?"

Darius had no idea. The wound was healed. The demon seemed otherwise utterly unharmed or phased. It was not until he began to draw the jewel encrusted rapier from his belt that Darius began to feel true terror.

"I need her whole!" Edous roared, and then began to laugh wildly. "Cruel! Cruel, cruel, cruel! Cruel are my mistresses! They ask of me, and I try. I try. I try. I try! And why? Why? Why? Why?"

Edous's steps were heavy, and his left hand flashed about as he spoke. Smoke rose from each footfall, and where he stepped, footprints of molten stone remained.

"Not enough. Not enough. Never enough. Not good enough for Father. No. Not for Mother dear. Not good. Never good." Edous was shaking now, both with laughter and manic sobs. "They are coming. They are there and near and here. I am become a god! Let me be!"

Edous screamed these last words, his voice causing the cave to shake once more. Darius tried to crawl back, to escape from the madman. But it was to no avail. Edous kicked Darius in the legs, sending him tumbling across the cavern floor. Sharp rocks cut at his skin, but those were ant bites compared to the pain from that kick. A hole was seared into his pants where Edous' foot touched him and his skin was red and blistered.

Darius raised a hand, calling once more for Stahlbak Hi'el. The axe lifted from the ground and rushed toward his open palm. Edous stepped once, but moved across the space between them, and swatted the axe from the air with his rapier.

"Don't touch that *thing!*" hissed Edous. "You weren't supposed to have that! She did it, didn't she? Damn her! To me. Why me?"

Darius wanted to curse the crazed lunatic, but he hadn't the strength. So, he did all he could, and spat on the fiend's foot.

"You insolent little—ugh, peasants!" Edous kicked Darius again, this time in the side where he had struck the table earlier. Pain encompassed all that Darius was as he flew through the air and into a stalagmite.

"I am going to enjoy draining your blood. And when I do, I will harvest the remains of our Blood Queen's soul from your flesh."

Upon hearing these words, the scar in Darius's chest seemed to resonate with inexorable fire, wracking Darius's body in further pain. It was as if it wanted to be free of him. As if it had know that this was a possibility now and yearned for release.

No! Darius grit his teeth. He could not let that happened. He had walked into this place to save Izebal, not resurrect the Blood Queen. But what could he do against such power? He had failed yet again. And this time, it would be the world that suffered for it.

"Talk, talk, talk. All you do is talk," laughed Edous as he loomed over Darius. "Let us finish what we started a millennium ago."

Darius needed to do something. Anything. But what?

"You aren't him," Darius grunted the words out. Blood spilled from his lips as he did so, dribbling into his beard. Why did it have to be speaking?

Edous's eyes widened. First there was anger, then confusion, then hatred. "Silence, worm! We are her consort! We are he! I, I am!" Edous's hands trembled, but he raised his sword all the same. "Let us see how quick that tongue is when I carve it out of your pretty little mouth, huh?" Every word was short and formed with a heavy breath.

"I killed him, with his own hammer," said Darius as he coughed blood and phlegm, sliding back away from Edous as he did so. "He was pathetic."

"Shut up! Shut up, shut up, shut up!" Edous shook his head in rage.

"I killed her too, your precious queen," laughed Darius. By Ordan's hammer, this was working. He just needed to get to Stahlbak Hi'el. "I watched her fall. Down into the Dimdreal."

"You insolent! I told you to be silent!" screamed Edous as he slapped Darius across the cheek with the flat of his blade. Despite the edge not striking him, pain seared his check as inky black tendrils of Antilight burned away his skin and hair.

It was only inches away. He had to act now.

Darius summoned all the strength he hand left and dove for Stahlbak Hi'el. To his surprise, he reached the axe without issue. He swung it at Edous's gaping face, and for a moment, hope blossomed inside his heart.

That hope was dashed away in an instant as something hot passed through his upper arm. The room seemed to slow to almost stillness. Darius watched in horror as his arm, along with his axe flew across the room. There was no blood. The blade of Edous's rapier had cauterized the wound as it passed through. But it was gone. Just like that. It was gone and so was any hope of survival.

"I see that I have disarmed you, Denathurias," Edous laughed coldly. "Now, I will carve her from your chest and she shall rise, vassal of the Forsaken Ones. And I, I will be consort to the very goddess of time immemorial!"

Edous plunged his blade toward Darius's chest. He closed his eyes and awaited death to take him.

Thunder shook the world as white lightning flashed just over Darius's body, sending a shockwave through his core. Before Darius could make heads or tails of the situation, something pushed him away from Edous. It hadn't been rough, but it was none too gentle either. But when he regained his focus, he felt awe overtake him.

A towering man with hair of flames and skin that shone with white light stood where Darius had been, and in his hands a colossal sword of white gold blocked Edous's blade. And on the man's back, as if an Aethereal specter, a dragon wound itself in a tight coil.

"What?" cried Edous in rage and shock.

"I am Fenron the Just, come to cleanse this place of the stain of your corruption," the blazing man thundered. "You will pay the penance of my father's retribution."

Darius could not believe his eyes. Standing before him was a literal god. A member of the Ellitheor pantheon. He could feel his power. This was no Blessed or mage or anything he had felt before.

Deep, ancient power was there. But also malice. A rage was in that man unlike anything Darius had ever known, dark and hateful.

Edous struck wildly at Fenron, his slender black blade striking like a viper while the massive two-handed sword of Fenron's moved in sweeping motions that left the air rippling with light. So fast and wild were the strikes that soon all Darius could see were blurs and all he could hear was the toll of a thousand bells being rung as metal struck metal.

Izebal!

The thought came to him in an instant. Darius leaned over to get up, but fell upon his chest. Surprise and then realization took him in waves. He had no right arm. It was gone. His left hand was there, the ring of his ancestors on his finger. His right burned with the same pain as the Itheanam's horn had caused. And when he looked at the stump, about a hands' breadth below the shoulder, his veins were already turning inky black.

He did not have much time. He had to act now. But when he tried to rise again, he found his body depleted of strength and the will to push on. He was spent. And he was going to die. The weight of it all hit him and pressed him further into the floor in grief and agony.

CHAPTER 38: SENDINGS

Una'pahu & Aellia

~Una'pahu~

Una'pahu stood on the beach next to Aellia, who did not look like she was faring well. The little white-haired Ordiatian woman was holding that mirror as if her life depended upon it, and perhaps it did. Perhaps all of their lives depended upon it. She had just sent Seamus through nothing. She had called it the Way. But there had been nothing. And now Seamus was gone into that nothing.

"How long till I can go?" Una'pahu asked impatiently. She hated sounding like this, but she needed to get to Seamus. He was struggling with things that no one understood. And how could they? He had bonded a dragon and a god, and they were both warring for his soul.

Aellia turned her sapphire eyes onto Una'pahu and said, "Be my guest if you think you could go faster, Westlander. But wait, you have not been able to awaken yourself, have you?"

Una'pahu felt her cheeks flush was anger. How dare this commoner speak to her like this. She was a Wakatiti. She had known that the Mainlanders had no sense of culture or decency, but to speak to a member of the Matriarch in such disdainful tones was deep offense. But she bit her tongue. Una'pahu was perhaps the most powerful Ta'ala Gau, mastering the Waterdance and the Way of the Waves. But this Mainlander could bend the will of the wind, not just direct their courses. She could manipulate it herself, becoming one with its very essence. And something within her own soul told her that if she followed this woman, she too could harness such power and come one with the seas and waters.

So, Una'pahu swallowed her pride, vowing that in time she would have her moment, and said, "Clearly, I have not."

"Then let me work."

Una'pahu nodded her head in acquiescence, doing her best to swallow the bile from how she had been spoken to, and marched to the seashore to stare at the frothing waves. As she stood in silence, arms folded and eyebrows furrowed, she relived the long days she and her friends had spent stranded upon this island. It had been a struggle for survival, but the feelings of camaraderie and closeness she had formed with Henri and Seamus, she would not trade that for the world. Seamus had always been Msa'oo, her lover. That part was still there, but fundamentally changed.

Seamus.

What was he? Dragon or god? How could he be both? How could he be either?

Only yesterday it seemed that he was a frizzle-haired deckhand with piercing green eyes and a freckled smile that made something in her stomach turn, and not in a bad way. She had grown so fond of his antics and the careless way he lived his life. Then, she had grown to love the man he had become, tall and lean, his body pressed to hers in the night. But now... now he was different. More, yet the same.

A fire burned in him, a twinned kindling of fire and light. At moments, she saw terror in his eyes, red flames lurking, stalking. At others, she saw self-righteous indignation, as if others were beneath him. Though neither of those were truly him. There were still sideways glances, cocky grins, and flippant words. He was still in there. She knew. She had to believe it.

"Oy," said Henri as he walked up beside her, his footfalls nearly silent.

Seamus's friend was still broad at the shoulders and held some belly, but he had leaned out so much. His once round face had become more squared, and his beard made him look twice the age of when they had left from Port Amandri. His glasses sat on his nose, still slightly crooked from being broken in the fight with Reylelan and her Biters. A shiver went down her spine at the mere thought of the witch.

"You alright?"

"I don't know," Una'pahu said with a sigh, her eyes turning back to the rolling waves.

Henri reached down and picked up a conch shell, a pink and white spiraling horn, and tossed it into the surf. "Crazy, in'it?"

"You can say that again," Una'pahu answered.

"I didn't believe none of it, never had a reason to I guess..." Henri said absently. His body stiffened as he set his shoulders back. When had he gotten so broad? "We're going to get him back."

"Ya."

"We are, Snapdragon, we're getting him back. We are all going home, just like we promised." Henri choked a little on the words, his bravado faltering as he spoke.

"Do you trust her?" asked Una'pahu as she tossed her head in Aellia's direction, eyes still upon the sea.

"Trust is a fickle thing," mused Henri.

Una'pahu could not hold back a dark chuckle at his words. She looked upon him now and smile warmly, trying her best to hold back the compounding weariness she felt. "Becoming quite the sage yourself. Not bad for being a deck boy."

His tanned skin reddened at the ears and cheeks. He raised a hand scratched at the back of his neck. His hair had grown shaggy and Una'pahu had to admit he did look far more fetching now. A

part of her heart warmed and she felt a sudden urge to encourage him now.

"He would not stop trying to help us," she said. "He loved you like a brother. We will do everything we can to help him, even if it means trusting whatever that thing up there is."

"She said you were like her, just not wholly yet." Henri said the words, and then looked as if he wished he could snatch them back out of the air.

Una'pahu had not handled it well when Aellia had stated she was most likely a Sage, pointing out her family's scepter and calling it an Oathrod. Una'pahu had been inclined to beat the nonsense out of the foreigner until Seamus had stepped in, speaking in that strange tone he did at times when his eyes blazed white-gold. He had said she was harboring the Sage of the Waves and Seas. Una'pahu had tried to push what he had said behind her, but when she heard him say her name... something resonated deep within her soul. And that terrified her more than she could admit, even to herself.

"I didn't mean—"

"She said it, not you," Una'pahu cut in. "Maybe I am, maybe not. That has nothing to do with now. I only hope we can trust what she's doing."

"We have to," answered Henri, his voice low and filled with dark dejection. "What other choice is there?"

"I don't know... I only wish that—"

"It's time!" shouted Aellia from a distance. "Hurry now!"

Una'pahu gave a final glance at Henri, who nodded his head before they both hurried back to where Aellia stood.

"The glass is still cracked, but I think I can get us all through this time. But, I need power from your Oathrod." Aellia spoke in nearly a shout and wind was whipping about her wildly, sending up grainy bits of sand and debris.

"Fine by me, just get us to Seamus, whatever it takes." Una'pahu answered as she reached for the scepter tucked into wide, cloth belt of her huvu'huvu. Her hand hesitated for just a moment.

Aellia turned her gaze upon her, and that dead eye of hers, the one that looked of grey jelly, had turned into a proverbial storm of azure light.

"Now is not the time for hesitation." Aellia's voice had been replaced yet again by that other one. And though it sounded young and bright, it was filled with the call of storms and the weight of ages past.

Una'pahu snatched the scepter and extended it, willing what channels of power she could through the Ta'ala Gau. She saw the change in her hands first, the ink beginning to shift from dull tones to vibrant greens smoldering with emerald light. Then she felt it, that ancient power flooding her body, clarifying her mind and suffusing her with strength. Just like the last time, Una'pahu touched the scepter's gemstone against the silver mirror and light arched between them.

"We will move fast," Aellia shouted. "Everyone, grab hold and ready yourself."

Una'pahu felt Henri grab at her left arm just has she extended her hand to Aellia's. Aellia touched the head of her scepter to the mirror.

A crashing sound like shattering glass emanated from the device, which burst apart before their very eyes. Una'pahu's grip faltered at the sudden explosion, but then she felt the hand that had been holding the mirror snatch her own.

Power unlike anything she had ever felt before surged through her body. Every fiber of her being felt as if it had been struck by lightning. She wanted to scream, but her muscles had seized, locking like iron. Fear of death pricked at her heart, only for a moment, and then she felt her flesh turn to mist.

Light.
There was only light.
No sound.
Sapphire light shone for all eternity, and it was glorious to behold.
There was no pain. No fear. No anguish of mind or soul.
There was understanding beyond comprehension.
Infinite existence unfolded in prismed patterns, baffling the mind.

Solid ground knocked the air from Una'pahu's lungs as she collapsed in a crumpled heap upon hard, wet stone. The light was gone. Everything felt so wrong now.

"Get up!" shouted a voice from a thousand miles away, from right by her ear.

Sight came slowly but surely. First, everything was a blur of dull colors smeared across her vision. Then they sharpened into walls, columns, and tunnels. Hearing came much faster. A fight was happening not far from where they were. Steel clattered against steel, and someone was screaming manically.

"We must go, now! Your friend is in danger." It was Aellia's voice, and she sounded panicked.

"What?" Una'pahu muttered as she tried, and failed, to heave herself off of the ground.

"He's here!"

"Wasn't that the point?" Una'pahu grunted as she successfully stood this time.

"Not Seamus, the one called Edous. I can feel him." Aellia spoke in tones of absolute dread.

The name sounded familiar, though Una'pahu could not put a finger on where she had heard it.

"Can't you fight?" Aellia asked as she shook Una'pahu's shoulders roughly.

Una'pahu wanted to be more frustrated at the woman's assault of her person, but the fact of the matter was, she could not even focus on her as her eyes were still swimming before her and her strength was practically nonexistent.

"Gallae take me!" swore Aellia. "Your friend is out cold. Think you can at least keep him from getting run through while I go and save your lover boy?"

Una'pahu went to make a snarky remark, but when she opened her mouth, it took everything she had to hold back a deluge of vomit that jumped to her throat. What had Aellia done to her?

Aellia rolled her one good eye; the other still shone with azure light. "Deep breaths. It'll pass." She reached into a pouch on her belt and withdrew a small bar wrapped in foil. "Eat it. Drafting takes it out of you, and what we did was a supercharged version of that. Just, deep breaths and join me when you can." Aellia tossed the bar at Una'pahu and then slid a wicked looking blade whose golden hilt was wrapped with red silk from a sheath before she rushed down a tunnel from which the sounds of fighting emanate the loudest.

Una'pahu's head fell back against something soft. A cursory glance, which took more strength than she wanted to admit, told her it was Henri's leg upon which she had landed.

Embarrassing. This was absolutely humiliating.

Una'pahu fought against tides of nausea and forced air into her lungs and blew it out through her nose as she fought with foil-wrapped bar. When she finally got it open, the reward was a mostly disfigured and melted bit of mushed brown with dried raisins and nuts mixed throughout. Her stomach lurched at the sight of it, but she fortified herself and took a bite. It was perhaps the single most delicious thing she had ever eaten. It was smooth as silk, save the extras, sweet and salty. She wanted more. Like an animal, she shoved the rest into her mouth and chewed ravenously.

How long had it been since she had eaten anything other than wild-caught fish and coconut flesh?

It took everything she had to suppress a moan of delight. And gods be damned, but if the breathing and bar hadn't brought clarity, energy, and focus. Seamus. She needed to get to Seamus. Henri was here, and the fight was there.

He would be fine, she told herself as she dragged his slack body behind a large stalagmite, concealing him from easy view of anyone that might run out of the cave. She did not want a repeat of the Scepter, who had vanished from the shore, though Una'pahu was certain it had been that crazed witch, Reylelan who had taken them.

Una'pahu did not have time for that now, she needed to act. With her scepter in her hand, she rushed toward the tunnel that Aellia had taken, ready to meet whatever foe lay at the end. Nothing in her life prepared her for what she saw as she made the final twisting descent that opened into a cavern as large as an amphitheater.

Seamus, wreathed in white light, shone like a beacon of heaven's glory. He swung that massive sword as if it were weightless, and where it struck, sparks ignited. Aellia swirled about him, like she was dancing, her curved sword flashing as she called lightning from her scepter. And they were both being driven back by a solitary figure whose eyes… whose eyes were just like Reylelan.

Una'pahu stiffened in fear. Her heart nearly leapt out her throat. She was not there. She was tied to a bed, Reylelan pulling at her will, assaulting her very mind. She saw Atura die to save her own life. She saw the way they feed on her, devouring her like animals. She felt Reylelan's cold, slender fingers sliding across her skin, touching her endlessly. She felt the pressure of her mind, her command, to love her. To adore her. To give herself to her.

Una'pahu was just about to collapse when she saw a forth person laying upon the ground. It was a man with black hair and beard, and he was missing an arm. Una'pahu gasped at the sight, but a certain will filled her, a need to get to him. And that was all she needed. A motivation to move. To escape.

Una'pahu latched onto that need and forced herself to make a step. If she could just do that. If she could make a single step, then she could make another. She hated Reylelan for what she had done to her, but this Edous had done something terrible to another, and with her abilities to heal, maybe she could save him, even if she hadn't been able to save herself.

Slowly she progressed forward, every step a colossal feat of will and strength. Maniacal laughter and shouts of battle echoed about her, but they were as froth on the waves, inevitable, unrelenting, but not important to Una'pahu. Not right now.

She knew Seamus was over there, fighting for his life. But what could she do against a foe that could hold whatever he was back and another who could control the very winds and storms? Una'pahu had been utterly helpless against Reylelan.

She froze for a moment, a heartbeat.

No! Push on, she screamed inside her own mind, fighting down that vestigial touch of Reylelan's power upon her.

As she drew closer, Una'pahu could make out more and more details of the man. He was older than her but not by too many years, though his beard had gone grey under his lip. No, not grey, silver. A second glance showed that the silver of his beard was not the strangest feature of the unconscious man. Dark lines covered his neck and face, as if his veins were bulging with black poison.

Una'pahu reached a hand out to touch his brow, but before she could even pace a finger upon him, she could feel the heat of his skin. He was burning up. And that wound. His arm had been hacked off, leaving only a stump of rotting, corrupted flesh. It was enough to make anyone's stomach turn, and Una'pahu was already on edge.

"I don't know if you can hear me," Una'pahu choked out as she pulled a waterskin from her waist. "But I am Una'pahu Mue'Mora Wakatiti and Ta'ala Gau. I am going to try and help you."

Una'pahu did not know why she was talking to the unconscious man, but something about it calmed her nerves, so she kept going as she prepared herself to cleanse the man. She had never healed something on this level before, but maybe...

Una'pahu grabbed at his tattered shirt, where dark stains of blood had formed, and pulled it away to begin the cleansing. "This is going to *ack!*"

Bright light flashed as a *whoosh* sent her hair flying from her face. Power jumped from where her fingertips had brushed his chest, coursing up her hand and into the Oathrod held in the other.

I accept this Oath, daughter of the waves and sea!

The whole world seemed to slow to a single instance as Una'pahu eyes were truly opened for the first time in her life. She could see every droplet of water, sense every pool and puddle. She could feel the moisture in the air, and perceive the very ebb and flow the seas beyond her physical understanding.

Una'pahu rose to her feet, the scepter still tight in her hand, and her eyes locked upon the man who was assailing her Msa'oo. The man whose eyes were the same as Reylelan's. Fear tried to bite her, to gnaw at her will. But she washed it away with waves of fury and oceans of resolve.

We are bounded, daughter, and we shall cleanse this world of corruption.

Una'pahu raised a hand and felt true power rise.

"Ka'ata ka!" she screamed, slamming her left foot down in a warrior's dance, the same dance she and Captain Atura had dance morning after morning in hopes of awakening even the most meagre semblance of power. Neither had ever dreamed of such power as this.

"Fa na kha!"

This time, all heads turned towards her as she swung her hands about, lifting a leg over her head, and then brought it down with a thunderous crash. A crash echoed by a torrent of water that had materialized above Edous and struck him to the ground.

The man's manic grin was washed from his face, replaced by tortured rage as rose to his feet and screamed, "Another one? What?"

~AELLIA~

Aellia and Iaenora were one, a thunderous, melodious blur of wind and lightning. They struck with force and precision, arcs of blue energy flowing off Tomo's sword and biting at Edous. However,

every strike was parried with seeming ease by the mutating demon. He had not appeared so...feral before.

He is being consumed by Iodaba's Touch.

"I figured," Aellia answered in her mind, trying not to split her focus from the fight. "How is he able to hold off both of us and Fen—Seamus at the same time?"

He has accepted death into his very essence, his very core is naught but Iodaba. His heart is more that of a dragon's than mortal man's.

"But we can kill him?" asked Aellia as she deflected a thrust from that black blade that wept darkness. "Iaenora, we can kill him, right?"

"Submit and be judged!" thundered Fernon as he drove down with a mighty two-handed strike.

The air warped as his blade descended and the ground shook upon impact. However, Edous remained upright, drenched as he was with Una'pahu's water strike, having caught Fenron's blade upon his own, sending a horrendous ringing throughout the cavern.

"Pathetic!" cackled Edous as he turned away Seamus's strike. "You are all pathetic children buying into a game with coins stolen from your betters!"

Aellia felt the heat of Edous's repost, felt the crackling negative energy flowing from his blade and into Seamus's side as his sword bit deep. She nearly lost her feet as Seamus let out a bellowing roar of agony as he dropped the two-handed sword and stumbled backward, his hands grabbing at the wound.

Una'pahu let out scream, her eyes going wide with shock and horror as Seamus began to roll upon the ground. She looked as if she were about to run toward him when she pulled up suddenly and turned to face the man who Aellia swore she recognized from... somewhere.

Keyholder!

No! It couldn't be... That man was thick and unkempt, with wild eyes and a scarred face. This man, albeit large, was lean of frame and, barring a missing arm, hadn't a scar on him.

Protect him, Iaenora urged inside Aellia's mind. *He has awakened Telanahr and she has bonded with the Ta'ala Gau. But he is fast fading. While Telanahr is an accomplished healer, she is not Zaevot.*

"What about Seamus?" Aellia asked, her attention pulled in two directions.

He can stand on his own for a moment. His is not our duty. Ours lays there, our only hope.

Aellia waisted no more time, but pushed herself forward, leaping across the cavern in a single motion. Wind whipped about her as she landed, sending dust and debris whirling away and leaving the cavern floor relatively clean.

Aellia was not sure what to expect—in truth, she had not expected anything out of the ordinary to happen—when she approached Una'pahu, but a wave of familial love passed between them that nearly took her breath away. She saw Una'pahu, but she also saw on a deeper level her sister Telanahr. Emotions long thought forgotten threatened to surface. Memories of her own brother, dying of the White Fever in her mothers arms. Her sister, on a battlefield of black sand and ash, searching for others. No, not her sister. Iaenora's sister.

This was about to get really weird, really quickly.

Aellia shoved those thoughts away. There would be time to work all this out later. That was, if they were able to heal this 'Keyholder', defeat Edous, and escape this cave before the crazed lunatic summoned the chained spirits of Morganna and Moranna into some unexpectant avatar chained onto a ceremonial table.

"What can I do?" Aellia asked through unsteady breaths.

"Watch my back," Una'pahu said, her voice echoing discordantly between her own and that of the Sage of Seas.

Aellia turned to face the approaching Edous, whose bleeding face shone with ferocious glee. She gripped Tomo's Di'kha and steadied herself. "I'll do what I can. But Una'pahu, don't take long."

~UNA'PAHU~

Una'pahu had never felt power like this before. It felt as if her entire body had been bathed in liquid fire. And she was much, much stronger for it. Then, there was that stranger's voice in the back of her mind. Strong and bold, like Atura, unshakable and commanding, speaking to her with perfect clarity.

You know the way of the cleansing. Push it through the Keyholder. He is filled with Iodaba's poison. He must be washed free of it, else all the world will suffer.

"Guide me," Una'pahu answered, surrendering her hands, her lips, and her mind to the Sage in her head.

Waters cleanse, tides rise, evil fades, yet light abides. Telanahr spoke in a singsong manner, her voice sweet as it was strong. *Wash free the evil, wash free the filth. Clear this man of darkness's silt.*

"Bit of a stretch there with the rhyme," Una'pahu said inside her mind.

It helps me focus. This not my path. Telanahr sounded affronted, but she huffed once and then went back to work, albeit silently this time.

Una'pahu watched as if she were in a dream, seeing her body move of its own accord without a single thought from herself in way of command. It was very disconcerting. However, the most frustrating part of it all was her inability to turn and look at the battle raging behind her between Aellia and Edous. But she did not have to look to know who was winning. The madman was laughing more and more, spewing jeering comments about Aellia, her heritage, and anything else that seemed to pop into his vulgar mind.

Be clean!

Una'pahu utter the words aloud, though not in her own voice, as she slammed two hands that had rivers of crystal clear water running around them down onto the Keyholder's chest. It was a primeval command, not just words. And the body responded accordingly. It jerked and twitched as tiny streams of glistening water flowed beneath his skin, excreting Iodaba's darkness through pores upon his flesh and from the stubby wound at the end of where his arm had been.

"Aghk!" cried the Keyholder, his eyes snapping open and he sat bolt upright.

"You have been hurt. We have removed much of Iodaba's Touch, but you are still weakened," Telanahr said from Una'pahu's mouth.

The man's eyes were wild, darting this way and that, and blazed with golden sunlight. When they fell upon something behind him, he went rigid as a ship's mast.

He moved his right stump. Blinked. Growled in a bestial manner. And then extended his left. The air seemed to inhale about Una'pahu, which was followed by a *whoosh* of air, and then the man was holding an axe in his off hand. He used the axe to lift himself to his full height and swore, "I'm going to carve that goddamn smile off his smug face."

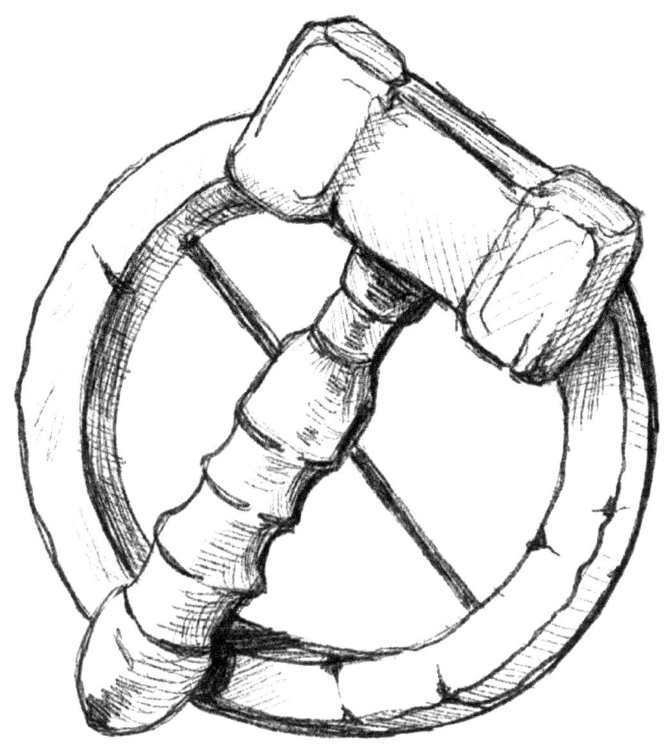

CHAPTER 39: THE END

Darius

Darius had not been out for more than a second or two, had he? It did not matter. Nothing mattered now other than carving that sack of walking bones into bloody pieces. He had stolen Little Ery from Eric and Sophie, he was certain he had orchestrated the attack on Izebal's troupe. He had killed Krunlan. And worst of all, he had taken Izebal right from under Darius's nose, while pinning him to a tree like he was nothing more than fodder.

Darius fed into the rage, stoking that fire. Yet again, he was under the earth with no means to call upon his Feroform. But this time, much to his surprise, he was not alone. There were two others here with him. One was the woman who had just healed him, and he understood somewhere in his mind that this young woman was the Sage of Water. This was only solidified as she nodded at his declaration of intent, raised herself up into the air on a jetstream of dark liquid, and shot toward Edous. The other was the young woman from the staircase all those long weeks ago. It seemed like a lifetime had passed since then, and looking at her now, he was almost certain it had. She had lost that girlish spunk, that condescending charm she had flaunted about so easily. Her face was lean and hard, and she bore a nasty scar of battle on her face.

Three on two, Darius liked those odds. Maybe he could actually do it. He looked at his axe. It was glowing as brightly as the day it had been forged. Apparently, the light from the Sage's Oathrods had suffused the twinned gemstone while he had been unconscious.

How long had he been out for?

That did not matter. He had one task, a singular purpose. Embed that axe into Edous's chest and release the full charge. It was cause an explosion he was not certain any one of them would survive. But if it meant the end of this demon, the end of one who could revive the Blood Queen, then it would all be worth it.

Darius crashed into the fray with no thought of life nor limb. What else had he to lose?

Edous met Darius's attack with unyielding strength. Somehow, the demon was holding his own. His sword moved like shadow, ringing loudly as it turned away sword and axe alike. His eyes smoldered with a darkness so black that it seemed to swallow the light from around him.

"Enough!" screamed Edous after he had simultaneously parried a thrust of the air Sage's sword and knocked away Darius's downward swing with the heel of his foot.

A pulse of darkness, echoed by a shattering sound, pushed all three of his assailants away. Edous's chest heaved with labored breaths, but he stood tall and proud.

"You are worms, each of you!" Edous's voice was full of scorn. "How dare you stand between me and my Mistresses' goals? Who do you think you are?"

A roar, not that of a man nor any beast Darius had ever heard, reverberated through the cavern. Edous turned his head, his left eye twitching as he peered across the empty space with contempt.

"I will feast upon your bones!"

That was enough to turn Darius's head. The voice was a landslide of crushing stone and breaking mountains. It was deep and ancient, filled with malice and hate. And the creature it was coming from looked like nothing Darius had ever seen before.

Vaguely humanoid in appearance, though one could argue there was little humanity there, was the beast. Tall and broad, with the right side of its body wrapped with red scales melting into ashen flesh. Great horns of black flame sprouted from its forehead as did bellowing wings sprout from its back. Its feet were clawed, as were its hands, and red fire blazed within its crazed, slitted eyes. It threw its head back, arching its back and flexing its arms, and let out a terrible roar.

"No..." muttered the Water Sage, who had been standing next to Darius.

"What?" Edous exclaimed, his voice rising in fury and confusion.

"Hurt!" thundered the beast, and Darius saw a stab wound with veins of inky black in its stomach. "I kill!"

The beast thrust itself forward, the air cracking around it in a clap of thunder, and barreled into Edous.

A hand grabbed Darius's shoulder, drawing his attention away from the spectacle. When he turned his attention away, he was met with green eyes filled with dread.

"We have to get him his sword," said the young woman.

Darius heard what she was saying, but when he looked back to where the two fought, he saw little need for a sword. The dragon was tearing into Edous without mercy. As a matter of fact, it looked like, given a few more blows, the dragon would tear Edous asunder. A wicked glee sank into Darius's heart.

"Please," the young woman urged. "He will consume—"

Darius stopped hearing her words as he looked on in horror. Edous landed a blow into the dragon's chest with his fist. The strike sent the beast tumbling backward and a shockwave of rancid, hot air cascading through the cavern. The beast crashed into the Sage of air, knocking them both onto the cavern floor in a heap.

That dark glee was snuffed out like a candle, replaced by grim determination as Darius took a split second to see the room. Edous's back was turned to him. He wobbled on his feet. That punch had been more than a physical thing, and he was weak. The water Sage was running toward that massive white-gold sword. Darius saw his opportunity and he took it.

"Ordan, grant me strength," said Darius under his breath as he burst into a dead run.

Edous wobbled as he turned. His eyes, though black, had lost that lightless power. Darius raised Stahlbak Hi'el over his head as he leapt into the air. Edous tried to raise his sword, but he was too late, too slow. Darius saw it in the fiend's eyes.

He was going to do it!

A beam of darkness struck Darius from the sky just as his axe was about to bite into Edous's chest, sending him toppling across the rocky ground. Tentacles of darkness jutted from behind where the bronze door had stood. They grabbed around Edous torso and head, yanking him backward into the darkness.

Darius raised his axe and hurled it into the darkness, to where he saw the demon vanishing. A circle of emerald runes burst into existence. Stahlbak Hi'el crashed into them and fell useless to the ground.

Eyes widening, Darius peered into the darkness, if only for a moment, and he felt his heart crack in half. Lit by runes of green light, he could make out Izebal. She stood holding onto Edous's writhing body, and he had something in his hand other than his sword, though Darius could not see what. Confusion washed over him as they made eye contact, but those were not the eyes he had come to know, the eyes he had come to love. Black as night they were, iris filled with circling storms of maroon lightning.

Izebal raised a hand to her neck, where her amulet had always hung. It was not there, but in its place, a red bolt of fabric bearing an upside-down golden eye. Sorrow filled her face, along with a torrent of other emotions. Emotions Darius could not understand.

Darius felt the strength leave his body as his limbs went numb and the sounds of blood pumping welled up in his ears.

Izebal muttered something. Her mouth moved, but Darius could not hear her. He could not hear her, nor anything other than his heart thundering, as if it were about to burst. Izebal took a step back and the air behind her warped and cracked.

Darius tried to stand, to run toward her. What was she doing? Why was she helping Edous?

Why.

That word consumed his whole being as the woman he had loved vanished from sight, clutching the man whom he hated more than anything else. With a final glance at Darius, Izebal raised a hand.

Black mist coalesced into a solid object, which she raised up to her face. When her hand fell away, a weeping mask of silver remained, concealing the face of the woman who had been.

Why?

Darius felt the walls begin to close in around him. The air suddenly had become so heavy. Why was the air so heavy? He could not breathe. He gasped. He stumbled. He gasped again as hot tears began to fall down his face.

Why?

Why was he crying?

What was happening to him?

He could not breathe.

How could she do this?

How could she do this to him?

He could not breathe.

Darkness came for him, and he did not allow himself to fall into it, to give way to the pain and the hurt. Darius felt his soul break over, and over again. He had failed.

Disconnected and confused, Darius watched with uncomprehending eyes as a second tear formed. A wolf of blue light leapt through, followed by a woman with glowing azure eyes. He could hear none of it, could sense no shift in power or presence. He just lay there, empty.

The two sages that had been there with him raced to meet this third, but Darius did not care. He could not feel anything at all. No pain from the wound in his shoulder. No pain from the gouge torn into his heart and soul at Izebal's betrayal. Nothing.

He felt nothing as the wolf of blue light walked to his side and placed its nose on his forehead. He felt nothing more than the faintest trickle of energy flow over him. And then the world warped and all vanished from sight.

***

"Is he okay?"

"By Ordan's beard..."

"Get him up. Let's go, laddie. Y'er gonna be alright."

Darius heard the words, but he could not comprehend what any of them meant. People who had not been there before were moving

around, but Darius could not focus on anyone or anything. He was vacant, his mind a hollow void.

Hands grabbed him. Strong, powerful hands that lifted him onto something like a bed. His body was this hoisted out of the cave on the makeshift bed.

The sky was still full of stars, though a pink haze was forming over the horizon. Dawn was coming. But Darius felt nothing other than the chill of the night. He did not even feel concern or apprehension as he was loaded into the back of Tyree's horseless wagon. He was empty, just a shell.

Others crowded in beside him, taking up the seats as he was laid upon the ground on his portable bed. It was not wide, and comfort seemed like a foreign idea, for Darius could not feel anything at all. Someone in the wagon was talking, saying this and that about some fight that had happened that night.

Two furry bodies laid down on either side of him. Darius could feel their restlessness, their warm, panting breaths. Something about this brought a slight comfort to Darius, though not enough to bring any semblance of clarity to his addled mind.

"Can you get us back to Talahmnas?"

"I can't," came the reply of someone who sounded as tired and strung out as Darius felt.

Tired. He was so tired.

He should sleep. That would help, wouldn't it?

"You've done enough, lassie," replied the man who had asked. He had a rich voice. Darius thought he had known it from somewhere long ago. "We're not too far from Dane, two days ride. Master Tyree, does this bucket of bolts have enough to get us there?"

"Aye, that it do."

"Hang in there, laddie," said the man as he laid a gentle hand on Darius's shoulder. Darius tried to look up, but his vision was nothing more than a blur. "We'll get y'er patched up. Just hold on."

"I. *Ugh*. Deceived." Darius grunted under the strain of trying to speak. It hurt, so bad. Not just the act of speaking, but what he was trying to say.

Izebal had betrayed them all. Used him. Deceived him.

Darius's mind rushed back over their time together. The moments, the memories. The camp where he had fought the huntsmen. Their eyes... they had been black, just like hers and Edous's had been. She had used that spell, the ink-black tentacles.

She had urged him to go about this path. Why? Why had she done it? Why?

"Save y'er strength laddie. Don't hurt y'erself."

"Izebal…" Darius tried to say anything, but just saying her name twisted something in his mind that broke his speech.

"We didn't see her," said the young woman.

"Memory. Mind." Darius tried to complete his thought but failed. He hoped that Lori could understand him. She could see his mind. Read his memories. They needed to be warned.

A knock sounded at the back of the horseless carriage. The man—who Darius was certain was Erik, though his addled brain was not putting two and two together—rose, as did Lori. "You sure we can trust these?"

"They're like me, Da," said Lori, trying to keep her breath steady. "I don't know how to explain it, but we're sisters."

"Seems simple enough," replied Erik in a whisper, though his voice was less than filled with reassurance.

"Room for three more?" That was the voice of the girl from the streets of Tur'Mor.

"We're headed to Dane, that be where ye want'n to go?" Erik asked, his body still blocking the door.

"Can't say want is the right word," the young woman continued. "But that one on the ground there, we're not done with him yet. Plus, we got another who could use some healing up, and my new sister here is short on Lifelight."

"I'm fine," grumbled a male voice.

"Easy Lightfoot, we'll get you taken care of," said the other.

"What about Seamus? Where is he?" the male asked.

There was an awkward silence that hung for a second too long before Erik broke it, saying, "We ain't got time. Y'er welcome now or never, but this carriage is leavin'."

"We'll take it," the Ordaitian girl said as she stepped up and into the carriage. There was a moment of grumbling outside, but eventually the other two clambered up as well.

"Let's be off then," said Erik firmly. "Master Tyree, to Dane. And let's be quick about it. I got a wife who'll have my hide if I delay, and a son who I almost lost who I'd like to see before his face fills with scruff."

"Krun?" grunted Darius, who had been lying silently on the ground, trying his best to make sense of what was happening around him.

"He lived," said Lori. Her voice was a mix of excitement and bone-deep weariness. "He was in bad shape. But with time, he should be fight'n again."

"Thank you, Darius," said Erik with uncommon solemnity. "Ye saved me family, yet again."

Darius wished that would have brought him peace and joy. But there was only emptiness. What was one family when Darius had put the whole world at risk?

"Y'er a hero laddie," Erik said as he slid back into his seat. "Now just hold on tell we can get ye patched up."

"Rest Darius, reserve y'er strength," said Lori as she touched a glowing palm to his forehead.

Darius faded back into shadow.

The End

EPILOGUE

Darius awoke in a bed. Not the makeshift thing he had been carried in on, but a full-sized bed that was soft and warm. His head felt as if had been placed between an anvil and smith's hammer, and the entire world was a haze of white light. His right hand itched something horrible, so he raised his left to scratch it. Reality came crashing down at the same moment his hand fell through empty space and onto the bed. His arm, from just below the shoulder down, was gone.

Memories, some vivid, while others were vague, washed over him in a deluge of information. The fight in the forest with an Itheanam that should not have been there. Traveling across the Way and his subsequent fight with Edous. Then the arrival of a god… no, that one must have been a figment of his imagination. But his arm was gone.

Panic began to well up in him, spreading so rapidly that Darius struggled not to scream. Try as he might, he could not keep his breath measured. He was trapped. His arm. His arm was gone.

Izebal!

No… not her. She couldn't have.

In a moment of pure hysteria, Darius reached out into the void, pulling at anything to bring him back to reality, to stop the ensuing madness.

The air warped around his extended left hand and his ring glinted with white light. A gust of air filled the room with a *whoosh* and Stahlbak Hi'el came crashing through the door that secluded him.

The haft of the axe had no sooner landed in his hand than when several footfalls filled the outer chamber. There was a clammer of voices, all of which were spoken in hurried whispers. The doorknob turned and in walked… well, Darius was not sure.

He was tall and lean, with straight hair pulled back in three loose strands and tied with silver wire to show sharpened cheek bones and large eyes. Eyes that held no irises, but looked like the heavens at night, lit with countless stars. He had strange tattoos under his eyes, a pointed beard that protruded from his chin, and a gemstone of opal in his forehead.

"Good morning, Darius," his voice was rich and melodic. "I see you have found my sisters. My name is Turtuk da'Varke, though the people of this time have come to know me by a rather ominous moniker that I quite enjoy: Apostle of Death. It is a pleasure to welcome you to my home. We have much to discuss."

"Aellia & Tomo – Only a Dream" Fan Art by: Anonymous

"Aellia" Fan Art by: M.T. Zimny   *"Darius" Fan Art by: Aaron Moschner*

...Until next time

ACKNOWLEDGEMENTS

First and foremost, I have to say a massive thank you to my wife, Heather. She has been by my side since we were in High School, and supported me every step of the way, reading the same chapters a thousand times, and listening to me monologue for hours. I cannot say I love you enough. Secondly, is to my mother. It was due to her influence that I fell in love with reading at a very young age. She opened the doors of my imagination and inspired me to seek the mystical and wonderful things of this life. Lastly, to all of my new friends at IFA, y'all rock my socks off!

ABOUT THE AUTHOR

DAVID ANDREW TROTTER was born in a small town in rural Arkansas. His mother provided much of his childhood education, and in doing so, instilled in him a love of reading and of learning. As a young man, David courted, and then married, the love of his life, Heather Scott. They now have three beautiful children, Oliver, Lily, and Theodore. David graduated from the University of Arkansas – Fort Smith with a degree in Business Administration.

David currently spends most of his time juggling a job, an active gym life, and his true passion, writing. This book was a culmination of years of hard work, effort, joyous moments, and bitter sorrows. This story, while you will never know, got him through some of the darkest times of his life, and he hopes that it will inspire and entertain each who dare to explore the wild, mystical world of his imagination.

https://www.facebook.com/david.a.trotter.3

https://www.instagram.com/datzme16/

Other Works

Birthrights

Azure Tides

The First Oath

Blessings of Blood

GLOSSARY

Aellia - *A-lee-a*
Orphaned after her father was imprisoned for assaulting an Upper, which he did not actually do, and her mother died of the White Fever, Aellia turned to the streets for survival. It was there that she met Felik and his Crew. Like her late mother, Aellia also contracted the White Fever, making her skin pale like porcelain and her hair straight and white. Despite her petite size, Aellia has spent most of her life running rooftops and fighting with knives, leaving her lean, muscular, and spattered with scars.

Alec Adelmo – *Al-ek A-dell-mow*
Brother of Xander, Mayor of Tur'Mor, Alec is a hook-nosed man with a desperation for power. He is man of mystery and shadows, clinging to the old ways.

Alessandro Tassi
Head of the Huntsmen. He has been brutally injured numerous times in his craft, resulting in a missing leg which was replaced by a prosthetic crafted by the Asterivians

Alyn Candius – *A-lin Candy-oos*
Is twin sister to Brei Candius and is a Blessed. She has the ability to Touch Aetora, which allows her to heal others of physical wounds and injuries.

Arrius Aldorian – *Are-E-oos Al-door-E-an*
A Midcouncilor of Tur'Mor and a pain in Felik's neck. He is responsible for maintaining civility in Southend but uses his power to abuse and coerce people into his bidding. He has become fat of power and wealth, his name being one of the oldest and 'purest' in Tur'Mor.

Aurelius Hallock – *uh-rail-E-oos*
Chief Inspector of Tur'Mor and friend of Alec Adelmo. His mutton chops and no-nonsense attitude are his defining features.

Auyxus
Sage spirit of Mind. She is thoughtful and quite reasonable, unless someone tries to harm her Bonded.

Avajan'Aluth – *ah-von uh-loo-th*
Also known as the Voice of the Aluth. This is a title appointed to the leader of the Aluth organization. The Avajan'Aluth is the only Aluth allowed to speak.

Belthazer Haadura – bell-th-u-z-ear HA-d-er-uh
Belthazer was a Zealot of the Dragon God Uuradan. He is a tall, darkly complected man who wears traditional Tuawtian garb as often as possible. He is one of the members of the Crew.

Betrugyn – bet-reh-geh-N
An assassin from Cogadh with one green eye, one black eye, and blonde hair speckled with red. While not a large man, Betrugyn is very deadly, and has a brooch that allows him to Touch Iodaba, granting him the ability of Metaphysical Transportation.

Brei Candius – *br-E candy-oos*
Is twin sister to Ayln Candius and is a Blessed. She has the ability to Touch Aetora and receive visions of the future.

Darius
Darius, True Name, Denathurias (den-ah-there-I-as), is a Feromage. The Feromage were called as the Guardians of Ethrea, instructed to protect the land against dark creatures, evil beings, and those perverted by the dark Touch of Iodaba. Darius is of the Iron Mountain Tribe and bears the branding of the Bear upon his right shoulder. He has the unique ability to Bind direct sunlight, something that no other person save a Feromage can do. There are three Bindings accompanied by three Oaths, each allotting Darius a unique set of abilities, though each come with increasingly severe consequences.

Diabhail – *Die-buh-hail*
High Priest of the Blood Queen Mireya, Diabhail is hell bent on serving his dark queen. He was tainted by the Touch of Iodaba from the Blood Queen's hand, granting him unnatural strength and speed. He fell by Denathurias's hand at the Battle of Morr, ultimately failing his queen and allowing her body to be cast into Dimdreal.

Edous – *E-dose*
The man with a face shrouded of flame. He is a master swordsman, trained in the arts of warfare from an early age. He is a noted leader in a secret organization, whose purposes are less than clear. He has the ability to both Decay and Metaphysically Transport. As part of his ensemble, he shrouds his face with Antilight, making it look like waves of heat are constantly engulfing his features, disguising himself from all who look upon him. His sword is tainted by Iodaba's power and if cuts anyone with it, the cut will continue to spread until it kills the inflicted.

Elcon Von'Harr - *L-Cone v-O' h-are*
High Priest of the Church of Ordan and Steward of the Congregation of Tur'Mor. He is old man who wears fine clothing and fancies himself a scholar of many studies. He is an extremely intellectual man who is in a position of vast power and control.

Erik Ruthvin –
Lord of the High Hall, the Wolf, Wielder of Aithne Lykos, Eric is a busy man, but never to busy for kin and clan. He is blonde haired and blue eyed, covered with tattoos that glow with Everlight, enhancing his body's strength and fortitude.

Felik – *Fee-lick*
The charismatic leader of a group of thieves and scam artists called The Crew. He is a muscular man with a scared face from a long forgone battle. He holds a dark secret, one which Midcouncilor Aldorian uses against him many times.

Felohme Yhzan – *fell-home yu-z-ah-n*
A fat Tuawtian man who escaped slavers and fled to Tur'Mor, where he joined Felik's Crew and became the negotiator and transporter of

the Crew. He is also an excellent cook and has an all-around jovial personality. He bears brandings on either temple of a dragon, the mark of the slaves.

Iaenora – *I-A-nora*
This is the name of one of the Sealed Sages who were prophesied to return to Bind the Forgotten Ones once more and forever.

Izebal – *is-uh-bal*
She is a Diju Speaker and knows many Words. She is a beautiful woman who is extremely powerful, as she can not only Speak Words, but also has access to Ria'Elahm through not one, but three Ra'el Aund. Her tokens of power are her dagger, her wand, and her amulet. These three sources allot her near limitless access to the Lifesource. Izebal has ink-black hair, dark, rich skin, and vibrant emerald eyes, whose irises are wild with green arcing flows of Ria'Elahm's touch. She has a tattoo on her neck of three emblems and a sinuous line winding between them. She is tall for a female, even of the Diju.

Khadais – *k-I-d-a-iss*
The Head of the Dorr A'Gadah.

Krarreack Pritfort – *Cray-rack*
Brother of Lady Sophie, Commander of the Skogortuers, and standing at nearly 7' tall, Krarreack is no small figure of Danelander society. He has flaming red hair and a dreadful personality.

Lady Sophie Ruthvin – Wife of Eric Ruthvin and sister of Krarreack. Tall and well built, poised and proper. She runs Talahmnas alongside her husband with efficiency and grace.

Lori Ruthvin – Eldest daughter of the Ruthvin Clan. Sworn into the Berzerk at the young age of 15, where she has risen to the head, leading the Oathsworn few.

Mikel Thanadius
Lion of Ordiatea, a General of the Ordiatian Army.

Mireya - *meer-E-yuh*
  Blood Queen of Morr

Mireya was the last known descendants of the blood of the Fallen Ones. She professes to be a descendent daughter of Moranna, who was said to have birthed seven daughters, as did her sister, Morgana, who of each birthed seven additional daughters, and thus filled the earth with the dark Touch of Iodaba. The Feromage spent most of their existence hunting and slaying the spawn of the Fallen Ones. It is also said than many of these descendent daughters would seek out their kin and slay them, using their Lifeblood as a means to Touch more of Iodaba's dark light.

Orrum Caldurius – *ore-um cal-dur-E-us*

High Patriarch of the Holy Church of Ordan. Caldurius is an old name, dating back the earliest days of the Republic. The title of High Patriarch is one of the only hereditary callings in all of the Republic. Orrum can trace his bloodline directly back to the first Patriarch of the Church, who, it was said, was to be touched by the finger of Ordan and the Holy Mother, Gallea, whispered into his ears all things that were, that are, and that would be. The High Patriarch is the only male Blessed.

Rahnaluz - ran-uh-law-z

The leader of the Kh'ar Robbers, also called ***Khall'ah Kh'ar***. He wears a mask to hide his true identity.

Shanavaral Lynak – *shawn-uh-var-all lin-ack*

High Priestess of Un'Mor, member of the Holy Council, Overseer of the Infirmary and Keeper of the Ancient Secret. She is a grey-haired woman of high poise. Priestess Shanavaral's features are sharp and angular, with no hint of humor or amusement.

Talendeal Un'Dar - *talon-deal oon'dar*

High Priest of Telnor and member of the Holy Council. He is primarily responsible for managing relationships with the Nation of Galacia. He is tall, dark skinned man, with thick brows that are salt and peppered with age.

Tomokorash Yukysa – *toe-mo-core-ah-sh U-ki-suh*
Also called, Tomo, is from Zau'fi. Suspicion grows as to her true state.

Tornak – *tore-nack*
A rarity, he is pale skinned with freckles on his face a head full of red hair. He is the youngest member of The Crew and is exceptional and forging documents and writs.

Tyree McDoogle
A crazy old man who is far more powerful than meets the eye. Burned and mangled, the left side of his body has left him wheelchair-bound, but it did nothing to dampen his spirits nor his mage abilities. His is a Master Mage, able to conjure and heal, cast visions, and even speak a few Words. Though how he learned those Words are a mystery.

Xander Adelmo – *zan-der A-dell-mow*
Xander is the mayor of Tur'Mor, elected for his charisma, progressive ideals, and his apparent love of the people. He was also a war hero and the second son of a rich noble house. His family is well informed and is an ancient name in Tur'Mor. He has broad shoulders, curly black hair, the titular Ordiatian olive skin tones, and a sharp beard with tight ringlet. While he does not talk much about it, he is an expert marksman, being the former Captain of the 34th Musketmen. He is also more than adapt at rapier fencing, saber fencing, poetry, dancing, wrestling, and the throwing of the discus.

Yemera Haldwen – *ya-meer-uh hal-d-when*
A member of the Holy Council and the High Priestess of Livitha. She is of Ordiatian blood and lineage, but is more reserved than her fellow Council Member, a Livithian trait, due to their negotiations with foreign dignitaries from outside the Republic.

<u>The Ellitheor:</u>

The Ellitheor are the gods of Ethrea, or at least, are recognized as the gods of several major nations, excluding the Zau'fi and Tuawtian Nations. The Ellitheor towered over mortal men during their time on Ethrea. They stood between eight and twelve feet tall, Fenron being the tallest of the Ellitheor. They are immortal beings, whose true origin is a topic of fierce debate amongst the devout worshipers and the theologians of Ethrea. What we do know, is that they came down from their dwellings on Vanherran upon silver sky ships, manned by the Daulkaefar.

Ordan

The High Father, Lord of Creation, Wielder of Ethra, the World Forger. He commands the power of Aetora and holds the Hammer, Ethra, in whose head is a fragment of Ria'Elahm itself. He is the only being able to access both Aetora and Ria'Elahm. He is a powerfully built, bald man with a great beard. He is often depicted in loose robes, with feet shod in golden sandals that wrap up the calf.

Gallea

The Holy Mother, the All-seeing, Mother of Crows and Sparrows, Mother of all Living, Vessel of Ria'Elahm. No physical description could be made that would not pale in comparison to her beauty. She had rich skin and liquid black hair and eyes the color of Ria'Elahm itself.

Moranna

Once Daughter of Fates, now Daughter of the Lost. She was gifted the ability to Touch Aetora. She forsook that ability to Touch Iodaba, whose corruption leeched the Light from her, replacing it with corrupted darkness. She took on the name, Fallen One.

Morgana

Once Daughter of Love, now Daughter of Lusts. She was gifted the ability to Touch Ria'Elahm. She forsook that ability to Touch Iodaba, whose corruption leeched the Light from her, replacing it with corrupted darkness. She took on the name, Fallen One.

Thaellan

Shepherd of the fields and steward of the seas. He is known for his fiery red hair and green eyes, a unique feature that none of his fellow Ellitheor share. He is also very quiet and almost followed his older sister's path, becoming a Fallen One. He was the first to return back to Vanherran and was not heard or seen from since his departure.

Fenron
The Honorable One, the White Knight, Zaufuine's Bane, Wielder of the Godsblade. Fenron is everything noble, grandiose, confident, and proud. He is the most skilled warrior of the Ellitheor, even surpassing his own father, Ordan. His sword is made of Endun'gar and Ellitheor Silver, with a peculiar white stone set in its cross-guard. The blade burns with white flame when in the presence of Iodaba's darkness. If he slays something with the blade, it becomes indestructible to that thing. He was last seen fighting Zaufuine, the Green Dragon of Galacia over three hundred years ago.

<u>**Organizations and Religions of Note**</u>

Aluth

A group of secret warriors, vowed to silence and the protection of the Church of Ordan. They were a special wrap about their heads called a Lo'Phandrak, a vest called a Han Ru Dhar, and boots made from a secret plant that grows in the Swamplands that muffles footfalls to absolute silence called Zhanrak.

Asterivians

A group of scholars, engineers, scientists, and theologians who have sworn to secrecy and fealty to their leader, known as The Illuminated One. Their main purpose is finding the key to immortality.

Berzerk

An elite group of female warriors sworn to the Lord of the High Hall. Skilled in both horseback and hand-to-hand combat, these select few pledge their loyalty to lord and country.

Church of Ordan

The Church's hierarchy is as follows: First comes the Holy Patriarch, who is the only male Blessed and has his own Sy'ey Aund, which allows him to receive Visions from the High Father. The Holy Patriarch sets as the Head of the Church and the Voice of the Holy Council. The Holy Council is comprised of the sitting High Priest or Priestesses from each of the major cities of Ordiatea and the Holy Patriarch. These council members oversee several priests, priestesses, and monks, each who have their own responsibilities in their given city and conclave. The Church is the oldest organization, with the Holy Patriarch being a blood descendant of those first men who fought alongside Ordan and Gallea in the Fall. The Church has massive amounts of wealth, power, and influence.

Diju

The Diju are a group of vagabonds who follow the Valean faith and are ever searching for the Forgotten Words of Lifesong, true names

of things as given by their Goddess, Ethenealal, the Earthmother. They mark themselves with inks to show their Path. They believe that Nkuaue, or the Stone Man, is responsible for the Breaking and for all the evils and sorrows of the world. They believe all life is a woven tapestry, knitted by the hand of Ethenealal herself. Lifesingers can Speak the ancient Words. Sparkdancers and Earthshakers can Touch Ria'Elahm, the first allowing for the ebbing forces like water, fire, and air; the later can manipulate earth, plants and foliage, metal, wood, and ore. The Diju are not of Ordiatea, though they are known to wander its forests, seeking out the forgotten Words. They are despised by the Danesmen, due to superstitions.

Huntsmen

A group of contractors who discreetly hunt and exterminate unwanted creatures of a mythic or paranormal nature, helping to uphold the current societal standards and belief systems. They are almost as obscure as the creatures and beings they hunt, more myth than men.

Kh'ar Robbers

A group of Noble-born individuals who seek to overthrow the democracy of Ordiatea and align themselves with the King of the Calun Nation. They were masks and meet in private, so as to hide their identities and ideals from the democratic government of Ordiatea.

Skogortuers

Elite soldiers of Talahmnas who are trained to protect their borders from foe human and fiend alike. Armed with weaponry crafted by the crazed mage, Tyree, these group of floppy-hatted warriors fear little.

Hierarchy of Ordiatian Government

Major City-states

Blackwater – Home to the Blackwater Clan, located east of Ranok and just north of Cogadh. Major export is fish and wood.

Dane – Capital City of Daneland, located in the northern-most mountain rage of Daneland. Major exports are ore and precious metals.

Livitha – This city-state is located in farthest southern reaches of Ranok, though not considered a part of the forest itself. It also is near the Dogtooth Mountains and is on the Potamae river. It is a primary producer of dyes, wools, and spices, as they are first on the Potamae and run steam powered barges up-river to trade with the other nations.

Talahmnas – Capital of Lower Daneland and home to the Ruthvin Clan. In its heart is the great Stone of the Ancestor, an ancient meteorite that struck the High Hill.

Telnor – The farthest city-state north, bordering the Iron Mountains. The people of Telnor are strongly akin to the Tuawtian and the Galacians who, during earlier periods of history, were not as welcome in Ordiatian society.

Tur'Mor – Capital City and heart of the Republic's Government. It houses over two million citizens, structures older than the Republic itself, and hundreds of tradesmen and thinkers who continually push the boundaries of what is possible.

Un'Mor – The city farthest south, bordering the Calun Nation's borders. This is where the primary force of Ordiatea's military resides. It also is where the infamous Infirmary is located.

<u>*Minor Cities of Note*</u>

Templetown – A quaint town formed around the base of a high hill in a half-moon pattern. This town is responsible for maintaining the Temple of Ordan. It is only a few miles northward of the Outer Walls of Tur'Mor.

Harbortown – Directly eastward of Tur'Mor, set on the Potamae River, Harbortown is where the Ordiatian Navy docks their fleet.

Outpost of Tur'Mor – A garrison is stationed here, bordered next to the Old Marsh. They are responsible for keeping guard of the eastern reaches of the land.

Ranok Outpost – A garrison is stationed here, bordering Ranok Forest. They are responsible for keeping guard on the road to Dancland, which cuts through the forest.

Furrow's Gap – A small town with only one inn. Often used by travelers heading to and from Daneland, though not many traverse that road anymore.

<u>*Government Officials*</u>

Rising Star

Head of the Republic of Ordiatea, which comprises of the Nations of Ordiatea, Galacia, and Daneland.

High Council

A group of dignitaries, each representing their home countries, that discuss all the geo-political intricacies that go into the running of a Republic.

Mayor

Each City-state of Ordiatea is overseen by an elected official called a mayor. They hold office for set term limits and are replaced via vote by those who own land.

Regents

Regents are unique to Tur'Mor, as the Capital is far larger than any other City-state in Ordiatea. There are four regents, and they each oversee a portion of Tur'Mor four quadrants.

Midcouncillors

Midcouncillors are voted upon officials, but typically only come from Houses of Name, high-born nobles. They are primarily responsible for different aspects of the city's functioning, schools, taxes, prisons, water supply, and so on. Tur'Mor has eighty-three Midcouncillors across the Four Quadrants and the inner court, known as the Valamour.

Royal Guard

The Royal Guard are responsible with the guarding and defending of the Noble Houses, the Valamour, Mayoral Family and the reports directly to the Rising Star. These are often referred to as Knights or Royal Knights, as they were once actual Knights, before the modernization of Ordiatea.

Inspectors

A subset of Royal Guards are those call Inspectors, who specialize in deduction and solving of high profile cases, including but not limited to, murder, rape, theft or harassment of any noble-born member of society.

City Guard

These are the policing body of Tur'Mor. They wear black jerkins with Silver Stars on their chests. They are charged with keeping the peace and promoting a city of harmony and cleanliness.

Artifacts and Items

Ra'el Aund
These were crafted for those born of the blood, but not powerful enough to directly access the True Source. They are unique in the fact that they are only bound by one Oath and only allow the wielder to use one of the Light Sources' three powers. The Blessed are most commonly known for using these.

Sy'ey Aund
Directional Items of Power. Rarer than Ra'el Aund, but less so than Tel'un Aund. The only thing that makes these lesser than the Tel'un Aund is these too, like the Ra'el Aund, can be forged by man. Though the process is far more complicated and dangerous. One must swear an oath of Unbreakable loyalty to craft such a weapon.

These requirc 3 things;
. An Unbreakable Oath
. A direct source from one of the Stone Keys (A perfect imbued gemstone to harness it)
. Either Ellitheor Silver, Dragon's Bone, or Endun'gar (white gold of Vanherran)

Tel'un Aund
Scepter of Sages / Oathrod
These Scepters, Tel'un Aund, were crafted in secret for the Seven Sages of Ordan, half endowed with the Everlight and half with Lifesource. Upon each are etched the words Ada'eha El-dached, the binding words of the Sages

Ellitheor Silver
The rings of the Feromage are the only known source of true Ellitheor Silver, though there is a near exact match of ore that is found in Talahmnas. What makes the difference? When Ellitheor Silver is forged, it must be mixed with three things; ore that can *only* be found on Vanherran, the power of Aetora and Ria'Elahm fused together, and lastly, the blood of an Ellitheor, dripped onto the billet while white hot. Once Ellitheor Silver is hardened and cooled, it cannot be broken or re-melted, unless unbonded by the blood of

the Ellitheor who sacrificed and all three Celestial Lights fusing into one destructive channel.

Fragtorch

Ra'el Aund with the specific use of shining blue light, but the users do not have to be Blessed, as they continually shine until the light dims and needs to be refueled at a Source.

The King's Jewel

A large amethyst that has been in the Royal Treasury since the founding of Tur, before it was Tur'Mor and only the Valamour existed, though it was only called Tur at the time.

Coinage of the Republic of Ordiatea
Siglat

Copper in make. Valued at 0.25 hours of labor. This is the lowest value coin in the common market. It is circular in shape, pressed with the crown and stars of Ordiatea.

Gram

Silver in make, and as the name denotes, contains one gram of silver. This is coin denotes 1 hour of labor. It is hexagonal and totes the image of the Rising Star and the three stars of Ordiatea.

Bar

Gold in make, bearing the bust of the first Lord of Tur'Mor. This is worth 10 hours of labor, or a full working day. This currency is rectangular in shape.

Buildings and Locales

Asterivae

The above ground part of the tower is a cylindrical building with a domed ceiling of brass, with great sheets of glass allowing for light. Beneath the dome is the Star Gazer, a massive telescope. Under that is the Library of Ages, where the Globe of Galaxies sets, tens of thousands of books gathered from seven nations and three ages fill this multi-leveled library.

Temple of Ordan

The Temple of Ordan is located atop a high hill overlooking Templetown. The temple is one of the oldest structures in Ordiatea, though it is constantly renovated and kept up. It is said that the temple was plotted out by a Patriarch who was given a vision from the High Father himself, which is why it does not look like any of the other buildings in Ordiatea.

Valamour

The Valamour is the name used for two separate things. Firstly, it is the name of the oldest structure in Tur'Mor, the tower at the heart of the city, which atop is carved the likeness of the First Three, the Founders of the Republic. The Valamour is also the name given to the Inner Court of Tur'Mor, a walled portion of the city where the ruling class resides. There are also grand gardens, expansive courtyards and gorgeous statues strewn throughout.

Darhdall Alley

Perhaps the wealthiest portion of Tur'Mor outside of the Valamour. These are permanent estates, owned by the upper echelon of Ordiatian society. It is located in Northend and is a gated community.

The Sanctuary

This is the largest Chapel of The Church of Ordan in Tur'Mor, located near the gateways from the Market District and Southend. It is a massive building with a domed ceiling, and four spires rising from the sides of the building. Its large, open-front doorway, is covered by a massive stone eave with dozens of carvings telling of the Ellitheor and the early Ordiatians.

The Loft

Once an academy of fine arts, the Loft was commandeered by Felik and is used as the Crew's hideout and base of operations.

The Monastery

The compound where the monks and priests of The Church of Ordan reside. It is located at the farthest portion of the Market District, butted against the dividing wall of Southend. And while it is a rather plain, stucco complex, it hosts its own courtyard, study, and private bathhouse.

Mayoral Residency

Located within the Valamour, this is where the sitting Mayor resides. It is a colossal estate, with expansive courtyards, viewing galleries, winery, and baths.

Mythical Creatures

Daulkaefar
Known as Elves, Angels, or Heralds, depending on who you ask. They have greyish skin, black eyes with star-like spots that act like pupils, granting them far-sight and night-sight, thus they prefer darkness as much as possible. They are immortal, super strong and fast, and can utilize a type of magic from Speaking Words.

Draugr
The basest form of a reanimated corps, mostly skeletal, and lacking any will of their own. These mindless creatures operate under the horde-mind, controlled by Redeye's persuasion.

Itheanam
Dark creatures created from the dead bodies of humans, fuscd to beasts by the souls sucked from living mortals. They come in all types and styles, depending on what beast(s) were used to form them, but they all have one thing in common, a central spike, driven through the skull, marked with runes, which tethers Iodaba's darkness to the beasts. Their skin appears almost tar-like, and if you look at it, you can see the souls of those trapped trying to escape from its body.

Morreans
Once human, Morreans are corrupted beings who have given up a portion of their soul to Touch Iodaba. This grants them unnaturally long life, enhanced speed and strength, but it comes with an insatiable bloodlust. It also turns their eyes black, extends their limbs, and causes various bones to protrude from their bleached flesh. Female Morreans are also said to release a pheromone that can cause males to become extremely aggressive and lustful.

Iarathor
The long-forgotten custodians of the subterranean world. Ancient and powerful, these elemental dwarves were powerful artificers and craftsmen, that was, until dragon fire consumed them and their homes.

Redeyes

Twisted creatures formed of human corpses, fused with Iodaba's corruption. They can steep the emotions in a room, causing people to lose their control and behave strangely.

The Three Celestial Lights

Aetora

Known as the Everlight or the Cognitive Light, the Light of Understanding. It is perceived in the Terral Realm as a brilliant blue light, wisping about like a fine mist. This light resides on Vanherran, sitting upon the throne of the House of Or. Its three attributes are as follows:

Iodaba

Known as Antilight or the Source of Death, Decay and Destruction. It is perceived in the Terral Realm as black in color with a maroon tint to it, flowing like liquid ink, but fracturing as cracked obsidian. The ultimate source of Iodaba is located in Halfak in the Seventh Level. Its three attributes are as follows:

Ria'Elahm

Known as the Lifesource or the Source of Material Creation. Ria'Elahm is seen in the Terral as a deep emerald color, vivid and wild. It sparks and jumps, like arcs of lightning, crackling and flowing. It is the power of nature and creation. Its three attributes are as follows:
Elemental Control
Repairing
Shielding / Warding

Localized Map of Ordiatea, including Talahmnas of Daneland

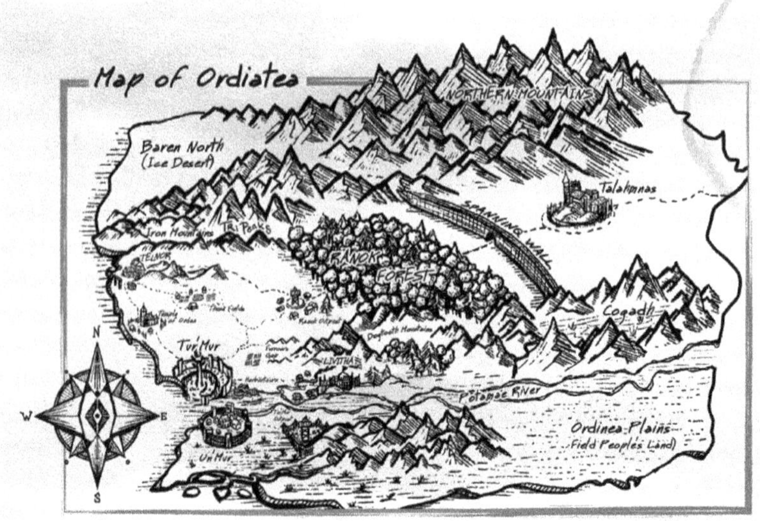

Coinage of the Republic of Ordiatea

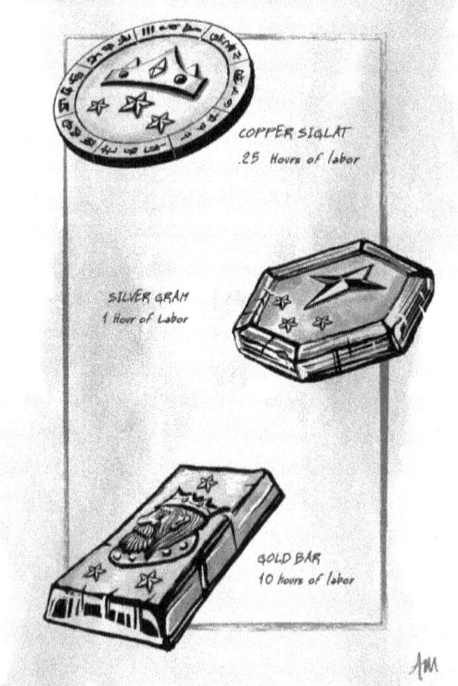

● Khundal'Khal - Elemental Dwarven (Iarathor) City beneath Duka'unka'falla, which was raided by the Great Wyrm, who killed all who stood before him. It is here that Fenron ran his holy blade through the heart of the wyrm, sealing them together in limbo.

● High King Dane Sterkamar VI - High King of all of Daneland

● Ulkeniheim - Danelander games of strength and valor

● Aithne Lykos - Flame of the Wolf

● Undraff - Dark Water Crashing

● Kantuund - Hammer of the Danes

● "Ghaz-kant jbron!" - She who walk with us

● Nip and Trip - Erik's two hounds

● Kroichae - black iron collar that siphons people's abilities to Touch sources.

● Krarraek - Sophie's brother and Erik's Brother-In-Law

● Yukta Śikhā - Name of a person that COULD be the Fire Sage

● Stahlbak Hi'el - Darius's axe

● Hurdy-gurdy - ADD THIS INSTRUMENT

● Talah'El - Stone of the Ancestors

● Lamdrean - whose Talent was earth and matter.

● Zaevot - gifted with Healings and Spirits.

● Telanahr - command the water in all its forms.

● Auedur - master of fire and flames, commanded all things that burned and consumed.

● Iaenora - the free-spirited one, whose Talent lay within the winds and endless skies.

● Auyxus, the Prudent - gifted the abilities of enlightenment and truth, whose Far Eye could see the future and the past